THE PENGUIN CLASSICS

FOUNDER EDITOR (1944–64): E. V. RIEU

HONORÉ DE BALZAC was born in Tours in 1799, the son of
a civil servant. He spent nearly six years as a boarder in a Vendôme school, then went to live in Paris, working as a lawyer's
clerk then as a hack-writer. Between 1820 and 1824 he wrote a
number of novels under various pseudonyms, many of them in
collaboration, after which he unsuccessfully tried his luck at
publishing, printing and type-founding. At the age of thirty,
heavily in debt, he returned to literature with a dedicated fury
and wrote the first novel to appear under his own name, *The
Chouans*. During the next twenty years he wrote about ninety
novels and shorter stories, among them many masterpieces, to
which he gave the comprehensive title the *Human Comedy*. He
died in 1850, a few months after his marriage to Eveline
Hanska, the Polish countess with whom he had maintained
amorous relations for eighteen years.

HERBERT J. HUNT was educated at Lichfield Cathedral Choir
School, the Lichfield Grammar School and Magdalen College,
Oxford. He was a Tutor and Fellow at St Edmund Hall from
1927 to 1944, then until 1966 he was Professor of French
Literature and Language at London University and from 1966
to 1970 was Senior Fellow of Warwick University. He
published books on literature and thought in nineteenth-
century France; he was also the author of a biography of Balzac,
and a comprehensive study of Balzac's writings: *Balzac's
'Comédie Humaine'* (1959, paperback 1964). His translation of
Balzac's *Cousin Pons* appeared in the Penguin Classics in 1968.
He died in 1973.

Honoré de Balzac

LOST ILLUSIONS

TRANSLATED
AND INTRODUCED BY
HERBERT J. HUNT

PENGUIN BOOKS

Penguin Books Ltd, Harmondsworth, Middlesex, England
Penguin Books, 625 Madison Avenue, New York, New York 10022, U.S.A.
Penguin Books Australia Ltd, Ringwood, Victoria, Australia
Penguin Books Canada Ltd, 2801 John Street, Markham, Ontario, Canada L3R 1B4
Penguin Books (N.Z.) Ltd, 182–190 Wairau Road, Auckland 10, New Zealand

—

Lost Illusions originally published in three parts 1837–43
This translation published 1971
Reprinted 1976, 1977

—

Copyright © the Estate of Herbert J. Hunt, 1971
All rights reserved

—

Made and printed in Great Britain
by Richard Clay (The Chaucer Press) Ltd,
Bungay, Suffolk
Set in Monotype Garamond

Contents

PART III: AN INVENTOR'S TRIBULATIONS

Introduction

THE HISTORY OF A LAW-SUIT

Introduction

HONORÉ DE BALZAC (born at Tours, 1799, died in Paris, 1850) was just past the middle of his writing career when he gave *Lost Illusions* to the world (*The Two Poets*, 1837, *A Great Man in Embryo*, 1839, *An Inventor's Tribulations*, 1843). After ten uneasy years (1819–1829) of initial efforts, interrupted between 1826 and 1828 by an abortive attempt to make his fortune as publisher, printer and type-founder, he had achieved his first relative success by producing the novel since known as *The Chouans* (1829), the first one he signed with his own name. By about 1830 he had already conceived the idea of presenting the social and moral history of his own times in a complex series of novels and short stories: he also intended it to be an interpretation of life and society as he saw it, and it was therefore backed by a certain number of 'philosophical novels', the most conspicuous of these being *The Skin* (1831), *Louis Lambert* (1832–1835) and *Seraphita* (1834–1835). He made a first collection of his works between 1834 and 1837, dividing them into three categories: *Studies of Manners*, *Philosophical Studies* and *Analytical Studies*. The *Studies of Manners* were sub-divided into various kinds of 'Scenes' – of Private, Provincial, Parisian, Political, Military and Country Life. But of course, as he went on writing, new novels had to be inserted into these compartments. After finding a general title for them in 1840 (*The Human Comedy*) he collected them again between 1842 and 1846. He continued to write with feverish energy until as late as 1847, and by 1850, when he died, the time was ripe for yet another collection; hence the appearance, between 1869 and 1876, of the so-called 'Definitive Edition'.

Since then the republication of these works – together with the publication of unfinished works and fragments, critical editions, his vast correspondence, etc – has become a major industry. Balzac's energy was unbounded and his productivity astounding. In fact he worked himself to death, one imperative motive for this being the urge to pay off the formidable debts he had contracted as a printer. Moreover his way of life was so extravagant that these debts went on increasing to the end. Another even more cogent motive was to bring forth all he had in him as the self-appointed 'secretary' of contemporary society. And yet he found time to lead an eventful, picturesque and tormented life, memorable for the incursions he made into fashionable, literary and artistic society and also for a series of love affairs which culminated in the lengthy court he paid to a woman who started as a 'pen-friend', became his mistress in 1834 and eventually, after keeping him on tenterhooks for many years, married him in May 1850, almost on the eve of his death: a Polish countess, Eveline Hanska. Naturally these sentimental adventures, his friendships, his animosities and his social relationships all furnished substance for his works, and one of the principal occupations of researchers has been to discover prototypes and models behind his characters (e.g., in Part II of *Lost Illusions*, the novelist George Sand behind Camille Maupin): not an unprofitable activity provided that one realizes that neither Balzac nor any other great writer carries real events and living persons into his fictions without fusing and transforming them.

Balzac may indeed have distinguished himself as a 'secretary' of society, but he was also a great creative artist, and from his study of contemporary society emerged, not a mere copy of the world around him, but a new world which may appropriately be called 'Balzacian': a vividly striking world, teeming with extraordinarily vital and energetic people, impressively real from one point of view, but so heightened and dramatized, so metamorphosed that it is difficult to say at what moment reality is transcended and imagination takes control. There has been much argument over Balzac as an observer of daily reality and Balzac as a 'seer' expressing his own vision of things. He certainly possessed remarkable powers of observation and a prodigious memory. But, as he himself frequently asserted, these faculties were supplemented by a strange gift of sympathetic intuition which he himself, taking a leaf from Scott, called 'second sight'. In fact he did regard himself as being specially if not preternaturally endowed. In any case no reader of his works will fail to see that he is not merely a 'historian' of society, but also a judge, a satirist and, within certain limits, a constructive thinker, although his philosophy is a curious one, a strange blend of science and occultism. As a novelist, he is, of course, a 'classic': that is to say that he tells a straightforward tale, creates his background, giving meticulous and often lengthy attention to localities, sites, buildings, furniture, physiognomy and dress, poses and develops his characters, and by so doing leads the action up to a climax which is usually rapid and eminently dramatic and moreover supported by lively and characteristic dialogue. He is then, in the main, an 'omniscient' narrator who knows where he is going and goes there. None the less, there are today quite a few exponents of the 'new novel', notably Michel Butor, who are far from thinking that the Balzac technique is antiquated in the twentieth century.

In its three parts *Lost Illusions* sits astride the *Scenes of Provincial Life* and the *Scenes of Parisian Life*. Broadly speaking, it has three main themes:

(1) A young man, born of a plebeian father and an aristocratic mother, after vainly trying to impose himself as a poet on the stupid and prejudiced 'high society' in his native Angoulême, is escorted to Paris by his patroness, Madame de Bargeton, for the purpose of making his name and fortune there. Such a migration and this bid for literary success in the metropolis were to some extent Balzac's own personal experience, one he several times used as a basis for his fictions, for example in *The Skin* and *Old Goriot*. But it was also a common experience, a particular case observed at close hand by Balzac being that of Jules Sandeau (though he did not turn out to be a complete failure), a budding author who provided some essential features for the character and career of Étienne Lousteau in *A Great Man in Embryo* and a few years later in *The Muse of the Department*. In 1835 Balzac's loyal friend Zulma Carraud, who had lived near Angoulême from 1831 to 1833, tried to interest him in a young protégé of hers, one Émile Chevalet, who had come to Paris for precisely the same pur-

pose. Balzac took stock of him and sent Zulma a devastating report. 'If he is without means, it will take him ten years to make a living by his pen . . . This young man is characteristic of our times. When one has no particular aptitude for anything, one takes to the pen and poses as a talented person.' But even for the exploitation of real talent, Balzac insists, long and patient effort is needed. And this point is persistently hammered home in the novel.

Lucien Chardon's case is similar to that of Chevalet although, according to Balzac's initial postulate, he does possess talent as both poet and prose-writer. The French title of this second part of *Lost Illusions* presents him as 'a great man from the provinces'. Perhaps 'a great man in embryo' would be better, and indeed, in 1838, Balzac was thinking of 'a great man in his apprenticeship' as an alternative title. Lucien's mother and sister, also his indulgent brother-in-law David Séchard, take him at his own valuation. So does Madame de Bargeton at first. What in effect are his claims to 'greatness'?

The specimens of his poetry proffered by Balzac – he extracted the sonnets from his friends, mostly minor poets except for Théophile Gautier, author of *The Tulip* – scarcely prove his case. It may not perhaps be fair to ask English readers to judge them by the translations offered, though the translator is not inclined to believe that his renderings are much worse than the originals. Then there is Lucien's review of the Panorama-Dramatique play – clever and vivacious, but hardly giving evidence of genius. Here we are indeed presented with a dilemma. Obviously the frequently appearing epithet '*grand homme*' is often used ironically. Yet there are many moments when Balzac seems to be using it seriously. The term 'poet' has of course a wider connotation than we should usually allow to it. Lucien and David Séchard are both called 'poets', though one is drawn to literature and the other to science, more specifically research into the processes of paper-making. Here a second theme appears to interfere with Balzac's basically satiric attitude and inspire him with a great deal of sympathy for Lucien.

(2) This second theme is the opposition Balzac draws between Paris and the provinces. Though he was himself a provincial by birth and early upbringing, he was proud of having become a Parisian, however whole-heartedly he might rail against Paris as being the heart and centre of the ruthless egoism and acquisitiveness which he looked on as the major vices of his time. And so, generally speaking, he adopts a contemptuous attitude towards provincial life. In 1833 he had written (in the preface to *Eugénie Grandet*): 'Things happen in Paris: they just glide by in the provinces. All is drab. Nothing stands out, though dramas are played through in silence.' And this Parisian sense of superiority is complicated with class snobbery. Balzac's family, peasant in its origins, had become solidly bourgeois. In the late eighteen-twenties, and more especially since 1830, he was priding himself on having made a triumphal entry into aristocratic society. At the same time he had taken to conservative views in politics and become a champion of 'Throne and Altar'. And so we shall always find Balzac striking an aristocratic pose (like Sixte Châtelet, he had awarded himself the 'particule' *de*) and mocking at the *bourgeoisie*. At the same time he never denies himself the pleasure of deriding the nobility for their pride of race and their unintelligent brand of conservatism – particularly in *The Old Maid* (1838) and *The Cabinet of Antiques* (1836–1839). As he portrays it, the aristocracy of Angoulême is at once arrogant, ignorant and petty-minded, and that is why he castigates its treatment of the potential 'great man' of Angoulême.

Once Lucien arrives in Paris he finds himself up against the more cultured aristocracy that has access to Court, represented by Madame d'Espard and her satellites – Balzac so often gives the list of them that there is no need to repeat it here. They treat him even more cruelly than the Saintots and Chandours of Angoulême. But they are well-dressed, elegant, full of *savoir-faire*, serenely satisfied with themselves and supposed to be devastatingly witty (Balzac's demonstrations of this wit may not be found altogether convincing). And so, in the second part of *Lost Illusions*, we become aware of further ambivalence in Balzac's attitude: he both admires and despises his *beau monde*. The denizens of the aristocratic Faubourg Saint-Germain are chillingly correct and supercilious, but they are so much more venomous and destructive because their action, once they embark on it, is far more effective than that of the gentry of Angoulême. They combine to dupe, ridicule and eliminate the poor, 'angelically' handsome young man – weak, vain and self-centred – who has hoped to attain to the social rank to which his mother's birth half entitled him.

(3) Once Lucien has been cast aside by Madame de Bargeton, he has to choose between two means of proving his worth: settling down to a long period of poverty and hard work, the course advocated and adopted by the austere d'Arthez, or taking to journalism and forcing himself upon the world of letters by the unscrupulousness which, according to Balzac, alone makes rapid success possible for an ambitious journalist. He decides on this second course but is too vulnerable to pull it off. This third theme can therefore also be regarded as the major theme of *A Great Man in Embryo*: Balzac's denunciation of journalism as one of the most pernicious knaveries of his time.

The first half of the nineteenth century witnessed the rapid rise to power of the periodical press. Journalism had been active – though dangerous to those engaged in it – during the Revolutionary period. Napoleon had kept the press under his thumb, as Giroudeau points out on page 235. The 'freedom' of the press was one of the most controversial issues both under the Restoration and the July Monarchy. Under Louis XVIII and Charles X the struggle between those who, like the Liberals and Bonapartists, wanted to keep the Revolutionary principles and gains intact, and the Conservatives of various hues, especially the 'Ultras', who wanted to put the political clock back, was an affair of major importance; likewise, under Louis-Philippe, the conflict between the spirit of stagnation and the parties in favour of 'movement'. Balzac's contention is that the majority of journalists under these three monarchs, instead of recognizing that they were called to a serious, even sacred mission, turned the Press into an instrument for self-advancement, prostituted principles to intrigue and used journalism merely as a means of acquiring money, position and power. He is reluctant to admit that there *were* great, responsible press organs, like *Le Journal des Débats*, *Le Conservateur*, *Le Constitutionnel* and, from 1824, *Le Globe*, which stood firm on principle; he is above all aware of the vogue which the *petits journaux* enjoyed after the fall of Napoleon, and of the role they played as political privateers.

The *petits journaux* were so-called because they were produced in smaller format than the important dailies or weeklies, which were more or less grave, staid and ponderous. They proliferated in Paris once the fall of the Empire had given a relative, though still precarious liberty to the Press – precarious because it was constantly threatened by the increasingly reactionary governments of the time. The politicians of the Right found it difficult to keep the newspapers under control even by such means as stamp-duty, caution-money, fines, suspensions and suppressions, the object of these being mainly to put obstacles in the way of would-be founders of hostile periodicals. The 'little papers', short-lived as they often proved to be, were much given to journalistic sharp-shooting. They preferred satire, personal attack, sarcasm and scandal-mongering to serious argument or the affirmation of ideals. They were mostly Opposition journals and were a constant thorn in the flesh of the Government. Balzac's aim was to expose their addiction to 'graft', intrigue, blackmail and the misuse of the *feuilleton*, namely the bottom portion of the first page or other pages generally reserved for critical articles and frequently devoted to the malicious task of slashing literary reputations. Andoche Finot – the prototype of such later newspaper magnates as Émile de Girardin and Armand Dutacq, pioneers in 1836 in the founding of cheap dailies which relied on advertisement and serialized novels as a chief source of income – acquires a large share in a big daily and hands on to the equally unprincipled Lousteau the editorship of the 'little paper' he already owns. Balzac probably had *Le Figaro* chiefly in mind, a periodical which was constantly going bankrupt or being suppressed but kept popping up again under different editors. Hector Merlin's royalist *Drapeau Blanc*, edited by Martainville, really existed, having been founded in 1819; so did *Le Réveil*. Other examples of 'little papers' before 1830 were *Le Nain Jaune* (Bonapartist), *Le Diable Boiteux* and *Le Corsaire* (both Liberal), *Le Voleur*, *La Mode*, *La Silhouette*, and, under Louis-Philippe, not only the phoenix-like *Figaro*, but also *La Caricature*, *Le Charivari* (ancestor of our English *Punch*), and once more *Le Corsaire*: a few among many. Louis-Philippe and his Cabinets were easy prey for these stinging gad-flies whose unremitting satire and innuendo remind one of the present-day *Canard Enchaîné*.

It is an amusing thought that, in the late twenties and early thirties, Balzac had himself been a contributor to these disreputable rags and sometimes had a hand in the running of them; for instance he had helped Philipon to found *La Caricature*. Throughout his career he contributed many novels in serial form to the more important newspapers, notably those founded by Girardin and Dutacq – *La Presse* and *Le Siècle*. But by the time he was writing *A Great Man in Embryo* he had left the *petits journaux* far behind him. He himself tried his luck as a newspaper-proprietor and editor: he bought *La Chronique de Paris* in 1836 and founded *La Revue Parisienne* in 1840. Both of these ventures failed. We can well imagine therefore what a large amount of bile was accumulating inside him. On the whole, reviews of his works appearing in periodicals had been hostile if not harsh. He suffered much from the disparagement of editors and critics such as Sainte-Beuve and Jules Janin respectively. He was always quarrelling with Émile de Girardin. And so he took his revenge. He had already made a preliminary attack on the periodical press in *The Skin*. And he followed up his attack of 1839 with his *Monograph of the Paris Press* (1842).

This information relative to Balzac's attack on the Press constitutes a bare minimum if we compare it to the discoveries made by researchers on the models used – both newspapers and personalities – but it should suffice to explain the importance he himself assigned to this third aspect of his novel. All this is centred round the person of Lucien Chardon, whose failure to prove his mettle as 'a great man' is due to his inexperience, feebleness of character and naivety, just as his failure to achieve legal status as 'Monsieur de Rubempré' is due to his self-conceit and readiness to be gulled by his ex-patroness Madame de Bargeton and her formidable cousin the Marquise d'Espard. The third part of *Lost Illusions* takes him back to Angoulême. David's failure as a printer (Balzac draws generously on his experience of 1826 for his knowledge of typography, its processes and difficulties) is now aggravated by his failure as the inventor of a cheap method of paper-manufacture. He has insuperable obstacles to cope with: the well-laid schemes of his competitors the brothers Cointet, supported by the Machiavellian wiles of the rascally solicitor Petit-Claud, the short-sighted meanness of his drunken father, the insolvency into which Lucien's forgery of bills of exchange plunges him and the renewed fatuousness of Lucien in supposing that he can reconquer Madame de Bargeton (now Madame la Comtesse du Châtelet) and obtain governmental subsidies which will enable David to complete his researches.

So *Lost Illusions* ends as it had begun, as a 'Scene of Provincial Life'. *An Inventor's Tribulations* shows in the main the same disparaging attitude to life in the provinces as *The Two Poets* had done. Angoulême, like Paris, is full of rogues and sharks; but the domestic harmony, unselfishness and integrity of the Séchard couple, naive and gullible as they are, does give a more pleasant colouring to the total picture and makes for some serenity of outlook at the end. After landing David in prison for debt, Lucien is reduced to such despondency that suicide seems to be the only way out. But at the last moment Balzac brings a *deus ex machina* into operation: the mysterious Spanish ecclesiastic and diplomat 'Carlos Herrera' who, after long harangues, takes Lucien under his wing and leads him back to Paris where he intends to make his fortune in a really effectual way. The scheme he adopts is to use another woman of easy virtue, Esther Van Gobseck, another Coralie (Balzac always kept a soft spot in his heart for such women), as a decoy for extorting money from an elderly, infatuated banker, the

Baron de Nucingen – readers of Balzac will know that, according to his ingenious system of 'reappearing characters', they are liable to meet the same persons time and time again in different novels – so that the Rubempré estates can be repurchased and the foundations laid for Lucien's ennoblement and success in political life. This project also fails. Lucien finds himself in prison under the accusation of murder and hangs himself in his cell.

All this takes place in the long sequel to *Lost Illusions* entitled *Splendour and Misery of Courtesans* (*A Harlot High and Low* in the Penguin Classics translation) which brings Lucien to his appointed end. This conclusion to his sorry career had obviously been in Balzac's mind since the beginning. There is a hint of it in Part I (page 60): 'Lucien, who did not know that his course lay between the infamy of a convict-prison and the palms awarded to genius, was soaring over the Mount Sinai of the Prophets without seeing that below him were the Dead Sea and the horrible winding-sheet of Gomorrha.' In 1838 he had published a fragment of *Splendour*. Once more Lucien was to prove feeble and ineffectual – mere putty in the hands of 'Carlos Herrera'. Who is this mysterious person? No Spaniard, but a character who had made his first appearance in *Old Goriot* in 1834; the master-criminal Vautrin, Jacques Collin, 'Trompe-la-Mort' – 'Cheat-Death': a man who has declared war on society and who, thanks to his homosexual tendencies, likes to take young men in hand and make a career for them (hence no doubt the allusion to Gomorrha in the above quotation). In *Old Goriot* he had failed to capture Eugène de Rastignac – Eugène found other ways of getting on – but Lucien becomes an easy prey. Vautrin is a fascinating figure, partly modelled on the notorious police-spy Vidocq of Napoleonic and Restoration times. He is also the prime mover in a drama – *Vautrin* – which Balzac produced in 1840. After Lucien's suicide, broken-hearted, he gives up his war on society and becomes its protector in the role of superintendent of police!

It goes without saying that *Splendour and Misery of Courtesans*, with such a plot as its basis, contains a strong element of melodrama, and this is foreshadowed in the last few chapters of *An Inventor's Tribulations*. But *Lost Illusions* is a genuine 'study of manners', even though it has a pronouncedly satirical bias. And, conversely, a sentimental one. It is a strange blend of cynical pessimism and Romantic emotionalism. Also a notable feature in Balzac's novels in general is his duality of attitude. There is the Balzac who participates and sympathizes, not only with his virtuous characters, rare enough in this novel (Eve, David, Madame Séchard, Marion, Kolb, Bérénice, Martainville), but also with his reprehensible ones – his treatment of Madame de Bargeton, Lucien and even Lousteau show this. Nor can he withold some admiration from rogues like Finot, the Cointets and Petit-Claud. There is also the Balzac who satirizes, admonishes and condemns. This ambiguity of attitude passes over into his style. At one moment he is crisp, pungent and objectively sardonic; at another moment inflated and pretentiously 'poetic'. Many of his more ambitiously stylistic passages, with his addiction to swollen metaphor and hyperbolic statement, invite criticism and are difficult to translate. As regards the present translation, it may be noted that in the first edition of the *Human Comedy* (1842 onwards) he had suppressed his original chapter divisions. Here they are restored. His paragraphs are sometimes inordinately long and transition is lacking from one order of ideas to another. I have therefore taken certain liberties in redividing them. Nor have I found it advisable to adhere slavishly to his system of punctuation.

Lost Illusions: this is of course the *leitmotiv* of the whole book. In Part I, Lucien quickly discovers that poetic ability gives no passport to social success with the Angoulême élite. On their arrival in Paris, he and his protectress soon find that there is no foundation for their mutual admiration. Etienne Lousteau, in Chapter Nine of Part II, disabuses Lucien about the likelihood of real talent making good in the literary world. Lucien's experience with publishers and editors emphasizes this truth. He has to face the brutal fact that, wherever he goes, only money and intrigue count. In Part III we are shown how Eve, David and Madame Chardon shed their illusions about their *grand homme de province*. Yet Lucien, after all the disasters which have overtaken him, is slow in shedding his illusions about himself. He still has a good opinion of himself as he returns, ragged and dejected, to the family homestead: 'I am heroic!' And, after further disasters, 'Carlos Herrera' comes along to restore his diminished morale. Gustave Flaubert, in 1869, was to renew the subject of 'lost illusions' in his *Sentimental Education*. The two novels are well worth comparing.

H. J. H.

Part One

THE TWO POETS

1. A provincial printing-office

AT the time when this story begins, the Stanhope press and inking-rollers were not yet in use in small provincial printing-offices. Angoulême, although its paper-making industry kept it in contact with Parisian printing, was still using those wooden presses from which the now obsolete metaphor 'making the presses groan' originated. Printing there was so much behind the times that the pressmen still used leather balls spread with ink to dab on the characters. The bed of the press holding the letter-filled 'forme' to which the paper is applied was still made of stone and so justified its name 'marble'. The ravenous machines of our times have so completely superseded this mechanism – to which, despite its imperfections, we owe the fine books produced by the Elzevirs, the Plantins, the Aldi and the Didots – that it is necessary to mention this antiquated equipment which Jérôme-Nicolas Séchard held in superstitious affection; it has its part to play in this great and trivial story.

Séchard had been one of those journeymen pressmen who, in the typographical jargon used by the workmen occupied in putting type together, are known as 'bears'. No doubt this nickname is due to the to-and-fro motion, resembling that of a caged bear, which carried the pressmen backwards and forwards between the ink-block and the press. In retaliation, the 'bears' call compositors 'monkeys' because of the antics these persons continuously perform in snatching up the letters from the hundred and fifty-two boxes which contain them. In the calamitous period of 1793, Séchard was about fifty, and a married man. His age and marital status saved him from the great call-up which bore off almost all working-men to the armed forces. The old pressman was the only hand left in the printing-office whose owner, known as 'the gaffer', had just died, leaving a childless widow. It looked as if the business was doomed to immediate extinction: the solitary 'bear' could not change into a 'monkey' because, being a mere pressman, he could neither read nor write. Taking no account of his incompetence, a 'Representative of the People', in a hurry to promulgate the eloquent decrees issued by the National Convention, invested the pressman with a licence as master printer and requisitioned the printing-press. After accepting this dangerous licence, Citizen Séchard indemnified his master's widow by paying over his own wife's savings, with which he bought the whole plant at half its value. So far so good, but the Republican decrees had to be accurately and punctually printed. Faced with this difficult problem, Jérôme-Nicolas Séchard was lucky enough to come upon a nobleman from Marseilles who did not relish the idea of losing his estates by emigrating or of risking his head by showing himself in public, and could only earn his daily bread by taking on some sort of employment. And so Monsieur le Comte de Maucombe donned the humble overalls of a foreman in a provincial printing-office. He set up, read and himself corrected the decrees which imposed the death penalty on citizens who gave concealment to noblemen; the 'bear', who had now become the 'gaffer', struck them off and posted them up; and both of them came through safe and sound. By 1795 the squall of the Terror was over, and Nicolas Séchard had to find another factotum as compositor, proof-reader and foreman. An Abbé, who was destined to become a bishop under the Restoration for having refused to conform to the Civil Constitutions, replaced the Comte de Maucombe until the day when the First Consul re-established the Catholic religion. Later the Count and the bishop were to find themselves both sitting on the same bench in the House of Peers. Although in 1802 Jérôme-Nicolas Séchard was no better at reading and writing than in 1793, his 'makings' were enough for him to be able to engage a foreman. The journeyman once so unconcerned about his future had become quite a martinet to his 'monkeys' and 'bears'. Avarice begins where poverty ends. No sooner had the printer espied the possibility of making a fortune than self-interest developed in him a material understanding of his craft, but he became greedy, wary and sharpsighted. With him practice made a long nose at theory. In the end he was able to appraise at a glance the cost of a page or folio according to the kind of character required. He proved to his ignorant customers that heavy type cost more to set than light; and when it came to the smaller type he averred that this was more difficult to handle. Composing being that part of printing of which he understood nothing, he was so afraid of undercharging that he never made anything but excessive estimates. If his compositors worked on a time-contract he never took his eyes off them. If he knew that a paper-manufacturer was in difficulties, he bought his stock for next to nothing and put it in store. And so by now he was already owner of the building which had housed the printing-office from time immemorial. He had every sort of good luck: he lost his wife, and had only one son, whom he sent to the town *lycée*, not so much in order to have him educated as to prepare the way for a successor: he treated him harshly in order to prolong the duration of his paternal authority; thus, during holidays, he made him work at the type-case, telling him that he must earn his living so that one day he might repay his poor father who was bleeding himself white in order to educate him. When the Abbé departed, Séchard chose a new foreman from among his four compositors, one whom the future bishop had singled out as being as honest as he was intelligent. He was thus in a position to look forward to the time when his son would be able to run the business so that it might expand in young and able hands. David Séchard was a brilliant pupil at the *lycée* of Angoulême. Although the elder Séchard was only a 'bear' who had made good without knowledge or education and had a healthy contempt for learning, he sent his son to Paris to study more advanced typography; but he so vehemently recommended him to amass a fair sum of money in the capital, which he called the 'working-man's paradise', and so often warned him not to count on dipping into his father's purse, that it was obvious that he looked on his son's sojourn in that 'home of sapience' as a means for gaining his own ends. While learning his trade in Paris, David completed his education: the foreman of the Didot works became a scholar. Towards the end of 1819 he left Paris without having cost his father a penny. The latter was now recalling him in order to hand over the management to him. At that time the Séchard press owned the only journal for legal notices that existed in the *département*. It also did all the printing for the prefectoral and episcopal administrations: these three clients were enough to give great prosperity to an energetic young man.

At that period precisely, a firm of paper-manufacturers, the brothers Cointet, purchased the second printer's licence in the Angoulême district. Up to then Séchard senior had managed to keep it completely inoperative by taking advantage of the military crisis which, during the Empire, damped down all industrial enterprise. For this reason he had not bothered to buy it himself and his parsimony was destined to bring ruin in the end to his ancient printing-press. When he learnt of this acquisition, old Séchard thanked his stars that the conflict likely to ensue between his own establishment and that of the Cointets would be sustained by his son, and not himself. 'I should have had the worst of it', he told himself. 'But a young man trained by the Didots will come out all right.' The septuagenarian was sighing for the moment when he could take his ease. His knowledge of high-class typography was scanty, but, to compensate for this, he was known as a past master in an art which workmen printers have jestingly dubbed *tipsiography*: an art held in great esteem by the divine author of *Pantagruel*, but one whose cultivation, persecuted as it is by so-called Temperance Societies, has fallen more and more into disrepute. Jérôme-Nicolas Séchard, true to the destiny which his patronymic marked out for him,[1] was endowed with an unquenchable thirst. This passion for the crushed grape – a taste so natural with 'bears' that Monsieur de Chateaubriand has discovered its effects in the genuine bears of North America – had for long been kept within just bounds by his wife; but philosophers have observed that habits contracted in early life attack old age with renewed vigour. Séchard's case confirmed this moral law: the older he

1. *Séchard*. The root-word is *sec*: dry. 'Séchard' could thus be translated as soaker.

6

grew, the more he loved imbibing. This passion left such marks on his ursine countenance as to make it truly unique: his nose had assumed the shape and contours of a capital A of triple canon size, while both of his veinous cheeks resembled the kind of vine-leaf which is swollen with violet, purple and often multi-coloured gibbosities: it made one think of a monstrous truffle wrapped round with autumn shoots. Lurking behind tufty eyebrows which were like two snow-laden bushes, his small grey eyes, sparkling with the cunning of avarice that was killing all other emotions, even fatherly affection, in him, showed that he kept his wits about him even when he was drunk. His cranium, completely bald on top, though it was still fringed with greying curls, called to mind the Franciscan friars in La Fontaine's *Tales*. He was short and pot-bellied like many of those old-fashioned lampions which consume more oil than wick – for excesses of every sort urge the body along its appointed path. Drunkenness, like addiction to study, makes a fat man fatter and a thin man thinner. For thirty years Jérôme-Nicolas Séchard had been wearing the famous three-cornered municipal hat still to be seen on the heads of town-criers in certain provinces. His waistcoat and trousers were of greenish velvet. Finally, he wore an old brown frock-coat, stockings of patterned cotton and shoes with silver buckles. This costume, thanks to which the artisan was still manifest behind the bourgeois, was so suited to his vices and habits, so expressive of his way of life, that he looked as if he had come into the world fully clad: you could no more have imagined him without his clothes than you could imagine an onion without its peel.

If this aged printer had not long since shown how far his blind cupidity could go, his plan for retirement would suffice to depict his character. In spite of the expert knowledge that his son must have acquired while training in the great Didot firm, he was proposing to strike a profitable deal with him – one which he had long been meditating. If the father was to make a good bargain, it had to be a bad one for the son. For this sorry individual recognized no father-and-son relationship in business. If in the beginning he had thought of David as being an only child, he later had only looked on him as an obvious purchaser whose interests were opposed to his own: he wanted to sell dear, whereas David would want to buy cheap; therefore his son was an enemy to be vanquished. This transformation of feeling into self-interest, which in educated people is usually a slow, tortuous and hypocritical process, was rapid and undeviating in the old 'bear', who thus showed how easily guileful *tipsiography* could triumph over expertise in typography. When his son arrived home, the old man displayed the commercial-minded tenderness which wily people show to their intended dupes: he fussed over him as a lover might have fussed over a mistress; he took him by the arm and told him where to step in order not to get mud on his shoes; he had had his bed warmed, a fire lit, a supper prepared. Next day, after trying to get his son intoxicated in the course of a copious dinner, Jérôme-Nicolas Séchard, by now well-seasoned, said to him: 'Let's talk business': a proposal so strangely sandwiched between two hiccoughs that David begged him to put it off until the following morning. But the old 'bear' was too expert at drawing advantage from his own tipsiness to delay so long-prepared a battle. Moreover, he said, having had his nose so close to the grindstone for fifty years, he did not intend to keep it there one single hour more. Tomorrow his son would be the 'gaffer'.

Here perhaps a word about Séchard's establishment is needed. The printing-office stood at the spot where the rue de Beaulieu runs into the Place du Mûrier, and had been set up in the building towards the end of the reign of Louis XV. And so a long time had elapsed since these premises had been adapted to the needs of this industry. The ground-floor consisted of one enormous room to which light came from the street through an old glazed window, and from an inner court through a large sash-frame. There was also an alley, leading to the master-printer's office. But in provincial towns the processes of printing always arouse such lively curiosity that customers preferred to come in by the front entrance, even though this meant walking down a few steps, since the workshop floor was below street level. Gaping visitors never minded the inconvenience of threading their devious way through the workshop. If they paid heed to the sheets of paper hanging like cradles from cords attached to the ceiling, they stumbled against rows of cases, or had their hats knocked off by the iron bars which supported the presses. If they watched the agile movements of a compositor plucking his letters out of the hundred-and-fifty-two compartments of type, reading his copy, re-reading the line in his composing-stick and slipping in a lead, they bumped into a ream of damp paper lying under its weights, or caught their hips against the corner of a bench: all to the great amusement of 'monkeys' and 'bears'. No one had ever arrived without mishap at the two large cages at the farther end of this cavern which formed two dismal annexes giving on to the courtyard and in which, on one side, the foreman sat in state and, on the other side, the master-printer. The courtyard walls were pleasantly decorated with vine-trellises which, given the owner's reputation, lent an appetizing touch of local colour. At the farther end a tumbledown lean-to, in which the paper was damped and cut, backed on to a jet-black party wall. There too was the sink in which, before and after the printing-off, the 'formes' were washed. From this sink seeped away a decoction of ink mingled with the household slops, and that gave the peasants passing by on market-days the idea that the Devil was taking his ablutions inside the house. On one side of the lean-to was the kitchen, on the other a wood-pile. The first floor of the house, which had only two attic bedrooms above it, contained three rooms. The first, which ran the whole length of the alley except for the well of the old wooden staircase and received its light from the street through a little wooden casement, and from a court-yard through a bull's-eye window, served both as antechamber and dining-room. Having no other decoration than white-wash, it exemplified the cynical simplicity of commercial greed; the dirty flags had never been washed; it was furnished with three rickety chairs, a round table and a sideboard standing between two doors which gave access, one to a bedroom, the other to the living-room; the

9

windows and doors were brown with grime; as a rule it was cluttered with blank or printed paper, the bales of which were often covered with the remains of Jérôme-Nicolas Séchard's dinner: dessert, dishes and bottles. The bedroom, whose leaded window-panes drew their light from the courtyard, was hung with some of those old tapestries which in provincial towns are displayed along the house-fronts on Corpus Christi day. The bed was a curtained four-poster with a coarse linen counterpane and a red serge coverlet over the foot; there were worm-eaten armchairs, two upholstered walnut chairs, an old writing-desk and a wall-clock hanging over the chimney-piece. This room owed its atmosphere of patriarchal simplicity and its abundance of brown tints to the worthy Rouzeau, Séchard's predecessor and former employer. The living-room had been modernized by the late Madame Séchard and shocked the eye with its appalling wainscots painted in wig-maker's blue; the panels were decorated with wall-paper depicting Oriental scenes in sepia on a white ground; the furniture consisted of six chairs with blue roan seats and backs in the shape of lyres. The two crudely-arched windows looking out on to the Place du Mûrier had no curtains; the chimney-piece was devoid of candelabra, clock and mirror. Madame Séchard had died when she was only half-way through with her plans for embellishment, and the 'bear', seeing no purpose in unproductive improvements, had abandoned them. It was into this room that Jérôme-Nicholas Séchard, *pede titubante*, ushered his son and pointed to a round table, on which was a statement of his printing-house stock drawn up by the foreman at his direction.

'Read that, my boy', said Jérôme-Nicolas as his besotted eyes rolled from the document to his son and from his son to the document. 'You'll see what a champion printing-office I'm giving you.'

'Three wooden presses supported by iron bars, with imposing-stone of cast iron . . .'

'One of my improvements,' said the old man, interrupting his son's reading.

'With all their appurtenances: ink-troughs, balls and

benches, etc. Sixteen hundred francs! . . . Why, father,' said David, letting the inventory fall, 'your presses are just old lumber, not worth three hundred francs. All they're fit for is firewood.'

'Old lumber, are they? . . .' Séchard senior exclaimed, 'Old lumber! Take the inventory and come downstairs! You'll see whether the new-fangled ironmongery they make nowadays works like these good, well-tried tools. And then you'll be ashamed to cry down honest presses which roll along like the mail-coaches and will go on running the rest of your life without needing the slightest repair. Old lumber! Yes, but good enough to keep your pot boiling! Old lumber which your father has been handling for twenty years and which helped him to make you just what you are!'

The old man clattered down the rugged, worn, rickety staircase without tumbling over himself, opened the alley door leading to the workshop, rushed to the first of his presses which he had been crafty enough to have oiled and cleaned, and pointed to the strong oaken side-pieces which his apprentices had polished.

'Isn't that a jewel of a press?' he asked. There was a wedding-invitation on it. The old 'bear' lowered the frisket on to the tympan and the tympan on to the carriage and rolled it under the press; he pulled the bar, unrolled the cord to draw back the carriage, and raised tympan and frisket with all the agility a young 'bear' might have shown. Thus handled, the press gave a pretty little squeak like that of a bird fluttering away after striking against a window-pane.

'Is there a single English press that can do such quick work?' said the father to his astonished son.

The old man ran to the second and third presses in succession and performed the same operation on each of them with equal adroitness. The last one revealed to his wine-blurred gaze a spot which his apprentice had overlooked: with a resounding oath the drunkard gave it a rub with his coat-tail, like a horse-coper smoothing the hide of a horse he wants to sell.

'With these presses, and without a foreman, you can earn

yourself nine thousand francs a year, David. As your future partner, I am against your replacing them by those accursed iron presses which wear out the type. You went into raptures in Paris over the invention of that damned Englishman, an enemy of France, trying to make a fortune for the typefounders. Oh yes! You wanted Stanhope presses! To hell with your Stanhope presses. They cost two thousand five hundred francs apiece, almost twice as much as my three beauties put together, and wear down the type because there's no give in them. I'm not educated like you, but bear this in mind: Stanhope presses may last longer, but they spell ruin for the type. My three presses will give you good service, the work will be pulled clean, and that's all the people in Angoulême will ask for. Print with iron or wood, gold or silver, they won't pay you a farthing more.'

'*Item*,' said David. 'Five thousand pounds of type from the Vaflard foundry . . .' The pupil of the Didots could not repress a smile on reading this name.

'All right, laugh away! After a dozen years, the characters are as good as new. There's a type-founder for you! Monsieur Vaflard is an honest man who turns out hard-wearing material; and in my opinion the best founder is the one you go to least often.'

'Valued at ten thousand francs,' David continued. 'Ten thousand francs, father! But that works out at forty sous a pound, and Messrs Didot only charge thirty-six sous a pound for their new pica. Your old batter is only worth the metal it's cast in – ten sous a pound.'

'So you call it better, do you? Bastard, italic and round type made by Monsieur Gillé, formerly printer to the Emperor: type worth six francs a pound, masterpieces of punch-cutting which I bought five years ago. And look, some of them still have the white of the casting on them!' Séchard senior caught up a handful of still unused 'sorts' and showed them to his son. 'I'm no scholar and can't read or write, but I know enough about it to guess that the English script types used by your precious Didots were cribbed from those of the Gillé foundry. Here's a *ronde*,' he added, pointing to a case and taking an M from it: 'a *ronde* in pica size which is still brand-new.'

David perceived that there could be no arguing with his father. He had to take it or leave it, accept or refuse the lot. The old 'bear' had included everything in the inventory, even the ropes in the drying room. The smallest job-chase, the wetting-boards, the basins, the stone and brushes for cleaning, everything was priced with miserly precision. The total amounted to thirty thousand francs, including the master-printer's licence and the good-will. David was mentally computing whether the transaction was feasible or not. Seeing his son musing in silence over the figure, Séchard senior grew anxious, for he preferred heated bargaining to mute acceptance. In this sort of dealing, bargaining denotes a business man capable of defending his interests. 'The man who never haggles never pays,' old Séchard used to say. As he watched his son closely to guess his thoughts, he ran through the list of his sorry utensils, all of them needed, he argued, for running a provincial printing-office. He took David round to a glazing-press and a trimmer for jobbing-work, and boasted of their usefulness and soundness.

'Old tools are always best,' he said. 'In the printing business they ought to fetch a better price than the new ones, as they do in the gold-beaters' trade.'

Hideous vignettes representing Hymens and Cupids, dead people pushing up the lids of their sepulchres and representing a V or an M, and enormous play-bill borders complete with mummers' masks were transformed, by virtue of Jérôme-Nicolas's wine-sodden eloquence, into articles of tremendous value. He told his son that provincial people were strongly rooted in their habits, and that any attempt to provide them with better products would be wasted. He, Jérôme-Nicolas Séchard, had tried to sell them better almanacs than the *Double Liégois*, which was printed on sugar-bag paper. Well, they had preferred the original *Double Liégois* to the most splendid almanacs. David would soon recognize the importance of such old-fashioned stuff, which would sell better than the most costly novelties.

'Ha! Ha! my boy! The provinces are one thing, Paris is another. If a man from L'Houmeau comes and orders wedding-cards, and if you print them without a Cupid and garlands, he won't think he's properly married: he'll bring them back to you if he only sees an M on them, as with your Messrs Didot. They are the glory of the printing-trade, but their new-fangled ideas won't take on in the provinces for a hundred years. And that's the truth.'

Generous souls make poor business men. David was one of those shy and sensitive people who shrink from argument and give way as soon as their opponent's foil pricks too near to their heart. His lofty sentiments and the deference he still paid to the old drunkard made him even less fit to hold his own in discussion with his father, particularly since he credited him with the best intentions – for at first he put down the pressman's voracious selfishness to affection for his tools. Nonetheless, since Jérôme-Nicolas Séchard had bought the entire concern from Rouzeau's widow for ten thousand francs in *assignats*, and since at present values thirty thousand francs was an exorbitant price, young David exclaimed:

'But father, you are bleeding me white!'

'I who brought you into the world . . .' said the old sot, with his arms raised towards the drying-poles. 'How much then do you reckon, David, for the printer's licence? Do you know what the *Advertising Journal* is worth at ten sous a line? It's a monopoly, and it brought in five hundred francs last month. My lad, take a look at the ledgers and see what comes in from the prefecture posters and registers and the work we do for the Mayor and the Bishop. You're a lazy-bones with no thought of getting on. You're boggling about the price of a horse which will carry you to some fine piece of property like the Marsac one.'

To the inventory was appended a deed of partnership between father and son. The benevolent father was letting his house to the firm for twelve hundred francs a year, although he had bought it for less than six thousand francs; and he was reserving one of the two attic rooms for his own use. Until such time as David Séchard had paid off the thirty thousand francs, profits were to be equally divided; once he had repaid this sum to his father, he would become the one and only owner of the printing-office. David computed the value of the licence, the good-will and the journal without taking the plant into account; he decided he would be able to make good and accepted the terms. His father, accustomed to the niggling cautiousness of the peasant class, and knowing nothing of the wider scope of Parisian calculations, was astonished at so prompt a conclusion.

'Can my son have made money?' he wondered. 'Or is he even now thinking of not paying up?' With this thought in mind, he questioned him in order to find out if he had money with him, so as to take it from him as a first instalment. The father's curiosity awakened the son's suspicions, and the latter remained as tight as a clam. The next day, Séchard senior ordered his apprentice to remove to the second-floor bedroom all the furniture which he planned to have transported to his country cottage in carts which would be returning there empty. He stripped the three first-floor rooms bare and handed them over to his son; he also put him in possession of the printing-works without giving him a farthing for the workmen's wages. When David asked his father, as a partner, to contribute to the outlay needed for their joint enterprise, the old pressman affected not to understand. He was not obliged, he said, to hand over money as well as the printing-office; his capital was already sunk in it. His son's logic became more pressing, and he replied that, when he had bought the printing-works from Rouzeau's widow, he had managed without a penny in his pocket. If he, a poor and completely ignorant workman, had succeeded, a pupil of the Didots would do better still. Moreover, David had been earning money thanks to the education his old father had paid for by the sweat of his brow, and now he could very well put it to use.

'What have you done with your earnings?' he asked, returning to the attack in order to clear up the problem which his son's silence had left unsolved the previous day.

'Well, I had to live, and I had to buy books,' David answered indignantly.

'Oh, you bought books! You won't do well in business. People who buy books can't be much good at printing them,' the 'bear' replied.

David experienced the most horrible of humiliations: a father's degradation. He had to endure the spate of mean, tearful, shifty, mercenary arguments which the old miser used to express his refusal. Realizing that he had to stand alone, without support, finding that he was dealing with a speculator instead of a father, he thrust back his grief and tried, out of philosophical curiosity, to get to the bottom of his character. He drew his attention to the fact that he had never asked him to render an account of his mother's fortune. Even if this fortune could not be set off against the price asked for the printing-works, it should at least go towards the running of the new partnership.

'Why', old Séchard replied, 'all your mother owned was her brains and beauty.'

At this reply, David saw through his father completely, and realized that, in order to extract such a reckoning from him, he would have to take legal proceedings, and that these would be interminable, costly and discreditable. The noble-hearted young man decided to shoulder the burden – a heavy one, for he knew what an effort it would be to discharge the obligations he was contracting towards his father.

'I will work hard,' he told himself. 'After all, if I find it heavy going, so did the old fellow. Besides, shall I not be working for myself?'

Séchard senior was worried by his son's silence. 'I'm leaving you a treasure,' he said.

David asked what this treasure was.

'Marion,' he replied.

Marion was a sturdy country girl, indispensable for the running of the printing-works. She wetted the paper and trimmed it, ran errands, did the cooking, washed the clothes, unloaded the paper from the vans, went round collecting debts and cleaned the ink-balls. Had she had been able to read, old Séchard would have made a compositor of her.

He set off on foot for the country. Although well pleased with his sale, which he was passing off as a venture in partnership, he was anxious about the way payment would be made. After the agony of making a sale, there always comes the agony of turning it into cash. All passions are essentially jesuitical. This man, who regarded education as useless, strove hard to believe in the effect it produces. His thirty thousand francs were so to speak lent out on mortgage, and the security for them was the sense of honour which education must have developed in his son. As a properly brought-up young man, David would sweat blood in order to meet his engagements; his knowledge of the trade would suggest ways and means; he had shown plenty of fine sentiments; he would certainly pay! Many fathers who act thus believe they have really been paternal, and old Séchard had managed to persuade himself of this by the time he reached his vineyard at Marsac, a little village some ten miles away from Angoulême. This domain, on which the previous owner had built a pleasant habitation, had grown in size from year to year since 1809, when the old 'bear' had acquired it. It was there that he exchanged the care of the printing-press for that of the wine-press and, as he used to say, he had had too much to do with wine not to know all about the vine.

For the first year of his retirement to the country, old Séchard showed a troubled countenance as he leaned over his vine-poles, for he spent all his time in his vineyard, just as formerly he had remained inside his workship. The unhoped-for thirty thousand francs went to his head even more than his cloudy September vintage: in his mind's eye he could already see himself fingering them lovingly. The less he deserved this money, the more he desired to lay hands on it. And so anxiety often brought him back from Marsac to Angoulême. He toiled up the slopes of the rock on whose pinnacle the town is perched and entered the workshop to see how his son was getting on. The presses were in their usual place. The one and only apprentice, with a paper cap on his head, would be cleaning the ink-balls. The old 'bear' could hear the press creaking over an invitation card, recognize his old type and see his son and the foreman, each in his cage, reading what he supposed to be the proofs of a book. After dining with David, he returned to his Marsac property, brooding over his fears. Avarice, like love, is endowed with second sight as regards

17

future contingencies; it sniffs them out and worries them. At a distance from the workshop where the sight of his apparatus fascinated him and carried him back to the days when he was prospering, the vine-grower could detect disquieting symptoms of inactivity in his son's demeanour. He took fright at the very name of *Cointet Brothers*, and could see it eclipsing that of *Séchard and Son*. In short the old man could scent misfortune in the wind, for misfortune was indeed hovering over the Séchard firm. But there is a divinity that looks after misers and, through a combination of unforeseen circumstances, this divinity was about to pour the proceeds of his usurious sale into the drunkard's lap.

The reason for the Séchard printing-office being on the decline in spite of factors making for prosperity was David's indifference to the religious reaction which set in under the Restoration government, equalled by his unconcern about the Liberal movement. He maintained in political and religious matters a neutrality which was most injurious to his interests. He was living in a period when provincial tradespeople had to line up with a party in order to get customers: in fact they had to choose between the patronage either of the Liberals or the Royalists. David had fallen in love; this, together with his scientific preoccupations and his inherent good nature, prevented his having that avidity for gain which goes to the making of a genuine business man and which might have induced him to study the differences existing between provincial and Parisian industry. Shades of opinion, which stand out so clearly in the *départements*, are obliterated in the great swirl of Parisian activity. The brothers Cointet adopted the views of the monarchist party, made an open show of keeping fast-days, haunted the Cathedral, cultivated the society of priests and brought out reprints of books of devotion as soon as they came into demand. Thus they took the lead in a lucrative side-line, and slandered David by accusing him of liberalism and atheism. How, they asked, could one give work to a man whose father had sided with the Terrorists, who was a drunkard, a Bonapartist, an old miser who sooner or later would surely leave piles of gold to his heir? They themselves

18

were poor men with large families, whereas David was a bachelor and would be rolling in wealth; that was why he was taking things easy. And so forth. Influenced by the accusations thus launched against David, the prefectoral and episcopal officials at length transferred their custom to the Cointets. Soon these greedy opponents, emboldened by their rival's indifference, founded a second advertising journal. All that the older press had left was jobbing-work from the townspeople; the profits from its advertising journal were reduced by half. Soon the Cointet firm, considerably enriched by the sale of prayer-books and works of piety, offered to buy the Séchard journal in order to monopolize the printing of departmental notices and judicial announcements. The moment David passed on the news to his father, the old vine-grower, appalled by the progress the Cointet firm was making, swooped down from Marsac to the Place du Mûrier with the swiftness of a crow scenting corpses on the battle-field.

'Leave me to deal with the Cointets,' he said to his son. 'You keep out of this.'

The old man was quick to see through the Cointet's intentions, and they were alarmed by his shrewd appraisal of the situation. His son, he said, was making a blunder, and he was going to prevent it. Where would their custom come from if the journal were handed over? Every solicitor, notary and tradesman in L'Houmeau was a Liberal. Well, the Cointets had tried to ruin the Séchards by making out they were Liberals. But this was as good as throwing out a life-line, for it meant that *Séchard and Son* would keep all the Liberal advertisements. Sell the journal? Just as well sell out completely, stock and printer's licence!

Thereupon he demanded sixty thousand francs of the Cointets for the printing-works, to save his son from ruin. He loved his son; he was protecting his son. The vine-grower made use of his son as peasants make use of their wives: his son wanted this, or he didn't want that, according to the propositions he extorted one by one from the Cointets. By this means he persuaded them, not without great effort, to pay twenty-two thousand francs for the *Charente Advertiser*. But

David was to undertake never to print any periodical whatsoever, under a penalty of thirty thousand francs' damages. This sale spelled suicide for the Séchard press, but the vine-grower cared little for that. Theft always leads to murder. The old reprobate counted on applying this sum to the recovery of his capital, and to lay his fingers on that he would have handed David over into the bargain, the more readily because this nuisance of a son had a right to one half of the unexpected windfall. By way of compensation, the generous father made over the printing-works to him – but he still kept the rent for the house at the prodigious figure of twelve hundred francs a year.

After this sale of the *Charente Advertiser* to the Cointets, the old man rarely came to town, alleging his great age; but the real reason was his lack of interest in a printing-office which no longer belonged to him. Nevertheless he was unable entirely to repudiate the long-standing affection he felt for his apparatus. When his concerns brought him to Angoulême, it would have been very difficult to decide what most attracted him to the house – his wooden presses or his son, whom he visited in order to make *pro forma* requests for his rent. His erstwhile foreman, who had now gone over to the Cointets, well knew what to make of this paternal generosity: the wily old fox, he said, was thus reserving to himself the right of intervening in his son's affairs, since the accumulation of unpaid rents made him a preferential creditor.

David Séchard's negligence was due to causes which will throw light on the young man's character. A few days after settling in at his father's printing-office, he had met one of his school friends, Lucien Chardon, a young man of about twenty-one, who at that time was living in the utmost poverty. He was the son of a former medical officer in the Republican armies who had been invalided out as a result of a wound. Nature had made a chemist of Monsieur Chardon senior, and chance had set him up as a pharmacist in Angoulême. Death overtook him just as he was working his way to a lucrative discovery after spending several years at scientific research. He was trying to find a cure for all kinds of gout.

Gout is a rich man's disease, and rich men will pay any price to recover their health once lost. And so, among all the problems which had given him subject for meditation, he had singled out this one for resolution. Divided between science and his practice as a pharmacist, the late Chardon had realized that science alone could bring him prosperity: he had accordingly studied the causes of the disease and based his remedy on a certain diet suited to every constitution. He died during a stay in Paris while soliciting the approval of the Academy of Science, and thus lost the fruit of his labours. Anticipating prosperous times, the pharmacist had spared no expense for the education of his son and daughter, so that budgeting for the family constantly ate away the income from his chemist's shop. Consequently, he not only left his children in poverty but also, unfortunately for them, he had brought them up in the expectation of a brilliant future, which his death extinguished. The illustrious doctor Desplein tended him in his last moments and watched him die in convulsions of rage. The prime motive for his ambition had been the ardent love he bore his wife, the last representative of the Rubempré family, whom he had miraculously saved from the scaffold in 1793. Without getting the girl's consent for the fiction, he had gained time by alleging she was pregnant. After having to some extent established the right to marry her, he did in fact marry her in spite of their mutual poverty. His children, like all love-children, inherited their mother's beauty and nothing more: a present which so often proves fatal when it goes with poverty. Madame Chardon's keen participation in her husband's hopes, labours and disappointments had made deep inroads into her beauty, just as her standard of living had suffered from the gradual deterioration which indigence inflicts; but her courage, and that of her children, proved equal to this adversity. The poverty-stricken widow sold the chemist's shop situated in the High Street of L'Houmeau, Angoulême's principal suburb. The proceeds allowed her to purchase an income of three hundred francs a year, a sum insufficient to provide even for her own needs; but she and her daughter accepted their situation without shame and went out to work to earn a living. The mother became a nurse for women in labour, and her gentle manners gained her the preference over all others in the rich households, in which she lived without costing her children anything and in fact earned twenty sous a day. To spare her son the humiliation of seeing his mother reduced to such humble employment, she had assumed the name of 'Madame Charlotte'. People in need of her services applied to Monsieur Postel, Chardon's successor. Lucien's sister worked in a laundry which handled fine linen and belonged to a neighbour, a very decent woman much esteemed in L'Houmeau, a Madame Prieur, and there she was earning about fifteen sous a day. She was in charge of the laundry-women and so enjoyed a sort of superiority which raised her somewhat above the class of working-girls. The meagre proceeds of their toil, added to Madame Chardon's income of three hundred francs, amounted to about eight hundred francs a year, which had to provide these three people with food, clothes and lodging. Even strict economy made this seem scarcely adequate, for it was almost entirely absorbed by Lucien's requirements. Madame Chardon and her daughter Eve believed in Lucien as fervently as Mahomet's wife believed in her husband: there were no bounds to the sacrifices they made for his future. This hard-up family lived in L'Houmeau in a dwelling rented for a very modest sum from Monsieur Chardon's successor; it lay at the further end of an inner court, over the dispensary. Lucien occupied a shabby room in the attic. Spurred on by his father who, with his passion for the natural sciences, had at first urged his son in the same direction, Lucien was one of the most brilliant pupils in the College of Angoulême; he had reached a senior class at the time Séchard was finishing his studies there.

When chance brought these two school friends together again Lucien, tired of drinking from the rudely-fashioned cup of poverty, was on the verge of making one of those drastic decisions which young men of twenty are apt to make. David offered to teach Lucien the art of proof-reading, although he had absolutely no need of a foreman, and paid him a wage of forty francs a month, which saved him from despair. The ties of a friendship dating from schooldays, thus renewed, were strengthened both by the similarity of their predicament and the differences in their characters. Both of them, full of varied ideas for making their fortune, were possessed of that soaring intelligence which makes a man capable of the highest achievements. Yet there they were, at the very bottom of the social ladder. The injustice of their lot forged a powerful bond between them. Moreover, each of them was a poet, although they had climbed different slopes on their way to Parnassus. Although he had been destined for the highest speculations of natural science, Lucien had an ardent thirst for literary glory, while David, whose meditative genius predisposed him to poetry, felt drawn towards the exact sciences. This interchange of roles engendered a kind of spiritual affinity between them. Lucien was not slow in communicating to David the lofty views transmitted to him by his father on the application of science to industry; and David opened Lucien's eyes to new paths in literature along which he might venture in order to make his name and fortune. In a few days the friendship between these two young people developed into the kind of passion that occurs only as one emerges from adolescence. David soon caught a glimpse of the beautiful Eve and fell in love with all the fervour natural to a melancholic and meditative spirit. The liturgical *Et nunc et semper et in secula seculorum* is the guiding maxim for those sublime, unknown poets whose only works are the magnificent epics which two hearts conceive but never consign to paper. When Eve's admirer fathomed the secret hopes which Lucien's mother and sister were setting on his handsome, poetic brow, when he became aware of their blind devotion, he found it sweet to draw closer to his beloved by sharing her hopes and self-denial. And so Lucien became a chosen brother to David. Like the 'Ultras' who were then trying to be more royalist than the King himself, David carried to excess the faith which mother and sister placed in Lucien's genius, and indulged him as a mother does her child. During one of the frequent conversations in which, under the stress of frustrating penury, they were ruminating as all young people do over means of prompt enrichment –

23

shaking the branches of all the trees which earlier marauders had already denuded of their fruit – Lucien remembered two ideas put forward by his father. Monsieur Chardon had talked of halving the price of sugar by the use of a new chemical reagent, and of a similar reduction in the cost of paper to be achieved by importing from America certain inexpensive vegetable substances analogous to those used by the Chinese. David recognized the importance of this problem over which the Didots had already cogitated, and he seized on the idea, seeing a promise of enrichment in it; and so he looked on Lucien as a benefactor whom he would never be able to repay.

Anyone will divine the incompetence of these two friends to manage a printing-press, obsessed as they were by their schemes and their cult of the inner life. Far from bringing in between fifteen and twenty thousand a year, as did the printing-office of the Cointet brothers, printers and publishers to the diocese, proprietors of the *Charente Advertiser*, which was now the only periodical in the *département*, the press belonging to young Séchard scarcely produced three hundred francs a month; and from this had to be deducted the proof-reader's salary, Marion's wages, taxes and rent; and that only left David with about one hundred francs a month. In enterprising and industrious hands the type would have been renewed, steel presses bought and a contract made with Paris publishers for cheap reprints of their books. But master-printer and foreman were so absorbed in their intellectual pursuits that they were content to carry out the orders placed by their sole remaining customers. The Cointet brothers were now so fully aware of David's character and manner of life that they slandered him no more; on the contrary, a wiser policy was to let his press rub along in honest mediocrity so that it should not fall into the hands of some rival to be feared; they themselves passed the so-called town custom on to it. Thus, without knowing it, David owed his commercial survival to the cunning calculation of his competitors. Pleased with what they called his mania, the Cointets made a show of rectitude and loyalty in their dealings with him; but in reality they were behaving like the Public Transport Service when it stages bogus competition in order to ward off a genuine one.

The outside of the Séchard premises was in keeping with the squalor reigning inside: the old 'bear' had never carried out any repairs. Rain, sun and every variety of inclement weather had made the door opening on to the alley look like an old tree-trunk, so deeply was it scored with cracks of unequal sizes. The house-front, an unsymmetrical medley of stone and brick, seemed to be drooping under the weight of a decrepit roof overladen with concave tiles such as are used for all roof-structures in the southern parts of France. The worm-eaten window-frames were furnished with the enormous shutters supported by thick cross-beams which the hot climate necessitates. It would have been difficult in the whole of Angoulême to find a building so full of cracks and so held together by the strength of its cement. Imagine the workshop itself, having light at both ends but dark in the centre, its walls plastered with posters, the lower half of them worn brown by the workmen who had been rubbing against them for thirty years, its ceiling encumbered with rope-tackle, its piles of paper, aged presses, stacks of stone slabs for flattening out the wetted sheets, rows of case and, at one end, the two cages in which master and foreman took their respective stances. This will show you what sort of existence the two friends led.

In 1821, in the early days of May, David and Lucien were standing by the window overlooking the court at about two in the afternoon, just as their four or five workmen were going off to dinner. When the master-printer saw his apprentice shutting the street door, which had a bell, he took Lucien out into the courtyard, as if he could no longer endure the smell of paper, ink-troughs, presses and old wooden utensils. The two of them sat down under the arbour from which they could descry anyone entering the workshop. The sunbeams frolicking among the vine-branches caressed the two poets and threw a halo of light around them. The contrast between the physiognomy and characters of the two men was so strongly accentuated that it might have tempted a painter to take up his brush. David had the physical conformation which nature bestows on beings predestined to arduous effort, whether spectacular or unobserved. His broad chest was set between robust shoulders which had the same fullness as all his members. His face, tanned brown, but florid and plump, rising from a sturdy neck, and framed in an abundant forest of black hair, reminded one at first of Boileau's cathedral canons, ruddy and glowing with health. But further inspection revealed, in the curve of his full lips, his cleft chin, the square cut of his nose with its sensitively chiselled nostrils – and above all in his eyes! – the steady flame of a first and only love, the sagacity of a thinker, the ardent melancholy of a mind capable of scanning the horizon from end to end and taking cognizance of all its undulations, one which readily found disillusion in imagined joys after subjecting them to the hard, clear light of analysis. If one could divine in this countenance the darting flashes of genius in eruption, one could also see the cinders lining the crater: the hope burning within it was damped down by a profound consciousness of the social obscurity in which humble birth and lack of means confine so many lofty spirits. In contrast with this needy printer nauseated with his occupation though it brought him so much in contact with intellectual activity, in contrast with this squat, ungainly Silene who drank as from a goblet deep draughts of science and poetry, seeking intoxication from them in order to forget the miseries of provincial life, Lucien had the grace of bearing with which sculptors have endowed the Indian Bacchus. His face had the distinction of line found in antique beauty: he had a Grecian brow and nose, the smooth whiteness of a woman's skin, and eyes of so deep a blue that they seemed to be black – eyes brimming with tenderness, their whites so limpid as to vie with those of a child. Above these fine orbs, edged with long, light brown lashes, were eye-brows such as a Chinese brush might have traced. A silky down gave a touch of colour to the cheeks and harmonized with that of his fair, naturally curly hair. An Olympian suavity shone forth on his golden-white temples. His short but gently curving chin bore the impress of incomparable nobility. The smile of a mourning angel hovered over lips whose coral was off-set by impeccably white teeth. He had the hands of a well-born man, elegant hands whose every gesture men felt constrained to obey and which a woman would have wanted to kiss. He was slender but of average height. Any man looking at his feet would have been tempted to take him for a girl in disguise, the more so because, like most men of subtle, not to say astute mind, he had a woman's shapely hips. This is usually reliable as a clue to character, and was so in Lucien's case, for his restless turn of mind often brought him, when he came to analyse the present state of society, to adopt the depravity of outlook characteristic of diplomats, who believe that any means however shameful they may be, are justified by success. One of the great misfortunes to which great intelligence is subjected is the necessity of comprehending all things, vice and virtue alike.

These two young people passed sovereign judgement on society the more readily because of the inferiority of their own status, for unappreciated men make up for their lowly position by the disdainful eye they cast upon the world. Moreover their despair was the more bitter because it made them press on more impetuously to what they regarded as their true destiny. Lucien had done much reading and much comparing; David did much thinking and much pondering. Although the printer seemed to enjoy the robust health of a peasant, he was a man of melancholic, even sickly genius and was lacking in self-confidence; whereas Lucien, possessing more initiative but less stability of mind, displayed an audacity which tallied ill with his languid, almost frail though femininely graceful physique. His was superlatively a Gascon temperament, bold, courageous, adventurous, overrating the bright and minimizing the gloomy side of things, never recoiling from a profitable misdeed and making light of vice if it served as a stepping-stone. These ambitious tendencies were so far kept in check by the beautiful illusions of youth which inclined him towards the nobler means which men enamoured of glory adopt in preference to any others. As yet he was at grips only with his own desires and not the difficulties of life, with his own potentialities and not that moral laxity which sets a terrible temptation to volatile spirits. Deeply fascinated by Lucien's brilliance of mind, David continued to admire him even while correcting the errors into which the *furia francese* flung him. The upright David's timidity of character was in conflict with his robustness of constitution, though he did not lack the doggedness of northern Frenchmen. Quick at discerning all difficulties, he was nevertheless ready to face them without losing heart; and he tempered the firmness of a truly apostolic rectitude with gracious and inexhaustible forbearance. In this long-established friendship, one of them loved the other to the point of idolatory: it was David. And so Lucien assumed control like a woman conscious of being loved, while David gave willing obedience. His friend's physical beauty implied an ascendancy which David acknowledged, believing himself to be uncouth and commonplace.

'The patient ox should draw the plough, the bird should be carefree,' the printer told himself. 'I will be the ox, Lucien shall be the eagle.'

For nearly three years therefore, the two friends had had one common destiny, one bright future ahead of them. They read the masterpieces which, once peace was proclaimed, loomed up on the literary and scientific horizon: the works of Schiller, Goethe, Lord Byron, Walter Scott, Jean-Paul Richter, Berzelius, Sir Humphry Davy, Cuvier, Lamartine etc. They drew warmth from these flaming hearths, made their own abortive writing efforts, took them up, laid them down, took them up again with ardour, toiling on continually without exhausting their unflagging youthful energy. Both were poor but fired with the love of art and science, and they forgot their present poverty in their efforts to lay the foundation of their future renown.

'Lucien, do you know what I have just received from Paris?' asked the printer, drawing a little 18mo volume from his pocket. 'Listen.'

And David read, as only a poet could read, André Chénier's bucolic poem entitled *Néère* and the one entitled *The Love-Sick Youth*, followed by the elegy on suicide which is couched in the style of antiquity, and finally Chénier's last two iambic poems.

'So that is what André Chénier is like!' Lucien exclaimed

again and again. 'It drives one to despair,' he repeated for the third time when David, too moved to go on reading, handed the volume over to him, – 'A poet discovered by another poet!' he cried, when he saw by whom the preface was signed.

'After writing all these poems,' David continued, 'Chénier still thought he had produced nothing worthy of publication.'

In his turn Lucien read out the epic passage from *The Blind Poet* and several elegies. When he came to the fragment:

Have they not bliss? Then there is none on earth,

he kissed the book, and the two friends wept, for they were both of them madly in love. The vine-shoots were coming into colour, the aged walls of the house, full of fissures and bulges, with ugly cracks running across them in irregular fashion, had been adorned with the fluting, the embossments, the bas-reliefs and the innumerable embellishments of some strange, faery architecture. Fantasy had scattered its blossoms and rubies over the dingy little courtyard. For David, André Chénier's Camilla had changed into his beloved Eve, and for Lucien into a great lady to whom he was paying court. Poetry had draped the majestic folds of its starry gown over the printing-office in which 'monkeys' and 'bears' were performing their antics. It was just on five o'clock, but the two friends were neither hungry nor thirsty; life was one golden dream, and all the riches of the world lay at their feet. They could descry that patch of blue on the horizon to which Hope points a finger for those whose life is overclouded, while saying with siren voice: 'Go, spread your wings: you will find escape from misery in that stretch of gold, silver or azure.' At this instant an apprentice named Cérizet, a Paris street-urchin whom David had brought to Angoulême, opened the little glass door from the workshop to the court, and indicated where the two friends sat to a stranger who came towards them and gave a bow.

'Monsieur,' he said to David, pulling an enormous copy-book from his pocket. 'Here is a memoir I should like to have printed. Would you give me an estimate of the cost?'

'Monsieur, we do not print such sizable manuscripts,' David replied without even glancing at the copybook. 'Go and see Messrs Cointet.'

'But we have a case of very pretty type which would be suitable,' Lucien added, taking the manuscript. 'Perhaps you would be good enough to come again tomorrow and leave us your work so that we may reckon up the cost of printing.'

'Is it not Monsieur Lucien Chardon whom I have the honour . . .?'

'Himself, sir,' answered the proof-reader.

'I am happy, sir,' the author said, 'to make the acquaintance of a young poet of such brilliant promise. I come from Madame de Bargeton.'

Lucien reddened on hearing this name and stammered a few words to express his gratitude for the interest Madame de Bargeton was taking in him. David noticed the blush and his friend's embarrassment, and left him in conversation with this country gentleman, who had written a memorandum on the culture of silkworms, and was impelled by vanity to get into print so that his colleagues of the Agricultural Society could read his monograph.

'Well, well, Lucien!' said David when the gentleman had gone away. 'Can it be that you're in love with Madame de Bargeton?'

'Desperately!'

'But there's a wider gulf of prejudice between you and her than if she were in Pekin and you in Greenland!'

'Where there's a will there's a way between people in love,' said Lucien, with his gaze turned down.

'You'll forget all about us,' replied the beautiful Eve's timorous admirer.

'On the contrary, it may be that I have given up my lady for your sake,' cried Lucien.

'What do you mean?'

'Although I love her, and in spite of the diverse interests which prompt me to obtain a footing in her house, I have told her I would never return there if a man whose talents are superior to mine, who is worthy of a glorious future, if David

Séchard, my brother and friend, were not accepted there. Her reply should be waiting for me at home. But although all the local aristocracy is invited there for this evening to a reading of my verses, if the reply is negative, I will never set foot again in Madame de Bargeton's house.'

David gave Lucien a vigorous handshake after wiping the tears from his eyes. The clock struck six.

'Eve will be getting anxious. Good-bye,' said Lucien abruptly. He made off, leaving David a prey to emotions which at his age alone are felt with such intensity, and above all in the case of two cygnets whose wings had not yet been clipped by life in the provinces.

'A heart of gold!' cried David, following Lucien with his eye as he walked through the workshop.

Lucien strode down to L'Houmeau through the handsome Promenade de Beaulieu, the rue du Minage and the Porte Saint-Pierre. You may know by the fact of his taking the longest way that Madame de Bargeton's house was situated on this route. It gave him so much pleasure to pass under her windows – even though she was unaware of it – that for two months he had not returned home by the Porte-Palet.

As he passed beneath the trees of Beaulieu, he surveyed the distance separating Angoulême from L'Houmeau. Local manners and customs had raised spiritual barriers between them which were much more difficult to cross than the slopes which Lucien was now descending. This ambitious young man, who had just gained admission to the Bargeton mansion by making his poetic reputation a bridge between town and suburb, was as anxious about his patroness's decision as can be a court favourite apprehensive of disgrace when he has tried to extend his power. These words must seem obscure to those who have not yet observed the manners peculiar to cities divided into an upper and a lower town; but it is all the more necessary at this point to make some remarks on Angoulême because they will help us to understand Madame de Bargeton, one of the most important characters in this story.

2. Madame de Bargeton

ANGOULÊME is an ancient town built on the summit of a cone-shaped rock towering over the meadows through which the river Charente runs. From the Périgord direction this rock forms a long ridge which terminates abruptly on the Paris–Bordeaux road, thus forming a sort of promontory marked out by three picturesque valleys. The importance of this town at the time of the religious wars is attested by its ramparts, its city gates and the ruins of a fortress perched on the peak of the rock. Its situation formerly made it a strategic point which was equally valuable to Catholics and Calvinists; but its erstwhile strength constitutes its weakness today; the ramparts and the excessive slope of the rock have prevented it from sprawling out over the Charente valley and condemned it to the direst stagnation. About the time when our story begins, the Government was trying to push the town forward into Périgord by building the prefectoral palace, a marine school and military establishments along the hill, and laying plans for roads. But commerce had moved in the opposite direction. Long since, the suburb of L'Houmeau had spread out like a bed of mushrooms at the foot of the rock and along the river banks, parallel to which runs the main road from Paris to Bordeaux. The paper-mills of Angoulême are well-famed: during the last three centuries they had of necessity established themselves along the Charente and its tributaries, where waterfalls were available. At Ruelle the State had set up its most important foundry for naval cannons. Haulage, post-houses, inns, wheelwrights' workshops, public transport services, all the industries which depend on roads and waterways clustered round the base of Angoulême in order to avoid the difficulties presented by access to the town itself. Naturally tanneries, laundries and all water-side trades remained within reach of the Charente, which was also lined with brandy warehouses, depots for all raw materials conveyed by water and in fact for all kinds of goods in transit. And so the suburb of L'Houmeau became a busy and prosperous town, a second Angoulême, arousing resentment in the upper town where the administration, the Bishop's palace, the courts of justice and the aristocracy remained. For this reason L'Houmeau, despite its increasing activity and importance, was a mere appendage of Angoulême. The nobility and the political authority held sway on high, commerce and finance down below: two social zones, everywhere and constantly hostile to each other; as a consequence, it is difficult to guess which of the two towns more cordially hates its rival. This state of things had remained fairly quiescent during the Empire; nine years of Restoration government had aggravated it. Most of the houses in Upper Angoulême are inhabited either by noble families or by long-established middle-class families living on their investments and constituting a sort of autochtonous nation to which strangers are never admitted. It is a rare occurrence if, even after living in the place for a couple of hundred years and contracting a marriage alliance with one of the original families, a family which has migrated from some neighbouring province is received into the fold: the native population still considers it a newcomer. Prefects, Receivers-General and civil service officials who have succeeded one another for forty years have tried to civilize these ancient families perched on their rock like so many watchful ravens: these families have attended their receptions and eaten their dinners, but they have persistently refused to welcome them to their own houses. Disdainful, disparaging, jealous and miserly, these houses intermarry and close their ranks to prevent anyone entering or leaving; they know nothing of the creations of modern luxury; in their view, to send a child to Paris is to seal its doom. Such prudence illustrates the antiquated manners and customs of these families, far gone in unintelligent royalism, fanatically devout though not genuinely pious, all of them as rigid in their way of life as the town itself and the rock on which it is built. And yet Angoulême enjoys a great reputation in the adjacent provinces for the education young people receive there. Neighbouring towns send their daughters to its boarding-schools and convents. It is easy to imagine the influence exerted by class-consciousness in Angoulême and L'Houmeau. Business people are rich, the aristocracy is generally impoverished. Each vents its spite on the other by an equal show of contempt. Even the middle classes in Angoulême join in this antagonism. A shopkeeper in the upper town cannot put enough scorn into his voice when he refers to a merchant of the suburb as a man from L'Houmeau. The Restoration, when it defined the status of the French nobility and awakened its hopes of something which only a general social upheaval could bring about, widened the moral gulf which, far more than the difference of locality, divided Angoulême from L'Houmeau. The aristocratic society of Angoulême, at that time at one with the Government, became more exclusive than anywhere else in France. Anyone living in L'Houmeau was virtually a pariah. Hence the deep, underground hatreds which were to inspire a terrible unanimity in those who engineered the insurrection of 1830 and destroyed the elements of a durable social community in France. The arrogance of the court nobility was a cause of alienation between the throne and the provincial nobility, and the latter alienated the middle-classes by wounding all their susceptibilities. It follows that to introduce a man from L'Houmeau, the son of a chemist, into Madame de Bargeton's circle constituted in itself a minor revolution. And who had started such ideas? Lamartine and Victor Hugo, Casimir Delavigne and Canalis, Villemain and Monsieur Aignan, Soumet and Tissot, Etienne and D'Avrigny, Benjamin Constant and Lamennais, Victor Cousin and Michaud: in short, all the older and younger literary celebrities, Liberals as well as Royalists. Madame de Bargeton was enamoured of art and letters, an extravagance of taste, a mania which Angoulême openly deplored; but some justification for it must be offered by sketching the life of this woman who was born for celebrity but whom an inevitable train of circumstances maintained in obscurity: her influence was to determine Lucien's destinies.

Monsieur de Bargeton was the great-grandson of an alderman of Bordeaux, Mirault by name, who in the reign of

Louis XIII had risen to noble status by virtue of his long-exercised function. Under Louis XIV his son, now Mirault de Bargeton, became an officer in the Household Guards and made such a lucrative marriage that, in the time of Louis XV, his son became purely and simply Monsieur de Bargeton. This Monsieur de Bargeton, grandson of the worshipful alderman, was so intent on behaving like a model nobleman that he squandered all the family property and checked its advance towards prosperity. Two of his brothers, great-uncles of the present-day Monsieur de Bargeton, reverted to commerce, so that there are still Miraults in business in Bordeaux. Since the Bargeton estate, situated in the province of Angoulême in dependency on the fief of La Rochefoucauld, was entailed, as well as a mansion in Angoulême which was called Bargeton House, the grandson of Monsieur de Bargeton the Squanderer inherited these two properties. In 1789 he lost all his effective feudal rights and had nothing more than the income from his land, which amounted to about ten thousand francs a year. If his grandfather had followed the glorious example set by Bargeton the First and Bargeton the Second, Bargeton the Fifth, who may be styled Bargeton the Silent, could have become the Marquis de Bargeton. He might have married into some great family and risen to be a duke and peer like so many others; whereas in 1805 he was very flattered to marry Mademoiselle Marie-Louise-Anaïs de Nègrepelisse, the daughter of a country gentleman who had long since been lost sight of in his manor-house although he belonged to the younger branch of one of the most ancient families in southern France. There was a Nègrepelisse among the hostages who stood surety for Saint Louis; but the chief of the elder branch bears the illustrious name of d'Espard, acquired under Henri IV through marriage with the heiress of that family. This gentleman, the younger son of a younger son, drew his subsistence from the property of his wife, a small estate near Barbezieux, which he exploited very successfully indeed by taking his own corn to market, distilling his own brandy and taking no heed of ridicule so long as he could fill his money-bags and enlarge his domain from time to time.

Circumstances which are unusual enough in the depths of the provinces had inspired in Madame de Bargeton a taste for music and literature. During the Revolution, a certain Abbé Niollant, the brightest pupil of the Abbé Roze, went into hiding in the little castle of Escarbas, bringing his musical compositions with him. He had amply paid for the old squire's hospitality by educating his daughter Anaïs, Naïs for short; without this lucky chance she would have been left to herself or, by a still greater mischance, her education would have been entrusted to some ignorant chamber-maid. The Abbé was not only a musician: he was well versed in literature and knew Italian and German. And so he taught these two languages – and counterpoint – to Mademoiselle de Nègrepelisse; he revealed to her the great literary works of France, Italy and Germany and fingered out with her the music of all the great composers. Finally, as an antidote to the inactivity resulting from the deep solitude to which political events condemned him, he taught her Greek and Latin, and gave her a smattering of the natural sciences. Her mother's presence in no way modified this masculine education of a young person whom life in the country already inclined to too great independence.

The Abbé Niollant, a man full of poetry and enthusiasm, was remarkable above all else for possessing that outlook peculiar to artists which, though in many respects commendable, rises superior to bourgeois ideas through its freedom of judgement and broad-mindedness. In mundane society, such intellectual boldness escapes censure because it is original and strikes deep, but in private life it may be found harmful on account of the deviations it may inspire. The Abbé was a man of feeling, and so his ideas were contagious for a girl whose exuberance of mind, so natural in the young, was encouraged by the solitude of country life. The Abbé imbued his pupil with his own spirit of enquiry and readiness to pass judgement; and it did not occur to him that qualities essential in a man can become defects in a woman destined to the humble occupation of wife and mother. Although he constantly reminded his pupil that additional graciousness and modesty should go with more extensive knowledge, Mademoiselle de

Nègrepelisse acquired an excellent opinion of herself and conceived a sturdy contempt for humanity at large. Surrounded by inferiors and domestics who were at her beck and call, she had all the haughtiness of great ladies but not their politeness in dispensing soothing blandishments. Flattered in every one of her particular vanities by a humble abbé who admired her as his own creation, she was so unfortunate as to find no criterion for self-criticism. Lack of company is one of the great drawbacks of country life. When no relationships exist which call for minor concessions in dress and deportment, we lose the habit of accepting inconvenience for the sake of others and a deterioration sets in which affects our inner and our outer selves. Subjected to no check from social exchange, Mademoiselle de Nègrepelisse's bold habits of thought passed into her manners and expression; she adopted that cavalier air which at first sight betokens originality but which is only fitting for women who lead an adventurous life. And so this kind of education, which would have had its rough edges smoothed down in higher social circles, was destined to bring ridicule on her in Angoulême, once her worshippers ceased to divinize her errors, which could appear graceful only in youth. As for Monsieur de Nègrepelisse, he would have given all his daughters' books to save a sick ox from dying; he was so miserly that he would not have allotted her a farthing more than the income to which she was entitled, even to the extent of buying the smallest thing needed for her education. The Abbé died in 1802, before his dear child was married – a match of which he would no doubt have disapproved. When the Abbé was dead, the old nobleman was at a loss to know how to deal with his daughter. He felt too weak to sustain the impending conflict between his avarice and the self-will of a daughter who had nothing to keep her busy. Like all young people who have left the beaten track which women ought to follow, Naïs had weighed up the idea of marriage: the prospect did not entice her. She objected to submitting her intelligence and her person to any of the men of poor calibre and negative personality who had come her way. She wanted to command and was expected to obey. Had the choice confronted her of yielding to the gross whims or incompatible tastes of a husband or elopement with a congenial lover, she would not have hesitated. Monsieur de Nègrepelisse was still aristocratic enough to fear an ill-sorted union. Like many fathers, he resolved to marry off his daughter, less for her sake than for his own peace of mind. He wanted to find an unintelligent nobleman or country squire, incapable of haggling over the account he must render to his daughter as custodian of her mother's estate, sufficiently devoid of wit and will for Naïs to be free to behave as she pleased, and unmercenary enough to marry her without a dowry. But how was he to find a son-in-law whom he and his daughter would both judge suitable? Such a man would be a paragon among sons-in-law. To serve this double purpose, Monsieur de Nègrepelisse took stock of the men in the province, and Monsieur de Bargeton seemed to be the only one who answered his requirements. Monsieur de Bargeton, a man in his forties, very much the worse for the amorous dissipations of his youth, was reckoned to be remarkably deficient in intelligence; but he had just enough common sense to manage his property, and good enough manners to live among the Angoulême *élite* without committing social solecisms or follies. Monsieur de Nègrepelisse quite bluntly explained to his daughter the negative value of the model husband he was offering her, and showed how conducive to her own happiness the match could be: she was marrying a coat of arms which was already two hundred years old, for the Bargetons bear *quarterly, or, three stag's heads caboshed gules, 2 and 1, alternant with three bull's heads sable, 1 and 2; barry of six azure and argent, the azure charged with six escallops or, 3, 2 and 1*. Thus furnished with a male chaperon, she would manage her fortune as she pleased under the ægis of a covering name and with the aid of relationships which her wit and beauty would procure for her in Paris. Naïs was much attracted by the prospect of such freedom. Monsieur de Bargeton thought he was making a brilliant marriage, reckoning that before long his father-in-law would leave him the landed property he was so lovingly rounding off. At the time however it looked as if Monsieur de Nègrepelisse might well have to write his son-in-law's epitaph.

Madame de Bargeton was by now thirty-six years old and her husband fifty-eight. This disparity of age stood out the more strongly because Monsieur de Bargeton looked like a man of seventy, whereas his wife could still, with impunity, give herself girlish airs, dress in pink and wear adolescent hair-styles. Although their income did not exceed twelve thousand francs a year, they were counted among the half-dozen wealthiest couples in the old town, merchants and administrative officials excepted. The need to keep on good terms with her father – Madame de Bargeton was waiting for his inheritance in order to move to Paris, and he was to keep her waiting so long that his son-in-law predeceased him – obliged the Bargeton couple to remain in Angoulême, where Naïs's brilliant mental qualities and the wealth of sensibility lying dormant in her heart were destined never to fructify, but rather, in course of time, to invite ridicule. Indeed, ridicule is most often incurred by the carrying of fine sentiment, good points and special ability to extremes. A haughtiness which is not toned down by intercourse with polite society takes on a certain rigidity when it can only find outlet in trivialities instead of expanding in contact with people capable of lofty feeling. Rapturous emotion, which is a virtue within virtue, which can turn women into saints and is the source of hidden devotion and splendid poetry, becomes mere pretentiousness when it expends itself on the petty trifles of provincial life. Far removed from the centre in which great minds scintillate, in which the very atmosphere is laden with ideas, in which everything is in constant renewal, education becomes out-dated, and taste grows as stale as stagnant water. For lack of grist, passions dwindle because they exaggerate the importance of insignificant things. That is the reason why avarice and scandal-mongering poison life in the provinces. Very quickly, the most distinguished person adopts the narrow ideas and unprepossessing manners of those around him. Thus perish men born with greatness in them and women who, under the discipline of social education and schooled by superior minds, might have been charming. Madame de Bargeton took up the lyre on the slightest occasion, making no difference between poems of personal inspiration and poems for public consumption. There are in fact feelings which others cannot understand and which one should keep to oneself. Certainly, a sunset is a great subject for poetry: but is a woman not ridiculous when she describes it in high-sounding words before a materially-minded audience? It affords delights which only two people, two poetic minds, two hearts can savour. Her weakness was to use long-winded sentences stiff with bombastic expressions, ingeniously called *tartines* (slices of bread and butter) in the jargon of journalism: newspapers serve them up every morning to their readers, who gulp them down however indigestible they may be. She was wonderfully prodigal of superlatives and weighted her conversation with them, so that the most trivial things assumed gigantic proportions. From that time onwards she squandered verbs like *typicize, individualize, synthesize, dramatize, superiorize, analyse, poeticize, prosaicize, collossify, angelify, neologize and tragicize*; for I must needs momentarily do violence to language in order to depict the eccentricities which are common to certain women. Her mind moreover suffered from the same inflammation as her language. Her feelings were as dithyrambic as her utterance. She had palpitations, went into ecstasies, waxed enthusiastic over every occurrence: a Grey Sister's act of self-devotion, the execution of the Faucher brothers, the publication of Victor d'Arlincourt's *Ipsiboé* or Lewis's *Anaconda*, Lavalette's escape from prison and the exploit of a friend of hers, a woman who had frightened burglars away by putting on a gruff male voice. In her estimation, everything was sublime, extraordinary, unheard-of, divine, marvellous. She became heated and wrathful, her spirits drooped, soared upwards and flagged again; she was elated or down in the depths; tears welled up into her eyes. She expended her vitality in perpetual admiration or consumed it in unaccountable disdain. She grew interested in the Pasha of Janina, would have been thrilled to fight for her virtue in his seraglio, thought it rather grand to be sewn up in a sack and thrown into the Bosphorus. She envied Lady Stanhope, that blue-stocking of the desert. She longed to become a Sister of Saint Camilla and go off to die of yellow fever while nursing the sick in

Barcelona: what a great, what a noble destiny! In short, she thirsted for everything but her own clear rivulet of life, hidden in the grass. She worshipped Lord Byron, Jean-Jacques Rousseau and all those who led poetic and dramatic lives. She had a tear for every misfortune and sounded a fanfare for every victory. She sympathized with Napoleon in defeat, she sympathized with Mehemet-Ali's massacre of the tyrants in Egypt. In short she put a halo round the heads of men of genius and believed they lived on fragrance and effulgence. Many people thought she was a crackpot, though not dangerously so; but certainly, to any perspicacious observer, all this would have looked like the debris of a magnificent love, a structure which had collapsed as soon as it rose from the ground: the ruins of a heavenly Jerusalem, in fact love without a lover. And they would have been right. The story of the first eighteen years of Madame de Bargeton's married life can briefly be told. For some time she lived on her own substance or on distant hopes. Then, once she recognized that the life in Paris to which she aspired was barred to her through the mediocrity of her fortune, she began scrutinizing the people about her, and her sense of isolation made her shudder. There was no man in her circle capable of inspiring her with one of those follies into which women fling themselves when spurred on by the desperation born of a life which has no outlet, which is uneventful and devoid of interest. She could count on nothing, not even on a chance event, for there are some lives in which chance never intervenes. At the time when the Empire was at the height of its splendour, when Napoleon passed into Spain and sent the flower of his armies there, this woman's hopes, hitherto frustrated, reawakened. Curiosity naturally prompted her to contemplate those heroes who, at the Imperial command, conquered Europe and renewed the fabulous exploits of the chivalric ages. Even the most parsimonious and refractory towns were obliged to give ceremonious welcome to the Imperial Guard, with mayors and prefects meeting it at the city gates and mouthing their ready-made speeches as if they were greeting royalty. Madame de Bargeton, attending a gala offered to the town by a visiting regiment, fell in love with a young gentleman, a subaltern whom the crafty Napoleon had lured with the prospect of a field-marshal's baton. This restrained, lofty passion, so different from the facile, ephemeral passions of those days, received a chaste hallowing from the hands of Death. At Wagram, a cannon-ball smashed the only portrait which testified to Madame de Bargeton's beauty, and which the Marquis de Cante-Croix had been carrying next to his heart. She long wept for this handsome young man, who had become a colonel after two campaigns, who was aflame with dreams of glory and love, who treasured letters from Naïs more than any military distinction. Grief cast a veil of sadness over her face: a cloud which only lifted as she reached that dreaded time of life when a woman begins to regret her years of beauty which have fled past without her enjoying them, when she sees her roses fading, when a yearning for love is reborn with the desire to prolong the smiling days of youth. All the qualities which set her apart began to sting like so many wounds at the moment when she was struck by the chill of provincial life. Like the ermine, she would have died of chagrin if perchance she had let herself be soiled by her contact with the men who, after a good dinner, thought only of gambling away a few sous in the evening. Her pride preserved her from the sorry intrigues of provincial love. Forced to choose between the empty existence of the men around her and non-existence, so superior a woman must needs have preferred the latter. And so she found marriage and social life as monotonous as life in a convent. She lived for poetry as a Carmelite lives for religion. The works of famous foreign writers, unknown until then, those published between 1815 and 1821, the great treatises of those two eagles among thinkers, Charles de Bonald and Joseph de Maistre, and finally even the less inspiring works of French literature, which was then putting forth such vigorous shoots, embellished her solitude but brought her no suppleness of mind or personality. She stood erect and sturdy like a tree which lightning has blasted but not brought down. Her dignity grew strained, her social ascendancy made her affected and over-refined. As with all those royalties who received the adulation of mediocre courtiers, she ruled by virtue of her shortcomings. Such was Madame de Bargeton's past: a chilling story which had to be told in order to explain her relationship with Lucien, who had come into her circle in rather singular circumstances. During the previous winter, a person had turned up in the town who had brought some brightness to Madame de Bargeton's dreary life. The post of Director of Indirect Taxes had fallen vacant, and Monsieur de Barante sent a man to fill it whose adventurous past pleaded sufficiently in his favour for feminine curiosity to provide him with a passport to the salon of the queen of Angoulême society.

Monsieur du Châtelet had been plain Sixte Châtelet when he came into the world, but in 1806 he had had the bright idea of assuming the particle. He was one of those agreeable young men who, under Napoleon, evaded conscription by dint of basking in the rays of the Imperial sunlight. The first post he occupied was that of private secretary to a princess of the Imperial family. Monsieur du Châtelet had all the varieties of incapacity which such a post required. He was well-built and good-looking, a good dancer, expert at billiards, skilled in all games, with a moderate talent for amateur theatricals and drawing-room ballads. He readily applauded other people's witticisms, was accommodating, compliant, envious, knowing everything and nothing. Though quite unmusical, he managed somehow or other to strum a piano accompaniment for any woman who could be reluctantly persuaded to warble a ballad which she had been laboriously practising for a whole month. Totally insensitive to poetry, he would boldly ask leave to take ten minutes' stroll in order to produce some impromptu poem, some quatrain as dull as ditch-water, with more rhyme than reason in it. Monsieur du Châtelet was also an adept at completing the pieces of tapestry on which the Princess had sketched the floral designs; with infinite grace he would hold up the skeins of silk for her to wind off, regaling her the while with small talk replete with thinly-veiled improprieties. Though ignorant of the art of painting, he could copy a landscape, hit off a profile in crayon, dash off

43

a dress design and colour it. In short he possessed all those minor talents which were a high road to fortune in an age when women were more influential in public affairs than people suppose. He had a great opinion of his skill in diplomacy, the science of those who lack any other and seem profound because they have nothing in them; a science however which it is useful to possess, since the fact of possessing it is demonstrated by the mere exercise of its major functions, since it allows ignoramuses to be reticent and to take refuge in mysterious shakings of the head; since, in short, the most accomplished votary of this science is the man who swims along with his head above the stream of events in such a way that he seems to be determining its course: it thus becomes a question of specific levity rather than gravity. In this sphere, as in the arts, you will find a thousand mediocrities for one man of genius. Yet, in spite of the services this Gentleman-in-Ordinary (and Extraordinary) rendered to her Imperial Highness, his protectress did not use her credit to get him into the Council of State. Not that he would not have made a delectable Master of Requests, like so many of his kind; but the Princess preferred to have him dancing attendance on her. However he was made a baron and was sent to Cassel as Envoy-Extraordinary, and indeed his appearance there was very extraordinary. In other words, Napoleon used him as diplomatic courier in the middle of a crisis. At the moment when the Empire collapsed, the Baron du Châtelet had been promised the post of chargé d'affaires at the court of Jerome in Westphalia. Having missed obtaining what he called a 'family' ambassadorship, despair took hold of him; he made a journey to Egypt with General Armand Montriveau. Separated from his companion by some strange mishaps, he had wandered about for two years from desert to desert and from tribe to tribe as a captive of the Arabs who successively sold him to one another without drawing the slightest advantage from his talents. At last he reached the territory of the Imam of Mascate while Montriveau was making for Tangiers; but at Mascate he was lucky enough to find an English vessel on the point of setting sail, and he managed to return to Paris a year before his travelling companion. His recent misfortunes, a few long-standing connections and services rendered to certain personages then in favour, brought him to the attention of the President of the Council, who appointed him to a post under Monsieur de Barante, with the prospect of succeeding to the first vacant directorship of taxes. The part Monsieur du Châtelet had played in her Imperial Highness's service, his reputation as a ladies' man, the singular events and sufferings attendant upon his travels in Egypt, all served to excite curiosity in the women of Angoulême. Having studied polite manners in the Upper Town, Monsieur le Baron Sixte du Châtelet adapted his conduct to them. He played the invalid and took on the role of a *blasé* and disillusioned man. He was for ever holding his head in his hands as if his sufferings gave him not a moment's respite – a little mannerism which reminded people of his travels and made him an interesting person. He visited the higher authorities, the General, the Prefect, the Receiver-General and the Bishop; but everywhere he went he was polite, cool and slightly disdainful, like all men who have not found their right place and are awaiting preferential treatment from the Government. He left his social talents to be divined, and they gained from not being known. Then, when he had brought people to desire his company without having wearied their curiosity, when he had recognized that the men were nonentities and expertly studied the women for several Sundays in the Cathedral, he discerned in Madame de Bargeton the person whose intimate circle it would suit him to join. He put his faith in music as an open sesame to this great house to which strangers found admission so difficult. He secretly purchased a *Mass* by Miroir and practised it on the piano; then, one fine Sunday when all Angoulême society was at mass, he enraptured the uninitiate by playing the organ, and revived the interest attached to his person by getting the minor clergy to commit the indiscretion of advertising his name. As Madame de Bargeton left the church, she paid him a compliment and expressed regret at not having had the opportunity of a musical evening with him. During the conversation thus carefully engineered, he naturally contrived to obtain the passport which no amount of asking would have procured him. The artful Baron went to call on the first lady of Angoulême and paid her compromising attentions. This elderly gallant – he was forty-five – perceived that the lady had all her youth to retrieve, rich talents to be fostered, and glimpsed the possibility of her becoming a widow with great expectations, in short of making a marriage alliance with the Nègrepelisse family, and so establishing a connection in Paris with the Marquise d'Espard, whose influence could help him to resume his political career. Naïs seemed to him like a fine tree ruined by a dark tangle of mistletoe and he resolved to tend it, prune it, encourage its growth and gather fruit from it. The nobility of Angoulême cried out against the introduction of a Giaour into the Kasba, for Madame de Bargeton's salon was a circle which admitted none but the purest social strain. Only the Bishop was an habitual visitor there; the Prefect was received only two or three times a year; the Receiver-General never set foot inside it – Madame de Bargeton attended his receptions and musical evenings, but never dined at his house. So that to exclude the Receiver-General while welcoming a mere Director of Taxes seemed like turning the hierarchy upside-down: this appeared inexplicable to the officials thus disdained.

Anyone able to form some idea of the petty snobbery which for that matter is to be found in every social sphere will surely understand what deference was paid to the Bargeton household by the bourgeoisie of Angoulême. For the inhabitants of L'Houmeau, the majesty of this small-scale Louvre, the glory which radiated from this provincial Hôtel de Rambouillet were as remote from them as the sun itself. All the people who gathered there had the most pitiable mental qualities, the meanest intelligence, and were the sorriest specimens of humanity within a radius of fifty miles. Political discussions consisted of verbose but impassioned commonplaces: the *Quotidienne* was regarded as lukewarm in its royalism; Louis XVIII himself was considered to be a Jacobin. The women were mostly stupid, devoid of grace and badly dressed; every one of them was marred by some imperfection; everything fell short of the mark, conversation, clothes, mind and body alike. Châtelet would not have put up with it if he had not had designs on Madame de Bargeton. Nevertheless, comportment and class consciousness, gentlemanly airs, the arrogance of the lesser nobility, acquaintance with the rules of decorum, all served to cloak the void within them. Royalist feeling was much more real there than in the upper reaches of Parisian life: a noteworthy attachment to the Bourbons, whatever their shortcomings, was much in evidence. A social group like this one might be compared, if such a simile is permissible, to a service of silver plate, antiquated in design, tarnished, and yet solid. The very rigidity of its political opinions was a kind of loyalty. The distance kept between it and the bourgeoisie and its relative unapproachability, placed it as it were on a pinnacle and gave it museum-piece value. The inhabitants of Angoulême set a certain price on each of these noblemen, in much the same way as cowrie shells take the place of silver currency among the negroes of Bambarra. Several women to whom du Châtelet paid flattering attention and who discerned in him a superiority of parts which the men of their own circle lacked, appeased the insurrection provoked by wounded self-respect: they all hoped to be next in succession to her Imperial Highness. The social sticklers opined that one would meet the intruder in Madame de Bargeton's salon, but that he would be received in no other house. He met with some impertinent treatment, but kept his end up by cultivating the clergy. Also he was indulgent to the defects which the social queen of Angoulême owed to her rural upbringing; he brought her all the latest books and read the newly-published poetry to her. They went into raptures together over the works of the young poets. Her raptures were genuine, but he was bored: he tolerated the Romantic poets, though, as a supporter of the Imperial school, he was incapable of understanding them. Madame de Bargeton, fired with enthusiasm for the literary renaissance due to Royalist influence, adored Monsieur de Chateaubriand for having hailed Victor Hugo as an *enfant sublime*. Saddened because she was only in remote touch with genius, she yearned

47

for Paris, where all the great men resided. Monsieur du Châtelet then imagined it would be a marvellous thing to inform her that there existed in Angoulême yet another *enfant sublime*, a young poet whose brilliance, though he was not yet aware of the fact, outshone that of the new constellations that were rising in Paris. A budding genius had been born in l'Houmeau! The headmaster of the college had shown the Baron some admirable lines from Lucien's pen. This poor and modest boy was positively a Chatterton, yet he had the right sort of political ideas and none of that ferocious hatred for social eminence which had prompted the English poet to lampoon his benefactors. Around Madame de Bargeton five or six persons clustered who shared her taste for art and letters, one of them because he could scrape the fiddle, another because his sepia drawings spoilt a good deal of blank paper, another in his capacity as president of the local Agricultural Society, and yet another because he had a bass voice which enabled him to sing *Se fiato in corpo avete* like a huntsman bawling a view-halloo. Amid these odd figures, she felt like a starveling at a stage banquet where every course is made of cardboard. And so her joy on hearing this piece of news was indescribable. She simply had to see this poet, this angelic being! She went into fits of ecstasy and raved about him for hours on end. Two days later the former diplomatic courier had arranged, through the headmaster, to introduce Lucien to Madame de Bargeton.

You alone, poor provincial helots for whom social gaps yawn wider than in Paris, where they are narrowing from day to day, you, whom inexorable barriers exclude from that fine world within which each social group anathematizes and cries *Raca* to the rest, you alone will understand what a turmoil seethed in Lucien Chardon's head and heart when his headmaster portentously announced that the doors of the Bargeton mansion were about to be opened to him! It was his fame that had made them turn on their hinges! He was to receive a warm welcome in that house whose ancient gables attracted his attention whenever he took his evening walks in Beaulieu with David, telling himself that never perhaps would their two names reach the ears of people who were deaf to science when it was of too lowly origin. His sister alone was let into the secret. Thanks to her careful housekeeping and her angelic foresight, she was able to draw a few gold coins from her savings-box in order to buy Lucien an elegant pair of shoes from the best shoe-maker in Angoulême and a new suit from the most fashionable tailor. She embellished his best shirt with a frill which she laundered and pleated herself. What joy she felt at seeing him thus accoutred! How proud she was of her brother! How much advice she gave him about all the stupid niceties of social behaviour which she was able to divine! Absorbed in meditation, Lucien had acquired the habit of putting his elbows on the table whenever he sat down, and he even used to pull the table towards him and lean on it. Eve warned him against such off-hand ways in the aristocratic holy-of-holies. She went with him as far as the Porte Saint-Pierre, and when they had arrived almost opposite the Cathedral, her eyes followed him as he walked down the rue de Beaulieu towards the Promenade where Monsieur du Châtelet was waiting for him. Then, poor girl, she stood there in such a state of emotion as if some great event had come about. It seemed to her that Lucien's admission to Madame de Bargeton's house heralded the dawn of prosperity. The saintly creature little knew that when ambition comes it puts an end to natural feeling.

When Lucien arrived at the rue du Minage, he found nothing striking in the external appearance of this 'Louvre' which his imagination had magnified. It was a house built in the soft stone peculiar to the region; time had given it a golden tint. It looked fairly gloomy from the street, and its inner aspect was very simple: a provincial courtyard, austere and neat; a sober, almost monastic style of architecture, but well preserved. Lucien walked up the old staircase with chestnut banisters; its stone treads changed to wooden ones once the first floor was reached. Crossing a shabby little anteroom and a large drawing-room, dimly lit, he found his sovereign lady in a small salon with wainscots of wood, carved in eighteenth-century style and painted grey. The upper parts of the door were painted in camaïeu. The panelling was decorated with old red damask, poorly matched. The old-fashioned furniture was apologetically concealed under covers in red and white check. The poet caught sight of Madame de Bargeton seated on a couch with a thinly-padded quilt, in front of a round table covered with green baize, on which an old-fashioned, two-candled sconce with a shade above it cast its light. The queenly lady did not get up, but she very graciously twisted round in her seat, smiling at the poet, who was much impressed by this serpentine contortion, which he thought distinguished.

Madame de Bargeton was struck by Lucien's exceptionally good looks, his shy demeanour and his voice. The poet was already poetry incarnate. By means of discreet side-glances the young man studied this woman whose appearance seemed to tally with her reputation. She was wearing, in conformity with the latest fashion, a slashed beret in black velvet, a kind of head-dress reminiscent of the Middle Ages and impressive to a young man because, so to speak, it made a woman more womanly still. From it there escaped a profusion of fairish red hair, golden where the light fell on it and auburn where it curled. The noble lady had the milk-white complexion which atones for the supposed disadvantage of such flaming hair. She had sparkling grey eyes under a white expanse of forehead which was bold in contour though it already showed some lines. The skin circling these eyes had a mother of pearl quality, and on either side of the nose two blueish veins emphasized the whiteness of this delicate surround. Her nose had a Bourbon curve which gave extra animation to her long face: a salient feature suggestive of a regal impetuosity akin to that of the Condés. Her hair did not completely hide her neck. Her dress, negligently crossed, afforded a glimpse of snowy flesh and gave the promise of a perfectly-shaped bosom. With her tapering, carefully-manicured, but rather bony fingers, she amiably beckoned the young poet to take the nearest chair. Monsieur du Châtelet sat down in an armchair. Lucien then perceived that the three of them were alone together.

Madame de Bargeton's conversation intoxicated the poet.

The three hours he spent near her were like a dream one would wish to last for ever. This woman seemed to him to be slim rather than thin, made for love but not in love, and delicate in spite of the strength in her. Her defects, exaggerated by her mannerisms, appealed to him, for young men begin by loving exaggeration, the kind of falsehood to which exalted souls are prone. He did not notice that her cheeks had lost their bloom and that there were flushed patches on her cheekbones to which vexations and suffering had imparted a bricklike tinge. What first seized his imagination was the flame of her gaze, her elegant curls shimmering in the light and the gleaming whiteness of her brow: luminous points in which he was caught like a moth in a candle. Also there was too much spiritual sympathy between them for him to appraise her as a woman. The liveliness of her feminine enthusiasm, the vivacity she put into the somewhat outmoded utterances which she had been repeating for so long but which he thought original, fascinated him all the more because he wanted to approve of everything in her. He had brought no poems to read out, but the question did not arise: he had left his poetry behind so that he might have cause to return, while Madame de Bargeton had not mentioned it so that she might persuade him to give a recital another day. Was this not tantamount to an initial understanding between them? Monsieur du Châtelet was displeased at her reception of Lucien. Belatedly, he sensed a rival in this handsome young man, and he escorted him back as far as the first slope turning down from Beaulieu with the idea of bringing his diplomacy into play. Lucien was more than mildly astonished to hear the Director of Taxes boasting of having introduced him and giving him advice on the strength of it.

'Heaven send that you may be better treated than I have been.' Thus Monsieur du Châtelet began. People at Court were less impertinent than this coterie of numskulls which inflicted deadly slights and meted out appalling disdain. The Revolution of 1789 would break out afresh if such people did not mend their ways. As for himself, if he still went to that house, it was because he was attracted to Madame de Bargeton, the only tolerable woman in Angoulême: he had paid court to her for want of occupation and then fallen madly in love with her. It could not be long before he won her, for there was every sign that she loved him. The subjugation of this haughty queen was the only vengeance he would exact from this stupid collection of minor gentry.

Châtelet expressed his passion like a man capable of killing any rival he found in his path. The old Imperial butterfly came down as heavily as possible on the poor poet by trying to crush him under the weight of his self-importance and to intimidate him. He puffed himself out by relating – and exaggerating – the perils he had encountered on his travels; but if this made its mark on the imagination of Lucien the poet, it certainly did not frighten Lucien the lover.

From that evening onwards, notwithstanding the threats and murderous scowls of this dandified old bourgeois, Lucien continued to visit Madame de Bargeton, first of all with the discretion proper to a denizen of L'Houmeau; then he began to take for granted what he had first of all looked on as an enormous favour and multiplied his visits. The people who frequented her circle regarded the chemist's son as a person of no consequence. If, in the early days, some gentlemen or a few ladies calling on Naïs encountered Lucien, they all treated him with the overwhelming politeness which correct people show to their inferiors. They all seemed very gracious at first to Lucien; but later on he became aware of the feeling which prompted their show of consideration. It was not long before he detected certain airs of condescension which stirred his bile and confirmed him in a resentful republicanism which many patricians-to-be adopt at their first contact with high society. But how many sufferings would he not have endured for the woman he heard addressed as Naïs – for among themselves the intimate members of this clan, both male and female, like the grandees of Spain and the cream of Viennese society, called one another by their Christian names: the motive behind this latest subtlety being to set up a distinction in the very heart of the Angoulême aristocracy.

Lucien's love for Naïs was that which any young man feels

for the first woman who flatters him, for she predicted a great future and immense glory for him. Madame de Bargeton used all the skill at her command in order to establish her poet in her salon: not content to exalt him to the skies, she also put him forward as a young man whom she wished to settle in life; she diminished his stature in order to keep him for herself. She made him her reader, her secretary; but she grew fonder of him than she thought possible after the frightful tragedy which had befallen her. She had a very bad conscience about it, and reminded herself that it would be madness to fall in love with a young man of twenty, one so far beneath her in station. Any show of familiarity was capriciously cancelled out by moods of *hauteur* inspired by her scruples. She was by turns aloof and patronizing, tender and caressing. And so Lucien, at first intimidated by this woman's high rank, experienced all the lively fear, hope and despair which, like so many hammer-strokes, dealing pain and pleasure alternately, beat down on first love and drive it so deep into the heart. For two months he looked upon her as a benefactress with a purely maternal interest in him. But confidential exchanges began. Madame de Bargeton called her poet 'dear Lucien', then simply 'dear'. Thus emboldened, the poet addressed the great lady as 'Naïs'. On hearing him call her by this name, she flew into one of those tempers which the young find so captivating; she scolded him for using the name by which everybody called her. The proud and blue-blooded Nègrepelisse offered her beautiful angel the only one of her names which no one had used, and consented to be 'Louise' for him alone. Lucien soared up to the third heaven of love. One evening Lucien came in while Louise was gazing at a portrait. She promptly slipped it into a drawer, and Lucien asked to see it. To calm the despair born of a first access of jealousy, Louise showed him the portrait of the young Cante-Croix and related, not without tears, the distressing story of her love, so chaste and so cruelly nipped in the bud. Was she making an essay of infidelity to her dead lover, or had she hit on the device of giving Lucien a rival in the shape of the portrait? Being too young to sift his lady's motives, Lucien fell into desperation, naïvely, because this was her opening move in the campaign on which women embark when they want a man to demolish the defence-work of scruples they have more or less ingeniously constructed. Women's discussions on duty, the proprieties and religion are as it were fortresses which they like to see taken by storm. The ingenuous Lucien did not need the spur of such coquetry: he would have joined battle in any case.

'*I* will not die. I will live for you,' Lucien was bold enough to say one evening; he wanted to be rid of Monsieur de Cante-Croix once and for all, and he gave Louise a look which plainly showed that his feelings for her had reached the passionate stage.

Alarmed at the progress which nascent love was making in her heart and that of the poet, she asked him for the lines he had promised for the first page in her album, with a view to starting a quarrel with him for his slowness in writing them. Imagine her state of mind when she read the two following stanzas which, naturally enough, seemed more beautiful to her than the best ones that Canalis, the poet of the aristocracy, had ever written:

> The faery brush and fancies of my muse
> Will not alone for ever spread their hues
>   On this receptive leaf.
> My love's shy pencil surely will confide
> To it her secret ecstasies, nor hide
>   Her still unspoken grief.
>
> One day with heavier fingers she will turn
> These yellowed pages and will seek to learn
>   What time has done with pleasure.
> Then, Cupid, grant sweet memory of the ways
>   We walked along in leisure,
> Blissful beneath blue skies and noontide rays!

'Am I really the person for whom these lines were written?' she asked.

This suspicion, inspired by the coquettishness of a woman who was enjoying playing with fire, brought a tear to Lucien's eyes. She pacified him with a kiss on the forehead – the first she had given him. Her mind was made up: Lucien was decidedly a great man for her to fashion; she would teach him Italian and German and perfect his manners; and this would be an excuse for having him always at hand, however much this might vex the bores who paid court to her. It would be her mission in life! She took up her piano-playing again in order to initiate her poet in the appreciation of music, and delighted him with her renderings of beautiful pieces from Beethoven; happy to see him half swooning with joy, she hypocritically asked him: 'Can we not be content with such happiness?' And the poor poet was fool enough to answer: 'Yes.'

Eventually matters reached this stage: the previous week Louise had had Lucien to dinner, with Monsieur de Bargeton as chaperon. In spite of this precaution, the news spread through the whole town, and it was regarded as so unheard-of that everyone wondered if it could be true. There was a terrible wagging of tongues. Some people felt that 'society' was about to be turned upside-down. Others exclaimed: 'That's what comes of Liberal doctrines!' Du Châtelet, a prey to jealousy, then learned that Madame Charlotte the midwife was none other than Madame Chardon, the mother of this Chateaubriand of L'Houmeau, as he put it – and this phrase was accepted as a witticism. Madame de Chandour was the first to come running to Madame de Bargeton.

'Do you know, dear Naïs,' she said, 'what everybody is saying in Angoulême? This little rhymster is the son of a Madame Charlotte who two months ago attended my sister-in-law's confinement.'

'My dear,' replied Madame de Bargeton, as haughtily as any royal personage. 'What is there surprising in that? Is she not a chemist's widow – a sorry predicament for one of Rubempré stock? Suppose we ourselves were penniless ... How should *we* make a living? How would *you* find food for your children?'

Madame de Bargeton's cool common sense silenced the lamentations of the nobility. Magnanimous souls are always inclined to discover virtue in misfortune. Moreover, one can derive supreme satisfaction from persevering in benevolence when it incurs censure: such blamelessness has all the piquancy of vice. At that evening's reception, Madame de Bargeton's salon was crowded with friends who had come to make remonstrance. She brought all her caustic wit into play, saying that if a man of noble birth could be neither Molière, nor Racine, nor Voltaire, nor Massillon, nor Beaumarchais, the tapestry-weavers, clock-makers and cutlers whose offspring became great men simply had to be accepted. She maintained that genius was always of gentle birth. She upbraided the gentry for their scant understanding of their true interests. In short she talked a lot of nonsense which might have enlightened less dim-witted people; but at least they paid tribute to her independence of mind. And so she blasted the storm away with her cannonade. When Lucien, at her summons, made his first entry into her faded, antiquated salon with its four tables set for whist, she gave him a gracious welcome and introduced him with queenly imperiousness. She called the Director of Taxes 'Monsieur Châtelet', thereby petrifying him by showing that she knew his assumption of the 'particle' to be illegal. From that evening onwards Lucien's abrupt introduction into Madame de Bargeton's social circle had to be accepted: but only as a poisonous substance which everyone undertook to eliminate by using the antidote of impertinence. Naïs had won her point, but her prestige suffered from it: there were certain dissidents who showed signs of emigrating. Taking advice from Monsieur Châtelet, Amélie (Madame de Chandour) decided to set up a rival altar by starting Wednesday soirées in her own house. But Madame de Bargeton held her salon every evening, and her visitors were so accustomed to the routine, so used to facing the same tapestries, playing their game of backgammon, seeing the same domestics and the same candelabra; so used to depositing their cloaks, their double-soled shoes and their hats in the same lobby, that they were as attached to the treads of the staircase as they were to the lady of the house. They all resigned themselves to putting up with 'the goldfinch of the sacred grove'[1] – another witti-

1. goldfinch: *chardonneret* – a pun on Lucien's plebeian surname, Chardon.

cism, perpetrated this time by Alexandre de Brebian, president of the Agricultural Society. He it was who finally calmed seditious spirits with the following inspired remark:

'Before the Revolution, the greatest noblemen admitted nobodies, people like this little poet from L'Houmeau, to their houses: Duclos, Grimm, Crébillon. But they did not admit tax-collectors, and after all, that is what Châtelet is.'

Thus du Châtelet became a scapegoat for Chardon and was cold-shouldered by everybody. Sensitive to this attack, the Director of Taxes, once Madame de Bargeton had called him plain Châtelet, had sworn to himself that he would possess her: he therefore supported the whims of the lady of the house, stood by the young poet and simulated benevolence. This great diplomat of whose services the Emperor had so maladroitly deprived himself made up to Lucien and claimed to be his friend. In order to launch him in society, he gave a dinner, attended by the Prefect, the Receiver-General, the colonel of the regiment then in garrison, the Director of the Naval Academy, the President of Assizes, in short all the highest administrative officials. Our little poet was so ceremoniously entertained that anyone save a young man of twenty-two would have strongly suspected that the praise lavished on him was a deceit and a hoax. At dessert, Châtelet called on his rival to recite his Ode on the death of Sardanapalus, his current masterpiece. After hearing it, the principal of the college, a phlegmatic man, clapped his hands and said that Jean-Baptiste-Rousseau had done no better. Baron Sixte Châtelet thought that sooner or later the little poetaster's reputation would burst like a balloon in this hot-house atmosphere of eulogy, or that, intoxicated with his anticipated glory, he would permit himself some impertinence which would thrust him back into his original obscurity. While he awaited the demise of this genius, he appeared to be laying his own pretensions as a burnt-offering at Madame de Bargeton's feet; but, with all the artfulness of a rake, he had drawn up his plan, was observing every move of the amorous pair with close strategic attention and watching for an opportunity to exterminate Lucien. From that time onwards, there arose in Angoulême and its environs a vague rumour which proclaimed that the province had given birth to a great man. On the whole, Madame de Bargeton was praised for the care she lavished on this eaglet. Seeing that her conduct was approved, she took steps to secure wide-spread approbation. She trumpeted throughout the *département* a forthcoming soirée complete with ices, cakes and tea – an impressive innovation in a town where tea was still sold in chemists' shops as a drug for the cure of indigestion. The flower of the aristocracy was invited to come and hear a great work which Lucien was to recite.

Louise had kept her favourite in the dark about the difficulties she had overcome, but gave him a hint of the conspiracy which had been hatched against him in her circle; for she did not want him to remain in ignorance of the dangers which beset the career of a man of genius and the obstacles which exceptional courage alone is able to surmount. Drawing a lesson from her victory, she pointed out that fame can only be won at the price of continual torment, told him of the martyr's stake which he had to face, and served this up with all the beautiful platitudes and pomposity of diction at her command; it was a counterfeit of the improvisations which mar Madame de Staël's *Corinna*. Louise's eloquence gave her such a sense of importance that her affection for the Benjamin who had inspired it grew stronger. She advised him boldly to repudiate his own father by assuming the noble name of Rubempré and to take no notice of any outcry provoked by this change of patronymic – moreover it would receive royal sanction. Louise claimed kinship with the Marquise d'Espard, a Blamont-Chauvry by birth, a lady who had much credit at Court, and she undertook to obtain this favour through her. This reference to the King, the Marquise d'Espard and the Court seemed like a firework display to Lucien, and convinced him of the need to submit to this baptism.

'Dear boy,' said Louise in a tenderly mocking voice, 'the sooner this is done, the sooner it will receive official approval.'

She peeled off one by one the successive layers of the Social State, and showed the poet how many rungs of the ladder he could step straight over by means of such a clever manoeuvre.

In a twinkling, she induced Lucien to abjure his low-class ideas about the chimerical equality preached in 1793, re-awakened in him the fever for social distinction which David's cool reasoning had calmed, and proved to him that high society was the only stage on which he could play his part. The resentful Liberal became a monarchist *in petto*. He tasted the apple of aristocratic luxury and glory. He vowed that he would lay a garland, even if it were stained with blood, at his lady's feet: he would win it at all cost, *quibuscumque viis*. In order to prove his courage, he told Louise of his present sufferings, which so far he had concealed from her at the bidding of that indefinable modesty which goes with first love and prevents a young man from displaying his more heroic qualities, so intent is he on being appreciated for himself alone. He depicted himself in the grip of poverty proudly endured, working in David's printing-office and spending his nights in study. This youthful ardour reminded Madame de Bargeton of her colonel at twenty-six, and her glance softened. Seeing that his stately lady was weakening, Lucien took hold of her hand, which she did not withdraw, and kissed it with the frenzy of a poet, a young man, a lover. Louise even permitted the apothecary's son to press his trembling lips on her brow.

'Child! Child! If anyone saw us I should look very ridiculous!' she said, awakening from her ecstatic torpor.

In the course of that evening, Madame de Bargeton's wit played great havoc with what she called Lucien's prejudices. According to her, men of genius had neither brothers and sisters nor fathers and mothers; the great works they were destined to construct forced them to appear selfish and sacrifice everything to their greatness. If his family suffered at first from the exorbitant imposts levied upon it by a titanic brain, it would later reap a hundred-fold reward for the many sacrifices necessitated by obstacles with which frustrated superiority has to contend in the early stages; it would share the fruits of victory. Genius was accountable only to itself; it alone knew what ends were to be attained and it alone could justify the means. Therefore it had to put itself above the laws which it was its mission to reshape; moreover, he who intends to dominate the times he lives in is entitled to take all and risk all, for all that is belongs to him. She reminded him how Bernard de Palissy, Louis XI, Fox, Napoleon, Christopher Columbus, Julius Caesar, had made their start in life, in company with all those illustrious gamblers who had begun by being riddled with debts, suffering indigence or misunderstanding, or held as madmen, bad sons, bad fathers and bad brothers, but who later had become the pride of their family, of their country, of the whole world.

These arguments responded to Lucien's secret failings and encouraged the progress of corruption in his heart; so ardent were his desires that he gave *a priori* assent to any means of advancement. But not to succeed is to commit the crime of social *lèse-majesté*. Has not a man who comes to defeat done to death all those middle-class virtues on which society is built? When it sees a Marius sitting among the ruins of them it drives him out with horror. Lucien, who did not know that his course lay between the infamy of a convict-prison and the palms awarded to genius, was soaring over the Mount Sinai of the Prophets without seeing that below him were the Dead Sea and the horrible winding-sheet of Gomorrha.

Louise was so successful in releasing her poet's heart and mind from the swaddling-bands in which provincial life had wrapped them that Lucien was eager to find out if he could conquer this lofty prey without suffering the humiliation of a refusal. The social evening which had been announced provided an opportunity to make this test. His love for her was mingled with ambition. He was in love and he wanted to rise; this two-fold urge is very natural in young people who have a heart to satisfy and indigence to fight against. Society's present-day habit of inviting all its children to one and the same banquet arouses their ambitions in the very morning of life. It robs youth of its graces and vitiates most of its generous sentiments by adulterating them with calculation. Poetic idealism would have it otherwise, but the fiction one would wish to accept is too often belied in reality for a more favourable picture to be given of young men as they are in the nineteenth century. Lucien felt that his calculation was motivated by a noble sentiment, his friendship for David.

He wrote a long letter to Louise, for he found boldness easier on paper than in speech. It took him twelve pages, which he recopied three times, to tell her of his father's genius, his baffled hopes and the terrible poverty in which he was forced to live. He depicted his beloved sister as an angel, David as a budding Cuvier who, although on his own way to greatness, was at once father, brother and friend to him. He would consider himself unworthy of being loved by Louise, who represented the peak of glory for him, if he did not ask her to do for David what she was doing for him. He would give up everything rather than betray David Séchard and wanted David to share in his success. It was one of those frantic letters in which young people threaten to shoot themselves if their request is refused, full of immature casuistry and the insensate logic of exalted minds; a delightful sample of word-spinning embroidered with the naïve declarations which come straight from the writer's heart without his knowing it, and which please women so much. After handing this letter to the lady's-maid, Lucien had spent the day at the printing-office, correcting proofs, superintending a number of jobs and dealing with certain minor printing-office matters. He had said nothing to David about the letter: at the time of life when one still has the heart of a child such noble reticence is natural. Moreover, he was perhaps beginning to be afraid of the Phocian's axe which David could wield expertly; perhaps he feared the keenness of a scrutiny which pierced through to his soul. After the Chénier reading, David's reproach, which felt to Lucien like a doctor's finger probing a wound, had touched him to the quick and made him divulge the secret which hitherto he had kept to himself.

One may readily imagine the thoughts which must have been running through Lucien's head as he walked down from Angoulême to L'Houmeau. Was the great lady annoyed? Would she welcome David to her house? Would not her ambitious admirer be hurled back into his sordid den in L'Houmeau? Although, before he kissed Louise's forehead, he had himself been able to gauge the distance separating a queen from her favourite, he had not stopped to consider that it was impossible for David, in the twinkling of an eye, to leap over the gulf which it had taken him five months to cross. Not knowing how absolute was the sentence of outlawry delivered against lowly people, he was unaware that a second venture of this kind would bring disaster to Madame de Bargeton. Branded and convicted for having so flagrantly demeaned herself, she would be forced to leave the town where her own caste would shun her as a leper was shunned in the Middle Ages. The clan of blue-blooded aristocracy and the clergy itself might well defend Naïs against all comers in the event of her allowing herself a lapse from virtue, but the crime of consorting with those beneath her would never be forgiven. The sins of royalty may be condoned, but once it abdicates they are condemned. And would she not indeed be abdicating if she received David at her house? Even though Lucien did not think out this aspect of the question, his aristocratic instinct gave him forebodings of many other difficulties, and he found them appalling. Noble feelings do not necessarily confer nobility of deportment. Racine looked like the noblest of courtiers, Corneille was very like a cattle-dealer, while Descartes could have passed for a worthy Dutch trader. Often, when visitors to La Brède met Montesquieu with a rake over his shoulder and wearing his night-cap, they took him for a common gardener. Knowledge of the ways of society, when it does not proceed from high birth, when it is not a *savoir-vivre* imbibed with one's mother's milk or transmitted through blood, is a matter of education, but education must be aided by the fortuitous possession of a certain elegance of manner, distinction of features and tone of voice. In David all these tremendous trifles were lacking, whereas his friend was endowed with them by nature. Lucien was of gentle extraction through his mother, and even his foot had the high arch of the Franks; whereas David Séchard had the flat feet of the Celt and the stocky build of his father the pressman. Lucien could anticipate the shower of raillery which would fall on David, and he could already see Madame de Bargeton repressing a smile. In short, without exactly feeling ashamed of his 'brother', he promised himself that he would never again give heed to a first impulse without turning it over in his mind.

And so, after the hour given to poetry and warm feeling, after a reading which had shown the two friends that a new sun was shining over the fields of literature, Lucien found that the time had come for policy and calculation. As he made his way back to L'Houmeau he regretted having sent the letter and would have liked to recall it; through a flash of intuition, he perceived how pitiless are the laws of society. Sensing how favourable to his ambition was the advantage he had already acquired, he was reluctant to withdraw his foot from the bottom rung of the ladder he had to scale in his assault on greatness. Then a picture of times past rose up before his eyes: the calm and simple life he had led as in a garden bright with the flowers of family love; David, so full of genius, who had nobly helped him and was ready to die for him if need arose; his mother, a great lady despite her lowly occupation; his sister, so graceful in the acceptance of her lot, the purity of her childhood and the immaculacy of her conscience; the hopes he cherished, which no biting wind had stripped of their petals. At such moments he told himself that it would be a finer thing to force his way through the serried ranks of the aristocratic or middle-class crowd by his own achievements than to reach success through a woman's favour. Sooner or later the genius in him would shine forth like that of so many men, his predecessors, who had brought society to heel. How women would love him then! The example of Napoleon, so baleful for the nineteenth century through the pretensions it inspires in mediocre people, came to Lucien's mind: he repented of his calculations and jettisoned them. Of such stuff was Lucien made: he veered as easily from bad to good as from good to bad. For the last month, the love a scholar feels for his retreat had given place in Lucien's mind to a kind of shame when he caught sight of the shop over which his family lived, with its sign written in yellow letters on the background of green:

POSTEL (LATE CHARDON) PHARMACIST

His father's name, thus displayed at a spot by which every carriage passed, was an eye-sore to him. On the evening when he had first emerged from the front door, adorned with a small iron grill in bad taste, in order to go and make his appearance at Beaulieu, where, with Madame de Bargeton on his arm, he was to find himself among the most elegant young people of the Upper Town, he had intensely deplored the obvious incompatibility between this habitation and the favour she was showing him.

'To love Madame de Bargeton, before long perhaps to possess her, and to be living in such a hole!' This was his thought as he passed through the alley into the little courtyard in which several bundles of drying herbs were hung out along the walls, in which the apprentice was scouring the laboratory cauldrons, in which Monsieur Postel, wearing his dispenser's apron, holding a retort, was inspecting a pharmaceutical product while keeping an eye on the shop: for even if he gave the closest attention to the drug, he kept his ear open for the sound of the door-bell. The odour of camomile, mint and various kinds of distilled plants filled the yard and the modest suite of rooms which were reached by climbing one of those narrow flights of stairs known as 'millers' ladders', with a pair of ropes doing duty for a handrail. Above it was the one and only attic bedroom, which Lucien occupied.

'Good-day to you, my boy,' said Monsieur Postel, who was the very epitome of a provincial shopkeeper. 'How goes it with you? I have just been carrying out an experiment with molasses, but it would have taken your father to discover what I am looking for. A fine man, he was! If I had known the secret of his cure for gout, we should both be rolling along in our carriages today!'

No week went by without the pharmacist, a man as stupid as he was good-natured, giving Lucien a little stab by reminding him of the disastrous prudence his father had shown in keeping quiet about his discovery.

'It's a great misfortune,' was Lucien's reply. He was beginning to find his father's pupil prodigiously vulgar, although he had often heaped blessings on his head: for more than once the honest Postel had given a helping hand to his master's widow and children.

'What's the trouble?' asked Monsieur Postel, laying his test-tube down on the laboratory bench.

'Has any letter come for me?'

'Yes, one which smells like balm! It's on the counter, beside my desk.'

The letter from Madame de Bargeton lying among a chemist's bowls! Lucien dashed into the shop.

'Hurry up, Lucien! Your dinner's been waiting an hour. It will get cold,' a soft musical voice called out through a half-open window. Lucien did not hear.

'He's a bit crazy, your brother, Mademoiselle,' said Postel, raising his head.

Unmarried himself, and very like a little brandy-cask on which a painter's whimsy has sketched a big, round, ruddy, pock-marked face, he assumed an air of ceremony and affability as he looked up at Eve, disclosing his thoughts of matrimony with his predecessor's daughter, although he had not yet resolved the conflict which was going on in his heart between love and thriftiness. That is why, with a smile, he so often repeated the same remark when Lucien passed to and fro: 'She's a real beauty, your sister! And you're not bad-looking either! Your father made a good job of everything.'

Eve was tall and olive-skinned, with black hair and blue eyes. Although she showed some signs of firmness of character, she was sweet-natured, tender and devoted. Her guilelessness, her simplicity, her tranquil submission to a life of toil, her unimpeachable modesty, had inevitably bewitched David Séchard. And so, since their first meeting, a mute, simple, Teutonic kind of passion, unostentatious and undemonstrative, had sprung up between them. The thoughts of each had gone out secretly to the other, as if they had been kept apart by some jealous husband to whom their fellow-feeling had given offence. Both of them hid it from Lucien, thinking that perhaps it might injure his prospects. David was afraid that Eve did not care for him, while Eve, for her part, gave way to the shyness which comes of poverty. A real working-class girl would have been bolder, but, like a girl of good family fallen upon evil days, she suited her behaviour to her unhappy circumstances. Though of modest demeanour, she had her pride, which would not allow her to show too much interest in the son of a man reputed to be rich. At that time, people aware of the increasing value of landed property reckoned that the Marsac domain was worth more than eighty thousand francs, quite apart from the plots of land which old Séchard, having saved up much money and being skilful in selling his produce, was no doubt adding to his possessions when favourable opportunities occurred. David was probably the only person who had no idea of his father's wealth. In his eyes, the house at Marsac was a shanty acquired in 1810 for some fifteen or sixteen thousand francs; he only went there once a year in the grape-picking season, when his father took him through the vineyards and bragged about his grape-harvests: but the young printer never saw these and thought little about them. The love of a studious young man, accustomed to solitude, whose feelings grew all the stronger because he overrated the obstacles in his path, stood in need of encouragement; for David regarded Eve with greater veneration than a simple clerk would regard a great lady. He was awkward and ill at ease in the company of the woman he worshipped, and as much in a hurry to leave as he had been to arrive; so he restrained his feelings instead of expressing them. Often, in the evenings, after inventing some excuse for going to consult Lucien, he walked down from the Place du Mûrier by the Porte-Palet to L'Houmeau; but when he got to the green door with the iron grill he made off again, in fear of having come too late or of seeming a nuisance to Eve, who he thought would have gone to bed. And yet, although the great love he bore her only expressed itself in trifling ways, Eve was well aware of it; she felt flattered, though without vainglory, at being the object of the deep respect so plainly visible in the looks he gave her, the words he spoke to her and his manners. But what Eve found most attractive in David was his fanatical attachment to Lucien: he had unwittingly discovered the best means of pleasing her. The mute joys of this love differed from tumultuous passion as the flowers of the field from the splendour of a garden bed. There were glances as soft and delicate as the blue lotus floating on the waters, expressions as fleeting as the faint perfume of wild roses, moments of melancholy as tender as velvety mosses: flowers put forth by two fine souls, and springing from a forever rich and fertile soil. On several occasions already Eve had divined the strength which lay behind this gentleness; she took the avowals which David dared not make so much into account that the slightest incident was likely to bring them to a more intimate spiritual understanding.

Eve had left the door open for Lucien. He sat down in silence at the place laid for him on a little table, with no cloth, standing on a trestle. The only silver cutlery this poor little household possessed consisted of three forks and spoons, and Eve put them all into use for her beloved brother.

'What are you reading?' she asked after taking a dish from the fire and setting it on the table, having put out the portable stove by covering it with the extinguisher.

Lucien gave no reply. Eve fetched a little plate daintily garnished with vine-leaves, and placed it on the table with a bowl full of cream.

'Look, Lucien, I got you some strawberries.'

Lucien was so absorbed in his reading that he did not hear her. Thereupon Eve came and sat near him without so much as a murmur; for one element in the love a sister feels for her brother is the tremendous pleasure of being treated unceremoniously.

'Whatever is the matter?' she cried as she saw tears glistening in her brother's eyes.

'Nothing, Eve, nothing,' he said. And, with surprising demonstrativeness, he put his arm round her waist, pulled her to him and kissed her brow, her hair and her neck.

'You're hiding something from me.'

'Well then, she loves me.'

'I knew very well that those kisses were not meant for me,' said poor Eve, in a hurt tone of voice, with a blush on her face.

'We are all going to be happy,' cried Lucien, swallowing his soup in great spoonfuls.

'We?' Eve replied. Inspired by the same presentiment as David had felt, she added: 'You won't love us now as much as you did.'

'How can you say such a thing? Don't you know me?'

Eve held out her hand to squeeze his; then she removed the empty plate, the brown earthenware soup-tureen, and pushed forward the dish she had prepared. Instead of eating, Lucien re-read Madame de Bargeton's letter, which Eve, discreetly, did not ask to see, so great was her respect for her brother. If he wished to tell her its contents, she would have to wait; if he did not, she could scarcely insist. She waited. This is how the letter ran:

Dear friend,

Why should I refuse to your brother in science the support I have given to you? In my view, all talent has equal rights. But you do not know how prejudiced are the people in my social circle. We shall not make those who belong to the aristocracy of ignorance recognize that intelligence confers nobility. If I am not influential enough to make them accept Monsieur David Séchard, I will readily give these sorry people up for your sake. It will be like one of the hecatombs of ancient times. But, dear friend, you would certainly not wish me to accept the company of a person whose mind and manners might be displeasing to me. The flattering remarks you make to me show me how blind friendship can easily become! Will you be cross with me if I make my consent subject to one reservation? I should like to see your friend, form my own judgement of him, and satisfy myself, for the sake of your future, that you are not under a delusion. Is not that an example of the maternal solicitude which must be shown to you, dear poet, by

LOUISE DE NÈGREPELISSE?

Lucien did not know with what art a 'Yes' is used in polite society to prepare for a 'No', or a 'No' as a preliminary to a 'Yes'. This letter spelt triumph for him: David would visit Madame de Bargeton and would shine with the majesty of genius. Intoxicated with a victory which persuaded him of the commanding influence he could exert over his fellow-creatures,

Lucien drew himself up with such pride, his features became so expressive of hope and so radiant with it, that his sister could not refrain from telling him how handsome he was.

'If this woman has any intelligence, she must certainly love you! In which case she's going to be very vexed this evening, for all the women will be trying to flirt with you! How fine you'll look as you read your *Saint John at Pathmos*! I should like to be a mouse and slip into the room! Come along, I've put your clothes out in Mother's bedroom.'

It was a room expressive of decorous poverty. There was a walnut bed furnished with white curtains, and under it a thin green carpet. The rest of the furniture consisted of a chest of drawers with a wooden top on which stood a mirror, and some walnut chairs. A clock on the mantelpiece was the sole reminder of bygone affluence. The window-curtains were white and the wall-paper grey, with a pattern of grey flowers. The floor, which Eve had stained and polished, was glistening with cleanliness. In the centre of the room, on a pedestal table, was a red tray patterned with gilt roses on which stood three cups and a sugar-bowl of Limoges porcelain. Eve slept in a small adjacent room no bigger than a ship's cabin containing a narrow bed, an old easy chair and a work-table close to the window. It was so tiny that the glazed door had always to be kept open for ventilation. In spite of the straitened means which these objects betokened, everything there was redolent of unassuming, studious life. To those who knew the mother and her two children, it made a moving and harmonious picture.

Lucien was tying his cravat when he heard David's step in the little courtyard, and the printer came in at once with the gait and appearance of a man in a hurry.

'There you are then, David,' cried the ambitious poet. 'Victory is ours! She loves me! she wants to see you.'

'No,' said the printer with some embarrassment. 'I have come to thank you for the proof of friendship you have given me. I have thought seriously about it. My way of life is settled, Lucien. I am David Séchard, a printer of Angoulême by royal appointment; my name can be read at the foot of the posters on every wall. In the eyes of people of her class, I am an artisan, a tradesman if you prefer, at any rate a man in business running a shop in the rue de Beaulieu, at the corner of the Place du Mûrier. As yet I have neither the wealth of a Keller nor the reputation of a Desplein, each of whom wields a kind of power which the aristocracy is still reluctant to acknowledge but which – I agree with them on this score – is of no account if the breeding and manners of a gentleman are lacking. What is there in me to justify this sudden elevation? I should be laughed at by bourgeois and nobility alike. As for you, yours is a very different situation. Being a proof-reader in no way ties you down – you are making an effort to acquire all kinds of knowledge which are indispensable to success; your present occupations can be explained in terms of your future. Besides, you might take up another career tomorrow: you might study law, or diplomacy, or go into the Civil Service. In short, you are neither ticketed nor docketed. Take advantage of being socially uncommitted: go forward alone and lay your hands on the prizes! Savour and enjoy all kinds of pleasure, even those which vanity procures. Be happy. I shall rejoice in your success: you will be my second self. Indeed, I shall be able to live your life in imagination. For you the pomp and circumstance of social life with its rapid wire-pulling and intrigues; for me the sober and industrious life of the tradesman and the time-consuming activities of science.'

'You shall be our aristocracy,' he added, with a glance at Eve. 'When your step falters, my arm will be there to sustain you. If you have some act of treachery to complain of, you will take refuge in our undying affection. Protection, favour, the good-will of others, if there were two people to share it, might flag, and we should do one another harm. Go on ahead: if I should need it, you can take me in tow. Far from envying you, I devote myself to your interests. What you have just done for me at the risk of alienating your benefactress, who may become your mistress, rather than leaving me in the lurch or repudiating me . . . this simple magnanimous act, well, Lucien, it would bind me to you for ever even if we were not already like brothers. Have no misgivings or scruples about taking the foremost role. It suits me thus to allow you the lion's share. In short, even if you caused me much anxiety, who can say that I should not still be under an obligation to you?'

As he said this, he cast the most timid of glances at Eve, whose eyes were full of tears, for she guessed all his motives.

'So then,' said David to his astonished friend. 'You are well-built, you have a graceful figure, you carry your clothes well, you look like a gentleman in your blue coat with yellow buttons and your plain nankeen trousers. In such a circle I should look like a working-man. I should be awkward, ill at ease. I should talk nonsense or else keep my mouth shut. Whereas you, in order to conform to the snobbery about patronymics, can adopt your mother's name and be known as Lucien de Rubempré. I am and always shall be David Séchard. Everything in the society you are entering is in your favour and my disfavour. Success awaits you. The women will worship you for your angelic beauty. Is that not so, Eve?'

Lucien threw his arms round David's neck and kissed him. David's modesty nipped many doubts and difficulties in the bud. Could Lucien have failed to show redoubled affection to a man who, out of friendship, had just made the same reflections as he had made through ambition? As an aspirant to fame and love he felt that his path was being smoothed; his heart overflowed with youthful and friendly exuberance. This was one of those rare moments in life when one's vital forces are agreeably tensed, when every cord vibrates and renders its full volume of sound. None the less David's high-souled wisdom awakened in Lucien the normal tendency a man has to view everything in terms of self. We all say, more or less, like Louis XIV: '*I* am the State!' The tenderness which his mother and sister lavished on him, David's devotion, and the habit of seeing the secret efforts of these three beings directed towards himself, gave him the defects to which children of good family are prone and bred in him the egoism which devours the nobility. Madame de Bargeton was fanning the flame by urging him to forget his obligations to his sister, his mother and David. He had not yet come to this; but was it not to be feared that, by widening the circle of his ambition, he might be forced to think only of himself in order to maintain himself within it?

Once the emotion had subsided, David observed to Lucien that his poem on Saint John of Pathmos was perhaps too biblical to be read in a circle which had little acquaintance with apocalyptic poetry. Lucien seemed upset at this, because he had to show his quality before the most critical public in the Charente valley. David advised him to take the André Chénier volume with him and exchange a dubious pleasure for a certain one. Lucien was a splendid reader, he would necessarily win applause, and this gesture of modesty would no doubt serve him well. Like most young people, they supposed that people in society were endowed with their own intelligence, and virtues. Youth, when it has not yet fallen from grace, may show no pity for others' faults, but it also credits them with its own magnificent ideals. In fact one needs much experience of life to realize, as Raphael so aptly put it, that to understand others is to rise to their level. Generally speaking, that special sense needed for the understanding of poetry is rare in France, where wit promptly dries up the holy well of ecstatic tears and where nobody will bother to break fresh ground, explore the sublime and discover the infinity it contains. Lucien was going to have his first taste of mundane ignorance and coldness of heart. He went to David's house to pick up the volume of poetry.

When David was alone with his beloved, he felt more embarrassed than ever before. A prey to a thousand terrors, he both wished for and feared a word of praise; he would have liked to run away, for even modesty has its special coquetry! Overwhelmed by love, he dared not utter a word which might make it seem that he was looking for gratitude; he felt that any remark he made would give him away, and so he kept quiet and looked as if he had committed a crime. Eve could guess to what torture his diffidence was putting him and found this silence enjoyable; but when he started twiddling his hat as a prelude to departure, she said with a smile:

'Monsieur David, since you are not spending the evening

with Madame de Bargeton, we can spend it together. The weather is fine. Shall we take a stroll along the Charente? We will talk about Lucien.'

David would have liked to throw himself at the feet of this delightful girl. Her very tone of voice gave him his unhoped-for reward: her affectionate accents had resolved the difficulties of the situation; her proposal was more than an eulogy, it was the first favour bestowed by love.

'Only,' she said, at the gesture which David made, 'let me have a minute or two to get ready.'

David had never in his life had an ear for a tune, but he went out humming one. This surprised the honest Postel and gave him violent suspicions about the relations between Eve and the printer.

3. *A social evening and a riverside stroll*

LUCIEN's character made him attentive to first impressions, and the most trivial incidents of this evening in society were to have a great effect on him. Like all inexperienced lovers, he arrived so early that Louise had not yet come into the drawing-room. Monsieur de Bargeton was there alone. Lucien had already begun his apprenticeship in the petty cowardice with which a married woman's admirer pays for his bliss and which shows women how far they can go in their demands; but he had not yet come face to face with Monsieur de Bargeton.

This noble gentleman had a small mind comfortably poised between an inoffensive vacuity which has some glimmer of comprehension and an arrogant stupidity which refuses either to give or take. Very conscious of his duties to society and doing his best to be agreeable, he had adopted the smile of a dancing-partner as his sole language. Content or dissatisfied, he smiled. He smiled on hearing a disastrous piece of news and also when a happy event was announced. This smile answered all purposes thanks to the variety of expression he gave it. If unhesitant approval was absolutely necessary, his smile was reinforced by a complaisant laugh; only in the last extremity would he utter a word. A tête-à-tête plunged him into the only kind of embarrassment which ever complicated his vegetative existence, for it obliged him to ransack the immense void within him in order to find something to say. He generally got over the difficulty by returning to the simple habits of childhood: he would think out loud and initiate you in the slightest details of his life; he would tell you of his needs or his aches and pains, and this was as near as he could get to expressing ideas. He was unable to chat about this or that, he abstained from the small talk in which imbeciles take refuge, and found matter for conversation in his most intimate private concerns. 'To please Madame de Bargeton,' he would say, 'I ate some veal this morning – she's very fond of it – and my stomach is completely upset. I knew it would be: it always takes me like that! Can you explain it?' Or else: 'I'm going to ring for a glass of lemonade. Would you like to join me?' Or else: 'I'm going riding to-morrow to see my father-in-law.' Brief sentences like these lent themselves to no discussion; they evoked a 'Yes' or a 'No', and the conversation fell flat. Monsieur de Bargeton then implored his guest's assistance by giving a westerly slant to his nose, which was like that of a wheezy old pug, and looked at you with his big eyes – they were of different colour – as if to ask: 'What were you saying?' Bores eager to talk of themselves he cherished: he listened to them with an honest and delicate attentiveness which made him so dear to them that the wind-bags of Angoulême credited him with a deep kind of intelligence and claimed that he was misjudged. And so, when they fell short of listeners, they would come to this gentleman to finish off their stories or their arguments, being quite sure of receiving an appreciative smile. Since his wife's drawing-room was always full, he usually felt at ease in it. He busied himself with the most trivial details. He watched for visitors coming in, smilingly bowed to them and led them up to his wife; he kept his eye open for parting guests, saw them out, and responded to their farewells with his eternal smile. When discussion was lively and he saw that everyone was busy talking, mute but happy, he stood perched like a stork on his two long legs and looked as if he were listening to a political debate; or he went over to study the hands at the card-tables, without understanding a thing about it, for he knew no card-games. Or he walked about taking his snuff and letting his dinner digest. Anaïs represented the bright side of life for him and afforded him unlimited enjoyment. When she was performing as mistress of the house, he relaxed in an easy chair and admired her, for it was she who did all the talking. Also he had come to take pleasure in trying to discern the wit in her remarks, and as quite often he only understood them long after they had been uttered, his face broke into smiles which went off like cannon-balls exploding underground. Moreover his respect for her amounted to adoration – and does not adoration of some sort make for happiness in life? As a person of wit and generosity, Anaïs had not exploited her advantage, for she discerned in her husband the easy-going temperament of a child who asks nothing better than to be ruled. She had taken care of him as one takes care of a favourite garment: she kept him spick and span and well-groomed, looked after him and humoured him. Monsieur de Bargeton, conscious of this humouring, this grooming, this attention, had contracted a dog-like devotion for his wife. Happiness is so easy to bestow when it costs nothing! Madame de Bargeton, realizing that good food was her husband's sole pleasure in life, had excellent dinners cooked for him; she pitied him; she had never uttered a complaint; and some persons who did not understand that her silence was due to pride credited Monsieur de Bargeton with hidden virtues. Besides this, she had subjected him to military discipline, and he gave passive obedience to his wife's commands. She would say to him: 'Call on Monsieur or Madame So-and-So,' and he went off like a soldier mounting guard. And so in her presence he remained rigidly at the shoulder-arms position. At the moment there was a question of getting this tongue-tied man elected to the Chamber of Deputies.

Lucien had not been frequenting the house long enough to

have lifted the veil behind which this unimaginable character sheltered. Monsieur de Bargeton, buried in his easy chair, seeming to hear everything and take everything in, achieving dignity by virtue of his silence, appeared to Lucien to be a prodigiously imposing person. Instead of taking him for what he was – a granite boundary-post – Lucien looked on this nobleman as an awesome sphinx, thanks to the tendency of imaginative minds to magnify all they see and to attribute a soul to everything in human shape; he deemed it advisable to flatter him.

'I am the first arrival,' he said, bowing to him with more respect than was usually accorded to the worthy man.

'That's quite natural,' replied Monsieur de Bargeton.

Lucien took this remark for the epigram of a jealous husband; his face reddened and he looked at himself in the mirror to keep himself in countenance.

'You live in L'Houmeau,' said Monsieur de Bargeton. 'People from far off always arrive earlier than those who live close by.'

'I wonder why that is,' said Lucien, trying to look affable.

'I don't know,' replied Monsieur de Bargeton, and he relapsed into immobility.

'You have not thought it worth while to find out,' replied Lucien. 'A man who can make such an observation is capable of discovering the cause.'

'Ah!' said Monsieur de Bargeton. 'Final causes! Ha! Ha! . . .'

Lucien racked his brains to revive the conversation, but it had petered out.

'No doubt Madame de Bargeton is dressing?' he asked, and shuddered at the silliness of the question.

'Yes, she is dressing,' the husband naturally replied.

Lucien looked up at the two exposed beams, painted grey, and the ceiling in between them, and could think of nothing further to say; but he then noticed, not without terror, that the small chandelier with its antique crystal pendants was stripped of its gauze and supplied with candles. The furniture covers had been removed, thus exposing the scarlet lampas with its faded flowers. These preparations indicated that the gathering was to be an exceptional one. The poet felt doubtful about the suitability of his attire, for he was wearing boots. In a daze of apprehension, he went and studied a Japanese vase which adorned a festooned Louis Quinze console-table; then he feared he might displease Louise's husband by not paying court to him, so he decided to find out if the worthy man had some pet subject on which he could draw him out.

'You don't often leave town, Monsieur?' he asked, returning towards Monsieur de Bargeton.

'Not often.'

Silence reigned once more. Like a wary cat, Monsieur de Bargeton was watching the slightest movements of this young man who was disturbing his repose. Each one was afraid of the other.

'Can he be suspicious about my attentions to Louise?' Lucien wondered. 'He seems definitely unfriendly.'

Just then, luckily for Lucien, who was finding it hard to sustain the uneasy glances Monsieur de Bargeton was casting at him as he paced to and fro, the old servant, wearing a livery, announced Monsieur du Châtelet. The baron came in, completely at ease, saluted his friend Bargeton, and gave Lucien the slight nod which was then in fashion, but Lucien thought it impertinent coming from a revenue official. Sixte du Châtelet was wearing a dazzlingly-white pair of trousers with straps under the feet to keep the crease. He had elegant shoes and stockings of Scotch thread. From his white waistcoat dangled the black ribbon of his monocle, and his black coat was commendable for its Parisian style and cut. He was just the sort of fop that past history would have led one to expect, but age had already endowed him with a rotund little belly which he found quite difficult to keep within the bounds of elegance. His hair and his side-whiskers, which the tribulations of his travels had turned white, were dyed, and that gave him a hard appearance. His complexion, once quite delicate, had taken on the coppery hue of people back from the Indies; but his general appearance, however ridiculous his undiminished pretensions might make it, still revealed something of the affable private secretary to an Imperial Highness.

He adjusted his monocle and scanned his rival from head

to foot, his nankeen trousers, his boots, his waistcoat and his blue coat, made in Angoulême. Then he coldly returned the monocle to his waistcoat pocket as if to say: 'Nothing to worry about.' Lucien, already abashed by the finance official's elegance, told himself he would have his revenge when the gathering saw him with his face radiant with poetry; nonetheless the keenness of his mortification increased the inner discomfort which Monsieur de Bargeton's apparent unfriendliness had caused him. The baron seemed to be bringing all the weight of his wealth to bear down on Lucien in order the better to humiliate him in his poverty. Monsieur de Bargeton, who had hoped to be spared further conversational effort, felt some consternation at the silence maintained by the two rivals as they looked each other up and down; but, whenever he found himself at his wit's end, there was one question which he kept in reserve – it was like a straw to a drowning man – and he judged that the moment had come to let fly with it, which he did, putting on an air of importance.

'Well, well, Monsieur,' he said to du Châtelet, 'What news is there? What are people talking about?'

'Why,' the Director of Taxes spitefully replied. 'Monsieur Chardon, he's the news. Apply to him. Are you not bringing us some pretty poem?' asked the sprightly baron, smoothing the lock of hair on one side of his temple which he felt had become disarranged.

'In order to know if I have succeeded, I ought to have consulted you,' said Lucien. 'You practised poetry long before I did.'

'Oh, merely a few pleasant ditties which I threw off by request, some occasional songs, some drawing-room ballads which were nothing without the music, and the grand Epistle I wrote for a sister of Buonaparte (what ingratitude to use this form of Napoleon's name!). They will give me no claim on posterity.'

At this instant Madame de Bargeton appeared in all the splendour of her carefully-studied *toilette*. She was wearing a Jewish turban embellished with an oriental brooch. A gauze scarf, with the gleaming cameos of a necklace visible underneath it, was gracefully draped around her neck. Her short sleaved dress of coloured muslin enabled her to display several rows of bangles arranged about her beautiful white arms. Lucien was charmed by this theatrical attire. Monsieur du Châtelet gallantly greeted this queenly person with nauseating compliments which drew a pleased smile from her, so happy she was to be praised in front of Lucien. She exchanged but one glance with her dear poet, and the politeness of her reply to the Director of Taxes was a virtual snub since it excluded him from the circle of her close acquaintances.

Just then the guests began to arrive. First of all the Bishop and his Vicar-General came forward: two dignified and portentous figures, who formed a violent contrast, for my lord was tall and thin, while his assistant was short and fat. Both of them had sparkling eyes, but the Bishop was pale and his Vicar-General had the rubicund face of a man blooming with health. Both of them were sparing of gesture and movement. Both seemed to be men of prudence; their reserve and silence were intimidating; they both passed for men of great wit.

The two clerics were followed by Madame de Chandour and her husband – extraordinary personages whom people unacquainted with life in the provinces would be tempted to regard as figments of the imagination. Stanislas de Chandour, Amélie's husband – she it was who posed as a social rival to Madame de Bargeton – was a man who tried to look younger than he was, being still slim at forty-five; he had a face like a sieve. His cravat was always knotted in such a way as to present two menacing points, one on a level with his right ear, the other drooping towards the red ribbon to which his Cross was attached. His coat-tails were sharply cut away. His very open waistcoat showed his bulging, starched shirt front and the ornately bejewelled pins which served as studs. In short, every detail of his costume was exaggerated and made him look so like a caricature that when strangers met him they could scarcely refrain from smiling. Stanislas was for ever scanning himself from head to foot, checking the number of buttons on his waistcoat, his gaze following the undulating lines of his close-fitting trousers, pausing fondly at his legs and coming amorously to rest on the tips of his boots. When he had finished this self-contemplation, he glanced round for a mirror to see if his hair had kept its curl, threw a contented look at the ladies to canvass their approval, thrust a finger into his waistcoat pocket and stood in three-fourths profile: this provoking, prize-cock posturing went down well with the aristocratic society of which he was the accredited lady-killer. More often than not, his discourse was punctuated with the kind of broad jests which had been current in the eighteenth century. This detestable mode of conversation brought him some success with the women and made them laugh. But Monsieur du Châtelet was beginning to give him some cause for anxiety. In fact the ladies, intrigued by the foppish revenue official's disdain, roused by the affectedness of his pretence that nothing could lift him out of his depression, and piqued by his languid sultan's tone of voice, gave him much livelier attention than at first, now that Madame de Bargeton was infatuated with the Byron of Angoulême. Amélie was a little woman with a clumsily theatrical manner, plump, with light skin and black hair, carrying everything to excess, loud-voiced, strutting about with her head laden with feathers in summer and flowers in winter; glib of tongue, but unable to wind up her periods without the accompaniment of wheezes caused by her un-avowed asthma.

Next appeared Monsieur Astolphe de Saintot, President of the Agricultural Society, a man of florid complexion, tall and stout, trailing after his wife, who in figure was very like a withered fern. They called her Lili, short for Elisa. This name, suggestive of something childlike in the person who bore it, squared ill with the character and manners of Madame de Saintot, who was solemn, extremely pious, crotchety and cantankerous at the card-table. Astolphe was reckoned to be a first-class scholar. Though he was an absolute ignoramus, he had contributed articles on sugar and brandy to a Dictionary of Agriculture, every detail of them pilfered from all the newspapers and out-of-date works dealing with these two products. Everyone in the *département* believed he was writing a treatise on modern methods of tilling. Although he remained shut up in his study every morning, he had not written so much as a couple of pages during the last twelve years. If anyone came to see him, they found him scrabbling among his papers, looking for a mislaid note or sharpening his quill; but he squandered the time he spent in his study, lingering over his newspaper, carving corks with his pen-knife, tracing fantastic doodles on his blotting-pad, skimming through his Cicero in the hope of lighting on a sentence or passage which might have some bearing on events of the day. Then, that evening, he would try to lead the conversation on to a subject which allowed him to say: 'There's a page in Cicero which could well be taken for a comment on what is happening today.' Thereupon he would recite the passage to the great astonishment of his listeners, who would repeat to one another: 'Really Astolphe is a mine of knowledge.' This interesting fact circulated through the whole town and gave support to its flattering beliefs about Monsieur de Saintot.

After this couple came Monsieur de Bartas, named Adrien, a baritone who had enormous pretensions as a musician. Self-conceit had seated him astride the diatonic scale: he had begun by admiring his own singing, then he had taken to talking music and in the end talked about nothing else. The art of music had become a kind of monomania with him; he only came to life when talking about it, and was in pain for the whole evening until he was asked to sing. Once he had boomed his way through one of his songs, he really began to live; he gave himself airs, stood on tip-toe when compliments came his way and made a show of modesty; nonetheless he passed from one group to another in quest of praise; then, when the last word had been said, he came back to music by starting a discussion about the difficulty of his song or by heaping praise upon the composer.

Monsieur Alexandre de Brebian, the hero of sepia, who made his friends' rooms hideous with his preposterous draw-ings and disfigured all the albums in the *département*, came in with Monsieur de Bartas. Each man had the other one's wife on his arm. Current scandal had it that this exchange of partners went the whole way. Both of the women, Lolotte (Madame Charlotte de Brebian) and Fifine (Madame Joséphine de Bartas), gave all their thoughts to wrappings and trimmings and the matching of unrelated colours; they were consumed with the desire to be taken for Parisians but gave no care to their homes which were in a lamentable condition. If these two wives, squeezed like dolls in home-made dresses too sparingly cut, afforded an outrageous exhibition of incompatible colour-schemes, their husbands, as devotees of the arts, allowed themselves a provincial slovenliness which made odd spectacles of them. Their crumpled coats gave them the appearance of extras brought on to the stage of a low-class theatre to play the part of high-society wedding guests.

Among the people who sallied forth into the salon, one of the most eccentric figures was that of Monsieur le Comte de Senonches, known to his social peers as Jacques: a great huntsman, haughty, spare, sunburnt, as amiable as a wild boar, as mistrustful as a Venetian, as jealous as a Turk. Yet he was on excellent terms with Monsieur du Hautoy, otherwise known as Francis, the friend of the family.

Madame de Senonches (Zéphirine) was tall and handsome, but some inflammation of the liver had already spoilt her complexion and given her the reputation of being a demanding woman. Her slim figure and delicate proportions provided an excuse for langourous airs which savoured of affectation but betokened the unfailingly satisfied passion and whims of a person who is loved.

Francis was a man of some distinction who had given up his consulship at Valencia and his hopes of a diplomatic career in order to come and live near Zéphirine de Senonches, also called Zizine. The ex-consul looked after the Senonches *ménage*, took over the education of the children, taught them foreign languages, and managed the estate of Monsieur and Madame de Senonches with entire devotedness. The nobility, the administrative officials and the bourgeoisie of Angoulême had long been commenting on the perfect unity of this household in three persons; but, as time went by, the mystery of this conjugal trinity appeared so rare and touching that

Monsieur du Hautoy would have seemed prodigiously immoral if he had shown any sign of getting married. Besides this, they were beginning to find something mysterious and disquieting in Madame de Senonches's excessive attachment to her god-daughter, Mademoiselle de la Haye, who acted as her lady's companion; and despite certain apparently insuperable chronological objections, they discovered striking resemblances between Françoise de la Haye and Francis du Hautoy. When Jacques went out hunting in the neighbourhood, everyone asked him for news about Francis, and he gave his unofficial major-domo precedence over his wife by reporting all his minor indispositions. Such blindness in a jealous person seemed so peculiar that his best friends enjoyed drawing him out and revealed this peculiarity to people unaware of it so that they too could enjoy the joke. Monsieur du Hautoy was a mincing dandy, and the little attentions he paid to his person had made him finicky and childish. He worried about his cough, his sleep, his digestion and his food. Zéphirine had encouraged her factotum to pose as a man of delicate health; she coddled him, muffled him up; she crammed him with titbits like a marquise's lap-dog; she prescribed or forbade him this or that sort of food; she embroidered waistcoats, cravat-ends and handkerchiefs for him; in the end she got him so much into the habit of wearing decorative trifles that she transformed him into a sort of Japanese idol. Moreover there was not even a shadow of misunderstanding between them: Zizine's glance turned to Francis on each and every occasion, and Francis seemed to take his ideas from Zizine's eyes. They were unanimous in blame or approval, and appeared to consult each other even before wishing anyone good-day.

The richest landowner in the district, a man envied by all, Monsieur le Marquis de Pimentel and his lady, whose joint income amounted to forty thousand francs a year, who always spent the winter in Paris, now arrived from the country in their barouche with their neighbours Monsieur le Baron and Madame la Baronne de Rastignac, accompanied by the Baron's aunt and their two daughters, charming young persons, well-bred, impoverished, but attired in that simplicity of dress which so much enhances natural beauty. These persons, who were beyond doubt the *élite* of the company, were received in chilly silence with a deference fraught with jealousy, especially when everyone saw the courtly welcome which Madame de Bargeton extended to them. Both these families belonged to the minority of provincials who hold aloof from gossip, do not mix with any clique, live in quiet seclusion and preserve an imposing dignity. Monsieur de Pimentel and Monsieur de Rastignac were addressed by their titles; no relation of familiarity existed between their womenfolk and those of the smart set in Angoulême – they were too close to the Court nobility to take any part in the inanities of provincial life.

Last of all came the Prefect and the General, accompanied by Monsieur de Séverac, the country gentleman who that morning had brought his memoir on silk-worm culture to David's office. He was, no doubt, the mayor of some canton or other, for which he possessed no other qualification than his rich estates; but his appearance and attire showed that he was completely out of his element in society, was ill at ease in the clothes he wore, was at a loss to know what to do with his hands, walked round and round any person he was talking to, stood up and sat down again when replying to any remark made to him, and looked as if he were ready to perform some menial task. He was obsequious, apprehensive and solemn by turns; he was in a hurry to laugh at any joke, listened with fawning attention, and sometimes put on an air of slyness when he thought anyone was making fun of him. Several times that evening, with his memoir lying heavy on his mind, Monsieur de Séverac tried to talk about silk-worms; but he was unlucky enough to light on Monsieur de Bartas who brought the subject back to music, and Monsieur de Saintot who quoted Cicero to him. Halfway through the evening the poor mayor managed to hit it off with a widow and her daughter, Madame and Mademoiselle du Broussard, who were by no means the two least diverting figures in this assembly. One word will explain their position: they were as poor as they were well-born. Their effort to appear well-dressed was indicative of concealed poverty. Very maladroitly and on all occasions Madame du Brossard sang the praises of her large and lanky daughter, a girl of seventeen who was supposed to be very good at the piano. She was at pains to show that any marriageable man and her daughter shared the same tastes, and once, on one and the same evening, in her anxiety to find a husband for her dear Camille, she had claimed that Camille loved both a wandering life in garrison towns and the settled existence led by gentlemen-farmers. They both had the prim and bitter-sweet dignity of persons whom everyone takes a delight in pitying, in whom people are interested out of egoism and who well know how empty are the soothing phrases with which society is pleased to greet the unfortunate. Monsieur de Séverac was fifty-nine and a childless widower; and so mother and daughter hung on his words with reverent admiration as he regaled them with all the details of his silkworm-breeding activities.

'My daughter has always loved animals,' said the mother. 'And so, since the silk which these little creatures spin interests us women, I will ask your leave to bring my Camille to Séverac for you to show her how silk is collected. Camille is so intelligent that she will grasp everything you tell her straight away. In fact, one day she was even able to understand the inverse ratio of the square of distances!' It was on this glorious note that the conversation between Monsieur de Séverac and Madame du Brossard came to an end, after Lucien's recital.

A few *habitués* drifted unceremoniously into the room; also two or three youths of good social standing, decked out in all their finery, but shy, tongue-tied, happy to have been invited on this impressive literary occasion. The boldest of them had a long chat with Mademoiselle de la Haye. All the women solemnly sat round in a circle with the men standing behind them. This gathering of odd people, with their strange assortment of dress and make-up, filled Lucien with awe, and his heart beat fast at finding himself the centre of attention. Bold as he was, he could hardly face this first ordeal without flinching, despite the encouragements of his patroness, who received the illustrious *élite* of the province with all the social graces of her repertoire. His initial embarrassment was prolonged by a circumstance easy to foresee, but one which was bound to perturb a young man still unfamiliar with the tactics of society. Lucien, who was all eyes and ears, heard himself styled 'Monsieur de Rubempré' by Louise, Monsieur de Bargeton, the Bishop and a few of the hostess's intimates, and 'Monsieur Chardon' by the greater part of this redoubtable gathering. Intimidated by the enquiring glances which curious people directed at him, he could read by the movement of their lips that they were articulating his bourgeois patronymic, and could guess in advance the judgements they were passing on him with that provincial candour which only too often verges on rudeness. These continual and unexpected pinpricks made him still more unsure of himself. He waited impatiently for the moment when he could begin his reading and take up a posture which would put an end to his torment of mind; but Jacques was telling Madame de Pimentel about his latest day in the hunting-field; Adrien was holding forth about Rossini, the new musical celebrity, to Mademoiselle Laure de Rastignac; Astolphe, who had learnt off by heart the newspaper description of a new kind of plough, was reeling it off to the Baron. The unhappy poet was unaware that with the exception of Madame de Bargeton poetry was a closed book to the minds of everyone present. They were all totally lacking in sensibility and had flocked together in a state of self-delusion about the kind of entertainment that awaited them. There are certain words which will always draw an audience like the trumpets, cymbals and big drum of mountebanks. The words beauty, glory, poetry have a magic appeal for the coarsest spirits.

When the company was complete, when the talking came to an end – not without many warnings given to the chatterers by Monsieur de Bargeton, whom his wife sent round like a church beadle smiting his wand on the flagstones – Lucien took his stance at the round table, with Madame de Bargeton by his side, in a state of violent mental turmoil. With quavering voice he announced that, so as not to disappoint the expectations of his audience, he was going to read the recently discovered masterpieces of a great but unknown poet. Although André Chénier's poems had been published in 1819, no one in Angoulême had heard of him as yet. Everybody interpreted this announcement as an expedient adopted by Madame de Bargeton in order to safeguard the poet's self-esteem and put the audience at its ease. Lucien started by reading *The Love-sick Youth*, which was received with flattering murmurs; then *The Blind Poet*, which was too long for these mediocre minds. While reading, Lucien was a prey to the excruciating suffering which can only be understood by artists or by those whose enthusiasm and high intelligence raise them to a similar level. If poetry, when read or when recited, is to be understood, devout attention must be paid to it. There must be a close bond between reader and listener, for without this the electric communication of feeling is impossible. If this cohesion between souls is lacking, the poet then feels like an angel trying to sing a celestial hymn amid the jeering laughter of demons. Now men of intelligence, in the sphere in which their faculties are developed, have the circumspective vision of a snail, the keen scent of a hound and the fine ear of a mole: they see, smell and hear everything around them. A musician or a poet as quickly senses admiration or incomprehension as a plant withers or freshens in a favourable or unfavourable atmosphere. Thanks to this acoustic sensibility, the whisperings of the men who had only come there as escorts to their wives and were talking of their own concerns resounded in Lucien's ears; he also noticed the reflex action of wide yawns and the consequent exposure of teeth which seemed to be mocking at him. And when like the dove from the ark he looked for a favourable spot on which his eye could rest, he encountered only the impatient gaze of people who had obviously been hoping that this gathering would have provided them an opportunity for exchanging views on matters of mutual interest. With the exception of Laure de Rastignac, two or three young people, and the Bishop, the whole assembly was bored. Indeed, connoisseurs of poetry try to allow the seed which the author's verse has sown to germinate in their soul; but this icy audience, far from absorbing the spirit of the poetry, did not even listen to the words. And so Lucien felt such profound discouragement that his shirt became damp with cold perspiration. He turned to look at Louise, and a fiery glance from her gave him enough courage to finish the reading; but his poet's heart was bleeding from a thousand wounds.

'Do you find that very entertaining, Fifine?' said the desiccated Lili to her neighbour – she had probably been expecting some spectacular display.

'Don't ask me my opinion, dear. I doze off as soon as I hear anyone reading.'

'I hope Naïs wont often give us poetry recitals in the evening,' said Francis. 'When I listen to reading after dinner, the attention I have to pay to it upsets my digestion.'

'Poor darling,' whispered Zéphirine. 'Have a glass of lemonade.'

'A very good recital,' said Alexandre. 'But I prefer whist.'

On hearing this remark which was regarded as witty because of the Irish meaning of the word,[1] a few ladies anxious for a game of cards made out that the reciter needed a rest. On this pretext, one or two couples slipped off into the boudoir. Then Lucien, at the request of Louise, the charming Laure de Rastignac and the Bishop, aroused attention once more by declaiming the spirited counter-revolutionary *Iambics*, which a few people, carried away by the verve with which Lucien recited them, applauded although they did not understand them. Such people can be influenced by vociferation just as coarse palates are excited by crude spirits. While ices were being passed round, Zéphirine sent Francis to have a look at the volume, and informed Amélie, who was sitting next to her, that the verses read by Lucien were in print.

'Well,' answered Amélie, with obvious pleasure. 'It's quite simple. Monsieur de Rubempré works at a printing-office. It's just like a pretty woman making her own gowns' – this she said with a side-glance at Lolotte.

1. 'Whisht!': hush!

'He has printed his poems himself,' the women said to one another.

'Why then does he call himself Monsieur de Rubempré?' asked Jacques. 'A gentleman should drop his name when he takes to manual labour.'

'He has in fact dropped his,' said Zizine. 'It was a commoner's name, and he has taken that of his mother, who is of gentle birth.'

'Since his lines are in print, we can read them for ourselves,' said Astolphe.

This stupidity confused the issue until Sixte du Châtelet deigned to explain to this ignorant gathering that Lucien's announcement had not been an oratorical precaution and that these fine poems had been written by the royalist brother of the revolutionary Marie-Joseph Chénier. This Angoulême assembly, with the exception of the Bishop, Madame de Rastignac and her two daughters, who had been impressed by the poetry, believed that it had been hoaxed and took offence at such deceit. There were low murmurs, but Lucien did not hear them. Isolated from this odious crowd by the enthralling melodies which were echoing through his mind, he was trying to convey them to his audience and so had only a misty view of people's faces. He read the sombre elegy on suicide, the one in which profound melancholy is expressed in the style of antiquity; then the one which contains the following line:

Your lines are sweet, I love to echo them.

And he finished up by reading the graceful idyll entitled *Néère*.

Steeped in delightful reveries, one hand passing through her curls which she had inadvertently ruffled, the other hanging inactive, with absent look, alone in the midst of her guests, Madame de Bargeton felt transported into her own rightful sphere for the first time in her life. Imagine then how disagreeable it was for her to be brought down to earth by Amélie, who took it upon herself to voice the general opinion.

'Naïs, we came here to listen to Monsieur Chardon's poems, and you are only giving us published poetry. Although these pieces are very pretty, the ladies here have enough local patriotism to prefer the local vintage.'

'Don't you think the French language is not very suitable for poetry?' Astolphe asked of the Director of Taxes. 'I find Cicero's prose a thousand times more poetic.'

'True French poetry is light poetry, the *chanson*,' replied du Châtelet.

'The *chanson* proves that our language is very musical,' said Adrien.

'I should very much like to hear the verses which have brought about Naïs's downfall,' said Zéphirine. 'But judging by the way she's treating Amélie's request, she doesn't feel inclined to give us a sample of them.'

'She owes it to herself to make him recite them,' answered Francis, 'After all, this young fellow's talent is his only justification for being here.'

'You have been in the diplomatic career, Monsieur du Châtelet,' said Amélie. 'Get him to do it.'

'Nothing could be easier,' replied the baron.

The former Secretary to her Imperial Highness was used to little manoeuvres of this kind: he went over to the Bishop and was able to bring him forward. At his Lordship's request, Naïs was forced to ask Lucien to recite some piece which he knew by heart. For his prompt success in this negotiation, the baron was rewarded by a languid smile from Amélie.

'Decidedly the baron has his wits about him,' she said to Lolotte.

Lolotte was remembering Amélie's feline remark about women who made their own dresses.

'How long is it since you began recognizing barons of the Imperial vintage?' she asked with a smile.

Lucien had attempted to deify his lady in an ode addressed to her under the kind of title young men invent on leaving school. This ode, over whose composition he had lingered so fondly and which was embellished with all the love he had in his heart, seemed to him to be the only work capable of rivalling that of Chénier. He gazed at Madame de Bargeton with a somewhat fatuous air and announced the title: TO HER!

Then he struck a lofty pose before declaiming this ambitious poem, for, with Madame de Bargeton to stand by him, he felt secure in his self-esteem as an author.

At this instant, Naïs's secret attachment became patent to the women present. Usually her high intelligence allowed her to dominate the people of her salon, but now she could not help feeling tremulous on Lucien's behalf. She was visibly embarrassed, and she looked round as if she were in some way asking for their indulgence. After which she had perforce to sit there with her eyes cast down and conceal her satisfaction as Lucien began to deliver the following stanzas:

TO HER

Often an angel, lily-tressed, takes flight
From Heaven's courts all radiant with glory
Where to Jehovah seraph choirs recite
Humanity's sad story.

Leaving the cohort of celestial legions
She lays aside her goldren sistrum, yields
Her silver wings, and droops through starry fields
To this world's darker regions.

Divine compassion moves her to assuage
The grief of genius; or, as winsome maid
In childhood's bloom bewitchingly arrayed,
Dispel the gloom of age.

Repentant vice she's quick to shrive and bless,
And whispers courage in a mother's ear.
Joy fills her heart when Dives sheds a tear
For Lazarus in distress.

One only of such envoys have we here,
Too fair, too loved for Earth to let her go.
Weeping, she lifts her gaze from here below
To the Paternal sphere.

'Tis not the splendours on her brow that shine
Need tell me from what Paradise she came;
Nor gleam of eye, nor yet the abundant flame
Of her virtue divine.

She is enhaloed, and my ravished soul
Would fain with her have saintly union found.
But archangelic armour girds her round
And frights me from my goal.

Shield then, shield from a lover's dazzled eyes
The shining seraph heavenwards returning!
Too soon would he the magic word be learning
That falls from twilit skies.

Then would you see us with exultant paean
Winging through cloud-rack to the empyrean
In close fraternal flight;
And sea-tossed sailors would descry the trace
Of spirits luminous soaring through space:
New stars to chart the Night!

'Do you understand this rigmarole?', Amélie asked of
Monsieur du Châtelet with a coquettish ogle.

'The sort of verse most of us scribbled when we left school,'
the baron answered, putting on an air of boredom in order to
sustain his role of sophisticated critic. 'Time was when we
went in for the mists of Ossian. We babbled of Malvinas, Fin-
gals, wraiths wrapped in clouds, warriors rising from their
graves with stars shining over their heads. Nowadays that kind
of poetic frippery has given place to Jehovah, sistrums, angels,
seraphs' wings and all the stock-in-trade of Paradise to which
words like 'immense', 'infinity', 'solitude' and 'intelligence'
have given a new lease of life. We deal in lakes, God speaking
through the clouds, a sort of near-Christian pantheism enriched with rare and far-fetched rhymes, like amethyst and
rainbow-kist, colocynth and labyrinth, and so forth. In short,
we have moved into new latitudes, from North to East: but
thick darkness still reigns.'

'The ode itself may be obscure,' said Zéphirine, 'but the
declaration seems clear enough to me.'

'And the archangelic armour is a fairly diaphanous muslin
garment,' said Francis.

Although politeness demanded that they should profess to
find the ode ravishing in order to please Madame de Bargeton,

the ladies, enraged at having no poet at their service to call them angels, rose from their seats with boredom written on their faces and murmured in icy tones: *Very good*; *lovely*; *perfect*.

'If you care at all for me, you will not congratulate the author or his angel,' said Lolotte to her dear Adrien with a despotic air which commanded obedience.

'After all, it's just verbiage,' said Zéphirine to Francis. 'Whereas love is poetry in action.'

'That's precisely what I was thinking, Zizine, but I couldn't have put it so neatly,' rejoined Stanislas, complacently surveying himself from head to foot.

'I would give quite a lot,' Amélie told du Châtelet, 'to bring Naïs down a peg or two. Letting a man call her an archangel! As if she were any better than us! And making us mix with such riff-raff: the son of a chemist and a sick-nurse, his sister a laundry-maid and himself a printer's assistant!'

'His father sold pills to cure flatulence,' said Jacques. 'He ought to have given some to his son!'

'He's carrying on his father's trade, for what he has just dispensed to us is very like a nostrum,' said Stanislas, assuming one of his most provocative poses. 'If I needed a nostrum, I could choose a better one.'

Immediately, of one accord, they set out to humiliate Lucien with their ironic and snobbish witticisms. Being a pious woman, Lili regarded this as an act of charity, proclaiming that it was time to enlighten Naïs and bring her to her senses. Francis the diplomat undertook to make a success of this stupid conspiracy, and all these petty-minded people threw themselves into it as if they were watching the last act of a play, and thought of it as a bit of sport they could tell their friends about the next morning.

The former consul, preferring to avoid a duel with the young poet who would be sent into a fury by a gibe uttered in the hearing of his patroness, realized that a non-secular weapon, one which excluded all possibility of retaliation, must be used in order to lay him low. He followed the example set him by the adroit du Châtelet when the question had arisen of asking Lucien to recite his verses. He went over to the Bishop, chatted with him, and pretended to share the enthusiasm which his Lordship had felt on hearing Lucien's ode. Then he maliciously intimated that Lucien's mother was a woman of superior talent and excessive modesty, and that it was she who had provided her son with the themes of all his poems. Lucien adored his mother, he said, and his greatest pleasure was to see other people paying just tribute to her. Once the Bishop had got this notion into his head, Francis calculated that the vagaries of conversation would lead up to a cruel witticism which he was hoping to elicit from the prelate.

When Francis and the Bishop rejoined the guests clustered round Lucien, those who had already been administrating small doses of hemlock to the wretched poet became doubly attentive. Having absolutely no experience of salon tricks and stratagems, Lucien could do nothing but gaze at Madame de Bargeton and give gauche answers to the gauche questions they asked him. He was ignorant of the names and titles of most of the persons present, and did not know how to hold his own in conversation with women whose inane remarks put him to shame. Moreover he felt worlds apart from these Angoulême divinities who at one moment called him Monsieur Chardon and at another Monsieur de Rubempré, while they addressed one another as Lolotte, Adrien, Astolphe, Lili and Fifine. His confusion was extreme when, taking Lili for a man's name, he called the brutal Monsieur de Senonches 'Monsieur Lili'. That Nimrod interrupted Lucien by calling him 'Monsieur Lulu', and Madame de Bargeton flushed up to the ears.

'One must be far gone in blindness to let in this little bounder and introduce him to us here,' he said under his breath.

'Madame la Marquise,' said Zéphirine to Madame de Pimentel in a low tone, but loud enough to be heard. 'Do you not notice a strong resemblance between Monsieur Chardon and Monsieur de Cante-Croix?'

'An ideal resemblance,' replied Madame de Pimentel with a smile.

'Glory can exert an attraction,' Madame de Bargeton said to the Marquise, 'which there is no shame in acknowledging. Some women are as susceptible to greatness as others are to pettiness,' she added with a side-glance at Francis.

Zéphirine missed the point of this, for she considered her consul a very great man; but the Marquise took sides with Naïs by breaking into laughter.

'You are a very fortunate man, sir,' Monsieur de Pimentel said to Lucien, correcting himself by calling him Monsieur de Rubempré after having called him Chardon. 'You can never be bored!'

'Do you work quickly?' asked Lolotte in the tone one would have used in asking a carpenter: 'Does it take you long to make a box?'

Lucien remained quite stunned after receiving this bludgeon blow; but he raised his head again when he heard Madame de Bargeton smilingiy reply: 'My dear, poetry doesn't spring up in Monsieur de Rubempré's head like grass in our courtyards.'

'Madame,' said the Bishop to Lolotte. 'We cannot show too much respect to those noble minds whom God has endowed with a beam of His own light. Indeed, poetry is a sacred thing. Poetry involves suffering. How many nights of silence have paid for the stanzas you admire! Pay a tribute of love to the poet who almost always leads an unhappy life and for whom God no doubt reserves a place in Heaven among his prophets. This young man *is* a poet,' he added, setting his hand on Lucien's head. 'Do you not see the mark of predestination on this handsome forehead?'

Happy at being so nobly defended, Lucien thanked the Bishop with a gentle glance, little knowing that the worthy prelate was about to become his executioner. The exultant glances which Madame de Bargeton darted at this hostile circle struck home like so many javelins into the hearts of her rivals and redoubled their fury.

'Ah! my Lord,' the poet replied, hoping to bring his golden sceptre down on the heads of these imbeciles. 'Common minds have neither your wit nor your charity. No one knows the grief we suffer or the toil we endure. A miner has less labour winning the gold from his mine than we have in wresting our imagery from the entrails of this most obdurate language of ours. If the aim of poetry is to bring ideas to the exact point at which the rest of the world can perceive and feel them, the poet must be for ever mounting and descending the ladder of men's intelligence in order to satisfy them all; he must conceal those mutually hostile forces, logic and sentiment, under the most vivid colours; he must concentrate a whole world of ideas in a single word and sum up whole philosophies in a single image; in short his verses are so many seeds which he sows in the furrows of personal feeling so that flowers may spring up in human hearts. Must he not have felt all there is to feel in order to give expression to it? And if one feels keenly, is not that suffering? Therefore poetry is only born after arduous journeys through the vast regions of thought and society. Are they not immortal, the works to which we owe those creations whose life becomes more authentic than that of people who have really lived – Richardson's Clarissa, Chénier's Camille, Tibullus's Delia, Ariosto's Angelica, Dante's Francesca, Molière's Alceste, Beaumarchais's Figaro, Walter Scott's Rebecca and the Don Quixote of Cervantes?'

'And what will you be creating for us?' asked du Châtelet.

'To put forth such conceptions,' Lucien replied, 'is it not tantamount to taking out one's patent as a man of genius? In any case, to give birth to such sublime conceptions demands a long experience of life, a study of human passions and interests that I could not yet have made. – But I am making a start,' he added bitterly as he threw a vengeful glance at the people around him. 'Ideas gestate a long time in the womb of thought.'

'You will have a painful delivery,' interrupted Monsieur du Hautoy.

'Your excellent mother will be able to help you,' said the Bishop.

This apparent witticism, so skilfully engineered, was the avenging shaft they had all been awaiting, and their eyes lit up with a gleam of delight. A smile of aristocratic satisfaction passed over everybody's face, and its effect was increased by Monsieur de Bargeton who, in his idiocy, gave vent to a belated laugh.

'My Lord, your wit is too subtle for us at this moment. These ladies do not understand you,' said Madame de Bargeton. This single word froze all laughter and made them turn their eyes on her with astonishment. 'A poet who draws all his inspiration from the Bible finds his true mother in the Church. Monsieur de Rubempré, read to us *Saint John at Pathmos*, or *Belshazzar's Feast*, in order to prove to my Lord Bishop that Rome is still the *magna parens* of Virgil.'

The women exchanged a smile on hearing Naïs pronounce these two Latin words.

On the threshold of life, men of the stoutest courage may well lose heart. At the first moment this affront cast Lucien down into watery depths; but he struck out and rose to the surface, vowing that he would dominate this gathering of people. Like a bull stung by a thousand darts, he pulled himself up in a rage and was about to do as Louise had said and recite *Saint John at Pathmos*; but most of the card-players, falling back into their routine habits, which afforded them a pleasure that poetry had not provided, returned to the whist-tables. Moreover, the irritated self-esteem of so many people would not have been fully avenged without the negative disdain for indigenous poetry which they displayed by deserting Lucien and Madame de Bargeton. They each had their special preoccupation: one of the men went and discussed the construction of a by-road with the Prefect; one of the women suggested that the evening's pleasure might be varied with a little music. The high society of Angoulême, fully incompetent to judge poetry, was anxious to know what the Rastignacs and the Pimentels thought of Lucien, and several persons gathered round them. On important occasions the prestige enjoyed by these two families in the *département* was always recognized: everyone envied them and paid court to them, for they all foresaw the possibility of needing their protection.

'What do you think of our poet and his poetry?' Jacques asked the Marquise, over whose lands he was allowed to shoot.

'Well,' she replied with a smile, 'it's not bad as far as provincial verse goes. Anyhow so good-looking a poet can't write anything bad.'

Everyone found this verdict adorable and went off to repeat it, but with greater malice than the Marquise had intended to put into it.

Then du Châtelet was asked to accompany Monsieur de Bartas as he massacred Figaro's great song. Now that the door was opened to music, they simply had to listen to du Châtelet's rendering of the chivalric ballad which Chateaubriand had written in Imperial days. Then came piano duets such as are played by little girls and called for by Madame du Brossard who wanted to show off her darling Camille's talent to Monsieur de Séverac.

Madame de Bargeton, wounded by the general display of contempt for her poet, returned disdain for disdain by retiring into her boudoir while the music was on. She was followed by the Bishop whose Vicar-General had explained to him the deep irony contained in his unintended epigram and who wanted to make up for it. Mademoiselle de Rastignac, captivated by the poem, slipped into the boudoir without her mother noticing. As Louise sat down on the quilted sofa to which she had brought Lucien, she was able, without being seen or heard, to whisper in his ear: 'Dear angel, they didn't understand you, but

Your lines are sweet, I love to echo them.'

Consoled by this flattery, Lucien forgot his grief for a moment.

'Renown can never be bought cheaply,' said Louise, taking and pressing his hand. 'You must suffer, really suffer, my friend; you will be great; grief is the price you must pay for immortality. I myself would love to have to endure the pains of conflict. God preserve you from the drabness of an existence free from struggles in which no eagle could ever spread his wings. I envy you your sufferings, for you at least are alive! You will put forth all your strength and have victory to hope for! Your struggle will be a glorious one. When you have climbed to that lofty sphere in which spirits of great intelligence are enthroned, be mindful of the poor folk whom fate has disinherited, whose intelligence is, morally speaking, stifled for lack of oxygen, who perish because, although they have always known what life can be, they have never lived; who have had keen eyes but have seen nothing; who have had delicate nostrils but have only known the scent of malodorous flowers. Sing then of the plant which withers deep down in the forest, choked by creeping ivies, by rampant and parasitic vegetation, never having felt the sun's caress, and dying without coming into bloom! Would not that be a poem of awe-inspiring melancholy, a real fantasy? What a superb composition that would make: the picture of a girl born under Asian skies or some child of the desert transported to a cold western country, crying out for the sunshine she adores, dying of sufferings that no one understands, perishing of cold and starved of love! It would be a symbol of many people's lives.'

'You would thus be picturing the soul remembering Heaven,' said the Bishop: 'a poem which must have been written in time past – I was pleased to find a fragment of it in the *Song of Songs*.'

'Do undertake it,' said Laure de Rastignac, expressing her simple faith in Lucien's genius.

'There is room in France for a great sacred poem,' the Bishop continued. 'Believe me, fame and fortune will come to a man of talent who will work for Religion.'

'He will undertake it, my Lord,' said Madame de Bargeton in a grandiloquent tone. 'Can you not see the idea of such a poem already dawning in his eyes like a glimmer of flame at day-break?'

'Naïs is treating us very badly,' Fifine was saying. 'What can she be doing?'

'Can't you hear her?' asked Stanislas. 'She's riding her hobby-horse – high-sounding words which nobody can make head or tail of.'

Amélie, Fifine, Adrien and Francis appeared at the door of

the boudoir with Madame de Rastignac, who was coming to look for her daughter and take her home.

'Naïs,' said the two women, delighted to disturb the private conversation going on in the boudoir. 'Won't you be kind and play something for us?'

'My dear child,' replied Madame de Bargeton. 'Monsieur de Rubempré is going to recite his *Saint John at Pathmos*, a splendid Biblical poem.'

'Biblical!,' echoed the astonished Fifine.

Amélie and Fifine returned to the drawing-room, and reported Louise's announcement as pabulum for mockery. Lucien excused himself from reciting the poem on the grounds of defective memory. When he reappeared, he aroused not the slightest interest. They were all chatting or playing cards. The poet had been stripped of all his radiance; the landed proprietors saw no use in him at all; the social climbers feared him as a powerful menace to their ignorance; the women, jealous of Madame de Bargeton – the Beatrice of this new Dante, according to the Vicar-General – threw glances of cold disdain at him.

'So that is the *beau monde*!' Lucien said to himself as he walked down to L'Houmeau along the slopes of Beaulieu, for there are moments in life when one likes to take the longest way home, so that walking may favour the train of thought which one wishes to pursue. Far from feeling discouraged, Lucien's fury at seeing his ambitions repulsed was giving him new strength. Like all men whom instinct drives upwards to a sphere which they reach before they are able to hold their own in it, he promised himself that he would stop at no sacrifice to maintain himself in high society. As he went along, he plucked out one by one the poisoned arrows which had been shot at him and, talking out loud to himself, he upbraided the ignoramuses he had had to deal with; subtle replies to their silly questions came to his mind, and he was exasperated at having thought of such witty retorts only when it was too late. As he reached the Bordeaux road which winds round the foot of the hill and skirts the banks of the Charente, he caught a glimpse in the moonlight of Eve and David, sitting on a log by the riverside, near a tannery: he followed the path which led down to them.

*

While Lucien was speeding towards his agony in Madame de Bargeton's salon, his sister had put on a pink multi-striped percaline dress, her stitched-straw hat and a small silk shawl: a simple attire which made her look well-dressed, as is the case with all persons in whom natural dignity sets off the slightest additional adornment. And so, having changed from her working dress, she had put David in a considerable flutter. Although the printer had resolved to propose to her, he was unable to utter a word when he gave the beautiful Eve his arm as they walked through L'Houmeau. Cupid is pleased with such deferential awe, not dissimilar to that which the glory of God arouses in His worshippers. The enamoured pair walked in silence towards the Pont Sainte-Anne in order to cross the left bank of the Charente. Eve found this silence embarrassing and paused half-way across the bridge in order to gaze at the river which, from that point to the place where the gunpowder factory was being built, forms a long pool on to which the setting sun was then casting a joyous stream of light.

'What a lovely evening!' she said in her search for a subject to talk about. 'The air is both warm and fresh, the flowers smell sweet, and there's a gorgeous sky.'

'Everything speaks to the heart,' replied David, trying to bring up the subject of love by way of analogy. 'People who love find infinite pleasure discovering the poetry which fills their soul in the undulations of a landscape, the transparency of the atmosphere and the scents which rise from the earth. Nature speaks for them.'

'She also loosens their tongues,' said Eve, laughingly. 'You were very quiet as we went through L'Houmeau. Do you know I felt really ill at ease?'

'You looked so beautiful that I was struck dumb,' David naïvely replied.

'So I am less beautiful now?'

'No; but I am so happy walking alone with you that . . . '

He was so nonplussed that he stood still and looked out over the hills with the Saintes road winding down them.

'If you are enjoying this walk I am delighted, for I feel I owe you this evening in exchange for the one you have given up for my sake. In refusing to go to Madame de Bargeton's house you have been just as generous as Lucien had been in running the risk of annoying her by the request he made.'

'Not generous, but wise,' David answered. 'Since we are alone under the sky, with no other witnesses than the reeds and bushes on the river bank, allow, me, dear Eve, to express some of the anxiety I feel about the course Lucien is following at present. After what I have just told him, you will regard my fears, I hope, as a mark of scrupulous friendship. You and your mother have done everything you could to give him ideas above his station; but by rousing ambition in him, have you not imprudently doomed him to great suffering? How will he maintain his position in the society to which his tastes attract him? I know him! He is of the kind who like to reap without sowing. Social commitments will take up all his time, and time is the sole capital of people whose future depends on their intelligence: he loves to shine, and society will intensify his desires, which no amount of money will be able to satisfy. He will spend money and earn none; in short, you have got him into the habit of thinking he's a great man; but society, before recognizing any sort of superiority, expects it to be strikingly successful. Now literary success is only achieved in solitude and through unremitting labour. What will Madame de Bargeton give your brother in return for so many days spent at her feet? Lucien is too proud to accept help from her, and we know he is still too poor to continue to mix with the society she keeps: a double source of ruin for him. Sooner or later this woman will abandon our dear brother after destroying his zest for work, after developing his taste for luxury, his contempt for our sober way of life, his love of enjoyment and his tendency to idleness, which is the kind of debauchery to which poets are prone. Yes, I tremble to think that his great lady may be using him as a plaything: either she loves him and he will forget all else; or she does not love him and will make him unhappy, for he's infatuated with her.'

'You chill me to the heart,' said Eve, stopping in front of the Charente dam. 'But so long as my mother has strength to carry on with her laborious profession, and so long as I live, the amount our work brings in will perhaps suffice for Lucien's expenditure and enable him to wait for the tide of fortune to change. I shall never be short of courage, for the idea of working for a person one loves' – Eve said this with heightened animation – 'takes all the bitterness and tedium from toil. I am happy when I consider for whom I am taking so much trouble – if indeed you can call it trouble. No, have no fear: we will earn enough money for Lucien to move in society. There lies prosperity for him.'

'There too lies disaster,' David rejoindered. 'Listen to me, dear Eve. The slow composition of works of genius calls either for a considerable ready-made fortune or a life of sublime unconcern lived in poverty. Believe me! Lucien holds the privations of indigence in such horror, he has so complacently sniffed the aroma of banquets, the perfume of success, his self-esteem has grown so big in Madame de Bargeton's boudoir that he will try anything rather than sink down again: the amount your work brings in will never be proportionate to his needs.'

'You are only a false friend after all!' Eve exclaimed in desperation. 'Or else you would not discourage us in this way.'

'Eve! Eve!' answered David. 'I wish I were indeed Lucien's brother. You alone can give me that title, which would enable him to accept everything from me and would give me the right to devote myself to him with the sacred love which you bring to the sacrifices you make – but also with the discernment of a level-headed person. Eve, my dear beloved child, make it possible for Lucien to possess a capital on which he can unashamedly draw. Will not a brother's purse be the same as if it were his? If only you knew all the ideas that Lucien's new situation has inspired in me! If he wants to visit Madame de Bargeton, he must cease to be my proof-reader; he must no longer live in L'Houmeau; you must no longer be a working-girl, and your mother must give up her employment. If you would consent to become my wife, the way would be made smooth. Lucien could live on my second floor while I built him a flat above the penthouse at the end of the courtyard, unless my father were willing to build a second storey. In this way we could arrange for him to lead a life free of care, a life of independence. The desire I have to stand by Lucien would give me, as regards my own future, an incentive which I should lack if I thought of myself alone; but it depends on you to sanction my devotion. One day perhaps he will go to Paris, the only theatre in which he can really make his *début* and where his talents can be appreciated and rewarded. Life in Paris is dear, and the three of us will not be too many to keep him going there. Besides this, do not both you and your mother need a support in life? Darling Eve, marry me for love of Lucien. Later perhaps you will come to love me when you see the effort I shall make to serve him and to make you happy. We are both of us equally moderate in our tastes, and our needs will not be great; Lucien's happiness will be our major concern, and his affection for us will be the savings-bank in which we shall invest our fortune, our feelings and our sensations – all we have in fact!'

'Convention is against us,' said Eve, who was touched to see such great love taking so humble a role. 'You are well-to-do and I am poor. One must be very much in love to rise superior to so great an obstacle.'

'Then you don't yet love me enough for that?' cried David in consternation.

'But perhaps your father would object . . .'

'That's fine,' David replied. 'If my father's consent is all that matters, you will be my wife. Eve, my darling Eve! You have just at this moment made my life very easy to bear. My heart, alas, was weighed down with feelings I dared not and could not express. Only tell me that you love me a little, and I shall have courage enough to tell you what else I have in mind.'

'Indeed,' she said, 'you are making me feel very shy. But

since we are confiding our feelings to each other, I will say that never in my life have my thoughts gone out to anyone but you. I have looked on you as one of those men to whom a woman may be proud to belong, and, as a poor working-girl with no prospects, I scarcely dared to hope for so happy a lot.'

'Say no more, say no more,' he said, and he sat down on the wall of the dam, for they had come back to it after pacing frantically to and fro over the same ground.

'Is there something the matter?' she asked, for the first time showing that graceful solicitude which women feel for someone who belongs to them.

'Nothing but good,' he replied. 'At the prospect of a life of complete happiness, one's mind is dazed, one's heart is full. Why am I the happier of us two?' he asked in a tone of melancholy. 'But I well know why.'

Eve looked at David with a coquettishly questioning air.

'Dear Eve, I am getting more than I am giving. And so I shall always love you more than you will love me, because I have greater reason for loving you: you are an angel, I am only a man.'

'That is too clever for me,' replied Eve with a smile. 'I really do love you.'

'As much as you love Lucien?' he broke in.

'Enough to become your wife, devote myself to you and try to spare you any sorrow in the life we shall spend together. It will be a hard life to start with.'

'Did you notice, darling, that I fell in love with you the very first day we met?'

'Is there any woman who cannot tell when a man loves her?'

'Then let me dispel the scruples you have about my supposed wealth. I am poor, dear Eve. Yes, my father has taken pleasure in ruining me; my work was as a matter of speculation for him, and he has acted like many so-called benefactors with those who are under an obligation to them. If I get rich it will be thanks to you. I am not talking as one who loves you, but as a thinking man. I must tell you of my shortcomings, tremendous ones for a man who has to make his career. My character, my habits, my favourite occupations make me unfit for anything connected with commerce and speculation, and yet we cannot get rich unless I develop some industrial ability. I may be capable of discovering a gold-mine, but I am singularly incapable of exploiting it. But you who, out of love for your brother, have been careful about the smallest things, who have a genius for thrift and the patient application of a real business woman, will be able to garner the harvest I shall have sown. Our predicament – I say "ours" because for long since I have considered myself to be one of the family – weighs so heavily on my heart that I have spent my days and nights looking for a means of making good. My knowledge of chemistry and the close watch I have kept on the needs of commerce have put me on the way to a lucrative discovery. I can't tell you anything about it yet, for I foresee that I shall have to go slowly. We shall have a hard life for several years perhaps; but in the end I shall hit on a process of manufacture for which others are searching as well as myself, but which, if I get in first, will bring us a large fortune. I have said nothing about it to Lucien, for his impulsiveness would spoil everything: he would look upon my hopes as realities, would live like a lord and perhaps get into debt. So keep this secret. Your dear, sweet companionship alone will be able to comfort me while I make these long experiments, just as the desire to enrich you and Lucien will give me steadiness and tenacity . . . '

'I too had guessed,' Eve interrupted, 'that you were one of those inventors who, like my poor father, need a woman to take care of them.'

'So you really love me! Oh! don't be afraid to tell me. Your very name has been a symbol of my love for you. Eve was once the only woman in the world, and what was literally true for Adam is a spiritual truth for me. Dear God! You love me?'

'I do,' she said, and these simple syllables were drawn out by her way of pronouncing them, as if to convey the magnitude of her feeling.

'Come then, let us sit down here,' he said, leading Eve by

the hand towards a long beam beneath the wheels of a paper-mill. 'Let me breathe in the evening air, listen to the croaking of the tree-frogs, admire the moonlight shining on the water. Let me take in this scene of nature, in every detail of which I feel that my happiness is written, and which I see for the first time in its splendour, illuminated by love, embellished by you, my dear, darling Eve! This is the first moment of sheer joy that fate has ever given me! I doubt whether Lucien can be as happy as I am!'

Feeling Eve's hand moist and trembling in his, David let a tear fall on it.

'Wont you tell me your secret?' asked Eve, in a coaxing voice.

'You have the right to know it, for your father was interested in this question, which is going to be an important one, for this reason: the collapse of the Empire is going to make the use of cotton stuffs almost general, thanks to the cheapness of this material compared to linen thread. At present paper is still made with hemp and linen rags; but this ingredient is dear, and its dearness is holding back the great momentum which the French Press will inevitably acquire. Now the supply of rags cannot be arbitrarily increased. It depends on the use of linen, and the population of a country only provides a limited quantity of it. This quantity can only be increased by a rise in the birth-rate. To bring about a notable change in its population, a country needs a quarter of a century and a great revolution in its manner of life, trade and agriculture. If therefore the needs of the paper-industry become greater than France's supply of rags, two or three times greater, for instance, in order to keep paper cheap, it would be necessary to make it out of some other material than rags. This argument is based on a fact which is happening here. In the paper-mills of Angoulême – they will be the last to make paper out of linen rag – the use of cotton for making pulp is increasing at an appalling rate.'

At a question from Eve, who had no idea what pulp was, David gave her some information about paper-making which will not be out of place in a work which owes its very existence as much to paper as to the printing-press: but no doubt this long digression between the two lovers will be better for being summarized.

Paper, which is no less wonderful a product than printing, of which it is the basis, had long been in existence in China when it penetrated through the underground channels of commerce to Asia Minor where, about 750 A.D., according to various traditions, they used paper made of cotton, pounded and reduced to a mash. The need of a substitute for parchment, which was exceedingly dear, led to the invention, in imitation of the 'bombycine' paper, as cotton paper was called in the East, of rag-paper, some say at Basel, in 1170, by refugee Greeks, others at Padua, in 1301, by an Italian named Pax. Thus the paper industry progressed slowly and obscurely, but it is certain that in the reign of Charles VI the pulp for playing-cards was being manufactured in Paris. When those immortal figures – Fust, Coster and Gutenberg – invented the printed book, certain artisans, unknown people like so many great artists in this period, adapted paper-making to the needs of typography. In this same fifteenth century, so vigorous and so ingenuous, the names given to the different sizes of paper, like those given to kinds of type, were characteristic of the ingenuousness of the times. Thus we have *Raisin, Jésus, Colombier, Pot, Ecu, Coquille, Couronne*, drawing their names from the grape-cluster, the image of Our Lord, the crown, the shield, the tankard, in short from the watermark stamped in the middle of the sheet; just as later, in Napoleon's time, they used an eagle: hence the paper called *Grand-Aigle*. Likewise they drew the names of types – Cicero, Saint Augustin, Gros-Canon – from the liturgical books, works of theology and the treatises of Cicero for which these characters were used at the beginning. The *italic* was invented by the Aldi of Venice: hence its name. Before the invention of machine-made paper of unlimited length, the largest formats were the *Grand-Jésus* and the *Grand-Colombier*; and as yet the latter was scarcely used except for atlases and engravings. In fact, the dimensions of printing-paper had to correspond to those of the press-stone. At the time when David was explaining all this, the idea of paper in reels still seemed fanciful in France, although Denis Robert d'Essone, in 1799 or thereabouts, had already invented a machine for making it which more recently Didot-Saint-Léger tried to perfect. The invention of vellum paper by Ambroise Didot only dates from 1780. This rapid glance amply demonstrates that all the great advances due to man's ingenuity and intelligence were only achieved exceedingly slowly and by means of imperceptible accretions, just as Nature proceeds. In order to reach perfection, writing and perhaps language itself passed through the same groping stages as typography and paper-making.

'In the whole of Europe,' said the printer by way of conclusion, 'rag-pickers collect rags and old linen and buy up the remnants from every kind of textile. These remnants are sorted out and stored by wholesale rag-merchants, and they supply the paper-mills. To give you some idea of this trade, I will tell you, Mademoiselle, that in 1814 a banker named Cardon, the owner of the pulping-troughs of Buges and Langlée, where Léorier de l'Isle attempted as early as 1776 to solve the same problem as your father, had a law-suit with a Monsieur Proust over an error amounting to two millions' pound weight of rags, a matter of ten million *livres*, that is to say about four million francs. The manufacturer washes his rags and boils them down to a clear pulp, and this is screened – just as a cook runs a sauce through the strainer – on to an iron framework called a mould, fitted with a fine wire gauze in the centre of which is the watermark which gives its name to the paper. Consequently the size of the paper depends on the size of the mould. Whilst I was with Messrs Didot, this problem was being investigated, and it still is; for the improvement your father was striving after is one of the most imperious needs of our time. And this is why: although the long-lasting quality of linen thread as compared to cotton thread makes the former cheaper than the latter in the long run, since poor people always have to draw a lesser or greater sum from their pockets, and since the weaker always go to the wall, they lose enormously by this. The middle classes do the same. Thus linen thread is in short supply. In England, where four-fifths of the population wear cotton instead of linen, paper is now made out of scarcely anything but cotton rags. This paper, which in the first place has the drawback of tearing and breaking, dissolves so easily in water that a book made of cotton paper would be reduced to a mash after a quarter of an hour in water, whereas an old book would not be ruined if it stayed in it for two hours. An old book could be dried; it might turn yellow and fade, but the text would still be legible and the work would not be destroyed. We are nearing the time when, as fortunes are equalized and so diminished, poverty will be wide-spread; we shall require cheap linen-wear and cheap books, just as people are beginning to require small pictures for lack of space in which to hang big ones. Neither the shirts nor the books will last, that's all. Sound products are disappearing everywhere. So then the problem facing us is of the highest importance for literature, the sciences and politics. That is why a lively discussion took place one day in my office over the ingredients used in China for the manufacture of paper. There, from time immemorial, thanks to the raw materials used, paper-making reached a perfection which is lacking in ours. Much interest was then being shown in Chinese paper, far superior to ours in lightness and fineness, for these precious qualities don't make it any less tough and, though thin, it is not at all transparent. A very well-informed proof-reader (in Paris some proof-readers are well up in science: at this moment Lachevardière employs Fourier and Pierre Leroux as proof-readers), namely the Comte de Saint-Simon, a proof-reader for the time being, came in while this discussion was on. He then told us that, according to Kempfer and Du Halde, *broussonetia* provided the Chinese with the material for their paper which, like ours, is entirely vegetable. Another proof-reader maintained that Chinese paper was chiefly made of animal matter, namely silk, so abundant in China. A bet was made in my presence, and as Messrs Didot are printers to the Institut de France, naturally the question was submitted to members of that scientific assembly. Monsieur Marcel, former director of the Imperial Printing Works, was selected as arbitrator, and he referred the two printers to Monsieur l'Abbé Grozier, the Arsenal Librarian. The Abbé Grozier's verdict was that both of them lost the bet. Chinese paper is made neither of silk nor of *broussonetia*: the pulp for it is made from bamboo fibre ground down. The Abbé Grozier possessed a Chinese book, a work which was both iconographical and technological, containing numerous plates illustrating paper-making in all its stages, and he showed us a first-rate sketch of a paper-factory in which coloured bamboo canes were heaped in a corner. When Lucien told me that your father, thanks to a sort of intuition peculiar to men of talent, had conceived of a method for replacing linen waste by an exceedingly common vegetable matter which territorial production could directly provide, as the Chinese do by using fibrous stalks, I sifted out all the attempts made by my predecessors and at last began to study the question. The bamboo is a reed; I naturally thought of the reeds which grow in our country. Labour costs nothing in China – three sous a day; and so the Chinese, once the paper is removed from the mould, can place it sheet by sheet between heated slabs of white porcelain, by which means they press it and give it a sheen, consistency, lightness and satiny softness which make it the finest paper in the world. Well, the Chinese hand-process must be replaced by some machine or other. The use of machinery will solve the problem of cheapness which the low cost of labour makes possible in China. If we succeeded in producing cheap paper of the Chinese quality we should reduce the weight and thickness of books by more than one half. A bound edition of Voltaire which, when printed on our vellum paper, weighs more than two hundred and fifty pounds, would not weigh fifty pounds on Chinese paper. And that would certainly be an achievement. Finding much-needed shelf-space in libraries will become a more and more difficult problem in a period when a general reduction in size – both things and men – is affecting everything, even human habitations. The great mansions and suites of rooms in Paris will sooner or later be demolished, for soon private fortunes will be no longer able to keep up the constructions of our forefathers. What a shame it is that our era cannot make books which will last! Ten years more, and Holland paper, that is to say paper made of linen rags, will be altogether unobtainable! Now your generous brother passed on to me your father's idea of using certain fibrous plants for the making of paper, and you see that if I succeed, you will be entitled to . . . ' At this moment Lucien came up to his sister and interrupted David's generous proposition.

'I don't know,' he said, 'if you have enjoyed this evening, but it has been a cruel one for me.'

'Why, my poor Lucien, what has happened?' asked Eve, noticing the excited expression on Lucien's face.

The exasperated poet told the tale of the anguish he had suffered, and poured into their sympathetic hearts the flood of thoughts with which he was tormented. Eve and David listened in silence, pained to watch this torrent of grief by which Lucien revealed both the greatness and the pettiness in his character.

'Monsieur de Bargeton,' concluded Lucien, 'is an old man who without doubt will soon be carried off by an attack of indigestion. Well, I will assert myself over this arrogant society, I will marry Madame de Bargeton. I read in her eyes this evening a love as great as mine. Yes, the humiliations I received wounded her too; she poured balm on my sufferings; she is as great and noble as she is beautiful and gracious! No, she will never betray me.'

'Is it not high time we made life smoother for him?' David whispered to Eve.

Eve quietly squeezed David's arm, and he, understanding her thoughts, made haste to tell Lucien the plans they had been considering. The two lovers were as wrapped up in their own concerns as Lucien was with his, so that Eve and David, eager to get his approval for their engagement, did not notice the start of surprise which the admirer of Madame de Bargeton gave when he learnt that David was to marry his sister. Lucien was dreaming of a fine match for his sister as soon as he had risen to some high position, in order that his ambitions might be furthered by the interest which an influential family might take in him. He was distressed to think that this union might prove one more obstacle to his social success.

'If Madame de Bargeton consents to become Madame de Rubempré, she will never want David Séchard as a brother-in-law!' This sentence briefly and clearly conveys the ideas which were gnawing at Lucien's heart. And the bitter thought came to him: 'Louise is right. People with a future are never understood by their families.'

If this alliance had been proposed to him at any other moment than when his imagination was putting Monsieur de Bargeton into his coffin, he would no doubt have evinced the liveliest joy. Had he reflected about his present situation and asked himself what kind of future Eve Chardon, a lovely but penniless girl, could hope for, he would have regarded this marriage as an unhoped-for piece of good luck. But he was living in one of those golden dreams in which young people, cantering along on their *ifs*, leap over all barriers. He had seen himself dominating society, and it wounded the poet in him to come down to earth so quickly. Eve and David supposed that their brother was silent because he was over-whelmed with so much generosity. For these two noble creatures, tacit acceptance was a proof of true amity. With warm and hearty eloquence the printer began to describe the happiness awaiting all four of them. In spite of remonstrances from Eve, he furnished his first floor with all the luxury a lover could imagine. With ingenuous good faith he constructed a second floor for Lucien and an upper storey of the penthouse for Madame Chardon, on whom he wanted to lavish all the care which filial solicitude can inspire. In short he prophesied such happiness for the family and such independence for his brother-in-law that Lucien fell under the spell of David's voice and Eve's caresses, and, as they took the road home under the shady trees along the calm and gleaming river, beneath the starry sky in the warm night air, he forgot the painful crown of thorns which Society had crammed down on his head. In short Monsieur de Rubempré acknowledged David. His volatile character quickly plunged him back into the pure, hard-working, middle class life he had led hitherto: he saw it

in fairer colours and free from care. The hubbub of aristocratic society moved farther and farther away. Finally, when
they were back on the paving-stones of L'Houmeau, the
ambitious young man clasped David's hand like a true brother
and adjusted his mood to that of the happy couple.

'If only your father doesn't stand out against your marrying,'
he said to David.

'You know well he doesn't bother about me! The old man
lives for himself alone. But tomorrow I'll go and see him at
Marsac, if only to persuade him to undertake the alterations
we need.'

David saw brother and sister home and asked Madame
Chardon for Eve's hand in marriage with the eagerness of a
man who can brook no delay. The mother took her daughter's
hand and joyfully put it in David's; the emboldened lover
kissed his beautiful fiancée on the forehead; she smiled at him
and blushed.

'This is the betrothal of poor folk,' the mother said, raising
her eyes as if to beseech the blessing of God. 'You are very
brave, my child,' she said to David, 'for we are badly off,
and I am afraid it may be contagious.'

'We shall be rich and happy,' said David solemnly. 'To
begin with, you will give up your work as sick-nurse, and you
will come and live with your daughter and Lucien in Angoulême.'

Thereupon the three young people lost no time in telling
the astonished mother of their wonderful project, abandoning
themselves to one of those impulsive family conferences in
the course of which one delights in harvesting crops only just
sown and relishing every joy in advance. It was time to send
David home, though he would have liked the evening to last
for ever. One o'clock was striking when Lucien escorted his
future brother-in-law as far as the Porte-Palet. The worthy
Postel, disturbed at these unusual comings and goings, was
standing behind his Venetian shutter; he had opened the
window and was asking himself, when he saw the light still
on in Eve's flat, 'What's happening at the Chardon's?'

'My boy,' he said as Lucien came in again. 'What on earth
is going on? Are you in need of me?'

'No, Monsieur,' replied the poet. 'But as you are our friend, I can tell you the news: my mother has just consented to my sister marrying David Séchard.'

Postel's only reply was to shut his window with a bang: he was in despair at not having proposed to Mademoiselle Chardon himself.

Instead of returning to Angoulême, David took the road to Marsac. He walked the whole way there and arrived at the vineyard running alongside his father's house just as the sun was rising. He caught sight of the old 'bear' poking his head over the hedge under an almond-tree.

'Good-day, father.'

'Oh, it's you, my lad. What brings you along so early? Go through there,' said the vinegrower, pointing to a little wicket-gate. 'My vines have all finished flowering, and not a single plant has been caught by the frost! They'll yield more than twenty casks to the acre this year, but what a lot of manure they've had!'

'Father, I've come to talk about an important matter.'

'Well, how are our presses going? You should be making a pile of money.'

'I shall do so, father. But at present I'm not rich.'

'They all blame me for overdoing the manure!' his father replied. 'The big folk here, Monsieur le Marquis, Monsieur le Comte, Monsieur this and Monsieur that make out that I spoil the quality of the wine. What's the good of education? It only gets you muddle-headed. Listen! These gentry get seven or sometimes eight casks to the acre and sell them at sixty francs each; and that comes to four hundred francs an acre at most in a good year. I get twenty casks and sell for thirty francs, making six hundred francs in all! Who are the simpletons? Quality, quality! What do I care about quality? Let these fine gentlemen keep their quality for themselves! Quality for me means money! . . . What were you saying?'

'Father, I'm getting married. I came to ask you . . . '

'Ask me for what? Nothing doing, my boy. Get married, all right. But as for giving you anything, I haven't a penny. Dressing the vines has cost me a fortune. The last two years I've been paying out for top-dressings, taxes and all sorts of expenses. The government grabs the lot; the best of it goes to the government! We poor vine-growers have made nothing for two years. Things don't look bad for this year. All right, but my miserable casks are already costing eleven francs apiece! It's the cooper that gets the profit. — Why get married before the grape-harvest?'

'Father, I have only come to ask for your consent.'

'Oh, that's different. Who are you reckoning to marry, by the way?'

'Mademoiselle Eve Chardon.'

'Who's she? What's she made of?'

'She's the daughter of the late Monsieur Chardon, the chemist of L'Houmeau.'

'You're marrying a girl from L'Houmeau, you, a well set-up business man? You, a printer by royal appointment? That's what comes of education! Some good sending your sons to college! — Come now, my boy, she's very well off then?' said the old vine-grower approaching his son with an ingratiating leer. 'For sure, if you're taking a girl from L'Houmeau, she must be worth thousands and thousands! Good, you'll be able to pay me your arrears of rent: two years and three months, my boy, and that makes two thousand seven hundred francs, and they'll come in the nick of time for me to pay my cooper. For anyone but my own son I could charge you interest: after all, business is business; but I'll let you off that. Well now, how much has she got?'

'She has just what my mother had.'

The old vine-grower nearly blurted out: 'What! she has only ten thousand francs!' But he remembered his refusal to render any account to his son, and he exclaimed: 'She's got nothing then!'

'My mother's fortune was her brains and her beauty.'

'You go and sell that on the market, and you'll see what you'll get for it! God help us! What bad luck fathers have with their children! When I married, David, all I had was a paper cap and my two hands. I was a poor "bear"; but with the fine printing-works I've given you, with all your hard work and your know-how, you ought to marry a respectable girl from the town, a woman with thirty or forty thousand francs. Stop being love-sick, and I'll find you a wife myself. A few miles away there's a miller's widow of thirty-two, worth a hundred thousand francs in property: that's the match for you! You can join her lands to the Marsac lands, they run side by side. Oh, what a fine estate we should have, and how well I'd look after it! They say she's going to marry Courtois, her chief hand, but you're a still better bargain for her! I'd run the mill, while she lived like a lady in Angoulême.'

'Father, I am committed.'

'David, you don't understand a thing about business. You'll come to ruin. Sure enough, if you marry this girl from L'Houmeau, I'll square accounts with you. I'll sue you for my rent, for I can see no good coming of this. Ah! my poor presses! You needed money to grease the works, to keep you going and get things moving. After this, only a good vintage can give me peace of mind.'

'Father, it seems to me that up to now I haven't caused you much worry . . .'

'And not paid much rent either,' the vine-grower retorted.

'I came to ask you not only to consent to my marriage, but also to build a second storey to your house and put up living premises above your penthouse.'

'Nothing doing. I haven't a sou, as you well know. Besides, it would be pouring money down the sink – what would it bring me in? So then, you got up at daybreak to come and ask me to do a building job that would bankrupt a king. I may have christened you David, but I'm not Solomon in all his glory. Are you crazy? You're not my child, you're a changeling.'

He broke in on his own discourse to show David a vine-stock. 'There's one,' he said, 'which will be loaded with grapes. That's the sort of child that doesn't disappoint its parents: give it manure and it pays you back. I sent you to school. I paid through the nose to make a learned man of you, I sent you to study with the Didots. And what comes of all this humbug? You give me a daughter-in-law from L'Houmeau without a penny in her stocking. If you hadn't studied, if I'd kept you here under my nose, you'd have done what I saw fit, and today you'd be marrying a miller's widow with a hundred thousand francs and a mill into the bargain. Oh yes! You're so brainy you think I'm going to foot the bill for these fine notions and build palaces for you! . . . To hear you talk, the house you're living in has been a pig-sty for two hundred years and isn't good enough for your girl from L'Houmeau to sleep in. Who is she? the Queen of France?'

'Very well, father, I shall build the second storey at my own expense and the son will enrich the father. It's the wrong way round, but it does happen sometimes.'

'What, my lad, you've money enough to build, but not enough to pay your rent? You young fox, you're trying to trick your father!'

Stated this way, the problem became difficult to solve, for the old man was delighted to manoeuvre his son into a position which enabled him to give him nothing at all while still talking like a father. And so David could get nothing else from him but plain and simple consent to the marriage and permission to build, at his own expense and in his father's own house, any accommodation he needed. The old 'bear', this paragon among thrifty sires, did his son the favour of not demanding the back rent and so not robbing him of the savings he had been so imprudent as to divulge. David returned home in a sad mood: he realized that if misfortune came he could not count on help from his father.

4. *Catastrophic sequels to provincial love*

THE Bishop's unintended shaft and Madame de Bargeton's retort were all that Angoulême could talk about. The slightest incidents were so distorted, exaggerated and improved upon that the poet became the hero of the moment. From the higher regions through which this rainstorm of scandal raged, a few drops fell down to middle-class levels. When Lucien passed through Beaulieu on his way to the Bargeton mansion, he noticed the envious attention with which several young men surveyed him, and his ear caught a few phrases which made him swell with pride.

'There's a lucky chap,' said a solicitor's clerk, an ugly young man named Petit-Claud, who had been at school with Lucien and with whom Lucien took on little airs of condescension.

'True enough. He's good-looking. He has talent and Madame de Bargeton is gone on him!' replied a youth of good social standing who had been present at the reading.

Lucien had waited impatiently for the time when he knew he could catch Louise by herself: this woman, who had become the arbiter of his destiny, had to be persuaded to accept his sister's marriage. After the events of the previous evening, she might perhaps feel more tenderly disposed, and from this tenderness might spring a brief spell of happiness. He was not mistaken: Madame de Bargeton welcomed him with an effusiveness which for a novice in love was a touching sign of mounting passion. She yielded her beautiful golden locks, her hand and her head to the burning kisses of the poet who had suffered so much the evening before.

'If you could have seen yourself as you were reading' – she used the affectionate 'thou', for they had reached that stage the evening before, when Louise, sitting on her sofa, had wiped away the drops of moisture gleaming like pearls on the brow on which she would have liked to set a wreath of laurels. 'Your lovely eyes were flashing, while from your lips I saw the golden chains unwind, the chains of words that poets use to bind men's hearts to them. You shall read me the whole of Chénier; he is the poet for lovers. You shall suffer no more, I will not allow you to! Yes, dear angel, I will put an oasis around you and in it you will live your poet's life – active, languid, indolent, industrious, pensive turn by turn. But never forget that you will owe your laurels to me, and that will be the splendid reward I shall reap for the pains I shall have to endure. Dear, dear boy, society will not spare me any more than it spares you – it takes its revenge for any happiness it does not share. Yes, I shall always be envied

– did you not see that yesterday? How quickly those gad-flies swarmed round to slake their thirst with blood from the pricks they had made! But how happy I was! I really lived! How long it is since every chord of my heart felt such vibrations!'

Tears were streaming down Louise's cheeks. Lucien took her hand, and the long kiss he gave it was his only reply. And so the poet's vanity was flattered by this woman as it had been by his mother, his sister and David. All those about him persisted in lifting him higher than ever on his imaginary pedestal. Everything, the adulation of his friends and the fury of his enemies, fanned the flame of his delusions and ambition; the atmosphere he moved in was bright with mirages. The imagination of young people is so inclined to eulogize, to foster such notions, and circumstances seem so eager to serve a handsome young man with a future before him, that more than one bitter and chilling lesson is needed to dissipate such illusions.

'So then, my beautiful Louise, you are willing to be my Beatrice – but a Beatrice who will let herself be loved?'

She raised her beautiful eyes – until then they had been drooping – and replied, with an angelic smile which gave the lie to her words:

'If you deserve it . . . later! Are you not happy? To have someone whose heart is yours! To be able to confide completely in someone you are sure will understand you! Surely that is happiness?'

'Yes,' he replied, but with the wry expression of a frustrated lover.

'Child that you are!', she said, teasingly. 'Come now, haven't you something to tell me? You looked quite worried as you came in, my Lucien.'

Lucien shyly told his darling of David's love for his sister, his sister's love for David, and the proposed marriage.

'Poor Lucien,' said Louise. 'He's afraid of being beaten and scolded, as if it were he who was getting married!'

'But what harm is there in that,' she continued, running her hands through his hair. 'What does your family matter

120

to me, since you are so much above it? If my father married his servant, would it worry you? Dear child, lovers are a whole family to themselves. Have I any interest in the world other than my Lucien? Become a great man, find the way to glory: that's all that concerns us!'

This egoistic response made Lucien the happiest man in the world. But just as he was listening to the extravagant arguments by which Louise was proving to him that they were alone in the world, Monsieur de Bargeton came in. Lucien knitted his eyebrows and seemed taken aback. Louise made him a sign, begged him to stay to dinner, and asked him to read some Chénier until the card-players and other regular visitors arrived.

'You will not only be giving her pleasure,' said Monsieur de Bargeton, 'but me as well. Nothing suits me better than to listen to reading after dinner.'

And so, coaxed by Monsieur de Bargeton as well as Louise, with the servants showing him the respect that servants feel for their employers' favoured guests, Lucien stayed on, accepting as his due all the enjoyments attached to a fortune which was to be his for the using. By the time the drawing-room had filled up, he felt so fortified by Monsieur de Bargeton's stupidity and so confident of Louise's love that he assumed a dominating attitude which his beautiful mistress encouraged and savoured the pleasures of the despotic power which Naïs had acquired and which she willingly shared with him. In short, he did his best during this soirée, to play the role of a country town 'lion'. Taking note of Lucien's new attitude, a few persons decided that he was, to use an old-fashioned expression, 'on the best possible terms' with Madame de Bargeton. Amélie, who had arrived with Monsieur du Châtelet and had joined the group of jealous and envious people gathered in a corner, affirmed that the worst had happened.

'Don't make Naïs responsible,' said Châtelet, 'for the vanity of a silly youth puffed up with pride at finding himself in company to which he never expected to be admitted. Can't you see that this Chardon is taking the gracious utterances of a society lady as advances? He hasn't yet learnt to distinguish between the silence of real passion and the patronizing language merited by his good looks, youth and talent! Women would be greatly to be pitied if they were blamed for all the desires they inspire in us. He is certainly in love, but as for Naïs ...'

'Oh! as for Naïs,' the perfidious Amélie repeated, 'Naïs is very happy to have inspired this passion. At her age, a young man's love has so many attractions to offer! His youthfulness is contagious; a woman becomes a girl again and takes on the scruples and affectations of a girl without realizing how ridiculous it is ... Just fancy! An apothecary's son strutting about as if he were master in Madame de Bargeton's house!'

Love's eyes are closed to social distances,

Adrien softly hummed.

The next day there was no house in Angoulême in which the degree of intimacy between Monsieur Chardon, *alias* de Rubempré, and Madame de Bargeton was not a matter for discussion. At most they had exchanged a kiss or two, and society was already accusing them of the most guilty relations. Madame de Bargeton was paying the penalty for her pre-eminence. Which of us has not observed the eccentricities peculiar to polite society, the capriciousness of its judgements and the extravagance of its demands? To some persons everything is permissible; their conduct may go far beyond the bounds of reason; all their actions are seemly; they are justified by all and sundry. But there are others to whom society is incredibly severe: they must make no mistakes, never falter or even utter a foolish remark. They are like venerated statues which are removed from their pedestals once the winter frost has nipped off a finger or chipped a nose; they are allowed no human feelings and must for ever remain god-like and perfect. A single glance at Lucien from Madame de Bargeton was equivalent to the twelve years' happiness enjoyed by Zizine and Francis. One hand-clasp was certain to bring down all the thunders of the Charente valley on the amorous couple.

David had brought back from Paris a secret nest-egg which he was earmarking for his wedding expenses and the construction of a second floor in his father's house. It was after all in his own interests to enlarge this house. It would come to him sooner or later, since his father was seventy-eight. And so the printer had Lucien's rooms half-timbered so as not to overload the cracked walls of this old building. He took pleasure in decorating and elegantly furnishing the first-floor flat in which his lovely Eve was to spend her days. It was a period of unmixed joy and happiness for the two friends. Weary as he was of the mean dimensions of provincial existence, tired as he was of the sordid economy which made a five-franc piece an enormous sum, Lucien uncomplainingly endured the cheese-paring and privation which poverty entails. The gloomy melancholy of his expression had given place to the radiancy of hope. A star was shining above his head; he had dreams of a bright future and was staking his happiness on the demise of Monsieur de Bargeton, who from time to time had stomach troubles and the happy mania of regarding his after-dinner indigestion as an ailment which after-supper indigestion could cure.

By the beginning of September, Lucien was no longer a proof-reader: he was Monsieur de Rubempré, sumptuously lodged in comparison with the wretched dormer-windowed attic the insignificant Chardon had occupied in L'Houmeau. He was no longer a man from L'Houmeau: he lived in Upper Angoulême and dined about four times a week with Madame de Bargeton. My Lord Bishop was friendly with him and received him at his palace. His occupations put him on a level with persons of the loftiest degree. In fact he was expected one day to rank among the most illustrious figures in France. Assuredly, as he paced through his elegant sitting-room, his charming bedroom and his tastefully decorated study, he could forgive himself for levying thirty francs a month on the painfully earned wages of his sister and mother, for he could look forward to the day when the historical novel at which he had been working for two years – *The Archer of Charles the Ninth*, and a volume of verse entitled *The Mar-*

guerites – would spread his renown through the world of literature and bring him enough money to pay his debt to his mother, sister and David. And so, feeling greater in stature, already hearing his name echoing down the corridors of the future, he was now accepting these sacrifices with a noble self-assurance: he could smile at the straits he suffered and enjoy his last days of poverty.

Eve and David had put their own happiness second to his. Their wedding had been postponed until the workmen could finish the furnishing, painting and paper-hanging on the first floor, for Lucien's concerns had been given priority. No one who knew Lucien would have been surprised at the devotion shown to him: he had such charming, such endearing manners! He so gracefully expressed his impatience and his desires! His cause was always won before he had opened his mouth. So fatal a privilege is disastrous rather than salutary to most young people. Accustomed to the attentions which their youth and good looks guarantee, and happy to receive the protection which humanity egoistically accords to any of its darlings in the same way that it gives alms to the mendicant who stirs its feelings and affords it emotional satisfaction, many of these overgrown children enjoy such favour but do not use it to advantage. Deceived as to the meaning and motives governing social relations, they always expect to be greeted with flattering smiles. But the moment comes when society discards them – perhaps on the threshold of a salon or at a street-corner – denuded, bald-headed, threadbare, worthless and destitute, like aging coquettes or worn-out garments.

Moreover Eve herself had desired this postponement because she wanted to cater as economically as possible for her future household needs. What could a loving couple refuse to a brother who, when he saw his sister at work, exclaimed with heart-felt sincerity: 'How I wish I could sew!' And David, grave and observant as he was, had joined in this conspiracy of self-sacrifice. None the less, since Lucien's triumph in Madame de Bargeton's salon, he was alarmed by the transformation he could discern in Lucien: he was afraid that he would come to despise their modest standard of living. Desiring to put his 'brother' to the test, he sometimes got him to choose between the patriarchal joys of family life and the pleasures of high society, and when he had seen Lucien giving up his vainglorious enjoyments for their sake, he had exclaimed: 'They won't succeed in spoiling him!' On various occasions the three friends and Madame Chardon went off on pleasure parties, as provincial people do. They took walks in the woods near Angoulême which run along the river Charente; they picnicked on the grass with provisions which David's apprentice brought to a certain spot at an agreed time; then they returned home in the evening, rather tired, but without having spent as much as three francs. On great occasions, when they dined at what is called a 'restaurât', a sort of rustic eating-house which is half-way between a provincial tavern and a Paris pleasure-garden, they went to the expense of five francs which David and the Chardons shared. David was infinitely grateful to Lucien for forgetting, during these rustic excursions, the satisfaction he drew from consorting with Madame de Bargeton and eating sumptuous society dinners. Each of them then wanted to fête the 'great man' of Angoulême.

At this conjuncture, just when all plans for the future household were practically complete, while David was making a journey to Marsac to prevail on his father to come to the wedding, in the hope that the old man would yield to his daughter-in-law's charm and contribute to the enormous expenditure necessitated by the alterations to the house, one of those events occurred which entirely change the look of things in a small town.

In the person of du Châtelet, Lucien and Louise had a close spy who, with the persistency of hatred mingled with passion and avarice, was watching for an opportunity to provoke a scandal. Sixte wanted Madame de Bargeton to declare herself so openly for Lucien as to become what one calls a 'lost woman'. He had posed as a humble confidant of Madame de Bargeton; but if, in her house in the Rue du Minage, he admired Lucien, he ran him down everywhere else. By imperceptible degrees he had gained the right to pay informal calls on Naïs, who was no longer suspicious of her elderly admirer; but he had staked too much on the love of Lucien and Louise which, to their very great regret, remained platonic. In fact there are passions which – put it as you will – are well or badly launched. Two persons make sentiment a matter of tactics, talk instead of acting, and fight in the open field instead of laying siege. As a result they often cool off towards each other because their desires spend themselves in a vacuum. Both lovers thus give themselves time to reflect and judge one another. Often passions which have taken the field with flying colours and fine array, with ardour enough to sweep all before them, end up by retreating to their quarters, with no victory gained, humiliated, disarmed, a laughing-stock for the vain stir they have made. These mischances are sometimes attributable to the timidity of youth and the temporisations with which women love to begin – for this kind of reciprocal deception happens neither to practised seducers nor to coquettes well versed in the strategy of passion.

Besides this, life in the provinces is singularly adverse to the satisfactions of love and favours passion only as a kind of intellectual debate. Also the obstacles it opposes to that sweet intercourse which so much binds lovers together drive ardent souls to extreme decisions. Provincial life is based on such meticulous espionage, it requires that private conduct shall be so open to inspection, it so reluctantly approves of any intimacy which consoles while not offending virtue, it so unjustly incriminates the most chaste relationship, that many women are stigmatized however innocent they may be. Thereupon some of them become angry with themselves for not having tasted all the felicity as well as the overwhelming unhappiness which a lapse from virtue brings. So that society, which without any serious examination blames or criticizes the overt act which brings long inward conflicts to an end, is primarily responsible for the ensuing scandal; but most of those people who rail against the supposedly shocking conduct of a few undeservedly calumniated women have never thought of the causes which have brought them into the open. Madame de Bargeton was to find herself in the same peculiar situation as many women who have fallen only after being unjustly accused.

In the early days of a passion, the inexperienced are intimidated by obstacles, and those which confronted the two lovers were very like the cords with which the Lilliputians tied up Gulliver. They were a multitude of trivialities which made all movement impossible and thwarted the most violent desires. So, Madame de Bargeton had always to remain in public view. If she had been 'not at home' at the time of Lucien's visits, there would have been nothing more to say: she might just as well have eloped with him. True, she received him in her boudoir, and he was so used to being there that he looked upon it as his domain – but Louise was scrupulous in keeping open house. Nothing went beyond the bounds of strict propriety. Monsieur de Bargeton bumbled about the house like a cockchafer and it never occurred to him that his wife might wish to be alone with Lucien. Had he been the only obstacle, Naïs could very easily have sent him off or kept him busy; but she was inundated with visitors, and the keener curiosity became, the more their number increased. Provincial people are by nature malicious and love to balk nascent passion. The servants passed to and fro through the house without being summoned and gave no warning of their presence, in conformity with the long-standing habits which a woman who had nothing to conceal had allowed them to acquire. To have made any changes in the domestic routine would have been tantamount to confessing a love intrigue which Angoulême continued to suspect. Madame de Bargeton could not set foot outside her house without the town knowing where she was going. To have gone for solitary walks with Lucien outside the town would have been a decisive step: there would have been less danger in shutting herself up with him in her house. If Lucien had stayed with her after midnight, with no other company present, tongues would have wagged the next morning. And so, indoors and out of doors, Madame de Bargeton's life was open to the public. These details give a complete picture of provincial life: a transgression is either openly avowed or made impossible.

Like all women involved in a love affair but lacking experience, Louise came to realize the difficulties of her situation one by one; they frightened her, and then the alarm she felt had its effect on those amorous discussions with which lovers, alone to themselves, most pleasantly while away the time. Madame de Bargeton had no estate to which she could take her beloved poet, like some women who cleverly manufacture some excuse for burying themselves in the country. Tired of living under the public gaze, exasperated by the tyranny whose yoke brought more vexation than her love afforded satisfaction, her mind turned towards L'Escarbas and she thought of paying her aged father a visit, so irritated she was with these miserable obstacles.

Châtelet did not believe in such great innocence. He kept an eye on the times at which Lucien visited Madame de Bargeton and called on her a few minutes later; and he was always accompanied by Monsieur de Chandour, the most indiscreet member of their circle, whom he was careful to let go in first, hoping that some lucky chance, obstinately awaited, would enable him to take the lovers by surprise. His role and his prospects of success were the more dubious because he had to remain neutral in order to manoeuvre the actors in the drama he wanted to stage. And so, in order to lull any suspicion in Lucien, whom he flattered, and Madame de Bargeton, who was not lacking in perspicacity, he had attached himself to the jealous Amélie for appearances' sake. So that a closer watch could be kept on Louise and Lucien, he had succeeded a few days since in starting a controversy about the two lovers between himself and Chandour. Du Châtelet claimed that Madame de Bargeton was playing with Lucien, that she was too proud and of too high rank to condescend to a chemist's son. This pretence of incredulity suited his plans, for he wanted to figure as Madame de Bargeton's champion. Stanislas de Chandour maintained that Lucien was by no means spurned as a lover. Amélie's eagerness to know the truth added heat to the discussion. Each party had a reasoned case. As is typical in a small town, intimate friends of the Chandours would often turn up during a conversation in which both du Châtelet and Stanislas were very competently upholding their point of view. It was not very difficult for either disputant to recruit partisans by asking his neighbour: 'What do *you* think about it?' This controversy kept Madame de Bargeton and Lucien under constant surveillance. Finally, du Châtelet one day remarked that whenever Monsieur and himself called on Louise and Lucien was there, no sign was revealed of a suspect relationship: the boudoir door remained open, people came and went, no mysterious exchanges gave any hint of guilty love-play between the two people, etc. Stanislas, who had more than his share of stupidity, undertook to steal in next day on tiptoe, and the perfidious Amélie expressed strong approval.

That next day was for Lucien one of those occasions when young lovers tear their hair and vow they will not go on with the silly business of wooing. He had grown used to his position. The poet who had so timidly taken a chair in the sacred boudoir of the 'queen' of Angoulême had been metamorphosed into an exacting lover. Six months had sufficed for him to regard himself as Louise's equal, and from then on he wanted to become her master. He left home that day promising himself that he would be very unreasonable, put his life to the hazard, bring all the resources of fiery eloquence into play, assert that his head was in a whirl and that he was incapable of conceiving an idea or writing a line. Now some women have a repugnance for deliberate decisions – and this does honour to their delicacy; they love to be swept off their feet rather than yield to stipulations; generally speaking, they will not have pleasure imposed on them. Madame de Bargeton observed on Lucien's brow, in his eyes, face and manner, that tenderness which betrays a fixed resolution. She decided to frustrate it, partly from contrariness, but also because she had an exalted conception of love. Like any woman given to exaggeration, she exaggerated her own value. In her eyes, Madame de Bargeton was a sovereign lady, a Beatrice, a Laura. She was sitting on a dais as in medieval times, watching the literary tournament, and Lucien had to win several victories before he could merit the prize: he had to outshine Victor Hugo, the *enfant sublime*, Lamartine, Walter Scott and Byron. The noble creature considered her love as an uplifting principle: the desires she inspired in Lucien were to incite him to glory. This feminine quixotism gives a dedicated quality to love which, when it is devoted to a worthy purpose, acquires some honour and dignity. Intent on playing the role of Dulcinea in Lucien's life for seven or eight years, Madame de Bargeton wished, like so many provincial women, that possession should be paid for by a kind of serfdom, a period of constancy which would enable her to gauge her lover's worth.

After Lucien had engaged battle with one of those violent outbursts of petulance which are laughed at by women who are still uncommitted but sadden women who know what love is, Louise assumed a dignified pose and began one of her long speeches abounding in high-flown phrases.

'Is that what you promised me, Lucien?' she asked at the end of it. 'Do not bring into the present, which is so sweet, a remorse which later would poison my life. Do not spoil the future! And – I say this with pride – do not spoil the present! Is not my heart all yours? What more can you want? Would you let your heart be dominated by your senses, when the finest privilege a woman has, if she is truly loved, is to impose silence on them? For whom then do you take me? If in your eyes I am not something more than a woman, I am less than a woman.'

'You wouldn't say anything else to a man you didn't love,' cried Lucien, in a rage.

'If you do not feel all the real love there is in my thoughts, you will never be worthy of me.'

'You are only casting doubt on my love in order to avoid responding to it,' said Lucien, throwing himself at her feet and weeping.

The poor young man wept in earnest on seeing that he was to remain so long at the gates of Paradise. His tears were those of a poet whose sense of power was humiliated, those of a child in despair at being refused a coveted toy.

'You have never loved me,' he cried.

'You don't mean what you are saying,' she replied, flattered at this vehemence.

'Then prove to me that you will be mine,' said Lucien, his hair all tousled.

At this moment, Stanislas arrived unheard, saw Lucien with bowed figure, his eyes full of tears and his head on Louise's lap. Satisfied with this sufficiently compromising tableau, Stanislas backed out towards du Châtelet, who was standing outside the drawing-room door. Madame de Bargeton quickly rushed forward, but failed to reach the two spies who, aware that they were intruding, had beaten a hasty retreat.

'Who were those people?' she asked her servants.

'Monsieur de Chandour and Monsieur du Châtelet,' answered Gentil, her old manservant.

She returned pale and trembling to her boudoir.

'If they saw you in that posture,' she said to Lucien, 'I am lost!'

'So much the better!' exclaimed the poet.

This selfish outburst, prompted by love, drew a smile from her. In the provinces an episode like this becomes worse in the telling. In no time at all, everyone knew that Lucien had been discovered on his knees before Naïs. Monsieur de Chandour, enjoying the importance which the affair conferred on him, went off to relate this great event to his cronies, after which he spread the news from house to house. Du Châtelet made haste to declare he had seen nothing; but while thus holding back he incited Stanislas to talk and improve on the details. Thinking himself witty, Stanislas added new ones each time he told the story. That evening Amélie's drawing-room was crowded, for by evening the most extravagant versions were circulating among the nobility of Angoulême, since everyone enlarged on Stanislas's story. Men and women alike were impatient to know the truth. The women who hid their faces in horror and talked most loudly of scandal and perversity were of course Amélie, Zéphirine, Fifine and Lolotte, who were all more or less involved in illicit relationships. All possible variations were sung on this cruel theme.

'Well now!' said one of them. 'Have you heard about poor

Naïs? I for one don't believe it; her life has been wholly blameless. She's much too proud to be more than a benefactress to Monsieur Chardon. But if it's true, I'm heartily sorry for her.'

'She's so much more to be pitied because she's making herself frightfully ridiculous. Why, she's old enough to be the mother of Monsieur Lulu, as Jacques called him. This little versifier is twenty-two at the most, and, between ourselves, Naïs is certainly forty.'

'Well,' said Châtelet, 'I believe that the very posture in which Monsieur was discovered proves that Naïs is innocent. You don't go down on your knees to get what you've had already.'

'That depends!' said Francis with a ribald air which earned him a disapproving glance from Zéphirine.

'But do tell us what the situation is,' Stanislas was asked as a secret conclave formed in a corner of the salon.

Stanislas had ended up by composing a little tale which was full of indecencies, and he accompanied it with gestures and postures which made the whole thing prodigiously incriminating.

'It's unbelievable,' they all repeated.

'In full daylight!' said one of them.

'Naïs is the last person I would have suspected.'

'What will she do now?'

There followed all sorts of commentaries and conjectures! . . . Du Châtelet defended Madame de Bargeton, but so clumsily that he fanned the flame of scandal-mongering instead of extinguishing it. Lili, in desolation at the disgrace which had fallen on the fairest divinity on the Olympus of Angoulême, went off in a flood of tears to retail the news at the Bishop's palace. As soon as the whole town was buzzing with the scandal, the happy du Châtelet went round to Madame de Bargeton's house where, alas, only one game of whist was in progress. He tactfully asked Naïs to come and talk with him in her boudoir. They both sat down on the little sofa.

'You of course know,' whispered du Châtelet, 'what all Angoulême is talking about? . . . '

'No,' she said.

'Well, I am too much your friend to leave you in ignorance. I must put you in a position to stop these slanders, no doubt invented by Amélie, who is conceited enough to consider herself your rival. I was coming to see you this morning with that ape Stanislas who was several paces in front of me, and when he got there' – he pointed to the boudoir door – 'he claims to have *seen* you with Monsieur de Rubempré in a situation which prevented him from entering; he came back to me quite scared and dragged me away without leaving me time to collect my wits; and we had got as far as Beaulieu before he told me why he had drawn back. If I had known why, I would not have stirred from your house before clearing the matter up to your advantage; but it would have proved nothing to have returned to your house once I had left it. Now then, whether Stanislas saw things inaccurately or was right, *he must be shown to be in the wrong.* Dear Naïs, don't let an imbecile gamble with your life, your honour and your future; get him silenced immediately. You know my situation here. Though I need to be on good terms with everybody, I am entirely devoted to you. I belong to you and my life is at your service. Although you have spurned me, my heart will always be yours, and I will miss no opportunity to prove to you how much I love you. Yes, I will watch over you like a faithful servant, hoping for no reward, solely for the pleasure it gives me to serve you, even though you are unaware of it. This morning, I told everybody I was outside your drawing-room door and had seen nothing. If you are asked who told you of the remarks made about you, refer to me. I shall be very proud to act as your avowed champion; but, between you and me, Monsieur de Bargeton is the only man who can call Stanislas to account . . . Even if this little Rubempré has committed an indiscretion, a woman's honour cannot be at the mercy of the first scatterbrain who flings himself at her feet. That is what I told them.'

Naïs inclined her head by way of thanks and remained pensive. She was sick to death of provincial life. At Châtelet's first word, her thoughts had flown to Paris. Her silence put her artful admirer into an embarrassing situation.

'I am at your service,' he said. 'I say that again.'

'Thank you,' she replied.

'What do you think of doing?'

'I shall see.'

A long silence ensued.

'Do you love this little Rubempré so much?'

A haughty smile flashed over her face, she folded her arms and fixed her gaze on her boudoir curtains. Du Châtelet went out without being able to read this proud woman's heart. When Lucien had gone, and also the four loyal old people who had come for their game of whist without concern for all these scandalous conjectures, Madame de Bargeton detained her husband as he was getting ready for bed and just about to say good night to her.

'Come this way, my dear. I want to talk to you,' she said with some show of solemnity.

Monsieur de Bargeton followed his wife into the boudoir.

'Monsieur,' she said, 'I have perhaps been mistaken in bringing to my protective care for Monsieur de Rubempré a warmth which has been as ill understood by the stupid people in this town as by himself. This morning Lucien flung himself at my feet and made a declaration of love to me. Stanislas came in at the moment I was bringing the boy to his feet. In contempt of the duties courtesy imposes on a gentleman towards a woman in any sort of circumstance, he claims to have surprised me in an equivocal situation with this boy whom I was then treating according to his deserts. If this hare-brained young man knew what slander his impetuosity has occasioned, I know him well enough to be sure he would go and provoke Stanislas and force him to fight. This action would be tantamount to a public avowal of his love. I need not tell you that your wife is chaste; but you will agree that there would be some measure of dishonour both for you and me if Monsieur de Rubempré took it upon him to defend her. Go this instant to Stanislas, and call him seriously to account for the insulting remarks he has made about me. Bear this in mind: you must not allow the matter to be settled unless he retracts his words in the presence of numerous and important witnesses. In this way you will acquire the esteem of all decent people; you will be behaving like a man of intelligence, a chivalrous man, and you will have a right to my esteem. I am going to send Gentil on horseback to L'Escarbas, for my father must be your second; old as he is, I know him to be the sort of man to trample underfoot this puppet who is blackening the reputation of a Nègrepelisse. The choice of arms is yours; fight with pistols, you are a marvellous shot.'

'I am going,' replied Monsieur de Bargeton, taking up his hat and cane.

'Very good, my friend,' his wife said with emotion. 'That is how I like men to be. You are a gentleman.'

She presented her forehead for a kiss, and the old man was proud and happy to kiss it. And she, who had a sort of motherly feeling for this grown-up child, could not repress a tear as she heard the outer door slam as it closed behind him.

'How he loves me!' she said to herself. 'The poor man is attached to life, and yet he would not regret losing it for my sake.'

Monsieur de Bargeton was not worried at the thought of having to fight a duel, of gazing coolly into the muzzle of a pistol levelled against him. One thing only embarrassed him, and he was shuddering as he made his way to the house of Monsieur de Chandour. 'What shall I say?' he was thinking. 'Naïs ought certainly to have primed me!' And he racked his brains in order to formulate a few sentences which would not appear ridiculous.

But people like Monsieur de Bargeton, who live in a silence imposed upon them by their paucity of wit and mental range, discover a ready-made dignity in an important crisis. Having little to say, they naturally utter few stupid remarks. Then, since they ponder much over what they have to say, their extreme mistrust of themselves leads them to rehearse their speeches so thoroughly that they express themselves amazingly well, a phenomenon similar to that which loosed the tongue of Balaam's ass. And so Monsieur de Bargeton conducted himself like an exceptional man. He justified the opinion of those who regarded him as a philosopher of the Pythagorean school. He arrived at Stanislas's house at eleven in the evening and found a large company gathered there. He went and bowed to Amélie in silence, and treated everyone to his inane smile which, in present circumstances, appeared to be profoundly ironical. Then a great silence fell, as it does in nature when a storm is brewing. Châtelet, who was there again, looked in turn, in a very significant manner, at both Monsieur de Bargeton and Stanislas, whom the injured husband politely approached.

Du Châtelet grasped the meaning of a visit made at so late an hour, when the old man was usually in bed: evidently Naïs was prodding this feeble arm into action; and since his standing with Amélie gave him the right of meddling in the affairs of her household, he took Monsieur de Bargeton aside and said: 'Do you want to speak to Stanislas?'

'Yes,' said the worthy man, happy at finding a go-between who would perhaps speak in his stead.

'Very well, go to Amélie's bedroom,' replied the Director of Taxes, happy at the prospect of this duel which might make Madame de Bargeton a widow and rule out the possibility of her marrying Lucien, the cause of the duel.

'Stanislas,' said du Châtelet to Monsieur de Chandour. 'Monsieur de Bargeton has no doubt come to call you to account for what you have been saying about Naïs. Come to your wife's room, and both of you behave like gentlemen. Let there be no uproar; make a great show of politeness; in short, be as coldly formal and dignified as an Englishman would be.'

Stanislas and du Châtelet came promptly up to Bargeton.

'Monsieur,' said the offended husband, 'You claim to have found Madame de Bargeton in an equivocal situation with Monsieur de Rubempré?'

'With Monsieur Chardon,' Stanislas sarcastically replied – he did not believe Bargeton to be a man of strong character.

'So be it,' the husband continued. 'If you do not take back this insult in the presence of all the company gathered in your house at this moment, I ask you to choose a second. My father-in-law, Monsieur de Nègrepelisse, will come to fetch you in the morning at four. Let us each make our arrangements, for the affront can only be settled in the manner I have just indicated. As I am the insulted party, I choose pistols.'

While making his way to the house, Monsieur de Bargeton had ruminated over this speech, the longest he had ever made. He delivered it without passion and with the simplest air in the world. Stanislas turned pale and asked himself: 'What *did* I see after all?' But, divided between the shame of eating his words in front of the whole town, in the presence of this mute but deadly serious person, and hideous fear, whose burning grip was tight about his neck, he opted for the less immediate peril.

'Very well, tomorrow,' he said to Monsieur de Bargeton, thinking that the matter might be smoothed out. Du Châtelet was smiling, Monsieur de Bargeton looked just the same as if he were at home; but Stanislas was pale. Seeing this, a few women guessed what the talk was about. The words: 'They are going to fight' were passed from mouth to mouth. One half of the assembly thought that Stanislas was in the wrong, since his pallor and bearing indicated that he had been lying; the other half admired Monsieur de Bargeton's decorum. Du Châtelet's demeanour was grave and mysterious. After staying for a few minutes to study people's faces, Monsieur de Bargeton withdrew.

'Have you any pistols?' du Châtelet whispered in Stanislas's ear. The latter shivered from head to foot.

Amélie took in the situation and felt ill; the women hurriedly carried her to her bedroom. The din was frightful, with everybody talking at once. The men remained in the salon and unanimously declared that Monsieur de Bargeton was in the right.

'Would you have thought the old fellow was capable of behaving like that?' asked Monsieur de Saintot.

'Why,' said the pitiless Jacques. 'When he was young he was one of the best of men with weapons. My father often told me about his exploits.'

'Bah!' said Francis to Châtelet. 'Put them twenty paces apart and they will surely miss one another if you choose cavalry pistols.'

When all the company had departed, Châtelet reassured Stanislas and his wife by explaining that all would be well, and that, in a duel between a man of sixty and one of thirty-six, the latter had all the advantage.

The next morning, just as Lucien was breakfasting with David, who had returned from Marsac without his father, Madame Chardon came in, in a fluster.

'Well, Lucien, have you heard the news that is going round, even in the market-place? This morning, at five o'clock, Monsieur de Bargeton nearly killed Monsieur de Chandour on the duelling-ground belonging, oddly enough, to a Monsieur Tulloye.[1] It seems that Monsieur de Chandour said yesterday that he had caught you making love to Madame de Bargeton.'

'That's a lie!' exclaimed Lucien. 'Madame de Bargeton is innocent.'

'A man from the country who told me the details had seen the whole thing from the top of his cart. Monsieur de Nègrepelisse had come as early as three o'clock to be Monsieur de Bargeton's second. He told Monsieur de Chandour that if any misfortune befell his son-in-law, he would take it upon himself to avenge him. A cavalry officer lent them his pistols, and Monsieur de Nègrepelisse tested them several times. Monsieur du Châtelet was opposed to the pistols being tried out, but the officer they had chosen as umpire said that unless they wanted to behave like children they must use serviceable weapons. The seconds posted the two adversaries twenty-five paces apart. Monsieur de Bargeton, who behaved as if he were out for a stroll, fired twice and lodged a bullet in Monsieur de Chandour's neck, and he collapsed without being able to return the fire. The hospital surgeon has just now declared that Monsieur de Chandour's neck will never be straight again for the rest of his days. I came to tell you about this duel to stop you from going to see Madame de Bargeton or showing yourself in Angoulême, for you might be challenged by some of Monsieur de Chandour's friends.'

At this moment, Gentil, Monsieur de Bargeton's valet,

1. Tulloye: *tue l'oie*: kill the goose.

came in on the heels of the printing-office apprentice, and handed Lucien a letter from Louise.

'You have doubtless heard, my friend, the upshot of the duel between Chandour and my husband. We shall not be receiving anyone today; be prudent and don't appear in public. I beg this of you in the name of the affection you bear me. Don't you think that the best way you can spend this sad day is to come and listen to your Beatrice, whose life is completely changed by this event and who has many things to say to you?'

'Fortunately,' said David, 'our wedding is fixed for the day after tomorrow. That will be an excuse for going less often to see Madame de Bargeton.'

'My dear David,' Lucien replied. 'She asks me to go and see her today. I think I must obey her. She will know better than we how I should behave in the present circumstances.'

'And so all the work is finished here?' asked Madame Chardon.

'Come and see,' cried David, happy to show her the transformation in the first-floor rooms, where everything was fresh and new. They breathed a spirit of calm such as often pervades young households, where orange blossom and the bridal veil are still the emblem of home life, with the springtime of love reflected in every object, where all is white, clean and bright with flowers.

'Eve will be like a princess,' said her mother. 'But you have spent too much money. You have been extravagant!'

David gave a smile but no reply, for Madame Chardon had put her finger on the raw place in a secret wound which was causing the poor lover considerable anguish: his estimates for the work had been so greatly exceeded that it was impossible for him to build over the lean-to, which meant that his mother-in-law would have to wait a long time for the apartment he wanted to give her. Generous persons feel the liveliest pain at not keeping those promises which to some extent constitute the minor vanities of tenderness. David was careful to hide his embarrassment in order to spare Lucien's feelings, for he might have felt overwhelmed by the sacrifice made for him.

'Eve and her friends have done their work well,' Madame Chardon was saying. 'The trousseau, the household linen, everything is ready. The girls are so fond of her that, without her knowing anything about it, they have put white twill covers edged in pink on the mattresses. It's beautiful! It makes you feel you want to get married!'

Mother and daughter had used up all their savings in furnishing David's house with articles the young never think about. Knowing to what expense he was going, for he had ordered porcelain china from Limoges, they had tried to match the things they were bringing with those which David was buying. This little rivalry in love and generosity was to bring the couple into tight circumstances from the very beginning of their marriage, surrounded though they were with all the appearances of middle-class ease which might pass as luxury in so backward a town as Angoulême then was. When Lucien saw his mother and David going into the bedroom, with whose blue and white hangings and dainty furniture he was familiar, he slipped away to see Madame de Bargeton. He found Naïs at breakfast with her husband, who had gained an appetite from his early morning outing and was eating without a thought for what had happened. The old country gentleman, Monsieur de Nègrepelisse, an imposing figure, a relic of the old French nobility, was sitting beside his daughter. When Gentil announced Monsieur de Rubempré, the white-haired old man eyed him with the curiosity of a father eager to pass judgement on the man his daughter has singled out. Lucien's extreme beauty made so lively an impression on him that he could not withhold a glance of approval; but he appeared to look on his daughter's liaison as a passing fancy, as a caprice rather than a durable passion. Breakfast was ending, Louise was able to rise from table and leave her father with Monsieur de Bargeton, beckoning Lucien to follow her.

'My friend,' she said in a voice which was at once sad and joyful. 'I am going to Paris, and my father is taking Monsieur de Bargeton to L'Escarbas, where he will remain during my absence. Madame d'Espard, a daughter of the Blamont-

Chauvry's, to whom we are related through the d'Espards, the elder branch of the Nègrepelisse family, has much power at present, both on her own account and through her relatives. If she deigns to acknowledge us, I hope to cultivate her a great deal: she might use her influence to obtain a post for Bargeton. My solicitations might get him thought of at Court as a possible deputy for a Charente constituency, and that will facilitate his nomination here. If he were elected deputy, that could further my plans in Paris. You it is, my darling child, who have inspired me to make this change in my existence. This morning's duel obliges me to shut up my house for some time, for some people will side with the Chandours against us. In a situation like ours, and in a small town, one must always absent oneself for a time in order to let rancours die down. But either I shall succeed and shall never see Angoulême again, or I shall not succeed and shall wait in Paris until the time comes when I can spend every summer at L'Escarbas and every winter in Paris. That is the only life for a society woman, and I have been too slow in taking it up. Today will be enough for us to make all our preparations; I shall set off tomorrow night and you will go with me, won't you? You will go on ahead. I will pick you up in my carriage between Mansle and Ruffec, and we shall soon be in Paris. It is there, my dear, that worthwhile people live. One can feel at ease only with one's equals; everywhere else one suffers. Besides, Paris, the capital of the intellectual world, is the stage on which you will find success! You must leap quickly over the gap which separates you from it! Don't let your ideas grow rancid in the provinces; get swiftly into contact with the men who will represent the nineteenth century. Draw near to Court and Government. Neither distinction nor high position go looking for talent wilting away in a small town. In any case tell me what fine works have been produced in the provinces! On the other hand think of the sublime but penniless Jean-Jacques Rousseau, irresistibly drawn to that radiant centre where men achieve glory through the fervour enkindled in them by the friction of rivalry. Must you not hasten to take your place in the constellation which rises in each generation?

You can scarcely imagine how useful it is for a talented young man to be brought into the limelight by high social connections. I will get you received into Madame d'Espard's salon, to which no one has easy access, and there you will meet all the celebrities of the day – ministers, ambassadors, Parliamentary orators, the most influential peers, wealthy and illustrious people. A handsome young man, full of genius, would have to be very maladroit not to arouse their interest. Men of great talent are not small-minded and will give you their support. When it is known that you move in distinguished circles, your works will acquire tremendous value. The great problem which artists have to solve is how to catch the eye of the public, but there you will find a thousand opportunities for making your way – sinecures, a subsidy from the privy purse. The Bourbons are devoted patrons of literature and the arts! Therefore you must be both a religious and a royalist poet. Not only will that be right and proper, but you will make your fortune into the bargain! Can you expect the Opposition or the Liberals to confer office and rewards or make a writer's fortune? And so, take the right road and reach the heights to which all men of genius aspire. I have let you into my secret: keep absolutely quiet about it, and get ready to follow me.'

'Don't you want to?' she added, astonished at her lover's silence. Dazed by the rapid glimpse of Paris which these seductive words had evoked, Lucien thought that never until then had he exercised more than half his mind and that only now was the other half of his brain coming to life with this enlargement of his prospects: he saw himself while living in Angoulême as a frog under a stone at the bottom of a swamp. He had a vision of Paris in all its splendour: Paris, an Eldorado to the imagination of every provincial; clad in gold, wearing a diadem of precious stones, holding its arms out to talent. He would receive a fraternal accolade from illustrious men. There genius was welcomed. There would be found no envious little gentry to humiliate writers with their cutting sarcasms and no parade of stupid indifference to poetry. There the works of poets gushed forth, were paid for and offered to the world. After reading the first few pages of *The Archer of*

Charles the Ninth the publishers would open their coffers and ask him: 'How much do you want?' In addition he reckoned that, as a result of the journey during which circumstances would make them man and wife, Madame de Bargeton would belong entirely to him. They would live together.

He replied with a tear to the question 'Don't you want to?', seized Louise round the waist, pressed her to his heart and enflamed her neck with the ardour of his kisses. Then suddenly he stopped short as one to whom memory returns and exclaimed:

'Good heavens! My sister is getting married the day after tomorrow!'

This exclamation was the expiring breath of his childhood purity and nobility. The powerful ties which bind young people's hearts to their family, to their earliest friend, to all their primitive feelings, were about to be dealt a severing blow.

'What of that?' cried the haughty Nègrepelisse. 'What connection is there between your sister's marriage and the furtherance of our love? Are you so keen on leading the choir at this middle-class, working-class wedding that you cannot sacrifice its noble joys to me? . . . A fine sacrifice!' she added contemptuously. 'This morning I sent my husband off to fight a duel on your behalf! Go away, Monsieur, leave me! I have been mistaken in you.'

She fell back in a swoon on to her sofa. Lucien rushed to her side and begged her forgiveness, anathematizing his family, David and his sister.

'I had such faith in you,' she said. 'Monsieur de Cante-Croix had a mother whom he idolized, but in order to obtain a letter from me in which I told him: *I am pleased with you!* he died in the firing-line. And you, when it is a matter of travelling with me, you can't even give up a wedding-breakfast!'

Lucien felt like suicide, and his despair was so sincere, so profound, that Louise forgave him; but she made it plain to him that he would have to atone for his fault.

'Go along then,' she said in the end. 'Be discreet, and wait at midnight tomorrow a hundred yards beyond Mansle.'

Lucien felt as if he were walking on air. He returned to

David's house with all his hopes at his heels – like Orestes pursued by the Furies – for he foresaw a thousand difficulties which were summed up in one terrible word: *money*. He was in such fear of David's perspicacity that he shut himself up in his elegant study to recover from the mental turmoil his changed situation was causing him. So then, he would have to leave this apartment which had been set up at such great expense; so many sacrifices would be rendered useless. But he reckoned that his mother would be able to live in it, and in this way David would save on the costs of the structure he had planned to build at the end of the courtyard. His departure would straighten out the family finances, and he discovered a thousand compelling reasons for departing: there is nothing so jesuitical as desire. He hurried at once to L'Houmeau to see his sister, tell her of his new prospects and discuss matters with her. As he passed by Postel's shop the thought came to him that, if other means were lacking, he could borrow enough money from his father's successor to last him a year.

'If I live with Louise,' he told himself, 'three francs a day will be as good as a fortune, and that only amounts to a thousand francs for a year. Well, in six months' time I shall be rich!'

Eve and her mother gave ear to Lucien's confidences under promise of deep secrecy. Both of them wept as they listened to the ambitious young man; and when he asked the reason for their sorrow, they informed him that all they possessed had been spent on table and household linen, Eve's trousseau and a multitude of purchases that David had not thought of making – and they had been happy to do it, for the printer was crediting Eve with a dowry of ten thousand francs. Lucien then imparted to them his idea of raising a loan, and Madame Chardon undertook to go and ask Monsieur Postel to lend them a thousand francs for a year.

'But Lucien,' said Eve – and the thought wrung her heart – 'will you not then be present at my wedding? Oh! come back for it; I can wait a few days! She will certainly let you come back here in a fortnight's time, once you have accompanied her to Paris! She will surely allow us a week, since we brought you up for her! Our marriage will turn out badly if you're not there . . .'

'But will a thousand francs be enough?' she suddenly broke off to ask. 'Your suit is wonderfully smart, but you've only one! You've only two fine linen shirts and the six others you have are of coarse holland. You have only three cambric cravats; the three others are of cheap jaconet. And your handkerchiefs aren't very good. Will you find a sister in Paris to launder your linen on the day you are to wear it? You need a lot more. You have only one pair of this year's nankeen trousers; your last year's are too tight, and so you will have to buy clothes in Paris, and prices in Paris are higher than in Angoulême. You have only two white waistcoats fit to wear; I have already mended the others. Look, I advise you to take two thousand francs with you.'

At this instant David came in. Apparently he had overheard this last remark, for he scanned brother and sister in silence.

'Tell me what this is all about,' he said.

'Well,' exclaimed Eve. 'He's going away with her.'

Madame Chardon entered without noticing David. 'Postel,' she said, 'is willing to lend the thousand francs, but only for six months, and he wants a bill of exchange from you endorsed by your brother-in-law, for he says you have no surety to offer.'

She turned round, saw her son-in-law, and all four of them stood there in deep silence. The Chardon family was conscious of having abused David's good nature. They were all ashamed. Tears came to the printer's eyes.

'So you won't be coming to our wedding?' he said. 'So you won't be living with us? And I have just squandered all I had. Oh, Lucien, I was bringing Eve her modest little wedding jewellery, not knowing' (he wiped his eyes and drew the cases from his pocket) 'that I should have cause for regretting having bought them.'

He laid the morocco-covered cases down on the table in front of his mother-in-law.

'Why do you bother about me so much?' asked Eve with an angelic smile which took the edge off her question.

'Dear Mamma,' said the printer. 'Go and tell Monsieur Postel I am willing to give my signature, for I can see by your face, Lucien, that your mind is set on going.'

Lucien gave a weak and regretful nod of assent, and the next moment he added: 'Don't think too badly of me, my beloved angels.' He took hold of Eve and David, kissed them, clasped them to him, and said:

'Wait for results, and you will learn how much I love you. David, what use would our high ideals be, if we were unable to disregard the trivial ceremonies in which the law ties up genuine feeling? Although far away, shall I not be present in spirit? Shall we not be together in our thoughts? Have I not my destiny to work out? Would the publishers come out here to get my *Archer of Charles the Ninth* and my *Marguerites*? Should I not still, a little sooner or a little later, have to do what I am doing today? Shall I ever meet with more favourable circumstances? Does not my whole future depend on making my beginnings in Paris in the Marquise d'Espard's salon?'

'He is right,' said Eve. 'Did you not tell me yourself that he ought to go to Paris without delay?'

David took Eve's hand, led her into the little cupboard of a room in which she had been sleeping for seven years, and whispered to her:

'He needs two thousand francs, as you were saying, my love. Postel will only lend one thousand.'

The agonized look which Eve gave her fiancé was expressive of all the torture she was suffering.

'Listen, Eve, my beloved. The beginning of our life together will not be comfortable. It's a fact, my expenditure has soaked up all I had. I have only two thousand francs left, and half of it is absolutely necessary for the running of the printing-office. If I give your brother a thousand francs, I shall be giving him our daily bread and compromising our tranquillity. If I were alone, I should know what to do. But there are two of us. You must decide.'

Beside herself, Eve threw herself into her lover's arms, gave him a tender kiss and, bathed in tears, whispered in his ear: 'Do what you would do if you were alone. I will go out to work to earn the money.'

In spite of a kiss as ardent as any ever exchanged between two fiancés, David left Eve completely dejected, and went back to Lucien.

'Don't worry,' he said. 'You will get your two thousand francs.'

'Go and see Postel,' said Madame Chardon. 'Both of you will have to sign the paper.'

When the two friends came back, they found Eve and her mother on their knees in prayer. Although the latter knew what great hopes ought to materialize on Lucien's return, at that moment they were conscious of all they were losing by his departure: they felt that happiness to come was being too dearly paid for by an absence which was going to break up their life and bring them endless fears for Lucien's future.

'If ever you forgot this scene,' whispered David to Lucien, 'You would be the most despicable of men.'

No doubt the printer deemed these grave words necessary, for he was no less appalled by Madame de Bargeton's ascendency over Lucien than by the fatal instability of character which could as easily fling him into evil ways as into good ones. It did not take Eve long to do Lucien's packing. This Fernando Cortez of literature had little to take away. He wore his best frock-coat, his best waistcoat and one of his fine linen shirts. All his linen, his famous suit, his appurtenances and manuscripts made up so slender a parcel that, to prevent Madame de Bargeton from setting eyes on it, David suggested sending it by stage-coach to a business acquaintance in Paris, a paper merchant, and writing to him to keep it with him until Lucien called for it.

In spite of the precautions taken by Madame de Bargeton to conceal her departure, Monsieur du Châtelet learnt of it and was curious to know whether she would be travelling alone or in Lucien's company; he sent his valet to Ruffec, with instructions to inspect all the vehicles changing horses at the post.

'If she takes her poet away with her,' he thought, 'she is mine.'

Lucien set off at dawn the next morning, accompanied by David who had hired a horse and trap, announcing that he was going to talk business with his father – a plausible little fiction in the circumstances. The two friends went to Marsac and spent the day with the old 'bear'; then, in the evening, they passed beyond Mansle in order to wait for Madame de Bargeton, who arrived towards morning. When he caught sight of the antiquated sixty-year-old barouche which he had so often looked at in the coach-house, Lucien experienced one of the liveliest emotions he had ever had. He flung himself into David's arms, and the latter exclaimed: 'Heaven send that this is for your good!'

The printer climbed back into his shabby trap, and his heart was heavy as he drove away, for he had horrible presentiments of the fate in store for Lucien in Paris.

Part Two

A GREAT MAN IN EMBRYO

First-fruits

NEITHER Lucien, nor Madame de Bargeton, nor Gentil, nor
Albertine the lady's maid ever talked about the incidents of
the journey, but one may well believe that the continued
presence of the servants made it very disagreeable for a lover
who was expecting all the delights of an elopement. Lucien,
who was travelling post for the first time in his life, was
flabbergasted to see almost the whole sum which was supposed
to last him for a year in Paris scattered by the wayside between
Angoulême and the capital. Like all men of vigorous talent
who have not shed the graces of childhood, he made the
mistake of expressing his naïve astonishment at the sight of
things which were new to him. A man must make a close
study of a woman before letting her see his emotions and
thoughts as they come to him one by one. A mistress as
tender as she is great-hearted smiles understandingly at ingenuousness; but if there is any vanity in her make-up she
will not forgive an admirer who shows himself to be callow,
vain or trivial. Many women so exaggerate their cult of love
that they always expect to find a god in their idol; whereas a
woman who loves a man for himself rather than for her own
sake adores the littleness as well as the greatness in him. Lucien
had not yet divined that in Madame de Bargeton love was
grafted on to pride. He ought to have caught the meaning
of certain smiles which escaped her during their journey
whenever, instead of containing his feelings, he expressed
them with the wonderment of a baby rat taking a first peep
outside its hole.

The travellers alighted before daybreak at the Hôtel du
Gaillard-Bois in the rue de l'Echelle. They were both tired
out and Louise wanted to go straight to bed. She did so after
ordering Lucien to ask for a room above the suite she took
for herself.

He slept till four o'clock in the afternoon. Madame de
Bargeton had him roused for dinner; when he learned how

late it was he threw on his clothes and joined Louise in one of those squalid rooms which are the disgrace of Paris where despite all its pretensions to elegance there is not yet a single hotel in which any wealthy traveller can feel at home. Although Lucien was still bleary-eyed from his sudden awakening, he found his Louise scarcely recognizable in this cold, sunless room with its faded curtains, its depressing, over-scrubbed tiles, its worn, tasteless, antequated or secondhand furniture. Indeed certain persons neither look nor are the same once they are detached from the faces, places and objects which constitute their normal environment. The physiognomy of living people has its own special aura, just as the chiaroscuro in Flemish pictures is needed to give life to the figures which the painter's genius has set in them. This is especially noticeable in the case of provincials. Moreover Madame de Bargeton seemed to be more on her dignity, more thoughtful than she should have been at the moment when a life of unrestricted happiness was opening before her. Lucien could make no complaint since Gentil and Albertine were serving them. The dinner lacked the abundance and basic wholesomeness characteristic of a provincial table. The dishes, parsimoniously reduced, came from a neighbouring restaurant; they were sparingly garnished and looked like measured rations. Paris is not generous in regard to the little commodities with which people of modest fortune have to be contented.

Lucien waited for the meal to end before he questioned Louise, who seemed to him to have unaccountably changed. He was not mistaken. A grave event – in the moral sphere reflection is an event – had occurred while he had been sleeping. About two in the afternoon, Sixte du Châtelet had presented himself at the hotel, awakened Albertine, expressed the desire to speak to her mistress and come back again after scarcely giving Madame de Bargeton time to make herself presentable. Anaïs, whose curiosity was aroused by Monsieur du Châtelet's unexpected appearance when she thought that her movements had been so well concealed, had received him at about three o'clock.

'I followed you at the risk of getting a reprimand from the

Administration,' he said as he greeted her, 'for I foresaw what is happening to you. But even if I lose my post, at least *you* shall not lose your good name!'

'What do you mean?' exclaimed Madame de Bargeton.

'I can well see that you love Lucien,' he continued with an air of tender resignation. 'You must indeed be in love to cast reflection aside and forget all the proprieties – you who are so well versed in them! Do you really believe, my dear, adored Naïs, that you will be admitted to Madame d'Espard's salon, or any other in Paris, once people know that you have practically fled from Angoulême with a young man, especially after the duel between Monsieur de Bargeton and Monsieur de Chandour? The fact that your husband is staying at L'Escarbas looks very like a separation. In cases like this, men of correct behaviour begin by fighting for their wives and leave them to their own devices afterwards. Love Monsieur de Rubempré, protect him, do what you will with him, but don't live with him! If anyone here knew you made the journey in the same carriage, you would be blacklisted by the very people you want to see. Besides, Naïs, don't make such sacrifices yet for a young man whom you've not yet compared with anyone else, who has been put to no test and may well desert you here for a woman of Paris whom he thinks more necessary to his ambitions than you are. I mean no harm to the man you love, but you must allow me to put your interests before his and to tell you: "Study him! Realize fully the steps you are taking." If you find doors are closed to you, if women refuse to receive you, at least make sure that these sacrifices will bring no regret and that the man for whom you are making them will always be worthy of them and appreciate them. Madame d'Espard is the more prudish and severe because she is herself living apart from her husband without anyone being able to fathom the reason for their separation. But the Navarreins, the Blamont-Chauvrys, the Lenoncourts and all her relatives have stood by her; the most strait-laced women go to her house and give her a respectful welcome in their own. The conclusion is: Monsieur d'Espard must be in the wrong. At the first visit you pay to her, you will realize how apt is my advice. I can certainly predict this, knowing Paris as I do: when you went to see the Marquise you would be lost if she knew that you were staying at the Hôtel du Gaillard-Bois with an apothecary's son, Monsieur de Rubempré though he would like to be. Here you will have rivals far more astute and cunning than Amélie: it won't take them long to find out who you are, where you are, where you have come from and what you are doing. I see you were counting on keeping your incognito, but you are one of those persons for whom this is impossible. Will you not come up against Angoulême wherever you go? – deputies from the Charente who are here for the opening of Parliament, or some general or other who is on leave in Paris. It would be enough if just one inhabitant of Angoulême should catch sight of you for strange conclusions to be drawn about you: you would simply be written off as Lucien's mistress. If you need me for any purpose, I am staying with the Receiver-General in the rue du Faubourg-Saint-Honoré, a few yards away from Madame d'Espard's house. I know the Maréchale de Carigliano, Madame de Sérizy and the Prime Minister well enough to introduce you to them. But you will meet so many people at Madame d'Espard's house that you will have no need of me. Far from having to desire admission to one or other of the salons, your presence will be desired in all of them.'

Du Châtelet was able to have his say without interruption from Madame de Bargeton: she was struck by the apropos of his observations. The first lady in Angoulême had indeed reckoned on keeping her incognito.

'You are right, dear friend,' she said. 'But what should I do?'

'Let me find you suitable apartments, completely furnished. That way you will live more cheaply than in any hotel, and you will be in your own home. If you take my advice you will sleep there tonight.'

'But how did you find out my address?'

'Your carriage was easy to recognize, and besides, I was following you. At Sèvres the postilion who was bringing you told mine your address. Will you allow me to be your quartermaster? I will soon write and tell you where I have found lodging for you.'

'Very well, do so,' she said.

This seemed a little thing to say, but it meant everything. The Baron du Châtelet had spoken like a man of the world to a woman of the world. He had come dressed with all the elegance of Parisian fashion in a smart and well-appointed cabriolet. It so happened that Madame de Bargeton was standing at her window to consider her situation, and from there she watched the old dandy's departure. A minute or two later Lucien, abruptly awoken and hastily dressed, appeared before her in his last-year's nankeen trousers and his shabby little frock-coat. He was handsome, but his clothes were ridiculous. If you put the Belvedere Apollo or Antinous in a water-carrier's costume, will you recognize him as the superb creation of a Greek or Roman chisel? The eye makes comparisons before the heart can rectify its rapid and automatic judgement. The contrast between Lucien and Châtelet was too blatant for Louise not to be struck by it. When, at about six o'clock, dinner was over, Madame de Bargeton motioned Lucien to come and sit beside her on the shabby sofa covered in yellow-flowered red calico.

'My Lucien,' she said. 'Don't you think that if we have committed an indiscretion equally disastrous to us both, there is reason for repairing it? We must not live together in Paris, dear child, nor let it be suspected that we came here together. Your future depends on my position, and I must do nothing to prejudice it. And so, from tonight onwards, I am going to lodge a short distance away; but you will stay in this hotel, and we can meet every day without criticism from anyone.'

Louise then expounded the laws of society to Lucien, who listened with wide-open eyes. Though he did not know that women who are going back on their indiscretions are going back on their love, he realized that for her he was no longer the Lucien of Angoulême. She only talked to him about herself, her own interests, her reputation, her place in society, and to palliate her selfishness she tried to persuade him that his own interests were also at stake. He had no rights over Louise, who had so promptly become Madame de Bargeton once more, and worse still he had no power either! And so he could not keep back the big tears which filled his eyes.

'If I am your hope and pride, you mean even more to me. You are my only hope and my whole future. I understood that if you were to share my success you would share my misfortunes too. And here we are, separating already.'

'You are judging my conduct,' she said. 'You do not love me.' Lucien looked at her with such a pained expression that she could not refrain from adding: 'Dear boy, I will stay here if you wish: it will spell ruin for both of us and we shall be without support. But when we are equal in misery and both of us are spurned, when failure – for we must foresee all possibilities – has relegated us to L'Escarbas, remember, my love, that I predicted this result, and that I proposed at the beginning that you should make your way in conformity with and obedience to the laws of society.'

'Louise,' he replied, putting his arms round her. 'It frightens me to see you so prudent. Remember that I'm very young and that I abandoned myself entirely to your dear will. I myself had wished to triumph over men and things by sheer force; but if I can succeed more quickly with your aid than by myself I shall be very happy to owe all my good fortune to you. Forgive me! I have staked too much on you not to be full of fear. For me, separation from you is a prelude to abandonment, and abandonment would kill me.'

'But my dear child,' she replied, 'Society does not ask a lot of you. It is merely a question of your sleeping here; you can spend the day in my flat without anyone taking exception.'

In the end a few caresses pacified Lucien. An hour later Gentil brought a note from Châtelet to tell Madame de Bargeton that he had found rooms in the rue Neuve-du-Luxembourg. She enquired where this street was situated – it was not very far from the rue de l'Echelle – and told Lucien: 'We shall be near one another.' Two hours later Louise took a carriage sent by du Châtelet in order to go to her flat. It was the kind of place that tapestry-makers furnish and let to rich deputies or important persons making a short visit to Paris: sumptuous but inconvenient. At about eleven o'clock Lucien returned to the little Hôtel du Gaillard-Bois, having so far seen nothing more of Paris than that part of the rue Saint-Honoré which runs between the rue Neuve-du-Luxembourg and the rue de l'Echelle. He went to bed in his sordid little room, which he could not help comparing with Louise's magnificent quarters. Just after he had left her, Baron Châtelet arrived there on his way back from the house of the Minister for Foreign Affairs, in all the splendour of his ballroom array. He had come to tell her of the arrangements he had made for her. Louise was worried: such luxury appalled her. Provincial ways of life had had their effect on her in the long run and she had become strict in her accounts, which she kept in such good order that in Paris she would have been taken for a miser. She had come away with a draft for twenty thousand francs from the Receiver-General, reckoning that this sum would more than cover her expenses for four years. She feared already that it was not enough and that she would fall into debt. Châtelet informed her that her flat would not cost her more than six hundred francs a month.

'A mere nothing,' he said as he saw Naïs give a shrug. 'You have at your disposal a carriage which will cost you five hundred francs a month: that makes little more than a thousand francs. After that you need only think of what you will spend on clothes. A woman who moves in society cannot settle things otherwise. If you want to get Monsieur de Bargeton made a Receiver-General or obtain a post for him in the King's household, you must not look like a pauper. Here gifts are made only to the rich. You are lucky to have Gentil to escort you and Albertine to dress you, for servants in Paris cost the earth. Launched in society as you will be, you won't often eat at home.'

Madame de Bargeton and the Baron chatted about Paris. Du Châtelet told her the latest news and the thousand and one niceties to be observed if one wishes to be accepted as a Parisian. He was not slow in giving Naïs advice about the shops she should patronize: he recommended Herbault for toques, Juliette for hats and bonnets; he told her where she could find a dressmaker to replace Victorine; in short he impressed on her the necessity of casting off everything to do with her Angoulême ways. As he was leaving, a happy inspiration came to him on the spur of the moment:

'Tomorrow,' he said in casual tones, 'I shall no doubt have a box at some theatre. I will pick you up, you and Monsieur de Rubempré, and take you to it. You will allow me, will you not, to show both of you a little of life in Paris.'

'He has more generosity of character than I thought,' Madame de Bargeton told herself on seeing Lucien invited.

In the month of September cabinet ministers have hardly any use for their boxes at the theatre: ministerial deputies and their constituents are busy with their grape-gatherings or their harvests, while their most exacting acquaintances are away in the country or travelling. And so, at this season, the finest boxes in the Paris theatres are filled with an assortment of guests whom the regular theatre-goers never see again and who make the audience look like a piece of patched tapestry. The idea had already come to du Châtelet that, thanks to this circumstance, and without much expense, he could procure for Naïs the kind of amusement most enticing to provincial visitors. The next day, when Lucien made his first call on Louise, he did not find her at home. She was out doing some indispensable shopping. Having written to tell the Marquise d'Espard of her arrival, she had gone to hold counsel with the grave and illustrious authorities on ladies' fashions whom du Châtelet had cited to her. Although Madame de Bargeton possessed the self-confidence which long-standing domination confers, she was terribly afraid of looking provincial. She had tact enough to know how much relations between women depend on first impressions, and though she knew she was capable of promptly rising to the level of superior women like Madame d'Espard, she felt the need to inspire good will at the first encounter, and was particularly anxious not to neglect anything which might contribute to success. She was therefore infinitely grateful to Châtelet for having indicated by what means she might get into step with the Parisian *beau monde*. By a strange chance the Marquise found herself in a situation which made her delighted to render service to some-one of her husband's family. The Marquis d'Espard had withdrawn from society for no apparent cause. He was taking no interest in his own affairs, or politics, or family concerns, or those of his wife.[1] Left thus to her own devices, the Marquise felt that she needed the approval of society; therefore she was happy to be able to replace the Marquis in this cir-cumstance by befriending his relations. Her intention was to put some ostentation into this patronage so that her husband might appear more obviously to be in the wrong. That very day she sent to 'Madame de Bargeton, née Nègrepelisse,' a note so nicely worded as to conceal from the cursory reader the shallowness of its contents.

She wrote that she was happy for a turn of events which was bringing a person whom she had heard mentioned and was desirous to know into closer connection with the family, for friendships in Paris were not so stable that she did not wish to have someone else on earth to love, and if this were not to come about she would have merely one more illusion to be interred with the rest. She put herself entirely at her cousin's disposal. She would have come to see her had an indisposition not kept her indoors; but she already regarded herself as being under an obligation to Madame de Bargeton because she had thought of her.

In the course of his first random stroll through the boule-vards and the rue de la Paix, Lucien, like all new-comers to Paris, took more stock of things than of persons. In Paris, it is first of all the general pattern that commands attention. The luxury of the shops, the height of the buildings, the busy to-and-fro of carriages, the ever-present contrast between extreme luxury and extreme indigence, all these things are particularly striking. Abashed at the sight of this alien crowd, the imaginative young man felt as if he himself was enor-mously diminished. People who in the provinces enjoy a

1. The explanation of this situation is to be found in *The Petition of Lunacy* (1836). The Marquise was trying to get her husband declared insane because he was anxious to repair an injury done by his ancestors.

certain amount of consideration and at every step they take meet with some proof of their own importance can in no wise accustom themselves to this sudden and total devaluation. Some transition is needed between the two states of being a somebody at home and of being a nobody in Paris; and those who pass too abruptly from the one to the other experience a feeling of annihilation. For a young poet used to having a sounding-board for all his feelings, an ear into which he could pour all his thoughts and a kindred soul to share his slightest impressions, Paris was to prove a fearsome desert. Lucien had not gone to fetch his fine blue coat, so that he felt embarrassed by the sorry, not to say ruinous, condition of his clothes as he was returning to Madame de Bargeton's flat at a time when he deemed she would be back. The Baron du Châtelet was already there, and he took them both out to dine at the Rocher-de-Cancale. Lucien, stunned by the rapid whirl of life in Paris, could say nothing to Louise, as all three of them were together inside the carriage. But he squeezed her hand, and she gave a friendly response to all the thoughts he was thus expressing. After dinner Châtelet took his two guests to the Vaudeville Theatre. Lucien felt secretly displeased to see du Châtelet and was cursing the ill-luck which had brought him to Paris. The Director of Taxes alleged his own ambition as an excuse for his arrival there: he was hoping to be appointed Secretary-General in a civil service department and to enter the Council of State as a master of requests; he had come to ask that the promises made to him should be honoured, for a man like himself could not remain a mere Director of Taxes; he would prefer to be nothing at all, become a deputy or return to a diplomatic career. He was puffing himself out, and Lucien vaguely recognized in the elderly fop the advantage which a man of the world enjoys in Parisian society; but above all he was ashamed to owe any enjoyment to him. Whereas the poet was anxious and ill at ease, the former Secretary to an Imperial Highness was altogether in his element. Just as old sea-dogs mock at greenhorn sailors who have not yet found their sea-legs, so du Châtelet smiled at his rival's hesitancy, his wonderment, the questions he asked and the little blunders he made through inexperience. But the pleasure which Lucien felt at his first visit to a theatre in Paris compensated for the annoyance which his blunders caused him. It was a memorable evening for him, thanks to his unvoiced repudiation of a great number of his ideas about life in the provinces. His little world was broadening out and society was assuming vaster proportions. The proximity of several beautiful Parisian women, so elegantly and so daintily attired, made him aware that Madame de Bargeton's *toilette*, though passably ambitious, was behind the times: neither the material, nor the way it was cut, nor the colours were in fashion. The hair-style he had found so seductive at Angoulême struck him as being in deplorable taste compared with the delicate inventiveness which lent distinction to the other women present. 'Will she remain like that?' he wondered, not knowing that she had spent the day preparing a transformation. In the provinces no occasion arises for choice or comparison: one sees the same physiognomies day by day and confers a conventional beauty on them. Once she has moved to Paris a woman accepted as pretty in the provinces commands not the slightest attention, for she is beautiful only by virtue of the proverb: 'In a community of the blind, one-eyed people reign supreme.' Lucien was observing Madame de Bargeton and making the same comparison as she had made the previous evening between Châtelet and himself. Madame de Bargeton too was indulging in strange reflections about her admirer. The poor poet was singularly handsome, but he cut a sorry figure. His frock-coat, too short in the sleeves, his cheap provincial gloves and his skimpy waistcoat gave him a prodigiously ridiculous appearance in comparison with the young men in the dress-circle: Madame de Bargeton found him pitiable to look at. The elegant Châtelet, who was giving her his undisguised attention and watching over her with such care as betokened deep passion, was as much at ease as an actor on the stage of his favourite theatre; he had taken only two days to recover all the ground he had lost in six months. Although it is not commonly admitted that feelings are subject to sudden changes, it is certain that two people in love often move apart more quickly than they have come together. In the case both of Madame de Bargeton and Lucien, mutual disenchantment was setting in, and Paris was the cause of it. The poet was seeing life on a larger scale and society was taking on a new aspect in Louise's eyes. With both of them, only a chance event was needed to sever the bonds between them. The axe was soon to fall and deal Lucien a terrible blow.

Madame de Bargeton set the poet down at his hotel and returned home in du Châtelet's company, which was horribly displeasing to the poor, susceptible young man. 'What will they be saying about me?' he wondered as he walked up to his dreary bedroom.

'That poor lad is incredibly boring,' said du Châtelet with a smile as he closed the carriage door.

'It is so with all those whose heart and brain contain a whole world of ideas. Men who have so much to express in fine, long-premeditated works profess a certain contempt for conversation, a commerce in which intelligence is converted into small change and frittered away.' So said the proud Nègrepelisse, still courageous enough to defend Lucien, though she did it less for Lucien's sake than for her own.

'I willingly grant you that,' replied the Baron. 'But we live with people and not with books. Listen, dear Naïs, I can see that as yet there is nothing between you and him, and I rejoice at this. If you intend to take up some interest in life which you have missed up to now, I entreat you, let it not be for this supposed genius. What if you were mistaken! What if, in a few days' time, comparing him to men of real talent, to the genuinely remarkable men you are about to meet, you realized that, like a beautiful shining Nereid, you had borne through the waves and brought ashore, not a poet with his lyre, but a little plagiarist with no manners and little range, stupid and conceited: one who may pass for a man of wit in L'Houmeau but who, once in Paris, turns out to be a very ordinary individual! After all, volumes of verse are published here every week, and the least of them is still worth more than all Monsieur Chardon's poetry. I beg you to wait and compare. Tomorrow, Friday, there will be Opera' – as he said this the carriage turned into the rue Neuve-du-Luxembourg – 'Madame d'Espard has at her disposal the box belonging to the First Gentlemen of the Bedchamber, and will no doubt take you there. In order to see you in all your glory, I shall go to Madame de Sérizy's box. They are performing *The Danaids*.'

She bade him good-night.

The next morning Madame de Bargeton did her best to assemble a morning outfit suitable for calling on her cousin, Madame d'Espard. The weather was rather cold, and all she could rummage out from her unfashionable Angoulême finery was an undistinguished green velvet dress with somewhat extravagant trimmings. As for Lucien, he felt he must retrieve his famous blue coat, for he now held his skimpy frock-coat in horror and wanted to be always smartly turned out, thinking that he might meet the Marquise d'Espard or pay her an impromptu visit. He took a cab so that he might bring his parcel straight back. In two hours he spent three or four francs, which gave him much subject for reflection on the cost of living in Paris. After dressing as elegantly as he could he went to the rue Neuve-du-Luxembourg, and there he met Gentil, in company with a footman in magnificent plumes.

'I was going to your hotel, Monsieur; Madame sent me this note to give you,' said Gentil, who was ignorant of the respectful phraseology current in Paris, accustomed as he was to the free and easy direct speech of the provinces.

The footman took the poet for a domestic. Lucien opened the note and learned that Madame de Bargeton was spending the day with the Marquise and was going to the Opera that evening; but she told Lucien to be there, for her cousin was allowing her to offer the young poet a seat in her box. The Marquise was delighted to give him this pleasure.

'Louise *does* love me then! My fears are absurd,' thought Lucien. 'She is introducing me to her cousin this very evening.'

He leapt for joy and decided to make the best of the time separating him from that happy evening. He dashed towards the Tuileries Gardens, with the idea of walking about until it was time to go and dine at Véry's restaurant. So then we see Lucien in high feather, with springy gait, treading on air, emerging on to the Terrasse des Feuillants, striding through it and studying the people walking along it: pretty women with their admirers, elegant couples arm in arm, greeting one another with a glance as they passed by. What a difference between this terrace and Beaulieu! How much finer than those of Angoulême were the birds on this magnificent perch! It was like the riot of colour blazing forth on ornithological species from India or America compared with the drab plumage of European birds. Lucien spent two hours of torment in the Tuileries: he angrily took stock of his own appearance and condemned it. In the first place, not one of these elegant young men was wearing a cut-away coat: if he saw one at all it was worn by some disreputable old man, or some poor down-at-heel, or a *rentier* from the Marais quarter, or a commissionaire. Having realized the difference between morning and evening wear, this highly sensitive and keen-sighted poet recognized the ugliness of his own apparel, which was fit only for the rag-bag, the out-of-date cut of his coat, its dubious blue, its outrageously ungainly collar and its tails nearly meeting in front through too long usage; the buttons were rusty and there were tell-tale white lines along the creases. Also his waistcoat was too short and so grotesquely provincial in style that he hastily buttoned up his coat in order to hide it. Lastly, only common people were wearing nankeen trousers. Fashionable people were wearing attractively patterned or immaculately white material! Moreover everyone wore gaitered trousers; the bottoms of his fell in ugly crinkles on the heels of his boots. He wore a white cravat with embroidered ends: his sister had seen Monsieur du Hautoy and Monsieur de Chandour wearing similar ones and had hastened to make some of the same kind for him. Only grave personages, a few aged financiers and austere public officials wore white cravats; worse still, the unhappy native of Angoulême saw a grocer's errand-boy with a basket on his head passing along the other side of the railings on the pavement of the rue de Rivoli, and he was wearing a cravat with its two ends embroidered by some adoring shop-girl. For Lucien this was like a blow in the chest, that ill-defined organ which is the seat of our emotions and to which, ever since man has had feeling, he lifts his hand in moments of great joy or great grief.

Lucien's reaction should not be dismissed as a manifestation of puerility. Rich people who have never known suffering of this kind may certainly think it petty and incredible; but the anguish caused by poverty is no less worthy of attention than the crises which turn life upside-down for the mighty and privileged persons on this earth. For that matter, is not an equal amount of pain felt in both cases? Suffering magnifies everything: suppose it were a question, not of a more or less handsome costume, but of a medal, a distinction or a title. Have not such apparent trifles tormented men in brilliant walks of life? The question of costume, moreover, is one of enormous importance for those who wish to appear to have what they do not have, because that is often the best way of getting it later on. Lucien broke out in a cold sweat at the thought that, the same evening, he was to appear in these clothes before the Marquise d'Espard, a kinswoman of a First Gentleman of the Royal Bedchamber, a woman whose salon was frequented by all sorts of exceptionally illustrious people.

'I look just like an apothecary's son, a mere shop-assistant!' he told himself, as he watched the passers-by, graceful, smart, elegant young men of the Faubourg Saint-Germain: all of them having a special *cachet*, all alike in their trimness of line, their dignity of bearing and their self-confident air; yet all different thanks to the setting each had chosen in order to show himself to advantage. The best points in all of them were brought out by a kind of *mise en scène* at which the young men of Paris are as skilful as the women. Lucien had inherited from his mother invaluable physical traits which, as he was fully aware, lent him some distinction, but this was only the ore from which the gold had to be extracted. His hair was badly cut. Instead of using flexible whalebone to keep his face well poised, he felt muffled up in his ugly shirt collar and his cravat was too lax to give support to his drooping head. Would any woman have guessed what dainty feet were imprisoned in the ungainly boots he had brought from Angoulême? Would any young man have envied him his slender waist, concealed as it was by the blue sacking he had hitherto taken for a coat? He saw around him exquisite studs on gleaming white shirts: his were russet-brown! All these elegant gentlemen had beautifully cut gloves while his were fit only for a policeman! One of them toyed with a handsome bejewelled cane, another's shirt had dainty gold cuff-links at the wrists. Another of them, as he chatted with a lady, twirled a charming riding-whip, and the ample folds of his slightly mud-spattered trousers, his clinking spurs and his small, tight-fitting riding-coat showed that he was about to mount one of the two horses held in check by a diminutive groom. And another was drawing from his waistcoat pocket a watch as flat as a five-franc piece and was keeping his eye on the time like a man who was too early or too late for a rendezvous. At the sight of these fascinating trifles which were something new to Lucien, he became aware of a world in which the super-fluous is indispensable, and he shuddered at the thought that he needed enormous capital if he was to play his part as a smart bachelor! The more he admired these young people with their happy, care-free air, the more conscious he grew of his un-couth appearance, that of a man who has no idea where he is making for, wonders where the Palais-Royal is when he is standing in front of it and asks a passer-by the way to the Louvre only to be told: 'You're looking at it.' Lucien saw that a great gulf separated him from such people and was wondering how to cross it, for he wanted to be like these slim young dilettantes of Paris. All these patricians were saluting divinely dressed and divinely beautiful women, women for whom, for the reward of a single kiss, he would have allowed himself to be hacked to pieces like the Countess of Königs-marck's page. In the dark recesses of his memory Louise, compared with these sovereign creatures, had the lineaments of an old woman. He encountered many ladies who will have their place in nineteenth century history, whose wit, beauty and love intrigues will be no less famed than those of by-gone queens. He saw pass by the ineffable Mademoiselle des Touches, so well known under her pseudonym of Camille Maupin, an eminent writer, as outstanding for her beauty as for her distinction of mind; her name was whispered round by men and women strolling along.

'Ah!' he thought. 'There goes poetry incarnate.'

What was Madame de Bargeton beside this seraph in the splendour of youth, hope and promise, with her soft smile, her dark eyes which were as deep as the heavens and as ardent as the sun! She was laughing and chatting with Madame Firmiani, one of the most charming women in Paris. Certainly a voice was crying within him: 'Intelligence is the lever which moves the world.' But another voice insisted that money is the fulcrum of intelligence. He was reluctant to linger among the ruins of his self-esteem at the scene of his discomfiture, so he made his way towards the Palais-Royal after asking his way there, for he did not yet know the topography of his quarter. He went into Véry's restaurant and, to initiate himself in the pleasures of Paris, ordered such a dinner as might console him in his despondency. A bottle of claret, oysters from Ostend, fish, a partridge, a macaroni dish and fruit were the *nee plus ultra* of his desires. While savouring this little orgy he bethought himself how he might give proof of his wit that evening in the company of the Marquise d'Espard and redeem the shabbiness of his odd accoutrement by the display of his intellectual wealth. He was torn from his dreams by the bill for his meal which relieved him of the fifty francs which he had thought would carry him a long way in Paris. His dinner had cost him as much as a month's existence in Angoulême. And so he reverently closed the door of this palace behind him with the idea of never setting foot in it again.

'Eve was right,' he said to himself as he went through the Stone Gallery on his way home for more money. 'Prices in Paris are not those of L'Houmeau.'

As he walked along he admired the tailors' shops thinking of the fine clothes he had seen that morning. 'No!' he exclaimed. 'I'll not go to Madame d'Espard's in such reach-me-downs.' He ran like a deer to his hotel, rushed upstairs to his room, took three hundred francs and returned to the Palais-Royal to re-equip himself from head to foot. He had noticed shoemakers, linen-drapers, waistcoat-makers and hatters at the Palais-Royal – a dozen shops from which he could pick out the requisites for future elegance. The first tailor he consulted made him try on as many coats as he was ready to sample and persuaded him that they were all in the latest fashion. He emerged with a green coat, white trousers and a fancy waistcoat. The total cost was two hundred francs. He soon found a pair of very elegant and well-fitting boots. After buying all he needed, he summoned a hairdresser to his hotel, to which he had already had his various purchases delivered. At seven in the evening he took a cab to the Opera-House, his hair waved like that of a Saint John in a procession, with a fine waistcoat and cravat, feeling however a little constricted in the close-fitting apparel he was wearing for the first time in his life. Following Madame de Bargeton's instructions, he asked for the box belonging to the First Gentlemen of the Bedchamber. At the sight of a man whose borrowed elegance made him look like a best man at a wedding, the attendant demanded to see his ticket.

'I haven't one.'

'Then you can't come in,' was the curt reply.

'But I am the guest of Madame d'Espard,' he said.

'How are we to know?' said the usher, unable to refrain from exchanging a smile with his fellow ticket-collector.

At that moment a carriage drew up under the peristyle. A footman, who was unknown to Lucien, pulled down the footboard of a brougham from which two ladies emerged in all their finery. Lucien, unwilling to receive from the ticket-collector an impertinent order to get out of the way, stood aside for the two women.

'This lady is the Marquise d'Espard, whom you claim to know,' said the ticket-collector ironically.

Lucien was the more taken aback because Madame de Bargeton did not appear to recognize him in his new plumage. But when he approached her, she gave him a smile and said: 'Ah! There you are! Splendid! Come along.'

The box attendants had recovered their gravity. Lucien followed Madame de Bargeton and, as they ascended the vast staircase of the Opera, introduced her Rubempré to her cousin. The First Gentlemen's box occupies one of the recesses at the back of the auditorium: in it one can see everyone and be seen by everyone. Lucien took a seat behind Madame d'Espard and was happy to be inconspicuous.

'Monsieur de Rubempré,' said the Marquise in a flattering tone of voice. 'This is your first visit to the Opera-House. Have a good look round. Take this seat, right in front. You have our permission.'

Lucien obeyed. The first act of the opera was coming to an end.

'You have made good use of your time,' Louise whispered to him in the first flush of surprise at Lucien's transformation.

Louise had remained the same. Proximity with a woman of fashion, the Marquise d'Espard, a Parisian Madame de Bargeton, was so prejudicial to her, her Parisian brilliance set in such strong relief the imperfections of her country cousin that Lucien, drawing two-fold enlightenment from the *beau monde* in this pompous assembly and the eminent Marquise, at last saw Anaïs de Nègrepelisse for what she was and as she was seen by the people of Paris: a tall, desiccated woman with freckled skin, faded complexion and strikingly red hair; angular, affected, pretentious, provincial of speech and above all badly dressed! In fact the very pleats of an outmoded Parisian dress can still reveal taste: one can make allowances and visualize it as it once was; but no allowances can be made for a superannuated up-country garment – it invites derision. Both the dress and the woman in it lacked grace and bloom: the mottled velvet went with a mottled complexion. Lucien was ashamed at having loved this cuttle-bone and promised himself to take advantage of Louise's next access of virtue by dropping her. His excellent eye-sight enabled him to see how many opera-glasses were levelled at their pre-eminently aristocratic box. The most elegant women were obviously scrutinizing Madame de Bargeton, for they were smiling as they chatted to one another. If Madame d'Espard realized from these feminine gestures and smiles who was the butt of their barbed comments, she took absolutely no notice of them. In the first place, everyone must have recognized her companion as a poor relation from the provinces, and any Parisian family can be similarly afflicted. Moreover, Louise had been discussing clothes with her cousin and expressing some misgivings; the Marquise reassured her, perceiving that Anaïs, once well-dressed, would soon have adopted Parisian manners. If Madame de Bargeton lacked social finesse, she had the native arrogance of a well-born woman and that indefinable something which can be called breeding. The following Monday therefore she would be able to take her revenge. Moreover, once the public had learnt that this women was her cousin, the Marquise knew that it would call a halt to mockery and make further inspection before passing judgement. Lucien could not guess what a change would be made in Louise's appearance by a graceful stole, an elegant dress, a pretty hair-style and guidance from Madame d'Espard. As they had been going upstairs the Marquise had already told her cousin not to hold her unfolded handkerchief in her hand. Good or bad taste depends on a thousand little niceties of this sort which an intelligent woman readily grasps, but which some women will never understand. Madame de Bargeton, already full of good intentions, had more intelligence than she needed to recognize her short-comings. Madame d'Espard, feeling sure that her pupil would do her credit, had not disdained to undertake her education. In short, their mutual interests had sealed a pact between them. Madame de Bargeton had promptly dedicated herself to the idol of the day, whose manners, wit and entourage had seduced, dazzled and fascinated her. She had discerned in Madame d'Espard the occult power which a great lady with ambition wields and she had promised herself success if she became the satellite of this star: hence the undisguised admiration she felt for her. The Marquise had been sensible of this naïve adoration and had become interested in her cousin, whom she found so weak and defenceless; it also suited her to have a pupil and to found a school; she asked nothing better than to acquire Madame de Bargeton as a sort of lady in waiting, a docile attendant who would sing her praises – and that is an even rarer treasure for a woman of Paris than a devoted critic is for the literary confraternity. In the meantime the flutter of curiosity was becoming too obvious for the social neophyte not to notice it, and Madame d'Espard tried politely to put her off the scent with regard to this commotion.

'If anyone comes to our box,' she said, 'we shall perhaps learn why those ladies are so interested in us.'

'I strongly suspect it's my old velvet frock and my rustic appearance that amuses these Parisian ladies,' said Madame de Bargeton with a laugh.

'No, it isn't you. There is some reason which I cannot fathom,' the Marquise added, with a glance at the poet, whom she now scanned for the first time and whom she seemed to find oddly dressed.

'There is Monsieur du Châtelet,' said Lucien at that moment, raising a finger to point towards Madame de Sérizy's box which the elderly dandy, now completely regroomed, had just entered.

At this gesture Madame de Bargeton bit her lips with vexation, for the Marquise could not refrain from a glance at Lucien and an astonished smile which plainly asked 'Where was this young man brought up?', and with so much disdain that Louise felt humiliated in her love – the most mortifying sensation for a Frenchwoman and one she does not forgive her lover for inflicting on her. In the social world trivial things are accorded such importance that a débutante could be ruined by a word or a gesture. The chief merit of fine manners and tone in high company is that they supply a harmonious effect in which everything is so well blended that there is no jarring note. Even those who through ignorance or by blurting out their thoughts break the rules of this science, ought to realize that in this matter a single dissonance, as in music, is a complete negation of the art itself, every canon of which must be meticulously observed if it is to remain an art.

'Who is that gentleman?' the Marquise asked, indicating Châtelet. 'Do you then know Madame de Sérizy already?'

'Ah! Is she the notorious Madame de Sérizy who has had so many adventures and yet is everywhere received?'

'It's amazing, my dear,' replied the Marquise. 'There *is* an explanation, but it has not been made! The men most to be reckoned with are friends of hers – but why? No one dares to probe this mystery. – Can that gentleman be the Lion of Angoulême?'

'Indeed, Monsieur du Châtelet,' said Anaïs, moved by vanity, now that she was in Paris, to grace her adorer with the title she had herself contested, 'is a man who has been much talked about. He went with Monsieur de Montriveau on his travels.'

'Ah!' observed the Marquise. 'I never hear that name without thinking of the poor Duchesse de Langeais, who has disappeared from sight like a shooting star.'[1]

'There,' she continued, pointing to another box, 'are Monsieur de Rastignac and Madame de Nucingen, the wife of a contractor, a banker, a business man, a large-scale broker, a man who imposes himself on Paris society through his wealth – and they say he has no scruples about the means he uses to increase it. He is taking the utmost pains to make people believe he is devoted to the Bourbons and has already tried to get me to receive him. His wife has taken Madame de Langeais's box, believing that with it she would take over her charm, wit and popularity! As usual, the fable of the jay decking itself with peacock's feathers!'

'But how do Monsieur and Madame de Rastignac whose income, as we know in Angoulême, is less than three thousand francs, manage to maintain their son in Paris?' Lucien asked of Madame de Bargeton in astonishment at the elegance and luxury which this young man's clothes displayed.

'It is easy to see that you come from Angoulême,' the

1. The tragic love affair between Montriveau and this lady is the subject of the novel entitled *La Duchesse de Langeais*.

Marquise replied with some irony, while still gazing through her opera-glasses.

Lucien did not understand. His attention was still riveted on the various boxes, and he was able to guess what judgements the occupants were passing on Madame de Bargeton and what curiosity he himself was arousing. Louise for her part was extremely mortified by the little impression her handsome Lucien was making on the Marquise. 'So he is not so handsome as I thought!' she said to herself. She had only a further step to take to find him less intelligent as well. The curtain had dropped. Châtelet, who had come to pay a call on the Duchesse de Carigliano in the next box to that of Madame d'Espard, gave a bow to Madame de Bargeton, who replied with a droop of the head. A woman of fashion sees everything, and the Marquise noticed how well-dressed du Châtelet was. At this moment four persons came one by one to the Marquise's box: four celebrities of Paris.

The first was Monsieur de Marsay, a man famous for the passions he inspired, conspicuous above all for a kind of girlish beauty: beauty of a languid, effeminate kind, though corrected by the way he looked at people: it was a steady look, calm, untamed and unflinching like a tiger's. He was liked, but he was feared. Lucien was no less good-looking, but his glance was so mild, his blue eyes so limpid that he could not be deemed likely to possess the strength and power by which so many women are attracted. Nor as yet had the poet anything advantageous about him, whereas Henri de Marsay had liveliness of wit, confidence in his ability to please and a style of dress so suited to his temperament that he crushed all rivalry around him. One can imagine what a poor impression Lucien, starched, stilted, stiff and raw like the clothes he was wearing, made in such company. De Marsay had won the right to utter impertinences by the wit he gave to them and the grace of manner which went with them. The welcome extended to him by the Marquise quickly enlightened Madame de Bargeton as to the prestige this personage enjoyed.

The second arrival was one of the two Vandenesse brothers

173

who had occasioned the Lady Dudley scandal,[1] a gentle, intelligent, modest young man whose success in society was due to qualities totally different from those on which de Marsay prided himself: he had been warmly recommended to the Marquise by her cousin Madame de Mortsauf. The third was General Montriveau, who had brought about the downfall of the Duchesse de Langeais. The fourth was Monsieur de Canalis, now one of the most illustrious of contemporary poets, a young man then only on the threshold of glory; prouder of his birth than of his talent, he made a pretence of dancing attendance on Madame d'Espard the better to conceal his passion for the Duchesse de Chaulieu. In spite of his airs and graces, already tainted with affectation, one could discern in him the tremendous ambition which later plunged him into the maelstrom of politics. His almost mincing beauty and his flattering smiles scarcely served to disguise the deep-seated egoism and perpetual calculation of a man who had yet to make his way; but the fact of having singled out Madame de Chaulieu, although she was over forty, was at that time putting him in favour at Court and winning him approval from the Faubourg Saint-Germain and insults from the Liberals, who dubbed him a 'poet of the sacristy'.

When she set eyes on these outstanding figures, Madame de Bargeton no longer wondered why the Marquise was paying little attention to Lucien. Then, when conversation began, when each of these subtle and delicate minds showed its mettle by shafts of wit which had more meaning and depth than anything Anaïs could have heard in a whole month in Angoulême; and particularly when the great poet gave vibrant expression to views which were positive and pertinent and yet had the gilding of poetry, Louise understood what du Châtelet had told her the evening before: Lucien counted for nothing here. Everyone looked on the unhappy stranger with such cruel indifference, his place there was so much that of a foreigner ignorant of the language, that the Marquise took pity on him.

1. Recounted in *The Lily of the Valley* (1835-6).

'Allow me, Monsieur,' she said to Canalis, 'to present Monsieur de Rubempré to you. You occupy too high a position in the literary world not to welcome a beginner. Monsieur de Rubempré is from Angoulême, and will no doubt need your sponsorship in his relations with the people in Paris whose mission it is to bring genius to light. As yet he has no enemies to make his fortune by attacking him. Would it not be a novel and worthwhile enterprise to help him to win through friendship what you owe to hostility?'

The four men of mark turned their gaze on Lucien while the Marquise was speaking. Although he was no more than two paces away from the newcomer, de Marsay lifted his monocle to look him over; his glance went from Lucien to Madame de Bargeton and from Madame de Bargeton to Lucien, and he sized them up with a mocking air which cruelly mortified them both; he was studying them with a smile as if they were a pair of curious animals. This smile was like a dagger-thrust to the provincial celebrity. Félix de Vandenesse gave him a kindly look, Montriveau an appraising glance which went right through him.

'Madame,' said Monsieur de Canalis with a bow. 'I shall obey you, despite personal interest which makes us disinclined to favour our rivals; but you have shown us that such miracles are possible.'

'Very well. Do me the pleasure of dining with me on Monday with Monsieur de Rubempré. At my house you will be more at ease talking of literary matters. I will try to recruit some of the despots and well-known patrons of literature, the authoress of *Ourika* and a few young poets with sensible views.'

'Madame la Marquise,' said de Marsay, 'if you sponsor Monsieur for his intelligence, I will sponsor him for his good looks. I will give him such advice as will make him the happiest elegant in Paris. After that, let him be a poet if he will.'

Madame de Bargeton thanked her cousin with a glance full of gratitude.

'I didn't know you were jealous of intelligent people,' said Montriveau to de Marsay. 'Happiness is mortal to poets.'

'Is that why you are thinking of marrying, Monsieur?' the latter continued, addressing Canalis in order to see if this shaft would get home to Madame d'Espard. Canalis gave a shrug, and Madame d'Espard, who was a friend of Madame de Chaulieu, merely laughed.

Lucien, whose tight-fitting clothes made him feel like a mummy in its case, was ashamed to have no reply to make. At last he said to the Marquise in a moved tone of voice: 'Your kindness, Madame, is so great that I am bound to be successful.'

At this moment du Châtelet came in, eager to seize the chance of meeting the Marquise through the support of Montriveau, one of the leaders of Paris society. He bowed to Madame de Bargeton and begged Madame d'Espard to pardon him for taking the liberty of invading her box: he had been so long separated from his travelling companion! This was the first time Montriveau and he had met since they had parted from one another in the heart of the desert.

'Fancy being parted in the desert and meeting next time in the Opera House!' said Lucien.

'A truly theatrical recognition!' said Canalis.

Montriveau introduced the Baron du Châtelet to the Marquise, who received the former Secretary of Her Imperial Highness's Commands with a welcome so much the more affable because she had already seen his cordial reception in three other boxes, because Madame de Sérizy only admitted people of good standing, and because he had been Montriveau's companion. This last qualification was of such great value that Madame de Bargeton was able to observe from the tone of voice, the expression and manners of the four gentlemen that they accepted du Châtelet without question as one of themselves. The reason for Châtelet's oriental affectations at Angoulême suddenly became clear to Naïs. Finally du Châtelet noticed Lucien and gave him one of those curt, cold nods with which one man disparages another and conveys to fashionable people how very low is the place he occupies in society. His salute was accompanied by a sardonic expression which seemed to say: 'What strange chance brings *him* here?'

Du Châtelet's point went home, for de Marsay leaned towards Montriveau and said in a whisper – but one audible enough to the Baron – 'Ask him who is that curious young man dressed like a tailor's dummy.'

Du Châtelet spent a minute or two talking softly to his companion as if he were renewing acquaintanceship with him, and no doubt he slashed his rival to pieces. Lucien was surprised at the ready wit and subtlety with which these men worded their remarks to one another; he was stunned by their sallies and epigrams, and above all by their lack of self-consciousness and ease of manner. That morning the sight of material luxury had reduced him to awe: now he was finding it again in the realm of ideas. He was wondering by what gift for impromptu these people hit on the piquant reflections and repartees which only long meditation would have enabled him to invent. And besides, these five men were not only easy in conversation, but also in the way they wore their clothes, which were neither new nor old. There was nothing gaudy about them and yet everything attracted attention. The luxury they displayed today was that of yesterday and would be the same tomorrow. Lucien sensed that his appearance was that of a man who had dressed up for the first time in his life.

'My dear,' de Marsay was saying to Vandenesse, 'little Rastignac is soaring up like a kite! There he is in the Marquise de Listomère's box. He's getting on, he's even eyeing us through his spy-glass! No doubt he knows you, Monsieur?' the dandy continued, speaking to Lucien but not looking at him.

'It is difficult,' Madame de Bargeton replied, 'to suppose that the name of the great man of whom we are so proud has not reached his ears: his sister recently heard Monsieur de Rubempré reciting some beautiful poetry to us.'

Félix de Vandenesse and de Marsay made their bow to the Marquise and went to the box occupied by Vandenesse's sister, Madame de Listomère. The second act began, and they all left the Marquise d'Espard, her cousin and Lucien to themselves. Some of them went to explain Madame de Bargeton to the women who were puzzled about her, the others told of the poet's arrival and made fun of his clothes. Canalis returned to the Duchesse de Chaulieu and remained there. Lucien was glad of the diversion which the performance provided. All Madame de Bargeton's fears in regard to Lucien were increased by the attention her cousin had vouchsafed to the Baron du Châtelet, since it was of quite different character from her patronizing politeness to Lucien. During the second act, Madame de Listomère's box remained crowded and appeared to be the scene of animated conversation about Madame de Bargeton and Lucien. Evidently the youthful Rastignac was the entertaining spirit in this box: he it was who took the lead in that typically Parisian derision which, moving to fresh pastures every day, is in a hurry to exhaust the topic in vogue by turning it into something old and stale in one brief moment. Madame d'Espard was anxious. She knew that the victims of slander are not allowed to remain long in ignorance of it, and she waited for the end of the act. As for Lucien and Madame de Bargeton, when people turn their feelings inwards upon themselves, strange things happen in a short time: the laws determining moral revulsions are rapid in their effects. Louise was remembering the sage and politic remarks du Châtelet had made about Lucien on the way home from the Vaudeville Theatre: every sentence had been a prophecy, and Lucien seemed intent on fulfilling every one of them. Losing his illusions about Madame de Bargeton while Madame de Bargeton was losing hers about him, the unhappy youth, whose destiny was a little like that of Jean-Jacques Rousseau, imitated him in this respect: he was fascinated by Madame d'Espard and fell in love with her immediately. Men who are young or who remember the emotions of their youth, will understand that this passion was extremely likely and natural. The pretty little ways, the delicacy of speech, the refined tone of voice and slender proportions of this woman, so well-born, so highly placed, so envied, in short this queenly person, made the same impression on the poet as Madame de Bargeton had made on him in Angoulême. His volatile character promptly impelled a desire in him for the protection of so lofty a person, and the surest means for this was to win her as a woman – all the rest would follow! He had been successful in Angoulême: why should he not succeed in Paris? Involuntarily, and despite his new found pleasure in the magic of opera, his glance, attracted by this splendid Célimène, was constantly roving in her direction, and the more he looked at her the more he wanted to go on looking! Madame de Bargeton intercepted one of these glances; she watched him and saw that he was more interested in the Marquise than in the performance. She would have gracefully resigned herself to being deserted for the fifty daughters of Danaus; but when one of his glances, more ambitious, more ardent and more significant than the others, showed her what was going on in Lucien's mind, she became jealous, though less for the future than because of the past. 'He has never looked at me like that,' she thought. 'Good heavens, Châtelet was right!' It was then that she realized her mistake in loving him. When a woman comes to repent of a weakness she passes a sponge as it were over her life in order to wipe everything out. Yet, although every one of Lucien's glances enraged her, she remained calm.

De Marsay returned at the interval, bringing Monsieur de Listomère with him. The staid Marquis and the young fop soon informed the haughty Marquise that the man got up as for a wedding whom she had been so unfortunate as to admit to her box had no more right to be called Monsieur de Rubempré than a Jew has a right to a Christian name. Lucien was the son of an apothecary named Chardon. Monsieur de Rastignac, well-informed about Angoulême matters, had already roused laughter in the two boxes, directed against that species of mummy whom the Marquise called her cousin and her precautions in taking a pharmacist about with her – no doubt in order that he might keep her artificially alive with drugs. Finally de Marsay retailed some of the thousand and one pleasantries in which Parisians are quick to indulge and which are promptly forgotten as soon as uttered; but behind all this was Châtelet, the begetter of this Carthaginian treachery.

'My dear,' Madame d'Espard whispered under her fan to

Madame de Bargeton, 'do tell me: is your protégé's name really Monsieur de Rubempré?'

'He has taken his mother's name,' said the embarrassed Anaïs.

'But what is his father's name?'

'Chardon.'

'And what did he do?'

'He was an apothecary.'

'I was very sure, my dear friend, that a woman sponsored by me could not be a target for mockery among the best people of Paris. I do not care to have my box filled with wags who are delighted to find me hobnobbing with an apothecary's son. Believe me, the best thing we can do is to leave together this very instant.'

Madame d'Espard assumed a noticeably supercilious air without Lucien being able to guess what he had done to cause this change of countenance. He told himself that his waistcoat was in bad taste, and that was true; that the cut of his coat was of an exaggerated style: that also was true. With bitterness in his heart he realized that he would have to visit a first-class tailor, and he firmly resolved to go the next day to the most fashionable one, so that, the following Monday, he could be on equal terms with the Marquise's other guests. Though he was lost in thought, he paid attention to the third act and kept his eyes fixed on the stage. But while he watched the splendour of this exceptional production, he continued to muse about Madame d'Espard. He was in despair over her sudden coldness, so strangely frustrating to the intellectual fervour with which he was embarking on this new love affair, unperturbed though he was about the tremendous difficulties he foresaw but which he was confident of overcoming. He emerged from his deep day-dream to look once more at his new idol; but as he turned his head he saw that he was alone. He had heard a slight stir, the door was closing and Madame d'Espard was slipping away with her cousin. Lucien was extremely surprised at this abrupt desertion, but he gave no prolonged thought to it, precisely because he found it inexplicable.

As the two women rolled along in their carriage through the rue de Richelieu towards the Faubourg Saint-Honoré, the Marquise said, in a tone of ill-concealed anger: 'My dear child, what are you thinking of? At any rate wait until the apothecary's son is really famous before you get interested in him. Even now the Duchesse de Chaulieu does not acknowledge her liaison with Canalis, and he *is* famous, and a gentleman as well. This young person is neither a son nor a lover to you, is he?' – as she asked this question the imperious woman cast a sharp and inquisitorial glance at her cousin.

'How lucky for me that I kept that little cad at arm's length and allowed him no liberties!' thought Madame de Bargeton.

'Very well,' continued the Marquise, taking the look in her cousin's eye for an answer. 'I strongly urge you to drop him. Why! to usurp an illustrious name is an audacity which society punishes. Admittedly it is his mother's name; but just think, my dear: the King alone has the right to confer by ordinance the name of Rubempré on the offspring of a daughter of that house; if she has married beneath her, the favour would be a tremendous one, and in order to obtain it one needs an immense fortune, also to have rendered services and to have influential protectors. The fact of his being dressed like a shopkeeper in his Sunday best proves that this young fellow is neither well-off nor a gentleman: he's good-looking, but to me he seems very stupid. He neither knows how to behave nor how to talk; in short he has no *breeding*. How comes it that you are taking him under your wing?'

Madame de Bargeton, now denying Lucien just as Lucien had inwardly denied her, felt terribly afraid that her cousin might learn the truth about her journey to Paris.

'My dear cousin, I am desperately sorry to have compromised you.'

'No one compromises me,' said Madame d'Espard with a smile. 'I am only thinking of you.'

'But you have invited him to dinner for Monday.'

'I shall be ill,' the Marquise quickly retorted. 'You will let him know, and I shall close my doors to him either as Rubempré or Chardon.'

During the interval, Lucien thought he might take a stroll in the *foyer* since everyone was flocking there. To begin with, not one of the men who had visited Madame d'Espard's box saluted him or seemed aware of his presence. Secondly, du Châtelet, whom he tried to buttonhole, kept a wary eye on him and took care to avoid him. Having become convinced, at the sight of the men who were wandering about the *foyer*, that he was more or less ludicrously dressed, Lucien reinstalled himself in a corner of his box and for the rest of the performance remained absorbed in watching the stately ballet of the fifth act with its celebrated *Inferno*, or scanning the audience from box to box and indulging in the profound reflections which the presence of Parisian society aroused in him.

'So that is my kingdom!' he said to himself. 'That is the society I have to tame.'

He returned to his hotel on foot, thinking of everything that had been said by the personages who had come to pay their respects to Madame d'Espard: their manners, gestures, the way they made their entry and took their leave, everything came back to his memory with astonishing accuracy. The next day, about noon, his first occupation was to visit Staub, the most celebrated tailor of that period. By dint of entreaties and cash payment, he persuaded Staub to get his clothes made in time for next Monday's dinner. Staub went so far as to promise him a delightful frock-coat, waistcoat and pair of trousers for that important occasion. Lucien ordered shirts, handkerchiefs, in fact quite a small trousseau, from a linen-draper, and was measured for shoes and boots by a well-known shoemaker. He bought a smart cane from Verdier, gloves and shirt studs from Madame Irlande; in short he tried to achieve the standards of the dandies. When he had satisfied every whim, he went to the rue Neuve-du-Luxembourg, only to find that Louise was out.

'She's dining with Madame la Marquise d'Espard, and won't be home till late,' said Albertine.

Lucien went and dined for two francs in a restaurant in the Palais-Royal and retired to bed early. The next day, which was Sunday, he was at Louise's rooms by eleven o'clock; she was not up. He returned at two.

'Madame is not seeing anyone yet,' said Albertine, 'but she has given me a note for you.'

'Not seeing anyone yet,' Lucien replied. 'But I am not *anyone*! . . .'

'What do I know about that?' Albertine asked with a very impudent air.

Lucien, less surprised at Albertine's reply than at receiving a letter from Madame de Bargeton, took the note, and when he was back in the street he read the following heart-breaking lines:

'Madame d'Espard is not well and cannot receive you tomorrow. I am not well either, but I am getting dressed in order to go and keep her company. I am desperately sorry about this little setback. But I trust in your talent. You will make your way without charlatanism.'

'And no signature!' said Lucien to himself. He was by now in the Tuileries, not realizing how far he had walked. The gift of second sight that talented people possess made him suspect the catastrophe which this cold missive announced. Lost in thought, he walked straight forward, gazing at the monuments in the Place Louis XV. It was a fine day. Fine carriages were constantly passing to and fro before his eyes as he made for the Grand Avenue of the Champs-Elysées. He followed the crowd of strollers and thus he saw the three or four thousand carriages which, on any fine Sunday, flow along this avenue and constitute a sort of impromptu Longchamp procession. Dazzled by the splendour of the horses, clothes and liveries, he went on and on until he arrived in front of the unfinished Arc-de-Triomphe. What were his thoughts when, on the way back, he saw Madame d'Espard and Madame de Bargeton in an admirable four-wheeled turn-out, behind which waved the plumes of the footman whose gold-embroidered green coat enabled Lucien to recognize the two ladies. The line of vehicles was held up by traffic congestion, and Lucien was able to take in Louise's transformation. She was unrecognizable: the colour-scheme of her clothes had been chosen to match her complexion; she was wearing a most attractive dress; the graceful arrangement of her hair became her well, and her hat, in exquisite taste, was conspicuous even beside that of Madame d'Espard, the leader of fashion. There is an indefinable way of wearing a hat: set it a little too far back and it looks too raffish; set it too far forward and it gives you a crafty appearance; set it to one side and you look too free and easy. Fashion-conscious women wear their hats at the angle that suits them and they always look just right. Madame de Bargeton had solved this interesting problem straight away. Her slender waist was girded with a pretty sash. She had adopted her cousin's gestures and deportment; sitting in the same posture as the latter, she was toying with an elegant perfume-box attached by a tiny chain to a finger of her right hand, which enabled her to display her shapely and daintily-gloved hand without seeming to do so deliberately. In short, she had modelled herself on Madame d'Espard without aping her; she was a worthy cousin of the Marquise, who seemed quite proud of her pupil. Women and men walking along the avenue gazed at the splendid carriage bearing the coat-of-arms of the d'Espard and the Blamont-Chauvry families with the two scutcheons addorsed. The large number of persons who saluted the two cousins astonished Lucien; he did not know that all the élite of Paris, comprising twenty salons, were already aware that Madame de Bargeton and Madame d'Espard were related. Young men on horseback, among whom Lucien could distinguish de Marsay and Rastignac, joined the barouche to escort the two cousins to the Bois de Boulogne. The gestures of the two dandies made it plain to Lucien that they were complimenting Madame de Bargeton on her metamorphosis. Madame d'Espard was sparkling with grace and health: evidently her indisposition had been a pretext for not receiving Lucien, since she was not postponing her dinner to another day. The poet, in a fury, approached the barouche, walking forward slowly, and as soon as he was visible to the two women, bowed to them. Madame de Bargeton pretended not to see him and the Marquise eyed him through her lorgnette, ignoring his salute. Disapproval meted out by the aristocracy of Paris was unlike that of the upper set in Angoulême: while doing their best to hurt Lucien's feelings, the gentry there acknowledged his prestige and took him for a human being, whereas he did not even exist for Madame d'Espard. She was not pronouncing a verdict but simply refusing him trial. The unhappy poet was seized with a mortal chill when he saw de Marsay staring at him through his monocle: the Parisian lion then let it fall in so singular a fashion that it seemed like the drop of the guillotine blade to Lucien. The barouche passed on. Rage and the lust for vengeance took hold of the man thus disdained: if he had had Madame de Bargeton in his grip he would have strangled her; he identified himself with Fouquier-Tinville in order to relish the enjoyment of sending Madame d'Espard to the scaffold; he would have liked to subject de Marsay to the kind of refined torture which savages have invented.

He saw Canalis pass by on horseback, as elegant as this most ingratiating of poets had to be, making his salaams to all the prettiest women.

'Great God! Gold at all cost!' Lucien was saying to himself. 'Gold is the only power which this society worships on bended knees.' But his conscience cried out: 'No! Not gold, but glory. And glory means hard work! Hard work! That's what David said. My God, why am I here? But I will win through! I will drive along this avenue in a barouche with a flunkey behind me! As for the Marquise d'Espard, I'll have plenty of her sort!'

While thus giving vent to his spite he was dining at Hurbain's restaurant for two francs. The next day he called on Louise at nine with the intention of reproaching her for her barbarous treatment of him. Not only was Madame de Bargeton not at home to him, but the concierge would not even let him go upstairs. He waited in the street, keeping watch, until noon. At noon du Châtelet emerged from Madame de Bargeton's flat, caught a glimpse of the poet and tried to escape. Greatly nettled, Lucien went after his rival. Du Châtelet, realizing that Lucien was close upon him, turned round and saluted him with the obvious intention of making off after this act of politeness.

'Of your kindness, Monsieur,' said Lucien. 'Grant me a

second, I have something to say to you. You did show me some friendliness, and I invoke it in order to ask you to do me a very slight service. You have just left Madame de Bargeton. Explain to me why I am in disgrace with her and Madame d'Espard.'

'Monsieur Chardon,' du Châtelet replied with feigned benevolence. 'Do you know why these ladies left you behind at the Opera House?'

'No,' said the wretched poet.

'Well, Monsieur de Rastignac did you a disservice at your first appearance. That young dandy, when questioned about you, said plainly and simply that your name was Monsieur Chardon and not Monsieur de Rubempré; that your mother was a midwife; that your father, when alive, was an apothecary in L'Houmeau; that your sister was a charming girl who was admirable at ironing shirts and that she was about to marry an Angoulême printer named Séchard. That's society all over. Put yourself on view and it discusses your case. Monsieur de Marsay came to Madame d'Espard to make fun of you, and the two ladies immediately took flight, believing they had compromised their reputation in entertaining you. Don't try to call on either of them. Madame de Bargeton would not be received by her cousin if she continued to see you. You are a man of genius: see if you can't avenge yourself. Society disdains you: disdain society. Take refuge in a garret, write masterpieces, acquire some sort of prestige and you will have society at your feet. Then you will pay it back for the wounds it inflicted on you here in Paris, the very place where they were inflicted. The more friendship Madame de Bargeton has shown you, the more she will hold aloof from you. That's how feminine feelings go. Anyway, at present there's no question of recovering Anaïs's friendship; all you have to do is to avoid having her as an enemy, and I will tell you how to do this. She has written letters to you: send them all back – she will appreciate such gentlemanly behaviour. Later on, if you need her, she will not be hostile. As for myself, I have so high an opinion of your prospects that I have defended you everywhere; and if I can do anything for you here in Paris, you will always find me ready to do you service.'

Lucien was so dejected, so pale, so undone, that he did not return the perfunctory salute which this elderly beau, rejuvenated in the atmosphere of Paris, gave him. He returned to his hotel, and there he found Staub in person, not so much in order to give him a fitting – which he did – as to learn from the hotel manageress something about the financial position of his unknown customer. Lucien had travelled post in his journey to Paris, and Madame de Bargeton had conveyed him back from the Vaudeville Theatre on Thursday last. This information was satisfactory. Staub called Lucien 'Monsieur le Comte' and showed him with what skill he had set off his fine figure.

'A young man in such clothes,' he said, 'has only to take a walk in the Tuileries and he'll marry a rich Englishwoman within a fortnight.'

The German tailor's pleasantry, the perfect cut of the clothes, the fine texture of the cloth, the elegance Lucien discerned in himself as he looked in the mirror, all these little things made him less sad. He played vaguely with the idea that Paris was the capital in which luck was everything, and for the moment he believed in luck. Had he not a volume of poems and a magnificent novel, *The Archer of Charles the Ninth*, in manuscript? He put his faith in destiny. Staub promised him the frock-coat and the rest of his outfit for the following day.

The next day the shoemaker, the linen-draper and the tailor returned, each of them armed with his bill. Having no idea how to get rid of them and being still conditioned by provincial customs, Lucien settled with them; but after paying them he had no more than three hundred and sixty francs left of the two thousand francs he had brought with him to Paris – and he had only been there one week! Nevertheless he put on his new clothes and went for a stroll along the Terrasse des Feuillants. There he took some sort of revenge. He was so well dressed, so graceful, so handsome that several women looked at him, and two or three were so struck by his beauty that they turned round to gaze at him. He studied the movements and manners of the young men and took a lesson in deportment while thinking all the time of his three hundred and sixty francs.

That evening, alone in his room, it occurred to him to clear up the problem of his expenditure in the Hôtel du Gaillard-Bois, where he was eating very simple food under the impression that he was economizing. He asked for his bill as if he were preparing to leave the hotel: it amounted to about one hundred francs. Next day he hurried to the Latin quarter, recommended to him by David as being cheap. After a long search he at last found, in the rue de Cluny, near the Sorbonne, a wretched lodging-house with furnished rooms where he rented accommodation for the price he was willing to pay. He immediately settled with the proprietress of the Gaillard-Bois and that same day took up his quarters in the rue de Cluny. His change of lodgings cost him only the fare for a cab. After taking possession of his shabby room, he gathered together all Madame de Bargeton's letters, made a packet of them, laid it on the table and, before writing to her, began to think over the events of that fatal week. He did not recognize that he had taken the initiative in rashly denying his love without knowing what would become of his Louise in Paris: he did not see the wrongs he had committed, but only his present plight. He blamed Madame de Bargeton: instead of enlightening him, she had ruined him. He grew angry and proud and began the following letter in a paroxysm of wrath:

What would you say, Madame, about a woman who took a fancy to some poor timid child, full of those noble beliefs which later are called illusions, and used all her coquettish graces, all her subtlety of mind and the most beautiful semblance of maternal love to divert him from his course? Neither the most affectionate promises, nor the castles in Spain which filled him with wonder, cost anything to her.

She takes him off with her, monopolizes him, scolds him for his lack of trust in her and flatters him turn by turn. When this child deserts his family and follows her blindly, she leads him to the shore of a boundless sea, smilingly entices him into a frail cockleshell and sends him forth helpless through the tempest. Then, from the rock on which she has remained, she bursts out laughing and wishes him good luck.

You are that woman; I am that child. But he holds in his hands a token which might be used to expose the crime you committed by your beneficence and the favour you showed him in casting him aside. You might have cause for blushing with shame when you saw that child struggling against the waves, once the thought came to you that you had held him to your bosom. When you read this letter you will be free to do as you like with such memories. You may forget them entirely if you will. After the bright hopes your finger pointed out to me in the heavens, I am facing the realities of poverty in the mire of Paris. While you, brilliant and adored, stride through the grand halls of society, to the threshold of which you led me, I shall be shivering in the miserable attic into which you have flung me. But perhaps remorse will come to you in the midst of your galas and pleasures; perhaps you will give a thought to the child you plunged into an abyss. Oh no, Madame! Spare yourself such remorse. From the depths of his misery this child offers you the only thing he has left as he looks his last on you: his forgiveness.

Yes, Madame, thanks to you, I have nothing left. But the world was made out of nothing. Genius must imitate God, and I begin by showing clemency, as He does, without knowing whether I shall have the strength He has. You need tremble only if I turn to evil ways, for then you will have been my accomplice in wrong-doing. Alas! I pity you because you can no longer have any part in the fame to which I aspire, with my work to lead me on.

After writing this letter, bombastic but full of that sombre dignity which an artist of twenty-one tends to overdo, Lucien's thoughts went back to the bosom of his family: in his mind's eye he saw the neat apartment which David had decorated for him by sacrificing a part of his resources. He had a vision of the peaceful, modest, commonplace joys he had tasted there. His mother, his sister and David gathered round him in shadowy outline. He heard anew the sound of their weeping at the moment of his departure. He too wept, for he was alone in Paris, friendless and unprotected.[1]

*

1. In the editions of 1837 and 1839, Part One had continued to this point.

A few days later, Lucien wrote as follows to his sister:

My dear Eve,

Sisters have the sad privilege of taking to themselves more sorrow than joy when they share the existence of brothers dedicated to Art, and I begin to fear that I shall become a grave liability to you. Have I not already imposed upon your generosity, you who have made such sacrifices for me? My memories of the past, so full of family joys, have fortified me in the solitude of my present position. With what swift flight, like an eagle returning to its eyrie, have I not winged my way back to you, to the haven of true affection, after suffering the first humiliations and disappointments of social life in Paris! Have the candles at home spluttered? Have the burning logs rolled over in the hearth? Have your ears tingled? Has my mother asked: 'Is Lucien thinking of us?' Has David answered: 'He is battling with men and things'? Dear Eve, I write this letter for your eyes alone. To you alone shall I dare tell of the good and the evil which will come my way, blushing for both of them, for here the good is as rare as the evil should be.

I have much to tell you in a few words. Madame de Bargeton has become ashamed of me, disavowed me, dismissed me, repudiated me nine days after our arrival. She has turned away at the sight of me; and I, in order to follow her into the society in which she had proposed to launch me, had spent seventeen hundred and sixty of the two thousand francs, so difficult to lay hands on, which I brought away from Angoulême. Spent them on what? you will ask. Dear sister, Paris is a strange, gaping maw. One can dine there for less than a franc, but the simplest dinner in a smart restaurant costs fifty francs. One can buy waistcoats and trousers for forty francs and forty sous, but a fashionable tailor charges you no less than a hundred francs for making them. You pay a sou to get over the street gutters when it's raining. And the shortest journey in a cab comes to thirty-two sous. After living in an elegant quarter, I am now at the Hôtel de Cluny in the rue de Cluny, one of the poorest and dingiest back-streets in Paris, squeezed between three churches and the ancient buildings of the Sorbonne. I have taken a furnished room on the fourth floor, a very bare and dirty one – but I still have to pay fifteen francs a month for it. I breakfast on a roll which costs two sous and a sou's worth of milk, but I dine quite well for twenty-two sous at the restaurant of a man called Flicoteaux, right in the square in front of the Sorbonne. Until winter comes my expenses will not exceed sixty francs a month all told – at least I hope not. Thus my two hundred and forty francs will last me the first four months. By then I shall no doubt have sold *The Archer of Charles the Ninth* and my *Marguerites*. And so don't be anxious about me. If the present is cold, bare and mean, the future is unclouded, rich and splendid. Most great men have gone through ups and downs: they affect me but do not overwhelm me. Plautus the great writer of comedies was a mill-hand. Machiavelli wrote *The Prince* in the evenings after spending the day in the company of workmen. Even the great Cervantes, who had lost an arm at the battle of Lepanto while making his contribution to that famous victory, and was called a 'disreputable old crock' by the scribblers of the time, unable to find a publisher, had to wait ten years before he could get the second part of that sublime work *Don Quixote* into print. We are not in so bad a position today. Unknown talent alone is subject to the vexations of poverty; once writers have made their name they grow rich. I shall be rich. Moreover I am living the life of a scholar. I spend half the day in the Sainte-Geneviève library where I am acquiring the education I lack, and without which I should not go far. And so today I feel almost happy. It took me only a few days to adjust myself cheerfully to my situation. From early morning I settle down to the work I love; my material life is assured; I do a lot of thinking, I study, and I don't see what can hurt me now that I have given up society, in which my vanity could have suffered pinpricks every moment of the day. Illustrious men of any age must live in isolation. They are like the birds of the forest. They sing, they add a charm to nature, and they must remain unseen. So shall I, if I am at all capable of realizing the ambitious plans my mind has conceived. I do not regret Madame de Bargeton. That woman did well to fling me into Paris and leave me to my own resources. Here is the habitat of writers, thinkers, poets. Here only can the seeds of fame be sown, and I know what fine harvests are being reaped today. Here only can writers find, in the museums and art collections, the immortal works of past genius to warm and stimulate the imagination. Here only vast libraries, always open, offer knowledge and sustenance for the mind. In short, in Paris, in the very air one breathes and the smallest details of existence, there is a spirit which permeates and makes its impress on the creations of literature. One learns more in half an hour, chatting in cafés and theatres, than one learns in the provinces in ten years. Here indeed all is spectacle, matter for comparison and instruction. Excessive cheapness, excessive costliness: such is Paris, where every bee can find a cell in which to store its honey, where every soul can assimilate the substance it needs. If then at this moment I am suffering, I am not repenting. On the contrary, I see a fine future ahead and my heart rejoices although it was bruised for a moment.

Good-bye, my dear sister. Don't expect letters from me regularly: a peculiar thing about Paris is that one really doesn't know where the time goes. Life rushes on with frightening rapidity. I embrace you all: Mother, David, and you more tenderly than ever.

2. *Flicoteaux*

FLICOTEAUX is a name inscribed in many memories. Few are the students who, having lived in the Latin quarter during the first twelve years of the Restoration, did not frequent this shrine of hunger and poverty. A three-course dinner then cost eighteen sous with a quarter-carafe of wine or a bottle of beer, and twenty sous with a bottle of wine. What has no doubt prevented Flicoteaux the friend of youth from making a colossal fortune is a certain feature in his programme (it figures also in capitals in his competitors' bills of fare) thus stated: BREAD AT YOUR DISCRETION – an in-discretion as far as restaurant-proprietors are concerned. Flicoteaux has been foster-father to a good many famous men. Certainly there are many amongst them who must feel innumer-able chords of memory stirring their hearts when they contemplate the front windows looking out on to the Place de la Sorbonne and the rue Neuve-de-Richelieu. Until the Revolution of July 1830, Flicoteaux the First and Flicoteaux the Second had respectfully preserved the small brown-tinted panes and the ancient, venerable appear-ance which denoted disdain for the pretentious exteriors devised by today's restaurant-keepers for appeal to the eye rather than the stomach. In lieu of heaps of stuffed game (not for consumption) or monstrous fishes justifying the comedian's joke 'I've discovered a fine carp: I'm saving up for it'; in lieu of the 'early' (better called 'yearly') fruit displayed in deceptive show-cases for the delectation of soldiers and their village girl-friends, the honest Flicoteaux set out variously-garnished bowls of stewed prunes to regale the customer's eye and assure him that the word 'dessert', too lavishly used on other menus, was not a take-in. Six-pound loaves, divided into four portions, substantiated the promise of BREAD AT YOUR DISCRETION. Such was the fine fare of an establishment which in his time Molière would have made famous, there being so many comic implications in the name itself. Flicoteaux's is still extant: it will live on as long as university students need to be kept alive. It's an eating-house, nothing less and nothing more. But its customers eat, as they also work, with a sombre or joyous zest according to character or circumstance. At that period this celebrated establishment consisted of two T-shaped dining-rooms, long, narrow and low, one of which drew its light from the Place de la Sorbonne, the other from the rue Neuve-de-Richelieu. Both are furnished with tables from some abbey refectory, for indeed their length gives them a monastic appearance; and the places are laid with the regular customers' napkins slipped into numbered shiny tinplate rings. Flicoteaux the First only changed the table-cloths every Sunday. But Flicoteaux the Second, so they say, started changing them twice a week as soon as his dynasty was threatened by competition. This restaurant is a workshop suitably equipped, and not an elegant banqueting-hall with pleasant amenities: customers are quickly served. Behind the scenes there is rapid activity. Waiters come and go without wasting time: they are all busy and much in demand. The food is not very varied, and always includes potatoes. There might not be a single potato in Ireland or anywhere else, but Flicoteaux would have a supply. For the last thirty years his potatoes have rejoiced in a Titian blond colouring. They are sprinkled with chopped green-stuff and enjoy a privilege which women envy: you saw them in 1814, and in 1840 they will look just the same. Mutton cutlets and fillet of beef are to the menu of this establishment what grouse and fillet of sturgeon are in Véry's restaurant, namely special dishes which have to be ordered in the morning. The female of the bovine species predominates and her calves proliferate, served up in the most ingenious disguises. When whiting and mackerel abound on the oceanic shores they are plentiful in Flicoteaux's restaurant. Everything there conforms to agricultural vicissitudes and the seasonal whims of the French climate, so that there one learns facts never suspected by the idle rich and those who take no interest in the phases of nature. Students herded together in the Latin quarter acquire a most accurate knowledge of what each season produces. They know when the crop of peas and beans is good, when the vegetable market is overstocked with cabbages, when lettuce is plentiful and the supply of beetroot scarce. A long-standing calumny, reiterated at the time Lucien was patronizing this restaurant, attributed the appearance of beefsteak to a rise in the death-rate of horses.

In few Paris restaurants will you witness so fine a spectacle. There you only find young people, faith in the future and poverty cheerfully endured, although in fact there is also no shortage of solemn, yearning, sombre and anxious faces. Usually there is a certain negligence of dress, and therefore regular customers who arrive in their best clothes invite attention. Everyone knows what this unusual attire signifies: a rendezvous with a mistress, a visit to the theatre or higher social circles. There, it is said, friendships have been formed between divers students who later have become famous men, as this story will confirm. Nevertheless, apart from young people from the same province gathered together at the end of a table, in general the diners have a gravity of bearing which does not readily unbend, thanks perhaps to the commonplace quality of the wine, which does not encourage expansiveness. Those who have frequented Flicoteaux's eating-house are able to recall various sombre and mysterious personages, wrapped in the mists of coldest indigence, who may have dined there for a couple of years and then disappeared without even the most inquisitive of customers gaining a glimmer of enlightenment about these Parisian will-o'-the wisps. Friendships initiated there were sealed in neighbouring cafés around a flaming punch-bowl or in the companionable warmth of small cups of coffee laced with some sort of brandy.

During the first days of his stay at the Hôtel de Cluny Lucien, like any newcomer, was shy and conventional in his behaviour. After the chastening experience of elegant life which had soaked up his capital, he plunged into his work with that initial ardour soon dissipated by the difficulties and diversions which Paris offers to every kind of existence, the most luxurious and the most denuded. To get the better of them, the savage energy of real talent or the grim will-power of ambition is needed. Lucien dropped into Flicoteaux's at about four-thirty, having observed that it paid to be among the first arrivals, for then the food was more varied and the customer could still obtain his favourite dishes. Like all those with poetic minds, he had taken to a particular place, and his choice of food betokened a fair amount of discernment. At his very first visit he had noticed a table near the cash-desk; he perceived from the physiognomy of its occupants and also their conversation, whose trend he readily grasped, that they belonged to the literary confraternity. Moreover, a kind of instinct told him that, being near to the cash-desk, he would be able to hold parley with the people who ran the restaurant. In the long run they would get to know him and at times of financial distress he would no doubt obtain the credit he needed. And so he had sat at a little square table beside the cash-desk, laid for only two people with two napkins without rings and probably intended for casual diners. Opposite Lucien sat a thin, pale young man, seemingly as poor as he was, whose handsome but already ravaged face announced that shattered hopes had seared his brow and left furrows in his soul in which sown seed had not germinated. Lucien felt drawn to this stranger by these lingering signs of idealism, also by an irresistible urge of sympathy.

The name of this young man, the first whom the poet from Angoulême was able to engage in conversation after a week of little acts of politeness and the exchange of words and observations, was Etienne Lousteau. Like Lucien, Etienne had come from the provinces: he had left his native town in Berry two years before. The vivacity of his gestures, the brilliance of his glance, the brevity of his occasional remarks, betrayed his bitter experience of literary life. Etienne had come from Sancerre with a tragedy in his pocket, spurred on by the same desire as Lucien – for fame, power and money. This young man, who at first dined regularly for several days, soon began to turn up only at long intervals. When, after five or six days' absence, he reappeared, Lucien hoped to see him again the next day, but the next day he would find Etienne's place taken by a stranger. When two young people have met the day before, the flame of yesterday's conversation casts its glow on that of today; but these intervals obliged Lucien to break the ice anew every time, and thereby delayed the progress of any intimacy between them during the first weeks. Lucien questioned the lady at the cash-desk and learnt that his future friend was on the staff of a 'little newspaper'[1], to which he contributed articles on new books and reviews of the plays performed at the Ambigu-Comique, the Gaiety Theatre and the Panorama-Dramatique. The young man suddenly became a somebody in Lucien's eyes and he counted on getting into rather more intimate conversation with him and making a few sacrifices in order to strike up a friendship, so necessary to a beginner. But the journalist remained absent for a fortnight. Lucien was unaware as yet that Etienne only dined at Flicoteaux's when he had no money, and that was what gave him his gloomy and disillusioned air and the iciness which Lucien tried to melt with flattering smiles and gentle words. Nevertheless such a relationship called for mature reflection, for this little-known journalist seemed to be leading an expensive existence in which glasses of cognac, cups of coffee, bowls of punch, visits to the theatre and suppers played their part. Now during the early days of Lucien's establishment in the Latin quarter, his conduct was that of a needy youth stunned by his first experience of life in Paris. And so, after studying the bill of fare and calculating the contents of his purse, Lucien dared not emulate Etienne's scale of living, for he was afraid of repeating the blunders which were still causing him

1. See Introduction, p. xv.

repentance. The yoke of his provincial loyalties still weighed upon him, and the figures of his two guardian angels, Eve and David, loomed up whenever a reprehensible thought came to him and reminded him of the hopes they placed in him, his responsibility for the happiness of his aging mother and all the promise of his budding genius. He was spending his mornings studying history in the Sainte-Geneviève library. His initial researches had made him conscious of appalling errors in his novel *The Archer of Charles the Ninth*. When the library closed, he returned to his damp, cold room to correct the work, stitching in new chapters and deleting others. After dining at Flicoteaux's he would go down to the Passage du Commerce and there, in Blosse's reading-room, he read works of contemporary literature, newspapers, collections of periodicals and books of poetry in order to keep up with the intellectual movement; he re-entered his miserable lodgings about midnight without having consumed any wood or tallow. This reading so enormously changed his ideas that he revised his collection of flower sonnets, his cherished *Marguerites*, and re-wrote them so completely that less than a hundred lines remained untouched. Thus, in the beginning, Lucien led the pure, innocent life of such poor, provincial immigrants as consider Flicoteaux's fare luxurious in comparison with that of their father's house, whose recreation consists of long walks along the Luxembourg avenues, looking yearningly at pretty girls from the corner of their eye, who never leave the quarter they live in and piously devote themselves to their work while dreaming of the future. But Lucien, a born poet, soon found himself a prey to vast longings and had no strength to resist the seduction of theatre-bills. The *Théâtre-Français*, the Vaudeville Theatre, *Les Variétés*, the *Opéra-Comique*, at all of which he stood in the pit, robbed him of about sixty francs. What student could resist the joy of seeing Talma in his famous roles? The theatre, first love of all poetic spirits, fascinated Lucien. The actors and actresses seemed to him to be imposing figures; he never thought it possible to go beyond the footlights and meet them on familiar terms. These people, the purveyors of his pleasure, were treated by the newspapers as figures of national importance, and he regarded them as marvellous beings! To be a dramatist, to have one's plays produced – what a dream to cherish! And for some bold spirits, Casimir Delavigne for example, this dream had come true!

These fecund thoughts, these moments of faith in himself, followed by moods of despair, stirred Lucien and kept him on the straight and narrow path of hard work and thrift, in spite of the underground rumblings of more than one insensate impulse. Through excess of prudence, he denied himself permission to enter the Palais-Royal, that place of perdition where in one single day he had spent fifty francs at Véry's and nearly five hundred francs on clothes. And so, whenever he yielded to the temptation to see Fleury, Talma, the two Baptistes or Michot, he restricted himself to the dim gallery for which he had to stand in a queue from half past five onwards, while late-comers had to go to the box-office to buy their seat for ten sous. Often, after they had queued for two hours, the cry 'Full house!' resounded in the ears of many a disappointed student. After the show Lucien used to return home with downcast eyes, paying no attention to the streets which at that hour were peopled with flesh and blood temptations. Perhaps there did come his way a few adventures of the kind which, extremely simple though they may be, occupy an enormous place in a young and timorous imagination. Startled at the dwindling of his capital one day when he was counting his money, Lucien broke out in a cold sweat and bethought him of the need to enquire about a publisher and look for some paid work. The young journalist of whom he had made a friend through his own initiative no longer came to Flicoteaux's. Lucien was waiting for some stroke of luck which did not come off. In Paris, such luck only comes to people who move around a great deal: the number of relationships increases the chances of success in every sphere, and moreover luck is on the side of the big battalions. Being a man in whom provincial caution still persisted, Lucien did not want the moment to come when he would have only a few francs left. He decided to accost the publishers.

3. Two varieties of publishers

ONE quite cold autumnal morning he walked down the rue de la Harpe with his two manuscripts under his arm. He made his way to the Quai des Augustins and strolled along the pavement, looking alternately at the flowing Seine and the booksellers' stalls as if his presiding genius were advising him to throw himself into the river rather than the career of letters. After anguished hesitations and an attentive scrutiny of the more or less kindly, enheartening, surly, merry or dreary faces he observed through the windows or on the door-steps, his eye caught a building in front of which shop attendants were packing up books. The walls were covered with posters:

ON SALE WITHIN

Le Solitaire, by Monsieur le Vicomte d'Arlincourt, 3rd edition.
Léonide, by Victor Ducange. 5 vols printed on fine paper.

Price 12 francs.

Inductions morales, by Kératry.

'They're lucky people!' Lucien exclaimed.

Posters, a new and original invention of the famous Ladvocat, were then flourishing on walls for the first time. Paris was soon to become a medley of colours thanks to the imitators of this method of advertisement, the source of one kind of public revenue. His heart bursting with excitement and anxiety, Lucien, once so important in Angoulême and now so small in Paris, sidled his way alongside the row of publishing-houses and summoned up enough courage to enter the shop he had noticed. It was crowded with assistants, customers and booksellers – authors too perhaps, Lucien supposed.

'I should like to speak to Monsieur Vidal or Monsieur Porchon,' he said to an assistant. He had read the shop-sign on which was written in large letters:

'Both of those gentlemen are engaged,' replied a busy assistant.

'I will wait.'

The poet was left alone in the shop, where he examined the batches of books. Two hours went by while he looked at the titles, opened the volumes and read pages here and there. In the end he leaned his shoulder against a glazed door draped with short green curtains behind which, he suspected, was either Vidal or Porchon. He overheard the following conversation:

'Will you take five hundred copies? If so I'll let you have them at five francs each and give you sixteen per cent on sales.'

'What price would that come to per volume?'

'A reduction of sixteen sous.'

'That would be four francs four sous,' said Vidal – or was it Porchon? – to the man who was offering his books for sale.

'Yes,' replied the vendor.

'On credit?' asked the buyer.

'You old humbug! And then I suppose you'd settle with me in eighteen months with bills postdated a year?'

'No, I'd settle straight away,' replied Vidal – or Porchon.

'To fall due when? In nine months?' asked the publisher or author who was evidently offering a book for sale.

'No, my dear man: in a year,' answered the wholesale bookseller. There was a moment's silence.

'You're bleeding me white!' cried the unknown.

'But surely you don't suppose we shall have got rid of five hundred copies of *Léonide* in twelve months,' the bookseller replied to Victor Ducange's publisher. 'If books sold as the publishers liked we should be millionaires; but they sell as the public likes. Walter Scott's novels bring us eighteen sous a volume, three francs sixty for the complete works, and you want me to sell your rubbishy books for more than that? If you want me to push your novel make it worth my while. – Vidal!'

A stout man left the cash-desk and came forward with a pen behind his ear.

'In the last trip you made,' Porchon asked him, 'how many of Ducange's books did you place?'

'I unloaded two hundred copies of *Le petit Vieillard de Calais*. But, in order to get them off my hands, I had to lower the price of two other works which were not bringing so much discount. They have turned into very pretty "nightingales".'

Later Lucien was to learn that the term 'nightingale' was applied by booksellers to works which stay perched up on shelves in the remote recesses of their store-rooms.

'Besides,' continued Vidal, 'you know that Picard is about to bring out some novels. We are promised twenty per cent discount on the retail price so that we may make a success of them.'

'All right. One year,' the publisher dolefully replied: he was dumbfounded by Vidal's last confidential remark to Porchon.

'It's agreed?' Porchon asked the publisher in a sharp tone.

'Yes.'

The publisher left, and Lucien heard Porchon saying to Vidal. 'We have orders for three hundred copies. We'll put off the date for settlement with him, sell the *Léonide* volumes at five francs each, demand payment for them in six months, and ...'

'And,' added Vidal, 'that's a profit of fifteen hundred francs.'

'Well, I could see he's getting into difficulties.'

'He'll be in the soup! He's paying Ducange four thousand francs for two thousand copies.'

Lucien halted Vidal by planting himself squarely in the doorway of this cage.

'Gentlemen,' he said to the booksellers. 'I have the honour of greeting you.'

The booksellers scarcely returned his salutation.

'I am the author of a novel on the history of France, after the manner of Walter Scott, entitled *The Archer of Charles the Ninth*, and I have come to propose that you should buy it.'

Porchon laid his pen on his desk and threw a tepid glance at Lucien. As for Vidal, he gave the author a brutal stare and replied: 'Monsieur, we are not publishing booksellers. When we produce books on our own account, that is an operation we only undertake with established authors. Besides that, we only purchase serious books, works of history and digests.'

'But mine is a very serious book. It reveals the true significance of the conflict between the Catholics, who stood for absolutism, and the Protestants, who wanted to found a republic.'

'Monsieur Vidal!' an assistant shouted. Vidal slipped away.

'I am not saying, Monsieur, that your book is not a masterpiece,' replied Porchon with a very discourteous shrug, 'but that we are only concerned with books which are already in print. Go and see the firms which buy manuscripts – Papa Doguereau, in the rue du Coq, near the Louvre. He is one of those who publish novels. If only you had told me earlier! you have just seen us talking to Pollet, a competitor of Doguereau and the publishers in the Wooden Galleries.'

'Monsieur, I have also a volume of poetry . . . '

'Monsieur Porchon!' came a voice from outside.

'Poetry!' Porchon angrily exclaimed. 'Who do you take us for?' He laughed in his face and vanished into the back premises.

Lucien crossed the Pont-Neuf a prey to innumerable reflections. By what he had understood of this commercial jargon he was able to guess that to these publishers books were like cotton bonnets to haberdashers, a commodity to be bought cheap and sold dear.

'I shouldn't have gone there,' he told himself; but he was none the less struck by the brutally materialistic aspect that literature could assume.

In the rue du Coq he espied a modest shop by which he had

already passed, and over which were painted, in yellow letters on a green background, the words DOGUEREAU, PUBLISHER.

He remembered having seen these words printed under the frontispiece of several novels he had read in Blosse's reading-room. He went in, not without inner misgivings such as men of imagination feel when they know they have a struggle before them. In the shop he discovered an extraordinary old man, an eccentric figure typical of a publisher of Imperial times. Doguereau was wearing a black coat with big square tails, long outmoded by the swallow-tails now in fashion. He had a waistcoat of common material, chequered in various colours, from the pocket of which hung a steel chain and copper key which dangled over an ample pair of black breeches. His watch was about the size of an onion. This costume was completed by iron-grey milled stockings and shoes graced with silver buckles. The old man's head was bare and adorned with greying hair, poetically sparse. Judging by his coat, breeches and shoes you would have taken Papa Doguereau, as Porchon had called him, for a professor of literature; judging by his waistcoat, watch and stockings, for a tradesman. His physiognomy did not belie this singular combination: he had the pedantic, dogmatic air and the wrinkled face of a teacher of rhetoric and the keen eyes, the wary mouth and the vague uneasiness of a publisher.

'Monsieur Doguereau?' asked Lucien.

'I am he, Monsieur,' said the publisher.

'I have written a novel,' said Lucien.

'You're very young,' said the publisher.

'But my age, Monsieur, has nothing to do with it.'

'That's true,' said the publisher, taking the manuscript. 'Ah, I do declare! *The Archer of Charles the Ninth*. A good title. Now, young man, tell me your subject briefly.'

'Monsieur, it's an historical work in the manner of Walter Scott which presents the conflict between Catholics and Protestants as a combat between two systems of government, involving a serious threat to the monarchy. I have taken sides with the Catholics.'

'Why now, young man: quite an idea. Very well, I will read your work, I promise you. I should have preferred a novel in the manner of Mrs Radcliffe, but if you are a hard worker, if you have some sense of style, power of conception, ideas and artistry of setting, I ask nothing better than to be useful to you. What do we need after all? Good manuscripts.'

'When may I return?'

'I am leaving town this evening and shall be back the day after tomorrow. I shall have read your book, and if I like it we can talk business that very day.'

Then Lucien, finding him so amenable, had the fatal idea of trotting out the manuscript of his *Marguerites*.

'Monsieur, I have also written a collection of poems.'

'Oh, so you're a poet! I no longer want your novel,' the old man said, holding out the manuscript. 'Rhymesters come to grief when they write prose. There are no stop-gaps in prose. One simply must have something to say.'

'But Walter Scott, Monsieur, also wrote verses.'

'True,' said Doguereau. He softened down, guessed the young man's penury and kept the manuscript. 'Where do you live? I will come and see you.'

Lucien gave the address without suspecting that the old man had any ulterior motive. He failed to recognize him for what he was – a publisher of the old school, a man belonging to the age when publishers liked to keep even a Voltaire or a Montesquieu under lock and key, starving in an attic.

'My way back takes me right through the Latin quarter,' said the old publisher after reading the address.

'What a kind man!' thought Lucien as he took his leave. 'So I have found someone who is friendly to the young, a connoisseur who knows something. There's a man for you! It's just as I said to David: talent easily makes good in Paris.'

He returned home happy and light-hearted, dreaming of glory. Thinking no more of the sinister remarks which had just now fallen on his ears in the office of Vidal and Porchon, he could see himself with at least twelve hundred francs in pocket. Twelve hundred francs meant one year's stay in Paris, a year during which he would get new works ready.

How many plans he built on this hope! How many pleasant dreams he indulged in as he foresaw a life given over to writing! He imagined himself living an orderly and settled existence: he only just managed not to go out and make some purchases. He could only curb his impatience by assiduous study in Blosse's reading-room. Two days later, Old Doguereau, surprised that Lucien had given such care to style in his first work, delighted at the exaggeration in character-drawing which was accepted in a period when drama was being developed, impressed by the impetuosity of imagination with which a young author always plans his first book – Papa Doguereau was not hard to please! – he came to the lodging-house where his budding Walter Scott was living. He was resolved to pay one thousand francs for sole rights in *The Archer of Charles the Ninth*, and to bind Lucien by a contract for several other works. But when the old fox saw the building he had second thoughts. 'A young man in such a lodging,' he told himself, 'has modest tastes; he's in love with study and toil. I need only pay him eight hundred francs.'

The landlady, when asked for Monsieur Lucien de Rubempré, replied 'Fourth floor!' The publisher looked up and saw nothing but sky above the fourth storey. 'This young man,' he thought, 'is a nice-looking boy, very handsome in fact. If he made too much money he would become a spendthrift and stop working. In our mutual interest, I will offer him six hundred francs – but in cash, not bills.' He mounted the staircase and gave three knocks at Lucien's door. Lucien came and opened it. The room was desperately bare. On the table were a bowl of milk and a small bread roll. The sight of genius in distress impressed the worthy Doguereau.

'Let him persevere,' he thought, 'in this simple way of life, this frugality, these modest requirements.' – 'It gives me pleasure to see you,' he said to Lucien. 'This, Monsieur, is how Jean-Jacques lived, and you will be like him in many respects. In such lodgings the flame of genius burns and great works are written. This is how men of letters ought to live instead of carousing in coffee-houses and restaurants and wasting their time, their talent and our money.'

He sat down. 'Young man, this isn't a bad novel. I have been a teacher of rhetoric and know French history: there are excellent things in it. In short you have a future before you.'

'Oh, Monsieur!'

'Yes, it's a fact. We can come to terms. I will buy your novel.'

Lucien felt his heart swelling and palpitating with joy. He was entering the world of literature; at last he was going to find himself in print.

'I will buy it for four hundred francs,' said Doguereau in honeyed tones, looking at Lucien with an air which seemed to indicate that he was carrying generosity to the straining-point.

'Per volume?' asked Lucien.

'No, for the novel,' said Doguereau, showing no astonishment at Lucien's surprise. 'But,' he added, 'cash down. You will undertake to write two novels per annum for six years. If your first novel is sold within six months I will pay you six hundred francs for the following ones. Thus, at two novels a year, you will earn a hundred francs a month, your living will be assured and you will be happy. Some of my authors only get two hundred francs for each of their novels. I pay two hundred francs for a translation from the English. In former times that would have been an extravagant price.'

'Monsieur,' said Lucien in icy tones. 'We cannot come to terms. Please give me back my manuscript.'

'Here it is,' said the aged publisher. 'You don't understand business, Monsieur. When an editor publishes an author's first novel he has to risk sixteen hundred francs for printing and paper. It's easier to write a novel than to find such a sum. I have a hundred manuscripts in my drawers, but less than a hundred and sixty thousand francs in my till. Alas! I have not made such a sum during the twenty years I have been a publisher. You can see then that the trade of printing novels doesn't bring in a fortune. Vidal and Porchon only take them from us on terms which daily become more onerous. You only invest your time, while I have to lay out two thousand francs. If things go wrong – for *habent sua fata libelli* –

I lose two thousand francs; as for you, all you have to do is to launch an ode against the stupidity of the public.

'After you have thought over what I have the honour of telling you, you will come and see me again. – You'll come back to me' – this the publisher repeated emphatically in response to a proudly defiant gesture from Lucien.

'Far from finding a publisher ready to risk two thousand francs for a young and unknown writer, you won't even find a publisher's assistant who'll take the trouble to read your scrawl. I have read it, and can point out several mistakes of French in it. You have written *observer* for *faire observer* and *malgré que . . . Malgré* takes a direct object.' Lucien looked humiliated. 'When I see you again, you will have lost a hundred francs,' he added, 'for then I shall only give you a hundred crowns.' He got up and bowed, but at the doorway he said: 'If you hadn't talent and promise, if I didn't take an interest in studious young people, I shouldn't have offered you such fine terms. A hundred francs a month! Think it over. After all, a novel tucked away in a drawer isn't like a horse in a stable: it doesn't need food. But it doesn't provide any either!'

Lucien took his manuscript, threw it on the floor and exclaimed:

'Monsieur, I would rather burn it!'

'That's a poet all over!' said the old man.

Lucien devoured his roll and gulped down his milk and went downstairs. His room was not spacious enough: if he had stayed in it he would have stalked round and round like a caged lion in the Paris Zoo.

4. *First friendship*

IN the Sainte-Geneviève Library, which Lucien was making for, he had noticed, sitting always in the same corner, a young man of about twenty-four who worked with that kind of steady application which nothing can distract or disturb and by which one may recognize real toilers in the literary sphere. This young man was no doubt a reader of long standing, for both the staff and the librarian himself were very obliging to him: the librarian let him take books home and Lucien used to see the studious stranger return them the next day: our poet felt that here was a brother in poverty and hopefulness. Short, thin and pale, this hard-working man had a fine forehead hidden behind a mass of black, somewhat unruly hair; he also had fine hands, and the eye of casual observers was drawn to him by his vague resemblance to the portrait of Bonaparte in the engraving taken from the painting by Robert Lefebvre. This engraving is a poem in itself: one of ardent melancholy, restrained ambition and concealed energy. Study it closely, and you will find that it breathes of genius, discretion, subtlety and grandeur. The eyes, like a woman's eyes, gleam with intelligence. They express a yearning for infinite space and a longing for difficulties to be overcome. Even if Bonaparte's name were not inscribed underneath, you would still gaze at it for just as long a time. The young man who was a replica of this engraving usually wore stocking-footed trousers, thick soled shoes, a frock-coat of coarse cloth, a black cravat, a grey and white cloth waistcoat buttoned right up and a cheap hat. His disdain for superfluous adornment was obvious. This mysterious stranger, marked with the stamp which genius imprints on the brow of its slaves was, as Lucien observed, •one of the most regular customers at Flicoteaux's. He ate sparingly, paying no attention to items on the menu, with which he seemed to be quite familiar, and drank water only. At the library or at the restaurant, in all he said or did, he manifested a kind of dignity which no doubt came from the consciousness that his life was dedicated to a great task, something which set him apart from other men. There was thought in the very look he gave. Meditation had its abode in that fine, nobly-shaped forehead. His bright black eyes, with their prompt and keen regard, betokened the habit of seeing into the heart of things. His gestures were simple and his countenance was grave.

Lucien felt an instinctive respect for him. Several times

already they had exchanged glances, as if they were about to speak to one another, on entering or leaving the library or the restaurant; but so far neither of them had ventured to do so. The young man worked in silence at the far end of the reading-room, in that part of it backing on to the Place de la Sorbonne. And so Lucien had not been able to make his acquaintance, although he felt drawn to this assiduous young student and the indefinable symptoms of exceptional talent that were evident in him. Both of them, as they acknowledged to each other later on, were naturally modest and timid and subject to all the tremors of self-consciousness which men of solitude tend to enjoy. Had it not been for their sudden meeting at the moment when disaster had just befallen Lucien, they might never perhaps have got into communication. But on entering the rue des Grès, Lucien caught sight of the young stranger as he was coming away from Sainte-Geneviève.

'The library is closed, Monsieur. I don't know why,' the latter said to him.

At this moment Lucien had tears in his eyes. He thanked the stranger with one of those gestures which are more eloquent than speech and induce young men to open their hearts to one another. They walked together down the rue des Grès in the direction of the rue de La Harpe.

'In that case I shall take a walk in the Luxembourg gardens,' said Lucien. 'Once one has left one's room it is difficult to go back and work.'

'True,' replied the stranger, 'one has lost the thread of necessary ideas. You seem downcast, Monsieur.'

'A strange thing has just happened to me,' said Lucien.

He recounted his visit to the quays, then the old publisher's visit to him and the proposals which had been put to him, giving his name and saying a few words about his predicament, telling him that in the course of about a month, he had spent sixty francs on food, thirty francs for his room, twenty francs on theatre tickets, ten francs for the reading-room: a hundred francs in all. He had only a hundred and twenty francs left.

'Monsieur,' said the stranger. 'Your history is mine and

that of a thousand or more young people who each year migrate from the provinces to Paris. And still we are not the unluckiest ones. You see that theatre?' – he pointed to the roof-tops of the Odéon – 'One day there came to live in one of the houses in the square a man of talent who had been plunged into the depths of poverty. He was married – an additional misfortune with which as yet neither of us is afflicted – to a woman he loved; he was blessed – if that is the word to use – with two children; he was riddled with debts but he trusted to his pen. He offered the Odéon a five-act comedy; it was accepted and put first on the waiting-list, the actors were rehearsing it, and the manager was speeding up the rehearsals: five strokes of luck, one might say five dramas even more difficult of accomplishment than the actual writing of his five acts. The poor author, lodging in a garret which you can see from here, used up his last resources in order to keep going while his play was being produced; his wife took her clothes to the pawnshop; their family lived on bread alone. On the day of the final rehearsal, the day before the first performance, he owed fifty francs in the district for household expenses – the baker, the milkman, the concierge. He had kept to the strict necessities of life: one coat, one shirt, one pair of trousers, one waistcoat and a pair of boots. Being sure of success, he came and embraced his wife and announced the end of their privations. "At last nothing stands in our way!" he cried. "Fire does," his wife replied. "Look, the Odéon is burning." Yes, Monsieur, the Odéon was on fire. And so do not complain. You have clothes, you have neither wife nor children, you happen to have a hundred and twenty francs in your pocket, and you owe nothing to anyone. Actually, the play in question ran to a hundred and fifty performances at the Louvois theatre. The King allotted a pension to the author. As Buffon said, genius is patience. Patience is indeed the quality in man which most resembles the process which Nature follows in her creations. And what is Art, Monsieur? It is Nature in concentrated form.'

By then the two young men were pacing up and down the Luxembourg gardens. Soon Lucien learned the name, which has since become famous, of the stranger who was striving to console him. He was Daniel d'Arthez, today one of the most illustrious writers of our time and one of those rare people who, as a poet has neatly expressed it, present

Fine talent matched with fine integrity.

'It costs a lot,' said Daniel in his gentle voice, 'to become a great man. The works of genius are watered with its tears. Talent is a living organism whose infancy, like that of all creatures, is liable to malady. Society rejects defective talent as Nature sweeps away weak or misshapen creatures. Whoever wishes to rise above the common level must be prepared for a great struggle and recoil before no obstacle. A great writer is just simply a martyr whom the stake cannot kill.'

'You bear the stamp of genius on your brow,' d'Arthez continued, summing Lucien up in a single glance. 'If at heart you have not the will-power and the seraphic patience needed, if, while the caprice of destiny keeps you still far from your goal, you do not continue on your path towards the infinite, as a tortoise in any country follows the path leading it back to its beloved ocean, give up this very day.'

'You also then expect to suffer great trials?' asked Lucien.

'Ordeals of every kind,' the young man replied in a resigned tone. 'Calumny, treachery, injustice from my rivals; effrontery, trickery, ruthlessness from the business world. If you are doing fine work, what does an initial setback matter?'

'Will you read and judge my work?' asked Lucien.

'I will,' said d'Arthez. 'I live in the rue des Quatre-Vents, in a house where once lived a most illustrious man, one of the brightest geniuses of our time, and a phenomenon in the world of science. He was Desplein, the greatest surgeon known, and here he first endured martyrdom as he battled with the initial difficulties of life and reputation in Paris. Remembering this every evening gives me the dose of courage I need every morning. I live in the room where often, like

Rousseau, but with no Thérèse, he fed on bread and cherries. Come in an hour's time. I shall be there.'

The two poets parted, clasping each other's hand with an indescribable effusion of melancholy tenderness. Daniel d'Arthez went and pawned his watch in order to buy two large faggots of wood so that his new friend might find a fire to warm him, for the weather was cold. Lucien arrived on time and his first view was that of an even less respectable-looking building than the one in which he was lodging, with a gloomy passage from the far end of which rose a dark staircase. Daniel d'Arthez's room on the fifth floor had two miserable windows, and between them was a bookcase of blackened wood, full of labelled filing cases. A narrow little bed of painted wood, like those used in schools, a secondhand night-commode and two armchairs upholstered in horsehair occupied the farther end of this room, whose walls were covered with chequered paper to which smoke and age had given a sort of varnish. A long table laden with papers stood between the fireplace and one of the windows. Opposite the fireplace was a shabby mahogany chest of drawers. The floor was completely covered with a carpet picked up at a sale, and this necessary luxury saved the expense of heating. In front of the table was a commonplace desk-chair covered in red sheepskin faded through long use; six poor-quality chairs made up the rest of the furniture. On the mantelpiece Lucien noticed an old branched sconce of the kind used at the card-table, furnished with four wax candles and a shade. When Lucien, discerning all round him the symptoms of stark poverty, asked why he used wax candles, d'Arthez replied that he could not bear the smell of burning tallow. This peculiarity indicated his very delicate physical sensitivity, which is also a sign of acute moral sensibility.

The reading lasted seven hours. Daniel listened with scrupulous attention without saying a word or making any remark – one of the rarest proofs of good taste that can be given by anyone who is himself an author.

'Well?' Lucien asked as he laid his manuscript on the mantelpiece.

'You are on the right and proper track,' the young man answered gravely. 'But you must reshape your work. If you don't want to ape Walter Scott you must invent a different manner for yourself, whereas you have imitated him. Like him, you begin with long conversations in order to pose your characters; after they have talked you proceed with description and action. The clash of wills necessary in any work of dramatic quality comes last. Let me see you reverse the terms of the problem. Replace these diffuse colloquies, at which Scott is magnificent but which lack colour in your novel, by the sort of description for which the French language is so well adapted. Let your dialogue be the expected sequel and the climax of your preparations. Launch yourself straight into the action. Let me see you attack your subject sometimes broadside on, sometimes from the rear. In short, vary your plan of action so as never to repeat yourself. You will thus blaze a new trail while adapting the Scotsman's drama in dialogue form to the history of France. Walter Scott lacks passion; it is a closed book to him; or perhaps he found it was ruled out by the hypocritical morals of his native land. Woman for him is duty incarnate. With rare exceptions, his heroines are absolutely identical; as painters say, he has only one pouncing pattern. His women all proceed from Clarissa Harlowe; reducing them all to one simple idea, he was only able to strike off copies of one and the same type and vary them with a more or less vivid colouring. Woman brings disorder into society through passion. Passion is infinite in its manifestations. Therefore, depict the passions and you will have at your command the immense resources which this great genius denied himself in order to provide reading matter for every family in prudish England. Dealing with France, you will be able to oppose to the dour figures of Calvinism the attractive peccadillos and brilliant manners of Catholicism against the background of the most impassioned period of our history. Every authentic reign from Charlemagne onwards will require at least one work, and sometimes four or five, as in the case of Louis the Fourteenth, Henry the Fourth and Francis the First. In this way you will write a pictorial history of France in which you will describe costume, furniture, the outside and inside of buildings and private life, whilst conveying the spirit of the times instead of laboriously narrating a sequence of known facts. You will find scope for originality in correcting the popular errors which give a distorted view of most of our kings. Be so bold, in your first work, as to rehabilitate that great and magnificent figure, Catherine de Medici, whom you have sacrificed to the prejudices which still cling to her memory. And then depict Charles the Ninth as he really was, and not as Protestant writers make him out to have been. After ten years of perseverance you will achieve fame and fortune.'

By then it was nine o'clock. Lucien emulated the unsuspected generosity of his future friend by inviting him out to dinner at Edon's restaurant, and it cost him twelve francs. While they were dining Daniel confided to Lucien the secret of his hopes and studies. D'Arthez would not allow that any talent could be exceptional without a profound knowledge of metaphysics. At present he was delving into and assimilating all the philosophic treasures of ancient and modern times. He wanted to be a profound philosopher, like Molière before he ever wrote a comedy. He was studying the world in writing and the living world: thought and fact. Among his friends were erudite naturalists, young medical men, political writers and artists: a confraternity of studious, serious and promising people. He made his way by writing conscientious and poorly-paid articles for biographical and encyclopaedic dictionaries or dictionaries of natural science. He kept such writing to the minimum required for earning his living and continuing his studies. D'Arthez had in hand an imaginative work which he had undertaken solely in order to explore the resources of language. This book, still unfinished, which he took up and laid down as the whim came, was reserved for his days of great penury. It was a psychological work of considerable scope cast in the form of a novel. Although Daniel was modest in his revelations, he seemed a gigantic figure to Lucien. When he left the restaurant at eleven o'clock, Lucien had conceived a lively friendship for this man of such unassuming virtue and, unwittingly, of so sublime a nature. Faithfully and unquestioningly he followed Daniel's advice. Daniel's fine talent, already matured by reflection and an original kind of criticism developed in solitude for his own especial purposes, had suddenly opened a door admitting Lucien to the most splendid palaces of the imagination. The lips of the provincial had been touched by a burning coal, and the words of the industrious Parisian had fallen on fertile soil in the brain of the poet from Angoulême. He began to reshape his novel.

5. The 'Cénacle'[1]

THE poet from the provinces was so happy to have found in the wilderness of Paris one soul abounding in generous feelings which accorded with his own that he acted like all young people starved of affection: he attached himself like a chronic malady to d'Arthez, called for him so that they could go to the Library together, went for walks with him in the Luxembourg gardens on fine days and escorted him home every evening to his wretched room after dining with him at Flicoteaux's. In short he clung as closely to him as a soldier huddling against his comrade in the icy steppes of Russia. During the early days of his acquaintance with Daniel, Lucien noticed, not without chagrin, that his presence created some embarrassment whenever Daniel and his bosom friends were together. At such times the conversation of these rare creatures, about whom d'Arthez talked to him with ardent enthusiasm, would be kept within the bounds of a reserve inconsistent with the warm friendship they so visibly felt for one another. On these occasions Lucien discreetly took his leave, feeling ill at ease because of the ostracism of which he was the object and the curiosity aroused in him by these unknown persons who addressed each other by their Christian

1. 'Cénacle', in French, is used in the special sense of a literary or artistic confraternity.

names only. Each of them, like d'Arthez himself, bore on his forehead the stamp of his own particular genius. After some secret resistance which Daniel fought without Lucien's knowledge, he was at last deemed worthy of admission to this high-minded confraternity, and from then on he came to know its members, united as they were by the closest sympathy and the gravity of their intellectual pursuits and meeting almost every evening in d'Arthez's room. All of them felt that d'Arthez was destined to become a great writer: they had regarded him as their leader ever since they had been bereaved of their first leader, a mystical genius, and one of the most outstanding intellects of that period who, for reasons it would be irrelevant to report here, had gone home to his native province, and whom Lucien often heard them refer to as Louis. It will be readily understood how much interest and curiosity was necessarily awakened in a poet by these persons if some information is given here about those of them who since that time, like d'Arthez, have risen to the peak of their reputation; for not all of them survived.

Among those still alive was Horace Bianchon, then a house-surgeon at the Hôtel-Dieu, who has since become a foremost luminary in the Paris School of Medicine: he is too well-known today for it to be necessary to give a portrait of him or to detail his character and mental qualities. Next came Léon Giraud, a profound philosopher and bold speculator who investigates all systems, judges them, expounds and formulates them and brings them to the feet of the idol he worships: HUMANITY. He is always great, even in the errors he commits, for these are ennobled by his good faith. This intrepid worker and conscientious scholar has become the leader of a moral and political school of thought on the merits of which only time will be able to pronounce. Even though his convictions have marked out a destiny for him in spheres alien to those into which his companions have ventured, he has none the less remained their faithful friend.

Art was represented by Joseph Bridau, one of the best painters of the young school. Were it not for the secret woes to which his too impressionable disposition condemns him,

Joseph, who for that matter has not spoken his last word, might well have carried on the tradition of the great Italian masters: he has Roman line and Venetian colour. But Cupid plays havoc with him. The shafts of love not only transfix his heart but also his brain, disturb the tenour of his life and set him off on the strangest of zigzag courses. If his mistress of the moment makes him too happy or too wretched, Joseph will sometimes exhibit sketches in which colour impairs purity of line, and sometimes pictures which he has persisted in finishing when weighed down with imaginary sorrows, and in these he has been so concerned with line that colour, with which he can achieve any effect he likes, is virtually absent. He is constantly disappointing both the public and his friends. Hoffmann would have adored him for his bold advances in the domain of art, for his caprices and his flights of imagination. When he displays all his qualities, he excites admiration and enjoys it and then he takes umbrage when he receives no praise for unsuccessful works, in which his inner eye sees all that the eye of the public finds lacking. Whimsical to a degree, he has been seen by his friends to destroy a completed picture to which he thought he had given too much finish. 'It's over-done,' he would say. 'It's beginner's work.' Occasionally original and sublime, he is capable of all the felicities and infelicities found in those nervous temperaments who are perfectionists to the point of morbidity. He has an intellect akin to that of Sterne but lacks Sterne's capacity for hard work. His witticisms and sallies of thought have unprecedented pungency. He is eloquent and knows what love means, but he brings the same capriciousness to affairs of the heart as to his style in painting. He was well-beloved in the 'Cénacle' for precisely those characteristics which philistines would have condemned.

Then there was Fulgence Ridal, one of the authors of our time most endowed with comic verve, a poet unconcerned with fame, tossing only his most commonplace productions on to the stage and jealously withholding his finest dramas from public scrutiny and keeping them for his own delectation and that of his friends, only requiring from the public the money he needed to preserve his independence and relapsing into idleness as soon as he obtained it. Lazy, as productive as Rossini, obliged, like all great comic poets, like Molière and Rabelais, to consider the obverse and reverse side, the pros and cons of everything, he was a sceptic, able to laugh at everything, as indeed he did. Fulgence Ridal is a great practical philosopher. His knowledge of people, his genius for observation, the contempt he feels for fame which he calls empty show, have not withered his heart. As active in others' interests as he is indifferent about his own, if he bestirs himself it is for a friend. In order not to give the lie to his truly Rabelaisian countenance, he does not hate good cheer but does not go out of his way to find it; he is at once melancholy and gay. His friends call him the 'regimental pet', and nothing describes him better than this sobriquet.

Three others, at least as outstanding as the four friends thus painted in profile, were destined to succumb one after the other: Meyraux first of all, who died after initiating the famous discussion between Cuvier and Saint-Hilaire over a momentous question which was to divide the world of scientists into two camps behind these men of equal genius. He died some months before the former, who stood out for narrow, analytical science as against the pantheistic Saint-Hilaire who is still alive and is revered in Germany. Meyraux was a friend of that Louis whom a predictable death was soon to snatch from the world of intellectuals. To these two men, both marked out for death, both of them little known today despite the immense range of their learning and genius, must be added Michel Chrestien, a republican with far-reaching ideas who dreamed of a European federation and in 1830 was to take a prominent place among the idealists of the Saint-Simonian movement. A political thinker of the calibre of Saint-Just and Danton though simple and gentle as a girl, gifted with a melodious voice which would have delighted Mozart, Weber or Rossini and whose rendering of some of Béranger's songs was sufficient to fire men's hearts with poetry, love or hope, Michel Chrestien, as poor as Lucien, Daniel and all his other friends, earned his living with the unconcern of a Diogenes. He drew up tables of contents for important books, prospectuses for publishers, but was as mute about his doctrines as the grave is mute about the secrets of the after-life. This gay bohemian of the intellectual life, a great political thinker who might perhaps have changed the face of the world, was to die like a common soldier in the massacre of the Cloister of Saint-Merri. A bullet fired by some tradesman or other killed one of the noblest creatures who ever trod on the soil of France. Michel Chrestien died fighting for doctrines other than his own. The federation he planned was a greater threat than republican propaganda to the aristocracies of Europe; it was more rational and less extravagant than the appalling ideas in favour of unbridled liberty proclaimed by those insensate young men who put themselves forward as the heirs of the National Convention. This noble plebeian was wept for by all who knew him, and there is no one among them who does not frequently think of this great, unknown politician.

These nine persons composed a fraternity in which esteem and friendship kept the peace between the most conflicting ideas and doctrines. Daniel d'Arthez, a nobleman from Picardy, was as convinced a supporter of monarchy as Michel Chrestien was a champion of European federalism. Fulgence Ridal made fun of the philosophical doctrines of Léon Giraud, who in his turn prophesied to d'Arthez the destruction of Christianity and the family. Michel Chrestien, who believed in the religion of Christ, the divine promulgator of the law of equality, defended the immortality of the soul against the scalpel-wielding Bianchon, a superlatively analytical mind. They all argued without quarrelling. They were without vanity, having no other audience than their own group. They told one another about their work and consulted one another with the amiable good faith of youth. If a serious matter was in dispute, the opponent gave up his own opinion in order to enter into his friend's ideas and was the better qualified to help him because he was unprejudiced about a cause or a work which was outside his speciality. Almost all of them were gentle and tolerant, and these two attributes gave clear proof of their superior quality. Envy, an ignoble accumulation of disappointed hopes, frustrated talents, failures and wounded pretensions, was unknown to them. Besides, they were all advancing along different paths. And so those newly admitted, like Lucien, to their society, felt quite at ease. Genuine talent is always simple and good-natured, open and unconstrained; its epigrams foster wit in others and never seek to injure self-esteem. Once the first shyness born of respect was dispelled, the company of these exceptional young men brought infinite satisfaction. Familiarity was no bar to the consciousness each one had of his own value, and each one held his neighbour in profound esteem; in short, since each of them felt that he might alternately do or be done good turns, none of them made any fuss about accepting them. Their conversation, full of charm and free of restraint, covered all sorts of subjects and their words went as lightly as winged shafts to the heart of the matter. Their great outward poverty stood in singular contrast to the splendour of their intellectual riches. None of them gave a thought to material realities except as an excuse for friendly pleasantries. One day when the cold weather had set in before its time, five of d'Arthez's friends came along, each prompted by the same thought, carrying logs under their cloaks, just as when at a country picnic each guest, being expected to provide some item of food, brings a pie. All of them being endowed with that moral beauty which transforms the outer man and, no less than labours and vigils, gives a divine glow to the faces of the young, they had those slightly irregular features to which chastity of life and the flame of thought impart shapeliness and purity. They were distinguished by a poetic breadth of forehead. Their bright, keen eyes bore witness to an unsullied life. The sufferings due to poverty, whenever they could be detected, were so gaily endured, so enthusiastically accepted by all, that they in no way impaired that serenity of countenance peculiar to young people still innocent of grave transgressions who have not stooped to any of those cowardly compromises which are wrested from men by poverty impatiently supported, the desire to succeed at all cost and the facile complacency with which men of letters accept or pardon acts of treachery. What makes friendships indissoluble and doubles their charm is a feeling not found in love – the feeling of certainty. These young people were sure of one another: the enemy of one became the enemy of all; they would have sacrificed their most urgent interests in obedience to the sacred solidarity which united their hearts. One and all were incapable of disloyalty; they could meet any accusation with a stout denial and defend one another without misgivings. Equally noble-hearted and equally strong in their convictions, they could think what they liked and say what they liked in matters both intellectual and scientific; hence the innocuousness of their intercourse and their gaiety in conversation. Since they were certain of understanding one another, they gave free reign to their wit, and so there was no formality between them: they confided their joys and sorrows to one another and freely expressed their thoughts and tribulations. The charming and delicate attentions which make La Fontaine's fable, *The Two Friends*, a treasure-trove for exalted souls were a matter of habit with them. Their circumspection in admitting a newcomer to their sphere is therefore understandable. They were too conscious of greatness and happiness to disturb it by admitting new and unknown elements.

This community of feeling and interests lasted for twenty years without any clash or misunderstanding. Death alone, in robbing them of Louis Lambert, Meyraux and Michel Chrestien, was able to diminish this noble constellation. When the latter succumbed in 1832 Horace Bianchon, Daniel d'Arthez, Léon Giraud, Joseph Bridau and Fulgence Ridal, despite the danger involved, went to move his body from Saint-Merri in order to pay him their last respects in defiance of political fanaticism. During the night they accompanied these cherished remains to the cemetery of Père-Lachaise. Horace Bianchon recoiled before none of the difficulties and broke through them all; he petitioned cabinet ministers, confessing his long-standing friendship with the departed federalist. It was a moving scene, which remained in the memory of the few friends who accompanied the five celebrities to Michel's grave. When you take a walk through that elegant cemetery you will see a plot purchased in perpetuity from which rises a mound of turf with a black wooden cross over it, and on this cross is engraved in red letters the name of Michel Chrestien. It is the only monument in this style. The five friends thought that such simplicity was the best homage they could pay to this simple man.

And so, in this cold garret, the finest dreams of fellow-feeling found expression. There a fraternal group, all of them equally proficient in their respective sphere of knowledge, enlightened one another in mutual good faith, withholding nothing, not even their less worthy thoughts, all of them being of wide learning and all tested in the crucible of adversity. Once admitted among these choice spirits and accepted as an equal, Lucien was the representative in it of poetry and beauty. He read sonnets to them and these were admired. They would ask him for a sonnet, just as he would beg Michel Chrestien for a song. Thus it was that Lucien discovered in the rue des Quatre Vents an oasis in the desert of Paris.

6. *The flowers of poverty*

AT the beginning of December Lucien, having used the remainder of his money to buy a few logs, found himself penniless while eagerly engaged in the task of re-writing his novel. Daniel for his part burned peat and heroically endured his poverty; he made no complaints, lived as steadily as an old maid and with so much method that he seemed like a miser. His courage stimulated that of Lucien who, as a newcomer to the Cénacle, was overwhelmingly reluctant to talk about the straits he was in. One morning he went to the rue du Coq in order to sell *The Archer of Charles the Ninth* to Doguereau, but failed to see him. Lucien did not know how indulgent great minds can be. Each of his friends was aware of the weaknesses peculiar to writers of poetry and the dejection resulting from the efforts of a mind overstrained by the contemplation of nature, the interpretation of which is the poet's function. These men, so sturdy in coping with their own troubles, showed a tender sympathy for Lucien in his sufferings. And so the members of the Cénacle added a crowning touch to one of those pleasant evenings given over to conversation, profound thinking, poetry, personal confidences, impetuous dashes through the fields of the intellect, international policy and the domains of history: they made a characteristic gesture which proved how slight was Lucien's understanding of his new friends.

'Lucien, my friend,' said Daniel. 'You didn't dine at Flicoteaux's yesterday, and we know why.'

Lucien could not prevent tears from streaming down his cheeks.

'You showed little trust in us,' said Michel Chrestien. 'We shall chalk a cross on the mantelpiece, and when we have reached the tenth . . . '

'We have each of us,' said Bianchon, 'done an extra piece of work. I looked after one of Desplein's wealthy patients for him. D'Arthez wrote an article for the *Revue Encyclopédique*. One evening Chrestien thought of going out singing in the Champs-Elysées with a scarf and four candles, but he was commissioned to write a pamphlet for a man with political ambitions and provided him with six hundred francs' worth of Machiavelli. Léon Giraud has borrowed fifty francs from his publisher. Joseph has sold some sketches and on Sunday Fulgence had his play performed before a full house.'

'Here are two hundred francs,' said Daniel. 'Take them and don't let us catch you out again!'

'Hanged if he isn't going to hug every one of us, as if we had done something extraordinary!' said Chrestien.

To show how delighted Lucien was to be in the midst of this living encyclopaedia of angelic spirits, this group of young men each bearing the impress of a special originality derived from his own line of research, it will suffice to record the replies which Lucien received the next day to a letter written to his family, a masterpiece of sensibility and good intentions, a heart-rending cry which his distress had wrung from him.

DAVID SÉCHARD TO LUCIEN

My dear Lucien,

You will find enclosed a draft in your name for two hundred francs, payable in ninety days. You can cash it with Monsieur Métivier, paper-merchant, our Paris correspondent, rue Serpente. My good Lucien, we are absolutely denuded. My wife has taken over the printing-office and is running it with a devotedness, patience and energy which make me thank Heaven for having given me such an angel for a wife. She herself has realized how impossible it is for us to send you any worthwhile help. But, my friend, I believe you are on so fine a path in the company of such great and noble hearts that a glorious destiny awaits you, aided as you are by people of almost divine intelligence like Messieurs Daniel d'Arthez, Michel Chrestien and Léon Giraud, with the counsels of Messieurs Meyraux, Bianchon and Ridal, whom your precious letter has made known to us. And so, without telling Eve, I drew this bill of exchange and will find some way of meeting it when it falls due. Do not turn aside from the road you are following: it will be hard going, but it will bring you fame. I would rather suffer a thousand ills than know you had fallen into any of the mud-pits of Paris – I saw so many of them when I was there. Have the courage to avoid, as you are doing, evil resorts, evil people, irresponsible persons and certain men of letters whom I learnt to appraise at their true value during my stay in Paris. In short, be a worthy emulator of those lofty minds who have become dear to me through you. You will soon reap the reward of such conduct. Good-bye, beloved brother: you have filled my heart with delight. I had not expected so much courage from you.

DAVID.

EVE SÉCHARD TO LUCIEN

My dear,

We all cried as we read your letter. Let those noble hearts to which your guardian angel led you know this: a mother and a poor young woman will pray to God for them night and morning; and if the most fervent prayers rise to His throne, they will obtain some favours for all of you. Yes, dear brother, their names are engraved in my heart. Oh, I shall meet them some day! If I have to walk the whole way I will come and thank them for showing you such friendship, for it has poured balm on my open wounds. Here, my darling, we are toiling like poor workmen. My husband, that unknown great man whom I love more every day as I discover, moment by moment, new treasures in his heart, is neglecting his printing-office, and I can guess why: your destitution, as well as ours and Mother's, worry him to death. Our beloved David is like Prometheus with grief, a yellow-beaked vulture pecking at his entrails. Noble as he is, he scarcely thinks of himself, for he is hoping to make a fortune. He spends all his time making experiments in the manufacture of paper; he has asked me to look after the business in his stead, but he gives me as much help with it as his preoccupation will allow. Alas, I am expecting a child. Such an event, which would have overwhelmed me with joy, makes me sad in our present situation. Our dear mother has become young again and found new strength for her tiring profession as sick nurse. Without our money troubles we should be happy. Old Séchard won't give his son a farthing. David went to see him to borrow a few coppers in order to help you, for your letter brought him to despair. 'I know Lucien', David said, 'he will lose his head and do something silly.' I gave him a good scolding. 'Would my brother fall short in any way?' I replied. 'Lucien knows I should die of grief.' Mother and I, without David suspecting it, have pawned a few articles which Mother will redeem as soon as any money comes in. In this way we raised a hundred francs which I am sending by post. Don't be cross with me, my dear, for not answering your first letter. We were in such a predicament that we worried night and day. Oh, I didn't know I was so strong. Madame de Bargeton is a soulless and heartless woman; even if she no longer loved you, she owed it to herself to help and protect you after snatching you away from us and flinging you into the terrible ocean of Paris, where God's blessing is needed for one to find true friends amid the rough seas of human self-interest. Have no regrets for her. I wanted you to have a devoted woman about you, a second myself; but now that I know you have friends who feel just as we do, my mind is easy. Spread the wings of your fine genius, darling. Our glory will be in you, as our love is already.

EVE.

My beloved child, after what your sister has written to you, I can only send you my blessing and assure you that my prayers and

225

thoughts are all, alas, for you alone, to the detriment of those around me. There are some hearts for whom absent people are always in the right: so it is with the heart of

YOUR MOTHER.

Thus, two days later, Lucien was able to pay back to his friends the loan they had so gracefully made him. Never perhaps had life seemed more beautiful to him, but this prompting of self-respect did not elude the searching glances of his friends.

'One would say that you were afraid of owing us something,' Fulgence exclaimed.

'Indeed,' said Michel Chrestien, 'the pleasure he manifests seems a grave thing to me. It confirms what I have already noticed: there is vanity in Lucien.'

'He's a poet,' said d'Arthez.

'Do you resent my having so natural a feeling?'

'We must give him credit,' said Léon Giraud, 'for not hiding it from us; but I fear that later on he may be afraid of us.'

'But why?' asked Lucien.

'Because we can read your heart,' Joseph Bridau replied.

'In you,' said Michel Chrestien, 'there is a diabolic spirit which will help you to justify in your own eyes things most contrary to our principles: instead of being a sophist in ideas you will be a sophist in action.'

'Indeed, I fear so,' said d'Arthez. 'Lucien, you will hold admirable discussions with yourself which will make you feel big, but they will lead to blameworthy deeds ... You will never be in tune with yourself.'

'What are your grounds for making such an accusation?' asked Lucien.

'Is your vanity so great, my dear poet,' exclaimed Fulgence, 'that it enters even into your friendships? All vanity of that kind betokens fearful egoism, and egoism poisons friendship.'

'Oh, good Heavens!' cried Lucien. 'So you don't know what great love I have for you?'

'If you loved us as we love you, would you have made such haste and fuss about returning to us what we had had so much pleasure in giving you?'

'Here we don't lend money to one another, we give it,' Joseph Bridau bluntly interposed.

'Don't think we are being harsh, my dear boy,' said Michel Chrestien. 'We are looking ahead. We are afraid that one day we may see you preferring the joys of petty requital to the joys of our pure friendship for you. Read Goethe's *Tasso*, the greatest work of that fine genius, and you will see there that the poet loves gaudy clothes, banquets, triumphs, outward show: well, be a Tasso without his follies. Are the world and its pleasures calling you? Stay here. Transfer to the realm of ideas all that you expect to gain from vanity. Exchange one folly for another: put virtue into your actions and vice into your fictions; instead, as d'Arthez said, of thinking well and behaving badly.'

Lucien let his head droop: his friends were right.

'I confess I have not strength such as yours,' he said, looking at them very appealingly. 'My back and shoulders are not sturdy enough to hold up Paris, to struggle courageously. Nature has given us different temperaments and faculties, and you know better than I do the reverse side of vices and virtues. I admit that I am already tired.'

'We will support you,' said d'Arthez. 'That is just what loyal friendship is for.'

'The help I have just received is precarious and everyone in my family is as poor as the rest; need will soon be on my heels again. Chrestien, depending as he does on casual earnings, has no influence with the publishers. Bianchon is outside this sphere of affairs. D'Arthez is only in touch with firms producing scientific and specialized treatises, which cut no ice with publishers looking for novelty. Horace, Fulgence Ridal and Bridau work in a region of ideas which keeps them a hundred leagues away from publishers. I must come to some decision.'

'Hold on to ours: endurance!' said Bianchon. 'Endure with courage and put your trust in hard work!'

'But what is only endurance for you means death for me,' Lucien quickly retorted.

'Before the cock has crowed three times,' said Léon Giraud with a smile, 'this man will have betrayed the cause of hard work for that of sloth and the vices of Paris.'

'How far has hard work taken you?' asked Lucien with a laugh.

'When you leave Paris for Italy, you don't find Rome midway,' said Joseph Bridau. 'You seem to expect your green peas to grow already cooked and served up with butter.'

'They only grow like that for the eldest sons of peers,' said Michel Chrestien. 'The rest of us sow them and water them and find them all the tastier.'

The conversation turned to jests and the subject was dropped. These shrewd minds and delicate hearts tried to make Lucien forget this little quarrel, but henceforth he realized how difficult it was to deceive them. There soon came to him an inner despair which he carefully concealed from his friends, for he believed them to be implacable mentors. His southern temperament, so apt to run up and down the gamut of emotions, caused him to vacillate between the most contrary resolutions.

On several occasions he talked of plunging into journalism, but his friends always said: 'For Heaven's sake don't.'

'That would be the end of the fine, gentle Lucien we love and know,' said d'Arthez.

'You wouldn't be able to stand steadfast against the constant antagonism between pleasure and toil of which a journalist's life consists, and steadfastness is the foundation of virtue. You would be so delighted to wield power, to pass sentence of life or death on the productions of thought, that you would become a hardened journalist in two months. To be a journalist is to become a proconsul in the republic of letters. The man who can say what he likes ends up by doing what he likes. This, as one might guess, was one of Napoleon's maxims.'

'But will you not still be with me?' asked Lucien.

'We shall no longer be with you,' Fulgence exclaimed. 'Once

a journalist, you would no more think of us than a brilliant, idolized Opera singer in her silk-lined carriage thinks of her native village with its cows and clogs. You only too obviously possess the qualities of a journalist: brilliance and versatility of thought. You would never deny yourself a shaft of wit, even if it reduced a friend to tears. I meet journalists in the theatre *foyers*, and they horrify me. Journalism is an inferno, a bottomless pit of iniquity, falsehood and treachery: one can only pass through it and emerge from it unsullied if one is shielded as Dante was by the divine laurels of Virgil.'

The more the Cénacle tried to turn Lucien away from this path, the more did his desire to brave the peril invite him to take the risk. He began to argue with himself: was it not ridiculous to let himself be once more overtaken by penury without doing anything to avert it? In view of the failure he had met with in regard to his first novel, Lucien felt little inclined to settle down to a second one. Besides, what would he have to live on while he was writing it? A month of privation had exhausted his stock of patience. Could he not do nobly what journalists did unworthily and without scruples of conscience? The mistrust of his friends was an insult to him, and he wanted to show them what mental vigour he had. Perhaps he might come to their help one day and be a herald of glory for them.

'Anyway, what sort of friendship is it that shies at complicity?' he asked one evening of Michel Chrestien as he was seeing him back home in company with Léon Giraud.

'We shy at nothing,' Michel answered. 'If you had the misfortune to kill your mistress, I would help you to conceal the crime and could still feel some respect for you. But if you took to espionage I should shrink from you in horror, for you would be adopting treachery and infamy as a system. That, in a word, is what journalism does. Friendship condones mistakes and the rash impulses of passion, but it must be implacable to anyone who decides to barter away his soul, his intellect and his thought.'

'Could I not take to journalism in order to sell my book of poems and my novel, and then give it up immediately?'

'That is how Machiavelli would behave, but not Lucien de Rubempré,' said Léon Giraud.

'Very well,' cried Lucien. 'I will prove to you that I am as capable as Machiavelli!'

'Ah!' cried Michel, clasping Léon by the hand. 'You have just sealed his doom.' – 'Lucien,' he added, 'You have three hundred francs, enough to live comfortably for three months. Very well, get to work, write a second novel. D'Arthez and Fulgence will help you to plan it, you will grow in stature, you will be a novelist. I instead will make my way into one of those mental brothels and become a journalist for three months. I will sell your books for you to some publisher after attacking his publications. I will write articles and get articles written about you. We will arrange a success for you, you will become a great man and you will still be our Lucien.'

'You really must despise me if you think that I should come to grief and that you will come through it unscathed!' said the poet.

'Lord forgive him! He's just a child!' cried Michel Chrestien.

7. *A newspaper seen from outside*

AFTER limbering up his wits during the evenings spent in d'Arthez's rooms, Lucien had studied the pleasantries and articles of the 'petits journaux'.[1] Sure that he could at least rise to the level of the wittiest contributors, he made secret attempts at these mental gymnastics, and sallied forth one morning with the exultant idea of requesting enlistment under one or other colonel of this light infantry of the Press. He put on his smartest clothes and crossed the Seine, thinking that authors, journalists, writers, in short the confraternity he hoped to join, would show more kindness and disinterestedness than the two types of bookseller-publishers who had previously dashed his hopes. He would meet congenial people

1. See Introduction, p. xv.

and find something like the benign and benevolent affection he had enjoyed at the Cénacle of the rue des Quatre Vents. Assailed by, giving heed to, yet combating the flutter of presentiments which count so much with men of imagination, he arrived at the rue Saint-Fiacre, near the Boulevard Montmartre, in front of the building which housed the offices of the 'little paper' he had selected: the sight of it set his heart beating furiously like that of a young man entering a house of ill-fame. Nevertheless he climbed the stairs to the mezzanine in which the offices were situated. In the opening room, divided into two equal portions by a partition half-boarded and half-latticed up to the ceiling, he found a one-armed ex-soldier who with his only hand was supporting several reams of paper on his head and holding between his teeth the registration-book prescribed by the stamp-duty administration. This poor man, whose face had a sallow tint and a crop of red blisters – hence his nickname Colocynth – pointed to the Cerberus of the newspaper who was the other side of the lattice. This individual was a retired army officer, bemedalled, with grey side whiskers curling round his nose, wearing a black silk cap, and buried under an ample blue frockcoat like a tortoise under its shell.

'From what date, Monsieur, do you wish your subscription to begin?' the Imperial officer asked him.

'I have not come to take out a subscription,' Lucien replied, looking towards a card on the door opposite the one through which he had entered: on it was written EDITORIAL OFFICE, with 'No admittance to the public' underneath.

'A complaint no doubt,' the Napoleonic soldier rejoindered. 'Yes indeed, we were hard on Mariette. Believe me, I still don't know why. But if you are demanding satisfaction I am ready,' he added, with a glance at an array of foils and pistols, an up-to-date panoply, bundled together in a corner.

'That still less, Monsieur. I have come for a word with the editor.'

'There's never anyone here before four.'

'Look here, Giroudeau old chap. My count is eleven

columns, and at five francs each that makes fifty-five francs. I've only had forty, therefore you still owe me fifteen francs as I said . . . '

These words came from a small, weasel face as pale as the white of an undercooked egg, from which gleamed two soft blue though alarmingly malicious eyes. They belonged to a slim young man concealed behind the ex-soldier's opaque body. This voice chilled Lucien to the marrow: it was a cross between the miaowing of a cat and the asthmatic choke of a hyena.

'Yes, my little militiaman,' the retired officer answered. 'But you are counting in the titles and the blanks. Finot told me to add up the total number of lines and divide it by the number required for each column. I have performed this garrotting operation on your article and find it is three columns short.'

'He doesn't pay for the blanks, the old screw, but he charges his partner for them in the overall cost of his copy. I'm going to see Etienne Lousteau, Vernou, and . . . '

'I can't go against orders, young man,' said the officer. 'What! For a matter of fifteen francs you bite the hand that feeds you – and you can toss off an article as easily as I can smoke a cigar! Come now, you'll stand your friends one bowl of punch less or win one game of billiards more, and all will be square!'

'Finot's cheese-parings will cost him dear,' the journalist retorted as he got up and went out.

'You'd think he was Voltaire and Rousseau rolled into one,' the cashier murmured to himself, casting his eyes on the provincial poet.

'Monsieur,' said Lucien, 'I will return at four o'clock.'

During the discussion, he had seen hanging on the walls the portraits of Benjamin Constant, General Foy, the seventeen illustrious spokesmen of the Liberal party and a medley of caricatures attacking the Government. Above all, he had been looking at the door of the sanctum in which, no doubt, was concocted the witty news-sheet which amused him every day, enjoying as it did the right of ridiculing kings and the gravest events of the day, in short of using a *bon mot* to call everything into question. He wandered along the boulevards – a new pleasure for him, but one so attractive that he saw the clock-hands in the jewellers' shops pointing to four without noticing that he had had no lunch. The poet promptly turned back down the rue du Fiacre, climbed the stairs, opened the door, found that the old officer had gone and saw the disabled pensioner sitting on his stamped paper munching a crust of bread and keeping watch over the editorial bureau as resignedly as he had formerly done his fatigue-duty, and having no more idea of what it was all about than he had understood the why and wherefore of the rapid marches ordered by the Emperor. The bold idea came to Lucien of stealing a march on this redoubtable functionary: he passed by him with his hat on and opened the door of the sanctum as if he belonged to the staff. The editor's office offered to his eager gaze a round table covered with a green cloth and six cherry-wood chairs with straw seats which were still new. The floor of this room was stained but not yet polished; it was however clean, and this indicated that few people were allowed in it. On the mantelpiece stood a mirror, a cheap clock covered with dust, two sconces into which two tallow candles had been carelessly thrust and, finally, a scattering of visiting cards. On the table rumpled old newspapers lay about an ink-stand in which the ink was dried as hard as lacquer and the quills on it twisted into circles. He read a few articles written in an illegible and almost hieroglyphic script on grubby scraps of paper torn length-wise by the printing-press compositors, for whom this serves as an indication that an article has been set up. Also, here and there, he gazed admiringly at witty caricatures sketched on grey paper by people who no doubt had sought to kill time by killing something else to keep their hand in. On the cheap, sea-green wall-paper were pinned nine different pen-and-ink sketches burlesquing *Le Solitaire*, a novel whose unprecedented success at that time was giving it a European reputation and whose abuse of inversions must have wearied the journalists.

'*The Solitary* in the provinces appearing the ladies astonishes.' – 'The effect of *The Solitary* on domestic pets.' – 'Among the savages, *The Solitary* explained, the most brilliant success obtains.' – '*The Solitary* translated into Chinese and presented, by the author, of Pekin to the Emperor.' – 'By Mont-Sauvage, Elodie raped.' (Lucien thought this caricature very indecent, but it made him laugh) – 'By the newspapers, *The Solitary* under a canopy carried round processionally.' – '*The Solitary*, bursting a press, the bears injures.' – 'Read backwards, astonishes *The Solitary* the Academicians by its exceptional beauty.'

Lucien noticed a drawing on a newspaper band representing a journalist holding out his hand, with 'Finot, my hundred francs!' written underneath and signed with a name which, though now well-known, will never be illustrious. Between the fireplace and the window stood a writing-desk with drawers, a document tray and an oblong hearth-rug: the whole was covered with a thick coating of dust. The windows had only short curtains. On the top of the desk were about twenty works which had been desposited there during the day, engravings, sheets of music, snuff-boxes with the 1814 Charter inscribed on the lid, a copy of the ninth edition of *The Solitary*, which was still the great joke of the moment, and a dozen sealed letters. When Lucien had inventoried this odd furniture and pondered lengthily upon it, and when it struck five, he returned to the pensioner to question him. Colocynth had finished his crust and was waiting as patiently as a soldier on sentry-go for the bemedalled officer, who was probably strolling about in the boulevard. At this moment, after the swish of a skirt and an easily recognizable feminine trip had been heard on the staircase, a woman appeared in the doorway. She was quite pretty.

'Monsieur,' she said, addressing Lucien. 'I know now why you cry up Mademoiselle Virginie's hats so much, and I have come to take out a subscription, for a year to start with. But tell me what the terms are . . . '

'Madame, I do not belong to the newspaper.'

'Oh!'

'A subscription to date from October?' asked the pensioner.

'What does Madame require?' said the old officer as he came in.

He began to confer with the fair milliner. When Lucien, tired of waiting, went back to the outer room, he heard this final sentence: 'But I shall be delighted, Monsieur. Mademoiselle Florentine can come to my shop and choose anything she wants. I have the ribbons in stock. So the matter is settled: you will say nothing more about Virginie. She's a bungler incapable of inventing a new shape. I'm a woman with ideas!'

Lucien heard a certain number of crown pieces tumbling into the cash-box. Then the officer began to make up his day's accounts.

'Monsieur, I have been here an hour,' said the poet with an air of annoyance.

'*They* haven't turned up,' said the Napoleonic veteran with a show of polite concern. 'I'm not surprised. I haven't seen them for some time. You see, it's the beginning of the month. The beggars only come on the 29th or the 30th for their pay.'

'And Monsieur Finot?' asked Lucien, having noted the editor's name.

'He's at his home in the rue Feydeau. – Colocynth, old boy, take him all that has come in today and get the copy off to the printer's.'

'Where then is the newspaper made up?' asked Lucien as if he were talking to himself.

'The newspaper?' said the cashier, taking the remainder of the stamp-money from Colocynth. 'The newspaper?' Hrrum! Hrrum! – Old boy, go to the printing-office to-morrow at six to see that the carriers get a move on. – The newspaper, Monsieur, is made up in the street, in the contributor's homes, in the printing-office, between eleven o'clock and midnight. In the Emperor's time, Monsieur, there were none of these waste-paper dumps about. *He* would have shaken all that off with a corporal and four men; *he* wouldn't have put up with all this claptrap. But I've said enough. If it suits my nephew's book and if they're writing for *his* son – Hrrum! Hrrum! – there's no harm in it after all. Well well!

Subscribers don't seem to be making a mass attack; I'm leaving the sentry-box.'

'Monsieur, you seem to know all about the editing of the newspaper.'

'The money side of it – Hrrum! Hrrum!' said the soldier, clearing his throat of all the phlegm it contained. 'It goes by talent: two or three francs for a column of fifty lines, each line having forty letters not counting the spaces. There you are! As for the contributors, they're a rum lot, these little whipper-snappers. I wouldn't have taken them on as rank-and-file soldiers. Because they cover blank paper with scrawl they seem to look down on an old captain of dragoons in the Imperial Guard, a retired battalion commander who went with Napoleon into every capital in Europe.'

Lucien, pushed towards the door by the Napoleonic veteran who was brushing his blue frockcoat and showing every intention of leaving, had the courage to block the exit.

'I have come for a job on the staff,' he said. 'And I assure you I have every respect for a captain of the Imperial Guard: they were men of bronze.'

'Well said, my little civvie,' the officer replied, giving him a tap on the stomach. 'But what class of contributors do you want to join?' the old trooper continued as he pushed by Lucien to go downstairs. He only halted in order to light his cigar at the concierge's lodge.

'Mother Chollet, if subscriptions come, take them in and make a note of them. – Subscriptions all the time, that's all I'm concerned with,' he added, turning to Lucien who had followed him. 'Finot's my nephew, the only one in my family who made things easier for me. And so whoever picks a quarrel with Finot finds himself up against old Giroudeau, captain of dragoons in the Imperial Guard, who started off as a cavalry trooper in the Sambre-et-Meuse army, and for five years was a fencing-master in the first Hussars, in the army of Italy. One, two! and the grouser's a gonner!' he imitated the lunge of a fencer as he said this.

'So then, young fellow, we have different corps in the editorial staff. There's the contributor who contributes and draws his pay, the contributor who contributes and draws no pay – what we call a volunteer; thirdly, there's the contributor who contributes nothing, and he's not the biggest fool among them: he never goes wrong, he pretends he's a writer, belongs to the newspaper, stands us dinners, loafs about in the theatres and keeps an actress; he's a very lucky one. Which do you want to be?'

'Why, a contributor who works well and therefore is paid well.'

'There you go, like all rookies who want to be field-marshals! Take old Giroudeau's advice: left wheel in single file, quick march, go and pick up nails in the gutter like that fine chap over there: you can see he's been in the service by the way he moves. Isn't it a scandal that an old soldier who's looked straight into the cannon's muzzle a thousand times should be picking up nails in Paris? God Almighty! You're a poor sort of God not to have stood by the Emperor! – In short, young man, the party you met this morning earned forty francs last month. Will you do better? And Finot says he's the cleverest man on his staff.'

'When you went into the battle of the Sambre-et-Meuse, were you told it was dangerous?'

'You bet I was!'

'Well then? . . .'

'Well then, go and see my nephew Finot, a fine chap, the straightest chap you'll meet – if you manage to meet him, for he darts about like a fish. In his trade, you see, he doesn't have to write but make other people write. It appears that these types prefer to dally with actresses rather than scribble on paper. Oh, they're a rum lot! Here's to our next meeting.'

The cashier thrust forward his fearful leaded cane – the sort that did good work at the first performance of *Germanicus* – and left Lucien standing in the street, as stupefied by this vision of an editor's office as he had been by the final results of literary effort in the office of Vidal and Porchon. He called ten times on Andoche Finot, the editor of the newspaper, in the rue Feydeau, without ever finding him. Early in the mornings, Finot was not yet back home. At midday he was out on business – he would be lunching, Lucien was told, at such and such a café. Lucien would go to that café and, overcoming his extreme repugnance, ask the barmaid for Finot: Finot had just left. Finally, worn out, Lucien looked on Finot as an apocryphal and fabulous personage, and found it simpler to watch for Etienne Lousteau at Flicoteaux's restaurant. No doubt this young journalist would explain the mystery over-hanging the existence of the newspaper to which he was attached.

8. The sonnets

SINCE that most blessed day when Lucien had made Daniel d'Arthez's acquaintance, he had changed his table at Flico-teaux's. The two friends dined side by side and chatted in a low voice about great literature, subjects to be treated and the manner of presenting, starting and finishing them. At present, d'Arthez was correcting the manuscript of *The Archer of Charles the Ninth*; he recast certain chapters, wrote the finest pages to be found in it and composed the splendid preface which perhaps overshadows the work but which brought so much illumination to writers of the new school. One day, just as Lucien was sitting down beside Daniel, who had been waiting for him, and while they were still shaking hands, he saw Etienne Lousteau turning the door-handle. He abruptly let go Daniel's hand and told the waiter he wanted to dine in his old place near the counter. D'Arthez looked at Lucien with one of those benign glances in which reproach is wrapped in forgiveness: it went so keenly to the poet's heart that he took hold of Daniel's hand and pressed it anew.

'This is a matter of importance for me,' he said. 'I'll tell you about it later.'

Lucien was in his former seat by the time Lousteau was taking his. He was the first to greet him, they soon got into conversation, and it was pursued with such animation that Lucien went off for the manuscript of *Les Marguerites* while

Lousteau finished his dinner. He had obtained leave to submit his sonnets to the journalist and was counting on his apparent benevolence in order to find a publisher or get a job with the newspaper. When he returned, Lucien saw Daniel in a corner of the restaurant, leaning sadly on his elbow and looking at him with melancholy; but Lucien was so poverty-stricken and so spurred on by ambition that he pretended not to see his brother of the Cénacle and followed Lousteau out.

Before evening fell, the journalist and the neophyte went and sat down under the trees in that part of the Luxembourg gardens which leads to the rue de l'Ouest from the broad Avenue de l'Observatoire. In those days this street was one long stretch of mud lined with boardings and marshes, with houses only beginning at the approach to the rue de Vaugirard. So few people passed along it that, at the dinner hour in Paris, a pair of lovers might well have a quarrel and start making it up without fear of being seen. The only possible spoil-sport was the veteran on sentry-go at the small gate opening on the rue de l'Ouest, if that venerable soldier took it into his head to increase the number of his monotonous rounds. It was in this alley, on a wooden bench, that Etienne listened to some samples chosen from *Les Marguerites*. Etienne, after two years of apprenticeship, had his foot in the stirrup as a newspaper man, and he counted some of the celebrities of that period among his friends: Lucien therefore found him an impressive figure. And so, as he unrolled the manuscript of *Les Marguerites*, the provincial poet deemed it necessary to deliver a sort of preface.

'The sonnet, Monsieur, is one of the most difficult forms of poetry and in general has been abandoned. No one in France has been able to rival Petrarch, whose native language, infinitely more supple than ours, allows conceits of thought repugnant to our *positivism* (if you will excuse the word). That is why I thought it original to begin with a collection of sonnets. Victor Hugo has taken to the ode, Canalis goes in for a wayward kind of poetry, Béranger monopolizes the *chanson*, while Casimir Delevigne has taken tragedy as his domain and Lamartine the "meditation".'

'Are you a classicist or a romantic?' asked Lousteau.

Lucien's air of surprise betokened such ignorance of the state of things in the Republic of Letters that Lousteau judged it necessary to enlighten him.

'My friend, you are coming into the thick of a fierce battle and must make a prompt decision. Literature is primarily divided into several zones; but our great men are split into two camps. The royalists are romantics, the liberals are classicists. Divergence in literary opinion is added to divergence in political opinion: hence war between fading and budding reputations, a war in which no weapons are barred: ink spilt in torrents, cutting epigrams, stinging calumnies, unrestrained abuse. By a strange anomaly, the romantic royalists call for literary freedom and the abrogation of laws which provide our literature with its conventional forms; while the liberals cling to the unities, regular rhythm in the alexandrine line and classical themes. And so in each camp literary opinions are at variance with political ones. If you stand aloof you will stand alone. Which side will you take?'

'Which is the stronger party?'

'The liberal press has far more subscribers than the royalist and ministerial press; nevertheless Canalis is making his way, even though he stands for monarchy and religion, even though he's protected by Court and Clergy. – Come now! Sonnets belong to the pre-Boileau literature,' said Etienne, seeing that Lucien was frightened at having to choose between two banners. 'Be a romantic. The romantics are all young folk and the classicists are *periwigs*: the romantics will win.'

The word 'periwig' was the latest epithet invented by romantic journalism for the adornment of the classicist.

'THE FIELD DAISY,' Lucien announced, choosing as a suitable beginning the first of two sonnets which justified the title of the collection:

> Not always for our vision's sole delight
> Field daisies, do you lavish your rich hues.
> There's poetry in them, and you, their Muse,
> Quicken our hopes and wake our inner sight.

Your golden stamens set in silver white
Are symbols of the treasures man pursues.
A thread of mystic blood your vein imbues
To show success is bought with pain and spite.

Was it to hail the Spring your buds unfurled
When Jesus, rising to a fairer world,
Showered forth virtues from His gracious wing?

And when you bloom afresh at Autumn's hour
Is it to tell us pleasures have their sting,
And radiant youth must fade like any flower?

Lucien's pride was piqued by Lousteau's complete un-responsiveness while listening to this sonnet. He was not yet acquainted with the disconcerting impassivity which hardened critics acquire and is a distinguishing mark in journalists equally tired of prose, drama and verse. Our poet, accustomed to receiving applause, gulped down his disappointment; he then read out the sonnet which was a favourite with Madame de Bargeton and some of his Cénacle friends.

'Perhaps,' he thought, 'this will wring a word from him.'

SONNET NO. TWO

THE MARGUERITE

I am the Marguerite. No fairer flower
Spangled the verdure of the velvet sward.
My simple beauty was its own reward
And morning freshness was my lasting dower.

Alas! against my will a new-born power
To me harsh fate was minded to award:
Prophetic gifts within my petals stored
Have brought me pain and death. O doleful hour!

No more in peace and silence do I live.
An answer to fond sweethearts must I give:
'He loves me, loves me not.' So runs the story

Torn from the gleaming whiteness of my gown.
– What other blossoms, thus despoiled of glory
But yield their secret to be trodden down?

When he had finished, the poet looked at his Aristarchus: Etienne Lousteau was contemplating the trees in the nursery plantation.

'Well?' asked Lucien.

'Well, my friend. Carry on. Am I not listening? In Paris, to listen without saying a word is high praise.'

'Perhaps you have had enough?' said Lucien.

'Continue,' was the journalist's reply.

Lucien then read the following sonnet; but he was filled with mortification, for Lousteau's inscrutable calm cast a chill on his recital. Had he had more experience of literary life, he would have known that, with writers, silence and curtness in such circumstances betoken the jealousy aroused by a fine work, just as their admiration denotes the pleasure they feel on listening to a mediocre work which confirms them in their self-esteem.

SONNET NO. THIRTY

THE CAMELLIA

Each flower's a word in Nature's book to read.
On love and beauty is the rose intent;
Sweet modesty the violets represent
And simple candour is the lily's screed.

But the Camellia, not of Nature's breed,
Unstately lily, rosebud void of scent,
To bloom in frigid seasons seems content
And chilly virgin's coquetry to feed.

Yet, in the theatre, when fair women lean
Over the balconies to view the scene,
Its alabaster petals give delight:

Snow-garlands, setting off the raven hair
Of love-inspiring ladies gathered there.
– No Phidias marble is more chastely white.

'What do you think of my poor sonnets?' Lucien asked in formal tones.

'Are you asking for the truth?' said Lousteau.

'I am young enough to love truth, and I am too anxious for success not to hear it without getting annoyed – but not without feeling despair.'

'Very well, my friend. The circumlocutions in the first one indicate a poem written in Angoulême, one which no doubt caused you too much effort for you to scrap it. The second and the third have more of a Paris atmosphere about them. But read me yet one more,' he added, with a gesture which the provincial prodigy found charming.

Encouraged by this request, Lucien was more self-confident in reading the sonnet which d'Arthez and Bridau liked best, perhaps because of the colour in it.

SONNET NO. FIFTY

THE TULIP

The Tulip I. From Dutch line I descend:
So exquisite and of so pure a strain
In brilliant hues on graceful stem I reign.
Flemings, to own me, half their substance spend.

To feudal ladyship I do pretend
And hold me stately like a châtelaine.
Gay colours doth my coat of arms contain:
Gules fessed with argent and with purple bend.

The heavenly Gardener tressed with loving hands
His sunbeam threads and royal purple strands
To weave for me a tunic soft and neat.

No flower in His own garden shows more fair,
Though in my cup of daintiest china-ware
Nature has stored no wealth of odours sweet.

'Well?' asked Lucien after a moment of silence which seemed to him inordinately long.

9. Good advice

'MY friend,' said Etienne Lousteau gravely, looking at the tips of the boots which Lucien had brought from Angoulême and which he was finishing wearing out. 'I advise you to black your boots with your ink in order to save boot-polish, to make toothpicks of your quill pens in order to give the appearance of having dined when, after leaving Flicoteaux's, you stroll along the beautiful walks in this garden, and look for some sort of job. Become a bailiff's man if you have pluck enough, a book-keeper if you prefer a sedentary life, or a soldier if you've a liking for military bands. You have the stuff of three poets in you; but, if you reckon to live on what your poetry brings in, you have time to die half a dozen deaths before you make your name. Now, judging by your rather youthful remarks, your intention is to coin money with your pen. I'm not passing judgement on your poetry: it's far better than all the volumes of verse which clutter up the bookshops. Almost all those "nightingales", marked at a slightly higher price than the others because they are printed on vellum, come fluttering down to the banks of the Seine, where you may go and study the songs they sing if one day you feel like making an instructive pilgrimage along the Paris quays from old Jérôme's secondhand bookstall on the Pont Notre-Dame as far as the Pont-Royal. There you will find all the *Essays in Poesy, Inspirations, Elevations, Hymns, Chants, Ballads, Odes,* in short all the clutches that have hatched out during the last seven years: muses covered with dust, spattered with mud by passing cabs, thumb-marked by all the idlers who want to look at the vignettes on the title-pages.

'You know nobody and have no access to any periodical: your *Marguerites* will still keep their petals chastely folded; they will never open their buds to the sunshine of publicity in the meadow of wide margins spangled with the floral designs which the illustrious publisher Dauriat, the monarch of the 'Galeries de Bois', lavishes on the works of his celebrities.

'My poor boy, like you I came here with my heart full of illusions, spurred on by the love of art, swept forwards by an invincible yearning for fame. I soon discovered the hard facts of the writer's trade, the difficulty of getting into print and the brutal reality of poverty. My enthusiasm, now deflated, and the effervescence of those early days made me blind to the mechanism which keeps the world moving: I had to see it in action, get caught up in the works, run foul of the shafts, get coated with grease and listen to the rattle of chains and fly-wheels. You will find out as I did that underneath your beautiful dream-world is the turmoil of men, passions and needs. You'll find yourself inevitably involved in the fearful struggles between one work and another, one man and another, one faction and another, and you'll have to wage systematic warfare to avoid being abandoned even by your own allies. These ignoble conflicts bring disenchantment to the soul, corruption to the heart and the weariness born of vain effort: for such effort often results in conferring glory on a man you hate, a man of second-rate talent put forward as a genius in spite of you. In literature, as in the theatre, much happens behind the scenes. Success, whether filched or merited, is what the pit applauds; the revolting tricks and dodges, the supernumeraries in their grease-paint, the hired clappers, the call-boys and scene-shifters, that's what it's not allowed to see. You are still watching from the pit. There's still time to abdicate before you set foot on the bottom step towards the throne for which so many people are fighting. Don't throw honour away, as I do, in order to live.'

Etienne Lousteau's eyes were moist with tears. 'Do you know how I live?' he continued with rage in his voice. 'The little money my family was able to give me was soon used up. I found myself penniless after getting a play accepted at the Théâtre-Français. At that theatre, even the patronage of a Prince or a First Gentleman of the Royal Bedchamber doesn't help one to jump the queue: the actors only give way to those who threaten their self-esteem. If you were able to spread a rumour that the *jeune premier* is asthmatic, that the *jeune première* has a fistula on some part of her body, that the *soubrette*'s breath is bad enough to kill flies on the wing, your play would be put on the very next day. I don't know whether in two years' time I myself shall be able to wield such power: one needs too many friends. Where, how and by what shifts was I to earn my daily bread? That was the problem which the pangs of hunger forced me to face. After many attempts, after writing an anonymous novel for which Doguereau – he didn't make much out of it – paid me two hundred francs, I plainly saw that I could only live by journalism. But how was I to get into the racket? I won't tell you of the steps I took and the applications I made in vain, nor of the six months I spent working as a supernumerary and being told I was scaring away the subscribers whereas in fact I was breaking them in. Let's pass over insults of that sort. Today I'm reviewing boulevard theatre plays, almost gratis, for the paper owned by Finot, that fat little man who still lunches two or three times a month at the Café Voltaire – a place you don't go to. Finot is the editor. I make my living by selling the tickets which the theatre managers give me to buy my benevolence as a subaltern member of his staff, also the books which publishers send me for review. Lastly, once Finot has had his cut, I make a bit out of the contributions in kind sent along by industrial concerns for or against which he allows me to launch articles. The makers of *Carminative Face-Lotion*, *Sultana Hand-Cream*, *Cephalic Oil* and *Brazilian Mixture* pay me twenty or thirty francs for a facetiously-worded commendation. I am forced to bark at the publisher who sends too few copies of his books to the paper: the paper takes two and Finot sells them; I also require two for sale. Even if he brings out a masterpiece, a publisher stingy with copies gets a drubbing. It's a dirty business, but I live by it, and so do hundreds of others. And don't imagine that the political world is much cleaner than the literary world: in both of them bribery is the rule; every man bribes or is bribed. When a publisher is bringing out a more or less important work, he pays me not to attack it. And so my income is in direct ratio to the prospectuses of forthcoming books. When prospectuses break out like measle spots money pours into my pocket and I stand my friends a meal. When there's nothing doing in the publishing line I dine at Flicoteaux's. Also actresses pay for the write-up we give them, though the wiliest ones pay merely to be criticized, for silence is what they fear most of all. And so a disparaging article, so worded that it can be turned inside out in another newspaper, is worth more and pays better than a dry commendation which is forgotten the next day. Polemics, my dear fellow, build a pedestal for celebrities. At this trade – as a hired assassin of ideas, industrial, literary and dramatic reputations – I make fifty francs a week; I can get a novel sold for five hundred francs and I'm becoming known as a man to be reckoned with. When, instead of living with Florine at the expense of a wholesale druggist who gives himself the airs of a lord, I settle down in a flat of my own, when I am promoted to a big newspaper and have my own daily article in it, on that day, my dear man, I shall make a great actress of Florine. As for me, I don't know what may be in store for me then: I may be a cabinet minister or even an honest man – anything may happen.'

He raised his downcast head and gazed up at the foliage of the trees with a look of despair which was both accusatory and frightening.

'And I have a fine tragedy which has been accepted! And I have among my papers a poem which will die on my hands! And once I was so kind and pure in heart! Now I have an actress at the Panorama-Dramatique for a mistress: I, who dreamt of splendid love affairs with the most distinguished women in high society! And lastly, because a publisher is one copy short in a book he sends to my paper, I run it down even though I admire it!'

Lucien, moved to tears, wrung Etienne's hand.

'Outside the literary world,' said the journalist, as they rose to their feet and made for the Grande Avenue de l'Observatoire which the two poets walked along as if to take more air into their lungs, 'there's not a single person who knows what a fearful Odyssey one has to pass through in order to acquire what one must call, according to the diversity of talents, popularity, vogue, reputation, renown, celebrity, public favour, the successive rungs on the ladder leading to fame – for which however they are never a substitute. The attainment of this brilliant zenith depends on so many and so rapidly varying chances that no example has occurred of any two men reaching it by the same route. Canalis and Nathan are two quite dissimilar cases, and they will not recur. D'Arthez, who is wearing himself out with work, will achieve fame by a different chain of events. Dame Reputation, whom so many men lust after, is almost always a crowned prostitute. Yes indeed, in relation to the lower kinds of literature she figures as the needy whore who stands shivering at street corners; in relation to second-rate literature, she's the kept woman who has come straight from the brothels of journalism – and I am one of her pimps; in relation to successful literature, she's the flashy, insolent courtesan with furnished apartments; she pays her taxes, is at home to eminent people and is kind or cruel to them by turns, has liveried servants and a carriage and is in a position to keep her anxious creditors waiting. Ah! those men who see in her – as I did yesterday, as you do today – an angelic creature with shining wings, clad in white tunic, with an evergreen palm in one hand and a flaming sword in the other, having some affinity both with the mythological abstraction that lives at the bottom of a well and the poor but honest maiden who lives in exile in a slum, whom only the beacon light of virtue and nobly courageous efforts lead to wealth, who flies back to Heaven with soul unsullied – unless of course she goes to her rest in a pauper's hearse, soiled, despoiled, raped and forgotten: those men, whose brains are circled with bronze, whose hearts still keep their warmth as they face the blizzards of experience, are rare in that place you see at your feet' – and he pointed to the great city with its smoke rising in the evening sky.

A vision of the Cénacle passed swiftly before Lucien's eyes and he felt moved, but he was swept along by Lousteau as the latter continued his appalling jeremiad.

'Such men are rare and sparse in this fermenting wine-vat, as rare as true lovers in the world of dalliance, as rare as honestly-acquired fortunes in the financial world, as rare as a man of integrity in journalism. The experience of the first person who told me what I am now telling you was wasted on me, just as mine no doubt will be useless to you. It's always the same story, every year the same enthusiastic inrush of beardless ambition from the provinces to Paris: an equal, indeed an increasing number of young men who leap forward, with high head and lofty heart, to their wooing of Fashion, the Princess Turandot of the *Thousand and One Days* to whom everyone would play Prince Calaf! But not one guesses the riddle and wins her. They all fall into the pit of misery, the mire of journalism, the morass of the book-trade. These mendicants go round like gleaners, picking up biographical articles, 'tartines', news-in-brief columns on the newspapers or else write books bespoken by the shrewd-minded pedlars of scrawl who prefer a piece of nonsense they can sell in a fortnight to a masterpiece which stays long on their hands. These caterpillars, squashed before they can turn into butterflies, live on shame and infamy: they're ready to bite or boost budding talent at the bidding of some pasha from the *Constitutionnel*, the *Quotidienne* or the *Journal des Débats*, on a hint from the publishers, at the request of a jealous colleague or often in return for a dinner. Those who get over the obstacles forget the squalor of their beginnings. I myself spent six months putting the best of my wit into some articles for a scoundrel who passed them off as his own and, on the strength of these samples, was put in charge of a *feuilleton*: he didn't take me on as a collaborator; he didn't even pay me five francs; and yet, when I meet him I'm obliged to shake hands with him.'

'But why?' Lucien asked with proud resentment.

'Because I may need to get a dozen lines into his *feuilleton*,' Lousteau coldly replied. 'In short, my friend, the key to success in literature is not to work oneself, but to exploit others' work. Newspaper-proprietors are contractors; we're their masons. And so, the more mediocre a man is, the sooner he arrives at success; he can swallow insults, put up with anything, flatter the mean and petty passions of the literary sultans like that newcomer from Limoges, Hector Merlin, who is already writing political articles in a Right Centre paper as well as working for our little rag: I have seen him stoop to pick up an editor's hat for him. By keeping on the right side of everybody, that fellow will edge in between rival ambitions while they are scuffling. I feel sorry for you. I see in you what I used to be, and I'm sure that in a year or two you'll be as I am now. You'll put this bitter advice down to some secret jealousy or self-interest, but it's prompted by the despair of a damned soul who can't get out of hell. No one else will dare to tell you what I'm shouting out to you with the grief of a disheartened man, like a second Job from his dung-heap: "Look upon my sores!"'

'I must fight; on this battle-field or another I must fight,' said Lucien.

'Then realize this!' continued Lousteau. 'It will be a fight to the death if you have any talent, for you'd have a better chance without it. The austerity of your conscience, which today is pure, will give way before those in whose hands you'll see that your future lies, those who with one word can give you life but will not speak that word: for, believe me, the author in fashion is harder and more insolent towards new-comers than the most brutal publisher: the one shows you out, the other tramples on you. In order to write fine works, my dear boy, you'll pump out in large penfuls all the tenderness, sap and energy in your heart, which you'll expose to view in the shape of passion, feeling and oratory. Yes, you'll write instead of acting, you'll sing instead of fighting, you'll do your loving, hating and living in the books you write; but when you've saved up your riches for your style, your gold and purple for your characters, when you walk in rags through the streets of Paris, happy to have launched on the world, in rivalry with the Registry Office, a creature named Adolphe, Corinna, Clarissa or Manon, when you've ruined your life and digestion giving birth to this creation, you'll see it slandered, betrayed, sold into slavery, deported to the salt marshes of oblivion by the journalists and committed to the grave by your best friends. Will you be able to wait for the day when your creation will spring to life once more –

resurrected by whom, when and how? There exists a magnificent book, the *cri du coeur* of incredulity, *Obermann*: it is languishing in solitude in the desert of the stock-rooms, and this is what the book-sellers ironically call a "nightingale". When will its Easter Day dawn? Who can tell? To start with, try and find a publisher daring enough to print *Les Marguerites*. It's not a question of getting paid for your poems, but of getting them into print. Do that, and you'll witness some curious scenes.'

This harsh tirade, delivered in tones varying with the passion it expressed, fell on Lucien like an avalanche of snow and chilled him to the heart. He stood there silent for a moment. At last, as though stimulated by the terrible poetry of difficulties ahead, he gave vent to a passionate outburst. Pressing Lousteau's hand, he exclaimed: 'I shall win through!'

'Well, well!' said the journalist. 'One more Christian going down into the arena to face the lions! My dear fellow, there's a first performance this evening at the Panorama-Dramatique. It doesn't begin till eight. It's six o'clock now. Go and put on your best clothes; in short, dress suitably. Come and call for me. I live in the rue de La Harpe, above the Café Servel, on the fourth floor. We'll visit Dauriat first of all. You really mean to go on with it? Right! I'll introduce you this evening to one of the kings of the book trade and a few journalists. After the show, we'll have supper in my mistress's flat with some friends, for the dinner we've had could scarcely be called a meal. There you'll meet Finot, the editor and owner of my paper. You know how Minette of the Vaudeville Theatre improved on the old proverb? *Time and bride wait for no man*. Well, luck might well be our bride: let's woo her!'

'I shall never forget this day,' said Lucien.

This affable friendliness, following the violent outcry of a poet describing the tactics of literary warfare, had as lively an effect on Lucien's mind as formerly, in the same spot, the grave, edifying words of d'Arthez had had. Excited by the prospect of an immediate wrestle between mankind and himself, the inexperienced young man had no idea how real was the spiritual degradation which the journalist had denounced.

He did not know he had to choose between two different paths, two systems for which the Cénacle and journalism respectively stood: the one way being long, honourable and certain, the other beset with reefs, dangerous, full of miry runnels in which his conscience was bound to get bedraggled. His nature urged him to choose the shorter and apparently more pleasant route, to snatch at rapid and decisive means. At this moment he could see no difference between d'Arthez's noble friendship and Lousteau's easy-going comradeship. His unstable mind looked on journalism as a weapon within his grasp, one he had skill enough to handle: he was resolved to take it up. Dazzled as he was by the proposals made by his new friend – the unceremonious handshake he gave as they parted seemed gracious to Lucien – how could he have known that, in the army of the Press, everyone needs friends as generals need soldiers! Lousteau, aware that Lucien's mind was made up, was recruiting him as a possible auxiliary. Lousteau was striking up a friendship for the first time and for the first time Lucien was taking to a patron. The one was out for a corporal's stripes, the other wanted to join the ranks.

10. A third variety of publisher

THE neophyte joyfully returned to his hotel, where he dressed up as carefully as on the disastrous day when he had tried to make a good impression in the Marquise d'Espard's opera-box. But his clothes already became him better – he had grown into them. He put on his fine, close-fitting, light-coloured trousers, some smart tasselled boots which had cost him forty francs, and his ball-room coat. He had his abundant, silky fair hair waved and perfumed, so that it streamed down in glistening curls. On his brow shone the audacity which he drew from the sense of his own worth and the future which lay before him. His woman's hands were carefully manicured, his almond-shaped finger-nails pink and well-shaped. His white, rounded chin offered a gleaming contrast to his black satin collar. Never did a more attractive-looking young man step down from the 'mountain' of the Latin quarter.

Handsome as a Greek god, Lucien took a cab, and at a quarter to seven he arrived at the door of the building which housed the Café Servel. The concierge invited him to climb four floors, giving him fairly complicated topographical instructions. Armed with this information, he found his way, not without difficulty, to an open door at the end of a long, dark corridor, and he recognized the sort of room typical of the Latin Quarter. Here, as in the rue de Cluny, in d'Arthez's room, in that of Chrestien and everywhere else, the poverty of youth dogged his footsteps. But everywhere poverty bears the distinctive mark imprinted on it by the character of its victim. In this room it was sinister. A walnut bed with no curtains, and under it a rucked-up, shabby secondhand carpet; at the windows, curtains yellowed by the smoke from a chimney which did not draw and also by cigar-smoke; on the hearth a Carcel lamp which Florine had given to Lousteau, but even that had come from a pawnbroker's shop; then a chest-of-drawers in discoloured mahogany, a table laden with papers, with two or three ruffled quill pens on it and no other books than those which had been brought in the evening before or on that very day: such was the furniture of this room, devoid of all articles of value, but presenting a tawdry collection of worn-out boots gaping in a corner, old socks full of holes; and in another corner cigar-stubs, dirty handkerchiefs, shirts which had run to two volumes and cravats which had reached their third edition. In short, it was a scribbler's camping-site, furnished with nondescript objects, of the strangest bareness imaginable. On the bedside table with its heap of books read that morning gleamed the red globe of a Fumade tinder-box. On the mantelpiece sprawled a razor, a pair of pistols and a cigar-box. On a wall panel Lucien saw some crossed foils under a fencing-mask. This furnishing was completed by three chairs and two armchairs hardly worthy of the cheapest tenement-house in the street. This room, at once dirty and dreary, gave evidence of a life lacking both repose and dignity: it was a place for sleeping in, for turning out scamped work; it was lived in of necessity, and one wanted nothing better than to get out of it. What a difference there was between this cynical disorderliness and the decent poverty in which d'Arthez lived! Lucien did not listen to the admonition this memory conveyed, for Etienne cracked a joke in order to gloss over the nudity of vice.

'This is my kennel: my show-place is in the rue de Bondy, in the new flat which our druggist has furnished for Florine; we have our house-warming this evening.'

Etienne Lousteau was wearing black trousers, well-polished boots and a coat which was buttoned up to the neck. His shirt – no doubt Florine provided him with a change of shirts – was concealed behind a velvet collar, and he was brushing his hat in order to give it a look of newness.

'Let's go,' said Lucien.

'Not yet. I'm waiting for a bookseller to give me some small change: there may be gambling. I haven't a farthing. And besides, I need some gloves.'

At this instant the two new friends heard steps in the passage.

'Here he comes,' said Lousteau. 'You're going to see, my dear fellow, what garb Dame Providence assumes when she manifests herself to poets. Before gazing on the fashionable publisher Dauriat in all his glory, you shall have seen the book-dealer of the Quai des Augustins, the one who discounts bills, the literary scrap-merchant, the wily Norman who was once a greengrocer. – Come in, you old Tartar!' cried Lousteau.

'Here I come,' said a man with a voice as quavering as that of a cracked bell.

'With money?'

'Money? There's none left in the book-trade,' replied a young man who, as he came in, looked at Lucien with an inquisitive air.

'To start with, you owe me fifty francs,' Lousteau went on. 'Next, here are two copies of *Travels in Egypt*, which is supposed to be marvellous: it's crammed with plates and will sell. Finot has been paid for the two articles I have to write on it. Next item: two of the latest novels by Victor Ducange, regarded by the readers of the Marais quarter as a first-rate author. Next item: two copies of the second work of a beginner, Paul de Kock, who writes the same kind of stuff. Next item, two copies of *Yseult de Dôle*, a pretty little provincial work. A hundred francs in all, list price. So you owe me a hundred francs, my little Barbet.'

Barbet looked over the books, carefully examining the edges and the covers.

'Oh! they're in perfect condition!' exclaimed Lousteau. 'The leaves of *Travels in Egypt* aren't cut, nor the Paul de Kock, nor the Ducange, nor the one on the mantelpiece, *Reflections on Symbolism*. I'll throw that one in, the mythology in it is so boring. I'll give it to you so that I needn't watch thousands of mites swarming out of it.'

'But,' asked Lucien, 'how will you write your reviews on them?'

Barbet gave Lucien a glance of profound astonishment and then looked back at Lousteau with a snigger. 'It's plain to see that this gentleman hasn't the misfortune to be a man of letters.'

'No indeed, Barbet. This gentleman is a poet who's going to wipe the floor with Canalis, Béranger and Delavigne. He'll go a long way – unless he jumps into the Seine, in which case he'll still get as far as Saint-Cloud.'[1]

'If I could offer a piece of advice to this gentleman,' said Barbet, 'it would be to give up verse and take to prose. There's no sale now for poetry on the quays.'

Barbet wore a shabby frock-coat fastened by a single button, a greasy collar, a hat which he kept on, and shoes; his waistcoat, agape, showed a good, coarse shirt of stout linen. Yet his round face, drilled with two greedy eyes, was not unprepossessing; but in his glance was the vague anxiety of people in the habit of being asked for money – and who in fact have money. He seemed straightforward and easy to deal with, so much was his astuteness padded round with plump-

1. I.e., to that part of the river to which corpses drifted and were fished up by the police.

255

ness. Having been first of all a shop assistant, he had, two years ago, taken over a wretched little stall on the quay; and from there he rushed to the journalists, authors and printers, buying up cheaply the complimentary copies of books sent to them and in this way earning from ten to twenty francs a day. Having saved up quite a lot of money, he scented out everyone's needs, kept his eye open for profitable bargains; for the benefit of hard-up authors, he discounted, at a rate of fifteen or twenty per cent, the bills which publishers had drawn for them; the next day he would go to these publishers in order to buy, at prices haggled over on a cash basis, a certain number of books in good demand; then he paid them with their own bills in lieu of money. He had had some schooling, and his education induced him to steer clear of poetry and up-to-date novels. He went in for small ventures – works of utility which he could buy up for a thousand francs and exploit as suited him, such as *A History of France for Children, Book-keeping in twenty Lessons, Botany for Girls*. He had already let two or three profitable books slip out of his hands after sending for their authors a score of times without making up his mind to buy their manuscripts. When he was blamed for his lack of courage, he instanced the report of a sensational law-suit, the manuscript of which, pirated from the newspapers, had cost him nothing but brought him two or three thousand francs.

Barbet was the cautious type of publisher who pinches and scrapes, draws few bills, niggles over invoices and pares them down, goes off Heaven knows where peddling his books himself, but disposes of them and gets paid for them. He was the terror of the printers, who didn't know how to cope with him: he demanded a discount on his payments and whittled down their charges, guessing that they were in urgent need of cash; then, for fear of them springing a trap on him, he gave no more orders to those he had fleeced.

'Well now,' said Lousteau. 'Let's get on with the business.'

'Look here, old boy,' said Barbet as one man to another. 'There are six thousand volumes for sale in my shop. Now, as an old bookseller said, books aren't bank-notes. The trade's in a bad way.'

'If you went to his shop, my dear Lucien,' said Etienne, 'this is what you'd find: an oak cash-desk, bought at some wine-merchant's bankrupt sale, and a tallow candle, never snuffed so that it may burn longer. In the dubious glimmer it gives, you'd see sets of empty shelves and, guarding this non-existent stock, a little boy in a blue jacket, blowing on his fingers, stamping his feet or flapping his arms like a coachman on his box. Look round and you'll see no more books than I have here. No one could guess what sort of trade goes on there.'

'Here's a bill for a hundred francs payable in three months,' said Barbet, unable to repress a smile as he pulled a stamped note of hand from his pocket. 'I'll take your books. Look, I can't pay in cash any more, sale being so difficult. I imagined you needed my help, I hadn't a penny, so I drew a bill to oblige you – and you know I don't like signing bills.'

'And what's more,' said Lousteau, 'you expect esteem and gratitude from me?'

'Paying drafts is no matter for sentiment,' Barbet replied. 'All the same, I don't mind having your esteem.'

'But I need gloves,' said Lousteau, 'and the shopkeepers won't have the courage to accept your bill. Come now, here's a superb engraving, here, in the top drawer of my chest. It's worth eighty francs. It's not out yet, but my article is, for I wrote an amusing one about it. It gave me a chance to get my teeth into Girodet's *Hippocrates refusing gifts from Artaxerxes*. Why now, this beautiful plate will be just the thing for all doctors who want to turn down the extravagant gifts of our Parisian satraps! And also you'll find about thirty drawing-room ballads below the engraving. Come on now, take the lot and give me forty francs.'

'Forty francs!' said the bookseller, squawking like a startled hen. 'Twenty at most. – And it might well be a dead loss to me,' he added.

'Out with your twenty francs,' said Lousteau.

'My goodness, I don't know if I have so much on me,' said Barbet, rummaging in his pocket. 'Here they are. You're stripping me bare . . . but you always get the better of me.'

'Come, let's get away,' said Lousteau, taking Lucien's manuscript and drawing a pen-stroke under the string.

'Have you anything more?' asked Barbet.

'Nothing, my little Shylock. But I'll put a splendid bit of business in your way.' – 'And,' he said in a whisper to Lucien, 'you'll go down three thousand francs on it. That'll teach you not to be such a skinflint.'

'But what about your review articles?' asked Lucien as they drove away to the Palais-Royal.

'Pooh! you've no idea how they're dashed off. Take *Travels in Egypt*: I opened the book and read a bit here and there without cutting the pages, and I discovered eleven mistakes in the French. I shall write a column to the effect that even if the author can interpret the duck-lingo carved on the Egyptian pebbles they call obelisks, he doesn't know his own language – and I shall prove it to him. I shall say that instead of talking about natural history and antiquities he ought only to have concerned himself with the future of Egypt, the progress of civilization, the means of winning Egypt over to France which, after conquering it and then losing it again, could still establish a moral ascendancy over it. Then a few pages of patriotic twaddle, the whole interlarded with tirades on Marseilles, the Levant and our trading interests.'

'But supposing he had done all that? What would you say then?'

'Well, I'd say that instead of boring us with politics he should have given his attention to Art and described the country in its picturesque and territorial aspects. Thereupon, as a critic, I fall to lamentation. We're snowed under with politics, I should say: it's boring, we can't get away from it. Then I should yearn for those charming travel books which explain all the difficulties of navigation, the thrill of winding through narrow straits, the delight of crossing the line, in short everything those who will never travel need to know. But, while commending them, one mocks at travellers who rhapsodize over a passing bird, a flying-fish, a haul of tunny, geographical points they have spotted and shallows they have recognized. One puts in a new claim for perfectly unintelligible scientific facts, which are so fascinating like everything which is profound, mysterious and incomprehensible. The reader laughs – he gets his money's worth. As regards novels, Florine is the greatest novel-reader in the world. She analyses them for me, and I knock off an article based on her opinion. When she's been bored by what she calls "literary verbiage" I take the book into serious consideration and ask the publisher for another copy. He sends it along, delighted at the prospect of a favourable review.'

'Great Heavens! But what about criticism, the sacred task of criticism?' said Lucien, still imbued with the doctrines of the Cénacle.

'My dear chap,' said Lousteau. 'Criticism's a scrubbing-brush which you mustn't use on flimsy materials – it would tear them to shreds. Now listen, let's stop talking shop. You see this mark?' he asked, pointing to the manuscript of *Les Marguerites*. 'I've inked a line in between the string and the paper. If Dauriat reads your manuscript, he certainly won't be able to put the string back along the line. So your manuscript is as good as sealed. It's not a bad dodge for the experiment you want to make. One more thing, just remember that you won't get into that sweatshop by yourself and without a sponsor: you'd be like those young hopefuls who go round to ten publishers before they find one who'll even offer them a chair ... '

Lucien had already tested the truth of this. Lousteau paid the cab-driver three francs, which left Lucien gaping, for he was surprised to see such prodigality after witnessing such great indigence. Then the two friends entered the Wooden Galleries, where the supposedly up-to-date publishers then reigned in all their glory.

11. The Wooden Galleries

At that period the Wooden Galleries constituted one of the outstanding curiosities of Paris. It will not be out of place to depict this disreputable bazaar, since for the last thirty-six years it has played so important a part in Parisian life that there are few men in their forties to whom the description of it – unbelievable to young folk – will not still give pleasure. On the site of the cold, lofty, broad Orleans Gallery, a kind of hot-house void of flowers, were shanties, or more exactly wood huts, poorly roofed, small, dimly lit on the court and garden side by lights of sufferance which passed for windows but which in fact were more like the dirtiest kind of aperture found in taverns beyond the city gates. A triple range of shops formed two galleries about twelve feet high. Shops sited in the centre looked out on to the two galleries, from which they borrowed their pestilential atmosphere and whose roofing allowed only a little light to filter through invariably dirty window-panes. These bee-hive cells had acquired so high a price thanks to the crowds which came there that, in spite of the pinched proportions of some of them – scarcely six feet wide and eight to ten feet long – they commanded a rent of three thousand francs a year. The shops drawing their light from the garden and court were hedged round with little fences of green trellis-work, perhaps in order to prevent the mob from rubbing against and demolishing the walls of crumbling plaster and rubble with which the shops were backed. So there was a space two or three feet wide in which vegetated the strangest botanical specimens – unknown to science – mingled with the varied, no less flourishing products of industry. Waste sheets of print hung round the tops of rose-trees in such a way that those flowers of rhetoric drew some scent from the stunted blooms in this untended garden watered only with fetid liquids. The foliage was beflowered with multicoloured ribbons or book-prospectuses. Vegetation was stifled by the flotsam and jetsam of fashion: you might find a bow of ribbon or a tuft of verdure, and you were disillusioned about the blossom you were inclined to admire when you found that what you thought was a dahlia was really a loop of satin. From court and garden alike this palace afforded a view of all the most bizarre products of Parisian squalor: anaemic colourwash, patched-up plaster-work, faded daubs, fantastic posters. Lastly, the green trellis-work in both garden and court was outrageously befouled by the Parisian public. Thus, on both sides, a disgraceful and nauseating fringe seemed calculated to keep any fastidious person from approaching the Galleries, but fastidious people no more recoiled from these horrors than the prince in a fairy tale recoils from dragons or any other obstacles interposed by some wicked genie between him and his princess. Then, as today, a passage ran through the middle of these Galleries, and, as today, you could go into it between the two peristyles still standing which had been begun before the Revolution but never completed for lack of funds. The fine stone gallery leading to the Théâtre-Français then formed a narrow passage, disproportionately high, and so badly roofed that the rain often came in. It was called the Glazed Gallery to differentiate it from the Wooden Galleries. The roofing of these hovels was moreover in such bad condition that the House of Orleans was sued by a dealer in cashmeres and other fabrics when he found that his merchandise had suffered considerable damage in the course of one night. He won his case. In some places a double tarpaulin provided the sole covering. The floor of the Glazed Gallery, where Chevet laid the foundations of his fortune, like that of the Wooden Galleries, was the natural soil of Paris, reinforced by the adventitious dirt brought in on the boots and shoes of passers-by. In all seasons, one's feet stumbled against mounds and depressions of caked mud; the shopkeepers were constantly sweeping them up, but newcomers had to acquire the knack of walking across them.

This sinister accumulation of refuse, these windows grimy with rain and dust, these squat huts with rags and tatters heaped around them, the filthy condition of the half-built walls, this agglomeration reminiscent of a gypsy camp or the booths on a fair-ground – the sort of temporary constructions which Paris heaps about the monuments it fails to build – this contorted physiognomy was wonderfully in keeping with the teeming variety of trades carried on beneath these brazenly indecent hutments, noisy with babble and hectic with gaiety, and where an enormous amount of business has been transacted between the two Revolutions of 1789 and 1830. For twenty years the Stock Exchange stood opposite, on the ground-floor of the Palais-Royal. There then public opinion was formed, reputations were made and unmade, political and financial affairs discussed. People met in these galleries before and after Stock Exchange hours. The Paris of bankers and merchants often encumbered the court-yard of the Palais-Royal and swarmed inside the building for shelter in rainy weather. It had sprung up haphazard in such a way as to become strangely like a sounding-board. It rang through and through with bursts of laughter. No quarrel could be started at one end of it without people at the other end knowing what it was about. It was the home ground of publishers, poets, pedlars of prose, politicians, milliners and, lastly the prostitutes who roamed about it in the evenings. There news buzzed and books by both young and established authors abounded. There Parliamentary conspiracies were hatched and publishers concocted their mendacities. There were sold the latest novelties which the public refused to buy elsewhere. There in one evening were sold several thousand copies of this or the other pamphlet by Paul-Louis Courier or *The Adventures of a King's Daughter*, the first broadside fired by the House of Orleans against the Charter of Louis XVIII. At the time when Lucien put in his first appearance there, a few shops had elegantly glazed front windows; but they belonged to the rows giving on to the garden or the courtyard. Until the day when this strange colony collapsed under the hammer of the architect Fontaine, the shops situated between the two galleries were entirely open and supported by pillars like booths in provincial fairs; the eye could see across the merchandise and the glass doors to the two galleries. Since heating was impossible, the shopkeepers had to put up with foot-warmers and were themselves responsible for the firemen's service, for, in a mere quarter of an hour, any careless act could start a fire in this commonwealth of timber dried by the sun, already smouldering, as it were, with the heat of prostitution, littered with gauze, muslin, paper, and ventilated by frequent draughts rushing through it.

The modistes' shops were full of unimaginable hats which seemed to be intended less for sale than for show, hanging in their hundreds on wire holders with mushroom knobs and decking the galleries with their manifold colours. For twenty years people strolling through the galleries have been wondering whose heads these dusty hats at last adorned. Seamstresses, usually ugly but free of speech, accosted women with artful words, adopting the manners and diction of the Parisian Covent Garden. A milliner's assistant, glib of tongue and bold of eye, would stand on a stool and harry passers-by: 'Won't you buy a pretty hat, Madame? Won't you let me sell you something, Monsieur?' Their rich and colourful vocabulary drew variety from their modulations of tone, the looks they gave and the jibes they made at passers-by. Booksellers and shopkeepers lived on good terms together. In the passage so pompously styled the Glazed Gallery the most singular avocations were to be found. There ventriloquists plied their trade, and charlatans of every kind, mountebanks who had nothing to show and others who showed you everything. There for the first time a man set up a concern by which he has made seven or eight thousand francs on the fair-grounds. The sign over his booth was a sun revolving in a black surround, and about it these words were inscribed in flaming red: *Here man sees what God cannot see. Price one penny*. The 'barker' never admitted one man by himself, nor ever more than two people. Once inside, you found yourself facing a large mirror. Suddenly a voice which might have terrified Hoffmann himself rang out like a mechanical contrivance when a spring is released: 'You see here, gentlemen, what through all eternity God cannot see, namely a fellow-creature. God has no fellow-creature!' You went out ashamed of yourself without daring to confess your stupidity. From behind every small door similar voices could be heard vaunting Cosmoramas, views of Constantinople, marionette shows, automata playing chess and dogs which could pick out the most handsome woman present. The ventriloquist Fitz-James had his heyday there, in the Café Borel, with Poly-technic students all around him, before he met his death in the fighting at Montmartre.

There were fruit-sellers and flower girls, and a famous tailor whose military embroideries glimmered through the dusk like so many stars. In the mornings, until two-thirty in the afternoons, the Wooden Galleries were mute, sombre and deserted. The shopkeepers chattered among themselves as if they were at home. The Paris population only began to congregate there at about three o'clock, when the Stock Exchange opened. Once the crowd arrived, young people hungry for literature but out of cash did their reading – gratis – at the booksellers' shopwindows. The assistants employed to watch over the books exposed for sale charitably allowed these poor young men to go on turning the pages. When it was a matter of a 12-mo volume of two hundred pages, as with *Smarra, Pierre Schlemilh, Jean Sbogar* or *Jocko*, it was devoured in two sessions. At that time there were no free public reading-rooms: one had to buy a book to read it, and so the number of volumes then sold would seem fabulous today. There was therefore something typically French in this charity shown to the juvenile intelligence, avid and poverty-stricken. As evening fell, this terrible bazaar became resplendent in its poetry. From every adjacent street there came and went a large number of prostitutes who were allowed to walk up and down without charge. From every direction street-walkers were hurrying along to 'do the Palais-Royal'. The Stone Galleries belonged to privileged brothels which paid for the right to parade gaudily dressed creatures between such and such an arcade and in the garden square into which they opened; but the Wooden Galleries were a happy hunting-ground for the commoner kind: they were supereminently 'The Palais', which at that time meant that they were the temple of prostitution. A woman could arrive there, go off with her capture and take him wherever she thought fit. Consequently, every evening, these women attracted so considerable a crowd to the Wooden Galleries that it was only possible to move along at a snail's pace, as in a procession or at a fancy-dress ball. This slow progress worried no one since it gave an opportunity for gaping. The clothes worn by these women are now a thing of the past. Their habit of wearing dresses cut low at the back and very low also in front; their quaint hair-styles devised to draw attention, here perhaps a Norman and there a Spanish *coiffure*; one street-walker all in curls like a poodle, another with sleek hair parted down the middle; legs enclosed in tight-fitting white stockings and displayed in various ways, but always to advantage: all this inglorious poetry has gone. The licentiousness of invitation and response, the open-air cynicism so in keeping with the locality are no longer to be found, not even in fancy-dress balls or the notorious public dances of our times. It was horrible but gay. The gleaming flesh of shoulders and bosoms stood out amid the almost invariably sombre hues of male costumes, producing the most magnificent contrasts. The hum of voices and the sound of pattering feet made a hubbub which could be heard from the middle of the garden as one continuous bass note punctuated with the shrill laughter of the prostitutes or shouts raised in occasional squabbles. Respectable persons and men of the greatest consequence rubbed shoulders with people who looked like gallows-birds. These monstrous gatherings had an indefinable piquancy which affected even the most insensitive persons. That is why the whole of Paris congregated there right up to the last moment and paced along the wooden flooring with which the architect of the new construction covered his basements. The demolition of these ignoble wooden erections aroused wide-spread and unanimous regret.

A few days previously the publisher Ladvocat had set up his premises at the corner of the passage running through the middle of the Galleries, opposite those of Dauriat, a now forgotten but very enterprising young man who blazed the trail which his rival so brilliantly followed. Dauriat's shop stood in one of the rows which gave on to the garden; Ladvocat's shop faced the court. Dauriat's shop was divided into two parts, one of which provided him with a vast storehouse for his books while the other served as his office. Lucien, arriving there that evening for the first time, was stunned at the sight of it, so irresistible was the impression it made on provincials and young men. He had soon lost touch with his guide.

'If you were as handsome as that boy over there, I'd return your love!' a trollop said to an old man as she pointed to Lucien.

This made Lucien as shy as a blind man's dog; he followed the torrent of people in a state of stupefaction and excitement difficult to describe. Harassed by the ogling of the women, tempted and dazzled by the white rotundity of shamelessly-exposed bosoms, he clung to his manuscript and held it tight against him for fear, poor innocent, of having it stolen!

'What do you want, sir?' he exclaimed as someone took hold of his arm – he thought that his poetry might have aroused some author's curiosity.

Then he recognized his friend Lousteau, who said to him: 'I knew very well you'd come this way in the end!'

12. A publisher's bookshop in the Wooden Galleries

LUCIEN was actually at the door of Dauriat's shop and Lousteau showed him in: it was full of people waiting to speak to the high and mighty Prince of the book-trade. Printers, paper-makers and cartoonists grouped round the assistants were questioning them about matters in hand or in prospect.

'Look. There's Finot, the director of my paper, chatting with a talented young man, Felicien Vernou, a little rascal who's as nasty as an unmentionable disease.'

'Well now, you've a first performance on tonight, old chap,' said Finot as he and Vernou came up to Lousteau. 'I've disposed of your box.'

'You've sold it to Braulard?'

'Well, why not? You'll find a seat. What have you come to ask Dauriat for? By the way, it's agreed that we cry up Paul de Kock: Dauriat has taken over two hundred copies of his book and now Victor Ducange is refusing him a novel. Dauriat says he wants to build up a new author in the same line. So you'll put Paul de Kock over Ducange.'

'But Ducange and I have a play on at the Gaieté,' said Lousteau.

'All right, you'll tell him I wrote the article. You'll make out I did a savage review and that you toned it down: he'll be grateful to you.'

'Couldn't you get Dauriat's cashier to discount this little hundred francs bill for me?' Etienne asked Finot. 'You know we're having supper together for the house-warming of Florine's flat.'

'Oh of course, you're standing treat,' said Finot, pretending to be making an effort of memory. 'Here, Babusson,' he added, taking Barbet's note of hand and presenting it to the cashier. 'Give this man ninety francs for me. – Endorse it, old chap.'

Lousteau took the cashier's pen while the latter was counting out the money and signed it. Lucien, all eyes and ears, lost not one syllable of this conversation.

'There's something else, my dear friend,' Etienne continued. 'I won't thank you: I'm yours through thick and thin. But I want to introduce this gentleman to Dauriat, and you might well get him to listen to us.'

'What about?' asked Finot.

'A collection of poems,' Lucien answered.

'Oh!' said Finot with a shrug.

'This gentleman,' said Vernou, looking towards Lucien, 'hasn't had much to do with the book-trade, otherwise he would already have locked his manuscript up in the remotest recesses of his domicile.'

At this moment a handsome young man, Emile Blondet, who had just made a beginning on the staff of *Le Journal des Débats* with articles of far-reaching importance, came in, shook hands with Finot and Lousteau and gave a light nod to Vernou.

'Come and have supper with us, at midnight, in Florine's flat,' said Lousteau to Blondet.

'Fine,' said the young man. 'But who'll be there?'

'Oh!' said Lousteau. 'Florine and Matifat the druggist, Du Bruel, the dramatist who gave Florine her first part; a little old man, Cardot senior and his son-in-law Camusot; also Finot . . .'

'Does he do things decently, your druggist?'

'He won't feed us on drugs,' said Lucien.

'Monsieur is very witty,' said Blondet, keeping a straight face as he glanced at Lucien. 'Will he be at the supper, Lousteau?'

'Yes.'

'We *shall* have fun!'

Lucien had blushed up to the ears.

'How long are you going to be, Dauriat?' asked Blondet, knocking on the window-pane through which one could look down on Dauriat's writing-desk.

'My friend, I'm just coming.'

'Good,' said Lousteau to his protégé. 'This young man, almost as young as you, is on the staff of the *Journal des Débats* and he's already a star critic: he commands respect, Dauriat will come and butter him up, and then we shall be able to state our business to this Pasha of vignettes and printing. Otherwise even at eleven o'clock we should still be waiting our turn. He'll be giving audience to more and more people as time goes on.'

Lucien and Lousteau then drew close to Blondet, Finot and Vernou went to form a group at the other end of the shop.

'What's he doing?' Blondet asked of Gabusson, the head assistant, who stood up to greet him.

'He's buying a weekly journal which he wants to ginger up to counteract the influence of the *Minerve Française* which is too devoted to Eymery's interests, and that of the *Conservateur* which is too blindly Romantic.'

'Will he pay well?'

'Of course, as always . . . too well!' said the cashier.

Just then there entered a young man who had recently

published a magnificent novel which had sold quickly and met with brilliant success: a second edition of it was being printed for Dauriat. This young man, got up in the quaint and extraordinary clothing which distinguishes the artistic temperament, made a vivid impression on Lucien.

'This is Nathan,' Lousteau whispered to the provincial poet.

Nathan, despite the independence and pride imprinted on his countenance, which was then in the bloom of youth, approached the journalists hat in hand and presented an almost humble demeanour to Blondet whom so far he only knew by sight. Blondet and Finot kept their hats on.

'Monsieur, I am glad of the opportunity which an opportune moment offers me . . . '

'He's so flustered he's committing pleonasms,' said Félicien to Lousteau.

' . . . of expressing my gratitude for the fine article you wrote about me in the *Journal des Débats*. Half the success of my book is due to you.'

'No, no, my friend,' said Blondet with an air of condescension disguised as geniality. 'You are a man of talent, damn it, and I am delighted to make your acquaintance.'

'Since your article is out, I shall not appear to be seeking your favour: we can now be on unconstrained terms with one another. Will you do me the honour and the pleasure of dining with me tomorrow? Finot will join us – and you, Lousteau, old man, you won't refuse me?' As Nathan said this he gave a handshake to Etienne. 'Oh indeed, Monsieur,' he said to Blondet, 'you've a fine career before you. You're carrying on the work of such men as Dussault, Fiévée, Geoffroi. Hoffmann was talking about you to Claude Vignon, one of my friends who was his pupil, and he told him he could die in peace, for the *Journal des Débats* would live for ever. They must pay you an enormous amount?'

'One hundred francs a column,' Blondet replied. 'It's not a great deal when one's obliged to read a hundred books in order to find one worth writing about – like yours. Your work gave me great pleasure, you have my word for it.'

'And it brought him fifteen hundred francs,' said Lousteau to Lucien.

'But you're writing on politics?' asked Nathan.

'Yes, a little here and there,' Blondet answered.

Lucien, feeling himself a tiro in this gathering, had admired Nathan's book, revered him as a god, and was stupefied at such a show of servility in front of this critic whose name and significance were unknown to him.

'Could I ever behave like this myself?' he asked himself. 'Must one really sacrifice one's dignity? – Put your hat on, Nathan! You've written a fine book and the critic has merely written an article.' Such thoughts made his blood boil. As one moment followed another, he saw timid young men, needy authors begging for a word with Dauriat, but who, seeing that the shop was full, despaired of gaining a hearing and went out saying: 'I'll come back.' Two or three politicians were talking of the summoning of Parliament and public affairs amid a group composed of political celebrities. The weekly journal whose purchase Dauriat was negotiating enjoyed the right of political discussion. In those days periodicals officially authorized to discuss politics were becoming rare. The privilege of running a newspaper was as much sought after as that of running a theatre. One of the most influential shareholders of *Le Constitutionnel* happened to be in the centre of this group of politicians. Lousteau was admirably acquitting himself of his task as cicerone. And so, as one sentence succeeded another, Dauriat became greater and greater in Lucien's estimation: it seemed to him that in this shop politics and literature converged. Our great man from the provinces learnt some terrible truths from the sight of an eminent poet prostituting the Muse to a journalist and thereby debasing Art, just as Woman was debased and prostituted in these squalid Galleries. Money! That was the answer to every riddle! Lucien felt that he was alone, a stranger, with only the thread of a dubious friendship to guide him to success and fortune. He blamed his tender and true friends of the Cénacle for having described the world to him in false colours, for having prevented him from throwing himself, pen in hand, into this battle. 'I might already be a Blondet,' he exclaimed to himself. Lousteau, who only recently had been crying out like a wounded eagle on the heights of the Luxembourg gardens and whom he had then considered so great, had by now dwindled to minimal proportions. In this place, the fashionable bookseller-publisher, the middleman in the life of all these men, seemed to him to be the really important figure. Clutching his manuscript, the poet was a prey to a trepidation which came close to fear. Inside this shop, on pedestals of wood painted to look like marble, he could see various busts – one of Byron, one of Goethe and one of Monsieur de Canalis, from whom Dauriat was hoping to extract a volume and who, on the day he had first visited the shop, had been able to gauge how highly his work was assessed in publishing circles. Involuntarily, Lucien felt less confident of his own worth, his courage weakened, he foresaw the influence Dauriat was to exert over his destiny, and he waited impatiently for him to appear.

13. *A fourth variety of publisher*

'WELL, children,' said a portly little man with a face rather like that of a Roman proconsul, though its expression was softened by an air of geniality which took in superficial observers. 'Here I am, the owner of the sole weekly on the market, one with two thousand subscribers.'

'Humbug!' said Blondet. 'It's seven hundred according to the stamp duty, and even that's nothing to sneeze at.'

'On my most solemn word of honour, there are twelve hundred. – I said two thousand,' he added *sotto voce*, 'to impress the paper-makers and printers here present. – I thought you had more tact, my boy,' he continued out loud.

'Are you taking partners?' asked Finot.

'That depends,' said Dauriat. 'Would you like a third share in it for forty thousand francs?'

'Agreed, if you'll take on the staff Emile Blondet – he's

here – Claude Vignon, Scribe, Théodore Leclerc, Félicien Vernou, Jay, Jouy, Lousteau . . . '

'And why not Lucien de Rubempré,' the provincial poet boldly interjected before Finot had finished.

'And Nathan,' said Finot, concluding his list.

'And why not all the people strolling about here?' rejoindered the publisher, knitting his eyebrows as he turned towards the author of *Les Marguerites*. 'To whom have I the honour of speaking?' he said, looking at Lucien with an insolent air.

'Just a minute, Dauriat,' Lousteau replied. 'It is I who have brought this gentleman to you. While Finot is considering your proposition, listen to me.'

Lucien felt hot under the collar as he observed the cold and frowning demeanour of this redoubtable Padishah of the publishing trade; a man who thou'd Finot although Finot addressed him as 'you', who called the much feared Blondet 'my lad' and who had offered his hand to Nathan in regal fashion and greeted him with a gesture of familiarity.

'A new piece of business, my lad,' Dauriat exclaimed. 'But do you know I have eleven hundred manuscripts to deal with? Yes, gentlemen,' he shouted. 'I've been offered eleven hundred manuscripts. Ask Gabusson. In fact I shall soon need an administrative staff to control the receipt of manuscripts and a reading committee to examine them; there'll be meetings to vote on their merit, with attendance vouchers and a permanent secretary to draw up reports for me. It's going to be like a branch of the French Academy, and my academicians will be better paid here in the Wooden Galleries than those at the Institut de France.'

'Quite an idea!' said Blondet.

'A bad idea,' Dauriat went on. 'It's not my business to sift the lucubrations of those among you who take to literature just because they can't be capitalists, bootmakers, army corporals, domestic servants, civil servants or bailiffs. There's no admittance here except to established reputations! Make your name, and gold will come flooding your way. In the last two years I've brought three people into the limelight, which means that I've brought triple ingratitude on myself. Nathan is claiming six thousand francs for the second edition of his book, which cost me three thousand francs in review articles and didn't bring me a thousand francs. As for Blondet's two articles, they cost me a thousand francs and a dinner which set me back five hundred francs . . . '

'And yet, Monsieur, if all the publishers talk like that, how can one get a first book into print?' asked Lucien, whose respect for Blondet diminished enormously when he learned how much Dauriat had paid him for the articles in the *Journal des Débats*.

'That's no concern of mine,' said Dauriat, fixing a murderous stare on the handsome Lucien who looked at him amiably in return. 'I don't publish books for fun. I don't risk two thousand francs just to get two thousand francs back. I'm a speculator in literature. I publish a work in forty volumes at ten thousand copies, just like Panckoucke and the Baudouin brothers. I use the power I have and the articles I pay for to launch a three hundred thousand francs venture rather than a volume in which only two thousand francs are invested. It costs as much effort to get a new name accepted – an author and his book – as to promote the success of works such as the *Masterpieces of Foreign Drama, French Victories and Conquests* or *Memoirs on the French Revolution*: and there's a fortune in them. I'm not here to be a springboard for future reputations, but to make money for myself and provide some for the celebrities. A manuscript which I buy for a hundred thousand francs costs me less than the one some unknown author expects me to buy for six hundred francs! Maybe I'm not quite a Mæcenas, but literature owes me some gratitude: I've already more than doubled the price which manuscripts fetch.'

'I'm explaining all this to you, young man,' said Dauriat to the poet, patting him on the shoulder with a gesture of revolting familiarity, 'because you're a friend of Lousteau. If I talked to all the authors who want me to publish their works, I should have to shut up shop – I should spend my time having extremely agreeable but much too expensive conversations. I'm still not rich enough to listen to all the monologues dictated by self-esteem. That only happens on the stage in classical tragedies.'

The luxury of this terrible man's apparel added emphasis, in the eyes of the provincial poet, to the cruel logic of his discourse.

'What *is* this manuscript?' Dauriat asked of Lousteau.

'A splendid volume of verse.'

At the word 'verse' Dauriat turned to Gabusson with a gesture worthy of the great actor Talma. 'Friend Gabusson, from now on, anybody who comes asking me to publish manuscripts . . . Take this in, the rest of you,' he said, addressing three shop-assistants who emerged from the piles of books on hearing the choleric tones of their employer, whose eyes were fixed on his finger-nails and his shapely hands. 'Whenever anyone brings manuscripts for me, you'll ask if they are in verse or prose. If they're in verse, get rid of them straight away. Verse will ruin the book-trade!'

'Well said! Dauriat's quite right,' the journalists cried out in chorus.

'It's a fact,' the publisher exclaimed, walking up and down his shop with Lucien's manuscript in his hand. 'You don't know, gentlemen, how much harm has been done by the success which came to Lord Byron, Victor Hugo, Casimir Delavigne, Canalis and Béranger. Their fame has brought us a new barbarian invasion. I'm sure that, at this very moment, publishers are having to cope with a thousand volumes of poetry which start off with disconnected stories of which you can't make head or tail, imitations of *The Corsair* and *Lara*. Under pretext of originality, young people go in for incomprehensible stanzas and descriptive poems, and this new school of poets claims originality by re-inventing Delille! During the last two years poets have multiplied like may-bugs. Last year I lost twenty thousand francs on them – ask Gabusson! The world may well be swarming with immortal poets – I've seen some with such fresh, pink faces that they haven't yet started shaving!' – he said this for Lucien's benefit – 'but as far as the book-trade is concerned, young man, there are only four poets: Béranger, Casimir Delavigne, Lamartine and

Victor Hugo. As for Canalis, he's been made a poet by the reviews he's had!'

Lucien did not feel courageous enough to pull himself together and stand on his pride in front of these influential men and their hearty laughter. He realized that he would cover himself with ridicule, but he felt a violent urge to leap at the publisher's throat, disarrange the insulting harmony of his knotted cravat, break the gold watch-chain glittering on his chest, stamp on his watch and tear him to pieces. Exasperated self-esteem opened the way to vengeful thoughts, and he vowed mortal hatred to the publisher while showing a smiling face.

'Poetry is like the sun: it makes the eternal forests grow but also engenders gnats, midges and mosquitos,' said Blondet. 'There's nothing good that doesn't bring something bad in its wake. Literature, for example, engenders publishers.'

'Journalists also!' said Lousteau.

Dauriat gave a great guffaw.

'Anyway, what's in it?' he asked, pointing to the manuscript.

'A collection of sonnets which would make Petrarch sing small,' Lousteau answered.

'What do you mean by that?' asked Dauriat.

'What anybody would mean,' said Lousteau, noticing that everybody's lips were curled in a sarcastic smile.

Lucien could not show how annoyed he was, but he was sweating like a horse under harness.

'All right, I'll read it,' said Dauriat with a princely gesture which showed what a great concession he was making. 'If your sonnets come up to the nineteenth-century standard I'll turn you out as a great poet, my lad.'

'If he's as intelligent as he's handsome, you're not taking a big risk,' said one of the most famous orators of the Chambre des Députés who was chatting with a member of the *Constitutionnel* staff and the director of the *Minerve*.

'General,' said Dauriat, 'fame costs twelve thousand francs in reviews and three thousand francs in dinners. Ask the author of *Le Solitaire*. If Monsieur Benjamin Constant is ready to write an article on this young poet, I'll not take long to do a deal.'

At the word 'General' and the mention of the illustrious name of Benjamin Constant, the book-shop took on the proportions of Olympus in the eyes of the provincial prodigy.

'Lousteau, I want a word with you,' said Finot. 'But I'll see you again at the theatre. Dauriat, it's a deal – but on certain conditions. Let's go into your office.'

'Come in, my boy,' said Dauriat, ushering Finot in. Making the gesture of a busy man to the dozen persons who were waiting for him, he was about to disappear inside when Lucien, feeling impatient, halted him.

'You are keeping my manuscript then. When can I expect your decision?'

'Well, my little poet, come back in three or four days. We'll see.'

Lucien was dragged off by Lousteau without being given time to take his leave either of Vernou, Blondet, Raoul Nathan, General Foy or Benjamin Constant, whose *Letters on the Hundred Days* had just appeared. Lucien scarcely caught more than a glimpse of his fair hair and fine head, his oblong face, his intelligent eyes, his attractive mouth, in short of the man who for twenty years had been the Potemkin of Madame de Staël and was making war on the Bourbons after making war on Napoleon, but whose fate it was to die from the shock of the victory he had won.

14. Behind the scenes

'What an emporium!' Lucien exclaimed when he had taken his seat in a cab beside Lousteau.

'To the Panorama-Dramatique, and drive fast – you'll get thirty sous for the journey,' said Etienne to the cabby. Then he replied to Lucien's remark, his self-esteem agreeably tickled at being able to pose as Lucien's mentor. 'Dauriat's a rogue who sells about fifteen or sixteen hundred thousand

276

francs' worth of books every year. His rapacity is just as great as Barbet's, but he operates on a massive scale. Dauriat has some civility, he can be generous, but he's vain. What wit he has is made up from what he hears people around him saying. His shop is an excellent meeting-place, and gives one a chance to chat with the best minds of our time. There, my friend, a young man learns more in an hour than he would in ten years poring over books. Articles are discussed, subjects are concocted, contact is made with famous or influential men who may prove useful. Today, in order to succeed, one needs to be in with such people. It's all a matter of chance, you see. The most dangerous thing is to churn out wit all alone in a corner.'

'But the insolence of the man!' said Lucien.

'Pooh! We all make fun of Dauriat. You need him and he tramples on you; but he needs the *Journal des Débats*, and Emile Blondet spins him round like a top. Oh! if you get into the writing racket you'll learn a lot more yet. Well now, didn't I tell you so?'

'Yes, you're right,' Lucien answered. 'In Dauriat's shop, I suffered even more cruelly than I expected according to your plan of action.'

'But why let yourself suffer? The thing we give our lives for, the subject we rack our brains over and wrestle with for nights on end, the race we run across the fields of thought, the monument we build with our heart's blood: editors regard all that as a good or a bad piece of business. Your manuscript will sell well or it won't. That's their whole problem. For them a book is merely a capital risk. The finer it is, the less chance it has of selling. Every exceptional man rises above the masses, and therefore his success is in direct ratio to the time needed for his work to prove its value. No publisher is willing to wait for that. Today's book must be sold out tomorrow. Following that policy, publishers refuse substantial books which can only gradually obtain the serious approval they need.'

'D'Arthez was right,' Lucien exclaimed.

'So you know d'Arthez,' said Lousteau. 'I know nothing

more dangerous than those lone spirits who think, as that fellow does, they can bring the world to their feet. By firing a young man's imagination with a flattering belief in the immense power which at first everyone feels he possesses, such seekers after posthumous glory prevent him from bestirring himself at an age when activity is possible and profitable. I'm all for Mahomet's policy: he commanded the mountain to come to him and then cried out: "If you won't come to me, I'll go to you!"

This sally, which had such forceful logic behind it, was of a kind to make Lucien waver between the system of resigned poverty preached by the Cénacle and the militant doctrine put forward by Lousteau. And so the poet from Angoulême relapsed into silence until they arrived at the Boulevard du Temple.

The Panorama-Dramatique, now replaced by a private house, was a charming theatre standing opposite the rue Charlot in the Boulevard du Temple. Two of its managing bodies in turn succumbed without scoring a single success, although Vignol, one of the actors who took over from Potier, made his *début* there, as well as Florine, the actress who was to become so famous five years later. Theatres, like men, are dependent on chance events. The Panorama-Dramatique had to compete with L'Ambigu, La Gaieté, La Porte-Saint-Martin and the musical comedy theatres: it was unable to hold out against their machinations, the restricted terms of its licence and the shortage of good plays. Authors were not inclined to fall out with established theatres in favour of one whose existence seemed problematical. However, the management was counting on the new play, a kind of comic melodrama by a young author, du Bruel, a man who wrote in collaboration with a few reputed authors but claimed to have written this one by himself. It had been composed for Florine's *début*: until then she had been an extra at La Gaieté, where for a year she had had walking-on parts in which she had drawn attention to herself without being able to secure an engagement; and so the Panorama had enticed her away from the neighbouring theatre. Another actress, Coralie, was also to make her *début* in this play.

When the two friends arrived, Lucien was amazed to see what power the Press wielded.

'This gentleman is with me,' said Etienne to the box-office man who bowed obsequiously to him.

'You'll find it very difficult to get seats,' said the chief ticket-collector. 'The only ones left are in the manager's box.'

Etienne and Lucien wasted some time wandering along corridors and parleying with box-openers.

'Let's go inside. We'll speak to the manager and he'll let us into his box. Besides, I want to introduce you to Florine, the star of the evening.'

At a sign from Lousteau, the orchestra usher took a small key and unlocked a concealed door in a large wall. Lucien followed his friend and passed suddenly out of the well-lit corridor into the black hole which in practically every theatre connects front and back-stage. Then, walking up a few damp steps, the provincial poet arrived behind the scenes, where the strangest of spectacles awaited him. The narrowness of the supporting struts, the height of the theatre, the ladders with their lamps, the flats, so ugly when seen from close quarters, the actors' heavy make-up, their costumes, so bizarre and made of such coarse material, the stagehands with their greasy jackets, the dangling ropes, the stage-manager striding about with his hat on, the extras sitting round, the hanging back-cloths, the firemen, all this array of ludicrous, dismal, dirty, hideous and tawdry objects was so unlike what Lucien had seen from out front that his astonishment was unbounded. They were finishing a good, broad melodrama entitled *Bertram*, a play copied from a tragedy by Maturin which was held in infinite esteem by Nodier, Lord Byron and Walter Scott, but fell flat in Paris.

'Keep hold of my arm unless you want to fall through a trap-door, bring a forest down on you, overturn a palace or run foul of a thatched cottage,' said Etienne to Lucien. – 'Is Florine in her dressing-room, my jewel?' he asked an actress who was attending to the play and getting ready to walk on.

'Yes, my love. Thank you for what you wrote about me. It was all the kinder seeing that Florine was starting here.'

'Come now, don't spoil your effect, little one,' Lousteau

said to her. 'Rush on, up with your hand! Try your *Hold,
unhappy wretch!* on me, for there are two thousand francs'
takings this evening.'

Lucien was staggered to see the actress strike a pose and
cry out *Hold, unhappy wretch!* in such a way as to make his
blood run cold. She was no longer the same woman.

'So that's the theatre,' he said to Lousteau.

'It's the same,' his new friend answered, 'as the bookshop
in the Wooden Galleries and any literary periodical: it's all
cooked up!'

Nathan appeared.

'What brings *you* here?' Lousteau asked him.

'Why, I'm doing the small theatres for the *Gazette* until
something better turns up.'

'Well then, have supper with us this evening, and give
Florine a good write-up in return.'

'I'm entirely at your service.' Nathan replied.

'You know she's now living in the rue de Bondy?'

'Who's the handsome young man you have with you,
Lousteau my pet?' asked the actress as she returned from the
stage to the wings.

'Ah! my dear, a great poet, a man who's going to be famous.
As you'll be supping together, Monsieur Nathan, let me
introduce Monsieur Lucien de Rubempré.'

'You bear a fine name,' said Raoul to Lucien.

'Lucien, this is Monsieur Raoul Nathan,' said Etienne to
his new friend.

'Upon my word, Monsieur, I was reading you two days
ago, and I couldn't conceive why, after writing such a book
and such a collection of poems, you should be so humble with
journalists.'

'Wait till *your* first book comes out,' Nathan replied with a
wry smile.

'Well well!' exclaimed Vernou as he caught sight of this
trio. 'Fancy Ultras and Liberals shaking hands!'

'In the mornings,' said Nathan, 'I hold the views of my
newspaper, but in the evenings I think as I like. *When editors
are away their staff will play.*'

'Etienne,' said Félicien Vernou, addressing Lousteau. 'Finot came with me, he's looking for you. And . . . here he is.'

'Hang it all! Isn't there a single seat left?' asked Finot.

'There's always one for you in our hearts,' said the actress, giving him a most pleasant smile.

'Well now, little Florville. So you've already got over your love affair? They were saying you'd been abducted by a Russian prince.'

'Do women get abducted today?' asked Florville, the actress who had declaimed *Hold, unhappy wretch!* 'We spent ten days at Saint-Mandé; my prince got away with it by paying compensation to the management. – The manager,' continued Florville with a laugh, 'is going to ask his Maker to send along lots of Russian princes: the compensation they pay would bring him takings without overheads.'

'And you, little one,' said Finot to a pretty girl in peasant costume who had been listening. 'Where did you steal those diamond ear-rings you're wearing? Have you been at work on an Indian prince?'

'No, just a shoe-polish merchant, an Englishman who's already left me. It isn't everybody that can hook millionaire businessmen bored with their home life, like Florine and Coralie. Aren't they lucky?'

'You'll miss your cue, Florville,' cried Lousteau. 'Your colleague's shoe-polish is going to your head.'

'If you want to make a hit,' said Nathan, 'instead of shrieking out your entry line *He is saved!* like a Fury, walk on quite sedately, go down to the footlights and say *He is saved!* in a chest voice, just as La Pasta sings *O patria!* in *Tancrède*. Off you go!' he added, giving her a push.

'It's too late, she's making a mess of it!' said Vernou.

'Why, what's she done? The audience is clapping like mad,' said Lousteau.

'She got down on her knees and showed her bosom. That's her angle,' said the actress who had been bereaved of her shoe-polish lover.

' – The manager's letting us have his box, you'll find me there,' said Finot to Etienne.

Lousteau then escorted Lucien behind the theatre through the maze of wings, corridors and staircases to the third storey and into a small room, where Nathan and Félicien Vernou arrived after them.

'Good day or good evening, gentlemen,' said Florine. 'Monsieur,' she said, addressing a short, stout man who was standing in a corner, 'these gentlemen are the arbiters of my destiny; they hold my future in their hands. But by tomorrow morning, I hope, they'll be under our table if Monsieur Lousteau hasn't forgotten anything . . . '

'Forgotten?' said Etienne. 'You'll have Blondet from the *Débats*, the real Blondet, Blondet in person, in short Blondet.'

'Oh! my dear little Lousteau! Here, I simply must give you a kiss!' she said, throwing her arms round his neck.

At this demonstration Matifat, the stout man, looked grave. At sixteen, Florine was thin. Her beauty, like a promising flower bud, could only please such artists as prefer a sketch to a finished picture. The features of this charming actress already had all their characteristic delicacy, and she reminded one of Goethe's Mignon. Matifat, a rich druggist from the rue des Lombards, had thought that a small-part actress in a boulevard theatre would not be expensive; but in eleven months Florine had cost him sixty thousand francs. Nothing seemed more extraordinary to Lucien than this honest and upright merchant stuck there like a statue in a corner of this ten-foot square nook, prettily papered, adorned with a swing-mirror, a couch, two chairs, a carpet, a mantelpiece, and stocked with wardrobes. A dresser had nearly finished putting the actress into a Spanish costume. The play was an imbroglio in which Florine was taking the part of a countess.

'In five years' time this creature will be the most beautiful actress in Paris,' said Nathan to Félicien.

'Well now, my loves,' said Florine, turning round to the three journalists, 'give me a good press tomorrow. In the first place, I've hired carriages for tonight, because I'm sending you back home as drunk as carnival revellers. Matifat has found some wines, oh! wines fit for Louis XVIII, and he's engaged the Prussian ambassador's chef.'

'We have only to look at Monsieur to hope for spacious fare,' said Nathan.

'Well, he knows he's entertaining the most dangerous men in Paris,' Florine replied.

Matifat cast an anxious glance at Lucien, for the young man's great beauty was arousing his jealousy.

'But there's one here I don't know,' said Florine, noticing Lucien. 'Which of you has brought the Apollo Belvedere from Florence? Monsieur is as handsome as one of Girodet's full-length portraits.'

'Mademoiselle,' said Lousteau. 'This gentleman is a poet from the provinces whom I neglected to introduce to you. You are so beautiful this evening that it's impossible to think of the trivial civilities of daily life.'

'I suppose he must be rich if he writes poetry,' said Florine.

'As poor as Job,' Lucien replied.

'That's some temptation for girls like us!' said the actress.

Du Bruel, the author of the play, suddenly came in. He was a young man in a frock-coat, small and slender, with something about him of the civil servant, the man of property and the stockbroker.

'My little Florine, you know your part well, I hope? No drying! Be careful with the scene in the second act: be caustic and subtle. Mind you say *I do not love you* in the way we agreed.'

'Why do you accept parts with such sentences in them?' Matifat asked Florine.

The druggist's question was hailed with a general peal of laughter.

'What does that matter to you, since it's not you I'm saying it to, silly old donkey? Oh! he tickles me to death with the nonsense he talks,' she added, looking towards the authors. 'On my word as a respectable girl, I'd like to pay him for every silly thing he says, except that I should soon be ruined.'

'Yes, but you look at me as you say that, just like when you're rehearsing, and it frightens me,' said the druggist.

'Very well then, I'll look at my little Lousteau when I say it,' she replied.

A bell rang out through the corridors.

'Off you go all of you,' said Florine, 'Let me read my part over again so that I can try and make sense of it.'

Lucien and Lousteau were the last to go. Lousteau kissed Florine's shoulders, and Lucien heard the actress say: 'Not a hope for this evening. The old idiot told his wife he was going into the country.'

'Isn't she a peach?' Etienne said to Lucien.

'But, my friend, this Matifat . . . ' Lucien exclaimed.

'Dear me, my boy, you still know nothing about life in Paris. There are certain things one has to put up with. It's as if you loved a married woman, that's all. What can't be cured must be endured.'

15. *A use for druggists*

ETIENNE and Lucien entered a stage-box on the ground floor, where they found the theatre manager and Finot. Matifat was in the box opposite with one of his friends named Camusot, a silk-merchant and protector of Coralie, accompanied by a decent little old man, his father-in-law. These three middle-class citizens were wiping the lenses of their opera-glasses while gazing down at the pit, disturbed by the flurry of movement they saw there. The boxes contained the quaint social medley usually present on first nights: journalists and their mistresses, demi-mondaines with their paramours, a few old playgoers with a liking for first performances and such society people as enjoyed the sort of emotions presented. In a first-tier box was the Director-General and his family, the man who had found a berth for Du Bruel in a finance department, a sinecure from which the writer of vaudevilles drew a salary. Since his dinner at Flicoteaux's, Lucien was moving on from one astonishment to another. Literary life, which for the last fortnight had seemed to him so wretched, so denuded, so horrible in Lousteau's room, so servile and yet so insolent in the Wooden Galleries, was opening out in strange splendour and revealing some singular aspects. This mixture of ups and downs, compromises with conscience, high-handedness and pusillanimity, treachery and dissipation, grandeur and servitude had put him in a daze like a man who is watching an extraordinary spectacle.

'Do you think Du Bruel's play will make money for you?' Finot asked the manager.

'It's a comedy of intrigue in which Du Bruel has tried to imitate Beaumarchais. The boulevard public doesn't like that kind of play: it wants its fill of emotion. Wit is not appreciated here. This evening everything depends on Florine and Coralie who are ravishingly graceful and beautiful. These two creatures wear very short skirts and do Spanish dances. The public may well be carried away. This performance is a toss-up. If the papers write me a few witty reviews – if the play succeeds – I may make three hundred thousand francs.'

'Plainly then it can only be a mild success,' said Finot.

'There's a conspiracy hatched by the three neighbouring theatres, so there'll be hissing in any case. But I've taken steps to thwart their evil schemes. I've paid extra to the *claqueurs* they're sending so that they'll hiss in the wrong places. Over there are three business men, and in order to get an ovation for Coralie and Florine, they've each taken a hundred tickets and given them to acquaintances capable of throwing the *claqueurs* out. The *claqueurs*, having received double pay, will let themselves be kicked out, and a bit of horse-play like that always puts the audience in a good mood.'

'Two hundred tickets!' cried Finot. 'What precious allies!'

'Yes. If I had two other pretty actresses as richly supported as Florine and Coralie I could make ends meet.'

For two hours it had been dinned into Lucien's ears that money was the solution to all problems. In the theatres as in the publishing-houses, in the publishing-houses as in editorial offices, there was no question of art or fame. These insistent tickings of the great Money pendulum throbbed through his head and heart. While the overture was being played, he could not help contrasting the clappings and hissings in the riotous pit with the scenes of calm and pure poetry he had enjoyed in David's printing-office and the vision they shared of the wonders of Art, the noble triumphs of genius and the shining wings of glory. A tear glistened in the poet's eye as he remembered the evenings spent with the Cénacle.

'What's wrong with you?' asked Etienne Lousteau.

'I see poetry being dragged through the mire,' he replied.

'Well well, my friend, so you still have your illusions!'

'But why should one grovel and submit to these vulgar Matifats and Camusots, as the actresses submit to the journalists and we ourselves submit to the publishers?'

'My boy,' Etienne whispered as he pointed to Finot, 'you see that stupid fellow there, without wit or talent but greedy, out for a fortune at all costs and clever at business: the man who, in Dauriat's shop, rooked me of forty per cent while pretending to oblige me? . . . Well, he's had letters in which various nascent geniuses have gone down on their knees to him for a hundred francs.'

Lucien was seized with heartfelt disgust and he remembered the drawing left on the green baize of the editorial table: *Finot, my hundred francs!*

'Better to die,' he said.

'Better to live,' Etienne retorted.

Just as the curtain rose, the manager went back-stage to give some orders.

'My dear fellow,' Finot then said to Etienne. 'I have Dauriat's word. I'm in for a third share in the ownership of the weekly paper. I've settled for thirty thousand francs cash down on condition I become editor and director. It's a splendid deal. Blondet tells me that laws are being drafted to muzzle the Press, and only existing newspapers will keep going. In six months a million will be needed to start a new paper. So I clinched the bargain without having more than ten thousand francs of my own. Listen. If you can get Matifat to buy the half of my share – one sixth – I'll make you editor of my little newspaper with a salary of two hundred and fifty francs a month. You'll be my figure-head. I want to maintain control of the editing and keep all my interests in it while appearing to have no hand in it. You'll get paid for all the articles at a rate of five francs a column: in this way you can reap a bonus of fifteen francs a day by only paying three francs a column and by saving on the unpaid articles. That amounts to another four hundred and fifty francs a month. But I want to be free to use the paper to attack or defend people and affairs as I see fit while leaving you free to satisfy your personal animosities and friendships so long as they don't hamper my policy. I may side with the ministry or the Ultras – I haven't decided yet; but I want, under cover, to keep my relations with the Liberals going. I'm telling you everything because you're a good chap. I may perhaps hand over to you the Parliamentary sessions in the *Constitutionnel* – I doubt whether I could go on doing them. And so, use Florine for this bit of wangling, and tell her to put pressure on the druggist: I have only two days for backing out if I can't raise the money. Dauriat has sold another third for thirty thousand francs to his printer and paper-maker. As for him, he gets his third for nothing, and makes ten thousand francs on the deal since the whole transaction only costs him fifty thousand francs. But in a year's time this newspaper will be worth two hundred thousand francs to sell to the Government if, as people make out, it has sense enough to buy up the periodicals.'

'You're a lucky man,' said Lousteau.

'If you had gone through all the bad times I have, you wouldn't say that. But at the present time, you see, I can't get over the misfortune of having a hatter for a father, one who still actually sells his hats in the rue du Coq. Only a revolution could make a successful man of me; and, short of a social upheaval, I need millions. I'm not sure that a revolution wouldn't suit me better. If I had a name like your friend's all would be plain sailing. Quiet! Here's the manager.'

'Good-bye,' said Finot, rising to his feet. 'I'm going to the Opera-House and maybe I'll have a duel on my hands to-morrow: I'm writing and signing F a devastating article on two dancers who have generals for lovers. I'm going all out against the Opera-House.'

'Really?' said the manager.

'Yes, they're all being stingy with me. One of them cuts down my boxes, another refuses to take out fifty subscriptions to my paper. I've sent an ultimatum to the Opera-House: I'm now demanding a hundred subscriptions and four boxes a month. If they accept, my paper will have eight hundred subscribers who'll get their copies and a thousand who'll merely pay for them. I know how I can arrange for yet another two hundred subscriptions: by January we shall have twelve hundred . . .'

'You'll be our ruin in the long run,' said the manager.

'You're not badly off, you, with your ten subscriptions. I got you two good articles in the *Constitutionnel*.'

'Oh, I'm not complaining,' the director exclaimed.

'I'll see you tomorrow evening, Lousteau,' Finot continued. 'You'll give me your answer at the Théâtre Français. There's a first performance and, as I can't review it, you'll occupy the box belonging to my paper. I'm giving you the preference: you've gone to no end of trouble for me, and I'm grateful. Félicien Vernou suggests going without his salary for a year and is offering me twenty thousand francs for a third share in the paper; but I intend to keep complete control of it. Good-bye.'

'He's well named Finot,[1] that man,' said Lucien to Lousteau.

'Oh, he's a gallows-bird who'll make his way,' replied Etienne, without caring whether he was heard or not by the clever man who was closing the door of the box behind him.

'Finot?' said the theatre manager. 'He'll be a millionaire; he'll enjoy universal consideration; perhaps he'll even have friends.'

'God in Heaven!' said Lucien. 'What a den of thieves! And you're going to involve that delightful girl in such a negotiation?' he asked, pointing at Florine who was throwing flirtatious glances in their direction.

'She'll bring it off,' Lousteau answered. 'You don't know how devoted and how clever these dear creatures are.'

The manager took up the story: 'They redeem all their

1. The adjective *finot* in French means artful and cunning.

shortcomings, they wipe out all their lapses from virtue by the infinite range of their love, when they do love. An actress's passion is so much more a thing of beauty because it stands out in such violent contrast with the people around her.'

'It's like finding a diamond in a dunghill, one fit to adorn the proudest of diadems,' Lousteau rejoindered.

'But look,' the manager continued. 'Coralie is wool-gathering. Our friend is making a conquest of Coralie without knowing it: he'll make her muff her best lines; she's losing her timing – twice already she hasn't taken a prompt. Monsieur, I beg of you, conceal yourself in the corner,' he said to Lucien. 'If Coralie has fallen in love with you, I'm going to tell her you have left the theatre.'

'Not at all,' cried Lousteau. 'Tell her this gentleman will be at the supper, that she'll do what she likes with him: then she'll act as well as Mademoiselle Mars.'

The manager went off.

'What, my friend,' said Lucien to Etienne. 'You have no scruples in getting Mademoiselle Florine to extort thirty thousand francs from this druggist for only a half-share in what Finot has bought for that sum?'

Lousteau gave Lucien no time to finish his argument. 'Why, where do you hail from, my dear boy? He's a cash-box which Cupid has provided.'

'But what about your conscience?'

'Conscience, my dear, is a kind of stick that everyone picks up to thrash his neighbour with, but one he never uses against himself. Devil take it, what are you grumbling about? In one day chance has worked a miracle for you that I've been waiting for these last two years, and it pleases you to find fault with the way it's done. Damn it all, you seem to me to have intelligence, you'll come by the independence of mind which intellectual adventurers have to possess in the world we're living in, and yet you're wading knee-deep in scruples like a nun accusing herself of having eaten her egg with concupiscence ... If Florine brings this off I become an editor, I get a fixed salary of two hundred and fifty francs a month, I take over reviews in the big theatres, I leave Vernou with the light comedy theatres, and you get your foot in the stirrup by taking over the boulevard theatres from me. So you'll get three francs a column and you'll write one every day, thirty a month, which will bring you ninety francs a month. You'll have sixty francs' worth of boxes to sell to Barbet; also you can demand ten tickets a month from your theatres, forty tickets in all, and you'll sell them for forty francs to the Barbet of the theatres, a man I'll put you in touch with. And so I can see you earning two hundred francs a month. By making yourself useful to Finot you could place a hundred francs article in his new weekly paper, if you managed to display exceptional talent – for there you sign your articles, and can't just toss things off as you can in the little newspaper. So then you'd have three hundred francs a month. My dear fellow, there are men of talent, like that poor devil d'Arthez who dines at Flicoteaux's every day, who don't earn three hundred francs in ten years. You'll make four thousand francs a year by your pen, without reckoning in your income from the publishers if you write for them. Now a Sub-Prefect only gets a salary of three thousand francs, and yet he has a high old time in his District. I won't mention free seats in the theatre, for this pleasure will quickly become a fatigue; but you'll have access to the wings in four theatres. Be hard and witty for a month or two, you'll be swamped with invitations and actresses' parties; you'll be courted by their lovers; you'll only dine at Flicoteaux's on the days when you haven't thirty sous in your pocket and are not dining out. At five o'clock this evening, at the Luxembourg, you didn't know what to do for yourself: now you're about to become one of the hundred privileged persons who foist their opinions on the French public. In three days' time, if we succeed, by printing thirty *bons mots* at the rate of three per diem you can make a man curse the day he was born; you can draw a regular income – in sensual pleasure – from all the actresses in your theatre; you can make a good play fall flat and send the whole of Paris flocking to a bad one. If Dauriat refuses to print your *Marguerites* without giving you something for them you can make him come to your rooms, humble and submissive, to buy them from you for two thousand francs. Use your talent and sling three articles into three different papers, each of them threatening murder to some of Dauriat's speculations or a book he's counting on, and you'll see him come crawling up to your garret and clinging round it like clematis. Finally there's your novel: the publishers, all of whom at present would show you the door more or less politely, will queue up outside your flat, and they'll bid up to four thousand francs for a manuscript which old Doguereau would price at four hundred francs! Those are the profits from the journalist trade. That's why we ward off all newcomers from the newspapers: one needs not only enormous talent, but also a lot of luck to get into them. And you're quibbling over your good luck!... Look now, if we hadn't met at Flicoteaux's today you might have gone on stagnating for three months or died of starvation, like d'Arthez, in an attic. By the time d'Arthez has become as learned as Bayle and as great a writer as Rousseau we shall have made our fortune, and his fortune and fame will be at our mercy. Finot will be a deputy in the Chamber and the owner of a great newspaper; as for us, we shall be whatever we have wanted to be: peers of France or languishing in a debtors' prison.'

'And Finot,' exclaimed Lucien, remembering the scene he had witnessed, 'will sell his great newspaper to the Ministers who make the highest bid, just as he sells his commendations to Madame Bastienne and disparages Mademoiselle Virginie, by proving that the former's hats are better than those the paper had cracked up first of all!'

'You're a simpleton, my dear,' Lousteau curtly replied. 'Three years ago Finot was down on his uppers, dined at Tabar's for eighteen sous, botched a prospectus for ten francs, and his coat hung on him by a miracle as incomprehensible as that of the Immaculate Conception. He's now the sole possessor of a newspaper valued at a hundred thousand francs. With the subscriptions paid for but involving no delivery, with the genuine subscriptions and the indirect contributions levied by his uncle, he's making twenty thousand francs a year; he eats the most sumptuous dinners every day; a month ago he bought himself a two-wheeler; and lastly, by tomorrow he'll be running a weekly paper, having a sixth share in it which cost him nothing, with a salary of five hundred francs a month to which he'll add a thousand francs' worth of articles contributed gratis but for which he'll charge his partners. You yourself, before anyone else, if Finot agrees to pay you fifty francs a page, will be only too happy to send him three articles for nothing. When you reach a similar position, then you can bring Finot to trial: one can only be tried by one's peers. Haven't you a great future before you if you fall in blindly with his official antagonisms, if you attack when Finot says "Attack!" and if you praise when Finot says "Praise!" When you want to wreak your spite on anyone, you can belabour your friend or your enemy by slipping a sentence in our paper every morning and saying to me: "Lousteau, let's kill that man!" Then you'll murder your victim all over again in a big article in the weekly paper. And finally, if it's matter of capital importance to you, after you've made yourself necessary to Finot, he'll let you deal the knock-out blow in a great newspaper which by then will have a thousand subscribers.'

'So you believe Florine will be able to persuade her druggist to make the deal?' asked Lucien, his brain in a whirl.

'I certainly think so . . . Here's the interval. I'm going to say a word or two to her, and it will be settled tonight. Once I've primed her, Florine will have all my wit at her command, as well as her own.'

'And this honest merchant is sitting there, gaping, admiring Florine without suspecting that he's going to be stung for thirty thousand francs . . . !'

'There you go again, more stupidity!' exclaimed Lousteau. 'One would think he was being robbed! Why, my dear man, if the Government buys the newspaper, in six months the druggist stands to get fifty thousand francs in return for his thirty thousand francs. Besides, Matifat won't worry about the paper, but only about Florine's interests. Once people know that Matifat and Camusot (for they'll go in together) are owners of a review, there'll be benevolent articles for Florine and Coralie in every paper. Florine will become famous and will perhaps get an engagement worth twelve thousand francs in another theatre. Lastly, Matifat will save on the thousand francs a month that presents and dinners to the journalists would cost him. You don't understand either people or business matters.'

'Poor man!' said Lucien. 'He's looking forward to a pleasant night.'

'What's more,' continued Lousteau, 'he'll be pestered with innumerable arguments until he's shown Florine a receipt for the sixth share bought from Finot. As for me, the day after, I shall be an editor earning a thousand francs a month. And that will be the end of all my troubles!' cried Florine's lover.

Lousteau went out, leaving Lucien dumbfounded, lost in deep thought as his mind flitted over the world as it is. Now that he had visited the Wooden Galleries and seen how publishers pull their strings and how literary reputations are concocted, the poet perceived the reverse side of the human conscience, the play of wheels within wheels in Parisian life, the machinery behind it all. He had been envying Lousteau for his good luck as he admired Florine's acting. For a few moments he had already forgotten Matifat. He stayed where he was for an indeterminate time, perhaps five minutes – but it seemed like eternity to him. His mind was aflame with perfervid thoughts and his senses caught fire at the sight of the actresses with their wanton eyes embellished with mascara, their gleaming necks, their provocatively short skirts sensually flounced, their legs displayed in red stockings with green clocks, in fact so hosed and shod as to throw any pit into a flutter. Two sorts of corruption were advancing towards him in parallel motion like twin sheets of water uniting to form a flood. They swirled over the poet as he sat reclining in his corner of the box, his arm resting on the red velvet of the rail, his hand hanging limp, his eyes glued to the curtain, feeling so much more vulnerable to the enchantments this kind of life offered with its alternations of lightning flashes and clouds because it was as dazzling as a firework display after the profound darkness of his own laborious, inglorious, monotonous existence.

16. Coralie

SUDDENLY an amorous glance streamed through a chink in the theatre curtain to meet Lucien's wandering regard. Awakened from his torpor, the poet recognized that this burning gaze was coming from Coralie; he lowered his head and looked at Camusot, who at that moment was returning to the box opposite.

This enthusiastic playgoer was a worthy, thickset, stout vendor of silk-stuffs in the rue des Bourdonnais, a judge in the Tribunal of Commerce, the father of four children, married for the second time and blessed with an income of eighty thousand francs, but fifty-six years old, wearing what looked like a thatch of grey hair and having the smug air of a man who is making the most of his remaining years and, after pocketing the thousand and one affronts of a commercial career, has no intention of taking leave of the world before he has enjoyed his full share of this life's pleasures. His forehead, which was the colour of butter fresh from the churn, and his monkish, florid cheeks did not seem broad enough to contain the beaming jubilation they expressed. Camusot's wife was not with him, and he intended to applaud Coralie vociferously. The many vanities of this rich bourgeois were summed up in Coralie, whom he patronized with all the lordliness of an eighteenth-century nobleman. At that moment he believed himself to be half responsible for Coralie's success, and he believed this all the more readily because he had paid for it. To give him countenance, he had his father-in-law beside him, a little old man with powdered hair and libidinous glance but none the less very respectable. Lucien's gorge rose once more, and he remembered the pure, idealistic love he had felt for Madame de Bargeton for a whole year. Love as poets conceive it immediately spread its white wings: innumerable memories, with their hazy blue contours, enveloped the great man of Angoulême and he sank back into reveries. The curtain rose. Coralie and Florine were on the stage.

'My dear, he's no more thinking of you than of the Grand Turk,' Florine whispered while Coralie was replying to a cue.

Lucien could not help laughing, and he gazed at Coralie. This girl, one of the most charming and delightful actresses in Paris, a rival of Madame Perrin and Mademoiselle Fleuriet whom she resembled and whose fate she was to share, was the type of woman who at will can exercise her powers of fascination upon men. Her face was of the perfect Jewish type: long, oval, of a light ivory tint, with a garnet-red mouth and a chin as delicately turned as the brim of a cup. Eyelids and curving lashes masked the gleam of jet-black pupils, and beneath them one divined a languorous gaze, aglint on occasion with the fire of oriental passion. Olive shadows circled her eyes; she had full and gracefully arched eyebrows. Her dusky forehead, with its divided crown of ebony hair, so glossy that it caught the sheen of the lights, suggested a generosity of thought which might have betokened genius. But like many actresses Coralie was without intelligence, although she could bandy ironic repartee in the wings, and she had no education despite her knowledge of boudoir life: all she had was the wit which the senses confer and the good nature of a woman amorously inclined. In any case, what did the moral side of things matter when men's eyes were dazzled by her smooth, round arms, her tapering fingers, the golden tint of her shoulders, such breasts as are sung of in the Song of Solomon, her neck with its rippling curves and her adorably shaped legs clad in red silk? This loveliness, truly poetic in its oriental charm, was set off by the conventional Spanish costume worn in the theatres. Coralie was the joy of the audience: all eyes were spanning her waist in its close-fitting basquine, caressing her Andalusian curves and the sensual undulations their movement transmitted to her skirt. The moment came when Lucien, as he saw that this creature was acting for him alone, feeling henceforth no more concerned with Camusot than an urchin in the gallery is concerned with his apple-peel, placed sensual love above pure love, enjoyment above desire, while the demon of lust whispered shocking thoughts in his ear.

'I know nothing,' he told himself, 'of the love which wallows in good cheer, wine and material joys. So far I have lived on ideals rather than realities. A man who wants to depict life must know all about it. This will be my first grand supper-party, my first orgy in unusual company: why should I not for once savour the much-vaunted delights into which the nobles of the last century flung themselves by living with wantons? Even if only to lift them on to the plane of true love, must I not experience the joys, ecstasies, transports, refinements and subtleties which the love of courtesans and actresses can offer? Is not this, after all, the poetry of the senses? Two months ago I looked on these women as divinities guarded by dragons one dared not approach. Here is one of greater beauty even than Florine, on whose account I was envying Lousteau. Why not take advantage of her whim, when the greatest lords pour out stores of wealth to buy one night with such women? When foreign ambassadors set foot in this underworld they think neither of yesterday nor tomorrow. What an idiot I should be to be more fastidious than princes, particularly since I'm not yet in love with anyone!'

By now Lucien had forgotten Camusot. After showing Lousteau the deep disgust he felt for this most odious sharing of women, he was falling into the same pit and was immersed in lustful desire, carried away by the sophistry of passion.

'Coralie has lost her heart to you,' said Lousteau as he came back. 'Your beauty, as rare as that of the most famous Greek sculptures, is doing unheard-of damage in the wings. You're in luck, my boy. Coralie is eighteen, and in a few days' time her beauty may bring her sixty thousand francs a year. She's still quite a good girl. Her mother sold her three years ago for sixty thousand francs, and so far she has reaped nothing but disappointment and is searching for happiness. She took to the theatre out of despair, for she loathed de Marsay, the man who bought her originally; and when she came out of the galleys – our prince of dandies soon dropped her – she happened upon the worthy Camusot. She doesn't lose any sleep over him, but since he's like a father to her she puts up with him and lets herself be loved. She has already turned down the most lucrative propositions and sticks to Camusot because he doesn't pester her. So you are her first love. Oh! one look at you was like a bullet in her heart, and Florine went to reason with her in her dressing-room where she's in tears because of your indifference. The play will be a failure. Coralie is forgetting her lines, so it's good-bye to the engagement Camusot was getting for her at the Gymnase.'

'Really? . . . Poor girl!' said Lucien, altogether flattered in his vanity at these words and feeling his heart swelling with self-satisfaction. 'My friend, more things are happening to me in one evening than ever did in the first eighteen years of my life.'

And Lucien told him of his love affair with Madame de Bargeton and his hatred for Baron Châtelet.

'Why now, our paper's short of an Aunt Sally, we'll stick our claws in him. This baron's an Empire beau and he sides with the Government. He'll suit us down to the ground. I've often seen him at the Opera-House. I can see your great lady from here: she's often in the Marquise d'Espard's box. The Baron's courting your ex-mistress, who reminds me of a cuttle-bone. Wait a minute! Finot has just sent me an urgent note telling me that the paper is short of copy: that's a trick played on him by one of our contributors, a nasty little man, Hector Merlin, because he's had his blank space cut down. In despair, Finot is knocking up an article against the Opera. Well then, my boy, write a review for this play: listen to it, ponder over it. As for me, I'm going to the editor's office to think up three columns on your man and your disdainful beauty. She won't feel much inclined for merry-making in the morning.'

'So that's how and where your paper is made up?'

'That's how – always,' Lousteau replied. 'I've been on it for ten months, and it's always short of copy at eight o'clock in the evening.'

In typographers' slang, they call 'copy' the manuscript to be set up, doubtless because the writers are supposed only to send a copy of what they have written. Perhaps also it may be an ironical rendering of the Latin word *copia* (abundance), for copy is never abundant.

'The great scheme which will never come off,' Lousteau continued, 'is to have a few numbers ready in advance. It's ten o'clock, and not a line is written. In order to give the number a brilliant finish, I'm going to tell Vernou and Nathan to lend us a score of epigrams on the deputies, Chancellor Cruzoé,[1] the Ministers and, if need be, our own friends. In such straits one is ready to murder one's father, one is like a corsair who loads his cannon with his prize money in order to stay alive. Make your article witty and you'll have done a lot to get into Finot's good books: he shows gratitude as a matter of calculation. His acquaintance is the best and soundest you can make – apart from the pawnbrokers of course.'

'But what sort of men are you journalists?' exclaimed Lucien. 'You mean one has to sit down at a table and pour out wit . . .?'

'Yes, it's absolutely like lighting a lamp: you burn it till there's no oil left.'

Just as Lousteau was opening the door of the box, the manager and and Du Bruel came in.

'Monsieur,' said the author of the play to Lucien. 'Allow me to tell Coralie on your behalf that you will go off with her after supper, or my play will fail. The poor girl doesn't know what she's saying or what she's doing; she'll be laughing when she should be crying and *vice versa*. There's already been some hissing. You might still save the play. In any case the pleasure which awaits you is no misfortune.'

'Monsieur, it's not my habit to tolerate rivals,' Lucien answered.

'Don't repeat that remark to Coralie,' cried the manager with a glance at Du Bruel. 'Coralie's the sort of girl to fling Camusot out through the window and would well and truly

1. The Chancellor Dambray, nicknamed Cruzoé (i.e. Crusoé, the French form of Crusoe) because, one day when Louis XVIII was expecting a visit from his favourite, Zoé du Cayla, Dambray knocked and Louis called out 'Come in, Zoé.' To the Opposition Press Dambray was henceforth known as Cruzoé (*Cru Zoé*, i.e. mistaken for Zoé).

ruin herself. The worthy proprietor of the Golden Cocoon allows Coralie two thousand francs a month and pays for all her dresses and *claqueurs*.'

'Since your promise would in no way bind me,' said Lucien with the air of an oriental potentate, 'carry on: save your play.'

'But don't give the impression of snubbing this charming girl,' said Du Bruel in supplicating tones.

'Very well then,' cried the poet. 'I see I must write the review of your play and smile on your leading lady. So be it!'

The author vanished after beckoning to Coralie, who from that moment acted with wonderful verve. Bouffé, who was playing the role of an elderly alcalde and for the first time revealing his talent for making up as an old man, came in front amidst a thunder of applause and said: 'Gentlemen, the play we have had the honour to perform is by Monsieur Raoul Nathan and Monsieur de Cursy.'[1]

'Well well!' said Lousteau. 'Nathan has had a hand in it. I'm no longer surprised he's here.'

The pit had risen to its feet. 'Coralie! Coralie' they all shouted.

From the box containing the two merchants a voice thundered out: 'And Florine!'

'Florine and Coralie!' a few voices repeated in response.

The curtain rose once more and Bouffé reappeared with the two actresses, to each of whom Matifat and Camusot threw a bouquet. Coralie picked up hers and held it out towards Lucien. The two hours he had spent in the theatre had been like a dream to him. His visit to the wings, horrible as they were, had begun the weaving of the spell. In them the innocent poet had caught the first whiff of disorderly and voluptuous life. In these dirty corridors encumbered with stage machinery and reeking with oil-lamps reigns a pestilence which destroys the soul. In them life has no longer anything sacred or real. Serious things are laughed at and impossible things seem true. This acted on Lucien like a narcotic, and Coralie completed the process by plunging him into a sort of joyful intoxication. The chandelier was put out. By then the

1. Du Bruel's *nom de plume*.

auditorium was empty save for the box-openers who were making an inordinate clatter as they removed the small benches and shut up the boxes. From the footlights, which had been snuffed out like a single candle, emanated a noisome odour. The curtain was raised. A lantern was let down from the flies. The firemen and theatre hands started their round. The magic of the scenery, the spectacle of pretty women filling the boxes, the blazing lights, the resplendent enchantment of back-cloths and new costumes gave place to coldness, desolation, darkness, emptiness. Everything looked hideous. Lucien's surprise was indescribable.

'Well well, are you coming, my boy?' said Lousteau from the stage. 'Jump up here from the box.'

Lucien reached the stage with one bound. He scarcely recognized Florine and Coralie in their undress, muffled up in their cloaks and coarse wraps, wearing hats with black veils, looking in short like butterflies which have reverted to the larval state.

'Will you do me the honour of giving me your arm?' Coralie asked in a tremble.

'Willingly,' Lucien replied. He did so, and felt her feeling the actress's heart beating against his like that of a bird.

The actress pressed close to the poet with the soft and ardent voluptuousness of a cat rubbing against her master's leg.

'So we are going to have supper together!' she said to him.

The four of them left the theatre and found two cabs waiting at the stage door opening on to the rue des Fossés-du-Temple. Coralie showed Lucien into the one in which Camusot and his father-in-law, the worthy Cardot, were already seated. Coralie offered the fourth seat to Du Bruel. The stage manager went off with Florine, Matifat and Lousteau.

'These cabs are frightful!' said Coralie.

'Why do you have no carriage?' asked Du Bruel.

'Why?' she cried bad-temperedly. 'I don't want to say why in front of Monsieur Cardot who has no doubt trained his son-in-law. Could you believe that, shrivelled and old as he is, Monsieur Cardot gives Florentine no more than five hundred francs a month – just enough to pay for her rent, her bread-and-butter and her footwear. The old Marquis de Rochegude, who has an income of six hundred thousand francs, has been offering me a coupé for the last two months. But I'm an artiste and not a street-girl.'

'You shall have your carriage the day after tomorrow, Mademoiselle,' said Camusot solemnly. 'But you never asked me for one.'

'Does one ask for such things? When one loves a woman, how can one leave her to pad about in the mire and run the risk of breaking her legs by going everywhere on foot? You have to be a Knight of the Yardstick to like a gown with mud on its hem.'

As she uttered these words, with a sourness which broke Camusot's heart, Coralie was feeling for Lucien's leg and pressing it between her own. She took his hand and squeezed it. Then she remained silent and seemed to become absorbed in one of those moods of infinite rapture which compensate these poor creatures for their past woes and disappointments and awake in them a kind of poetic feeling unknown to other women – those who, fortunately for them, are not subject to such violent revulsions of feeling.

'In the end your acting was as good as that of Mademoiselle Mars,' said Du Bruel to Coralie.

'Yes,' said Camusot, 'something seemed to be worrying Mademoiselle Coralie at the beginning; but from the middle of the second act she swept the audience off its feet. She can claim half the credit for your success.'

'And I for hers,' said Du Bruel.

'You're both talking nonsense,' she said in a changed tone of voice.

The actress took advantage of a moment of darkness to raise Lucien's hand to her lips and kiss it and wet it with her tears. This stirred Lucien to the marrow of his bones. There is a splendour of humility in a love-stricken courtesan which can give points to the angels.

'You will be writing the article, Monsieur,' said Du Bruel to Lucien. 'You will be able to work in a charming paragraph about our dear Coralie.'

'Oh yes! Do us that little service,' said Camusot in the tones of a man on his knees before Lucien. 'You'll find in me one well disposed to serve your interests at all times.'

'By why can't you leave this gentleman to do as he likes?' cried the actress, exasperated. 'He'll write as he sees fit. Papa Camusot, you may buy me carriages, but not praise.'

'You'll have it at a very cheap price,' was Lucien's polite reply. 'I have never written for the newspapers. I'm not well up in their way of doing things and you'll have the virginity of my pen.'

'That will be quite amusing,' said Du Bruel.

'Here we are in the rue de Bondy,' said the puny old Cardot, whom Coralie's outburst had reduced to stupefaction.

'If I have the first fruits of your pen, you will have those of my heart,' said Coralie during the brief instant she was alone with Lucien in the carriage.

17. How a news-sheet is edited

CORALIE rejoined Florine in her bedroom in order to put on the clothes she had sent there in advance. Lucien knew nothing of the expense lavished on actresses or mistresses by prosperous merchants who want to enjoy life. Although Matifat, who had not so considerable a fortune as his friend Camusot, had done things in a slightly parsimonious way, Lucien was surprised to see a tastefully decorated dining-room tapestried in gilt-studded green cloth, brightly lit with fine lamps, furnished with well-stocked *jardinières*; and a drawing-room hung with yellow silk embellished with motifs in brown and resplendent with the furniture then in fashion, including a chandelier by Thomire and a Persian carpet. Clock, candelabras and fire-place were all in good taste. Matifat had arranged for all the decoration to be done by Grindot, a young architect who was building him a house and who, knowing the purpose of these apartments, gave particular attention to his task. That is why Matifat, always the business man, seemed to be continuously thinking of the bills and regarded these extravagances as so many jewels imprudently removed from their casket.

'And that's what I shall be obliged to do for Florentine.' This thought could be read in old Cardot's eyes.

Lucien suddenly understood why the condition of his room gave no concern to Lousteau, the journalist whom Florine loved. As he was the unsuspected lord of the feast, Etienne could enjoy all these beautiful things. And so his pose was that of the master of the house as he stood in front of the hearth chatting with the theatre manager, who was congratulating Du Bruel.

'Copy! Copy!' shouted Finot as he came in. 'There's nothing in the newspaper letter-box. The compositors have my article and will soon have finished it.'

'We're coming round to it,' said Etienne. 'We shall find a table and a fire in Florine's boudoir. If Monsieur Matifat would be so kind as to provide us with paper and ink, we'll throw the newspaper together while Florine and Coralie are changing.'

Cardot, Camusot and Matifat disappeared, hurrying to find quills, pen-knives and everything the two writers required. At this moment one of the prettiest dancers of the time, Tullia, rushed into the room.

'My dear child,' she said to Finot. 'You've got your hundred subscriptions. They'll cost the management nothing, for they're already allotted – the singers, the orchestra and the corps de ballet have had to take them. Your paper is so amusing that no one will complain. You'll get your boxes. In fact, here's the money for the first quarter' – and she handed him two banknotes. 'So don't pull me to pieces.'

'I'm done for,' cried Finot. 'I no longer have the leading article for my number, since I shall have to go and cancel my infamous diatribe.'

'How gracefully you move, my divine Laïs,' exclaimed Blondet, following the dancer in with Nathan, Vernou and Claude Vignon whom he had brought with him. 'You'll stay to supper with us, dear love, or I'll have you squashed like the butterfly you are. Since you're a dancer, there'll be no rivalry here over talent. And as far as beauty's concerned, you all have too much sense to be jealous in public.'

'For Heaven's sake, my friends, Du Bruel, Nathan, Blondet, save me!' cried Finot. 'I need five columns.'

'I'll fill two of them with the review,' said Lucien.

'I've a subject for one,' said Lousteau.

'Well then, Nathan, Vernou, Du Bruel, provide me with some pleasantries for the last page. Our good Blondet can easily supply the two small columns on page one. I must run to the printer's. Fortunately, Tullia, you have your carriage with you.'

'Yes, but the Duke's in it with the German envoy,' she said.

'Let's invite the Duke and the envoy,' said Nathan.

'A German! He'll drink well, listen hard, and we'll say so many outrageous things that he'll write to his Court about them,' cried Blondet.

'Which, of all of us, is a sufficiently grave personage to go down and speak to him?' asked Finot. 'Come, Du Bruel, you're one of our bureaucrats: bring up the Duc de Rhétoré and the envoy, and give your arm to Tullia. Goodness! how beautiful she is this evening!'

'We shall be thirteen at table!' said Matifat, turning pale.

'No, fourteen,' cried Florentine on entering. 'I *must* keep an eye on my lord Cardot!'

'Besides,' said Lousteau, 'Blondet has brought Claude Vignon along.'

'I brought him for a drink,' replied Blondet as he annexed an inkpot.

'Now then, the rest of you,' he said, addressing Nathan and Vernou. 'You must have sparkle enough for the fifty-six bottles of wine we're about to drink. And mind you stir up Du Bruel: as a writer of vaudevilles, he can very well produce a number of malicious quips. Squeeze some epigrams from him.'

Fired with the desire to win recognition in the presence of so many people of mark, Lucien wrote his first article on the round table in Florine's boudoir under the gleam of the pink candles which Matifat had lit.

PANORAMA DRAMATIQUE

First performance: 'The Alcalde in Difficulties', im- broglio in three acts. – Mademoiselle Florine's début. – Mademoiselle Coralie. – Bouffé.

People come and go, talk and walk, look round for something and find nothing: all's bustle and hustle. The alcalde can't find his daughter but he has found the cap he had lost. But the cap doesn't fit. It must belong to some thief or other. But where's the thief? People come and go, talk and walk and search more frantically than before. The alcalde ends up by finding a man, but no daughter; then his daughter, but no man, which satisfies the magistrate though not the audience. Calm returns; the alcalde wants to question the man. The old alcalde sits down in a big alcaldic arm-chair and adjusts his alcaldic sleeves. Spain is the only country where alcaldes are attached to flowing sleeves and where you see alcaldes' necks surrounded with the ruffs which, on the Paris stage, it's one half of an alcalde's job to wear. This alcalde, who had been so busy trotting about with the short steps of a wheezy old man, is Bouffé: Bouffé the successor of Potier, a young actor who is so good in old men's parts that he makes the oldest men laugh. There's a future for a hundred old men in that bald forehead, that quavering voice, those spindle-shanks trembling under the body of a Gerontius. He's so old, this young actor, that he frightens people: they fear his oldness may be passed on like a contagious disease. And what an admirable alcalde! What a charming, anxious smile, what fussy stupidity! What stupid dignity! What magisterial hesitancy! How well this man knows that anything may be true or false alternately! How worthy he is to be the minister of a constitutional monarch! At each question the alcalde puts, the stranger puts a question to him; Bouffé replies, in such wise that, answers coming in shape of questions, the alcalde clears things up by the questions he asks. This superlatively comic scene, which has a touch of Molière in it, set the audience rocking. Everybody on the stage seems to have reached agreement, but I'm not competent to sort it all out. The alcalde's daughter was there, played by a real Andalusian girl, with Spanish eyes, Spanish complexion, Spanish waistline and Spanish gait: a Spanish girl from head to foot, with a dagger in her garter, love in her heart and a cross dangling from the end of a ribbon over her bosom. At the end of the act someone asked me how the play was going. I told him: 'It's wearing red stockings with green clocks; it has the tiniest foot (in patent shoes) and the finest leg in Andalusia!'

Ah! this alcalde's daughter makes you drool with love and arouses wicked thoughts. You want to leap on to the stage to offer her your heart and your hearth, or maybe an income of thirty thousand francs and your pen. This Andalusian is the loveliest actress in Paris. Coralie, since that's the name she goes by, is capable of playing the countess or the shop-girl. There's no knowing in which part she would be more attractive. She will be what she wants to be. She has it in her to play any part: is not that the best thing one can say of any actress in the boulevard theatres?

In the second act a Spanish girl arrives from Paris with her cameo face and bewitching eyes. I asked a question in my turn: where did she come from? I was told she had come from the slips and that her name was Florine; but really I couldn't believe it, there was so much fire in her movements and so much fury in her love. This rival of the alcalde's daughter is the wife of a hidalgo in a cloak cut to Almaviva's style, with enough material in it to clothe a hundred hidalgos of the boulevard theatres. If Florine had neither red stockings with green clocks nor patent shoes, she had a mantilla and a veil which she turned to admirable purpose, great lady that she is! She showed wonderfully well that a tigress may turn into a she-cat. I gathered from the stinging repartee of these two girls that there was some drama of jealousy between them. Then, when everything was almost settled, the alcalde's stupidity threw everything back into confusion. All that world of torches and tapers, valets, Figaros, hidalgos, alcaldes, girls and women began it all anew: searchings, comings, goings and turnings. Then the plot was pieced together again and I left it at that, for the two women, the jealous Florine and the happy Coralie entangled me once more in the folds of their basquines and their mantillas, and I could see nothing but their dainty little feet.

I was able to get to Act III without making any disturbance, without the police being called in or the audience being scandalized, and from now on I believe in the power of public and religious morality which the Chamber of Deputies worries so much about that you might suppose there's no morality left in France. I was able to understand that it's all a matter of one man loving two women without being loved by them, or being loved by them without returning their love, who doesn't love alcaldes or isn't loved by alcaldes; but he's undoubtedly a worthy hidalgo who loves someone, himself – or God as a makeshift, for he becomes a monk. If you want to know more, hurry along to the Panorama-Dramatique.

'You now know quite well that you must go there for the first time in order to get acclimatized to those triumphant red stockings with red clocks, that dainty, promising little foot, those eyes sparkling with sunbeams and the wiles of a Parisienne disguised as an Andalusian or an Andalusian disguised as a Parisienne. Then you must go a second time to enjoy the play: the old man will send you into fits of laughter and the lovelorn hidalgo will bring you to tears. In both respects the play's a hit. The author, they say, wrote it in collaboration with one of our great poets; he has aimed at success by bringing you a pair of amorous girls, one in each hand, thereby lifting the pit to the seventh heaven of emotional turmoil. The legs of these two young ladies seemed to have more wit than the author. Nevertheless, once these two rivals left the stage, one discovered that the dialogue was scintillating, and that is a convincing proof of the excellence of the play. The author was acclaimed amid a clamour of applause which gave some anxiety to the architect who built the theatre; but the author, who is accustomed to the rumblings of the intoxicated Vesuvius seething under the chandeliers, was not alarmed. His name? Monsieur de Cursy. As for the two actresses, they danced the famous Seville bolero which, in former times, found favour with the Fathers of the Council and which has passed the censor despite the perilous provocations of its postures. This bolero has enough in it to attract all the elderly gentlemen who don't know what to do with the remnants of their love-life. I am charitable enough to advise them to keep the lenses of their operaglasses from getting blurred.

While Lucien was writing these pages, which started a revolution in journalism by the revelation it gave of a new and original style, Lousteau was writing his article, a so-called sketch of manners, entitled *The Ex-Beau*, which began thus:

The Empire beau is always a slender and elongated man, well preserved, who wears stays and sports the cross of the Legion of Honour. His name is something like Potelet and, in order to be in with the Court of today, this Imperial beau has awarded himself a

307

du: he is du Potelet, but he may become plain Potelet again in the event of a revolution. He's also a man who serves two purposes like his name: he pays court to the Faubourg Saint-German after having been the glorious, useful and amiable train-bearer of a sister of the man whom a sense of decorum forbids me to mention. If du Potelet now repudiates the services he rendered to Her Imperial Highness, he still sings the drawing-room ballads of the benefactress with whom he was so closely linked . . .

The article consisted of a tissue of personalities in the taste of the time; they were passably stupid, for this kind of literary exercise was later brought to notable perfection, particularly by *Le Figaro*. It included a clownish parallel between Madame de Bargeton, to whom Baron Châtelet was paying court, and a cuttle-bone: this amused readers without their needing to know the two persons so derided. Châtelet was compared to a heron. The loves of the heron and his inability to swallow the cuttle-fish, which broke into three pieces when he dropped it, provoked irresistible laughter. The same pleasantry was carried on in further articles and created an enormous stir in the Faubourg Saint-Germain, and was one of the thousand and one causes for the further severity of the laws passed against the Press.

One hour later, Blondet, Lousteau and Lucien returned to the salon, where the guests were chatting – the Duke, the German envoy, the four women, the three merchants, the theatre manager, Finot and the three authors. An apprentice printer, wearing his paper cap, had already come to collect the copy for the newspaper.

'The compositors will knock off if I don't bring them something,' he said.

'Look, here are ten francs, and tell them to wait,' Finot replied.

'If I give them that, Monsieur, they'll take to typsiography, and good-bye to the paper!'

'That lad has appalling good sense,' said Finot.

It was while the envoy was predicting a brilliant future for this urchin that the three authors came in. Blondet read out an exceedingly witty article attacking the Romantics. Lousteau's article raised laughter. The Duc de Rhétoré recommended him to slip in a piece of incidental praise for Madame d'Espard so as not to antagonize the Faubourg Saint-Germain too much.

'And you, read to us what you have written,' said Finot to Lucien.

When Lucien, trembling with fear, had finished, the company broke into loud applause, the actresses kissed the neophyte and the three merchants nearly strangled him with their embraces. Du Bruel took him by the hand and a tear came to his eye; finally, the theatre manager invited him to dinner.

'Children have ceased to exist,' said Blondet. 'Since Monsieur de Chateaubriand has already applied the epithet *enfant sublime* to Victor Hugo, I am obliged to tell you quite simply that you are a man of wit, feeling and style.'

'Monsieur de Rubempré is now on the staff of the paper,' said Finot, thanking Etienne and throwing him the shrewd glance of a man used to exploiting talent.

'What clever things have you written?' asked Lousteau of Blondet and Du Bruel.

'These are by Du Bruel,' said Nathan.

Seeing the amount of attention Monsieur le Vicomte d'A . . . is receiving from the public, Monsieur le Vicomte Démosthène said yesterday: 'Perhaps they'll leave me in peace now.'[1]

A lady said to an Ultra who was criticizing Chancellor Pasquier's speech because it leaned too much to the left: 'Never mind, he has truly monarchical calves.'[2]

'If it starts like that,' said Finot, 'I don't need to hear any more. – Hurry along with all that,' he said to the apprentice. 'The paper's a bit patchy, but it's our best number'; and he turned to the group of writers who were already casting looks of sly appraisal at Lucien.

1. A jibe against Victor d'Arlincourt, a pretentious but insipid historical novelist of the time (see above, page 233–4) and Sosthène de La Rochefoucauld, the Director of Fine-Arts, a much ridiculed figure.

2. Pasquier was unpopular with the Ultras for his liberal tendency. 'Monarchical calves' is an impudent reference to the obesity of Louis XVIII.

'He has wit, that young fellow,' said Blondet.

'It's a good article,' said Claude Vignon.

'Dinner's ready!' shouted Matifat.

The Duke gave his arm to Florine, Coralie took Lucien's; the dancer had Blondet on one side and the German envoy on the other.

18. *The supper*

'I DON'T understand why you're attacking Madame de Bargeton and Baron Châtelet; they say he has been made prefect of the Charente and a Master of Requests.'

'Madame de Bargeton got rid of Lucien as if he had been a tramp,' said Lousteau.

'Such a handsome young man!' said the envoy.

The dinner, served in new silver-plate, in Sèvres porcelain on linen damask, was lavishly sumptuous. Chevet had supplied the food and the wines had been chosen by the most famous merchant in the Quai Saint-Bernard, a friend of Camusot, Matifat and Cardot. Thus, for the first time, seeing Parisian luxury in full swing, Lucien met with one surprise after another, but concealed his astonishment like the man of wit, feeling and style he was – according to Blondet's testimony.

As they crossed the salon, Coralie had whispered to Florine: 'Get Camusot so thoroughly drunk that he'll be forced to sleep in your flat.'

'So you've *made* your journalist?' asked Florine, using a word from the vocabulary peculiar to women of the street.

'No, my dear, I love him!' Coralie rejoindered with an enchanting little shrug.

These words were carried to Lucien's ears by the fifth of the deadly sins. Coralie was superbly dressed, every detail of her attire artfully setting off her special charms – each woman's beauty has its own particular perfections. Her dress, like Florine's, was all the prettier for being made of a delicate material which was then new – silk muslin, the exclusive use of it belonging for a few days to Camusot, whose large orders from Paris, in his capacity as head of the 'Golden Cocoon', were a godsend to the Lyon factories. Thus both love and adornment, which are as paint and perfume to a woman, enhanced the happy Coralie's seductiveness. A pleasure awaited with a feeling of certainty holds a tremendous power of seduction for young people. Perhaps such certainty is what constitutes in their eyes the attraction of evil haunts. Therein perhaps lies the secret of long-lasting fidelity. Pure and sincere love, first love in fact, in conjunction with the impetuous infatuations which assail these poor creatures, also the admiration Coralie felt for Lucien's great beauty, endowed her with the wit which comes from the heart.

'I should love you even if you were ugly and ill!' she murmured to Lucien as they sat down to table.

What words for a poet to hear! Camusot vanished and Lucien no longer saw him when he looked at Coralie. Could a man whose every instinct was for enjoyment and sensation, bored with the monotony of provincial life, drawn into the vortex of Parisian society, weary of poverty, tormented by enforced continence, tired of his monastic seclusion in the rue de Cluny and his unfruitful labours, could such a man have held aloof from this glittering banquet? Lucien had one foot in Coralie's boudoir and the other caught in the bird-lime of the daily press which he had run after so hard without succeeding in catching up with it. After vainly standing sentry so often in the rue du Sentier, here he found the Press sitting at table, drinking deep, jovial, good-humoured. All his grievances had just been avenged by an article which the very next day would pierce two hearts into which he had vainly sought to pour all the fury and pain with which his cup had been filled. Looking at Lousteau, he thought: 'There's a friend!' without suspecting that Lousteau already feared him as a dangerous rival. Lucien had made the mistake of expending too much wit: a dull article would have served him admirably. Blondet counterbalanced the envy that was gnawing at Lousteau by telling Finot that one had to surrender to such forceful talent.

This verdict determined Lousteau's conduct: he resolved to remain friendly with Lucien and come to an understanding with Finot in order to exploit so dangerous a newcomer by keeping him in a state of need. This decision was rapidly taken by these two men and its significance was fully implied in two muttered phrases:

'He's a man of talent!'

'He'll want too much.'

'Oh!'

'Right!'

'I never sup without trepidation with French journalists,' said the German diplomat, with calm and dignified good nature, as he glanced towards Blondet whom he had met in the Comtesse de Montcornet's salon. 'There's a prophecy of Blucher which it will be your business to fulfil.'

'What did he say?' asked Nathan.

'When Blucher arrived at the heights of Montmartre with Saacken in 1814 – forgive me, gentlemen, for taking you back to so disastrous a day for you – Saacken, who was a brutal man, said: "And so we are going to burn Paris!" – "Take care you don't. Down below there is what will be the death of France!" Blucher replied, pointing to the enormous cankerous growth they saw at their feet, fiery and smoke-laden, in the valley of the Seine.'

'I thank God there are no newspapers in my country,' the minister continued after a pause. 'I haven't yet got over my fright at the sight of that little fellow in his paper cap. He's only ten, but he reasons like a hardened diplomat. And so, this evening, I feel as if I were supping with lions and panthers who are doing me the honour of sheathing their claws.'

'It is clear,' said Blondet, 'that we can tell Europe, and prove it, that your Excellency had disgorged a serpent this evening and has only just missed injecting its venom into Tullia, our loveliest dancer. On that theme we could make glosses about Eve, the Bible, the first and the last sin. But have no fear: you're our guest.'

'It would be quite an amusing thing to do,' said Finot.

'We could print scientific dissertations on all the serpents found in the human heart and body before they reach the diplomatic corps,' said Lousteau.

'We could show there's some sort of a serpent in that jar of brandied cherries,' said Vernou.

'In the end you'd come to believe it yourself,' said Vignon to the diplomat.

'Gentlemen,' said the Duc de Rhétoré, 'don't unsheathe your claws: they're so nicely padded at the moment.'

'The influence and power of newspapers are only just dawning,' said Finot. 'Journalism is in its infancy; it will grow up. In ten years from now, everything will be subject to publicity. Thought will enlighten the world . . . '

'It will blast the world,' said Blondet, interrupting Finot.

'That's saying something,' said Claude Vignon.

'It will bring forth kings,' said Lousteau.

'And bring down monarchies,' said the diplomat.

'Therefore,' said Blondet, 'if the Press didn't exist, it would be folly to invent it. But it's here, and we live on it!'

'You'll die of it,' said the diplomat. 'Don't you see that the superiority of the masses, supposing that you were to enlighten them, will make it difficult for the individual to achieve greatness? By sowing the seeds of argument in the minds of the lower classes you'll reap a harvest of revolt, and you will be its first victims? What do they smash in Paris when there's a riot?'

'Street-lamps,' said Nathan. 'But we are too modest to have any apprehensions: we shall only get a few slight cracks.'

'The French are too intelligent to let any kind of government get firmly into the saddle,' said the diplomat. 'Otherwise you would start conquering Europe all over again; a conquest which you were unable to maintain with your swords.'

'Newspapers are an evil,' said Claude Vignon. 'An evil which could be utilized, but the Government wants to fight it. There'll be a conflict. Who will go under? That's the question.'

'The Government,' said Blondet. 'I'm shouting myself hoarse saying this. In France wit is a most potent weapon, and the papers have not only all the wit which witty men have, but the hypocrisy of Tartuffe into the bargain.'

'Blondet! Blondet!' said Finot. 'You're going too far. Some of our subscribers are present.'

'You're the owner of one of those poison warehouses. No doubt you're afraid; but I don't care a rap for any of your news-shops although I make my living by them.'

'Blondet is right,' said Claude Vignon. 'Instead of being a priestly function, the newspaper has become a political party weapon; now it is becoming merely a trade; and like all trades it has neither faith nor principles. Every newspaper is, as Blondet says, a shop which sells to the public whatever shades of opinion it wants. If there were a journal for hunch-backs it would prove night and morning how handsome, how good-natured, how necessary hunchbacks are. A journal is no longer concerned to enlighten, but to flatter public opinion. Consequently, in due course, all journals will be treacherous, hypocritical, infamous, mendacious, murderous; they'll kill ideas, systems and men, and thrive on it. They'll be in the happy position of all abstract creations: wrong will be done without anybody being guilty. I shall be Vignon, you will be Lousteau, you Blondet, you Finot: a bunch of Aristides, Platos, Catos, disciples of Plutarch. We shall all be innocent, we shall all be able to wash our hands of all infamy. Napoleon gave the explanation of this phenomenon – moral or immoral, whichever you like – in a superb aphorism dictated to him by his study of the Convention: *In corporate crimes no one is implicated*. A newspaper can behave in the most atrocious manner and no one on the staff considers that his own hands are soiled.'

'But the Government will bring in represssive laws,' said Du Bruel. 'It's already drawing them up.'

'Bah!' said Nathan. 'What can the law do against French wit, the most subtle of all dissolvents?'

'Ideas,' Vignon continued, 'can only be neutralized by ideas. Terror and despotism alone can stifle the French genius, whose language lends itself admirably to allusion and *double entendre*. The more repressive the law becomes, the more will wit spurt forth like steam through a safety-valve. Thus, when the King does something good, if the newspapers are against him it will be the minister who has done it all, and *vice versa*. If a newspaper invents some outrageous calumny, it attributes it to information received. If a private person complains it will get off with an apology for the liberty taken. If it is hauled before the courts, it complains that it was not asked to rectify its statement. But ask it for a rectification and it will laughingly refuse, making light of the crime it has committed. Finally, if the victim wins his case, it ridicules him. If a penalty is imposed, if the damages are too high, it will pillory the plaintiff as an enemy of liberty, his country and enlightenment in general. It will show up Monsieur So-and-So as a thief while making out that he is the most honest man in the kingdom. So its crimes are trifles, those who attack it are monsters! And in a given space of time it can make its readers believe anything it wants. Also, nothing it doesn't approve of can be patriotic and it is never in the wrong. It will use religion to attack religion and the Charter to attack the King; it will scoff at the judicial bench when the judicial bench offends it and praise it when it has pandered to popular passions. In order to get subscribers it will invent the most moving fables; it will play the clown like Bobèche. A newspaper will serve up its father raw, with no other seasoning than its jokes, rather than fail to interest or amuse its public. It will be like an actor putting his son's ashes into the cinerary urn so that he can weep real tears, or like a mistress sacrificing everything to her lover!'

'In short it's the common people in folio size,' Blondet exclaimed, interrupting Vignon.

'Yes,' Vignon continued, 'but a common people which is hypocritical and ungenerous. It will put a ban on talent, just as Athens put it on Aristides. We shall see the newspapers, which originally were run by men of honour, fall subsequently into the hands of the greatest mediocrities possessing the patience and india-rubber faint-heartedness lacking in men of fine genius, or into the hands of grocers with money enough to buy the products of the pen. We can already see this happening! But in ten years' time any urchin fresh from school will believe he's a great man; he'll climb on to the column of a newspaper in order to kick his predecessors in the teeth; he'll pull their feet from under them in order to get their place. Napoleon was very right to muzzle the Press. I would wager that, under a government which they had themselves brought into power, the Opposition news-sheets would use the same arguments and the same articles to topple it over as they now use to attack the King's ministry, once it refused them anything whatsoever. The more concessions are made to the journalists, the more demanding they'll become. The journalists who have made the grade will give place to famished and poverty-stricken journalists. It's an incurable sore which will become more and more cancerous, more and more insufferable; and the greater the evil, the more it will be tolerated, until the day comes when, thanks to their abundance, the newspapers will be in a confusion like that of Babel. We know, the whole lot of us, that the papers will go further in ingratitude than kings, further in speculation and calculation than the dirtiest kind of commerce, that they will rot our intelligences by selling us their mental fire-water every morning. But we shall all write for them, like the people who work a quicksilver mine knowing that they'll die of it. Look at the young man over there, sitting beside Coralie – what's his name? Lucien. He's handsome, he's a poet and, what is worth more for him, a man of wit. Well, he'll enter one of those intellectual brothels called newspapers, throw his best ideas into it, dry up his brains, corrupt his soul, commit those anonymous acts of treachery which, in the war of ideas, stand in lieu of stratagems, pillages, arson, shifts and tacks in the wars waged by bandits. When he, like a thousand others, has been at great expense of genius for the profit of the shareholder, these vendors of poison will let him die of hunger if he's thirsty, and of thirst if he's hungry.'

'Thank you,' said Finot.

'But, Heaven forgive me,' said Claude Vignon. 'I knew all that. I'm in the same convict prison, and the arrival of a new convict gives me pleasure. Blondet and I have more in us than Monsieur X and Monsieur Y who batten on our talent. None the less we shall always be exploited by them. We have some feeling underneath our intelligence, but we haven't enough ferocity to qualify as exploiters. We're lazy, contemplative, meditative, critical of all and sundry: they'll suck out our brains and then accuse us of loose living.'

'I thought you men would be a bit more amusing,' cried Florine.

'Florine is right,' said Blondet. 'Let's leave the cure of public ills to the quacks – our statesmen. As Charlet said: "One never spits into the wine-vats."'

'Do you know what Vignon puts me in mind of?' said Lousteau, turning to Lucien. 'One of those gross women in the rue du Pélican who tells a schoolboy: "Little man, you're too young for a place like this ..."'

This sally raised a laugh and amused even Coralie. The merchants listened as they went on eating and drinking.

'What a nation!' said the envoy to the Duc de Rhétoré. 'So much good and so much evil in conjunction! Gentlemen, you are spendthrifts who cannot come to ruin.'

Thus it happened, by the blessing of chance, that no information was lacking to Lucien about the precipice over which he was to fall. D'Arthez had set the poet on the noble path of toil by inciting in him the feeling which overcomes all obstacles. Even Lousteau had, for a selfish motive, tried to stave him off by showing journalism and literature in their true light. Lucien had been reluctant to believe in so much hidden corruption; but now at last he was hearing journalists crying out in pain and could see them at work disembowelling their foster-mother as they predicted the future. In the course of that evening he had seen things as they were. Instead of feeling horror-stricken as he looked into the very heart of Parisian corruption so well characterized by Blucher, he was enjoying this witty company to the point of intoxication. It seemed to him that these extraordinary men, under the damascene armour of their vices and the glittering helmet of their cold analysis, were superior to the grave and austere brethren of the Cénacle. Besides, he was savouring the first delights of affluence, he was under the spell of luxury and the tyranny of sumptuous fare; his wayward instincts were reviving, he was drinking choice wines for the first time, he was sampling the exquisite products of first-class cooking; he saw a minister, a duke and his little dancer mingling with the journalists and admiring the atrocious power they wielded; he felt a terrible itch to dominate this world of potentates and believed he had the power to overcome them. Finally there was Coralie who had been made happy by only a few sentences from him: he had examined her in the light of the festive candles through the steam arising from the dishes and the mists of intoxication, and she was so beautified by love that she seemed sublime to him! Moreover this girl was the prettiest, the most beautiful actress in Paris. The Cénacle, that celestial sphere of noble intelligence, was bound to lose the battle against such wholesale temptation. Lucien's vanity, a vanity peculiar to authors, had just been flattered by men of experience; he had received praise from his future rivals. The success of his article and his conquest of Coralie were two triumphs which might well have turned an older head than his. During the discussion, everyone had eaten and drunk well. Lousteau, sitting next to Camusot, three or four times poured kirsch into the merchant's wine without anyone noticing and played on his vanity to get him to drink copiously. This manoeuvre was so carefully carried out that the merchant was unaware of it: he thought that in his particular line he was as sprightly as the journalists.

An exchange of sharp pleasantries began as the dessert delicacies and the wines went round. The diplomat, a man of much intelligence, made a sign to the Duke and the dancer as soon as he heard the buzz of nonsensical remarks which, as this man of acumen well knew, herald the grotesque scenes that bring orgies to an end, and all three of them departed. As soon as Camusot's wits became fuddled, Coralie and Lucien who, during the supper, had been behaving like amorous adolescents, fled downstairs and jumped into a cab. Camusot was under the table, and Matifat thought he had disappeared with the actress. He left his guests smoking, drinking, laughing, bickering, and followed Florine when she went off to bed. As daylight overtook the combatants, or rather Blondet, this intrepid wine-bibber, the only one still capable of speech, invited the sleepers to drink a toast to rosy-fingered Dawn.

19. An actress's apartments

LUCIEN was unused to Parisian orgies; he was still in possession of his reasoning faculties as he went downstairs, but the open air made him feel hideously drunk. Coralie and her maid had to help the poet up to the first floor of the fine house in the rue de Vendôme where the actress lived. On the staircase Lucien nearly collapsed and was disgustingly sick.

'Quick, Bérénice,' cried Coralie. 'Tea, make some tea!'

'It's nothing. It's the fresh air,' said Lucien. 'Also, I've never drunk so much.'

'Poor child! he's as innocent as a lamb,' said Bérénice, a stout woman from Normandy, as ugly as Coralie was beautiful.

At last Lucien, without realizing it, was put into Coralie's bed. With the help of Bérénice the actress had undressed her poet with the loving care of a mother for her small child. He kept on saying: 'It's nothing. It's the fresh air. Thank you, Mamma.'

'How sweet the way he says "Mamma"!' exclaimed Coralie, kissing his hair.

'What a pleasure to love such an angel, Mademoiselle. Where did you pick him up? I never thought that a man could be as handsome as you are beautiful.'

Lucien wanted to sleep, not knowing where he was or what was going on. Coralie made him swallow several cups of tea and then left him sleeping.

'The concierge didn't see us, or anyone else?' asked Coralie.

'No, I was waiting up for you.'

'Victorine knows nothing about it?'

319

'Not likely,' said Bérénice.

Ten hours later, at about noon, Lucien woke up under Coralie's gaze. She had been watching him as he slept! The poet in him understood. She was still in her fine dress, abominably stained, but she was going to treat it as a relic. Lucien recognized the devotion and delicate attentiveness of true love awaiting its reward: he gave Coralie one look. She undressed in an instant and slipped like a grass-snake into bed beside Lucien. By five o'clock the poet was again asleep, sunk deep in voluptuous pleasure. He had caught a glimpse of the actress's bedroom, a ravishingly luxurious creation in white and pink, a wonderland of choice and dainty objects excelling those which Lucien had already admired in Florine's flat. Coralie was now up, since she had to be at the theatre by seven in order to play her Andalusian role. She had again been contemplating her poet as he slept off his sensual enjoyment; she had been enthralled and could never be sated with this noble love which united heart and senses and enraptured both. The deification which makes it possible to feel as two separate people on earth and to love as one single person in heaven was like a priest's absolution to her. For that matter, who would not have found exoneration in Lucien's more than human beauty? As she knelt by the bed, happy to love for love's sake, the actress felt a sort of sanctification. This state of delight was disturbed by Bérénice.

'Here comes Camusot. He knows you are here,' she called out.

Lucien stood up, his innate generosity prompting him to do no harm to Coralie. Bérénice drew aside a curtain, and Lucien retreated into a charming dressing-room where Bérénice and her mistress brought him his clothes with extraordinary rapidity. When the merchant appeared, Coralie caught sight of the poet's boots, which Bérénice had put in front of the fire to warm after covertly polishing them. Both servant and mistress had forgotten these incriminating boots. Bérénice departed after exchanging an anxious look with her mistress. Coralie threw herself on to her settee and invited Camusot to sit down in a gondola chair facing her.

The good man, who adored Coralie, was looking at the boots and dared not lift his eyes to his mistress.

'Ought I to make a fuss and leave Coralie on account of this pair of boots? It would be a trifling thing to get angry about. There are boots everywhere. These would look better in a shoemaker's shop-window or strolling about on a man's legs in the boulevards. Here however, with no legs in them, they tell a tale which doesn't argue for fidelity. I'm fifty, that's true: I have to be as blind as Cupid.'

There was no excuse for this cowardly monologue. The pair of boots were not half-boots like those in use today and which might in some measure be invisible to an unobservant man; they were, as fashion then ordained, full-length boots, very elegant, with tassels, the sort which glistened above close-fitting, almost invariably light-coloured trousers and reflected objects as in a looking-glass. So these boots were staring the honest silk-merchant in the face and, we must add, breaking his heart.

'What's the matter?' asked Coralie.

'Nothing,' he replied.

'Ring the bell,' said Coralie, smiling at Camusot's cowardice. 'Bérénice,' she said to her Norman maid as she entered, 'find me some button-hooks so that I can try these wretched boots on again. And don't forget to bring them to my dressing-room this evening.'

'What? Are they *your* boots?' Camusot asked, breathing more easily.

'My goodness, what do you think?' she said with a haughty air. 'You great silly, you surely don't believe? ... Oh yes, he would believe it!' she said to Bérénice. 'I've a man's role in What's-his-name's play, and I've never dressed as a man before. The theatre shoemaker brought me those boots to practise walking in them while I was waiting for the pair he measured me for. He helped me on with them, but they hurt me so much I took them off; none the less I must try them again.'

'Don't put them on again if they're uncomfortable,' said Camusot, who had found them very uncomfortable indeed.

'That would be more sensible,' said Bérénice, 'instead of Mademoiselle torturing herself as she did. It made her cry, Monsieur, and if I were a man I'd never let a woman I loved cry! It would be better if they were made of morocco leather. But the management is so stingy! Monsieur, you ought to go and order some for her ... '

'Yes, I will,' said the merchant. – 'You're only just getting up,' he said to Coralie.

'This very minute. I didn't get to bed till six o'clock, after looking for you everywhere. You made me keep my cab waiting for seven hours. That's all the care you take of me! Neglecting me for the bottle! I had to take care of myself, seeing that I shall now be performing every evening so long as *The Alcalde* makes money. I don't want to belie that young man's article!'

'He's handsome, that boy,' said Camusot.

'You think so? I don't like men of that kind: they're too much like women. And besides they don't know how to love like you silly old business men who find life so boring!'

'Will Monsieur be dining with Madame?' asked Bérénice.

'No. My mouth's all furred up.'

'You got nicely sozzled last night. Oh, Papa Camusot, let me tell you I don't like men who drink ... '

'I suppose you'll give that young man a present,' said the merchant.

'Indeed yes, I prefer to pay them that way, instead of doing what Florine does. Well then, you bad lot, I love you, but you'd better leave me – or else give me a carriage so that I needn't waste time in future.'

'You'll have it tomorrow for the dinner with your manager at the Rocher de Cancale. Sunday evening the new play won't be on.'

'Come along, I'm going to dine,' said Coralie; and she took Camusot off.

An hour later Lucien was released by Bérénice. She had been Coralie's childhood companion and she was as sharp and nimble-minded as she was corpulent.

'Stay here. Coralie will come back alone. She's even ready

to get rid of Camusot if he worries you,' said Bérénice to Lucien. 'But, dear child of her heart, you're too much of an angel to ruin her. She told me she's made up her mind to give everything up and leave this paradise to go and live with you in your garret. Oh! jealous and envious people have made it plain to her that you hadn't a penny to bless yourself with and that you lived in the Latin quarter. Mind you, I'd go with you and do your housework. But I've managed to cheer the poor child up. Isn't it a fact, Monsieur, that you've too much sense to do anything so idiotic? You'll see all right that that lump of a man will only get the carcase and that you'll be the pet, the beloved, the idol she'll give her soul to. If you knew how good she is when I put her through her parts! A perfect darling! She well deserved that God should send her one of his angels, she was so disgusted with life. She was very unhappy with her mother, who used to beat her and then sold her! Yes, Monsieur, a mother selling her own child! If I had a daughter I'd look after her as I do my little Coralie; she's been like my own child to me. This is the first good time I've seen her having, the first time she's had lots of applause. It seems that because of what you wrote about her, they're getting up a fine claque for the next performance. While you were asleep Braulard came to work things out with her.'

'Who's Braulard?' asked Lucien, under the impression that he had already heard this name mentioned.

'The leader of the clappers. He's been arranging with her about what spots to clap loudest at in her part. Florine makes out she's her friend, but she's quite capable of doing her a bad turn and stealing the show. The whole boulevard's in a stir on account of your article. – There's a bed for you, fit for a prince to make love in!' she added as she spread a lace coverlet over it.

She lit the candles. In the light they gave, Lucien was dazzled and indeed fancied he was in a fairy palace. Camusot had picked out the richest stuffs the Golden Cocoon could provide for the wall hangings and the window draperies. The poet was treading on a carpet fit for royalty.

The light gleamed and shimmered in the carvings of the

rosewood furniture. The white marble mantelpiece was resplendent with most costly trifles. The bedside rug was of swansdown edged with ermine. Black velvet slippers lined with crimson silk spoke of the pleasures awaiting the author of *Les Marguerites*. An exquisite lamp hung from the silk-draped ceiling. All around were wonderful *jardinières* filled with choice flowers, pretty white heather and scentless camellias. The whole room was a picture of innocence. How could one imagine an actress and the morals of the theatre in such a setting? Bérénice noticed Lucien's amazement.

'Isn't it lovely?' she asked in a wheedling tone of voice. 'Won't you be better off making love here rather than in an attic? ... Don't let her do anything silly,' she continued, leading Lucien to a magnificent pedestal table spread with food abstracted from her mistress's dinner so that the cook might not suspect the presence of a lover.

Lucien had an excellent dinner, presented by Bérénice in a service of chased silver with decorated plates worth twenty francs apiece. This luxury had the same effect on him as a girl of the streets with her bare flesh and dainty sheer stockings has on a boy in his teens.

'How lucky this Camusot is!' he cried.

'Lucky?' Bérénice retorted. 'Why, he would give all he has to be in your place and swap his old grey thatch for the fair hair of a young man like you.'

After pouring out for him some of the most delicious wine that Bordeaux ever prepared for the wealthiest Englishman, she urged Lucien to go back to bed while waiting for Coralie and take a little nap; and in fact Lucien was only too ready to lie in this wonderful bed. Bérénice had read this desire in the poet's eyes and was pleased for her mistress's sake. At half-past ten he awoke under a gaze which was brimming over with love. Coralie was there, in her most voluptuous night attire. Lucien had slept, and was no longer drunk – only with love. Bérénice withdrew with the question: 'What time tomorrow?'

'Eleven. Bring our breakfast up to bed. I'll see no one before two o'clock.'

At two the next afternoon, the actress and her lover were dressed and sitting face to face as if the poet had come to pay a visit to his protégée. Coralie had bathed Lucien, brushed and combed his hair and dressed him; she had sent out to Colliau's to get him a dozen fine shirts, a dozen cravats and a dozen handkerchiefs; also a dozen pairs of gloves in a cedar box. When she heard the rumble of a carriage at the street-door, she rushed to the window with Lucien. They both saw Camusot getting out of a magnificent coupé.

'I didn't think,' she said, 'that one could hate a man so much . . . and luxury too . . . '

'I'm too poor to allow you to ruin yourself,' said Lucien, thus passing under the Caudine Forks.

'My precious darling,' she said, pressing against Lucien's heart, 'then you really do love me? – I asked Monsieur to come and see me this morning,' she said, presenting Lucien, 'thinking that we might go for a ride in the Champs-Elysées to try out the carriage.'

'You must go without me,' said Camusot sorrowfully. 'And I can't dine with you. I'd forgotten it's my wife's birthday.'

'Poor Musot! How bored you'll be!' she said, giving the merchant a hug.

She was wildly happy at the thought that she and Lucien together would be the first to ride in this fine coupé, that she could go alone with him to the Bois de Boulogne; in her outburst of joy she seemed to be really fond of Camusot and heaped caresses on him.

'I wish I could give you a carriage every day,' said the poor man.

'Let's go, Monsieur, it's two o'clock,' said the actress to the shame-faced Lucien whom she consoled with an adorable gesture.

Coralie rushed downstairs dragging Lucien behind her; he heard the merchant lumbering along behind them like a seal, unable to catch up with them. The poet experienced the most intoxicating delights: Coralie, radiant with happiness, displayed to the ravished eyes of all who beheld her an attire which was the last word in taste and elegance. The Paris of the Champs-Elysées admired the pair of lovers. In one of the lanes of the Bois de Boulogne their coupé encountered the barouche of Mesdames d' Espard and de Bargeton who gazed at Lucien with astonishment: he darted at them the contemptuous glance of a poet who foresees the fame in store for him and intends to exploit his power. The instant when a single glare directed at these two women enabled him to convey some of the vengeful thoughts which, thanks to them, were gnawing at his heart, was one of the sweetest moments in his life, and perhaps decided his destiny. Lucien became once more a prey to the fury born of pride: he wanted to reappear in society and take a spectacular revenge; all the petty social snobbery which as a hard-working man and the friend of the Cénacle he had trampled underfoot once more took possession of him. He now realized the full purport of the attack Lousteau had made on his behalf. Lousteau had pandered to his passions, whereas his mentors of the Cénacle seemed bent on repressing them in favour of dull virtue and toil, which Lucien was now beginning to find unprofitable. Hard work! . . . Does it not spell death to temperaments avid for enjoyment? Hence the readiness of writers to sink into a *dolce far niente* attitude, take to good cheer and the luxurious delights of the life lived by actresses and women of easy virtue. Lucien felt an irresistible longing to continue the frantic life of the last two days.

The dinner at the Rocher de Cancale was exquisite. Lucien found Florine's guests there, except for the envoy, the Duke, the dancer and Camusot; these were replaced by two actors and Hector Merlin with his mistress, a delightful women who went by the name of Madame du Val-Noble, the most beautiful and elegant of those women who then constituted a special world in Paris, the women who today are decorously dubbed *lorettes*.[1] Lucien, who for the last forty-eight hours had been living in Paradise, learnt of the success of his article. Seeing himself lionized and envied, the poet felt self-assured; he sparkled with wit and became the Lucien de Rubempré who for a few months was to be a shining light in the literary and artistic

1. Women of easy virtue, supposedly called *lorettes* because they lived in the neighbourhood of the church of Notre-Dame de Lorette.

world. Finot, a man of uncontestable skill in divining talent, who could nose it out as an ogre scents raw flesh, cajoled Lucien in an attempt to recruit him for the squad of journalists under his command. Lucien nibbled at the bait of his flattery, but Coralie observed the tactics of this man who battened on other people's intelligence and tried to put Lucien on his guard.

'Don't commit yourself, my love,' she said to the poet. 'Wait. They want to exploit you. We'll talk about it this evening.'

'Don't worry,' Lucien answered. 'I feel I can be as spiteful and cunning as they are.'

Finot, who no doubt had not definitively fallen out with Hector Merlin over the blank spaces, introduced him and Lucien to one another. Coralie and Madame du Val-Noble fraternized and overwhelmed each other with caresses and attentions. Madame du Val-Noble invited Lucien and Coralie to dinner.

Hector Merlin, the most dangerous of all the journalists present at the dinner, was a spare little man with pinched lips, inordinate ambition and unbounded jealousy. He delighted in all the evil he saw done around him and took advantage of the hostilities which he himself fostered; he had much wit and little will-power, but in lieu of that he had the instinct which guides upstarts to the regions where money and influence serve as beacon lights. Lucien and he took a dislike to each other, and it is not difficult to explain why. Merlin was tactless enough to talk out loud to Lucien while Lucien was quietly thinking. By the time dessert was served, the bonds of the most moving friendship appeared to unite all these men, though each of them thought himself a cut above the rest. As a newcomer Lucien was the object of their flattering attentions. They chatted freely. Hector Merlin alone remained serious. Lucien asked him the reason for this.

'Well, I see that you are entering the world of literature and journalism with your illusions intact. You believe in friendship. We are all friends or enemies according to circumstances. We are the first to belabour one another with the weapons we ought only to use on other people. You'll soon perceive that you'll get nowhere with fine sentiments. Are you kind-hearted? Become ill-natured. Be cross-grained on principle. Perhaps no one has told you of this overriding law: I'm disclosing it to you, and it's by no means an unimportant disclosure. If you want to be loved, never leave your mistress without making her weep a bit. To make your fortune in literature, always hurt everybody's feelings, even those of your friends. Wound their self-esteem: everybody will fawn on you.'

Hector Merlin was happy to see by the neophyte's air that his words had gone home like the thrust of a dagger. They played cards. Lucien lost all his money. Coralie took him away, and the delights of love made him forget the terrible emotions of the gaming table, to which, later, he was to fall a victim. The next day, as he left her rooms and walked back to the Latin quarter, he found that she had put in his purse the money he had lost. This attention saddened him at first, and he thought of returning to the actress to give back her humiliating present; but he had already reached the rue de La Harpe and went on his way to the Hôtel Cluny. As he walked along he thought over Coralie's kind act and saw in it a proof of the maternal love which women of her sort mingle with their passions, for with them passion includes all kinds of sentiment. As one thought followed another, Lucien found in the end an excuse for accepting. He said to himself: 'I love her, we'll live together as husband and wife and I'll never leave her!'

20. Last visit to the Cénacle

WHO, unless he were a Diogenes, would not understand Lucien's feelings as he climbed the muddy, smelly stairs of his hotel, as the key grated in the door-lock and as he looked once more on the dirty tiles and pitiable mantelpiece of this horribly bare and squalid room? On the table he found the manuscript of his novel and a note from Daniel d'Arthez:

'Our friends are almost satisfied with your work, dear poet.

You can offer it with increased confidence, they say, to friends and enemies alike. We have read your charming article on the Panorama-Dramatique play: you must be arousing as much envy in the literary world as regret in us.'

'Regret? What does he mean?' cried Lucien, surprised at the tone of politeness prevailing in this note. Was he then a stranger to the Cénacle? After devouring the delicious fruit which the Eve of the greenroom had offered him he was even keener on keeping the esteem and friendship of the brethren of the rue des Quatre-Vents. For a few moments he remained plunged in meditation, comparing his present life in this room with the future awaiting him in Coralie's flat. Oscillating between honourable and corrupting thoughts, he sat down and began to examine his work in the state in which his friends had returned it to him. How great was his astonishment! From chapter to chapter, the skilful and devoted pen of these great but as yet unknown men had changed dross into rich ore. A full, close, concise and vigorous dialogue had been substituted for the conversations which he now realized were idle chatter compared with a discourse breathing the very spirit of the times. His portraits, somewhat woolly in outline, had been brought into strong and colourful relief; all of them were linked up with the interesting phenomena of human life by means of physiological comments, due no doubt to Bianchon, expressed with subtlety and infusing life into them. His verbose descriptions had taken on substance and vividness. In place of the misshapen, ill-clad child of his imagination he found an entrancing white-robed maiden with rose-coloured girdle and scarf, a ravishing creation. When night came, it caught him with streaming eyes, overwhelmed at this greatness of heart, realizing the value of such a lesson, admiring these emendations which taught him more about literature and art than his four years of reading, comparison and study had done. The correction of a badly-sketched cartoon by masterly touches taken direct from life always reveals far more than theories and observations.

'What friends! What hearts of gold! How fortunate I am!' he exclaimed as he locked the manuscript up.

Carried away by an impulse natural to poetic and excitable

natures, he rushed to Daniel's room. However, as he mounted the staircase, he felt less worthy of these great-hearted men whom nothing was able to divert from the path of honour. A voice was telling him that, if Daniel had loved Coralie, he would have refused to share her with Camusot. He was also aware in what deep horror the Cénacle held journalists, and he knew that he was already on the way to being one. He found his friends, except Meyraux, who had just left, a prey to the despair written on their faces.

'What's the matter, my friends?' asked Lucien.

'We have just heard of a terrible catastrophe: the greatest intellect of our time, our dearest friend, who had been our guiding light for two years . . . '

'Louis Lambert,' said Lucien.

' . . . is in a state of catalepsy which leaves no hope,' said Bianchon.

'He will die with no feeling in his body and his head in the clouds,' Michel Chrestien added with solemnity.

'He will die as he has lived,' said d'Arthez.

'Love, thrown like a burning torch into the vast realm of his intelligence, has set it on fire,' said Léon Giraud.

'Yes,' said Joseph Bridau, 'it has raised him to such a state of rapture that we have lost contact with him.'

'We are the ones to be pitied,' said Fulgence Ridal.

'But perhaps he will get better,' cried Lucien.

'According to what Meyraux has told us, no cure is possible,' Bianchon replied. 'His brain is possessed by phenomena which are beyond medical control.'

'But surely medicinal treatment is possible,' said d'Arthez.

'Yes,' said Bianchon. 'Now he's only cataleptic: we can make an imbecile of him.'

'Oh! Why can't we offer the evil spirit another brain in exchange! I would willingly give mine!' cried Michel Chrestien.

'And what would become of the federation of Europe?' asked d'Arthez.

'Ah! That's true,' Michel Chrestien replied. 'Before belonging to an individual, one belongs to Humanity.'

'I came here,' said Lucien, 'with my heart full of gratitude towards all of you. You have changed my bullion into gold currency.'

'Gratitude? Who do you take us for?' asked Bianchon.

'We were happy to do it,' said Fulgence.

'So then, you're a journalist?' said Léon Giraud. 'The report of your *début* has even reached the Latin quarter.'

'I'm not one yet,' answered Lucien.

'Ah! So much the better!' cried Michel Chrestien.

'I told you so,' d'Arthez continued. 'Lucien has the heart of one who knows the value of a pure conscience. Is it not a tonic and a viaticum to lay one's head on one's pillow at night still able to say: "I have not passed judgement on other people's work; I have caused affliction to no one; my wit has not been plunged like a dagger into an innocent person's heart; no one's happiness has been sacrificed to my pleasantries; they have not even disturbed the self-complacency of fools or put an unjust strain on genius; I have disdained the facile triumphs of the epigram; in short I have not given the lie to my convictions." '

'But,' said Lucien. 'I believe one can be like that even when working on a newspaper. If I had positively no other means of subsistence I should certainly have to come to it.'

'Oh! Oh! Oh!,' said Fulgence, his tone of voice rising at each exclamation. 'We are capitulating!'

'He will become a journalist,' said Léon Giraud gravely. 'Ah! Lucien, if you were willing to become one with us – we are going to bring out a journal in which neither truth nor justice will ever be outraged, in which we shall disseminate doctrines useful to humanity – perhaps . . . '

'You won't have a single subscriber,' Lucien interjected with Machiavellian malice.

'They will have five hundred subscribers who will be worth five hundred thousand others,' replied Michel Chrestien.

'You'll need a lot of capital,' Lucien answered.

'No,' said d'Arthez, 'only self-devotion.'

'He smells like a scent-shop,' cried Michel Chrestien, sniffing at Lucien's hair with a comical gesture.

'We saw you in a superlatively-gleaming carriage, drawn by horses worthy of a Beau Brummell, with a mistress worthy of a prince: Coralie.'

'Well,' said Lucien. 'Is there anything wrong in that?'

'You say it as if there were,' Bianchon exclaimed.

'I could have wished Lucien might have had a Beatrice,' said d'Arthez. 'A noble-hearted woman who would have been his inspiration through life.'

'But Daniel,' said the poet. 'Is not love everywhere alike?'

'Ah!' said the republican. 'In this matter I'm an aristocrat. I couldn't love a woman whose cheek is kissed in public by an actor, a woman addressed as "darling" in the wings, who cheapens herself in front of the groundlings and smiles on them, who dances with lifted skirts and puts on male attire in order to display what I want to be the only man to see. Or, if I loved such a woman, she would give up the theatre, and my love would purify her.'

'And supposing she could not give up the theatre?'

'I should die of disappointment, jealousy and a thousand other ills.'

'But one cannot wrest love from one's heart as if one were pulling out a tooth.'

Lucien became sombre and pensive. 'When they know that I tolerate Camusot, they'll despise me,' he was saying to himself.

'Look now,' the fierce republican said to him with cruel frankness. 'You may become a great writer, but you'll never be anything but a little humbug,' and taking up his hat he went out.

'He's a hard man, Michel Chrestien,' said the poet.

'Hard and salutary like the dentist's forceps,' said Bianchon. 'Michel foresees your future, and perhaps even now is weeping for you in the street.'

D'Arthez was gentle and consoling and tried to cheer Lucien up. After an hour the poet left the Cénacle, tortured by his conscience which was crying out to him: 'You'll be a journalist!' as the witch cries out to Macbeth: 'Thou shalt be king hereafter.'

From the street he looked up at the long-suffering d'Arthez's casement window, through which shone a dim light, and returned to his room, sad at heart and unquiet of soul. A kind of presentiment told him that he had been clasped to the heart of his true friends for the last time. On entering the rue de Cluny via the Place de la Sorbonne, he caught sight of Coralie's carriage. In order to see her poet for one moment and simply to wish him good-night, the actress had covered the distance from the Boulevard du Temple to the Sorbonne. Lucien discovered his mistress in tears at the sight of his garret; she wanted to share her lover's destitution; she wept as she stowed away his shirts, gloves, cravats and handkerchiefs in the hideous lodging-house chest of drawers. Her despair was so genuine, so great, and expressed so much love that Lucien, who had been reproached for associating with an actress, thought of Coralie as a saint who would not hesitate to wear the hair-shirt of poverty. In order to come to him, this adorable creature had invented the pretext of informing her friend that Camusot, herself and Lucien were jointly to return hospitality to Matifat, Florine and Lousteau by giving them supper, also of asking Lucien if he had any invitation to suggest which might be useful to him. Lucien replied that he would talk it over with Lousteau. After a few moments the actress hurried off, without revealing that Camusot was waiting for her downstairs.

21. *A variety of journalist*

THE next morning at eight o'clock Lucien called on Etienne, found he was out and hurried over to Florine's rooms. The journalist and the actress received their friend in the dainty bedroom in which they were conjugally installed, and all three had a splendid lunch.

'Well, my boy,' said Lousteau when they were at table and when Lucien had mentioned the supper to be given by Coralie. 'I advise you to come with me to see Félicien Vernou, to invite him and to strike up a friendship with him in so far as one can do so with such a character. Félicien will perhaps get you into the political journal for which he concocts a daily *feuilleton* and in which you may be able to spread yourself in serious articles for the top columns. This news-sheet, like ours, belongs to the Liberal party: you'll be a Liberal, that's the popular party. Moreover, if you thought of going over to the ministerial side you'd join it to greater advantage for having shown them you're a man to be reckoned with. – Haven't you and Coralie been invited to dinner with Hector Merlin and his Madame du Val-Noble, whose salon is visited by a number of great lords, young dandies and millionaires?'

'Yes,' replied Lucien. 'You'll be there too with Florine.' We may note that Lucien and Lousteau, during their carousals at the Friday supper and the Sunday dinner, had arrived at the stage of 'thouing' each other.

'Well, we shall meet Merlin at the editorial office: he's a chap who'll follow close behind Finot. You'll do well to cultivate him and get him and his mistress to join you at the supper. He'll perhaps be useful to you before long, for men who are haters need everybody, and he'll be serviceable to you if he has your pen to call upon.'

'Your first article caused enough sensation for you not to meet with any obstacle,' Florine said to Lucien. 'Lose no time in taking advantage of it, or else you'll soon be forgotten.'

'As for the deal,' continued Lousteau, 'the great deal has come off! This Finot, a man of no talent, is director and editor of Dauriat's weekly, the owner of a sixth part of it which is costing him nothing, and he draws a salary of six hundred francs a month. As from this morning, my dear, I'm editor of the little paper. Everything happened as I presumed it would the other evening: Florine was splendid – she could give points to Prince Talleyrand.'

'Oh well,' said Florine, '*we* get hold of men through their pleasures, whereas diplomats only work on their self-conceit. The diplomats see men giving themselves airs and we see them making fools of themselves: so we get the best results.'

'As he clinched the deal,' said Lousteau, 'Matifat perpetrated

334

the only witticism he'll ever utter in his career as a vendor of quackeries: "This affair," he said, "remains in my line of business!"'

'I suspect Florine of having prompted him,' Lucien exclaimed.

'And so, my dear boy,' continued Lousteau, 'you have your foot in the stirrup.'

'You were born lucky,' said Florine. 'How many insignificant young people we see dragging along in Paris for years without getting an article into a paper! You will have pushed ahead like Emile Blondet. In six months from now, I can see you being all upstage,' she added, using a phrase from her theatre slang and casting him a mocking glance.

'Haven't I been in Paris for three years?' said Lousteau. 'And only yesterday did Finot offer me a fixed stipend of three hundred francs a column and a hundred francs for a page in his weekly.'

'Well now, have you nothing to say?' Florine exclaimed, looking at him.

'We shall see,' said Lucien.

'My dear,' Lousteau answered with an air of pique. 'I've arranged everything for you as if you were my brother. But I don't answer for Finot. Finot will be got at by sixty rogues who'll be offering their services to him at reduced prices in the next two days. I promised you the job: you'll refuse it if you see fit. – You don't know how lucky you are,' he continued after a pause. 'You'll belong to a set whose members attack their enemies in various papers and look after one another's interests.'

'Let's go and see Félicien Vernou first of all,' said Lucien, in a hurry to get in touch with those redoubtable birds of prey.

Lousteau sent for a cab and the two friends went to the rue Mandar, where Vernou lived in a house along an alley, in a second-floor flat. Lucien was very astonished to find this sour, disdainful, strait-laced critic in a dining-room of extreme vulgarity, hung with nasty, cheap wallpaper in imitation brickwork blotched at equal intervals with patches of mildew, decorated with aquatint engravings in gilt frames, at table with a woman who was too ugly not to be his lawful wife and two infants perched on very high chairs with bars to keep the little rascals in. Taken by surprise in a dressing-gown made out of pieces left from one of his wife's printed calico dresses, Félicien did not look very pleased.

'Have you had lunch, Lousteau?' he asked, offering Lucien a chair.

'We have just left Florine's apartments,' said Etienne, 'and we lunched there.'

Lucien could not take his eyes off Madame Vernou. She looked very like a fat cook, tolerably clean, but superlatively common. She was wearing a scarf over a sleeping-bonnet tied so tightly that her cheeks bulged. Her dressing-gown, which had no girdle and was fastened at the neck by a button, fell round her in great folds and was so ill-fitting that it was impossible not to compare her to a boundary-stone. She looked exasperatingly healthy, had almost purple cheeks and hands with fat, pudgy fingers. At the sight of this woman, the reason for Vernou's embarrassed attitude in social gatherings became clear to Lucien. This writer, nauseated with married life, too weak-willed to leave his wife and children but imaginative enough always to feel ashamed of them, was bound to resent other people's success and be discontented with everything while still remaining discontented with himself. Lucien now understood the sour expression which chilled this envious countenance, the harshness of the repartees with which the journalist punctuated his conversation and the acerbity of his remarks, as pointed and elaborately-wrought as a stiletto.

'Come into my study,' said Félicien, getting up from table. 'No doubt you want to talk about literary matters.'

'Yes and no,' Lousteau replied. 'Old boy, it's a matter of a supper.'

'I came,' said Lousteau, 'to invite you on Coralie's behalf . . .'

At this name Madame Vernou raised her head.

'. . . to come to supper this day week,' Lucien continued. 'You'll meet the same company as at Florine's, with Madame du Val-Noble, Merlin and a few others in addition. There will be cards.'

'But, my dear,' said Vernou's wife, 'That's the day we have to go to Madame Mahoudeau.'

'Well, what does that matter?' said Vernou.

'If we didn't go, she'd be hurt, and you're glad enough to get her to discount your publisher's notes of hand.'

'My friends, here's a wife who doesn't understand that supper beginning at midnight doesn't prevent one attending a soirée which ends at eleven. Madame Mahoudeau and I work together,' he added.

'You have a fertile imagination!' Lucien replied, and by this single remark he made a mortal enemy of Vernou.

'All right,' Lousteau continued. 'You'll come. But that's not all. Monsieur de Rubempré is joining us, so push him in your paper. Introduce him as a young fellow capable of writing serious literature so that he can get in at least two articles a month.'

'Yes, if he wants to be one of us, attack our enemies as we shall attack his and stand by our friends, I'll speak for him this evening at the Opera.'

'Very good, see you tomorrow, my boy,' said Lousteau, shaking Vernou's hand with every sign of lively friendship. 'When does your book come out?'

'Well', said the paterfamilias, 'that depends on Dauriat. I've finished it.'

'Are you satisfied? . . .'

'I am and I'm not . . .'

'We'll give it a good write-up,' said Lousteau as he rose and and bowed to his colleague's wife.

This abrupt departure was necessitated by the bawlings of the two children who were squabbling, hitting one another with the spoons and throwing bread pudding in each other's face.

'You have just met, my child,' said Etienne, 'a woman who, unwittingly, will do a lot of damage in the literary world. Poor Vernou! He can't forgive us for the wife he has. We ought to rid him of her – in the public interest of course –

and then we should be spared a deluge of ferocious articles and epigrams aimed at everybody who's successful and doing well. What prospects has he with such a wife and two such horrible brats? Have you seen Rigaudin in Picard's play: *La Maison en loterie?* Well, like Rigaudin, Vernou won't do any fighting but he'll make others fight; he's capable of cutting off his nose to spite his best friend's face. You'll see him treading on every corpse, smiling at everyone's misfortune, attacking princes, dukes, marquises and nobles because he's a plebeian; attacking the reputation of celibates because he's married himself, and always moralizing and pleading in favour of domestic joys and civic duties. In short this very moral critic can be kind to no one, not even children. His life in the rue Mandar is divided between a woman who could take the part of the Grand Panjandrum in Molière's *Would-be Gentleman* and two ugly, scruffy little Vernous; he likes to sneer at the Faubourg Saint-Germain in which he'll never set foot and he makes duchesses talk like his wife. That's the man who'll howl at the Jesuits, insult the Court, accuse it of wanting to re-establish feudal dues and the law of primogeniture, and preach some sort of crusade in favour of equality, while he won't have it that anybody else is his equal. If he were a bachelor, if he mixed with society, if he could swagger along like a royalist poet with a pension and the cross of the Legion of Honour, he'd be an optimist. There are a thousand cases of journalists starting off like that. Journalism's a huge catapult with petty hatred to let it off. – After all that, do *you* feel like marrying? Vernou no longer has a heart: he's bursting with bile. Consequently he's the journalist *par excellence*, a two-legged tiger whose claws rend everything as if his pen had rabies.'

'A misogynist,' said Lucien. 'Has he any talent?'

'He has the wit necessary for turning out articles. Vernou secretes articles, he'll always produce articles and nothing but articles. No amount of dogged toil will ever enable him to graft a book on to his prose. Félicien is incapable of turning out a work, co-ordinating its constituent parts and grouping his characters in a well-balanced plot which begins, develops and moves forward to a climax; he has ideas, but no knowledge of facts; his heroes will be two-legged abstractions, philosophical or liberal; lastly, he labours after originality of style, but his inflated periods would collapse under the pinpricks of criticism. And so he goes in deadly fear of the newspapers, like all those who need bladders and blarney to keep their heads above water.'

'You're composing quite an article!' cried Lucien.

'One can say such things, my boy, but one must never write them down.'

'Why not? You're an editor now,' said Lucien.

'Where do you want me to set you down?' asked Lousteau.

'At Coralie's.'

'Ah! we're in love,' said Lousteau. 'It's a mistake! Do with Coralie what I do with Florine: treat her as a housekeeper, but be as free as a mountain goat!'

'You'd bring the saints to damnation!' said Lucien, laughing.

'Demons are past being damned,' Lousteau replied.

His new friend's light and brilliant tone, the way he reacted to life, his paradoxes mingled with the characteristically Machiavellian maxims current in Paris, had their effect on Lucien without his knowing it. In theory, the poet recognized the danger underlying such thoughts, but he found them useful for application. When they arrived at the Boulevard du Temple, the two friends agreed to meet again, between four and five, in the newspaper office, where no doubt Hector Merlin would be found.

22. *Boots can change one's way of life*

LUCIEN was effectually in the grip of the sensual delights afforded by genuinely enamoured courtesans, who fasten on to the tenderest parts of the soul, lend themselves with incredible pliancy to each and every desire and favour the habits

339

of lax self-indulgence from which they draw their strength. He was already thirsting for the pleasures of Paris: he loved the ease, abundance and sumptuousness of life in the actress's flat. On arriving he found Coralie and Camusot in transports of joy. The Gymnase theâtre had proposed, as from the coming Easter, an engagement on clearly defined terms which went beyond Coralie's expectations.

'This triumph is due to you,' said Camusot.

'Oh, undoubtedly,' said Coralie. 'But for him *The Alcalde* would have failed; there would have been no review, and I should have been stuck in a boulevard theatre for six more years.'

She flung her arms round his neck in front of Camusot. There was an indescribable gracefulness and sweet impetuosity in the actress's swift, effusive gesture: she was in love! Like all men at moments of great sorrow, Camusot lowered his gaze to the floor and discerned, along the seam of Lucien's boots, the coloured thread used by fashionable shoemakers which stood out in deep yellow against the glossy blackness of the uppers. The special colour of this thread had captured his attention during his silent reflections on the inexplicable presence of a pair of boots in front of Coralie's hearth. He had read in black letters printed on the soft white leather of the lining the address of a celebrated shoemaker of the period: 'Gay, rue de la Michodière.'

'Monsieur,' he said to Lucien. 'You have a fine pair of boots.'

'Everything he has is fine,' Coralie rejoindered.

'I should very much like to get my boots from the same shop.'

'Oh!' said Coralie. 'How much that smacks of the rue des Bourdonnais to ask for tradesmen's addresses! Are you going to wear young men's boots? A fine figure you'd cut! Stick to your top-boots. They're just the thing for a staid man with a wife, children and a mistress.'

'In short, if this gentleman would pull off one of his boots he would be doing me a signal service,' said the obstinate Camusot.

'I couldn't put it on again without a button-hook,' said Lucien, turning red.

'Bérénice will fetch one; it won't be out of place here,' said the merchant with an unpleasant leer.

'Papa Camusot,' said Coralie, throwing him a look of scathing contempt. 'Don't be afraid to show what a coward you are! Come on, speak your mind. You think this gentleman's boots are like mine, don't you? I forbid you to take off your boots,' she said to Lucien. 'Yes, Monsieur Camusot, yes: these boots are the very ones which were standing empty in front of my fire-place the other day. This gentleman was hidden in my dressing-room waiting to put them on: he had spent the night here. That's what you think, isn't it? All right, that's what I want you to think. It's the simple truth. I'm deceiving you. So what? That suits me down to the ground.'

She sat down without anger and with the airiest manner, looking straight at Camusot and Lucien, neither of whom dared to look at the other.

'I'll only believe what you want me to believe,' said Camusot. 'Don't make fun of me. I was in the wrong.'

'Either I'm a shameless hussy who has suddenly fallen for this gentleman, or I'm a poor, wretched creature who for the first time has felt that true love which all women long for. In either case, you must leave me or accept me as I am.' This she said with an imperious gesture which made the merchant cower.

'Can this be true?' asked Camusot. He could see by Lucien's demeanour that Coralie was serious. He was only begging her to go on deluding him.

'I love Mademoiselle Coralie,' said Lucien.

At this statement, made in a moved tone of voice, Coralie fell on the poet's neck, clasped him in her arms and turned her head towards the silk-merchant to show him what a wonderful picture she and Lucien made as a loving couple.

'Poor Musot, take back all you have given me. I want nothing from you. I'm madly in love with this young man, not for his brains but for his beauty. I prefer poverty with him to millions with you.'

Camusot sank down into an armchair, put his head in his hands and remained silent.

'Do you want us to leave this flat?' she asked him with incredible ferocity.

A cold shudder ran down Lucien's back at the prospect of having a woman, an actress and a household on his hands.

'Stay here and keep everything, Coralie,' said the merchant in a weak voice expressive of heart-felt grief. 'I don't want anything back. All the same the furniture here is worth sixty thousand francs, but I couldn't bear the idea of my Coralie living in penury. And yet it won't be long before you *are* living in penury. Whatever great talents this gentleman may possess, they won't be enough to provide for you. That's what we old men must expect! Coralie, allow me the right to come and see you sometimes: I can be useful to you. For that matter I confess it would be impossible for me to live without seeing you.'

The poor man's meekness, stripped as he was of his happiness at what he had thought was the happiest moment of his life, moved Lucien keenly: but not Coralie.

'Do come, my poor Musot,' she said. 'Come here as much as you like. I shall be all the fonder of you for not deceiving you.'

Camusot seemed content not to be banished from his terrestrial paradise, in which no doubt he was sure to suffer; but he hoped later on to recover all his rights in it by trusting to the hazards of Parisian life and the seductions with which Lucien would be surrounded. The wily old merchant thought that sooner or later this handsome young man would permit himself some infidelities, and he wanted to remain friendly with the pair in order to spy on Lucien and discredit him in Coralie's eyes. Lucien was appalled to see a man so far gone in passion and yet so spineless. Camusot offered them dinner at Véry's restaurant in the Palais-Royal, and they accepted.

'What happiness!' cried Coralie when Camusot had left. 'No more garret in the Latin quarter for you. You'll live here, we'll not leave one another. For appearance's sake you'll rent a little flat in the rue Charlot, and come what may!'

She started to perform her Spanish dance with a gusto expressive of indomitable passion.

'With hard work I can earn five hundred francs a month,' said Lucien.

'I can earn just the same at the theatre, without counting extras. Camusot still loves me and will keep me in clothes. With fifteen hundred francs a month we shall be living in clover.'

'But what about the horses, the coachman and the serving-man?' asked Bérénice.

'I'll run up debts,' cried Coralie.

She started dancing a jig with Lucien.

'I must accept Finot's proposition straight away,' exclaimed Lucien.

'Come along then,' said Coralie. 'I'll get dressed and take you to your newspaper office, and I'll wait for you down below in the carriage.'

Lucien sat down on a sofa, watched the actress as she got ready and gave himself over to the gravest reflections. He would have preferred to leave Coralie her freedom rather than to be pitch-forked into the obligations which such a union entails, but she was looking so beautiful, so shapely, so alluring that he was captivated by the picturesque aspects of this Bohemian life, and threw down the gauntlet to Fortune. Bérénice was instructed to take charge of Lucien's house-moving and settling in. Then the exultant, lovely and happy Coralie dragged off her cherished lover, her poet, and crossed the whole of Paris in order to arrive at the rue Saint-Fiacre.

23. The arcana of journalism

LUCIEN sprang lightly up the staircase and stalked confidently into the newspaper offices. Colocynth (with his stamped paper still on his head) and old Giroudeau once again hypocritically told him that no one was there.

'But the staff must meet somewhere to edit the newspaper,' he said.

'Probably. But the editing's not my concern,' said the captain of the Imperial Guard, and he went on checking his wrappers and repeating his eternal *Hrrum! Hrrum!* At this moment, as good or bad luck would have it, Finot arrived to inform Giroudeau of his fictitious abdication and recommend him to look after his interests.

'No beating about the bush with this gentleman. He's on the newspaper,' said Finot to his uncle as he took and clasped Lucien's hand.

'Ah! Monsieur is on the paper!' cried Giroudeau, surprised at his nephew's gesture. 'Well, Monsieur, so you had no difficulty in getting on to it.'

'I want to fix things up so that you won't get bamboozled by Etienne,' said Finot with a sly look at Lucien. – 'This gentleman will have three francs a column for everything he writes, including theatre reviews.'

'You've never made such terms with anyone else,' said Giroudeau, glancing at Lucien with astonishment.

'He'll have the four boulevard theatres, and you'll take care he isn't done out of his boxes and that his theatre tickets come to him. All the same,' he added, turning to Lucien, 'I advise you to have them sent direct to you. – This gentleman is undertaking to write, in addition to his reviews, ten articles of *Varieties* of about two columns each for fifty francs a month for a year. Does that suit you?'

'Yes,' said Lucien, whose hand was being forced by his new circumstances.

'Uncle,' said Finot to the cashier. 'Draw up the contract and we'll sign it when we go down.'

'Who is this gentleman?' asked Giroudeau, rising and removing his black silk bonnet.

'Monsieur Lucien de Rubempré, who wrote the article on *L'Alcalde*.'

'Young man,' cried the old soldier, tapping Lucien on the forehead, 'You've got a gold-mine there. I'm not a literary man, but I read your article and liked it. I ask you! What gaiety! So I said: "That will bring us subscribers!" And subscribers came. We sold fifty numbers.'

344

'Is my contract with Etienne Lousteau copied in duplicate and ready to sign?' Finot asked his uncle.

'Yes,' Giroudeau replied.

'Put yesterday's date on the contract I'm signing with this gentleman, so that Lousteau will be bound by its terms.' Finot took his new colleague by the arm with a semblance of friendliness which beguiled the poet. He led him to the stairs and said:

'In this way you have a settled position. I'll introduce you myself to the members of my staff. And this evening Lousteau will get you known at the theatres. You can earn a hundred and fifty francs a month on our little paper which Lousteau is going to run; so try and get on with him. The rogue will bear me a grudge for having tied his hands with regard to you, but you have talent, and I don't want you to be exposed to the whims of an editor. Between ourselves, you can bring me up to two sheets a month for my weekly Review, and I'll pay you two hundred francs for them. Don't tell anyone about this arrangement: I should be open to vengeance from all those whose self-esteem is wounded at the sight of a newcomer's good fortune. Make four articles of your two sheets, sign two of them with your own name and two with a pen-name so that you won't appear to be taking the bread out of other people's mouths. You owe your position to Blondet and Vignon who see a future before you. And so don't blot your copy-book. Above all, don't trust your friends. As for you and me, let's keep on terms of good understanding. Serve me, and I'll serve you. You have forty francs' worth of theatre boxes and tickets to sell, and sixty francs' worth of books to flog. That and your writing will give you four hundred and fifty francs a month. If you use your wits you can get at least two hundred francs more from what the publishers will pay you for articles and prospectuses. But you'll stand by me, won't you? I can count on you?'

Lucien clasped Finot's hand in a spasm of unprecedented joy.

'Don't let's appear to have come to an understanding,' Finot whispered to him as he pushed open the door of a garret on the fifth floor of the building, situated at the end of a long corridor.

Lucien then perceived Lousteau, Félicien Vernou, Hector Merlin and two other contributors whom he did not know, all sitting on chairs or arm-chairs round a table covered with green baize in front of a good fire, smoking and laughing. The table was loaded with paper, and on it was a real, full inkpot, also some quills which though of poor quality were good enough for the staff. It became plain to the new journalist that it was there the great work was carried out.

'Gentlemen,' said Finot, 'the purpose of this meeting is to install our friend Lousteau in my lieu and stead as editor of the newspaper I am obliged to relinquish. But although my opinions are undergoing a necessary transformation so that I can take over the editorship of the Review of whose destinies you are aware, my convictions remain the same and we are still friends. I belong entirely to you, just as you will belong to me. Circumstances vary, principles don't change. Principles are the pivot on which the pointers of the political barometer turn.'

A burst of laughter came from the assembled staff.

'Who taught you that sort of language?' asked Lousteau.

'Blondet,' Finot replied.

'Wind, rain, storm, set fair,' said Merlin. 'We'll go together through all of them.'

'Anyway,' Finot continued. 'Don't let's get muddled up with metaphors: anyone who has a few articles to bring me will find Finot again. – This gentleman,' he said, introducing Lucien, 'is one of you. I have settled things with him, Lousteau.'

Each one complimented Finot on his rise in status and his new destinies. 'There you are, astride of us and the other people,' said one of the journalists whom Lucien did not know. 'You're becoming a Janus!'

'Let's hope he doesn't become a Janot,' said Vernou.[1]

'You'll let us attack our *bêtes noires*?'

'As much as you like!' said Finot.

1. Janot was a type of uncouth clown in eighteenth century French comedy.

'Indeed,' said Lousteau, 'the paper can't go back on itself. Monsieur Châtelet has got annoyed, and we're not going to leave him in peace for a week.'

'What happened?' asked Lucien.

'He came to demand satisfaction,' said Vernou. 'The ex-fop of Imperial days found old Giroudeau here, and he, in the coolest possible manner, indicated that Philippe Bridau had written the article, and Philippe requested the baron to choose his time and weapons. The matter went no further. We are busy drawing up an apology to the baron for tomorrow's number: every sentence in it is a dagger-thrust.'

'Get your teeth into him, he'll come along to me,' said Finot. 'I shall seem to be doing him a service by pacifying you, he's a Government man, and we shall get our hooks on something – an assistant professor's post or a tobacconist's licence. It's lucky for us he took offence. Which of you would like to write an article on Nathan for my new paper?'

'Give it to Lucien,' said Lousteau. 'Hector and Vernou will be writing articles in their respective papers . . .'

'Good-bye, gentlemen,' said Finot with a laugh. 'We'll meet again face to face on the battlefield!'

Lucien received a few compliments on his admission to the redoubtable corps of journalists, and Lousteau presented him as a man on whom they could count.

'Lucien invites you one and all, gentlemen, to supper with his mistress, the fair Coralie.'

'Coralie is going to the Gymnase,' said Lucien to Etienne.

'Well then, gentlemen, it's agreed that we push Coralie, is it not? Put a few lines in all your papers about her new engagement and praise her for her talent. You can credit the Gymnase with tact and cleverness. Can we credit it with intelligence also?'

'Yes, that too,' Merlin replied. 'It's putting on a play Frédéric is writing with Scribe.'

'Oh! Then we'll say that the manager of the Gymnase is the most foresighted and perspicacious of speculators,' said Vernou.

'By the way, don't write your articles on Nathan's book before we have put our heads together,' said Lousteau. 'I'll

347

tell you why. We want to be useful to our new comrade. Lucien has two books to publish: a collection of sonnets and a novel. The power of the paragraph must make him a great poet within three months! We'll use his *Marguerites* in order to decry Odes, Ballads and Meditations, in fact all Romantic poetry.'

'It would be a joke if the sonnets were worthless,' said Vernou. 'What is your opinion of your sonnets, Lucien?'

'Yes, how do you like them yourself?' asked one of the unnamed journalists.

'Gentlemen,' said Lousteau. 'On my word, they are good.'

'Well, I'm glad of that,' said Vernou. 'I'll use them to trip up the sacristy poets. I'm tired of them.'

'If Dauriat doesn't accept the *Marguerites* this evening, we'll bombard him with articles against Nathan.'

'But what will Nathan say?' cried Lucien.

The five journalists burst out laughing.

'He'll be delighted,' said Vernou. 'You'll see how we shall arrange matters.'

'So this gentleman is going in with us!' said one of the contributors unknown to Lucien.

'Yes, yes, Frédéric. No tricks. – You see, Lucien,' said Etienne to the neophyte, 'how we are treating you: you won't draw back when occasion demands. We all like Nathan, but we're going to attack him. Now let's carve up the empire of Alexander. Frédéric, would you like the Théâtre Français and the Odéon?'

'If these gentlemen agree,' said Frédéric.

They all nodded assent, but Lucien saw gleams of envy in their eyes.

'I shall keep the Opera, the Italians and the Opéra-Comique,' said Vernou.

'Right. Hector will take the Vaudeville theatre,' said Lousteau.

'Don't I get any theatres then?' exclaimed the other contributor unknown to Lucien.

'Let's see now,' said Lousteau. 'Hector will leave you the Variétés and Lucien the Porte-Saint-Martin. – Let him have the Porte-Saint-Martin,' he said to Lucien. 'He's mad on

Fanny Beaupré. You can take the Cirque-Olympique in exchange. I shall take Bobino, the Funambules and Madame Saqui. What have we for tomorrow's number?'

'Nothing.'

'Nothing?'

'Nothing!'

'Gentlemen, be at your brightest for my first number. Baron Châtelet and his cuttle-bone won't last a week. The author of *The Solitary* is worn threadbare.'

'Sosthenes-Demosthenes isn't funny any longer,' said Vernou. 'He's common property now.'

'Oh! We need some new Aunt Sallies,' said Frédéric.

'Gentlemen,' cried Lousteau, 'how about ridiculing the virtuous men of the Right? Suppose we said that Monsieur de Bonald has smelly feet?'

'Let's start a series of portraits of the Government orators,' said Hector Merlin.

'You do that, my boy,' said Lousteau. 'You know them. They belong to your party. You can satisfy some of the grudges they bear against one another. Get your claws into Beugnot, Syrieys de Mayrinhac and others. If the articles can be written in advance, we shan't get stuck for copy.'

'How about inventing a few refusals of burial licences in more or less aggravating circumstances?' asked Hector.

'No, don't let's follow in the footsteps of the great constitutional dailies which have their "clergy files" full of *canards*,' Vernou retorted.

'*Canards?*' Lucien enquired.

'What we call a *canard*,' Hector replied, 'is a story which looks as if it were true but which is invented to ginger up 'News in Brief' when it's a bit colourless. It was one of Franklin's lucky finds: he invented lightning-conductors, republican government and *canards*. As a journalist he so easily took in the Encyclopaedists by his *canards* from overseas that in his *Philosophical History of the Indies* Raynal proffered two of them as authenticated facts.'

'I didn't know that,' said Vernou. 'What are the two *canards?*'

'The story of the Englishman who sold a negress who had

349

saved his life, but first he got her with child in order to make more money out of the sale. Also the sublime speech of a pregnant girl conducting her own defence and winning her case. When Franklin came to Paris he confessed to these *canards* in Necker's salon, to the great confusion of the French *philosophes*. And that's how the New World twice corrupted the old one.'

'A newspaper,' said Lousteau, 'accepts as truth anything that is plausible. We start from that assumption.'

'Criminal justice proceeds on just the same lines,' said Vernou.

'Well well. We meet here this evening at nine,' said Merlin.

Each of them got up, shook hands, and the meeting was closed with manifestations of the most touching familiarity.

'What did you do to Finot,' Etienne asked Lucien as they went downstairs, 'for him to make a deal with you? You're the only man with whom he's made a binding agreement.'

'I did nothing,' said Lucien. 'He proposed it himself.'

'In any case, I'm delighted that you've come to an agreement. It puts both of us in a stronger position.'

On the ground-floor, Etienne and Lucien came upon Finot who drew Lousteau aside into the official editorial office.

'Sign your contract so that the new editor will believe that the matter was settled yesterday,' said Giroudeau, presenting two stamped documents to Lucien.

As he read through this contract, Lucien overheard a fairly sharp discussion between Etienne and Finot about the products in kind accruing to the newspaper. Etienne wanted his share in these imposts levied by Giroudeau. No doubt a compromise was reached by Finot and Lousteau, for the two friends left the building in complete agreement.

'Eight o'clock, at the Wooden Galleries, in Dauriat's office,' said Etienne to Lucien.

A young man turned up and applied for a post on the newspaper with the same timid and anxious air that Lucien had formerly had. Lucien felt a secret pleasure as he saw Giroudeau practising on this neophyte the same pleasantries which the old soldier had used to deceive him; self-interest enabled him perfectly to understand the necessity for these stratagems, which set impassable barriers between beginners and the attic to which only the elect had access.

'Even as things are, there's not such a lot of money for the staff,' he said to Giroudeau.

'The more there were of you, the less each one would get,' the captain replied. 'So there it is!'

The old veteran twirled his leaded cane, went out grunting his *hrrum-hrrum* and looked surprised when he saw Lucien getting into the fine carriage which was waiting in the boulevard.

'Nowadays it's you who are the military men, and we the civilians,' the soldier said to him.

24. *Re-enter Dauriat*

'UPON my word, these people seem to be very decent fellows,' said Lucien to Coralie. 'Here I am, a journalist sure of being able to earn six hundred francs a month if I work like a Trojan; also I shall get my two books accepted and write others, for my friends are going to organize a success for me! So I say as you do, Coralie: come what may!'

'You'll succeed, darling. But don't be as good as you are beautiful: you'd come to ruin. Be hard on people – that's the way to get on.'

Coralie and Lucien went for a drive in the Bois de Boulogne, and there they once more met the Marquise d'Espard, Madame de Bargeton and Baron Châtelet. Madame de Bargeton gave Lucien a seductive glance which could well be taken for a salutation. Camusot had ordered the best of all possible dinners. Coralie, now that she knew she was rid of him, was so charming to the wretched silk-merchant that he could not remember her having been so gracious or attractive during the fourteen months of their relationship.

'Come now,' he said to himself. 'Why not keep on with her in spite of what's happened?'

He proposed on the quiet to Coralie that he should buy her six thousand francs' income in Government stock – which his wife would know nothing about – if she would continue to be his mistress; he would be willing to turn a blind eye on her affair with Lucien.

'Would I betray such an angel?... Take a look at him, you old scarecrow, and then at yourself!' she said, pointing to the poet, whom Camusot had plied with drink to make him slightly tipsy.

Camusot decided to wait for indigence to give him back the woman whom indigence had delivered over to him once before.

'Very well, I'll just be your friend,' he said, kissing her on the forehead.

Lucien left Coralie and Camusot in order to go to the Wooden Galleries. How changed in mind he was since his initiation into the mysteries of journalism! He mingled boldly with the swirling crowd in the Galleries, assumed an insolent air because he had a mistress and made a free and easy entrance into Dauriat's shop because he was a journalist. He found a great gathering there and exchanged handshakes with Blondet, Nathan, Finot and all the literary men with whom he had been fraternizing for a week. He felt important and flattered himself that he outshone his companions; the modicum of wine he had taken had a wonderfully stimulating effect on him: he was witty and showed that he was able to howl with the pack. None the less, Lucien did not receive the tacit approval, mute or spoken, on which he was counting: he sensed an initial surge of jealousy in this gathering, as yet not so much anxious as curious to know how highly this talented newcomer would rate among them and how big a slice he would grab of the journalistic cake. Finot, who looked on Lucien as a mine to be exploited, and Lousteau, who believed he had a claim on his gratitude, were the only ones, so it seemed to the poet, who smiled on him. Lousteau, who had already taken on the airs of an editor, tapped smartly on the window-panes of Dauriat's office.

'One moment, my friend,' the publisher replied, raising his head above the green curtains and recognizing him.

This moment lasted an hour, after which Lucien and his friend entered the sanctum.

'Well now,' the new editor asked. 'Have you thought over our friend's piece of business?'

'Indeed I have,' said Dauriat, leaning forward in his arm-chair like an oriental potentate. 'I've glanced through the collection of poems and got a man of taste, a good judge, to read them, for I don't claim to be a connoisseur in poetry. I, my friend, buy ready-made reputations as an Englishman buys ready-made love. You are as great a poet, my boy, as you are a handsome youngster. On my word as an honest man – I don't mean as a publisher, mind you – your sonnets are magnificent and you've put good work into them, a rare enough thing when one has inspiration and verve. In short, you know how to rhyme – one of the qualities of the modern school. Your *Marguerites* make a fine book, but there's no money in them, and I can only go in for very big undertakings. My conscience won't let me take your sonnets; it would be impossible for me to push them, and there's not enough to be made out of them for what it would cost to make a success of them. Moreover you won't go on writing poetry: your book is a book apart. You're a young man! You're bringing me the eternal collection of early poems that all literary men compose on leaving school; they're keen on them to start with, and later on they make fun of them. Your friend Lousteau no doubt has a poem stowed away somewhere. Lousteau, haven't you a poem you laid great store by?' asked Dauriat, throwing Etienne an astute glance of complicity.

'Well now, *could* I have been expected to write in prose?' asked Lousteau.

'There you are, you see!' Dauriat continued. 'And yet he's never mentioned it to me, but our friend here knows all about publishing and business. The question for me,' he said to Lucien in oily tones, 'is not whether you're a great poet. You have much, but much merit: if I were a beginner in the book-trade, I should make the mistake of publishing your volume. But today, in the first place, my sleeping partners and shareholders would cut off funds – it's enough for me to have lost twenty thousand francs last year to turn them against poetry, and they are my masters. Nevertheless that's not the crux of the matter. I admit that you may be a great poet, but will you be productive? Will you turn out sonnets regularly? Will you run to ten volumes? Will you be a business proposition? Indeed no: you'll make a delightful writer of prose and you've too much intelligence to spoil it with padding; you stand to make thirty thousand francs a year in journalism, and you won't barter them for the three thousand francs you'd find it hard to rake in with your hemistichs, stanzas and similar trash!'

'You know, Dauriat,' said Lousteau, 'that this gentleman is on our paper.'

'Yes,' answered Dauriat. 'I've read his article and – in his own interest, be it understood – I refuse the *Marguerites*. Yes, Monsieur, you'll get more money from me in the next six months for the articles I shall ask from you than you would for your unsaleable poetry.'

'But what about my reputation as a writer?' cried Lucien. Dauriat and Lousteau burst out laughing.

'God save us!' said Lousteau. 'The man still has his illusions.'

'Reputation as a writer,' Dauriat replied, 'means ten years' perseverance and the alternative of a hundred thousand francs' loss or gain for the publisher. If you find people crazy enough to print your poems, in a year from now you'll think well of me when you learn the result of the operation.'

'Have you the manuscript with you?' asked Lucien, coldly.

'Here it is, my friend,' replied Dauriat, who was now adopting singularly sugary tones with Lucien.

Lucien took the scroll without looking to see the position of the string, so certain it seemed that Dauriat had read the *Marguerites*. He went out with Lousteau without appearing either dismayed or discontented. Dauriat walked through the shop with the two friends, talking about his newspaper and that of Lousteau. Lucien was unconcernedly toying with the manuscript of the *Marguerites*.

'Do you believe Dauriat read your sonnets or had them read?' Etienne whispered to Lucien.

'Yes,' said Lucien.

'Look at the "seals"!'

Lucien perceived that the ink-lines and the string were in a state of perfect conjunction.

'Which sonnet did you most particularly notice?' Lucien asked the publisher, turning pale with suppressed rage.

'They are all worthy of notice, my friend,' Dauriat replied. 'But the one on the marguerite is delicious and ends with a very subtle and delicate thought. By that I divined what success your prose is bound to obtain. And so I recommended you straight away to Finot. Write articles for us – we'll pay well for them. You see, it's all very fine thinking of reputation, but keep your feet on the ground and take everything that comes your way. You'll be able to write verses when you're rich.'

The poet made an abrupt exit into the Galleries in order not to explode: he was furious.

25. The battle begins

'Well, my child,' said Lousteau as he followed him out. 'Keep calm, take men for what they are: a means to an end. Do you want to get your own back?'

'At all cost,' said the poet.

'Here's a copy of Nathan's book that Dauriat has just handed me. The second edition comes out tomorrow; read it again and knock off an article tearing it to shreds. Félicien Vernou can't stand Nathan because he thinks his success is jeopardizing the future success of his own work. It's a mania of little minds like his to imagine that there's no place in the sun for two successes. And so he'll get your article into the big daily he works for.'

'But what can one say against the book? It's a fine book!' Lucien exclaimed.

'Oh come, my dear, learn your trade,' said Lousteau with a laugh. 'Even if the book's a masterpiece, your pen must prove that it's a piece of stupid nonsense, a dangerous and unwholesome work.'

'How can I do that?'

'By making every quality a defect.'

'Such a *tour de force* is beyond me.'

'My dear, a journalist is an acrobat, and you must get hardened to the drawbacks of the profession. Look now, I'm a decent chap, and I'll tell you what to do in such a case. Pay attention, my boy.'

'You'll begin by saying it's a fine work: after that you can enjoy yourself saying what you like about it. The public will say: "This critic isn't jealous, he'll certainly be impartial." From then on it will regard your criticism as conscientious. Having thus acquired your reader's esteem, you'll regret to have to cast blame on the system which such books are going to inaugurate in French literature. Does not France, you will ask, hold intellectual sway over the whole world? Until now, century after century, French writers have made Europe keep to the path of analysis and philosophical enquiry through the power of style and the originality of form they have given to ideas. And here you slip in – for the bourgeois reader – some praise for Voltaire, Rousseau, Montesquieu, Buffon. You'll explain how inexorable the French language has been and prove that it puts a polish on thought. You'll fire off axioms like this: in France a great writer is always a great man; his native tongue always constrains him to think; this is not the case in other countries, and so forth. You'll prove your contention by comparing Rabener, the German satirist of manners, to La Bruyère. There's nothing like talking about an unknown foreign writer to give standing to a critic – Cousin has used Kant as a springboard. Once you've set foot on that territory, you launch an aphorism which sums up and explains for halfwits the system of our eighteenth century men of genius by calling their literature a *literature of ideas*. Using this term as a weapon, you fling all the illustrious departed at the head of living authors. Then you explain how in our day a new literature is being produced which misuses dialogue, the most facile of literary forms, and description, which exempts people from thinking. Over against the novels of Voltaire, Diderot, Sterne and Lesage, so substantial, so incisive, you'll set the modern novel which renders everything in images and to which Walter Scott has given far too *dramatic* a character. In such a genre there's room only for truly original minds. The Scott type of novel is a genre and not a system, you'll say. You'll blast this baneful genre in which ideas are thinned down and flattened out, a genre which every type of mind can exploit, a genre which makes it easy for anyone to become an author, a genre which in short you'll call the *literature of imagery*.

'You'll direct this line of argument against Nathan and show he's an imitator with only a semblance of talent. His book lacks the great, closely-woven style of the eighteenth century; and you'll show that the author has put events in the place of feelings. Life is not merely movement; ideas are not merely pictures! Reel off maxims like that and the public will repeat them. Despite the merit of the work then, it appears disastrous and dangerous to you; it opens the gates of the Temple of Fame to the mob – and you'll give a far-off glimpse of a host of minor authors eager to imitate so facile a form. From then on you can let yourself go in thunderous lamentations about the decadence of taste, and you'll slip in words of praise for Messrs Etienne, Jouy, Tissot, Gosse, Duval, Benjamin Constant, Aignan, Baour-Lormian and Villemain, all of them leading spokesmen of the Liberal Napoleonic party whose protection Vernou's paper enjoys. You'll show this glorious phalanx resisting the invasion of the Romantics, standing out for ideas and style against imagery and verbiage, continuing the Voltairian school and opposing the Anglo-German school, in the same way as the seventeen orators of the Left are fighting for the nation against the Ultras of the Right. Under the ægis of these names, venerated by the immense majority of Frenchmen who will always side with the left-wing Opposition, you can pulverize Nathan whose work, though it contains traits of superior beauty, gives freedom of the city to a literature devoid of ideas.

'From now on, the point at issue – do you take my meaning?

357

– is no longer Nathan and his book, but the glory of France. It's the duty of every honest and courageous writer to react vigorously against these importations from abroad. In that way you flatter the subscriber. Your line is that France is wise to all these tricks and not easy to take in. If the publisher, for reasons you don't want to go into, has calculated on getting away with it, the real public has promptly done justice to the errors committed by the five hundred dolts who constitute the publisher's vanguard. You'll say that after being lucky enough to sell one edition of this book, he's overreaching himself by bringing out a second one, and you'll regret that so shrewd a man should know so little about the instincts of the nation. That's your main line of attack. Put a sprinkling of wit into these arguments, season them with a dash of vinegar, and you'll have Dauriat sizzling in the journalistic frying-pan. But don't forget to wind up with a show of pity for Nathan's mistake in taking the wrong road: once he leaves it, contemporary literature will be indebted to him for some fine works.'

Lucien was stupefied as he listened to Lousteau's words: the scales fell from his eyes and he became alive to literary truths of which he had not even guessed.

'But what you tell me,' he exclaimed, 'is full of reason and relevance.'

'If it were not, how could you make an attack on Nathan's book?' said Lousteau. 'That, my boy, is Article Number One for the demolition of a work. It's the critic's pickaxe. But there are lots of other recipes! You'll learn as you go on. When you're obliged to speak in unqualified terms about a man you don't like – sometimes newspaper-owners and editors have their hands forced – you'll bring into play the negative gambits of what we call a leading article. You head the article with the title of the book you're expected to review; you begin with generalities enabling you to talk about the Greeks and the Romans, and then you say at the end: "These considerations bring us to Monsieur So-and-So's book which will be the subject of a second article." And the second article never appears. Thus you smother a book between a couple of promises. What you're writing here isn't an article against

Nathan, but one against Dauriat: that calls for a pickaxe. A pickaxe glances off a fine work, but it cuts right through to a bad one: in the first case, it hurts only the publisher; in the second case it does the public a service. These forms of literary criticism are used just as much in political criticism.'

Etienne's cruel lesson was opening shutters in Lucien's imagination and he caught on admirably to the tricks of the trade.

'Let's go to the office,' said Lousteau. 'We shall find our friends there and we'll settle how to drive home the attack on Nathan. You'll see how they'll laugh!'

Arriving at the rue Saint-Fiacre, they climbed together to the attic in which the newspaper was being made up, and Lucien was as surprised as he was delighted to see the kind of glee with which his colleagues agreed to demolish Nathan's book. Hector Merlin took a square of paper and wrote the following lines which he carried off to his newspaper:

A second edition of Monsieur Nathan's book is announced. We reckoned on keeping silent about the work, but this semblance of success obliges us to publish an article, not so much on the work itself as on the direction new literature is taking.

At the head of the jibes selected for the next day's issue, Lousteau set this sentence:

The publisher Dauriat is bringing out a second edition of Monsieur Nathan's book. So he doesn't know the legal saw: NON BIS IN IDEM? All honour to courage in distress!

Etienne's words had served as a torch to Lucien, in whom the desire for vengeance on Dauriat stood in lieu of conscience and inspiration. At the end of three days during which he did not stir from Coralie's room, where he worked at the fire-side, with Bérénice to serve his meals and a quiet, attentive Coralie to fondle him in his moments of weariness, he finished off a critical article of about three columns in which he rose to amazing heights. He hurried off to the newspaper office at nine in the evening, found the editorial staff assembled and read out his work to them. They listened attentively.

Félicien took the manuscript without saying a word and rushed downstairs.

'What's got hold of him?' asked Lucien.

'He's taking your article to the press!' said Hector Merlin. 'It's a masterpiece: not a word to cut out or a line to add!'

'One only had to show you the way!' said Lousteau.

'I'd like to see Nathan's face tomorrow when he reads that,' said another member of the staff whose face was beaming with satisfaction.

'It pays to be friendly with you,' said Hector Merlin.

'It's all right then?' asked Lucien with lively concern.

'Blondet and Vignon will be green with envy,' Lousteau replied.

'Here,' Lucien went on, 'is a little article I've knocked together for you: if it goes down well it might provide material for a series of similar compositions.'

Lucien then read to them one of those delightful articles which ensured success for this *petit journal*: in two columns it depicted one of the minor facets of Parisian life, a figure, a type, an everyday event or something out of the ordinary. This sample, entitled 'People one sees in the streets of Paris' was written in a new and original style, so that thought was provoked by the mere clash of words and the reader's attention stimulated by the jingle of adverbs and adjectives. This article was as different from the grave and penetrating article on Nathan as the *Lettres Persanes* is from *L'Esprit des Lois*.

'You're a born journalist,' Lousteau told him. 'It will go in tomorrow. Write as many of them as you like.'

'Great fun!' said Merlin. 'Dauriat is furious at the two bombshells we've thrown into his shop. I've just been there. He was breathing out fire and slaughter. He was mad with Finot, who told him he'd sold his paper to you. As for me, I drew him aside and whispered these words in his ear: "The *Marguerites* will cost you dear! A man of talent comes to you, and you send him about his business while we welcome him with open arms."'

'Dauriat will be thunderstruck by the article we've just been listening to,' said Lousteau to Lucien. 'You see now, my boy, what a newspaper can do! Incidentally your private revenge is getting on fast! Baron Châtelet came along this morning to ask for your address: there was a murderous article on him this morning; this ex-fop has a soft skull and he's in despair. Didn't you read the paper? It's quite a comical article. Look: *The Heron's funeral procession with the Cuttle-fish as chief mourner.* Madame de Bargeton is now definitely known in society as the *Cuttle-bone* and Châtelet is no longer called anything but *Baron Heron.*'

Lucien took the paper and could not help laughing as he read the little masterpiece of banter from Vernou's pen.

'They'll hoist the white flag,' said Hector Merlin.

Lucien joyfully contributed his quota to some of the witticisms and shafts with which they finished off the paper as they chatted and smoked, related the day's adventures, poked fun at their colleagues or revealed new details about their characters. This eminently mocking, witty, spiteful conversation brought much enlightenment to Lucien about morals and personalities in the literary world.

'While the paper's being set up,' said Lousteau, 'I'm going to take you round a bit, introduce you to all the ticket-offices and wings of the theatres in which you have right of entry. Then we'll pick up Florine and Coralie at the Panorama-Dramatique and frolic with them in their dressing-rooms.'

And so both of them, arm in arm, went from theatre to theatre for Lucien to be enthroned as reviewer, complimented by the managers, ogled by the actresses who all knew what importance a single article from him had just conferred on Coralie and Florine, since they had secured engagements, one at the Gymnase at twelve thousand francs a year, the other at the Panorama at eight thousand francs. Each visit was a minor ovation which magnified Lucien in his own eyes and taught him the measure of his power. At eleven o'clock, the two friends arrived at the Panorama-Dramatique, where Lucien assumed a nonchalant air which worked wonders. Nathan was there. He offered his hand to Lucien who took it and clasped it.

'Well now, my masters,' he said, looking at Lucien and Lousteau. 'So you're intending to get me dead and buried.'

'Just wait till tomorrow, my dear, and you'll see how Lucien has laid about you! Upon my word, you'll be satisfied. When criticism is as serious as that, a book gains by it.'

Lucien turned red with shame.

'Does it hit hard?' asked Nathan.

'It's an impressive article,' said Lousteau.

'Then it won't do me any harm?' Nathan continued. 'But Hector Merlin said in the Vaudeville *foyer* that it slashed me to pieces.'

'Pay no heed to him, just wait,' cried Lucien, and he took refuge in Coralie's dressing-room, following her in at the moment when she was leaving the stage, her attractions enhanced by the glamour of her costume.

26. *Dauriat pays a call*

The next day, while Lucien was lunching with Coralie, he heard in the quiet street below the brisk rattle of a cabriolet, suggestive of an elegant carriage drawn by a horse whose easy trot and way of pulling up indicated purity of breed. Lucien looked out through the window and in fact caught sight of Dauriat's splendid English thoroughbred, and Dauriat himself, handing the reins to his groom before jumping down from the vehicle.

'It's the publisher,' Lucien called out to his mistress.

'Keep him waiting,' Coralie immediately said to Bérénice.

Lucien smiled at her self-possession and the way she so admirably identified herself with his interests, and he turned back to embrace her with genuine fervour: she had shown presence of mind.

The insolent publisher's haste in appearing, the sudden self-abasement of this prince of charlatans was prompted by circumstances almost forgotten today, so violent is the transformation which has taken place in the book-trade during the last fifteen years. From 1816 to 1827, a period when reading-rooms, first established for the perusal of newspapers, undertook to supply readers, for a fee, with newly-published books, and when the exorbitant taxes imposed on the periodic press forced it to turn to advertisement, the book-trade had no other means of publicity than articles inserted either in the *feuilletons* or the main text of the newspapers. And yet, until 1822, French newspapers were printed on pages of such limited size that the leading journals scarcely exceeded the dimensions of the 'little papers' of today. In their resistance to journalistic tyranny, Dauriat and Ladvocat were the first to invent posters, by means of which they could bring their books to the attention of Parisians with a display of fancy type, a quaint use of colours, vignettes and, later, lithographs, thus making posters a poem for the eyes and often a drain on amateurs' purses – for some of them were so original that one of the maniacs known as *collectors* owns a complete set of Parisian posters. This means of publicity, restricted first of all to shop-windows and those of the big boulevard establishments, was abandoned in favour of advertisement in the press. Nevertheless posters, which continue to strike the eye when both the advertisement and often the work itself are forgotten, will always survive, above all now that the device has been adopted of painting them on walls.

Advertisement, which is accessible to all those who can pay for it and has made the fourth page of the newspaper as lucrative for the Exchequer as it is for speculators, was born of the rigours of stamp-duty, postal charges and caution-money. These restrictions, invented during the ministry of Monsieur de Villèle, who could easily have killed the newspapers by letting them multiply, had the contrary effect of creating a sort of monopoly by making it almost impossible to launch a newspaper. In 1821 then, the newspapers exercised the right of life and death over the conceptions of thought and the enterprises of publishers. A short notice inserted in 'News in Brief' was terribly expensive. There was such a multiplicity of intrigues inside the editorial offices and in the evenings on the battle-field of the printing offices at the time when the process of page-setting determined the admission or rejection of such and such an article, that the important publishing-houses employed a 'man of letters' paid to draw up these little articles in which many ideas had to be conveyed in few words. These obscure journalists, who were paid only after the insertion, often spent the whole night at the printing-offices to witness the setting-up of either the big articles – of curiously varied provenance – or a modicum of lines which were then given the name of *puffs*. Today the standard of morals in literature and the book-trade has changed so much that many people would dismiss as fables the tremendous efforts, the acts of enticement and treachery and the intrigues that the need for obtaining these 'puffs' inspired in publishers, authors, martyrs in the cause of fame and all such galley-slaves condemned for life to heap success upon success. Dinners, cajolery and presents were all a common practice in journalistic circles. The following anecdote will better exemplify the close alliance between criticism and the book-trade than all the assertions just made:

An eminent man of letters, still young, who was aspiring to a political career, a ladies' man and editor of a leading newspaper, had gained favour with a well-known publishing-house. One Sunday this opulent firm was regaling the principal newspaper editors in a mansion in the country. The lady of the house, young and pretty at that time, took the illustrious writer out into her park. The head clerk of the firm, a cold, grave, methodical Teuton, with a mind only for business, was walking round it with a *feuilleton* writer and chatting with him about a project on which he wanted to consult him. Their conversation led them out of the park and they reached the woods. Deep down in a thicket, the German caught a glimpse of someone who was very like his employer's wife. He raised his *lorgnette*, made a sign to the young journalist to keep quiet and come away, and himself cautiously retreated the way he had come.

'What did you see?' asked the writer.

'Nothing much,' was the reply. 'Our big article will go

through. Tomorrow we shall have at least three columns in the *Journal des Débats*.'

Yet another fact will explain the power such articles wielded. Monsieur de Chateaubriand's book on the last of the Stuarts was languishing in a warehouse, unsaleable. Thanks to a single article written by a young man in the *Journal des Débats*, the book was sold out in a week. At a time when if one wanted to read a book one had to buy it instead of borrowing it, ten thousand copies of certain Liberal works, provided they were lauded by the Opposition news-sheets, could find a market; but then of course Belgian pirating had not yet come into existence. The preparatory attacks made by Lucien's friends, and Lucien's article, would be sufficient to stop the sale of Nathan's book. Nathan would only suffer in his self-esteem; having been paid, he had nothing to lose; but Dauriat stood to lose thirty thousand francs. In fact the trade in books styled *livres de nouveauté* can be summed in this commercial theorem: a ream of blank paper is worth fifteen francs; once printed it is worth five francs or three hundred francs according to the success it obtains. In those times, a favourable or hostile article often decided this question of finance. Therefore Dauriat, having five hundred reams to sell, had hurried along to make terms with Lucien. The sultan among publishers had become a slave.

After waiting for some time, grumbling, making as much noise as possible and parleying with Bérénice, he was allowed access to Lucien. The haughty publisher assumed the smiling demeanour of a courtier entering the royal presence; but it was a blend of self-conceit and affability.

'Don't let me disturb you, my dear loves!' he said. 'Aren't they sweet, these two turtle-doves! In fact, you're just like a pair of doves! Who would suppose, Mademoiselle, that this young man with his maidenly air is a tiger with claws of steel who'll tear a reputation as easily as no doubt he tears off your dressing-gown when you're slow in removing it . . .' And he began to laugh without finishing the jest. 'My boy,' he continued, sitting down beside Lucien. Then he broke off and added: 'Mademoiselle, I am Dauriat.' – Coralie was giving him such a cold reception that he found it necessary to fire off his name like a pistol-shot.

'Monsieur,' said the actress, 'have you had lunch? Would you like to join us?'

'Indeed yes, we can chat more cosily at table,' Dauriat replied. 'Moreover, by accepting your lunch, I shall win the right of having you to dinner with my friend Lucien, for henceforth we must be hand in glove together.'

'Bérénice! Oysters, lemons, fresh butter and champagne,' said Coralie.

'You're a man of too much intelligence not to know what brings me here,' said Dauriat, looking at Lucien.

'You've come to buy my collection of sonnets?'

'Precisely,' Dauriat answered. 'First of all, let's both of us lay down our arms.'

He pulled out an elegant pocket-book, drew three thousand-franc notes from it, put them on a plate and offered them to Lucien with the obsequiousness of a courtesan and said: 'Does that satisfy you, Monsieur?'

'Yes,' said the poet. A wave of bliss hitherto unexperienced swept over him at the sight of this unexpected sum. He held himself in, but he wanted to sing, to leap up and down. He believed in the existence of wizards and Aladdin's wonderful lamp; in short he believed he had a genius at his command.

'So the *Marguerites* will belong to me?' asked the publisher. 'But you'll never attack any of my publications?'

'The *Marguerites* are yours, but I can't pledge my pen. It belongs to my friends, just as theirs belongs to me.'

'But after all, you are becoming one of my authors. All my authors are my friends. You'll do no damage to my affairs without my being warned of any attacks so that I can forestall them?'

'Agreed.'

'Here's to your future fame!' said Dauriat, raising his glass.

'Obviously you've read the *Marguerites*,' said Lucien.

Dauriat was not disconcerted.

'My boy, buying the *Marguerites* without knowing them is the finest flattery a publisher can permit himself. In six months you'll be a great poet; articles will be written about you. People are afraid of you, so I need do nothing to get your book sold. I'm the same business man today as I was four days ago. It's not I who have changed, it's you. Last week I wouldn't have given a fig for your sonnets, but your position today turns them into something rich and rare.'

'Oh well,' said Lucien, being now in a mocking and charmingly provocative frame of mind since he felt all the pleasure of a sultan in possessing a beautiful mistress and in being assured of success. 'Even if you haven't read my sonnets, you've read my article.'

'Yes, my friend. Otherwise should I have come along so promptly? Unfortunately it's very fine, this terrible article. Oh! you have tremendous talent, my boy. Believe me, make the most of the vogue you're enjoying.' He said this with a show of good feeling which concealed the utter impertinence of this compliment. 'But have you had the newspaper, have you read it?'

'Not yet,' said Lucien. 'Nevertheless this is the first time I've published a great piece of prose. But Hector must have sent it to my address in the rue Charlot.'

'Here it is: read it,' said Dauriat, in the declamatory tones of Talma taking the part of Manlius.

Lucien took the sheet, but Coralie snatched it from him. 'You know well,' she said laughingly, 'that I claim as mine the first-fruits of your pen.'

Dauriat was singularly flattering and deferential; he feared Lucien, and therefore invited him and Coralie to a grand dinner he was giving to the press towards the end of the month. He went off with the manuscript of the *Marguerites* and told 'his' poet to drop in when convenient at the Wooden Galleries to sign the contract which he promised to have ready. Still maintaining the regal ceremoniousness with which he tried to impose on superficial minds and to pass for a Maecenas rather than a publisher, he left the three thousand francs behind without taking a receipt, refusing Lucien's offer of one with a gesture of nonchalance, and departed after kissing Coralie's hand.

'Well now, my love, would you have seen many of these scraps of paper if you had stayed in your hovel in the rue de Cluny and gone on ransacking your old books in the Sainte-Geneviève Library?' asked Coralie, to whom Lucien had related his life story. 'Why, your little friends in the rue des Quatre-Vents strike me as being a rare lot of simpletons!'

His friends of the Cénacle regarded as simpletons! Yet Lucien laughed as he listened to this verdict. He had read his article in print and had just savoured the ineffable bliss, the initial joy which comes but once to flatter an author's self-esteem. As he read and re-read the article he became more alive to its scope and purport. A manuscript in print is like a woman on the stage – her beauties and her defects are revealed; she can suffer destruction or gain a new lease of life; a flaw leaps to the eye as vividly as a brilliant idea. Lucien was thrilled and thought no more about Nathan, who was merely a stepping-stone for him. He was overjoyed and could see wealth ahead of him. For a youngster who not long ago had strolled modestly down the slopes of Beaulieu in Angoulême on his way back to L'Houmeau and Postel's garret where the whole family lived on twelve hundred francs a year, the sum which Dauriat had handed over was a Potosi mine. A still vivid memory, but one which the continual enjoyments of Parisian life were to efface, took him back to the Place du Mûrier. He recalled to mind his lovely and noble sister, his David, his poor mother; he immediately sent Bérénice to change one of his notes, and in the meantime wrote a short letter to his family. Then he made Bérénice hurry off to post, fearing that if he lingered he might not be able to give his mother the five hundred francs he was sending to her address. To him and to Coralie this restitution seemed to be a good deed. The actress kissed Lucien, thought of him as a model son and brother and heaped caresses on him, for such traits of character delight those good-natured girls who wear their hearts on their sleeves.

'We now have,' she said, 'a dinner booked for every evening this week and can afford a little treat. You've done enough work.'

Then Coralie, as a woman who wanted to enjoy the beauty of a man whom all other women would envy her, took Lucien back to Staub's shop, for she had decided he was not sufficiently well-dressed. From there the two lovers went to the Bois de Boulogne and returned to dine with Madame du Val-Noble. There Lucien found Rastignac, Bixiou, Des Lupeaulx, Finot, Blondet, Vignon, the Baron de Nucingen, Beaudenord, Philippe Bridau, Conti the great musician, a whole world of artists and financiers – such people as look for strong emotions to compensate for great labour. They all gave Lucien a wonderful welcome. Sure of himself, Lucien gave as free play to his wit as if it had not been a saleable commodity, and was proclaimed *un homme fort*, an eulogy then in fashion among these specious friendly persons.

'Ah well, we shall have to see what stuff he has in him,' said Théodore Gaillard to a poet enjoying Court patronage who then was thinking of founding a royalist 'little paper' later to be dubbed *Le Réveil*.

After dinner the two journalists accompanied their mistresses to the Opera, where Merlin had a box in which the whole company installed themselves. Thus Lucien reappeared in triumph in the place where, some months before, he had had so heavy a fall. He showed himself in the *foyer* arm in arm with Merlin and Blondet, outfacing the dandies who formerly had made a fool of him. He now had Châtelet at his mercy! De Marsay, Vandenesse, Manerville, the lions of the day, exchanged a few insolent stares with him. Undoubtedly the handsome and elegant Lucien had been the subject of conversation in Madame d'Espard's box, to which Rastignac paid a long visit, for the Marquise and Madame de Bargeton were eyeing Coralie through their opera-glasses. Was Lucien arousing some regret in Madame de Bargeton's heart? His mind was preoccupied with this thought: at the sight of the Corinna of Angoulême a desire for vengeance stirred his heart as on the day when, in the Champs-Elysées, she and her cousin had treated him with contempt.

27. *A study in the art of recantation*

'DID you come from your province with a lucky charm?' Blondet asked Lucien several days later when he called on him at eleven and found him still in bed. 'His good looks,' he said to Coralie, kissing her on the forehead and pointing to Lucien, 'are causing havoc from cellar to garret, high and low.'

'I have come to requisition you, dear friend,' he said as he shook hands with the poet. 'Yesterday, at the Théâtre des Italiens, Madame la Comtesse de Montcornet desired that I should take you to see her. You'll not refuse this to a young and charming woman at whose house you'll meet the élite of fashionable society?'

'If Lucien's a nice boy,' said Coralie, 'he won't go to see your countess. What need has he to go trailing his cloak in society? He'd be bored.'

'Do you want to keep him in close confinement?' asked Blondet. 'Are you jealous of fashionable women?'

'Yes,' cried Coralie. 'They're worse than we are.'

'How do you know that, my little puss?' said Blondet.

'By their husbands,' she replied. 'You forget that I had de Marsay for six months.'

'Do you imagine, my child,' rejoindered Blondet, 'that I am very keen on introducing so handsome a man as yours into Madame de Montcornet's salon? If you're against it, take it that I've said nothing. But it's less a question, I think, of feminine concerns than of obtaining peace and mercy from Lucien for the poor devil who's become a butt for his newspaper. Baron Châtelet is stupid enough to take articles seriously. The Marquise d'Espard, Madame de Bargeton and the Comtesse de Montcornet take an interest in the Heron, and I have promised to reconcile Laura and Petrarch, that is to say Madame de Bargeton and Lucien.'

'Ah!' cried Lucien, who felt new blood coursing through all his veins and experienced the heady joy of satisfied vengeance. 'So I have them at my feet! You give me cause for venerating my pen, my friends and the inexorable power of the Press. I haven't yet written an article on the Cuttle-Fish and the Heron. I'll go there, my friend,' he said, taking Blondet by the waist. 'Yes, I'll go, but only when the pair of them have felt the weight of this very light object!' – He took up and brandished the pen with which he had written the Nathan review. 'Tomorrow I'll fling two little columns at their heads. After that we'll see. Don't worry, Coralie. It's a question, not of love, but of revenge, and I intend it to be complete.'

'Spoken like a man!' said Blondet. 'If you knew, Lucien, how rare it is to meet with such fire and fury in the *blasé* society of Paris, you'd realize your own value. – You'll be a devil of a fellow,' he added, expressing himself in rather more vigorous terms. 'You're on the road to power.'

'He'll reach it,' said Coralie.

'Well, he's already gone a long way in six weeks.'

'And when nothing but the width of a corpse separates him from the sceptre within his grasp, he can use Coralie's body to step over.'

'The love of you two reminds me of people in the Golden Age,' said Blondet. 'I congratulate you on your great article,' he continued, looking at Lucien. 'It's full of originality. You're already out of your apprenticeship.'

Lousteau came along with Hector Merlin and Vernou to see Lucien, who was prodigiously flattered to be the object of their attentions. Félicien was bringing a hundred francs to Lucien in payment for his article. The newspaper had felt it necessary to remunerate so well-written a work in order to get a hold on the author of it. In view of this conclave of journalists, Coralie had ordered lunch from the Cadran-Bleu, the nearest restaurant; when Bérénice came to tell her the meal was ready she ushered them all into her beautiful dining-room. Half-way through, when the champagne had gone to everyone's head, the reason for the visit of Lucien's colleagues became clear.

'You don't want to make an enemy of Nathan, do you?'

said Lousteau. 'Nathan's a journalist, he has friends, he could play a nasty trick on you at your first publication. Haven't you *The Archer of Charles the Ninth* to sell? We saw Nathan this morning. He's in despair; but you'll write an article in which you'll squirt showers of praise in his face.'

'What! After my article attacking his book, you want me to . . .' asked Lucien.

Emile Blondet, Hector Merlin, Etienne Lousteau and Félicien Vernou all cut him short with a burst of laughter.

'Haven't you invited him to supper here the day after tomorrow?' said Blondet.

'Your article,' said Lousteau, 'wasn't signed. Félicien, who's not such a greenhorn as you, didn't fail to put a C at the foot of it: you can use it henceforth to sign your articles in his paper, which is entirely left-wing. We all belong to the Opposition. Félicien has been tactful enough not to commit you to any line of opinion. In Hector's rag, which is right-centre, you can sign with an L. Attacks are anonymous, but it's all right to sign when you're handing out praise.'

'Signing doesn't worry me,' said Lucien, 'but I can see nothing to say in favour of the book.'

'So you wrote what you thought?' Hector asked Lucien.

'Yes!'

'Ah, my boy,' said Blondet. 'I imagined you had more in you. Really, upon my word, looking at your forehead, I credited you with the omnipotence of a great mind, of those who have mettle enough to see everything from two points of view. My dear boy, in literature, every idea has its front and reverse side, and no one can presume to state which side is which. Everything is bilateral in the domain of thought. Ideas are two-sided. Janus is the tutelary deity of criticism and the symbol of genius. Only God is triangular! What puts Molière and Corneille in a category apart is their ability to make Alceste say yes and Philinte say no, and likewise with Corneille's Octave and Cinna. In *La Nouvelle Héloïse* Rousseau wrote one letter for and another against duelling: would you dare to take it upon yourself to declare his true opinion? Which of us could decide between Clarissa and Lovelace or between Hector and Achilles? Who was Homer's true hero? What did Richardson really mean? Criticism must examine every work in all its various aspects. In short we are great relativists.'

'So you stand by what you have written?' said Vernou in a bantering tone. 'But we are vendors of phrases and we live by our trade. When you decide to write a great and fine work, a book in short, you can put your ideas and your whole soul into it, stand up for it, defend it; but articles written today and forgotten tomorrow are only, in my view, worth what we get paid for them. If you attach any importance to such stupid trifles, you'll be making the sign of the cross and invoking the Holy Spirit whenever you write a prospectus.'

All of them seemed astonished at Lucien's scruples and proceeded to demolish his garb of pretence and put him into the more manly toga of the journalist.

'Have you heard the epigram Nathan consoled himself with after reading your article?' asked Lousteau.

'How could I?'

'He exclaimed: *Art is long but articles are fleeting!* The man will be coming to supper here two days hence. He'll have to grovel before you, fawn on you and tell you what a great man you are!'

'It certainly would be comical,' said Lucien.

'Comical?' retorted Blondet. 'It's necessary!'

'I am willing, my friends,' said Lucien, slightly tipsy. 'But how do I do it?'

'Well,' said Lousteau. 'Write three fine columns for Merlin's paper refuting what you said before. We enjoyed Nathan's fury, but we've just told him that he ought rather to thank us for the close piece of polemics by means of which we were intending to get his book sold out in a week. At the moment he looks on you as a traitor in the camp, the scum of the earth, a scoundrel: the day after tomorrow you'll be a great, level-headed man, a nineteenth century Plutarch! He'll clasp you to his bosom. Dauriat came to you and gave you three thousand francs: the trick had worked. Now you must get Nathan's esteem and friendship. The publisher's the only man to be taken in. Only our enemies must be sacrificed and harried. In the case of someone who had made his name without our help, whose talent incommoded us, who had to be wiped out, we shouldn't stage such a come-back; but Nathan's one of our friends. Blondet had had the first edition of his book attacked in the *Mercure* for the pleasure of retorting in the *Journal des Débats*. So it sold like hot cakes!'

'Honestly, my friend, I'm incapable of writing two words of praise about this book.'

'You'll get another hundred francs,' said Merlin. 'Nathan will already have brought you in two hundred francs, without counting the article you can write for Finot's Review: Dauriat will pay you a hundred francs for it and so will the Review. Total: four hundred francs.'

'But what can I say?' asked Lucien.

'This is how you can manage it, my boy,' replied Blondet, collecting his thoughts. 'Envy, you will say, which fastens on to all fine works like a maggot to fruit, has tried to bore its way into this book. In order to find defects in it, a critic was forced to invent theories and distinguish between two kinds of literature: that which devotes itself to ideas and that which takes refuge in imagery. At this point, my boy, you'll say that the ultimate achievement of the literary art is to impress the idea on the image. By attempting to prove that poetry consists wholly of imagery, you'll complain that our tongue gives little scope for poetry, you'll talk of the reproaches foreigners make to us about the *positivism* of our style, and you'll praise Monsieur de Canalis and Nathan for the service they are rendering to France by relieving the language of its prosiness. Demolish your previous argument by showing that we're in advance on the eighteenth century. Invent *Progress* – a delightful hoax to play on the bourgeois! The new literature goes in for tableaux in which all the genres are concentrated, comedy as well as drama, description, character-drawing and dialogue for which the brilliant complexities of an interesting plot provide a setting. The novel, which requires feeling, style and imagery, is the most tremendous creation of modern times. It's taking the place of comedy which, with its antiquated rules, is no longer possible in modern conditions of life. The novel includes both facts and ideas in its inventions, which call for the wit and incisive moral insight of La Bruyère, character-drawing as Molière understood it, the grandiose stage effects of Shakespeare and the depiction of the most delicate shades of passion, which is the sole treasure our forerunners have bequeathed to us. And so the novel is far and away superior to the cold mathematical discussion and the arid analysis of the eighteenth century.'

'The novel, you will say sententiously, is an amusing form of epic. Quote from *Corinne*, lean on Madame de Staël. The eighteenth century brought everything into question, the task of the nineteenth century is to give the answers. This it will do by recourse to reality, but a reality which lives and moves; in fine, it is bringing passion into play, an element unknown to Voltaire. Work in a tirade against Voltaire. As for Rousseau, all he did was to put clothes on arguments and systems. Julie and Claire are abstractions, not creatures of flesh and blood. You can then make a switch and state that we are indebted to the peaceful Bourbon regime for a fresh and original literature: remember you're writing in a right-centre journal. Mock away at system-makers. Finally, in a burst of eloquence, you can exclaim: those then are the many errors, the many falsehoods perpetrated by our colleague! And why? In order to disparage a fine work, deceive the public and establish this conclusion: a book which is selling isn't selling. *Proh pudor!* (let fly with a *Proh pudor!* – this honest expletive will stir the reader). Lastly, proclaim the decadence of criticism! By way of conclusion: there's only one kind of literature, the kind which diverts. Nathan is exploring a new path, he has understood the times and is responding to its needs. Drama is what is needed today. A century in which politics are a non-stop dumb-show performance cries out for drama. Have we not seen in the course of twenty years, you will ask, the four dramas of the Revolution, the Directory, the Empire and the Restoration? From then you reel out a dithyramb of eulogy and the second edition will be sold out . . .'

'And this is how you'll work it: next Saturday, you'll

write a page in the *Mercure*, and you'll openly sign it DE RUBEMPRÉ. In this third article you'll say: "The property of fine works is to arouse ample discussion. This week such and such a newspaper said such and such a thing about Nathan's book, such and such another has given an energetic reply." You criticize the two critics C and L, you pay me a passing compliment on the first article I wrote in the *Débats*, and you end up by insisting that Nathan's work is the finest the period has produced. That's as good as saying nothing at all – they say it about every book. Your week will have earned you four hundred francs as well as the pleasure of having told the truth somewhere or other. People of sense will agree with C or L or Rubempré, perhaps with all three! Mythology, certainly one of the greatest human inventions, placed Truth at the bottom of a well: doesn't one need a bucket to pull it out? You'll have given the public three buckets instead of one. There you are, my child. Get on with it!'

Lucien was in a daze. Blondet kissed him on both cheeks and said: 'I'm off to my shop.'

Everyone went off to his 'shop'. For these hardy types, the newspaper was just a 'shop'. They were all to meet that evening in the Wooden Galleries, where Lucien was to sign his contract with Dauriat. Florine and Lousteau, Lucien and Coralie, Blondet and Finot were dining at the Palais-Royal, where Du Bruel was giving dinner to the manager of the Panorama-Dramatique.

'They are right!' exclaimed Lucien, once he was alone with Coralie. 'Men must serve as tools in the hands of competent people. Four hundred francs for three articles! Doguereau scarcely offered as much for a book which cost me two years' labour.'

'Write reviews,' said Coralie. 'Get some fun out of it! Shall I not myself be posing this evening as an Andalusian, wearing gypsy costume tomorrow and trousers another day? Do as I do: make faces at them for their money, and let's live happily.'

Lucien, taken with this paradox, put his wit astride the skittish mule which is the offspring of Pegasus and Balaam's she-ass. He began to gallop through the fields of thought during his ride in the Bois de Boulogne; he discovered original and attractive features in Blondet's thesis. He dined as happy men dine, went to Dauriat's office and signed the contract ceding all rights in the manuscript – without seeing the drawbacks of this – then he made a trip to the newspaper office, where he threw two columns together, and went back to the rue de Vendôme. Next morning, it turned out that the previous day's ideas had germinated, as happens with all minds which are bursting with sap and whose faculties have as yet had little exercise. Lucien derived pleasure from thinking out this new article and set about it with enthusiasm. From his pen flowed all the fine sallies born of paradox. He was witty and mocking, he even rose to new reflexions on feeling, ideas and imagery in literature. With subtle ingenuity, in order to praise Nathan, he recaptured the first impressions about the book he had had at the reading-room in the Cour du Commerce. After being a harsh and scathing, a bantering and humorous critic, he became quite poetic in a few final periods whose majestic balance was like that of a perfume-laden censer swinging before an altar.

'There's a hundred francs, Coralie!' he cried, holding up the eight sheets which he had written while she was dressing.

In this state of verve, he dashed off the terrible article against Châtelet and Madame de Bargeton which he had promised Blondet. That whole morning he enjoyed in secret one of the liveliest pleasures known to journalists, that of whetting the epigram, polishing the cold blade which finds a sheath in the victim's heart and carving the handle of it for the readers' delectation. The public admires the intellectual craftsmanship which has gone to the making of this dagger-hilt and sees no harm in it, not knowing that the steel of a vengeful witticism artfully probes and burrows into someone's self-esteem and inflicts innumerable wounds. This horrible pleasure, sombre and solitary, savoured in secrecy, is like a duel fought with an absent person who is killed from a distance with the shaft of a pen, as if the journalist had the fantastic power of wish-fulfilment accorded to the possessors of talismans in Arabian tales. An epigram is wit prompted by hatred, and hatred springs from man's evil passions just as all his good qualities are distilled from love. And so there is no man who fails to be witty when avenging himself for the same reason that there is no man who fails to obtain enjoyment from love. Despite the facility and vulgarity of this kind of wit in France, it is always well received. Lucien's article was destined to put, and it did put, the finishing touch to the reputation for malice and spitefulness which his newspaper acquired: it struck through to the heart of two people, grievously wounding Madame de Bargeton, his erstwhile Laura, and Baron Châtelet, his rival.

'Well now,' Coralie said to him. 'Let's take a ride in the Bois: the horses are harnessed and stamping. You mustn't kill yourself with work.'

'Let's take the Nathan article to Hector. Decidedly a newspaper's like the lance of Achilles, which cured the wounds it had inflicted,' said Lucien, emending a few phrases in his script.

The two lovers set off and made a splendid parade in the Paris which, not long since, had repudiated Lucien and was now beginning to take notice of him. The fact of commanding notice in Paris, having realized its immensity and the difficulty of making an impression there, put Lucien in a state of elation which went to his head.

'My darling,' said the actress, 'let's call at your tailor's to get your clothes pressed or try on the new ones if they're ready. If you go to your fine ladies' houses, I want you to wipe the floor with such people as the monster De Marsay, little Rastignac, Ajuda-Pinto, Maxime de Trailles and the Vandenesse brothers, in fact all those foppish creatures! Don't forget that Coralie is your mistress! And remember not to aim any darts at her!'

28. Journalistic grandeurs and servitudes

Two days later, the evening before the supper offered by Lucien and Coralie to their friends, the Ambigu theatre was putting on a new play which Lucien was to review. After dining, Lucien and Coralie went on foot from the rue de Vendôme to the Panorama-Dramatique via the Boulevard du Temple in the direction of the Café Turc: at that time this was a favourite spot for walking. Lucien heard people vaunting his good luck and his mistress's beauty. Some said that Coralie was the most beautiful woman in Paris and others remarked that Lucien was worthy of her. The poet felt at home in his new milieu. This was the life for him! The Cénacle scarcely came into his line of vision. He wondered if those great minds which, two months earlier, he had so much admired, were not in fact too ingenuous with their puritanical ideas. The word 'simpletons' which Coralie had carelessly let fall had germinated in Lucien's mind and was already bearing fruit. He took Coralie to her dressing-room and wandered into the wings where he sauntered about like an oriental despot and where all the actresses wooed him with their ardent glances and their flattering remarks.

'I must go and do my job at the Ambigu,' he said. There was a full house at the Ambigu and no seat for Lucien. He went back-stage and bitterly complained at there being no reserved seat for him. The stage-manager, who did not know him as yet, told him that two tickets had been sent to his newspaper and washed his hands of him.

'I shall write about the play according to the amount of it I've heard,' said Lucien with an air of pique.

'Are you crazy?' the leading lady said to the stage-manager. 'He's Coralie's lover.'

The stage-manager immediately turned to Lucien and said: 'Monsieur, I'll go and talk to the house-manager.'

Thus the slightest incidents showed Lucien how powerful the Press was and flattered his vanity. The house-manager went and asked the Duc de Rhétoré and Tullia, the *prima donna*, who were in a stage-box, to take him in with them. The duke recognized Lucien and consented.

'You have brought two people to despair,' the young man said to him, referring to Baron Châtelet and Madame de Bargeton.

'What will they feel like tomorrow then?' asked Lucien. 'Up to now my friends have merely been sharp-shooting at them, but tonight I'm firing off a red-hot cannon-ball. Tomorrow you'll see why we make fun of Potelet. The article is entitled: "Potelet in 1811 and Potelet in 1821." Châtelet will be exposed as one of those types who have betrayed their benefactor by rallying to the Bourbons. After I've shown them all I can do, I'll go to Madame de Montcornet's salon.'

In the conversation which ensued Lucien displayed sparkling wit: he was intent on showing this aristocrat what a gross mistake Madame d'Espard and Madame de Bargeton had made in spurning him. But, when the duke maliciously called him Chardon, he gave himself away by attempting to establish his right to bear the name of Rubempré.

'You ought,' the duke said to him, 'to become a royalist. You have proved you are a man of wit: now prove you're a man of good sense. The only way to get a royal ordinance restoring the title and name of your maternal ancestors is to ask for it as a reward for services rendered to the Château. The Liberals will never make you a count! Mark my words, in the long run the restored monarchy will get the better of the Press, the only power to be feared. There has been too much delay: the Press ought to be muzzled. Take advantage of its last moments of freedom to show you're a man to be reckoned with. In a few years' time a name and a title will be a more stable form of wealth than talent. So you can have everything: intelligence, noble rank and good looks, and the world will be at your feet. At present therefore be a Liberal only in order to put a better price on your royalism.'

The duke begged Lucien to accept the invitation to dinner which would be coming from the envoy with whom he had supped in Florine's rooms. Lucien was immediately won over by the nobleman's reflexions and was charmed to see opening before him the doors of the salons from which he had believed a few months ago that he was permanently excluded. He marvelled at the power of ideas: evidently the Press and intellectual ability were a passport in present-day society. He appreciated the possibility that Lousteau regretted having opened the gates of the Temple to him; he was already, for personal reasons, aware of the need for setting up barriers which ambitious people rushing up to Paris from the provinces found it difficult to clamber over. If a young poet came and appealed to him as impetuously as he had appealed to Lousteau, he scarcely dared ask himself what sort of reception he would give him. The young duke perceived that Lucien was meditating deeply on these matters and was in no doubt as to their cause: he had revealed the whole political vista to this ambitious youth, unstable of will but unbounded in his desires, just as the journalists, like the Devil tempting Jesus, had taken him to the pinnacle of the Temple and shown him the kingdoms and riches of the world of literature. Lucien did not suspect that a little conspiracy was being woven against him by those who were at that moment suffering from the newspaper attacks, or that Monsieur de Rhétoré had a finger in the pie. The latter had alarmed Madame d'Espard's coterie by talking of Lucien's wit in their presence. Commissioned by Madame de Bargeton to sound the journalist, he had been hoping they would meet at the Ambigu-Comique. Neither polite society nor the journalists should be credited with deep schemes or well-concerted treachery. Neither the one nor the other plan their campaigns in advance: their Machiavellism lives so to speak from hand to mouth and consists in always being on the spot, ready for anything, ready to take what comes, good or evil, and to watch for moments when passion puts a man at their mercy. During Florine's supper, the duke had sized up Lucien's character: now he had captured him by playing on his vanity and was practising his diplomatic ability on him.

When the play was over, Lucien hurried to the rue Saint-Fiacre to write his review of it. His criticism was deliberately harsh and mordant: it pleased him to try out his power. This melodrama was better than that of the Panorama-Dramatique; but he wanted to find out if he was capable, as he had been told he was, of damning a good play and bringing success to a bad one. Next day, at lunch with Coralie, he unfolded the newspaper, after telling her that he had torn the Ambigu-Comique play to shreds. He was more than mildly astonished to read, after his article on Madame de Bargeton and Châtelet, a review of the Ambigu play that had been so toned down during the night that, while his witty analysis of it remained intact, a favourable verdict emerged from it. The play was sure to fill the theatre coffers. His fury was indescribable: he decided to thrash the matter out with Lousteau. He believed himself to be indispensable and resolved that he would not let himself be dominated and exploited like a nincompoop. In order to put his power on a firm footing, he wrote an article in which he summed up and counterbalanced all the opinions about Nathan's book set forth in Dauriat's and Finot's respective Reviews. Then, once his blood was up, he tossed off one of his 'Variétés' articles due for the little paper. In the first flush of enthusiasm, young journalists give loving care to their articles and in this way, very imprudently, they use up all their ammunition. The director of the Panorama-Dramatique was giving the first performance of a vaudeville in order to leave Florine and Coralie a free evening. It was to be played before the supper began. Lousteau came for Lucien's article on it; he had written it in advance, having attended the dress rehearsal so that there need be no anxiety about the paper being set up in time. When Lucien had read him one of those charming little articles on Parisian foibles – which brought success to the newspaper – Etienne kissed him on both eyes and hailed him as the Providence of the daily press.

'Why then do you amuse yourself changing the gist of my articles?' asked Lucien, who had only written this brilliant article in order to give greater cogency to his grievances.

'Who, I?' exclaimed Lousteau.

'Well then, who was it altered my article?'

'My dear,' Etienne replied with a laugh. 'You're not yet

au fait as concerns business. The Ambigu provides us with twenty subscribers, and the paper is only delivered to nine of them: the director, the orchestra conductor, the stage-manager, their mistresses and three joint owners of the theatre. In this way each of the boulevard theatres pays the newspaper eight hundred francs. There's the same amount of money in boxes allotted to Finot, without counting the subscriptions taken out by actors and actresses. So the rascal reaps eight thousand francs from the boulevard theatres. That being the case with the small theatres, guess what the big ones bring in! Do you understand? We have to show a great deal of indulgence.'

'What you mean is that I'm not free to write what I think.'

'Why, what matter, if you make a good thing out of it?' asked Lousteau. 'Besides, my dear, what have you got against this theatre? You must have some motive for slashing yesterday's play. If we slashed for the fun of it we should endanger the paper. If we made well-deserved attacks it would lose all its power. Has the manager fallen short with you?'

'He hadn't kept a seat for me.'

'Right!' said Lousteau. 'I'll show the manager your article and tell him I softened it down: you'll get more out of it than if it had appeared. Ask him for some tickets tomorrow: he'll give a blank signature for forty per month, and I'll take you to a man with whom you'll come to an arrangement for unloading them; he'll buy them from you for half the price of the seats. You'll meet another Barbet, a leader of the *claque*. He doesn't live far away. We've time enough. Come on.'

'But, my dear man, Finot is plying a scandalous trade by thus levying indirect taxes on the products of thought. Sooner or later . . .'

'Get along with you! Where were you born? cried Lousteau. 'What do you take Finot for? Underneath his false good nature, his hypocritical airs, his ignorance and stupidity you'll find all the astuteness of the hatmaker from whose loins he sprang. Didn't you see in his den in the newspaper office an old Empire veteran, his uncle? This uncle is not only a respectable man, he's lucky enough to pass for a numskull.

It's he that's involved in all the pecuniary transactions. An ambitious man in Paris is very well off when he has at his side a catspaw who lets himself be involved like that. In politics as in journalism there are lots of cases in which the chiefs must never get entangled. If Finot went into politics, his uncle would be his secretary and rake in on his own account the levies made in ministerial bureaux on important affairs. Giroudeau, whom you'd take at first glance for a simpleton, has just enough cunning to be a stooge who can't be caught out. He's on sentry-go to save our ears from being deafened with complaints, objections and pestering by would-be recruits. I don't believe you'll find his like on any other newspaper.'

29. The playwrights' banker

'He plays his part well,' said Lucien. 'I've seen him at it.'

Etienne and Lucien went to the rue du Faubourg-du-Temple, and there the editor halted in front of a fine-looking house.

'Is Monsieur Braulard in?' he asked the concierge.

'Why *monsieur*?' asked Lucien. 'Do you call a claque leader a *monsieur*?'

'My dear, Braulard has an income of twenty thousand francs. He holds the signature of the dramatists who write for the boulevard theatres, all of whom have an account with him, as with a banker. There's a traffic in authors' tickets and complimentary tickets. Braulard disposes of this merchandise. Do a bit of statistics – it's a fairly useful science when it's not misused. Fifty complimentary tickets for each evening performance in five theatres comes to two hundred and fifty a day; if they average out at two francs each, Braulard pays the authors a hundred and twenty-five francs a day and stands a chance of gaining the same amount. Thus, authors' tickets alone bring him nearly four thousand francs a month, totalling forty-eight thousand francs a year. But reckon on a loss

384

of twenty thousand francs, for he can't always get rid of his tickets.'

'Why not?'

'Well, seats which people pay for at the box-office are sold competitively with the complimentary tickets for which there are no reserved seats. In short the theatre keeps its booking rights. There are fair-weather days and there are bad shows. And so, Braulard perhaps makes thirty thousand francs a year by these sales. Then he has his *claqueurs*, and that's a different racket. Florine and Coralie pay their tribute to him: if they didn't subsidize him they wouldn't get their applause when they come on and go off stage.'

Lousteau had been explaining this matter in a low voice as they climbed the stairs.

'Paris is a singular place,' said Lucien, who was finding vested interests squatting in every corner.

A smart little serving-maid ushered the two journalists into Braulard's apartments. The ticket-merchant, sitting in an office chair in front of a large roll-top desk, stood up on seeing Lousteau. Braulard, wrapped in a grey duffle frockcoat, was wearing footed trousers and red slippers, for all the world as if he were a doctor or a barrister. To Lucien he looked like a working-class man grown rich: a coarse face, two very astute eyes, the hands of a professional *claqueur*, a complexion over which orgies had flowed like rain on the roof-tops, pepper-and-salt hair and a somewhat choked voice.

'You come no doubt on behalf of Mademoiselle Florine, and this gentleman on behalf of Mademoiselle Coralie,' he said. 'I've often seen you about. Don't worry, Monsieur,' he said to Lucien. 'I buy the clientèle at the Gymnase, I'll look after your mistress and warn her of any tricks they might play on her.'

'We wouldn't say no to that, my dear Braulard,' said Lousteau. 'But we have come about the tickets the newspaper has at all the boulevard theatres: I as editor, this gentleman as reviewer in each theatre.'

'Ah yes, Finot has sold his paper. I heard about the deal. He's doing well, Finot. I'm dining him at the week-end. If

385

you will do me the honour and pleasure of coming, you can bring your ladies: it will be quite an occasion. We shall have Adèle Dupuis, Ducange, Frédéric du Petit-Méré and Mademoiselle Millot, my mistress. We shall have plenty of fun! And even more to drink!'

'Ducange must be in difficulties, he's lost his lawsuit.'

'I've lent him ten thousand francs, for which the success of *Calas* will recoup me; so I've given him a leg-up. Ducange is a man of intelligence, a man of resource . . .'

Lucien thought he must be dreaming when he heard this man weighing up the talent of authors.

'Coralie has made good,' Braulard said to him with the air of a competent judge. 'If she behaves nicely, I'll give her my secret support against the intrigues when she makes her *début* at the Gymnase. Listen: for her I'll have men posted in the gallery who'll make little hums of approval in order to start applause. That's a manœuvre which gives an actress a send-off. I like Coralie, and you must be pleased with her; she's a woman of feeling. Oh! I can get anyone I want hissed off the stage.'

'But let's settle this matter of tickets,' said Lousteau.

'All right. I'll come and get them from this gentleman in the early days of each month. He's your friend. I'll treat him the same as you. You have five theatres, you'll have thirty tickets: that will be something like seventy-five francs a month. Perhaps you'd like an advance?' asked the ticket-merchant going back to his desk and pulling out a well-filled cash-box.

'No, no,' said Lousteau. 'We'll keep that in reserve for rainy days.'

'Monsieur,' said Braulard, turning to Lucien. 'I'll go and arrange things with Coralie fairly soon. We shall come to a good understanding.'

Lucien was looking round, not without astonishment, at Braulard's office in which he saw a library, engravings and decent furniture. As he passed through the drawing-room, he observed that the furniture in it struck a compromise between shoddiness and ostentation. The dining-room seemed to him to be the best-kept room, and he made a joking remark about it. 'Why, Braulard's a gastronome,' said Lousteau. 'His dinners, which get mentioned in plays, are in keeping with his cash-box.'

'I have some good wines,' was Braulard's modest reply. 'Hallo, here are my lamp-lighters,' he cried as he heard the sound of husky voices and footsteps clumping upstairs.

As Lucien went out, he saw filing in front of him the evil-smelling squad of *claqueurs* and ticket-touts, all wearing caps, well-worn trousers, threadbare frockcoats, with hangdog, dirty blue, dirty green, muddy, scraggy faces, long beards, and eyes which were at once ferocious and fawning: a nauseous population which lives and swarms in the Paris boulevards, sells safety-chains and 'gold' jewellery for twenty-five sous in the mornings, and in the evenings claps its hands under the theatre chandeliers; which in short adapts itself to all the unclean exigencies of Parisian life.

'There go the "Romans"!'[1] said Lousteau with a laugh. 'There goes fame for actresses and dramatists. Seen from close to, it's no more prepossessing than our own.'

'It's hard,' answered Lucien as they returned to his rooms, 'to keep one's illusions about anything in Paris. Everything is taxed, everything is sold, everything is manufactured, even success.'

30. A journalist's christening-party

LUCIEN'S guests were Dauriat, the manager of the Panorama-Dramatique, Matifat and Florine, Camusot, Lousteau, Finot, Nathan, Hector Merlin and Madame du Val-Noble, Félicien Vernou, Blondet, Vignon, Philippe Bridau, Mariette, Girou-deau, Cardot with Florentine, and Bixiou. He had invited his friends of the Cénacle. The dancer Tullia who, it was said, was not cruelly disposed to Du Bruel, was also of the party

1. Professional applauders having been first employed in Imperial Rome, this ironical euphemism for *claqueurs* was in current usage at the time.

(though without her duke), as well as the owners of the newspapers for which Nathan, Merlin, Vignon and Vernou worked. The guests formed an assembly of thirty persons: Coralie's dining-room could hold no more.

About eight o'clock, in the light of the chandeliers, furniture, hangings and flowers, this abode assumed the festive air which lends a dream-like appearance to Parisian luxury. Lucien experienced an indescribable thrill of happiness, satisfied vanity and hopefulness on beholding himself the master in these premises, being no longer able to fathom how or by whose agency this stroke of the magic wand had come about. Florine and Coralie, dressed with the extravagant care and artistic lavishness typical of actresses, smiled on the poet like two angels whose task it was to open the gates of a dreamland palace to him. In fact Lucien was practically in a dream. In a few months his life had been so abruptly transformed, he had so swiftly passed from extreme indigence to extreme opulence that at moments he was seized with anxiety like people who, while they are dreaming, are aware they are asleep. Nevertheless, at the sight of this splendid reality, his eye expressed a kind of self-confidence which envious people would have described as self-complacency. He had changed in himself. Having known happiness every day, he had lost some of his colour, there was a moist and langorous expression in his eyes; in short, to use a phrase of Madame d'Espard, he had the very look of a man who is loved. He was all the more handsome for that. Consciousness of the power and strength he possessed was discernible in a countenance illumined by love and the experience he had gained. He was at last face to face with the literary and social world and believed he could stride about in it as a dominating figure. To this poet, whom only the weight of misfortune was to bring to reflection, the present seemed to hold no cares. The sails of his skiff were bellying out with success, and the instruments needed for the course he was to steer were at his command: a well-furnished house, a mistress whom the whole of Paris envied him, carriage and horses, and finally incalculable sums to be drawn from his pen. His heart, mind and soul had undergone a like metamorphosis:

he no longer thought of quibbling about the means in view of the great ends achieved.

His scale of living will seem so rightly suspect to thrifty minds with some knowledge of life in Paris that it will not be superfluous to reveal the foundation, slight as it was, on which the material well-being of the actress and her poet was based. Without committing himself, Camusot had instructed the furnishers to give Coralie credit for at least three months. Horses and servants and everything else were to be available as if by magic to these two children eager for enjoyment and enjoying everything blissfully. Coralie took Lucien by the hand and allowed him an initial glance at the theatrical splendour of the dining-room adorned with a magnificent dinner-service, the candelabras with their forty branches, the royal delicacies of the dessert and the menu itself, which Chevet had produced. Lucien kissed Coralie's brow and clasped her to his heart.

'I shall succeed, my child,' he told her, 'and I will reward you for so much love and devotion.'

'Never mind that,' she said. 'Are you contented?'

'If I weren't I should be hard to please.'

'Well, a smile from you pays for everything,' she replied, and with a sinuous grace she brought her lips to his.

They found Florine, Lousteau, Matifat and Camusot arranging the card-tables. Lucien's friends were arriving – all these people already called themselves Lucien's friends. They played cards from nine to midnight. Luckily for him, Lucien knew no card-games; but Lousteau lost a thousand francs and borrowed them from Lucien who did not feel he could refuse the loan to a friend. At about ten o'clock Michel, Fulgence and Joseph turned up. Lucien withdrew into a corner to chat with them, and he noticed a fairly cold and serious, not to say constrained expression on their faces. D'Arthez had been unable to come as he was finishing his book. Léon Giraud was attending to the publication of the first number of his Review. The Cénacle had sent along its three artists as being less likely than the rest to feel out of place in festivities of this kind.

'Well, my dears,' said Lucien putting on a little tone of superiority, 'You'll see that the *little humbug* may yet become a *great politician.*'

'I ask nothing better than to be proved wrong,' said Michel.

'You're living with Coralie until something better turns up?' asked Fulgence.

'Yes,' Lucien continued with an attempt at simple candour. 'Coralie had a poor old silk-merchant who worshipped her: she threw him out. I'm luckier than your brother Philip,' he added, turning to Joseph Bridau, 'who doesn't know how to cope with Mariette.'

'In short,' said Fulgence, 'You're as good as any other man now; you'll make your way.'

'I'm a man who'll always be the same to you in whatever situation he may be,' Lucien replied.

Michel and Fulgence looked at each other and exchanged a mocking smile which Lucien noticed: it made him realize how absurd his remark had been.

'Coralie is wonderfully beautiful,' exclaimed Joseph Bridau. 'What a splendid picture one could make of her!'

'She's kind-hearted too,' answered Lucien. 'Upon my word, she's angelic. But you shall do her portrait: take her, if you like, as the model for your *'Venetian girl brought to the senator by an old woman.'*

'All women in love are angelic,' said Michel Chrestien.

At this moment Raoul Nathan swooped down on Lucien with a frenzied show of friendliness, took his hands and clasped them.

'My good friend, not only are you a great man, but also a man of heart, and today that's more rare than genius,' he said. 'You're devoted to your friends. In short, I'm yours for life and death and shall never forget what you've done for me this week.'

Lucien, at the height of joy on seeing himself so flattered by a man of renown, again assumed a superior air as he looked at his three friends from the Cénacle. Nathan's arrival was due to the fact that Merlin had shown him the proof of the article praising his book, which was to appear in the next day's newspaper.

'I only agreed to write the attack,' Lucien whispered to Nathan, 'on condition that I replied to it myself. I'm on your side.'

He turned back to his three Cénacle friends, delighted at having had an opportunity to justify the remark which had drawn a laugh from Fulgence.

'Let d'Arthez's book appear, and I'm in a position to serve his interests. The mere chance of this would induce me to stick to journalism.'

'But have you a free hand?' asked Michel.

'As free as one can have when one is indispensable,' Lucien replied with a poor pretence at modesty.

By midnight the guests were at table and the festivities began. Conversation was freer in Lucien's than it had been in Matifat's flat, for no-one suspected the divergence of out-look which existed between the three deputies of the Cénacle and the representatives of the Press. The latter, with their young minds so depraved by their addiction to pros and cons, came to grips and flung at one another the most deplorable axioms of the sophistical code which journalism was then engendering. Claude Vignon, who wanted criticism to pre-serve its august character, held forth against the tendency of the *petits journaux* to indulge in personalities, and asserted that later on writers would reach the point of discrediting themselves. Whereupon Marlin and Finot openly embarked on a defence of the policy of what is called *blague* in journalistic slang; he maintained it would be a means for hall-marking talent.

'All those who can survive the test will be men of really stout calibre,' said Lousteau.

'Besides,' said Merlin, 'while great men are receiving their ovations, a concert of insults *must* be raised around them, as at the Roman triumphs.'

'But then,' said Lucien, 'all the writers who get mocked at will believe they're attending their own triumph!'

'Mightn't one say that applies to you?' cried Finot.

'But our sonnets,' said Michel Chrestien, 'would they not bring us a crown of gold, as to Petrarch?'

'Crowns of gold have already come into this,' said Dauriat. This word-play aroused general acclamation.

'*Faciamus experimentum in anima vili*,' Lucien retorted with a smile.

'Anyway,' said Vernou. 'Woe to those whom the press doesn't challenge and those to whom it throws garlands when their first work comes out! Such people will be consigned like saints to their niches and nobody will pay them the slightest attention.'

'They'll be told, as Champcenetz told the Marquis de Genlis when he was looking too lovingly at his own wife: "Move on, friend, you've had your turn!"' said Blondet.

'Success is mortal in France,' said Finot. 'We're too envious of one another not to want to forget other people's triumphs and make sure everybody else forgets them.'

'As a matter of fact, the opposition of views gives life to literature,' said Claude Vignon.

'As in Nature,' exclaimed Fulgence, 'in which life emerges from two opposing principles. The victory of one spells death for the other.'

'As in politics too,' added Michel Chrestien.

'We have just seen the proof of it,' said Lousteau. 'This week Dauriat will sell two thousand copies of Nathan's book. Why? Because his book, having been attacked, will be well defended.'

'How could an article like this one,' asked Merlin, taking out the proofs of the next day's newspaper, 'not sell off an edition?'

'Read me the article,' said Dauriat. 'I'm always a publisher, even at supper.'

Merlin read out Lucien's triumphant article, and all the gathering applauded.

'Now *could* this second article have been written without the first one?' asked Lousteau.

Dauriat drew from his pocket the proof of the third article

and read it. Finot listened attentively, since it was destined for the second number of his Review; and, in his capacity as editor, he expressed exaggerated enthusiasm.

'Gentlemen,' he said. 'If Bossuet were alive in our century he would not have written in different vein.'

'You're right there,' said Merlin. 'Today Bossuet would be a journalist.'

'Here's to Bossuet the Second!' said Claude Vignon, raising his glass with an ironic bow to Lucien.

'Here's to my Christopher Columbus!' Lucien replied, drinking a toast to Dauriat.

'Bravo!' Nathan shouted.

'Who are you calling a bravo?' asked Merlin spitefully, looking both at Finot and Lucien.

'If you go on like this,' said Dauriat, 'we shan't be able to follow your drift, and these gentlemen' – he pointed to Matifat and Camusot – 'won't understand you. Joking is like cotton thread: it breaks when it's too finely spun. That's what Bonaparte said.'

'Gentlemen,' said Lousteau. 'We are the witnesses of a grave, inconceivable, unprecedented and truly surprising event. Don't you wonder at the rapidity with which our friend has changed from a provincial into a journalist?'

'My children,' said Finot, standing up with a bottle of champagne in his hand, 'we have all protected and encouraged our host's beginnings in a career in which he has surpassed our expectations. In two months he has won his spurs with the fine articles we have all read. I propose we give him his authentic christening as a journalist.'

'And put a wreath of roses round his head in order to register his double victory!' shouted Bixiou with a glance towards Coralie.

Coralie beckoned to Bérénice who went and fetched some old artificial flowers from the actresses' boxes. A garland of roses was soon woven once the bulky chamber-maid had brought the flowers, with which the drunkest among them decked themselves grotesquely. Finot, the high priest of these ceremonies, poured a few drops of champagne on Lucien's fine fair head and with delightful gravity pronounced these sacramental words;

'In the name of the Stamp-Duty, the Caution-Money and the Laying-on of Fines, I baptise thee journalist. May thy articles sit lightly upon thee!'

'... And be paid for without deduction for the blank spaces!' added Merlin.

At this juncture Lucien observed the saddened faces of Michel Chrestien, Joseph Bridau and Fulgence Ridal who took up their hats and left amid jeering hurrahs.

'Chrestien and Christians, they're queer cattle!' said Merlin.

'Fulgence *was* a good chap,' Lousteau replied. 'But they've corrupted his morals.'

'Who are they?' asked Claude Vignon.

'Some solemn young men,' answered Blondet, 'who gather together in a philosophical and religious conventicle in the rue des Quatre-Vents where they worry about the general destinies of Humanity.'

'Oh! Oh! Oh!'

'... They're trying to find out whether humanity revolves on its own axis,' Blondet continued, 'or whether it's moving forward. They were hard put to it to decide between rectilinear and parabolic motion, discovered that the Biblical triangle was nonsensical, and then some prophet or other rose among them who pronounced in favour of the spiral.'

'Men may well league together to invent more dangerous absurdities,' cried Lucien, trying to defend the Cénacle.

'You may take such theories for idle words,' said Félicien Vernou, 'but the time comes when they are translated into rifle-shots and guillotines.'

'As yet,' said Blondet, 'they're still searching for the providential idea behind champagne, the humanitarian meaning of trousers and the tiny insect that makes the world go round. They put great men who have fallen – Vico, Saint-Simon, Fourier – on their feet again. I'm very much afraid they're turning poor Joseph Bridau's ideas upside-down.'

'They're responsible,' said Lousteau, 'for Bianchon, who comes from the same province and college as myself, giving me the cold shoulder.'

'Are mental gymnastics and orthopædy taught there?' asked Merlin.

'That could be,' Finot replied, 'since Bianchon is inclined to take to their moonshine.'

'All the same,' said Lousteau, 'he'll make a great doctor.'

'Isn't d'Arthez their nominal leader,' said Nathan, 'a young fellow who's destined to swallow us up in one gulp?'

'He's a man of genius!' cried Lucien.

'I'd rather have a glass of sherry,' said Claude Vignon with a smile.

By this time, everyone was explaining his character to his neighbour. When intelligent people come to the stage of wanting to explain themselves, to open their hearts to one another, it is certain that they are riding at full speed towards intoxication. An hour later, all the guests, having become the best friends in the world, were accepting one another as great men, men of mark, men with a future before them. In his capacity as host, Lucien had retained some clarity of mind; he listened to certain sophistries which impressed him and added the final touch to his demoralization.

'My children,' said Finot. 'The Liberal party is obliged to liven up its polemics, for at present it has nothing to say against the Government. So you can imagine what a quandary the Opposition is in. Which of you would like to write a pamphlet demanding the re-establishment of the right of primogeniture in order to raise an outcry against the secret designs of the Court? The pamphlet will be well paid for.'

'I'll do it,' said Hector Merlin. 'That's in my line of opinion.'

'Your party would say you're compromising yourself,' Finot retorted. 'Félicien, you can take on this pamphlet. Dauriat will publish it. We won't let on.'

'How much?' asked Vernou.

'Six hundred francs. You'll sign it "Count C".'

'It's a deal!' said Vernou.

'So you're going to lift the *canard* into the field of politics?' asked Lucien.

'It's the Chabot affair transferred to the sphere of ideas,' Finot replied. 'You accuse the Government of having certain intentions, and thus unleash public opinion against it.'

'It will always cause me the deepest astonishment to see a government giving up the guidance of ideas to scoundrels like us,' said Claude Vignon.

'If the Cabinet is so stupid as to step into the arena,' Finot replied, 'we've got it on the run. If it gets riled we enflame the discussion and stir up the masses against it. The Press never runs any risk, whereas the Government stands to lose everything!'

'France is non-existent until the day the Press is outlawed,' said Claude Vignon. 'You're going further every day,' he said to Finot. 'You'll be like the Jesuits, but without their faith, their stability of thought, their discipline and unity.'

They all returned to the card-tables. The candle-light soon became dim under the glimmering light of early dawn.

'Your friends from the rue des Quatre-Vents were as gloomy as condemned criminals,' said Coralie to her lover.

'No,' the poet answered. 'It's they who were the judges.'

'Judges are more fun,' said Coralie.

31. Polite society

LUCIEN lived for a month with his time taken up by suppers, dinners, lunches, soirées, and was dragged by an irresistible current into a whirlpool of pleasure and facile labour. He gave up calculating. The power to calculate amid the complications of life is the mark of a strong will which poets and weak or purely intellectual people can never counterfeit. Like most journalists, Lucien lived from hand to mouth, spending his money as fast as he earned it, giving no thought to the periodical expenses of Paris life which all Bohemians find so crushing. His clothes and appearance rivalled those of the most celebrated dandies. Like all doting women, Coralie loved to dress up her idol; she ruined herself in order to provide her beloved poet with the elegant outfit of a man about town for which he had so much yearned when he first wandered through the Tuileries. And so Lucien had wonderful canes, a dainty lorgnette, diamond studs, rings for his morning cravats, signet-rings, and finally a sufficient number of fabulous waist-coats to match the colour of his clothes. The day he betook himself to the party given by the German diplomat, his metamorphosis aroused a kind of repressed envy among the young men present, those who reigned supreme in the realm of fashion, like De Marsay, Vandenesse, Ajuda-Pinto, Maxime de Trailles, the Duc de Maufrigneuse, Beaudenord, Manerville etc. Men of the world are as jealous of one another as women. The Comtesse de Montcornet and the Marquise d'Espard, in whose honour the dinner was given, had Lucien between them and overwhelmed him with coquettish attentions.

'But why did you withdraw from society?' the Marquise asked him. 'It was so ready to welcome you and make much of you. I have a bone to pick with you: you owed me a call, and I'm still waiting for it. I saw you the other day at the Opera and you didn't even deign to see me or greet me.'

'Your cousin, Madame, had dismissed me in no uncertain terms, and . . .'

'You don't understand women,' Madame d'Espard broke in. 'You have wounded to the heart the most angelic and noblest person I know. You have no idea what Louise intended to do for you, and with what subtlety she had drawn up her plan. Oh yes, she would have succeeded,' she said in response to a mute objection from Lucien, 'was not her husband, who has now died, as he was sure to die, of dyspepsia, bound to leave her free sooner or later? Do you think she wanted to become Madame Chardon? The title "Comtesse de Rubempré" was well worth the trouble of acquiring. You see, love is a great vanity which must come to terms – particularly in marriage – with all the other vanities. Suppose I were madly in love with you, that is to say enough to marry you, I should find it very hard to be called "Madame Chardon". Don't you agree? Now that you have seen how difficult life is in Paris, you know how many twists and turns one must make in order to reach one's goal. Well, you must admit that for a man without name or fortune, Louise was aspiring to an almost unattainable favour, and so she had to leave nothing to chance. You have a lot of intelligence, but when a woman loves she has more of it than even the most intelligent man. My cousin wanted to make use of this absurd Châtelet . . . I have much pleasure to thank you for – your articles against him gave me many a laugh!,' she said by way of parenthesis.

Lucien no longer knew what to think. Initiated as he was in the perfidies of journalism, he knew nothing of those of society. And so, despite his perspicacity, he was due for some hard lessons.

'What, Madame,' said the poet, his curiosity now keenly aroused, 'are you not giving your support to the Heron?'

'Why, in society one is forced to show politeness to one's cruellest enemies and pretend to be amused by boring people, and often one has to seem to be sacrificing one's friends the better to serve them. You must still be very inexperienced. You are to be a writer, and yet you are unaware of the deceptions current in society? If my cousin appeared to be sacrificing you to the Heron, wasn't that necessary in order to exploit his influence for your benefit? The man's in very good odour with the present Ministry. And therefore we pointed out to him that to some extent your attacks did him service, so that one day we might be able to reconcile the two of you. Châtelet has been compensated for your persecution of him. As Des Lupeaulx said to the Ministers, while the newspapers ridicule Châtelet, they leave the Ministry in peace.'

'Monsieur Blondet gave me the hope that I might have the pleasure of seeing you at my house,' said the Comtesse de Montcornet while the Marquise was leaving Lucien to his reflections. 'You will find a few artists there, some writers and a woman who most keenly desires to meet you: Mademoiselle des Touches, a woman whose talent is rarely found in our sex; no doubt you will be going to visit her. Mademoiselle des Touches – or Camille Maupin if you prefer – has one of the most remarkable salons in Paris and is fabulously rich; she has been told you are as handsome as you are witty and she's dying to meet you.'

Lucien could only thank her profusely, and he threw an

envious glance at Blondet. There was as much difference between a woman of the style and quality of the Comtesse de Montcornet and Coralie as there was between Coralie and a woman of the streets. This Comtesse, young, beautiful and sprightly, had as a special brand of beauty the extremely fair complexion of Northern women. Her mother was the Princess Scherbellof by birth, and for that reason, before dinner, the German envoy had lavished the most respectful attentions on her.

By this time the Marquise had finished disdainfully toying with a chicken wing. 'My poor Louise,' she said to Lucien, 'was so fond of you! She confided in me about the fine future she was dreaming about for you. She would have put up with a lot of things, but what contempt for her you showed by sending her back her letters! We can forgive cruelty – to wound a person means that one still has faith in her – but not indifference! Indifference is like ice at the poles, it deadens everything. Come now, let's agree on this: you have wilfully thrown away treasures. Why had you to break with her? Even if you had been disdained, had you not your fortune to make and your name to recover? Louise was thinking of all that.'

'Why did she tell me nothing about it?'

'Goodness me, it was I who advised her not to take you into her confidence. Look: between ourselves, seeing you so unaccustomed to society, I was afraid of you. I feared that your lack of experience, your impetuous fervour might destroy or disturb her calculations and our plans. Can you remember now what you were like then? Acknowledge that if you could see yourself now as you were then you would be of my opinion. You and your former double are no longer alike. That's the only wrong we committed. Tell me, is there one man in a thousand who combines so much intelligence with so marvellous an aptitude for falling into step? I didn't think you were so surprisingly exceptional. Your metamorphosis was so swift, you found it so easy to conform to Parisian manners that I didn't recognize you in the Bois de Boulogne a month ago!'

Lucien was listening to the great lady with inexpressible satisfaction: she uttered her flattering words with so confiding, so playful, so naive an air, she seemed so deeply interested in him that he believed some miracle was happening like that of his first evening at the Panorama-Dramatique. Since that happy evening, everyone had smiled on him and he believed that his youthfulness worked like a charm. So he decided to test the Marquise, promising himself the while that he would not let himself be duped.

'What then, Madame, were those plans which today have become chimerical?'

'Louise wanted to obtain from the King an ordinance which would allow you to bear the name and title *de Rubempré*. She wanted to bury the *Chardon*. This first success, so easy to obtain then, one which your opinions now make almost impossible, would have made your fortune. You may think these ideas are visions and airy nothings; but we have some knowledge of life, and we know what substance there is in the title of "count" borne by an elegant and charming young man. Announce here and now in front of any young English millionairess or any heiress: *Monsieur Chardon* or *Monsieur le Comte de Rubempré*: there would be two very different reactions. Even if he were in debt, the Count would find open hearts and his beauty would be enhanced like a diamond in a rich setting. Monsieur Chardon would simply not be noticed. We haven't invented these ideas: we find them reigning everywhere, even among the bourgeois. At present you are turning your back on fortune. Look at that attractive young man, the Vicomte de Vandenesse, one of the King's private secretaries. The King is quite fond of young men of talent, and he, when he came from his native province, was just as lightly-equipped as you. You have infinitely more intelligence than he: but do you belong to a great family? Have you a name?

'You know Des Lupeaulx? His family name, Chardin, is similar to yours. But he wouldn't sell his little farmstead – Les Lupeaulx – for a million francs. One day he'll be the Comte des Lupeaulx, and his grandson will perhaps be high up in the nobility. If you keep to the wrong track, the one you are following, you haven't a hope. See how much more reasonable Emile Blondet is than you. He's got into a newspaper which supports the Government: all the powers that be approve of him; he can consort with the Liberals without danger since he has orthodox opinions. And so, sooner or later, he'll get where he wants; but he made a careful choice both of opinions and patrons. The pretty little lady next to you is a Mademoiselle de Troisville with two peers of France and two members of the Chamber in her family. Her name enabled her to make a rich marriage. Her salon is much frequented, she'll have influence and she'll stir up the political world in favour of this little Monsieur Emile Blondet. What will a Coralie bring you? You'll find yourself loaded with debts and sated with pleasure in a few years' time. Your love for her is a bad investment and you're planning your life badly. That is what the woman whose feelings you like to hurt told me the other day at the Opera. When she deplored the misuse you're making of your talent and the best days of your youth, she was thinking, not of herself, but of you!'

'Ah! if only you were right, Madame!' cried Lucien.

'What motive have I for falsehood?' asked the Marquise, throwing Lucien a cold and haughty look which brought him down to earth again.

Abashed, Lucien did not continue the conversation and the offended Marquise spoke to him no more. He was piqued, but recognized that he had been clumsy and promised himself he would make amends. He turned to Madame de Montcornet and talked to her about Blondet, lauding the merit of this young writer. The countess took this in good part and, at a gesture from Madame d'Espard, invited him to her next soirée, asking him if it would not give him pleasure to meet Madame de Bargeton again there, for, despite her widowhood, she would be present. It was not to be a grand reception – just an intimate and friendly occasion.

'Madame la Marquise,' said Lucien, 'maintains that I alone am in the wrong. Is it not for her cousin to be gracious to me?'

'Call a halt to the absurd attacks being made on her – in any case they compromise her strongly with a man she derides – and a peace treaty will soon be signed. You thought she had played with you, so they tell me, but I could see she was very sad at your having abandoned her. Is it true that she left her province with you and for you?'

Lucien looked at the Countess with a smile, without venturing to reply.

'How could you mistrust a woman who made such sacrifices for you? For that matter, beautiful and intelligent as she is, she ought to be loved *despite everything*. Madame de Bargeton loved you even more for your talent than for yourself. Believe me, women love intelligence more than good looks.' As she said this, she stole a glance at Emile Blondet.

At the Envoy's party Lucien recognized the differences existing between high society and the marginal society in which he had been living for some time: two spheres of outward show between which there was no similarity and no point of contact. The loftiness and the arrangement of rooms in this residence, one of the richest in the Faubourg Saint-Germain, the antique gilding in the salons, the grand scale in which the decoration was carried out, the lavish attention to every detail, all this was new and strange to him; but the so swiftly acquired habit of moving in luxurious surroundings prevented him from showing any astonishment. His demeanour was as far removed from self-assurance and fatuousness as it was from complaisance and servility. The poet behaved in a seemly manner and found favour with those who had no reason for showing hostility, unlike the young men who were jealous because of his sudden introduction into high social circles, his success and his good looks.

When they rose from table, Lucien offered his arm to Madame d'Espard, who accepted it. Rastignac, seeing that Lucien was thus courted by the Marquise, availed himself of the fact that they both belonged to the same province and reminded him of their first meeting in the salon of Madame du Val-Noble. The young nobleman seemed inclined to cultivate acquaintance with the great man from his province by inviting him to lunch at his flat one morning and offering to put him in touch with the young men of fashion. Lucien accepted this proposal.

'Our dear Blondet will be with us,' said Rastignac.

The minister plenipotentiary came and joined the group formed by the Marquis de Ronquerolles, the Duc de Rhétoré, De Marsay, General Montriveau, Rastignac and Lucien.

'Very good,' he said with the Teutonic simplicity under which he concealed a formidable astuteness. 'You have made peace with Madame d'Espard, she is enchanted with you, and we all know,' he said, looking round at each man in turn, 'how difficult she is to please.'

'Yes, but she adores wit,' said Rastignac, 'and my illustrious fellow-countryman has plenty to spare.'

'It won't take him long to realize what a bad line of business he's in,' said Blondet with some asperity. 'He'll come over, he'll soon be one of us.'

A chorus chimed up round Lucien on this theme. The men of graver status launched a few profound observations in portentous tones, while the young men made fun of the Liberal party.

'I'm sure he tossed up head or tails,' said Blondet, 'whether he should plump for the Left or the Right; but now he'll really make his choice.'

Lucien was moved to laughter as he remembered the scene with Lousteau in the Luxembourg gardens.

'He took as his mentor,' continued Blondet, 'a certain Etienne Lousteau, a *petit journal* swashbuckler who looks on a newspaper column merely as a five-franc piece, whose political creed is that Napoleon will come back and – this seems to me more stupid still – believes in the gratitude and patriotism of the left-wing gentry. As a Rubempré, Lucien is bound to have aristocratic leanings; as a journalist, he is bound to side with the Government, otherwise he'll never either be Rubempré or come to be a secretary-general.'

The diplomat proposed that Lucien should take a hand at whist: there was great surprise when Lucien confessed that he did not understand the game.

'My friend,' Rastignac whispered to him, 'come to my

rooms early the day you will be sharing my paltry lunch and I'll teach you whist. You are disgracing our royal borough of Angoulême. I'll repeat a remark of Monsieur de Talleyrand: if you know no whist, you're saving up for a miserable old age.'

Des Lupeaulx was announced. He was a Master of Requests much in favour who served the Government in a clandestine way, an astute and ambitious man who insinuated himself everywhere. He greeted Lucien whom he had already met at Madame du Val-Noble's party, and his greeting had a semblance of friendliness which was to take Lucien in. Finding the young journalist at this gathering, Des Lupeaulx, who made it his policy to be everybody's friend in order not to be caught napping by anyone, realized that Lucien was likely to reap as much success in society as in literary circles. He detected an ambitious man in the poet and showered protestations of friendship and benevolence on him so as to make their acquaintance to appear of longer standing than it actually was and to deceive Lucien as to the value of his words and promises. Des Lupeaulx's principle was to get a good knowledge of those he might wish later to shake off once he found they were rivals. Thus Lucien was well received in this society. He realized how much he owed to the Duc de Rhétoré, the Envoy, Madame d'Espard and Madame de Montcornet. He went over and chatted with each of these ladies for a few moments before leaving, and he gave them a graceful display of wit.

'What a fatuous man!' said Des Lupeaulx to the Marquise, when Lucien had taken his leave of her.

'He'll go rotten before he's ripe,' de Marsay said to the Marquise with a smile. 'You must have hidden reasons for turning his head like this.'

Lucien found Coralie ensconced in her carriage in the courtyard, where she had come to wait for him. This attention moved him, and he told her how the evening had passed. To his great astonishment, she approved of the new ideas which were already running through Lucien's head, and she strongly urged him to enrol under the ministerial banner.

'You'll get nothing but knocks from the Liberals: they're conspirators, they killed the Duc de Berry. Will they overturn the Government? Never! You'll get nowhere with them, whereas if you go over to the other side you'll become the Comte de Rubempré. You can make yourself useful, become a peer of France and marry a rich woman. Be an Ultra. In any case it's the done thing,' she added, voicing what was for her an ultimate argument. 'That Val-Noble woman I've been to dinner with told me that Théodore Gaillard was definitely founding a royalist *petit journal*, to be called Le Réveil, as a counter-blast to the sneers of your paper and Le Miroir. Judging by what he says, Monsieur de Villèle and his party will be in power before the year's out. Try and make something out of this change of ministry by getting on their side while they're still nobodies; but say nothing to Etienne or his friends – they're quite capable of playing a nasty trick on you.'

A week later, Lucien called on Madame de Montcornet, and was once more thrown into a violent turmoil when he met again the woman he had so much loved and whom his pleasantries had cut to the quick. Louise also was transformed. She had become more what she would always have been if she had not lived in the provinces: a great lady. Her mourning apparel showed a grace and refinement which indicated a contented widowhood. Lucien believed that her stylishness was partly aimed at him; nor was he mistaken in this; but having, like an ogre, tasted human flesh, he remained the whole evening undecided between the beautiful, loving and voluptuous Coralie and the dry, haughty and cruel Louise. He could not make up his mind to sacrifice the actress to the great lady. Madame de Bargeton, now feeling attracted once more to Lucien on finding him so witty and handsome, waited the whole evening for him to make this sacrifice. Her efforts, her subtle words and coquettish airs proved to be labour in vain, and when she left the salon she was to take with her an unappeasable desire for vengeance.

'Well, dear Lucien,' she said in a kind tone full of Parisian graciousness and magnanimity, 'you were to be my pride, and you chose me for your first victim. I have forgiven you, my child, at the thought that there were still signs of love in such vindictiveness.'

By this remark and the queenly air which went with it Madame de Bargeton was re-asserting her position. Lucien, who thought all the right to be on his side, felt that he was being put in the wrong. No question arose of the terrible farewell letter by which he had broken with her or of the motives for the rupture. Women in high society have a marvellous talent for attenuating the wrong they have done by making light of it. They can and do wipe it all out with a smile or a question affecting surprise. They remember nothing, explain everything, express astonishment, cross-examine, make commentaries, amplify, argue and end up by rubbing out the wrongs they have done as one rubs out a stain with a touch of soap: you knew that the stains were black, but suddenly you see that everything was immaculately white. You yourself are exceedingly lucky not to find yourself guilty of some unforgivable crime. In a single moment, Lucien and Louise had recovered their illusions about each other and were talking in friendly language; but Lucien, intoxicated with vanity, intoxicated with Coralie who, let us admit, was making life easy for him, was unable to give a straight answer to the question which Louise put to him with a hesitant sigh: 'Are you happy?' A melancholy 'No' would have settled his future. He explained his position with regard to Coralie – intelligently as he thought. He said he was loved for himself, in short he uttered all the idiocies of a man in love. Madame de Bargeton bit her lips. All was over.

Madame d'Espard came to her cousin with Madame de Montcornet. Lucien saw himself so to speak as the hero of the evening; he was flattered, cajoled, fêted by these three women who spun their web round him with infinite art. And so, he thought, his success in this fine and fashionable world was no less great than in the world of journalism. The beautiful Mademoiselle des Touches, so famous under her pen-name of Camille Maupin, to whom Madame d'Espard and Madame de Bargeton introduced Lucien, invited him to one of her Wednesday dinners, and seemed to be impressed by his so justly vaunted good looks. Lucien tried to prove that he had even more wit than good looks. Mademoiselle des Touches gave expression to her admiration with the naïve playfulness and the winning impetuosity of superficial friendliness which deludes all those who are not familiar with life in Paris, where mere habit and continuity in social enjoyment make people avid for novelty.

'If she found me as attractive as I find her,' said Lucien to Rastignac and de Marsay, 'we could make a quick romance of it . . .'

'You are both of you too clever at writing romances to be inclined to live one,' Rastignac replied. 'Can authors ever love each other? There always comes a moment when they make cutting little remarks to each other.'

'It would not be a nightmare for you,' said de Marsay, laughing. 'This charming lady is thirty, it's true, but she has an income of almost eighty thousand francs a year. She's adorably whimsical, and her beauty is of the long-lasting type. Coralie, my dear, is a little idiot: good enough for a start, since a handsome young man shouldn't be without a mistress. But in the long run, if you don't make some fine conquest in society, this actress will spoil your chances. Come, dear fellow, cut out Conti, who's about to sing with Camille Maupin. In every age poetry has had precedence over music.'

While Lucien listened to Mademoiselle des Touches and Conti, his hopes flitted away.

'Conti is a fine singer,' he said to Des Lupeaulx.

He went back to Madame de Bargeton, who took him into the salon in which the Marquise d'Espard was sitting.

'Well,' Madame de Bargeton asked her cousin, 'are you willing to take an interest in him?'

'That's all very well,' said the Marquise with a mixture of arrogance and mildness, 'let Monsieur Chardon put himself into a position to be protected without embarrassing those who protect him. If he wishes to obtain the ordinance which will enable him to exchange his father's insignificant name for that of his mother, must he not at least be one of us?'

'In two months I shall have arranged all that,' said Lucien.

'Very well,' said the Marquise. 'I will see my father and my uncle who are in service with the King: they will talk to the Chancellor about you.'

The diplomat and the two women had easily touched on Lucien's sensitive spot. Thrilled by the glamour of aristocracy, the poet felt unspeakable mortification at hearing himself called Chardon when he saw that the salons only admitted men who bore high-sounding names with titles to set them off. On various occasions, wherever he presented himself, he experienced the same distress. No less disagreeable was the sensation he felt when he stooped once more to his menial occupations after having spent the previous evening in high society, with Coralie's carriage and footmen to enable him to make a presentable appearance. He took lessons in riding so that he could gallop up to the carriage windows of Madame d'Espard, Mademoiselle des Touches and the Comtesse de Montcornet, a privilege he had so much envied on his arrival in Paris.

Finot was delighted to procure for his most important contributor free entry into the Opera, and there Lucien wasted many evenings; but henceforth he belonged to a special world, that of the elegant young men of the period. Our poet returned a splendid lunch to Rastignac and his fashionable friends, but committed the error of giving it in Coralie's apartments. He was too young, too much of a poet and too self-confident to appreciate certain niceties of decorum. How could an actress, an excellent creature no doubt, but devoid of education, teach him the ways of the world? The immigrant from the provinces gave ample evidence to these young men, who were very ill-disposed towards him, of the fusion of interests between the actress and himself: a thing which all young people secretly envy but none the less stigmatize. The person who that very evening made the cruellest jests about him was Rastignac, although he maintained himself in society by similar means; but he kept up appearances so well that he was able to dismiss back-biting as slander.

Lucien had been quick to learn whist. Card-playing became a passion with him.

32. The 'viveurs'

To stave off any rivalry, Coralie, far from disapproving of Lucien's dissipations, favoured them with the blindness peculiar to totally committed passion which never looks beyond the present and sacrifices everything, even the future, to the pleasure of the moment. A characteristic of true love is its enduring resemblance to childhood: in both are found the same heedlessness, imprudence, prodigality, laughter and tears.

There flourished at this period a society of young people, rich or poor, all of them idle, known as *viveurs*: they did in face *live* with incredible recklessness, were doughty trencher-men and even doughtier drinkers. Spendthrifts to a man, they led not merely a wild but a frenzied existence in which the most uncouth buffoonery played a part. They shrank from no extravagance of conduct and gloried in their misdeeds which nevertheless they kept within certain bounds: their escapades were seasoned with such originality of wit that it was impossible not to condone them.

No other fact brings out so patently the helotism to which the Restoration had condemned young people. So full of sap and vital exuberance were the men of the young generation that, having no outlet for their energy, they not only flung it into journalism, conspiracies, literature and art, but frittered it away in the strangest excesses. When it was industrious, this fine youth of France wanted power and pleasure; when artistic, it aimed at masterpieces; when unoccupied, it craved for the excitement of passion; in any case it wanted a part to play, and it was allowed none at all in politics. The *viveurs* were almost all people endowed with outstanding faculties which some of them wasted by leading this enervating life, while others were proof against it. The most celebrated and keen-witted of these *viveurs*, Rastignac, under the guidance of De Marsay, embarked in the end on a serious career and distinguished himself in it. The fooleries in which these young folk indulged made such a stir that they provided the matter for several light comedies.

Launched by Blondet into this dissipated company, Lucien became one of its shining lights, together with Bixiou, one of the most malicious wits of his time and the most indefatigable of practical jokers. Lucien's life was one long bout of intemperance punctuated with the facile labours of journalism; he continued his series of short articles and made prodigious efforts from time to time to produce a few fine pages of carefully thought-out criticism. But study became exceptional with the poet and he only gave himself to it under the spur of necessity. Lunches, dinners, carousals, social evenings and gambling took up most of his time, and Coralie devoured the rest. Lucien would not allow himself to think of the future. Moreover he saw his so-called friends all behaving as he did, paying their way with well-remunerated publishers' prospectuses and bonuses given for certain articles needed for advertizing hazardous speculations, living from hand to mouth and careless of what was to come. Once admitted on a footing of equality into the set of journalists and writers, Lucien took note of the tremendous obstacles to be overcome in the case of his trying to rise higher: everyone consented to have him as an equal, but no one wanted him as a superior. By slow degrees then he gave up hope of literary fame, believing it easier to come by success in politics.

'Intrigue arouses less hostile passions than talent, its underground manœuvres attract no one's attention.' So Châtelet, with whom Lucien had become reconciled, said to him one day. 'Besides, intrigue is superior to talent: it makes something of nothing, whereas most of the time the immense resources of talent only serve to make a man unhappy.'

And so, while living a life in which Tomorrow always trod close on the heels of a Yesterday ending in revelry and never carried out its promised tasks, Lucien proceeded with his main idea: he regularly frequented society, paid court to Madame de Bargeton, the Marquise d'Espard, the Comtesse de Montcornet, and did not miss a single one of Mademoiselle des Touche's soirées. He came to these gatherings on the way to a party, after a dinner given by authors or publishers; he left the salons to go to a supper which he had won by some bet. The strain of Parisian conversation and gambling absorbed the few ideas, the little strength which his excesses left him. Henceforth the poet no longer possessed the lucidity of mind and cool-headedness needed for looking about him and displaying the consummate tact which upstarts must employ at every instant; it was impossible for him to detect at what moments Madame de Bargeton was moving towards him again, recoiling with wounded feelings or condemning him anew. Châtelet computed the chances his rival still had and became Lucien's friend in order to encourage him in the dissipation which sapped his energy. Rastignac, jealous of his fellow-countryman and moreover finding a more useful and reliable ally in the baron, espoused Châtelet's cause. It was for that reason that Rastignac, a few days after the interview between the Petrarch and Laura of Angoulême, had reconciled the poet with the old Empire fop in the course of a magnificent supper at the Rocher de Cancale.

Lucien, who never came home until morning and got up at mid-day, could not resist the love which was ready to hand and always available. Thus the mainspring of will-power in him, constantly weakened by the sloth which made him indifferent to the fine resolutions taken at moments when he had an inkling of his real situation, lost all resilience and soon responded no longer even to the strongest pressure of poverty. The kind and tender Coralie, having at first been very happy to see Lucien amusing himself, having indeed encouraged him in dissipation because it seemed a sure guarantee that his attachment and the bonds of dependence she wound around him would be of lasting quality, had courage enough to urge her lover not to forget his work; several times she was obliged to tell him he had earned little money during the month. Lover and mistress piled up debts with alarming rapidity. The fifteen hundred francs remaining from the price of the *Marguerites*, together with the first five hundred francs Lucien had earned, had promptly been swallowed up. In three months the poet's articles did not earn him more than a thousand francs, and yet he thought he had done an enormous amount of work. But he had already adopted the ridiculous sophistry of rakes in the matter of debts. The debts of young people of twenty-five have their attractive side: later on no one condones them. It is to be noticed that some souls with real poetry in them, but whose will-power is dwindling, who give themselves over to sensation so as to translate it into images, are essentially lacking in the moral sense which should accompany all observation. Poets prefer to be at the receiving end of impressions rather than to get into other people's skins and study the mechanism of feeling. So Lucien made no enquiry of the *viveurs* about those among them who faded out; he did not foresee that a future awaited these alleged friends, some of whom had inheritances, others definite expectations, others acknowledged talent, others the most intrepid faith in their destiny and a set purpose of getting round the law. Lucien believed in his own future and trusted in the profundity of Blondet's axioms, as for instance that 'Everything works out in the long run – Nothing goes wrong with penniless people – The only fortune we can lose is the one we haven't yet made – Drift with the current and you'll get somewhere in the end – A man of wit with a foothold in society makes his fortune when he wants to!'

The winter which brought him so many pleasures was needed by Théodore Gaillard and Hector Merlin for finding the capital required for the foundation of *Le Réveil*, the first number of which did not appear until March 1822. The affair was negotiated in Madame du Val-Noble's rooms. This elegant and witty courtesan, who used to say, as she displayed her sumptuous apartments, 'This is the balance account of the *Thousand and One Nights*,' exerted a certain influence on the bankers, prominent noblemen and writers of the royalist party, all of whom were accustomed to meeting in the salons in order to negotiate certain affairs which could not be dealt with anywhere else. Hector Merlin, to whom the editorship of *Le Réveil* was promised, was to have Lucien, now his close friend, as his right-hand man; the *feuilleton* of one of the Government newspapers was also promised him. Lucien's change of front was being secretly prepared under cover of a life of pleasure. He was sufficiently immature to credit himself with great statesmanship in concealing this dramatic stroke, and laid great hopes on ministerial largesse to put his accounts in order and dispel Coralie's secret worries. The actress kept on smiling and covered up her distress; Bérénice was bolder and told Lucien how things stood. Like all poets, the great man in embryo showed a momentary concern for their disastrous situation, promised to work, forgot his promise and drowned his passing cares in debauchery. One day when Coralie noticed that her lover's brow was clouded, she scolded Bérénice and told her poet that all was going well. Madame d'Espard and Madame de Bargeton professed that they were awaiting Lucien's conversion before they persuaded Châtelet to ask for the much-desired ordinance legalising his change of name. Lucien had promised to dedicate his *Marguerites* to the Marquise, who appeared to be very flattered by a distinction which authors have rarely conferred since they became a power in the land.

When Lucien went one evening to ask Dauriat how the book was getting on, the publisher brought forth excellent reasons for postponing the printing of it. He had such and such a transaction on his hands which was taking up all his time; a new volume of Canalis was about to be published and the two ought not to clash; Monsieur de Lamartine's *Nouvelles Méditations* were in the press and two important collections of poems ought not to coincide; moreover the author ought to trust in his publisher's flair. Meanwhile Lucien's needs became so pressing that he had recourse to Finot who paid him advances on his articles. When one evening at supper the journalist-poet explained his situation to his fast-living friends they drowned his misgivings in buckets of champagne iced with pleasantries. Debts? Why, every man of character has his debts! Debts betoken satisfied needs and demanding vices. A man only succeeds when squeezed in the iron grip of necessity.

'Grateful pawnbrokers should drink a toast to great men!' cried Blondet.

'To want all is to owe all!' said Bixiou.

'No. To owe all is to have had all!' retorted Des Lupeaulx.

These *viveurs* succeeded in persuading the young man that his debts would be the magic spur with which he would prick on the steeds harnessed to the chariot of his fortune. Then Julius Caesar always came up with his forty millions of debt, Frederick the Great with the one ducat a month his father allowed him, and always the famous, demoralizing examples of great men extolled for their vices and not for the omnipotence of their courage and conceptions.

Finally Coralie's carriage, horses and furniture were distrained by various creditors for sums amounting to four thousand francs. When Lucien applied to Lousteau for the return of the thousand francs he had lent him, Lousteau showed him writs of distraint establishing in Florine's flat a situation analogous to the one in Coralie's; but Lousteau was grateful enough to propose taking the necessary steps for getting *The Archer of Charles the Ninth* accepted for publication.

'But how has Florine got into such a situation?' asked Lucien.

'Friend Matifat got cold feet,' Lousteau replied. 'We've lost him. But if Florine feels like it we can make him pay dear for letting us down! I'll tell you all about it.'

33. *A fifth variety of publisher*

THREE day's after Lucien's fruitless approach to Lousteau, lover and mistress were sadly eating their lunch by the fireside in their handsome bedroom; Bérénice had fried some eggs on the fire, for the cook, the coachman and other servants had gone. It was impossible to dispose of the furniture under distraint. The household no longer contained anything in gold or silver or anything of intrinsic value: for every object however there was a corresponding pawn-ticket, and all of these together would have made a very instructive little octavo volume. Bérénice had kept enough cutlery for two. The *petit journal* was rendering inappreciable services to Lucien and Coralie by maintaining the tailor, the milliner and the dressmaker, all of whom trembled at the thought of displeasing a journalist capable of bringing their establishments into disrepute.

Lousteau arrived during lunch, shouting 'Hurrah! Long live *The Archer of Charles the Ninth*! I've flogged a hundred francs' worth of books. Let's share out!'

He handed fifty francs to Coralie and sent Bérénice out for a more substantial lunch.

'Yesterday, Hector Merlin and I dined with some publishers, and we paved the way for the sale of your novel by making guileful insinuations. We said you're negotiating with Dauriat, but that he's being stingy and won't give more than four thousand francs for two thousand copies, whereas you want six thousand francs. We made out you are twice as great as Sir Walter Scott. Indeed, we said, you have some incomparable novels up your sleeve: it's not one book you're offering, but a business proposition. You're not the author of one more or less ingenious novel: you'll produce a whole collection! The word 'collection' went home. So don't forget your cue: you have among your manuscripts *The Duchesse de Montpensier*, or *France under Louis XIV*, *Petticoat the First* or *The Early Years of Louis XV*, *The Queen and the Cardinal* or *Paris in the time of the Fronde*, *The Son of Concini* or *a Richelieu Plot!* ... These novels will be announced on the jacket. This manœuvre we call bluffing our way to success. You crack up your books on the jacket until they become famous, and thus you make a greater name by the books you haven't written than by those you have. *In the press* is as good as a mortgage in literature! Come, aren't you amused? Have some champagne. You can guess, Lucien, that our publishers had eyes like saucers ... By the way, have you any saucers left?'

'They are under distraint,' said Coralie.

'Point taken. I'll go on. Publishers will believe in all your manuscripts if they see a single one. In the book-trade, they ask to see the manuscript and pretend they're going to read it.

Let's allow the publishers their fatuous make-believe: they never do read any books, otherwise they wouldn't publish so many! Hector and I have hinted that for five thousand francs you'd agree to three thousand copies in two editions. Give me the manuscript of *The Archer*. The day after tomorrow we'll have lunch with the publishers and get them where we want them.'

'Who are they?' asked Lucien.

'Two partners, two decent chaps, straight enough: Fendant and Cavalier. One of them was once a chief clerk in the Vidal and Porchon firm, the other's the smartest travelling salesman in the Quai des Augustins. They've been going for a year. After losing a small amount of capital publishing novels translated from the English, these fellows are now wanting to exploit the home-grown product. Rumour has it that these two dealers in inky paper only risk other people's capital, but I don't imagine you're going to bother about where the money they give you comes from.'

Two days after, the two journalists were invited to lunch in the rue Serpente, in the quarter where Lucien had formerly lived and where Lousteau still kept his room in the rue de La Harpe. Lucien picked his friend up there and saw that it was in the same state as on the evening of his introduction to the literary world. But he was not astonished: his education had initiated him into the vicissitudes of a journalist's life, which held no further secrets for him. Our great provincial had pocketed, gambled with and lost the advance fee for more than one article while also losing the desire to write it; he had written many a column according to the ingenious recipes that Lousteau had prescribed as they had walked down from the rue de La Harpe to the Palais-Royal. Having become dependent on Barbet and Braulard, he trafficked in books and theatre-tickets; by now he had no scruples about eulogizing or attacking; at the moment he was feeling quite gleeful at the thought of getting the most he could out of Lousteau before turning his back on the Liberals, whom he was planning to attack the more effectively for having studied them closely. As for Lousteau, he was extracting – to Lucien's prejudice –

the sum of five hundred francs in cash from Fendant and Cavalier, as a kind of commission for having procured this future Walter Scott for the two publishers in quest of a French Scott.

The firm of Fendant and Cavalier was one of those publishing houses founded without any sort of capital, like many which were then being founded and will still be founded while paper-manufacturers and printers persist in giving credit to the book-trade for as long as it takes to deal out seven or eight of those rounds of cards called publications. Then as today, works were bought from authors in bills drawn to fall due in six, nine or twelve months' time – a payment based on the nature of the sale which publishers settle among themselves by means of even longer-termed values. The publishers paid the paper-manufacturers and the printers in the same currency; in this way the latter had on their hands, unremuneratively, a whole library of anything from a dozen to a score of works. Reckoning on two or three successes, the profit from the sound propositions paid for the bad ones, and they kept going by grafting one book on to another. If all their operations were dubious or if, by bad luck, they happened upon good books which could only be sold after being savoured and appreciated by the real public; if the discounts levied on their bills were onerous, if creditors of theirs became bankrupt, they calmly filed their petitions without turning a hair, being prepared in advance for such a result. Thus every chance was in their favour, since they staked other people's funds, not their own, on the big green baize cloth of speculation. Fendant and Cavalier were in this situation, Cavalier having contributed his practical experience and Fendant his cunning. Their 'corporate' funds richly deserved this title, for they consisted of the few thousand francs their mistresses had painfully saved, out of which both men had each assigned themselves fairly substantial emoluments: they very scrupulously spent them on dinners offered to journalists and writers, or on theatre shows at which, they alleged, business was transacted. These semi-scoundrels, it was admitted, both knew their way about, but Fendant was more wily than Cavalier.

True to his name, Cavalier travelled in books, while Fendant looked after the Paris end of the business. This partnership was what such partnerships will always be between two publishers: a duel.

The two partners occupied the ground-floor of one of the old houses in the rue Serpente; their office was situated at the far end of vast salons which had been converted into shops. They had already published many novels, such as *A Tour in the North*, *The Merchant of Benares*, *The Well in the Sepulchre*, *Takeli*, and the novels of Galt, an English author who had no success in France. Walter Scott's success was drawing the attention of the book-trade so strongly to English productions that publishers, like true Normans, were giving all their thought to the conquest of England: they were on the look-out for Walter Scotts, just as, later on, speculators were to look for asphalt in shingly terrain, bitumen in marshes, and so draw profit from the railroads then being planned. One of the major stupidities of Parisian commerce is that it hopes to achieve success by sticking to the same lines of enterprise as have paid off before, whereas success goes by contraries. In Paris more than anywhere, success kills success. And so, under the title of such a work as *The Strelitz Family or Russia in the last century*, Fendant and Cavalier boldly inserted in capital letters, 'after the manner of Walter Scott'. Fendant and Cavalier were athirst for success: one good work could help them to get rid of their stocks of paper, and they had been tempted by the prospect of having reviews in the newspapers. At that time sales were absolutely dependent on this, for very rarely is a book bought for its intrinsic value, having almost always been published for other reasons than its merit. As far as Fendant and Cavalier were concerned, Lucien was a journalist, and his book was a commodity whose early sales would tide them over their end-of-the-month obligations.

Lousteau and Lucien found the partners in their office with the contract ready and the bills of exchange already signed. Lucien marvelled at such promptitude. Fendant was a skinny little man of sinister physiognomy: he looked like a Kalmuck with his small receding forehead, his squat nose, his tight mouth, his tiny alert eyes, the tortured contours of his face, his coarse complexion and his voice which sounded like a cracked bell. To sum up, his entire appearance was that of a consummate rogue; but these defects were compensated by the honeyed tone of his utterance, for it was by his discourse that he attained his ends. Cavalier, a bluff individual whom one would have taken for a stage-coach driver rather than a publisher, had reddish hair, a wine-flushed complexion, the thick-set build and the volubility of a commercial traveller.

'There's nothing to discuss,' said Fendant to Lucien and Lousteau. 'I've read the book; it has literary qualities and suits us so well that I have already sent the manuscript to the press. The contract is drawn up on the agreed basis; for that matter, we never deviate from the terms we have stipulated. Our drafts are payable in six, nine or twelve months; you'll find it easy to get them discounted and we shall repay you the discount. We have reserved the right to give the work a different title. We don't like *The Archer of Charles the Ninth*: it isn't enough to excite the reader's curiosity. There were several kings named Charles and so many archers in the Middle Ages! Why now, if you said *A Soldier of Napoleon*! But *The Archer of Charles the Ninth*? . . . Cavalier would have to give a course of lectures on French history in order to sell a single copy in the provinces.'

'If you knew the people we have to deal with!' cried Cavalier.

'*The Saint Bartholomew Massacre* would be better,' continued Fendant.

'*Catherine de Medici or France under Charles the Ninth*,' said Cavalier.

'Well, we'll decide that when the work is printed,' Fendant concluded.

'As you will,' said Lucien, 'provided the title suits me.'

When the contract was read, signed and duplicates exchanged, Lucien put the bills of exchange in his pocket with unparalleled satisfaction. Then all four went up to Fendant's apartment where they ate the coarsest kind of lunch: oysters, beef-steaks, kidneys done in champagne and Brie cheese;

but these foods were accompanied by exquisite wines procured by Cavalier, who knew a traveller in wines. As they were sitting down to table the printer commissioned for the novel turned up and gave Lucien a surprise by bringing him the first two proof-sheets of his book.

'We want to get on with it,' said Fendant to Lucien. 'We're counting on your book and we're badly in need of a success.'

The lunch had begun at midday, but it was not over until five o'clock.

'Where can we cash the bills?' Lucien asked Lousteau.

'Let's go and see Barbet,' Etienne replied.

The two friends, somewhat heated with wine, went down towards the Quai des Augustins.

34. Blackmail

'CORALIE'S extremely surprised to hear of Florine's loss. Florine only told her about it yesterday and blamed you for this misfortune: she seemed embittered to the point of leaving you,' said Lucien to Lousteau.

'True enough,' said Lousteau, casting prudence aside and unburdening himself to Lucien. 'My friend – you, Lucien, are really my friend, for you lent me a thousand francs and so far have only once asked for them back – beware of gambling. If I didn't gamble I should be happy. I'm in debt to all and sundry. At this moment I have the bailiffs on my heels. In short I'm obliged, when I go to the Palais-Royal, to double some dangerous capes.'

In *viveur* slang, 'doubling a cape' in Paris means making a detour, either in order not to come upon a creditor or to avoid the places where one might meet him. Lucien, who himself had to be careful about what streets he went through, was familiar with this manoeuvre without knowing what it was called.

'So you owe a lot?'

'A paltry amount!' replied Lousteau. 'Three thousand

francs would put me right. I wanted to go steady and give up gambling, and in order to get solvent I tried a bit of *chantage*.'

'What's *chantage*?' asked Lucien who had not met this word.

'Blackmail: an invention of the English press recently imported into France. Blackmailers are people in a position to manipulate the newspapers. A newspaper director or editor is never supposed to dabble in blackmail, and so he employs people like Giroudeau or Philippe Bridau. These ruffians approach a man who, for certain reasons, doesn't want to be talked about. Many people have peccadilloes – more or less original ones – on their conscience. Many fortunes in Paris are suspect, having been acquired by methods of questionable legality and often by criminal practices. Delightful anecdotes could be told about them. For instance, Fouché's gendarmes closing in on spies employed by the commissioner of police who, not having been let into the secret of the forging of English bank-notes, was about to arrest the printers who, with the connivance of Fouché as Minister of Police, were illicitly producing them. Then there's the story of Prince Galathione's diamonds, the Maubreuil affair, the Pombreton legacy, etc. The blackmailer has laid hands on some paper, some important document, and makes an appointment with the man who's feathered his nest. If the man thus compromised doesn't pay a certain sum, the blackmailer points out that the Press is ready to set to work on him and unmask him. The rich man is frightened and pays up: the trick's done. You embark on some sticky operation which a series of articles can bring to failure: a blackmailer is detailed to propose that you buy them off. There are some Ministers to whom blackmailers are sent and who stipulate with them that the paper shall only attack their political acts and not their persons; or they may deliver up their persons and cry quarter for their mistresses. That nice little master of requests, Des Lupeaulx whom you know, is perpetually busy carrying out negotiations of that sort with journalists. The rogue has already made a wonderful position for himself among the powers that be through his relationships: he's at once the Press mandatory and the ministers' ambassador; he has shady dealings with people who don't want to lose their reputations; he even extends this commerce to political affairs, buys the newspapers' silence about such and such a loan, such and such a concession granted without competition or publicity in which the Liberal banking sharks are given their share. You did a bit of blackmail with Dauriat, who gave you three thousand francs to stop you from running Nathan down. In the eighteenth century, when journalism was in its infancy, blackmail was operated by means of lampoons which royal favourites and great lords paid to have destroyed. The inventor of blackmail was Aretino, a very great Italian who levied imposts on kings just as in our days such and such a newspaper levies imposts on actors.'

'How have you been working on Matifat in order to get your three thousand francs?'

'I had Florine attacked in six newspapers and Florine complained to Matifat. Matifat asked Braulard to find out the reason for these attacks. Braulard was taken in by Finot, for whose profit I was doing the blackmailing, and he told the druggist that you were demolishing Florine in Coralie's interests. Giroudeau went and intimated to Matifat that everything could be settled if he would sell his sixth share of Finot's Review for ten thousand francs. Finot was to give me three thousand francs if the trick worked. Matifat was about to clinch the deal, happy to get back ten of his thirty thousand francs which seemed to him a bad risk because Florine had been telling him for several days that the Review wasn't doing well and that instead of pocketing a dividend he might have to face a new call for capital. But the director of the Panorama-Dramatique, before filing his petition, needed to negotiate a number of bills, and in order to get Matifat to place them, he informed him of the trick Finot was playing on him. Matifat, who's a smart business man, gave up Florine, kept his sixth share and now he knows what we're up to. Finot and I are howling with despair. We've had the misfortune to attack a man who won't stand by his mistress, a soulless and heartless wretch! Unfortunately Matifat's business gives no handle to the Press; his interests are unattackable. You can't criticize a druggist as you criticize hats, millinery, plays and art products. Cocoa, pepper, paint, dye-woods and opium can't go down in price. Florine's at the end of her tether, the Panorama closes down tomorrow, and she's at her wit's end to know what to do.'

'As a consequence of the theatre closing down,' said Lucien, 'Coralie is starting at the Gymnase in a few days' time. She might be of use to Florine.'

'Don't you believe it!' said Lousteau. 'Coralie hasn't much brain, but she's still not idiot enough to give herself a rival! Our affairs are in a terrible mess. But Finot's in such a hurry to get his sixth share back . . .'

'Why?'

'It's an excellent piece of business, my dear. There's a chance of selling the paper for three hundred thousand francs. Finot would then own a third of it, plus a commission allotted by his partners which he'd share with Des Lupeaulx. And so I'm going to suggest that Finot and I do a bit of blackmailing together.'

'So blackmail means "Your money or your life!"'

'Far better: "Your money or your good name!" The day before yesterday a *petit journal*, whose owner had been refused credit, alleged that a repeater-timepiece ringed with diamonds belonging to a prominent person in the capital had fallen in some strange manner into the hands of a soldier of the King's Guards, and he promised the full story of this event, one worthy of the *Thousand and One Nights*. The prominent person concerned lost no time in inviting the editor to dinner. The editor certainly made something out of it, though the story of the watch is now lost to contemporary history. Every time you see the Press hounding influential people, be sure that underneath it there's some case of discounts refused or some service they wouldn't render. Blackmail with regard to private life is what wealthy Englishmen most dread, and that largely accounts for the secret revenues of the British Press, which is infinitely more depraved than ours. We are babes in the matter! In England a compromising letter is bought for two or three hundred pounds so that it can be sold back.'

'How are you planning to get your grip on Matifat?'

'My dear,' Lousteau continued. 'This paltry grocer wrote some extremely interesting letters to Florine: the ultimate in hilarity as regards spelling, style and ideas. Now Matifat goes in great fear of his wife. Without naming him, without his being able to squeal, we can get at him in the very stronghold of his *lares et penates* where he thinks he's safe. Imagine his fury when he reads the opening chapter of a novel of manners entitled *A Druggist's Amours* after he has been loyally informed of the chance event which has put such and such a newspaper in possession of letters in which he talks of 'baby Cupid', writes *gamet* for *jamais* and tells Florine she's helping him to cross the desert of life – it might look as if he takes her for a camel. In short, this screamingly funny correspondence has enough in it to make readers split their sides for a fortnight. He'll be put in fear of an anonymous letter telling his wife about this little joke. But will Florine agree to let it appear that she's persecuting Matifat? She still has principles, that is to say hopes. Perhaps she's keeping the letters for herself and wants her share. She's my pupil, and therefore pretty smart. But when she realizes that bailiffs are no joke, when Finot has made her a suitable present or given her the hope of an engagement, she'll hand over the letters to me and I shall pass them on to Finot – for a consideration. Finot will hand over the correspondence to his uncle, and Gireaudou will bring the druggist to heel.'

This piece of confidence sobered Lucien. His first thought was that he had exceedingly dangerous friends. Then he reflected that he must not fall out with them, for he might stand in need of their terrible power in case Madame d'Espard, Madame de Bargeton and Châtelet broke faith with him. By then Etienne and Lucien had reached Barbet's sordid bookstall on the Quai des Augustins.

'Barbet,' said Etienne to the book-seller, 'we have five thousand francs from Fendant and Cavalier falling due in six, nine and twelve months. Will you discount the bills?'

'I'll take them at three thousand francs,' said Barbet with imperturbable calm.

'Three thousand francs!' cried Lucien.

'No one else will take them,' the bookseller replied. 'Those gentlemen will go bankrupt within three months. But I know they have two good works whose sale is dragging; they can't afford to wait, so I shall settle for them on the spot – with their own bills. In that way I shall get the goods for two thousand francs less.'

'Are you ready to lose two thousand francs?' Etienne asked Lucien.

'No!' cried Lucien, appalled by this first transaction.

'You're making a mistake!' Etienne replied.

'You won't get their paper cashed anywhere,' said Barbet. 'This gentleman's book is the last card Fendant and Cavalier can play. They can only print it by depositing the copies with their printer; if it's a success it will only give them six months' grace, for sooner or later they'll crash. People like them do more elbow-lifting than book-selling. Their bills are a matter of business for me, and so you can get better terms from me than the discounters will give, since they'll figure out how much each signature is worth. Discount-broking consists in knowing if three signatures will each of them yield thirty per cent in case of bankruptcy. To start with, you only offer me two signatures, and neither of them is worth more than ten per cent.'

The two friends stared at each other, surprised to hear this villainous man giving a concise analysis of the discounters' point of view.

'Speechifying apart, Barbet,' said Lousteau. 'What money-broker can we go to?'

'Old Chaboisseau at the Quai Saint-Michel – you know him – he dealt with Fendant's last monthly account. If you refuse my offer, try him; but you'll come back to me, and then I shall only give you two thousand five hundred francs.'

Etienne and Lousteau went along the Quai Saint-Michel to a little house at the end of an alley, where Chaboisseau, one of the discount-brokers for the book-trade, lived. They found him on the second floor, in rooms furnished in a most bizarre fashion. This petty banker, who was none the less a millionaire, was enamoured of the ancient Greek style. The bedroom cornice was an imitation of this. The bed, of purely classical design, had purple drapings and was arranged along the wall in Greek fashion as in the background of a canvas by David: it dated from Imperial days when this was the predominant taste. The arm-chairs, tables, lamps, sconces and the smallest oddments, no doubt patiently collected in the furniture shops, were redolent of the fine, slight and elegant grace of antiquity. This mythological *ensemble* contrasted strangely with the discounter's manners. It is to be noted that the most eccentric types are found among men given over to the pursuit of money. They are, in a sense, libertines in the realm of thought. Able to turn everything into gold and surfeited therewith, they go to enormous efforts to shake free of satiety. A shrewd observer can always detect in them some mania, a vulnerable spot in their hearts. But Chaboisseau seemed to be entrenched in Antiquity as in an impregnable fortress.

'No doubt he conforms to his background,' Etienne said to Lucien with a smile.

Chaboisseau, a little man with powdered hair, a drab green frockcoat and a nut-brown waistcoat set off with black breeches, patterned stockings and shoes with creaking soles, took the bills and examined them; then he solemnly returned them to Lucien.

'Messrs Fendant and Cavalier are charming and very intelligent young men, but I'm out of money,' he said in a mild voice.

'My friend will be accommodating about the discount,' Etienne replied.

'I wouldn't take those bills at any price,' said the little man, and this dismissal of Lousteau's proposition was like the blade of a guillotine sliding towards a criminal's neck.

The two friends withdrew. As they crossed the anteroom, through which Chaboisseau prudently escorted them, Lucien noticed a heap of books which the broker, a former bookseller, had bought up and among which the novelist's eye suddenly lit on the architect Ducerceau's work on the royal palaces and famous châteaux of France, a book in which the plans are drawn with the greatest accuracy.

'Would you sell me this work?' asked Lucien.

'Yes,' said Chaboisseau, becoming a bookseller once more.

'How much?'

'Fifty francs.'

'It's a stiff price, but I need it. I could only pay you with the bills you won't take.'

'You have one for five hundred francs due in six months. I'll take that one,' said Chaboisseau, who no doubt had an unpaid account with Cavalier for that sum.

The two friends went back to Chaboisseau's Greek room, where the money-broker wrote out a little invoice at six per cent interest with six per cent commission, which amounted to a deduction of thirty francs. He put to his account the fifty francs for the Ducerceau and drew four hundred and twenty francs from his cash-box, which was full of glittering crowns.

'Come now, Monsieur Chaboisseau! These bills are all good or they're all bad. Why can't you discount the rest of them?'

'I'm not discounting. I'm taking payment for a sale,' the man said.

Etienne and Lucien were still laughing – uncomprehendingly – at Chaboisseau when they arrived at Dauriat's where Lousteau asked Gabusson to tell them of another money-broker. The two friends hired a cab and drove to the Boulevard Poissonnière, armed with a letter of recommendation from Gabusson, who had foretold that they would be meeting the oddest of men, a 'queer fish', to quote his expression.

'If Samanon won't take your bills,' he had said, 'no one else will.'

Samanon was a second-hand bookseller on his ground floor, an old clothes merchant on his first floor, a dealer in prohibited engravings on his second floor; he was also a pawnbroker. No character from the tales of Hoffmann, no one among Scott's sinister misers could be compared to what Nature in social and literary garb had ventured to create in this man – if indeed Samanon could be called a man. Lucien could not repress a start of fright when he saw this small, wizened greybeard, whose bones seemed to be forcing their way through the perfectly tanned hide of a face spotted with numerous green or yellow blotches, like a painting by Titian or Paul Veronese when viewed from close up. Samanon had one eye fixed and glazed, the other sharp and glittering. This man, who appeared to use the dead eye for discounting and the other for selling obscene prints, wore a small flat wig of a rusty black, under which his white hair poked up. His yellow forehead had a menacing expression, his protruding jaws emphasized the hollowness of his cheeks and his lips, drawn back from his still white teeth, made him look like a neighing horse. The contrast between his eyes and his grimacing mouth, everything in fact gave him quite a ferocious appearance. The stiff, sharp bristles of his beard must have been as prickly as pins. A small threadbare frockcoat which had become as dry as tinder, a cravat of faded black rubbed through by his beard, disclosing a neck as wrinkled as a turkey's, gave little evidence of a desire to let care of his person compensate for his sinister physiognomy.

The two journalists found this man sitting at a horribly dirty counter busily pasting tickets on the backs of a few old books bought at a sale. After exchanging a glance by which they asked each other the numerous questions which the very existence of such a character inspired, Lucien and Lousteau saluted him and presented Gabusson's letter together with Fendant and Cavalier's bills of exchange. While Samanon was reading, there came into the shop a highly intelligent-looking man wearing a short coat so stiffened by the many foreign substances which had been worked into it that it seemed as if it had been cut out of a piece of zinc.

'I need my coat, my black trousers and my satin waistcoat,' he said, offering Samanon a numbered ticket.

Samanon pulled at the copper knob of a bell and a woman came in whose fresh, bright pink cheeks suggested she came from Normandy.

'Lend this gentleman his clothes,' he said, holding out a hand to his customer, who was an author. 'Dealing with you is a pleasure, but one of your friends brought me a young chap who took me in completely.'

'So he can be taken in!' said the writer to the two journalists, pointing to Samanon with a profoundly comical gesture.

Like an Italian beggar fetching his best clothes out of pawn for one day, the great man handed over thirty sous which the broker grabbed with a yellow, chapped hand and dropped into the cash-box under his counter.

'What extraordinary trade are you carrying on?' asked Lousteau of this great artist, an opium addict living in a dream-world of enchanted palaces who was neither willing nor able to do any creative work.

'This man lends more money on pledgeable articles than the State pawn-shop,' he replied. 'What's more, he's so appallingly charitable that he lets you have them back for occasions when you have to dress up. This evening I'm dining with my mistress at the Keller's. I can more easily find thirty sous than two hundred francs, and I've come for my wardrobe which has brought in a hundred francs to this charitable userer during the last six months. Samanon has already eaten away my library book by book and franc by franc.'

'And sou by sou,' said Lousteau with a laugh.

'I'll pay you fifteen hundred francs,' Samanon told Lucien.

Lucien gave a leap as if the discounter had plunged a red-hot skewer into his heart. Samanon was looking carefully through the bills and examining the dates.

'Even so,' said the dealer, 'I shall have to go and see Fendant who'll have to deposit some books with me. – Your credit's no good,' he said to Lucien. 'You're living with Coralie and your furniture is under distraint.'

Lousteau looked at Lucien who took up his bills and rushed out into the street exclaiming: 'He must be the devil incarnate!' For a few minutes the poet gazed at the little shop, which could only have drawn smiles from passers-by – so pitiable it looked, so mean and dirty were its little boxes with their labelled books – and made them wonder: 'What sort of business goes on there?'

A few moments later the anonymous great man, who ten years later was to take part in the vast but unrealistic enterprise of Saint-Simonism, emerged in fine clothes, gave the two journalists a smile and with them made for the Passage des Panoramas to complete his transformation by having his shoes polished.

'When Samanon goes to see a bookseller, a paper-merchant or a printer, you may know they're on the rocks,' said the artist to the two writers. 'At such times Samanon is like an undertaker coming to measure someone for a coffin.'

'There's no hope now of getting your bills discounted,' said Etienne to Lucien.

'When Samanon refuses,' said the stranger, 'no one accepts: he's the *ultima ratio*! He acts as a stooge for Gigonnet, Palma, Werbrust, Gobseck and the other crocodiles who infest the Paris money-market; any man with a fortune to make or un-unmake comes up against them sooner or later.'

'If you can't get your bills discounted at fifty per cent,' continued Etienne, 'you'll have to change them for cash.'

'But how?'

'Give them to Coralie, and she'll take them to Camusot.'

'. . . That revolts you,' Etienne went on, after a start from Lucien had cut him short. 'What childishness! Can you let such nonsense weigh against your future?'

'In any case I'll take this money to Coralie,' said Lucien.

'Another piece of stupidity!' said Lousteau. 'You'll get nowhere with four hundred francs when you need four thousand. Let's keep enough to get drunk with in case we lose, and try our luck at the tables.'

'Good advice,' said the anonymous great man.

With Frascati's only a few yards away, these words had magnetic power. The two friends dismissed their cab-driver and climbed up to the gambling-den. First they won three thousand francs, dropped to five hundred, then won back three thousand seven hundred francs; then they got down to five francs, worked up again to two thousand and staked then on *Pair* in order to double them at one stroke: *Pair* had not shown up for five rounds, and they punted the whole sum on it. *Impair* came up again. Then Lucien and Lousteau tumbled down the stairs of this celebrated pavilion after wasting two hours in a fever of excitement. They had kept a hundred francs. As they stood on the steps of the little peristyle whose double pillars outside the building supported a small iron porch which many eyes have lovingly or despairingly contemplated, Lousteau said as he saw Lucien's flushed countenance: 'Let's dine on fifty francs.'

The two journalists remounted the stairs. In an hour they rose again to three thousand francs. They put them on the Red, which had come up five times, trusting in the chance to which they owed their previous loss. Black came up. It was six o'clock.

'Let's keep only twenty-five francs for our food,' said Lucien.

This new attempt was short-lived, the twenty-five francs being lost in ten throws. Raging, Lucien threw his last twenty-five francs on the number representing his age and won: who could describe how his hand shook as he took the rake to pull in the crowns that the banker threw down one by one? He gave Lousteau ten louis and said: 'Run off to Véry's.'

Lousteau understood and went off to order dinner.

Lucien, now gambling on his own, put his thirty louis on Red and won. Emboldened by the hidden voice which gamblers sometimes hear, he left it all on Red. Red came up again, and he felt as if he had live coals inside him. Heedless of the voice, he put the hundred and twenty louis on Black and lost. Then he experienced the delicious sensation which comes to gamblers once their terrible excitement is over, when they have nothing more to stake and leave the glaring palace in which their fleeting dreams have faded. He rejoined Lousteau at Véry's where he 'fell to with a will', to use a popular expression, and drowned his cares in wine. By nine he was so completely drunk that he was unable to understand why the concierge in the rue de Vendôme sent him off to the rue de la Lune.

'Mademoiselle Coralie has left her apartments and moved to another house, the address is written on this piece of paper.'

Too drunk to be surprised at anything, Lucien got back into the cab which had brought him and had himself taken to the rue de la Lune, amusing himself by making puns on the name of the street. That very morning the bankruptcy of the Panorama-Dramatique had become public news. The frightened actress had hastened to sell all her furniture, with the consent of her creditors, to little Père Cardot who, in order not to change the purpose this flat had served, installed Florentine in it. During this operation, which she called 'getting the washing done', Bérénice was having indispensable articles of second-hand furniture moved into a little three-roomed flat on the fourth floor of a house in the rue de la Lune, close to the Gymnase. There Coralie was waiting for Lucien. All she had saved from the wreck was her unsullied love and the modest sum of twelve hundred francs.

Lucien drunkenly related his misfortunes to Coralie and Bérénice. 'You did right, my angel,' the actress said to him, throwing her arms round him. 'Bérénice will manage to negotiate your bills with Braulard.'

36. A change of front

THE next morning Lucien awoke to the enchanting joys which Coralie lavished upon him. The actress was more loving and tender than ever, as if she wanted to make up for the poverty of their new ménage with the richest treasures of her heart. She was ravishingly beautiful; her hair was peeping out

432

from a scarf wrapped round her head; she was immaculate and fresh, with laughing eyes and speech as gay as the beams of the rising sun stealing through the windows to gild this charming penury. The room, still in decent condition, was hung with a sea-green wall-paper with a red border and adorned with two mirrors, one over the mantelpiece, the other over the chest of drawers. A second-hand carpet, which Bérénice had bought with her own slender resources despite Coralie's orders, covered the bare, cold tiles. There was room enough in the chest of drawers and a mirror-fronted wardrobe for the clothes of the two lovers. The mahogany furniture was upholstered in a blue cotton material. From the wreckage Bérénice had saved a clock, two porcelain vases, four silver forks and spoons and six small spoons. The dining-room, which led to the bedroom, would have been suitable for a government clerk earning twelve hundred francs a year. The kitchen was opposite the landing. Above was an attic room in which Bérénice was to sleep. The rent was not more than three hundred francs. This squalid house had a false *porte-cochère*, and behind one of its leaves, permanently closed, the concierge had his lodge. A small window had been let into it through which he kept watch on his seventeen tenants. Such beehives are called 'investment properties' in the language of notaries. Lucien perceived a desk, an arm-chair, ink, pens and paper. The gaiety shown by Bérénice, who was reckoning on Coralie's *début* at the Gymnase, and by Coralie who was studying her part – half a dozen sheets of paper with a bit of blue ribbon tied round them – banished the anxiety and sadness of the now sober poet.

'So long as no one in society knows anything of this comedown,' he said, 'we shall get over it. After all, we can look forward to four thousand five hundred francs a year! I shall make the most of my position in the royalist newspapers. Tomorrow we are launching *Le Réveil*. I now know all about journalism and shall settle down to it.'

Coralie, discerning nothing but love in these words, kissed the lips which had spoken them. Bérénice had set the table near the fire and had just served a modest lunch of scrambled eggs, two cutlets and coffee with cream. There was a knock at the door. Lucien's three candid friends, d'Arthez, Léon Giraud and Michel Chrestien appeared before his astonished eyes. Keenly moved, he asked them to share his lunch.

'No.' said d'Arthez. 'We know everything, having just left the rue de Vendôme, but we have come for a more serious motive than mere condolence. You know my views, Lucien. In any other circumstances I should rejoice to see you adopting my political convictions; but, in the situation you have put yourself into by writing for the Liberal press, you simply cannot join the ranks of the Ultras without permanently staining your character and besmirching your life. We have come to conjure you in the name of our friendship, however much it may be impaired, not to sully your reputation. You have been attacking the Romantics, the right wing and the Government: you cannot now start defending the Government, the right wing and the Romantics.'

'What I am doing is determined by far-reaching considerations: the end will justify the means,' said Lucien.

'Perhaps you don't understand the present situation,' said Léon Giraud. 'The Government, the Court, the Bourbons, the absolutist party or, if you like to include everything in a comprehensive term, the system opposed to the constitutional system, divided though it is into several divergent factions once the question arises about the methods to be followed for stamping out the Revolution, is at least of one mind about the need for abolishing the Press. All these papers, *Le Réveil*, *La Foudre* and *Le Drapeau Blanc*, have been founded as a counterblast to the calumnies, insults and mockery of the Liberal press. – I do not approve of it,' he added by way of parenthesis, 'because the failure to recognize the greatness of our mission is precisely what has led us to launch a grave and reputable newspaper whose influence will soon command respect and make itself felt by its weight and dignity – Well, this royalist and ministerial artillery is a first attempt at reprisals against the Liberals, shot for shot and wound for wound. What do you think will happen, Lucien? Subscribers to the left wing newspapers are in a majority. In the Press, as in war, victory will be on the side of the big battalions! You Royalists will be branded as infamous men, liars, enemies of the people: those on the other side will be defenders of the fatherland, honourable men and martyrs, though perhaps they'll be more hypocritical and perfidious than you yourselves. By this means the pernicious influence of the Press will be increased and its most odious enterprises legitimized and hallowed. Insult and personal attack will become one of its public rights, will be adopted for the benefit of subscribers and taken for granted as a practice followed by both sides. When the full extent of this evil is made plain, restrictive and prohibitive laws, in a word censorship, first applied when the Duc de Berry was assassinated but removed at the opening session of the Chamber of Deputies, will return. Do you know what the French people will conclude from this conflict? It will accept the insinuations of the Liberal press, it will believe that the Bourbons intend to attack vested interests established by the Revolution, will rise one fine day and drive the Bourbons out. Not only are you making your own life unclean: one day you'll find that you've joined the losing side. You're too young, too much of a newcomer to the Press; you know too little about its ulterior motives and wirepulling. You have excited too much jealousy in the Liberal newspapers to be able to stand the hue and cry it will raise against you. You'll be swept along in the raging current of party strife: partisan fever is still at its height, though now it expresses itself not in brutal acts as in 1815 and 1816, but in quarrels over ideas, verbal conflicts in the Chamber and wrangles in the Press.'

'My friends,' said Lucien. 'I am not the featherbrain poet you like to take me for. Whatever may happen, I shall have won an advantage that the triumph of the Liberal party could never give me. By the time you have won your victory I shall have made good.'

'We shall cut off your . . . hair!' said Michel Crestien with a laugh.

'By then I shall have children,' Lucien replied. 'Even cutting off my head would make no difference!'

The three friends failed to understand Lucien, in whom relations with society had developed pride of caste and aristocratic vanity to the highest degree. The poet foresaw – with some reason – an immense fortune to be made out of his beauty and his wit, with the name and title of Comte de Rubempré to support them. Madame d'Espard, Madame de Bargeton and Madame de Montcornet held him by this thread as a child holds a cockchafer. The words 'He's one of us, he has the right ideas!' uttered three days before at Mademoiselle des Touches's reception, had intoxicated him; so also had the congratulations he had received from the Duc de Lenoncourt, the Duc de Navarreins, the Duc de Grandlieu, Rastignac, Blondet, the lovely Duchesse de Maufrigneuse, the Comte d'Esgrignon, Des Lupeaulx and members of the royalist party who were the most influential and most in favour at Court.

'Well, there's no more to be said,' d'Arthez rejoindered. 'You'll find it harder than any other man to keep yourself unsullied and preserve your self-esteem. I know you, and you'll suffer a lot when you see yourself despised by the very people to whom you have devoted yourself.'

The three friends took their leave of Lucien without giving him a friendly handshake. For a few moments Lucien remained pensive and sad.

'Come along now, forget all about those ninnies,' said Coralie, jumping on to Lucien's knees and throwing her lovely cool arms round his neck. 'They take life seriously, and life's a joke. Besides, you'll be the Comte Lucien de Rubempré. If necessary, I'll flirt with people at the Chancellery. I know how to deal with that rake Des Lupeaulx and make him get your ordinance signed. Haven't I told you that if you need one more stepping-stone in order to reach your prey, you can step on Coralie's dead body?'

The next day, Lucien allowed his name to be included among the contributors to Le Réveil. His name was announced in the prospectus as an acquisition, and the Government had a hundred thousand of these prospectuses distributed. Lucien went to the triumphal banquet – it lasted nine hours – at Robert's restaurant, quite near Frascati's, and the leading lights of the royalist press were there: Martainville, Auger, Destains and a crowd of authors, still with us in 1839, who at that time 'stood by Throne and Altar' as the stock phrase went.

'How we'll let fly at the Liberals!' said Hector Merlin.

'Gentlemen!' replied Nathan, who was enlisting under this standard because he firmly believed it was better to have the authorities for him rather than against him in the theatre enterprise on which he was proposing to embark. 'If we are to make war on them, let's do it in real earnest. Let's not shoot popguns at them! Let's go for all the classicist and Liberal writers without distinction of age or sex. They shall run the gauntlet of our mockery, and we'll give no quarter.'

'But let's be honourable and not be won over with copies of books, presents, publishers' bribes. Let's put journalism on its feet once more.'

'Very good,' said Martainville. '*Justum et tenacem propositi virum!* Let's be implacable and mordant! I'll show Lafayette up for what he is: Tom Fool the First!'

'As for me,' said Lucien, 'I'll take on the heroes of *Le Constitutionnel*: Sergeant Mercier, Monsieur Jouy's *Complete Works* and the illustrious orators of the Left!'

A fight to the death was resolved on and voted for unanimously, at one in the morning, by this band of journalists who drowned all their differences in a flaming bowl of punch.

We've given our meerschaums a splendid monarchical and clerical colouring! said one of the most celebrated writers of the Romantic movement as he left the room.

This historic witticism appeared the next day in *Le Miroir*. It had been divulged by a publisher present at the dinner, but this leakage was laid at Lucien's door. His defection was the signal for a fearful uproar in the Liberal papers: Lucien became their *bête noire* and was flayed in the cruellest manner. They related the unhappy story of his sonnets, told the public that Dauriat preferred to lose three thousand francs rather than sell them and called him 'the sonnetless sonneteer'.

One morning, in the same paper in which Lucien had made so brilliant a start, he read the following lines directed solely at him, for the public could scarcely be expected to understand the joke:

If Dauriat the publisher persists in not publishing the future French Petrarch's sonnets, we will act like generous adversaries and open our columns to these poems, which must be quite piquant, judging by the following, which a friend of the author has communicated to us.

And under this terrible announcement, the poet read the sonnet in question, which brought him to bitter tears:

> One morning in a well-stocked flower-bed
> Sprang up a sickly, unattractive plant.
> 'How fair my bloom will be, how elegant!'
> It bragged, 'in one so exquisitely bred!'
>
> Kindly received, on vanity it fed,
> And soon no charm of colour would it grant
> To other flowers. – 'Since you're so arrogant,
> Come, prove your lineage!' its neighbours said.
>
> Its blossom opened: ne'er was any clown
> More mocked, derided, hissed and shouted down
> Than this coarse weed, so vulgar its display.
>
> The gardener tore it out – well-earned dismissal.
> Its only requiem was a donkey's bray:
> Only an ass is partial to a THISTLE.[1]

Vernou wrote of Lucien's passion for gambling and pilloried *The Archer* in advance as an unpatriotic work in which the author took sides with the Catholic cut-throats against their Calvinist victims. Within a week the quarrel became envenomed. Lucien was counting on his friend Lousteau, who owed him a thousand francs and with whom he had come to a secret understanding. But Lousteau became Lucien's sworn enemy for the following reasons:

For the last three months Nathan had been in love with Florine and was wondering how he could steal her from

1. Readers will already know that *chardon* is the common noun for a thistle.

Lousteau, for whom moreover she was playing the role of Providence. The actress was in such distress and despair at finding herself without an engagement that Nathan, being a colleague of Lucien, went to see Coralie and begged her to offer Florine a part in a play of his own, undertaking to procure a conditional engagement at the Gymnase for the out-of-work actress. Florine, intoxicated with ambition, did not hesitate. She had had time to weigh up Lousteau. Nathan was a man of both literary and political ambition, one whose energy was equal to his needs, whereas Lousteau's vices were sapping his will-power. The actress, desirous of making a glamorous return to the stage, handed the druggist's letters over to Nathan, and Nathan forced Matifat to buy them back with the sixth share in the newspaper which Finot coveted. Florine thus obtained a magnificent flat in the rue Hauteville and accepted Nathan as her 'protector' in the teeth of the journalistic and theatre world. Lousteau was so cruelly hurt by this event that he burst into tears at the end of a dinner his friends gave to console him. The guests at this feast judged that Nathan had played his cards well. A few journalists like Finot and Vernou were well aware of the dramatist's passion for Florine, but they were all agreed that Lucien had hatched the plot and thus violated the sacred laws of friendship. According to them, party spirit and the desire to serve his new friends had driven this newly-fledged royalist to unpardonable conduct.

'Nathan is swept away by the logic of passion,' cried Bixiou, 'whereas the provincial great man, as Blondet calls him, is acting in cold blood!'

And so the destruction of Lucien, the intruder, the little scoundrel who wanted to make one meal of all and sundry, was unanimously resolved and deeply meditated. Vernou hated Lucien and undertook to give him no respite. In order to avoid paying three thousand francs to Lousteau, Finot accused Lucien of having prevented him from gaining fifty thousand francs by letting Nathan into the secret of the operation against Matifat. Nathan, on Florine's advice, had contrived to get Finot's support by selling him his 'little sixth' for fifteen thousand francs. Lousteau, having lost his three thousand francs, never forgave Lucien for the enormous damage done to his interests. Wounds of self-esteem become incurable once oxide of silver gets into them.

37. *Finot's finesses*[1]

No words, no description can depict the fury of writers when their *amour-propre* is wounded, nor the energy they can tap when they feel the prick of the poisoned darts of mockery. But those who are stung to energetic resistance under attack are quickly defeated. Only men of calm mind, who base their policy on the deep oblivion into which an insulting article falls, display real literary courage. Thus, at first glance, the weak appear to be strong; but their resistance does not endure.

For the first fortnight the maddened Lucien poured forth a torrent of articles in the royalist newspapers in which he and Hector Merlin shared the burden of literary cirticism. Every day, from the battlements of *Le Réveil*, he maintained a steady fire of wit, and was supported in this by Martainville, the only man who served him without ulterior motives, knowing nothing of the bargains struck during bouts of revelry, or in Dauriat's office in the Wooden Galleries or the theatre green-rooms, between journalists of both parties who were secretly hand in glove. When Lucien entered the Vaudeville *foyer* he was no longer treated as a friend. Only the people of his own party shook hands with him, whereas Nathan, Hector Merlin and Théodore Gaillard unashamedly fraternized with Finot, Lousteau, Vernon and a handful of journalists graced with the label of 'decent types'. In this period, the Vaudeville was a centre for literary slander, a kind of sanctum frequented by people of all parties, politicians and magistrates. On one occasion, after administering a reprimand in a certain Chamber of the Council, a presiding magistrate who had scolded one of his colleagues for sweeping round the green-rooms in his magisterial gown, found himself rubbing gowns in the Vaudeville *foyer* with the very person he had reprimanded. After a time, Lousteau became friends once more with Nathan when he met him there. Finot was there nearly every evening. When the opportunity occurred, Lucien studied the attitude of his enemies, and the unfortunate young man always discerned implacable coldness in them.

At that time the party spirit engendered much more serious hatred than it does today. Springs have been so over-stretched today that in the long run animosity has weakened. Criticism of today, after making a burnt-offering of a man's book, proffers a hand to him. The victim must embrace the officiating priest under penalty of running the gauntlet of pleasantry. If he refuses, a writer passes for an unsociable man, quarrelsome, eaten up with self-conceit, unapproachable, resentful, full of rancour. Today, when an author has received treacherous stabs in the back, avoided the snares set for him with infamous hypocrisy and suffered the worst possible treatment, he hears his assassins wishing him good-day and putting forth claims to his esteem and even his friendship. Everything is condoned and justified in a period when virtue has been transformed into vice and certain vices have been extolled as virtues. Camaraderie has become the holiest of freedoms. The leaders of diametrically opposed opinions talk to one another in dulcet tones and with courtly conceits. Formerly, as may perhaps be remembered, it needed courage for certain Royalist writers and some Liberal writers to meet in the same theatre. The most provocative taunts were made for everybody to hear. Looks exchanged were like loaded pistols and the slightest spark could set off a quarrel. What man has not overheard his neighbour's imprecations at the entry of certain persons who were special targets for the attacks of one or the other two parties? For indeed there were then only two parties, Royalists and Liberals, Romanticists and Classicists: an identical hatred in different guise, a hatred great enough to explain why guillotines had been set up under the National Convention.

And so Lucien, now an out-and-out Royalist and Romantic, after having begun as a rabid Liberal and Voltairian, found himself under the same weight of enmity as hung over the man most abhorred by the Liberals at that period: Martainville, the only man who stood by him and liked him. The fellowship between them did harm to Lucien. Parties are ungrateful to those on outpost duty and readily abandon them as forlorn hopes. In politics especially, those who want to succeed must move with the main body of the army. The most spiteful tactics the *petits journaux* could adopt was to couple the names of Lucien and Martainville. The Liberal faction threw them into each other's arms. This friendship, whether false or genuine, brought down upon them articles steeped in gall from the pen of Félicien, whom Lucien's success in high society exasperated and who believed, like all the poet's former comrades, that he was about to be elevated to higher status. And so the poet's alleged betrayal was characterized in more envenomed terms and embellished with all kinds of aggravating circumstances. Lucien was known as *Judas the Less* and Martainville as *Judas the Greater*, for Martainville was rightly or wrongly accused of having surrendered the Seine bridge at Pecq to the invading Prussians in 1815. Lucien laughingly replied to Des Lupeaulx that he for his part had assuredly surrendered the *pons asinorum*. Lucien's luxurious way of living, unsubstantial as it was and built upon expectations, revolted his friends who could forgive him neither for his now non-existent carriage – they fancied he was still running one – nor the splendour of his life in the rue de Vendôme. They all instinctively felt that a handsome, intelligent young man whom they themselves had schooled in corruption might rise to any heights: so they used all possible means to strike him down.

A few days before Coralie's first appearance at the Gymnase, Lucien went arm in arm with Hector Merlin to the Vaudeville *foyer*. Merlin was scolding his friend for having served Nathan's ends by helping Florine.

'You have made two deadly enemies in Lousteau and Nathan. I gave you good advice and you didn't take it.

You've dealt out praise and done good turns right and left, but you'll be cruelly punished for your kind deeds. Florine and Coralie will never be on good terms now they're acting on the same stage: one of them will want to score off the other. You have only our newspapers to defend Coralie. In addition to the advantage which his profession as a dramatist gives him, Nathan has the Liberal papers at his disposal in the matter of theatres, and he has been in journalism rather longer than you!'

This remark was an echo to Lucien's secret misgivings: neither Nathan nor Gaillard treated him with the candour that he had the right to expect. Yet he could not complain – he was so recent a convert! Gaillard overwhelmed him by telling him that newcomers had to give proof of loyalty for a long time before their party could trust them. Among the staff of the royalist and ministerial newspapers Lucien met with unexpected jealousy, that kind of jealousy which arises between all men who have any sort of cake to share and makes them like dogs quarrelling over a bone: growls, posture and character are the same in both cases. These writers played a thousand underhand tricks in order to discredit one another with the Government, accused one another of lukewarmness and hatched the most perfidious intrigues in order to get rid of rivals. The Liberals had no motive for internecine conflicts because they were far removed from power and the favours it can confer. When Lucien acquired some glimmering of this inextricable tangle of ambitions, he had not the courage to take a sword to cut through the knots, nor did he feel patient enough to untie them. He did not have it in him to be the Aretino, or the Beaumarchais, or the Fréron of his age, but clung to his one desire – to get his ordinance, realizing that with his name restored he could make a fine marriage. His fortune would then only depend on a stroke of luck which his beauty would help to bring about. Lousteau, who had been on such confidential terms with him, knew his secret, and as a journalist was able to aim a deadly thrust at the Angoulême poet's most vulnerable spot. Accordingly, on the very day when Merlin brought Lucien to the Vaudeville

Theatre, Etienne had set a horrible trap for him – one into which in his naïvety he was destined to fall and perish.

'Here's our handsome Lucien,' said Finot, dragging Des Lupeaulx, with whom he was chatting, up to Lucien whose hand he grasped with a truly feline affectation of friendship. 'I know of no other example of such a rapid rise to fortune as his,' said Finot, looking in turn at Lucien and the master of requests. 'In Paris there are two kinds of fortune: one is a material commodity – money, which anyone can pick up; the other is immaterial – relationships, position, access to the kind of society which certain persons cannot enter whatever their material fortune. My friend . . .'

'. . . Our friend,' said Des Lupeaulx, throwing a flattering glance at Lucien.

'. . . Our friend,' Finot continued, tapping Lucien's hand between his own, 'has made a brilliant fortune in this respect. In truth, Lucien has more resourcefulness, more talents, more wit than all those who envy him, and he's ravishingly good-looking. His former friends can't forgive him for his success and so they say he's merely been lucky.'

'Such luck,' said Des Lupeaulx, 'never comes to fools or incompetents. After all, can one call Bonaparte's destiny a matter of luck? There were a score of top generals before him in command of the armies of Italy, just as at present there are a hundred young men who want to be admitted to the salon of Mademoiselle des Touches, who's already regarded as your future wife in social circles, my dear!' He clapped Lucien on the shoulder. 'Oh! you're in great favour. Madame d'Espard, Madame de Bargeton and Madame de Montcornet are infatuated with you. Aren't you going this evening to Madame Firmiani's reception, and tomorrow to the Duchesse de Grandlieu's at-home?'

'Yes,' said Lucien.

'Allow me to introduce a young banker to you, Monsieur du Tillet, a man worthy of you who has made a fine fortune, and in a short time.'

Lucien and Du Tillet greeted each other, entered into conversation, and the banker invited Lucien to dinner. Finot and

Des Lupeaulx, two men of equal depth who knew each other well enough to keep on terms of friendship, made a show of resuming a conversation they had begun, left Lucien, Merlin, Du Tillet and Nathan chatting together, and moved off towards one of the divans with which the Vaudeville *foyer* was furnished.

'Well now, my dear friend,' said Finot to Des Lupeaulx, 'tell me the truth. Is Lucien getting serious patronage? He has become the *bête noire* of all my staff; and before supporting them in their conspiracy, I wanted to consult you in order to know whether it would be better to foil it and serve him.'

At this point the master of requests and Finot, for a moment or two, gazed at each other with deep attention.

'My friend,' said Des Lupeaulx, 'how can you imagine that the Marquise d'Espard, Châtelet and Madame de Bargeton, who has had the baron appointed Prefect of the Charente and made a Count as a preparation for their triumphal return to Angoulême, have forgiven Lucien for his attacks? They have thrown him into the royalist party in order to eliminate him. This very day they are all looking for motives for refusing what has been promised to this childish creature: find some, and you'll have rendered the most tremendous service to these two ladies, one for which they'll remember you sooner or later. I'm in their confidence, and they detest the little fellow to an amazing extent. This Lucien might have reconciled himself with his cruellest enemy, Madame de Bargeton, by ceasing his attacks, but on terms which all women love to carry out – you understand me? He's handsome, young, he could have drowned this hatred under torrents of love, he would then have become the Comte de Rubempré and the 'cuttle-fish' would have obtained some post for him – some sinecure – in the King's household. Lucien would have proved a very charming reader for Louis XVIII, been put in charge of some library or other, appointed master of requests *pro forma* or made a director in some department of the Privy Purse. The little idiot has missed his chance. That's perhaps what they haven't forgiven him for. Instead of dictating terms he's had them dictated to him. The day when Lucien let himself be

445

duped by the promise of an ordinance, Baron Châtelet took a great step forward. Coralie has ruined that young man. If she hadn't been his mistress, he would have wanted the 'cuttle-fish' back – and he'd have got her.'

'Then we can lay him low,' said Finot.

'How are you going to do it?' Des Lupeaulx asked him with a casual air: he wanted to win credit for this service with the Marquise d'Espard.

'He has a contract which obliges him to work with Lousteau's *petit journal*, and it will be all the easier to get him to write articles because he hasn't a penny. If the Keeper of the Seals sees himself baited in a humorous article, and if we can prove that Lucien wrote it, he will regard him as a man unworthy of the King's bounties. In order to get this provincial prodigy a bit flustered, we are engineering a flop for Coralie: he'll see his mistress hissed off the stage. Once the ordinance is kept pending for an indefinite period, we shall then chaff our victim about his aristocratic pretensions, talk of his mother, a midwife, and his father, an apothecary. Lucien's courage is only skin-deep: he'll cave in, and we'll send him back where he came from. Nathan got Florine to sell me Matifat's sixth share in the Review, I've bought the paper-manufacturer's share, and so am in it alone with Dauriat. We can come to an agreement, you and I, to take the newspaper over to the Court party. I only sided with Florine and Nathan on condition that I got back my sixth share: they sold it to me, and I must serve them. But, beforehand, I wanted to know what Lucien's chances were.'

'You're living up to your name!' said Des Lupeaulx with a laugh. 'Believe me, I like people of your sort.'

'Well then,' said Finot to the master of requests, 'can you get a definite engagement for Florine?'

'Yes; but let's get rid of Lucien, for Rastignac and De Marsay want to hear the last of him.'

'Sleep in peace,' said Finot. 'Nathan and Merlin will go on writing articles which Gaillard has promised to insert. Lucien won't be able to produce a line, and in this way we shall cut off his supplies. He'll only have Martainville's paper for

446

defending himself and Coralie: one paper against all the rest. He won't be able to stand up to it.'

'I'll tell you some of the Minister's tender spots. But let me have the manuscript of the article you're making Lucien write,' Des Lupeaulx replied, taking care not to inform Finot that the ordinance promised to Lucien was a hoax.

Des Lupeaulx left the *foyer*. Finot went over to Lucien and, with the tone of geniality which took in so many people, explained why he could not forgo the copy due to him. He shrank, he said, from the idea of a law-suit which would ruin the hopes his friend was placing in the royalist party. He liked people who were strong-minded enough to make a bold change of front. Had not Lucien and he to rub shoulders with each other through life? Would not each of them have innumerable little services to render the other? Lucien needed a reliable man in the Liberal party in order to launch attacks on the ministerialists or Ultras if they refused to serve his interests.

'Suppose they fool you, what will you do then?' Finot concluded. 'If some minister, believing he has you tied to the halter of your apostasy, ceases to be afraid of you and sends you about your business, won't you have to set a few dogs on him to bite him in the calf? Well now, you're at daggers drawn with Lousteau who's out for your blood. You and Félicien are no longer on speaking terms. I'm the only one you have left! One of the rules of my profession is to live on good terms with really able men. You can do for me, in the society you frequent, equivalent services to those I shall do for you in the Press. But business before all else! Send me some purely literary articles: they won't compromise you, and you'll have discharged your obligations.'

Lucien saw nothing but friendliness, mingled with artful calculations, in Finot's proposals. Flattery from him and Des Lupeaulx had put him into a good humour: he thanked Finot!

447

38. *The fateful week*

In the lives of ambitious people and all those whose success depends on the aid they get from men and things for a plan of campaign more or less concerted and perseveringly followed out, a cruel moment comes when some power or other subjects them to severe trials. Everything goes wrong at once, on every side threads break or become entangled and misfortune looms at every point of the compass. When a man loses his head amid this moral chaos, he is lost. People who can stand up to these initial reverses, who can brace themselves against the storm, who can save themselves by making a formidable effort to climb above it, are the really strong men. So then, to every man who is not born rich comes what we must call his fateful week. For Napoleon it was the week of the retreat from Moscow.

This cruel moment had come to Lucien. Everything had gone too happily for him in the social and the literary world; he had been too lucky, and was to see men and things turning against him. The first blow was the sharpest and most grievous of all: it reached him in what he thought to be an invulnerable spot, his heart and his love. Coralie might not be keen-witted, but she had shining qualities of soul and the gift for revealing them in the sudden impulses which are characteristic of great actresses. These strange manifestations, so long as they have not become a matter of habit through long use, are subject to whims of character, and often to a praiseworthy modesty which dominates actresses who are still young. Inwardly naive and timid, outwardly bold and uninhibited as a player has to be, Coralie, still in love, felt her woman's heart reacting against the mask she wore as an actress. The art of counterfeiting sentiment, a sublime sort of insincerity, had not yet triumphed over nature in her. She was ashamed of giving to the public what love alone could rightfully claim. Also she had a weakness peculiar to women who are truly feminine. Whilst knowing that her vocation was to reign as a sovereign on the stage, she yet stood in need of success. Incapable of facing an audience with which she was not in sympathy, she always trembled as she walked on; and then she might well be frozen by a cold reception. Thanks to this terrible sensitivity, each new part she played was like a first appearance for her. Applause induced a sort of intoxication in her which had no effect on her self-esteem but which alone could give her courage: a murmur of disapproval or the silence of a listless public upset her completely; a large and attentive audience, eyes focused on her with admiration and benevolence, galvanized her, and then she could enter into communication with the nobler qualities in all their souls and felt she had the power to elevate and move them. This dual effect accentuated both the sensitiveness of the genius in her and its constitutive elements, and also laid bare the poor girl's delicacy and tenderness.

Lucien had come to appreciate the treasures stored in her heart and realized that his mistress was still very much of a girl. Unskilled in the insincerities common to actresses, Coralie was incapable of defending herself against the backstage rivalries and machinations which were a matter of habit with Florine, as dangerous and depraved a young woman as Coralie was simple and generous. It was necessary for roles to come Coralie's way: she was too proud to go begging to authors and submit to their degrading terms, or to give herself to the first pen-pusher who tried to blackmail her into sleeping with him. Talent, rare enough in the strange art of histrionics, is only one condition of success; for a long time talent is even a drawback unless there goes with it some genius for intrigue: this Coralie absolutely lacked. Foreseeing what sufferings lay in store for his mistress when she began at the Gymnase, Lucien wanted at all cost to procure a triumph for her. The money left over from the sale of furniture and that which Lucien earned had all gone in costumes, equipment for her dressing-room and all the expenses an opening performance entails. A few days beforehand, Lucien took a humiliating step under the stimulus of love: he went with Fendant and Cavalier's bills to the Golden Cocoon in the rue des Bourdonnais to propose that Camusot should discount them. The poet was not yet so corrupted as to be able to advance coolly to this encounter. The road he took became littered with many sorrows and paved with the most dire reflections as he vacillated between 'I will! – I won't!' Nevertheless he arrived at the cold and dark little office, which drew its light from an inner court, where he found, gravely seated, no longer the man in love with Coralie, the compliant, ineffectual libertine, the doubting Thomas he had known, but the solemn paterfamilias, the smooth, self-righteous business man wearing the respectable mask of a magistrate in the Tribunal de Commerce, entrenched as head of a firm behind an authoritative coldness, surrounded by clerks, cashiers, green filing cabinets, invoices and samples, with his wife on guard and his daughter, a simply-dressed girl, near by. Lucien trembled from head to foot as he approached, for the worthy merchant cast at him the glance of insolent unconcern he had already seen in the eyes of the discounters.

'Here are some securities; I should be infinitely obliged if you would take them from me, Monsieur,' he said as he remained standing in front of the seated merchant.

'You have taken something from me, Monsieur,' said Camusot. 'I remember that!'

Thereupon Lucien explained Coralie's situation, in a low voice and whispering in the silk-merchant's ear, so close that the latter could hear the humiliated poet's heart-beats. It was not in Camusot's intentions that Coralie should suffer failure. As he listened, the merchant looked at the signatures with a smile: he was a judge in the Tribunal de Commerce and knew in what predicament the publishers stood. He gave Lucien four thousand five hundred francs on condition that he endorsed the bills: *for values received in silk-stuffs*. Lucien immediately went to see Braulard and paid handsomely to make sure of a fine success for Coralie. Braulard promised to come, and indeed came, to the dress rehearsal in order to settle at what points in the play his 'Romans' should bring their horny hands into action and carry the house with them. Lucien handed the remaining money to Coralie without telling her

450

of the approach he had made to Camusot; he calmed her anxiety and that of Bérénice: they were already hard put to it to make ends meet. Martainville, one of the most knowledgeable men of the time in theatre matters, had come along several times to help Coralie learn her part. Lucien had obtained the promise of favourable articles from several royalist journalists and so had no forebodings of misfortune.

Then, the evening before Coralie's opening, a disaster befell Lucien. D'Arthez's book had come out. The editor of Hector Merlin's newspaper gave the work to Lucien as the man most competent to review it: he owed his fatal reputation in this field to the articles he had written on Nathan. The office was full of people, and all the staff of journalists was there. Martainville had come to settle a detail concerning the general policy adopted by the royalist newspapers in their polemics against the Liberal press. Nathan, Merlin and all the collaborators on *Le Réveil* were in conference about the influence which Léon Giraud's twice-weekly journal was exerting, an influence so much more pernicious because its language was prudent, sage and moderate! They started talking about the Cénacle of the rue des Quatre-Vents, which they called a 'conventicle'. It had been decided that the royalist papers should wage a systematic war to the death on these dangerous adversaries – who were in fact to pave the way for the 'Doctrinaires', the sect whose fatal activities, from the day when the meanest of vengeful motives brought the most brilliant royalist writer into alliance with it, were destined to overthrow the Bourbons. D'Arthez, of whose absolutist opinions the journalists were unaware, fell under the anathema pronounced against the Cénacle and was to be the first victim. His book was to be 'flayed', to use the stereotyped term.

Lucien refused to write the article, and his refusal excited the most violent scandal among the important members of the royalist party present at the meeting. They roundly declared to Lucien that a new convert had no will of his own; if it did not suit him to adhere to Throne and Altar he could rejoin his former party. Merlin and Martainville drew him aside and

451

amicably remarked to him that he was exposing Coralie to the hostility which the Liberal papers had vowed against him, and that she would no longer have the royalist and ministerial papers to defend her. If matters remained as they were, her performance would no doubt give rise to heated polemics which would bring her the renown for which every actress yearns.

'You don't know the ropes,' said Martainville. 'For three months her acting will be subject to the cross-fire of our articles, and she'll pick up thirty thousand francs in the provinces during her three months' vacation. For a mere scruple which will prevent your entry into politics, one which you should tread underfoot, you're going to destroy Coralie and your own future: you're throwing away your livelihood.'

Lucien saw that he must choose between d'Arthez and Coralie: his mistress would be ruined if he did not slaughter d'Arthez in the big newspaper and *Le Réveil*. The unhappy poet returned home sick at heart, sat down by the fire in his bedroom and read the book: it was one of the finest in modern literature. His tears fell on one page after another and he hesitated for a long time, but in the end he wrote a mocking article of the kind at which he was so skilful and laid hold of the book as children lay hold of a beautiful bird to pluck its feathers and torture it. His terrible banter was bound to do the book harm. As he re-read this fine work, all Lucien's better feelings were reawakened; at midnight he went across Paris, arrived at d'Arthez's apartment and perceived, flickering through the window-panes, the chaste and modest glimmer at which he had so often gazed with feelings of admiration which were truly deserved by the noble constancy of this really great man. Lacking the courage to go upstairs, he sat for a few moments on a boundary-stone. At last, urged on by his good angel, he knocked, and found d'Arthez reading, with no fire in his room.

'What has happened to you?' asked the young author at the sight of Lucien, guessing that only some terrible misfortune could have brought him there.

'Your book is sublime,' cried Lucien, his eyes full of tears, 'and they've ordered me to attack it.'

'Poor boy, you're making a hard living,' said d'Arthez.

'I ask you only one favour: keep my visit a secret, and leave me to my occupations as a damned soul in my particular hell. Perhaps one arrives nowhere without acquiring callouses in the most sensitive places of one's heart.'

'You haven't changed!' said d'Arthez.

'You think I'm a coward? No, d'Arthez, no! I'm a child madly in love.'

And he explained his situation.

'Let me see the article,' said d'Arthez, moved at all that Lucien told him about Coralie.

Lucien gave him the manuscript. D'Arthez read it, and could not refrain from smiling. 'What a disastrous way of using one's wit!' he exclaimed; but he stopped as he saw Lucien sunk into an armchair, overwhelmed with genuine grief. 'Will you let me correct it? I'll return it tomorrow. Mockery brings dishonour on a book, while grave and serious criticism is sometimes praise. I can make your article more honourable both to you and to me. Besides, I alone am thoroughly aware of my own shortcomings.'

'When climbing an arid slope, one sometimes finds fruit to slake the torment of a raging thirst. That fruit I find here!' said Lucien, throwing himself into d'Arthez's arms and imprinting a kiss on his brow with the words: 'I feel as if I were entrusting my conscience to you, so that you may give it back to me one day!'

'I regard periodic repentances as a great hypocrisy,' said d'Arthez solemnly, 'for repentance is then only a bonus given to evil deeds. Repentance is a virginity which our souls owe to God: a man who twice repents is therefore a reprehensible sycophant. I'm afraid you only look on penitence as a prelude to absolution.'

The words left Lucien thunderstruck as he walked slowly back to the rue de la Lune. Next day the poet took his article, revised and returned by d'Arthez, to the newspaper; but from that day he was eaten up with a melancholy which he was not always able to disguise. When that evening he saw that the Gymnase auditorium was full, he felt the terrible emotions which a first night at the theatre arouses; in his case they were intensified by all the power of love. All his vanity was at stake. He scrutinized every face as a man in the dock gazes at the faces of the jurymen and magistrates. Any murmur of disapproval made him start; any trivial incident on the stage, Coralie's entrances and exits, the slightest vocal inflexions were bound to perturb him beyond measure. The play in which Coralie was appearing was one of those which fail but bounce up again: it failed. When Coralie came on stage she was not applauded, and the coldness manifested in the pit came as a blow to her. She received no applause from the boxes – except that of Camusot. Persons posted in the balcony and the gallery quietened the silk-merchant with repeated cries of 'Hush!' The gallery imposed silence on the *claqueurs* whenever they gave forth salvoes which were obviously overdone. Martainville was stout in his applause, and the hypocritical Florine, Nathan and Merlin followed suit. As soon as the play had collapsed, Coralie's dressing-room was crowded; but this crowd made matters worse by the consolations they offered her. The actress fell back in despair, less on her own account than on Lucien's.

'Braulard has let us down,' he said.

Coralie was so heart-broken that she developed an acute fever. The next day it proved impossible for her to act: she felt she was cut short in her career. Lucien hid the newspapers from her by opening them in the dining-room. All the *feuilleton* writers blamed Coralie for the play's failure. She had overrated her ability, they said. She was the delight of the boulevard theatres but out of place at the Gymnase. A laudable ambition had driven her there, but she had disregarded her limitations and had misinterpreted her role.

Lucien then read various paragraphs about Coralie concocted according to the hypocritical recipe of his articles on Nathan. He burst into a rage worthy of Milo of Croton when he felt his fingers caught in the oak-tree which he himself had split open; he became livid. Those friends of his were giving Coralie most perfidious advice in admirably kind, indulgent and sympathetic phraseology. She ought, they said, to play parts which the unprincipled authors of these infamous *feuilletons* knew well were entirely unsuited to her talent. This from the royalist papers, no doubt schooled in their role by Nathan. As for the Liberal papers and the *petits journaux*, they came out with the perfidies and banterings that Lucien himself had practised. Coralie heard one or two sobs, leapt out of bed to go to Lucien, caught sight of the papers and read them. After reading them she went back to bed and remained silent. Florine was in the plot, had foreseen the outcome and learned Coralie's part, Nathan having coached her for it. The theatre management stood by the play and wanted to give Coralie's part to Florine. The manager came to see the wretched actress, who was weeping and dejected; but when he told her in Lucien's presence that Florine had learnt the part and that the play simply must go on that evening, she sat up and jumped out of bed.

'I *will* play my part,' she screamed.

But she fell back in a faint. And so Florine took over her part and made her reputation in it, for she saved the play. All the Press gave her an ovation, as a consequence of which she became the great actress who is well-known today. Her triumph exasperated Lucien in the highest degree.

'. . . A wretched creature who owes you her daily bread! Let the Gymnase buy you out of your engagement if it wants to. I shall be the Comte de Rubempré. I shall make a fortune and marry you!'

'That would be foolish,' said Coralie, throwing a wan look at him.

'Foolish?' cried Lucien. 'Well then, in a few days you'll be living in a fine house, you'll have a carriage, and I'll write a part for you!'

He took two thousand francs and ran off to Frascati's. The unhappy man stayed there seven hours, a prey to all the furies, though outwardly calm and cool. During the whole day and a part of the night he had the most varying luck: he won as much as thirty thousand francs and left without a penny. When he got home, he found Finot there waiting for his 'little articles'. Lucien made the mistake of complaining.

'Oh, life's not a bed of roses,' Finot replied. 'You were so sudden with your half-right turn that you were bound to lose the support of the Liberal press, which has much more power than the ministerial and royalist press. You should never move from one camp into another before making a good bed in it, one in which you can console yourself for losses you must expect. But in any case a wise man goes and sees his friends, explains his motives and gets their advice about his abjuration. Then they become his accomplices, pity him, and then they agree, as Nathan and Merlin did with their cronies, to take in one another's washing. Wolf doesn't eat wolf. You yourself, in this affair, displayed the innocence of a lamb. You'll have to show your teeth to your new party if you want to get a cut of the joint out of them. And so it's not surprising that they've sacrificed you to Nathan. I won't hide from you the noise, scandal and uproar your article against d'Arthez is raising. People are saying that Marat was a saint compared with you. They're getting ready to attack you, and your book won't survive it. How's your novel going?'

'There are the last pages,' said Lucien, pointing to a batch of proofs.

'Unsigned articles against little d'Arthez in the ministerial and Ultra papers are being attributed to you. Every day now *Le Réveil* is sticking pins into the people in the rue des Quatre-Vents; their gibes are funny, and therefore all the more murderous. Yet there's a whole political clique, a grave and serious one, lined up behind Léon Giraud's paper – they'll get into power sooner or later.'

'I haven't set foot in *Le Réveil* for a week.'

'Well, think about my little articles. Write fifty straight away and I'll make one payment for the lot. But mind they conform to the tone of the paper.'

Thereupon Finot nonchalantly gave Lucien the subject for a humorous article against the Keeper of the Seals, telling him a spurious story which, he said, was going round the salons.

To make good his gambling losses Lucien, despite his depression, recovered his verve and mental agility, and composed thirty articles, each one amounting to two columns.

456

That done, he went to see Dauriat, sure of finding Finot there and wanting to hand them over quietly. He also wanted to hear the publisher explain why his poems were not in print. The shop was full of his enemies. At his entry, there was complete silence; all conversation ceased. Seeing himself sentenced as an outlaw, Lucien felt his courage redoubled, and he told himself, as he had done in the Luxembourg alley, 'I *will* win through!'

Dauriat was neither patronizing nor kind; he was facetious, and stood firm on his rights: he would publish the *Marguerites* in his own good time and would wait until Lucien's position could ensure their success, since he had bought the entire rights in them. When Lucien objected that Dauriat was obliged by the very nature of the contract and the status of the contracting parties to publish the collection, the publisher maintained the contrary view and said that in law he could not be held to an operation which he deemed ill-advised: he alone was the judge of its timeliness. Moreover there was a solution of which all the courts would approve: Lucien was entitled to return the three thousand francs, take his work back and get it published by a royalist firm.

Lucien withdrew, more vexed by the moderate tone Dauriat had adopted than he had been with his autocratic pompousness at their first interview. And so the *Marguerites* would no doubt only be published at the moment when he had on his side the auxiliary strength of an influential caucus or when he himself became a power to be reckoned with. The poet went home slowly, a prey to such discouragement as might have led him to suicide if action had followed thought. He found Coralie in bed, pale and ill.

'Get her a part, or she'll die,' Bérénice said to Lucien while he was dressing to go to the house where Mademoiselle des Touches lived in the rue du Mont-Blanc: she was giving a soirée where he was to find Des Lupeaulx, Vignon, Blondet, Madame d'Espard and Madame de Bargeton.

It was being given in honour of Conti, the great composer who was renowned as one of the best singers outside the theatre, La Cinti, La Pasta, Garcia, Levasseur and two or three illustrious amateur singers belonging to society. Lucien moved smoothly towards the spot where the Marquise, her cousin and Madame de Montcornet were sitting. The unhappy young man assumed a light, contented, happy air; he made jokes, displayed himself as he had been in his days of splendour and tried not to appear as if he needed the support of high society. He expatiated on the services he was rendering to the royalist party and offered as proof the cries of hate which the Liberals were raising.

'You will be very amply rewarded, my friend,' said Madame de Bargeton, directing a gracious smile at him. 'Go to the Chancellery the day after tomorrow with the Heron and Des Lupeaulx, and there you'll find your ordinance signed by His Majesty. Tomorrow the Keeper of the Seals is taking it to the Château; but the Council is sitting, and he'll be late coming back. Anyway, if I heard the result in the evening, I'd send word to you. Where are you living?'

'I'll come for it,' answered Lucien, ashamed to have to say that he lived in the rue de la Lune.

'The Duc de Lenoncourt and the Duc de Navarreins have spoken of you to the King,' said the Marquise, taking up the tale. 'They spoke highly of your absolute and entire devotion, such devotion as merits an outstanding reward to requite you for the persecutions of the Liberal party. For that matter, the name and title of the Rubemprés, to which you have a right through your mother, will become illustrious through you. In the evening the King told the Lord Chancellor to bring him an ordinance authorizing Monsieur Lucien Chardon to bear the name and titles of the Comtes de Rubempré in his quality as grandson of the last Count through his mother. "Let us encourage the song-birds[1] of Pindus," he said after reading your sonnet on the lily, which happily my cousin remembered and which she had given to the Duke. Monsieur de Navarreins replied: "Particularly since Your Majesty can perform the miracle of changing song-birds into eagles."'

Lucien's effusive gratitude might have softened any woman

1. In the text, *chardonneret* (gold-finch); more word-play on Lucien's patronymic.

less deeply offended than Louise d'Espard de Nègrepelisse. The more handsome Lucien was, the more she thirsted for vengeance. Des Lupeaulx had been right: Lucien had no flair. He was unable to guess that the alleged ordinance was only a hoax with Madame d'Espard's hall-mark on it. Emboldened by his success and the flattering distinction which Mademoiselle des Touches showed him, he stayed at her house until two in the morning in order to speak to her privately. He had learnt in the royalist newspaper offices that Mademoiselle des Touches was secretly collaborating in a play with a part for the star of the moment, little Léontine Fay. Once the salons were deserted, he took Mademoiselle des Touches to a sofa in the boudoir, and so movingly related Coralie's misfortune and his own that the illustrious hermaphrodite[1] promised to have the chief part given to Coralie.

The morning after, just as Coralie, cheered by this promise, was coming back to life and lunching with her poet, Lucien was reading Lousteau's newspaper, which contained the epigrammatical account of the fabricated anecdote about the Keeper of the Seals and his wife. The King himself was cleverly portrayed in it and ridiculed without the Public Prosecutor being able to intervene.

Here is the story to which the Liberal party tried to give the appearance of truth, but which was merely one more of the many clever slanders it spread abroad.

Louis the Eighteenth's passion for amatory and musk-scented correspondence, full of madrigals and scintillating conceits, was interpreted in this article as the final phase in a love-life which had by now become theoretic: he was passing, it said, from deeds to ideas. His illustrious favourite, so cruelly lampooned by Béranger under the name of Octavie, had conceived some very serious misgivings. Her correspondence with His Majesty was languishing. The more sparkle Octavie displayed, the colder and duller her lover became. It was not long before Octavie discovered why she

1. In *Béatrix*, published only a few weeks before, Mademoiselle des Touches plays a prominent part, and Balzac calls attention to some disconcertingly masculine traits in her. Hence the term 'hermaphrodite'.

was out of favour: her power was threatened by the piquant first-fruits of a new correspondence between the royal penman and the wife of the Keeper of the Seals. This excellent lady was reputed to be incapable of writing a love-letter, and therefore must purely and simply be a go-between acting for some boldly ambitious person. Who could be hiding behind these petticoats?

After making some enquiries, Octavie discovered that the King's correspondent was his own Chancellor. She laid her plans. With the help of a dependable friend, she one day had the Minister detained by a stormy debate in the Chamber of Deputies and contrived a tête-à-tête during which she outraged the King's self-esteem by showing that he was being duped. Louis XVIII fell into a characteristically royal and Bourbon rage, stormed at Octavie and refused to believe her. Octavie offered immediate proof by asking him to write a note which called peremptorily for a reply. The unhappy wife, thus taken by surprise, sent someone to fetch her husband from the Chamber. But this had been foreseen, and at that moment he was making a speech. His wife sweated blood, summoned up all her wit and replied with what little she had been able to muster.

'Your Chancellor can tell you the rest!' Octavie exclaimed, laughing at the King's discomfiture.

Mendacious as this article was, it stung the Keeper of the Seals, his wife and the King to the quick. It is said that Des Lupeaulx, whose secret Finot never divulged, had invented the anecdote. This lively and mordant article delighted the Liberals and the party led by the King's brother. It had amused Lucien without him thinking it to be anything else than a very pleasant *canard*. He went next day to pick up Des Lupeaulx and the Baron du Châtelet, who wished to convey his thanks to the Lord Chancellor for having been appointed a Councillor of State with special functions, made a Count and promised that he should be Prefect of the Charente as soon as the present Prefect had eked out the few months he needed to complete his term of office so that he could qualify for the maximum pension. The Comte du Châtelet – for the *du* was inserted into the ordinance – took Lucien in his carriage and treated him as an equal. Had it not been for Lucien's articles, he would perhaps not have been so promptly raised to such eminence: persecution by the Liberals had proved to be a stepping-stone for him. Des Lupeaulx was already at the Ministry in the Secretary-General's cabinet. When he caught sight of Lucien, this official gave a start of astonishment and looked at Des Lupeaulx.

'What! You dare to come here, sir?' said the Secretary-General to the stupefied Lucien. 'The Lord Chancellor has torn up the ordinance prepared for you. There it is!' He pointed to some paper or other which had been torn to shreds. 'The Minister wanted to know who had written yesterday's appalling article – here is a copy of the issue,' said the Secretary-General, tendering to Lucien the pages of his article. 'You call yourself a royalist, sir, and you contribute to that infamous newspaper which is making the Ministers' hair turn white, causing vexation to the Centre parties and working for our downfall. You lunch on the *Corsaire*, the *Miroir*, the *Constitutionnel* and the *Courrier*; you dine on the *Quotidienne* and the *Réveil*, and you have supper with Martainville, the most terrible antagonist the Ministry has: he's urging the King towards absolutism, and that would lead to revolution as quickly as if he went over to the extreme Left. You are a journalist of great wit, but you'll never be a politician. The Minister denounced you to the King as the author of the article, and in his anger the King reprimanded Monsieur le Duc de Navarreins, his first gentleman-in-waiting. You have made enemies, so much the more to be feared because they were favourably disposed to you! What may seem natural coming from an enemy is appalling when it comes from an ally.'

'Why, you've behaved like a child, my dear,' said Des Lupeaulx. 'You've compromised me. Mesdames d'Espard and de Bargeton, and Madame de Montcornet, who had answered for you, must be furious. The Duke will certainly have vented his wrath on the Marquise and the Marquise will have scolded her cousin. Better keep away from them and wait.'

'The Lord Chancellor is coming. Please leave,' said the Secretary-General.

Lucien found himself in the Place Vendôme, as stunned as a man who has just been hit on the head with a bludgeon. As he walked back along the boulevards he tried to judge his own actions. He saw himself as the plaything of envious, avid and perfidious men. What was he in that ambitious world? A child running after the pleasures and enjoyments of vanity and sacrificing everything to them; a poet with no depth of thought, flitting like a moth from candle to candle, having no settled plan, the slave of circumstance, thinking sensibly but acting foolishly. He was suffering endless torments of conscience. To sum up, he was penniless, he felt worn out with toil and grief, and his articles were taking second place to those of Nathan and Merlin.

He went along in a haphazard fashion, lost in his reflections. As he made his way he saw, in several of the reading-rooms which were then beginning to supply books as well as periodicals, a notice on which his name stood out underneath a strange and to him unknown title: *By Monsieur Lucien Chardon de Rubempré*. His novel was out, he had been ignorant of the fact, and the newspapers were saying nothing about it. He stood there with his arms hanging down, motionless, and did not notice a group of most elegant young men, among them Rastignac, De Marsay and a few others of his acquaintance. Nor did he observe that Michel Chrestien and Léon Giraud were approaching him.

'You are Monsieur Chardon?' asked Michel in a voice which vibrated inside Lucien like the chords of a harp.

'Don't you know me?' he answered, turning pale.

Michel spat in his face.

'There's an honorarium for your article against d'Arthez. If everybody, in his own cause or that of his friends, behaved as I am doing, the Press would still be what it ought to be: a priestly function, respectable and respected.'

Lucien had staggered back. He leaned on Rastignac, and said to him and to De Marsay: 'Gentlemen, you could scarcely refuse to be my seconds. But first I want to make the score even and the matter irreparable.'

He gave Michel a sharp and unexpected slap in the face. The dandies and Michel's friends interposed between the republican and the royalist to prevent this conflict from degenerating into a street brawl. Rastignac took hold of Lucien and led him to his own flat in the rue Taitbout, a few yards away from this scene, which had taken place in the Boulevard de Gant in the dinner hour. Thanks to this circumstance, no crowd had gathered round as is usual in such cases. De Marsay came to seek out Lucien, and the two dandies forced him to dine gaily with them at the Café Anglais, where they got drunk.

'Are you good at épée?' De Marsay asked him.

'I have never handled a sword.'

'With fire-arms?' asked Rastignac.

'I have never in my life fired a single pistol-shot.'

'You have chance on your side,' said De Marsay. 'You are a formidable opponent: you might kill your man.'

39. Skulduggery

VERY fortunately Lucien found Coralie in bed and asleep. She had taken an impromptu part in a minor play and had vindicated herself by obtaining legitimate and unsubsidized applause. This performance, which took her enemies by surprise, decided the theatre manager to give her the chief role in Camille Maupin's play, for he had now discovered the reason for Coralie's failure on her first night at the Gymnase. Angered by the plot Florine and Nathan had hatched to bring disgrace on an actress he valued, he had promised that the management would stand by her.

At five in the morning Rastignac came for Lucien. 'My friend, your lodging is in keeping with the street you live in.' This was all he said to him by way of greeting. 'Let us be first at the rendezvous on the Clignancourt road. That will show good taste, and we must set a good example.'

'These are the proceedings,' said De Marsay as soon as their cab turned into the Faubourg Saint-Denis. 'You are fighting with pistols at a distance of twenty-five paces, and are free to walk towards one another to a distance of fifteen paces. Thus each of you has five steps to take and three shots to fire – no more. Whatever happens, you undertake both of you to advance no further. We are to load your opponent's pistols and his seconds will load yours. The weapons have been chosen at an armourer's by the four seconds together. I promise you, we have given some assistance to chance: you will fight with cavalry pistols.'

Life had become a nightmare to Lucien; he cared not whether he lived or died. And so the courage special to suicides enabled him to make a brave show in the eyes of those who were watching the duel. He did not move forward but maintained his stance. This unconcern was taken for cool calculation and they considered the poet to be a very level-headed person. Michel Chrestien advanced to his full limit. The two opponents fired simultaneously since the insults had been regarded as equal on both sides. At the first shots Chrestien's bullet grazed Lucien's chin while the latter's passed ten feet over his adversary's head. At the second shot Michel's bullet lodged in the collar of the poet's coat, which fortunately was padded and stiffened with buckram. At the third shot, Lucien was hit in the chest and fell flat.

'Is he dead?' asked Michel.

'No,' said the surgeon, 'He'll pull through.'

'So much the worse,' Michel retorted.

'Yes indeed, so much the worse,' Lucien repeated, bursting into tears.

Midday found the unhappy young man in bed in his room; it had taken five hours and great care to transport him there. Although his condition was not dangerous, cautious treatment was needed: a fever might bring about unwelcome complications. Coralie kept her despair and affliction in control. So long as her lover was in danger, she stayed up at nights with Bérénice, conning her parts. Lucien was in danger for two months. Coralie, poor girl, was sometimes playing roles demanding gaiety, whilst her inner self was saying: 'Perhaps my dear Lucien is dying at this moment.'

During this period, Lucien was tended by Bianchon: he owed his life to the devotion of this friend whom he had so heinously offended but to whom d'Arthez had confided the secret of Lucien's visit, thus vindicating the unhappy poet. During one moment of lucidity, Lucien told him he had written no other article on d'Arthez's book than the solemn and pondered article inserted into Hector Merlin's paper.

At the end of the first month, Fendant and Cavalier filed their petition. Bianchon told the actress to hide this frightful news from Lucien. The famous *Archer of Charles the Ninth*, published under an eccentric title, had not met with the slightest success. In order to scrape up some more money before filing his petition Fendant, without Cavalier's knowledge, had sold the whole stock of the work to some philistines who resold it at a reduced price through the book-pedlars. At this moment Lucien's novel was gracing the parapets of the bridges and quays of Paris. The bookshop on the Quai des Augustins, which had taken a certain quantity of copies, stood therefore to lose a considerable sum thanks to the sudden drop in price: the four 12mo volumes which it had bought for four francs fifty centimes were being offered for two francs fifty. The trade made a loud outcry, but the newspapers continued to maintain the deepest silence. Barbet had not foreseen that the work would be so promptly scrapped, since he believed in Lucien's talent. Forsaking his usual practice, he had pounced on two hundred copies, and the prospect of a loss drove him frantic: he said horrible things about Lucien. Then he made a heroic decision: with the pigheadedness peculiar to misers, he stored his copies in a corner of his shop and let his colleagues unload theirs at a very low price. Later, in 1824, when d'Arthez's fine preface, the intrinsic worth of the book and two articles written by Léon Giraud had restored it to its real value, Barbet sold his copies one by one for ten francs each.

Despite the precautions taken by Bérénice and Coralie, they were unable to prevent Hector Merlin from visiting his moribund 'friend', and he made him drink, drop by drop, this bitter bowl of 'broth', a word used in the book-trade to describe the baleful operation which Fendant and Cavalier had embarked on in publishing the work of a beginner. Martainville, the only man loyal to Lucien, wrote a magnificent article in favour of the work, but Liberals and Ministerials alike were so exasperated with the editor of the *Aristarque*, the *Oriflamme* and the *Drapeau Blanc* that the efforts of this sturdy athlete, who always repaid the Liberal party with ten insults for one, did some damage to Lucien. No newspaper took up the gauntlet of polemics, however sharp the attacks made by the royalist bravo. Coralie, Bérénice and Bianchon shut the door on all Lucien's so-called friends, who made loud protests; but it was impossible to stave off the bailiffs. Fendant and Cavalier's bankruptcy made their bills immediately due by virtue of a provision in the Commercial Code, which inflicts maximum damage on third parties because it deprives them of the benefits of forward deals.

Lucien found that Camusot was taking vigorous proceedings against him. On seeing his name cited, the actress realized the terrible and humiliating step her poet, in her opinion so angelic, had been forced to take; she loved him ten times more for it, and was unwilling to beg Camusot to relent. When the bailiff's men came for their prisoner, they found him in bed and recoiled at the idea of taking him away. They went to see Camusot before asking the President of the Tribunal to state in which hospital they were to deposit the debtor. Camusot immediately hurried to the rue de la Lune. Coralie went downstairs and came up again with the documents of the proceedings which, on the strength of Lucien's endorsement, made him out to be a tradesman. How had she obtained these papers from Camusot? What promise had she made? She maintained the most gloomy silence, but she looked half dead as she mounted the stairs.

Coralie performed in Camille Maupin's play and contributed much to the success achieved by the illustrious hermaphrodite writer. Her creation of this role, however, proved to be the last flicker from this lovely lamp. At the twentieth performance, just when Lucien, restored to health, was beginning to take his food and walk about, and was talking of getting back to work, Coralie fell ill: she was devoured by a secret sorrow. Bérénice was persuaded that she had promised to return to Camusot in order to save Lucien. Coralie had the mortification of seeing her role given to Florine, for Nathan threatened war on the Gymnase in the event of Florine not taking Coralie's place. By performing her part till the last moment in order not to let her rival rob her of it, Coralie overtaxed her strength; the Gymnase had advanced her some money, and she could not ask for any more from the theatre coffers; in spite of his willingness, Lucien was still not fit for work, moreover he was nursing Coralie in order to relieve Bérénice. And so this poverty-stricken household came to absolute destitution, although it was lucky enough to find in Bianchon a skilful and devoted doctor who obtained credit for it at the chemist's. Coralie's and Lucien's situation soon became known to tradespeople and the landlord. The furniture was seized. The dressmaker and the tailor, no longer fearing him as a journalist, took merciless proceedings against the Bohemian couple. In the end, only the pork-butcher and the chemist allowed credit to the unhappy pair. Lucien, Bérénice and their patient were obliged for about a week to eat nothing but pork in all the varied and ingenious forms which pork-butchers give to it. Pork-butcher's meat, which causes inflammation of the intestine, aggravated the actress's malady.

This indigence forced Lucien to go and ask Lousteau for the thousand francs owed to him by this treacherous man, his former friend, and amid all his woes this was the step it cost him most to take. Lousteau could no longer return to his room in the rue de La Harpe: he was being sued for debt and tracked down like a hare. It was only in Flicoteaux's restaurant that Lucien was able to find the man who had so disastrously introduced him into the literary world. He was dining at the same table as when Lucien had met him – to his misfortune – on the day when he had moved away from d'Arthez. Lousteau offered him dinner – and Lucien accepted!

After leaving Flicoteaux's, Claude Vignon, who was dining there that day, Lousteau, Lucien and the anonymous great man whose clothes were kept stored in Samanon's pawnshop thought of going to the Café Voltaire for coffee, but they were simply not able to put thirty sous together from among the coppers jingling in their respective pockets. They strolled through the Luxembourg gardens hoping to meet a publisher there, and in fact they came upon one of the best known printers of the time, of whom Lousteau requested forty francs which he produced. Lousteau divided the sum into four equal portions, each of the writers taking one. Indigence had extinguished all pride and feeling in Lucien; he wept in front of these three men of letters as he told them of his plight; but each of his companions had just as cruel and terrible a drama to relate to him: when each one had told his sad tale, the poet found he was the least unfortunate of the four. And so they all felt the need to forget both their misery and the thoughts which made it twice as black. Lousteau rushed off to the Palais-Royal to gamble with the nine francs left out of his ten. The anonymous great man, although he had a ravishing mistress, went to a low-down brothel in order to wallow in the mire of dangerous pleasures. Vignon betook himself to the Petit Rocher de Cancale, intending to down two bottles of claret in order to abdicate both reason and memory. Lucien parted from Claude Vignon at the door of the restaurant, refusing to share Vignon's supper. The hand-shake which the provincial celebrity gave to the only Liberal journalist who had not been hostile to him was accompanied by a horrible feeling of depression.

'What am I to do?' he asked him.

'One has to take what comes,' said the celebrated critic. 'Your book's a fine one, but it has made people envious; you've a long, hard struggle before you. Genius is a terrible malady. In every writer's heart is a monster which devours all feelings like a tapeworm the moment they are born. Which will prevail, the malady over the man, or the man over the malady? One must certainly be a great man to keep the balance between genius and character. As talent increases the heart dries up. Short of being a colossus, short of having the shoulders of Hercules, one remains either without heart or without talent. You are of slight and slender build, you'll lose the battle,' he added as he disappeared into the restaurant.

Lucien returned home pondering over this terrible pronouncement, the profound truth of which gave him a luminous view of literary life.

'Money! Money!' a voice cried out within him.

He wrote out three bills for a thousand francs, payable to himself, each to fall due after one, two and three months, making a perfect forgery of David Séchard's signature. He endorsed them. Then, next day, he took them to Métivier, the paper-merchant in the rue Serpente, and Métivier discounted them without demur. Lucien wrote a few lines to his brother-in-law to inform him of this inroad on his capital and made the usual promise to meet the bills at maturity. When Coralie's debts and his own were paid, there remained three hundred francs which the poet handed over to Bérénice, telling her to refuse him if he asked for money: he feared that he might be seized with the desire to return to the gambling-den.

40. Farewells

UNDER the stimulus of a sombre, cold and speechless fury, Lucien began to compose the wittiest articles he had yet written, as he watched over Coralie by lamplight. When he had to search for ideas, his eye fell on that adored creature, white as porcelain, beautiful as dying persons can be, smiling at him with her two pale lips, showing him eyes which were shining like those of all women struck down both by sickness and sorrow. Lucien sent his articles to the newspapers; but as he could not go to the offices to pester the editors, the articles did not appear. When he did decide to go to his newspaper office, Théodore Gaillard, who had made him advance payments and later was to make a profit from these literary gems, received him coldly.

'Better look to yourself, my dear,' he said. 'You've lost your sparkle. Don't get disheartened. Show some spirit!'

'Our little Lucien only had his novel and his earliest articles inside him,' exclaimed Félicien Vernou, Merlin and all those who hated him, whenever there was talk of him at Dauriat's or in the Vaudeville theatre. 'He's sending us pitiable stuff.'

To have nothing inside you – a stock phrase in journalistic parlance – amounts to a sovereign judgement against which it is difficult to appeal once it is pronounced. The phrase, which was being peddled everywhere around, was destroying Lucien without his knowing it, for at that time his trials were greater than he could bear. In the midst of his overwhelming labours, he was sued in respect of the David Séchard bills: he went to draw on Camusot's experience. Coralie's former lover was generous enough to take his part. This fearsome predicament lasted for two months during which summonses were showered on him; on Camusot's recommendation, Lucien sent them to the barrister Desroches, a friend of Bixiou, Blondet and Des Lupeaulx.

At the beginning of August Bianchon told the poet that Coralie was beyond hope and had only a few days to live. Bérénice and Lucien spent these fateful days weeping, and were unable to hide their tears from the poor girl, who for Lucien's sake was in despair at dying. By a strange reversion, Coralie insisted that Lucien should bring a priest to her. She wished to be reconciled with the Church and die in peace. Her repentance was sincere, and she made a Christian end. Her agony and death robbed Lucien of his last shreds of strength and courage. The poet remained in a state of complete dejection, sitting in an armchair at the foot of Coralie's bed, not ceasing to gaze on her until the moment when he saw her eyes covered with the film of death. It was then five in the morning. A bird flew down on to the pots of flowers standing outside the window and twittered a few notes. Bérénice, on her knees, was kissing Coralie's hand as it grew cold under her tears. There were then only eleven sous on the the chimney-piece. Lucien went out in such a state of despair that he was ready to beg for alms in order to bury his mistress, or to go and throw himself at the feet of the Marquise d'Espard, the Comte du Châtelet, Madame de Bargeton, Mademoiselle des Touches or the terrible dandy De Marsay.

He felt he had no pride or strength left in him. He would have enlisted as a soldier in order to get a little money! He walked towards Camille Maupin's house with the stooping and shuffling gait characteristic of deep unhappiness, went in without paying attention to the slovenliness of his attire and asked the man-servant to beg her to receive him.

'Mademoiselle didn't go to bed till three this morning,' the footman told him, 'and no one would dare to go to her room before she rings.'

'When does she ring for you?'

'Never earlier than ten o'clock.'

Lucien then wrote one of those appalling letters in which men once elegant, but now reduced to beggary, throw their self-respect to the winds. One evening, when Lousteau was telling him of the requests made by talented young men to Finot, he had expressed doubt about the possibility of such self-abasement; yet now his pen perhaps carried him beyond the limits to which his predecessors had been driven. As he returned through the boulevards in a state of feverish stupefaction, without suspecting what a masterpiece despair had just dictated to him, he met Barbet.

'Barbet, let me have five hundred francs,' he said, holding out his hand.

'No, two hundred,' the publisher replied.

'Oh, have you no heart?'

'Yes, but I also have a business to run. I'm losing money through you,' he added after telling him the details about Fendant and Cavalier's bankruptcy. 'And so earn me some more.'

Lucien shuddered.

'You're a poet and must be able to write all kinds of verse,' the publisher continued. 'Just now I need some ribald songs to mix up with *chansons* I've borrowed from different authors, so as not to be prosecuted for infringement of copyright and so that I can sell a pretty collection of *chansons* in the streets for ten sous. If you like to send me tomorrow ten good drinking or spicy songs ... you know what I mean! ... I'll pay you two hundred francs.'

Lucien went home: there he found Coralie laid out stiff

on a trestle-bed, wrapped in a shabby bed-sheet in which Bérénice was sewing her. The fat Norman woman had put a lighted candle at each corner of the bed. On Coralie's face gleamed the bloom of beauty which speaks so eloquently to living people because it expresses absolute calm: she looked like a girl afflicted with chlorosis, and it seemed at moments that those two purple lips were about to open and murmur 'Lucien!', whose name, together with the name of God, she had murmured with her dying breath. Lucien asked Bérénice to go to the undertaker's and order a funeral costing no more than two hundred francs, inclusive of a service at the mean little church of Bonne-Nouvelle.

As soon as Bérénice had gone, the poet sat down at his table near the body of his mistress and composed the ten songs, which called for gay thoughts and popular tunes. He went through agonies before he could begin the task; but in the end intelligence came to the help of necessity, just as if he had known no suffering. He was already giving effect to Claude Vignon's terrible judgment on the divorce which occurs between heart and mind. What a night this poor young man spent racking his brains for poems to be sung at smoking-parties, while he scribbled in the light which fell from the tapers at the side of the priest who was praying for Coralie's soul! Next morning Lucien had finished the last song, and was trying to adapt it to a then popular tune. As they heard him singing, Bérénice and the priest were afraid he had gone mad.

> My friends, we'll have no sermons here
> While we're imbibing wine or beer.
> Can there be any rhyme or reason
> In moralizing out of season?
> A song goes better, so I'm thinking,
> When jolly souls are busy drinking.
> This all the epicures assert:
> Apollo is no welcome guest
> When Bacchus give us of his best.
> Laugh! Quaff!
> The devil take the rest!

If you would live a hundred years
– Hippocrates is my authority –
Drink lustily and drown your fears
Before and after your majority.
What matter if our tottering legs
Can't reach our Mollies or our Megs?
So long as we can crack a jest
And pour good liquor down our chest?
Laugh! Quaff!
The devil take the rest!

The place we came from well we know:
Of such a thing there is no question.
But as for knowing where we'll go
How now could that help our digestion?
Then thank the gods and live in clover,
Taking no thought until it's over.
True, life is short, but why protest?
Enjoy it while you may, with zest.
Laugh! Quaff!
The devil take the rest!

Just while the poet was singing the last dreadful couplet,
Bianchon and d'Arthez entered and found him in a paroxysm
of despondency. He was shedding floods of tears, and had not
even the strength to make a fair copy of the songs. When,
torn with sobs, he explained his predicament, he saw tears in
the eyes of his listeners.

'This,' said d'Arthez, 'atones for many misdeeds.'

'Happy they who find their hell here below,' said the priest
in grave tones.

The sight of this beautiful corpse smiling on eternity, her
lover paying for her funeral with indecent rhymes, Barbet
paying for her coffin, the four tapers round an actress whose
basque skirt and red stockings with green clocks had once
put a whole auditorium into a flutter of excitement, and, at
the door, the priest who had brought her back to God returning to the church to say mass for one who had loved so
much! – this grandeur and this infamy, so much grief, ground
under the heel of poverty, chilled the hearts of the gifted writer

473

and the talented doctor, who sat down without being able to utter a word. A man-servant appeared and announced Mademoiselle des Touches. This great-hearted and beautiful woman took in everything, moved swiftly towards Lucien, clasped him by the hand and slipped two thousand-franc notes into it.

'It's too late,' he said, with the look of a dying man.

D'Arthez, Bianchon and Mademoiselle des Touches did not leave Lucien before they had soothed his despair with the kindest of words; but he was a completely broken man. At midday the Cénacle – except Michel Chrestien, although he had been enlightened on the question of Lucien's guilt-assembled in the little church of Bonne-Nouvelle; also Bérénice and Mademoiselle des Touches, two extras from the Gymnase, Coralie's dresser and the unhappy Camusot. All the men escorted the actress to the Père-Lachaise cemetery. Camusot, weeping hot tears, solemnly swore to Lucien that he would buy the burial plot in perpetuity and erect a tombstone with the inscription: CORALIE, and underneath this: *Died August 1822, aged nineteen.*

Lucien lingered until sunset on this hill-top from which his gaze took in the whole of Paris. 'Who could possibly love me?' he asked himself. 'My real friends despise me. Whatever my misdeeds, all I did appeared good and noble to the one who lies there! All I have now is my sister, David and my mother! What are they thinking of me at home?' The wretched provincial prodigy returned to the rue de la Lune, where his feelings were so excruciatingly painful as he looked round the flat, that he took lodgings in a mean hotel in the same street. The two thousand francs which Mademoiselle des Touches had given him, with the price he got for the furniture, settled all his debts. Bérénice and Lucien had a hundred francs between them and these kept them going for two months, during which Lucien remained in a state of morbid dejection: he could neither write nor even think. He abandoned himself to his grief, and Bérénice took pity on him.

'If you went back home, how would you travel?' she asked

in response to an exclamation from Lucien, who was thinking of his sister, his mother and David Séchard.

'On foot,' he said.

'But you'll still need food and lodging on your journey. If you do thirty miles a day, you'll need at least twenty francs.'

'I'll get them,' he said.

He took his clothes and fine linen, only keeping on what was strictly necessary, and went to Samanon who offered him fifty francs for all his cast-off finery. He entreated the usurer to give him enough to go by stage-coach, but was unable to soften him. Enraged, Lucien went hot-foot to Frascati's, tried his luck there and came back without a farthing.

Back in his miserable room in the rue de la Lune, he asked Bérénice for Coralie's shawl. This kind woman eyed him and realized – he had confessed his loss at the gaming tables – that this poor desperate poet was minded to hang himself.

'Are you crazy, Monsieur?' she asked him. 'Go for a walk and come back at midnight. I shall have earned the money you need. But stay in the boulevards and keep away from the riverside.'

Lucien walked about the boulevards, stupefied with grief, watching the carriages and passers-by. He felt dwarfed and isolated in this crowd swirling about him, driven along by the multifarious interests to which Parisians are inclined. Returning in thought to the banks of his native Charente, he thirsted for family joys; then there came to him one of those flashes of inspiration by which all such half-feminine natures are duped: he would not throw up the sponge before he had unburdened himself to David Séchard and taken counsel of his three remaining guardian angels.

While he was wandering about, he saw Bérénice in her best clothes, chatting with a man in the muddy Boulevard Bonne-Nouvelle, where she had taken up her stance at the corner of the rue de la Lune.

'What are you doing?' cried Lucien, aghast at the suspicion which the sight of the Norman woman aroused in him.

'Here are twenty francs. The price may be dear, but you'll

be able to go home,' she replied, slipping four five-franc coins into the poet's hand.

Bérénice made off without Lucien seeing which way she had gone. Be it said in his favour, this money burned his fingers and he wanted to return it. But he was forced to keep it as the last stigma with which life in Paris was branding him.

Part Three

AN INVENTOR'S TRIBULATIONS

INTRODUCTION

1. The doleful confession of a 'child of the age'[1]

THE next day Lucien obtained a visa for his passport, bought himself a holly stick, went to the Place Denfert and boarded a local omnibus which for ten sous took him to Longjumeau. After his first day's tramp he slept in a farm stable five miles away from Arpajon. When he reached Orleans he already felt tired and worn-out; but for three francs a bargee took him as far as Tours, and during this trip he only spent two francs on food. He walked from Tours to Poitiers in five days. By the time he was well beyond Poitiers he had only five francs left, but he mustered his remaining strength so as to continue his journey. One day, having reached a plain when night overtook him, he decided to sleep in the open. And then he espied, deep down in a ravine, a barouche which was climbing a slope. Unnoticed by the postilion, the travellers and a flunkey seated on the box, he managed to squeeze into the boot between two packages and, squatting in such a way as to soften the effect of the jolts, he fell asleep. The next morning, awakened by the sun in his eyes and the sound of voices, he recognized the little town of Mansle where, eighteen months before, he had gone to wait for Madame de Bargeton with a heart full of love, hope and joy. Finding himself covered with dust, with a ring of postilions and bystanders around him, he realized that he had laid himself open to a charge. He leapt to his feet and was about to speak when two travellers who had got down from the barouche cut him short: he saw before him the new Prefect of the Charente – the Comte Sixte du Châtelet – and his wife, Louise de Nègrepelisse.

'If only we had known what a fellow-traveller chance had given us!' said the Comtesse. 'Climb up with us, Monsieur.'

1. For this chapter-heading Balzac had in mind a novel by Alfred de Musset: *The Confession of a Child of the Age* (1836).

479

Lucien coldly saluted the couple with a look which was both humble and menacing, and plunged into a by-road ahead of Mansle, in order to reach a farm where he might make a breakfast of bread and milk, rest and have a quiet think about his future. He had three francs left. The author of *Les Marguerites* sped on feverishly for a long time, following the river downstream and examining the lay-out of the country which was becoming more and more picturesque. About mid-day he reached a spot where the wide stream, banked with willows, formed a kind of lake. He paused to contemplate the pastoral grace of this fresh, leafy grove, and was much moved. A house adjoining a mill astride a branch of the river showed amid the tree-tops its thatched roof grown over with house-leeks. The front of this simple dwelling had no other ornament than a few clumps of jasmine, honeysuckle and hops, and all around was a blaze of phlox in bloom and luxuriant thick-leaved plants. On the stone-work, supported by rough piles, which kept the causeway above the highest floods, he saw nets spread out in the sun. Ducks were swimming in the clear pool beyond the mill between two currents roaring over the sluice-gates. The mill was giving forth its grating rumble. On a rustic bench the poet perceived a good, fat housewife knitting and watching over a child who was teasing the hens.

'Good lady,' said Lucien, stepping forward. 'I am very tired, I have a fever, and only three francs. Will you put me up for a week? I can feed on brown bread and milk and sleep on straw. That will give me time to write to my relations so that they can send me money or come here to fetch me.'

'Willingly,' she said, 'so long as my husband agrees. – What do you say, goodman?'

The miller emerged, looked at Lucien and took his pipe from his mouth to say: 'Three francs for a week? Might as well take nothing.'

'Perhaps I shall end up as a miller's lad,' the poet thought as he gazed at the delightful landscape before lying down in the bed the miller's wife made for him. He slept so soundly in it that his hosts grew alarmed.

'Courtois, just go and see if the young man is alive or dead,' said the miller's wife at about noon next day. 'He's been lying there for fourteen hours and I daren't go myself.'

'I believe,' the miller answered as he finished spreading out his nets and fishing tackle, 'that this nice-looking young man might well be some little sprig of a strolling-player without a penny to bless himself with.'

'What makes you think that, husband?' she asked.

'Well, he's no prince, or minister, or deputy or bishop, and yet he's got white hands like a man who doesn't work.'

'I'm very surprised then that hunger doesn't wake him up,' said the miller's wife, who had been getting a meal ready for the guest chance had sent them the previous day. ' – An actor?' she continued. 'Where would he be going? It's too early for the Angoulême fair.'

Neither the miller nor his wife had any idea that, besides actors, princes and bishops, there exists a kind of man who is both prince and actor, a man who discharges a splendid sacerdotal function: the Poet, who seems to be doing nothing but nevertheless reigns over Humanity once he has learnt how to depict it.

'What *can* he be then?' Courtois asked his wife.

'Could it be risky to take him in?' asked the miller's wife.

'No fear! Thieves have more go in them. He'd have already robbed us by now.'

'I'm neither prince, nor robber, nor bishop, nor actor,' said Lucien sadly, suddenly showing himself – no doubt he had heard the colloquy between man and wife through the casement. 'I'm a poor tired young man who has walked all the way from Paris. My name is Lucien de Rubempré, and I'm the son of Monsieur Chardon, who owned the chemist's shop in L'Houmeau before Postel. My sister married David Séchard, the printer in the Place du Mûrier in Angoulême.'

'Let's see,' said the miller. 'Isn't that printer the son of the old fox who's running a vineyard at Marsac?'

'The very man,' Lucien answered.

481

'Well now,' Courtois went on. 'He's a funny sort of father. They say he's making his son sell up, and he owns more than two hundred thousand francs' worth of land, without counting what he keeps in his crock.'

When body and soul have been broken in a long and painful struggle, the hour at which a man's strength reaches exhaustion is followed either by death or by a state of annihilation similar to death; but at that juncture constitutions capable of resistance find their strength renewed. Lucien, assailed by a crisis of this sort, looked as if he were about to expire at the moment when he learned, though in vague terms, of the catastrophe which had befallen David Séchard, his brother-in-law.

'Oh! my sister!' he cried. 'My God, what have I done? I'm an infamous wretch.'

Then he collapsed on to a wooden bench, as pallid and prostrate as a dying man. The miller's wife hurried to him with a bowl of milk which she forced him to drink; but he begged the miller to help him back to his bed, asking his forgiveness for the embarrassment his death would cause, for he thought his last hour had come. Faced with the spectre of death, the handsome poet was seized with religious ideas. He asked to see a priest, make his confession and receive the Sacraments. Such a plaintive request, made in a failing voice by a young man with such grace of features and figure, went straight to Madame Courtois's heart.

'Look now, husband, take the mare and find Monsieur Marron, the doctor at Marsac. He'll see what's wrong with this young man, who looks very poorly to me. Fetch the Curé too. Maybe they'll know better than you how things stand with the printer in the Place du Mûrier — Postel is Monsieur Marron's son-in-law.'

When Courtois had gone, his wife, imbued like all country folk with the notion that sick people must have food, administered refreshment to Lucien, who took what he was given, now abandoning himself to violent remorse which, acting like a poultice on a sore, produced a revulsion and saved him from total apathy.

Courtois's mill was two or three miles away from Marsac,

the chief town in the canton, half-way between Mansle and Angoulême. So the good miller was not slow in bringing back the doctor and the parish priest of Marsac. Both of them had heard of Lucien's liaison with Madame de Bargeton, and since everybody in the Charente valley was at that time gossiping about that lady's marriage and her return to Angoulême with the new Prefect, the Comte Sixte du Châtelet, when they learned that Lucien was staying at the mill, both doctor and priest were intensely curious to know what had prevented Monsieur de Bargeton's widow from marrying the young poet with whom she had eloped, and also to find out if his motive for coming home was to rescue his brother-in-law. And so both curiosity and humane feelings brought prompt help to the moribund poet. Consequently, two hours after Courtois's departure, Lucien heard the country doctor's rickety gig clattering along the stony roadway leading to the mill. The two Marrons – they were uncle and nephew – came in immediately. Thus, at that moment, Lucien met two people who were as closely connected with David Séchard's father as neighbours in a little vine-growing hamlet can be. When the doctor had examined the sick man, felt his pulse and inspected his tongue, he looked towards the miller's wife with a smile calculated to dissipate any anxiety.

'Madame Courtois,' he said. 'If, as I don't doubt, you've a good bottle of wine in your cellar and a nice eel in your tank, serve them both to your sick man. He's suffering from stiffness, that's all. If you do that, our great man will be on his legs again in no time!'

'Ah, Monsieur,' said Lucien. 'I'm suffering from a spiritual, not a physical ailment, and these good people have dealt me a mortal blow by telling me of the disasters which have befallen my sister, Madame Séchard. In Heaven's name, you who have, according to Madame Courtois, married your daughter to Postel must know something about David Séchard's affairs!'

'He's probably in prison,' the doctor replied. 'His father refused to help him . . . '

'In prison!' Lucien repeated. 'But why?'

'Why? For drafts issued from Paris which no doubt had slipped his memory – he doesn't seem to know very well what he's doing.'

'I beg you to leave me with Monsieur le Curé,' said the poet, whose countenance had become very grave.

The doctor, the miller and his wife went out. When Lucien was alone with the old priest, he exclaimed: 'Monsieur le Curé, I deserve the death which I feel to be approaching. I am the greatest of sinners and nothing is left to me but to throw myself into the arms of the Church. It is I, father, who have brought this affliction on my sister and brother – for David Séchard is a true brother to me. I drew some bills which David has not been able to meet . . . I have ruined him. The abject misery I was in made me forget this crime. The suit to which these bills gave rise in Paris was settled through the intervention of a millionaire and I thought he had paid them off. But he can't have done so.'

Thereupon Lucien told the priest of all his misfortunes. When he had finished this tragic story, a feverish narration truly worthy of a poet, he entreated the priest to go to Angoulême to enquire of Eve, his sister, and Madame Chardon, his mother, how things really stood, so that he might know if he still might make amends.

'Until your return, Monsieur le Curé,' he said, weeping bitterly, 'I may live on. If my mother, my sister and David don't cast me out, I shall not die!'

Lucien's eloquence, the tears he shed during his lamentable confession, the sight of such a handsome young man, pale and half-dead with despair, this tale of mishaps putting too great a strain on human endurance, all excited interest and pity in the clergyman.

'In the provinces, Monsieur, as in Paris,' the Curé replied, 'one must believe only half of what one is told. Don't be alarmed about a rumour which, half a dozen miles away from Angoulême, is probably quite false. Old Séchard, our neighbour, left Marsac a few days ago, and so he may be busy settling his son's affairs. I will go to Angoulême, and when I come back, I shall be able to tell you if you can return to your family. Your confession and your repentance will help me to plead your cause with them.'

The Curé did not know that, during the last eighteen months, Lucien had repented so many times that his repentance, however heart-felt it seemed, had no other value than that of a well-enacted scene – and yet one enacted in good faith!

After the priest, the doctor had his turn. Diagnosing an attack of nerves whose danger was receding, the nephew was as consoling as the uncle had been: his final recommendation was that his patient should take plenty of nourishment.

2. *Back-kick from a donkey*

THE priest, who knew the locality and its inhabitants, had made for Mansle, through which the public conveyance from Ruffec to Angoulême was due to pass; he obtained a seat in it. The old man counted on asking information about David Séchard from his grand-nephew Postel, the chemist in L'Houmeau, the printer's former rival for the hand of the beautiful Eve. Seeing the care the little apothecary took in helping the old man to dismount from the frightful rattletrap which at that period plied from Ruffec to Angoulême, the most obtuse observer could have guessed that Monsieur and Madame Postel were staking their prosperity on inheriting his money.

'Have you had lunch? Would you like something? We weren't expecting you, what a pleasant surprise!'

They showered questions on him. Madame Postel was certainly cut out to be the wife of a L'Houmeau chemist. Small in stature like Postel, she had the rubicund face of a country-bred girl. Her figure was common enough, and all her beauty consisted in the freshness of her complexion. Her red hair, falling very low over her forehead, her manners and style of speech, well suited to the simplicity engraved in every feature of her round face, her pale-brown eyes, everything about her in fact announced that she had been married only for her expectations. And so, after a year as housewife, she already ruled the roost and seemed to have gained complete control of Postel, who was only too happy to have married an heiress. Madame Léonie Postel, née Marron, was breast-feeding her son, whom the old priest, the doctor and Postel adored – an unattractive infant who took after both his father and his mother.

'Well now, Uncle,' said Léonie. 'What can you be doing in Angoulême, since you won't take anything and talk of leaving no sooner than you have got here?'

As soon as the worthy priest had uttered the names of Eve and David Séchard, Postel turned red, and Léonie treated the little man to the glance of obligatory jealousy which a woman entirely in command of her husband never fails to throw back upon his past in the interest of her own future.

'But what have those people done for you, Uncle, that you should be bothering about their affairs?' Léonie asked with visible tartness.

'They are in misfortune, my daughter,' he answered, and he described to Postel the state in which he had found Lucien at the Courtois's mill.

'Ah! So that's the plight he's in on his return from Paris!' cried Postel. 'Poor lad! And yet he had his wits about him, and he was ambitious! He went after the wheat and comes back without even the chaff. But what's he here for? His sister's living in appalling poverty, for all these men of genius, David no less than Lucien, are hopeless when business is concerned. We discussed his case at the Tribunal of Commerce and, as one of its members, I had to sign the judgement against him...! It went to my heart! I'm not sure whether, in the present circumstances, Lucien can go to his sister's house; but in any case the little room he lived in here is unoccupied, and I'm ready to offer it to him.'

'Very good, Postel,' said the priest, putting on his three-cornered hat and preparing to leave the shop after kissing the child who was asleep in Léonie's arms.

'You will surely dine with us, Uncle,' said Madame Postel.

'It will take you a long time if you want to sort out these people's troubles. My husband will take you back home in his pony and trap.'

Husband and wife watched their precious uncle as he departed for Angoulême.

'He's pretty spry for his age,' the apothecary remarked.

While our venerable cleric climbs the slope towards Angoulême, it will not be irrelevant to unravel the skein of interests in which he was about to get involved.

THE HISTORY OF A LAWSUIT

3. The problem at issue

AFTER Lucien's departure for Paris, David Séchard, sturdy and intelligent like the ox which painters represent as the Evangelist's companion, set out to make the great and rapid fortune that he had wished for – less for himself than for Eve and Lucien – that evening on the banks of the Charente when, as he sat with Eve on the weir, she had given him her hand and heart. To raise his wife to the sphere of elegance and wealth in which she was entitled to live and to give strong-armed support to his brother's ambition: such was the programme written in letters of fire in his mind's eye. Newspapers and politics, the tremendous strides made in the production and marketing of books, the advance of science, the prevalent tendency to make every national interest a matter for public discussion, in fact the entire social movement which got under way once the Restoration regime seemed settled, was sure to demand almost a ten-fold increase in the supply of paper compared with the quantity on which the celebrated Ouvrard, guided by motives similar to David's, had based his speculations in the early days of the Revolution. But by 1821 there were too many paper-mills in France for anyone to hope to acquire a monopoly in them, as Ouvrard had done by buying up all they produced and then the chief factories themselves. Moreover, David had neither the audacity nor the necessary capital for such speculations. At that moment, machines for making paper of unlimited length were being put into production in England. So it was vitally necessary to adapt paper-making to the needs of French civilization, which was threatening to extend discussion to all subjects and to take its stand on a never-ending manifestation of individual thought – a real misfortune, for the more a people deliberates the less active it becomes. And so, curiously enough, while Lucien was getting caught in the cogwheels of the vast journalistic machine and running the risk of it tearing his honour and intelligence to shreds, David Séchard, in his distant printing-office, was surveying the expansion of the periodical press in its material consequences. He wanted to provide the means for the end towards which the spirit of the age was tending. For that matter, he was so perspicacious in seeking a fortune from the manufacture of cheap paper that the upshot was to justify his foresight. During the last fifteen years, the Patent Office has received over a thousand applications relating to alleged discoveries of new substances to be used in the manufacture of paper.

And so, after his brother-in-law's departure for Paris, being more certain than ever of the usefulness of such a discovery, an unspectacular but immensely profitable one, David fell into such a state of constant mental preoccupation as the problem was bound to produce in one anxious to solve it. Since he had exhausted all his resources in order to get married and to meet the expenses of Lucien's journey to Paris, he found himself reduced to utter poverty at the very beginning of his wedded life. He had kept back a thousand francs for the needs of his printing-office, and he owed a bill for a like sum to the apothecary Postel. Thus a double problem confronted this extremely thoughtful man: he had to invent a cheap paper, and that promptly; he also had to adapt the profits from the discovery to the needs of his household and his business. Now, what epithet can one apply to a brain capable of rising above the cruel anxieties whose cause was three-fold – an indigence which had to be concealed, the sight of a starving family and the daily demands of a profession calling for meticulous accuracy – and all the while surveying the regions of the unknown with the fervour and enthusiasm of a scientist in pursuit of a secret which from day to day eludes the most subtle researches? Alas! As will be seen, inventors have many other ills to endure, not to mention the ingratitude of the masses who are told by idlers and incompetents: 'He was born to be an inventor and couldn't do anything else. There's no more point in showing grati-

tude for his discovery than one does to a man for being born
a prince! He's doing what he was meant to do! And besides, the
work he does brings in its own reward!'

4. *A plucky wife*

MARRIAGE brings about profound physical and psychological disturbances in a young girl. Furthermore, if she marries
a middle-class husband with a business to run, she has to give
her mind to an entirely new range of interests and get a
grounding in business matters. She must therefore spend
some time taking things in before she can play an active part.
Unfortunately, David's love for his wife retarded her education, for until some days or even weeks after the wedding
he did not dare to tell her how their finances stood. In spite of
the dire straits to which his father's avarice had brought him
he had not the heart to spoil their honeymoon period by putting her through the dismal apprenticeship of his exacting
profession or by teaching her the things a tradesman's wife
has to know. And so the thousand francs – all the money he
had – were spent on household needs instead of workshop
expenses. David's apathy and his wife's ignorance lasted four
months, and then they had a rude awakening! When the bill
of exchange which David had drawn on Postel fell due, there
was no money left for the housekeeping, and Eve knew only
too well how this debt had been incurred not to sacrifice her
wedding jewellery and her silver to its settlement. The very
evening when this draft was paid off, Eve tried to make David
talk about the business, for she had noticed that he was neglecting the printing-office and applying himself to the project
he had explained to her some months before.

Before he had been married two months David was
spending most of his time in the shed at the bottom of the
courtyard, in the small room which he used for moulding his
rollers. Three months after his arrival in Angoulême David
had replaced the old-fashioned ink-balls with a table and rollers

made of glue and molasses which gave a smooth and even distribution of ink. The value of this early improvement in typography was so incontestable that the Cointet brothers adopted it as soon as they saw it in action. Against the party wall of this kitchen-laboratory David had built a fireplace and boiler on the pretext that he would thus need less fuel for recasting his rollers; but the rusty moulds stood ranged along the wall and the rollers were never cast a second time. Not only had David provided this room with a stout oak door lined with sheet-iron on the inside; he had also replaced the dirty window-panes with fluted glass so that they would admit less light and prevent people outside from seeing what he was about.

At the first remark which Eve made to David on the subject of their future, he gave her a worried look and stopped her short with these words: 'My dear, I know what your feelings must be when you see the workshop deserted and our business dwindling almost to nothing. But look,' he continued as he led her to their bedroom window and pointed to his mysterious recess, 'there our fortune lies . . . We must suffer for a few more months; but let's suffer in patience. Leave me to solve the industrial problem you know about, and all our tribulations will come to an end.'

David was so good-hearted, his devotion was so much to be taken for granted, that his poor wife, though concerned like all wives with the daily budget, took it upon herself to spare her husband all domestic worries. So she quitted the pretty blue and white bedroom where she had been content to do needlework while chatting with her mother and went down to one of the two wooden cages situated at the end of the printing-office so that she might study the practical side of typography. This in itself was an act of heroism on the part of an already pregnant woman. During these first months David's presses had been idle, and the workmen required until then had one by one deserted. Snowed under with work, the brothers Cointet not only employed such journeymen in the district as were enticed by the prospect of working full time at their presses, but a few also from Bordeaux; and from there it was easy to obtain apprentices who thought they were clever enough to wriggle out of their articles. When she looked into the resources at their disposal Eve found that there were only three hands left: Cérizet, the apprentice David had brought with him from Paris, Marion, tethered to the firm like a watchdog, and Kolb, an Alsatian who had once been an odd-job man in the Didot firm. Having been called up for military service, Kolb happened to be stationed in Angoulême when David spotted him at a military review, just when his period of service was coming to an end. Kolb came to see David and fell in love with the bulky Marion, finding that she possessed all the qualities a man of his class looks for in a woman: the vigorous health which tans the cheeks, the masculine strength which enabled her to lift a type-forme with ease, the scrupulous honesty by which Alsatians lay great store, the devotion to one's masters which is a sign of good character, and finally the thriftiness which had brought her a nest-egg consisting of one thousand francs, linen, clothes and personal effects of a truly provincial cleanliness. Marion was big and fat and thirty-six. She was flattered to receive attentions from a cuirassier who was five feet seven inches in height, well-built, and as strong as a fortress. He naturally conceived the idea of becoming a printer. As soon as the Alsatian had obtained his discharge from the army, Marion and David made quite an efficient 'bear' of him, although he could neither read nor write.

The composition of the 'town work', as it was called, was not too abundant during these three months for Cérizet not to have coped with it. Being at one and the same time compositor, page-setter and senior hand in the printing-office, Cérizet achieved what Kant calls the 'phenomenal triplicity': he set up and corrected his settings, entered the orders and drew up the bills; but more often than not having no work to do, he sat in his cage at the back of the office reading novels while waiting for orders to come in – a poster or an invitation card. Marion, whom Séchard senior had trained, cut the paper, damped it, helped Kolb to print it, laid it out and trimmed it. None the less she also cooked the meals after doing the marketing in the early morning.

When Eve asked Cérizet for the first six months' accounts,

493

she discovered that receipts only came to eight hundred francs. Expenditure, at a rate of three francs a day for Cérizet and Kolb – the one drawing a daily wage of two francs, the other of one franc – amounted to six hundred francs. Now, since the cost of material needed for work done and delivered amounted to something over a hundred francs, it was clear to Eve that during the first six months of his wedded life David had failed to cover his rent, the interest on capital based on the value of his stock and his printer's licence, Marion's wages, ink and finally the profits a printer should make: an accumulation of items expressed in printers' language by the word *stuffs*, an expression derived from the cloth and silk used to soften the pressure of the clamping-screws on the type by the insertion of a square of 'stuff' (the 'blanket') between the platen of the press and the paper which is being printed. Having roughly computed the means at their disposal and the results they yielded, Eve could easily guess how small were the resources offered by their presses which were almost brought to a standstill by the voracious activity of the brothers Cointet who were at once paper-manufacturers, newspaper proprietors and appointed printers to the Bishop, the Prefect and the municipal authorities. The newspaper which, two years before, Séchard father and son had sold for twenty-two thousand francs, was now bringing in eighteen thousand francs a year. Eve saw through the calculations concealed behind the apparent generosity of the brothers Cointet, who were leaving the Séchard press just enough work to subsist on but not enough for it to compete with them.

Taking over the business side, Eve began by drawing up an exact inventory of all the stock. She set Kolb, Marion and Cérizet to the task of tidying, cleaning and putting the workshop in order. Then, one evening when David was returning from a ramble in the fields, followed by an old woman who was carrying an enormous bundle wrapped in linen, Eve asked his advice as to how they could make use of the lumber left by old Séchard and promised him she would look after the business herself. At her husband's suggestion she decided to use up all the remnants of paper she had found and sorted

494

out by printing, in double columns and on one single sheet, the illustrated folk-tales which peasants paste up on the walls of their cottages: the story of the Wandering Jew, Robert the Devil, the Fair Maguelonne and various legends of the saints. Eve turned Kolb into a pedlar. At first Cérizet wasted no time: from morning to night he set up these ingenuous broadsheets with their crude illustrations, and Marion pulled them off. Madame Chardon took charge of all domestic tasks while Eve coloured the engravings. In two months, thanks to Kolb's activity and honesty, Madame Séchard sold three thousand sheets over an area of thirty miles round Angoulême. They cost her thirty francs to produce and brought in three hundred francs at a penny apiece.

But by the time every cottage and tavern wall was papered with these legends, they had to think of some other speculation, for the Alsatian was not allowed to travel outside the Department. After rummaging round the workshop Eve discovered a collection of figures required for the printing of a so-called Shepherds' Almanac, in which objects are represented by signs, pictures and symbols in red, black and blue. Old Séchard, illiterate as he was, had formerly made a lot of money by printing this little book intended for equally illiterate people. An almanac of this kind costs only a penny and comprises a hundred and twenty-eight pages of very small format. Delighted at the success of her broadsheets – the sort of production which is a speciality with small provincial presses – Madame Séchard decided to print the Shepherds' Almanac on a large scale by putting her profits into it. The paper used for the Shepherds' Almanac, sold annually in France in its millions, is coarser than that used for the Liège Almanac and costs about four francs a ream. Madame Séchard resolved to use up a hundred reams on a first run: that would make fifty thousand almanacs to dispose of and two thousand francs' profit to reap.

Preoccupied as a man so deeply engrossed must be, David nevertheless felt some surprise when he looked in at the office and heard a press groaning and saw Cérizet busily setting type under Madame Séchard's direction. When he came in one day to survey the operations Eve had undertaken, it was a great triumph for her to win her husband's approval. He thought the Almanac an excellent piece of business, and promised advice on the use of the various coloured inks needed for the figures in a production whose appeal was only to the eye. In fact, he decided that he would himself recast the rollers in his mysterious workshop so that he might, as far as possible, help his wife in her fine little venture.

While this bustling activity was in its beginnings there came the heart-rending letters in which Lucien told his mother, sister and brother-in-law of his failure and financial difficulties in Paris. It is therefore easy to see that, in sending three hundred francs to the spoilt child, Eve, Madame Chardon and David had offered the poet their very heart's blood. Overwhelmed at the news Lucien gave them and in despair at earning so little while working so courageously, Eve was awaiting with some trepidation an event which in most cases brings a young couple to the highest pitch of joy. Realizing that she was about to become a mother, she said to herself: 'If my dear David has not reached his goal by the time of my confinement, what will become of us? ... And who will look after the new ventures of our unfortunate printing-press?'

5. A Judas in the making

THE Shepherds' Almanac ought to have been ready by the first of January, but Cérizet, who was responsible for all the composing, was now working at it so slowly that Madame Séchard was reduced to despair, the more so because she did not know enough about printing to be able to scold him: all she could do was to keep an eye on the young man from Paris. Cérizet was an orphan from the great Foundling Hospital in Paris and had been articled as apprentice to the Didot firm. From the age of fourteen to seventeen he had been devoted to David, who had him trained by one of his best journeymen while keeping him under his wing as printer's devil. He naturally became interested in Cérizet because he found him intelligent, and he won his affection by giving him occasional enjoyments and treats which he was too poor to pay for himself. Blessed with an attractive though sly little face, reddish hair and cloudy blue eyes, Cérizet had brought his Paris street-arab ways with him to Angoulême. In this provincial capital his sharp, caustic and spiteful turn of mind made him a person to be feared. In Angoulême he was less under David's surveillance, either because his mentor felt he could trust him now he was older, or because he thought that provincial life would have a salutary influence on him. He little guessed that Cérizet was playing the role of a plebeian Don Juan to three or four working-class girls and had gone to the bad completely. His moral code, a product of Paris taverns, made self-interest a law unto itself. And besides, the following year Cérizet was to 'draw his number', as the expression goes, for conscription, and so he could see no career for him and began to run up debts with the thought that he would be a soldier in six months' time and beyond the reach of creditors. David still maintained some authority over this young man, not because he was his employer, nor because of the interest he had taken in him, but because the former street-urchin of Paris realized that David was a highly intelligent man. Cérizet soon began to fraternize with the Cointets' workmen, attracted to them as he was by the prestige of the journeyman's jacket and blouse, in fact by that *esprit de corps* which perhaps carries more weight among the lower than the upper classes. In their company Cérizet lost the few moral scruples that David had instilled in him. Nevertheless, when they chaffed him about the 'old clogs' in his printing-office – a contemptuous term applied by the 'bears' to the Séchards' antiquated presses – and showed him the dozen fine steel presses at work in the Cointet's immense printing-office, where the only wooden press remaining was used for striking off proofs, he still sided with David and proudly flung the following taunt at the scoffers: 'With his "old clogs" my boss will go further than yours with their cast-iron contraptions which can turn out nothing but mass-books! He's working on a new process which will make all the printers in France and Navarre queue up for it!'

'All very fine, you miserable little twopenny-halfpenny type-setter,' they would retort, 'but your real boss is a laundry-woman!'

'Never mind!' Cérizet would reply. 'She's pretty. She's nicer to look at than your bosses' ugly mugs!'

'Does looking at her keep you in food and drink?'

From the public bars or perhaps from the printing-office door where these friendly wranglings went on, some inkling of the situation of the Séchard press came through to the Cointet brothers: they learnt of Eve's speculative venture and decided that an enterprise which might set the unfortunate woman on the way to prosperity ought to be nipped in the bud.

'We must give her a rap over the knuckles and put her off the taste for business,' the two brothers told each other.

The particular Cointet who ran the printing-office got in touch with Cérizet and suggested that he should do some proof-reading for them at so much per proof, in order, they said, to relieve their own proof-corrector who could not cope with all the jobs in hand. In this way, by putting in a few hours in the evenings, Cérizet was able to earn more with the Cointets than he earned the whole day with David. This meant that the Cointets were in contact with Cérizet: they discerned great possibilities in him and condoled with him for being in a situation so unfavourable to his interests.

'You might well,' one of the Cointets told him one day, 'rise to being foreman in an important printing-office and earn six francs a day; and with your intelligence you might well acquire an interest in the business.'

'How would it help me to have a good job?' Cérizet replied. 'I'm an orphan. I'm in next year's call-up, and if I don't draw a lucky number who'll pay for a substitute for me? . . . '

'If you make yourself useful,' the affluent printer replied, 'why should not someone advance you the money needed to buy you out?'

'You don't imagine my boss would do it?'

'Why not? perhaps by then he will have discovered the secret he's looking for.'

Cointet made this remark in such a way as to arouse the worst possible thoughts in his listener's mind, and Cérizet darted a look at the paper-manufacturer which was as eloquent as the most searching question.

'I don't know what he's after,' he answered warily, seeing that the master-printer was holding back. 'But he's not the sort of man to be looking for capitals in his lower case.'

'Look here, my friend,' said Cointet, taking up six sheets of the diocesan prayer-book and offering them to Cérizet. 'If you can correct all that for us by tomorrow, you'll have eighteen francs tomorrow. We're being very decent, since we're putting our competitor's foreman in a way to make a bit of money. As a matter of fact, we could allow Madame Séchard to go all out for her Shepherds' Almanac and then ruin her. Well, you have our permission to tell her that she won't be the first in the market . . . '

The reader will now understand why Cérizet was being so slow in composing the Séchard almanac. When Eve learnt that the Cointets were upsetting her poor little venture she was seized with terror, and though she tried to see a proof of loyalty in Cérizet's somewhat hypocritical divulgation of the competition awaiting her, she soon noticed that this man, her only compositor, was showing signs of too lively a curiosity. She tried to believe that it was due to his youthfulness.

'Cérizet,' she said one morning, 'you plant yourself on the doorstep and you wait for Monsieur Séchard to pass through so as to find out what he's doing. You stare into the courtyard when he comes out of the workshop where the rollers are cast instead of getting on with the setting-up of our almanac. You ought not to do that, particularly when you see that I, his wife, respect his secrets and spare no effort to leave him free to get on with his work. If you hadn't wasted time the almanac would be finished, Kolb would already be selling it, and the Cointets could do us no harm.'

'All very well, Madame,' Cérizet replied. 'For the two francs a day I earn here, don't you think it's good enough if

I do five francs' worth of setting? Why, if I hadn't proofs to read in the evening for the Cointets, I should be living on air!'

'You've soon learnt to be ungrateful, you'll make your way all right,' answered Eve, less heart-stricken at Cérizet's reproaches than by his coarse tone of voice, his truculent attitude and his aggressive stare.

'May be. But not while my boss is a woman. There's too much pulling the devil by the tail.'

Outraged by this affront to her womanly dignity, Eve froze Cérizet with a look and went up to her room. When David came in for his dinner, she asked him: 'My dear, have you any confidence in that little rogue Cérizet?'

'Cérizet?' he replied. 'Well, he was my printer's devil. I trained him, made him my copy-holder, put him on case-work. In fact I taught him everything he knows. You might as well ask a father if he trusts his own child.'

Eve informed her husband that Cérizet was proof-reading for the Cointets.

'Poor boy! he's got to live,' David answered with the humility of an employer who feels that he himself is to blame.

'Yes. But, my dear, look at the difference between Kolb and Cérizet. Kolb travels fifty miles a day, keeps his expenses down to less than a franc, and brings home seven, eight or sometimes nine francs for the sheets he has sold, and only asks for his twenty sous over and above his expenses. Kolb would cut off his right hand rather than pull off a single sheet on the Cointet presses; not for thousands of francs would he look at the things you throw away in the yard, whereas Cérizet picks them up and studies them.'

Great-hearted people find it difficult to believe in evil or ingratitude and need rude lessons before they recognize the lengths to which human baseness can go; and even when their education in this respect is complete they rise to an indulgence which marks the highest degree of contempt. David was content to exclaim: 'Pooh, that's merely the nosiness of a Paris street-arab.'

'Very well, my dear, do me the pleasure of going down to the office, see how much composing your street-arab has done this last month and tell me if, during that month, he ought not to have finished our almanac.'

After dinner, David recognized that the almanac should have been set up in a week. Then, learning that the Cointets were preparing a similar one, he came to his wife's help. He suspended Kolb's sale of the sheets of pictures and took over complete control of the office. He himself got one forme ready for Kolb to strike off with Marion while he struck off the other one with Cérizet and attended to the colour printing. Various colours are used and each colour has to be printed separately so that four different inks need four strikings-off. Thus, with four printings to one page, the Shepherds' Almanac costs so much to set up that it is only produced in provincial workshops where labour is cheap and overheads are almost nil. Such a publication therefore, crude as it is, is not a paying concern for presses which turn out first-class work. And so, for the first time since old Séchard's retirement, two presses could be seen working away in the old workshop. Although the almanac was a masterpiece of its kind, Eve was none the less obliged to sell it for two and a half centimes because the Cointets let the pedlars have theirs for three centimes. By having them hawked round she managed to cover expenses and make a profit on Kolb's hand-to-hand sales; but her venture was a failure. Cérizet, seeing that he had awakened distrust in his beautiful mistress, bore a grudge against her in his heart of hearts and muttered under his breath: 'You don't trust me. I'll get my own back!' The Paris urchin is made like that.

And so Cérizet accepted from Messrs Cointet a wage which was clearly too high for mere reading of proofs, which he fetched from their office every evening and returned the next morning. He had more and more talk with them every day, got on close terms with them and in the end glimpsed the possibility, which they held out to him as a bait, of being exempted from military service. Far from having to bribe him, the Cointets heard from his own mouth the first intimation that he was spying on David and trying to discover the secret process at which he was working.

Eve's anxiety increased when she saw how little faith she could put in Cérizet, and realizing she could not hope to find a second Kolb she decided to dismiss her sole compositor, whom her second sight as a loving wife showed her to be a traitor; but as this meant that the printing-office would have to close down she made a valiant decision: she sent a letter to Monsieur Métivier, who acted as Paris correspondent for David, the Cointets and almost all the paper-manufacturers in the Angoulême district, and requested him to insert the following advertisement in the Publishers' Journal in Paris:

For sale, a printing-office in running order, with stock and licence, situated in Angoulême. For terms of sale apply to Monsieur Métivier, rue Serpente, Paris.

6. The two Cointets

AFTER reading the number of the Journal in which this advertisement appeared, the Cointets said to one another: 'That little woman has her head screwed on right. It's time we took control of her printing-office by providing her with the wherewithal to live. Otherwise we might get real competition from David's successor. It's in our interest to keep a constant eye on that workshop.'

With this thought in mind the Cointet brothers came for a talk with the Séchards. They asked to see Eve, and she felt the liveliest joy on seeing how quickly her ruse had worked, for they came straight out with the proposal that Monsieur Séchard should do some printing on their account: they were encumbered, they said, with orders, their presses could not cope with the jobs in hand, they had been looking for workmen even in Bordeaux and undertook to keep David's three presses busy.

'Gentlemen,' Eve said to the two brothers while Cérizet went to inform David of his rivals' visit, 'my husband knew some excellent, honest and hard-working journeymen at the Didot's: no doubt he will choose his successor from the best of them . . . Is it not better to sell our business for a matter of twenty thousand francs, which will yield us a thousand francs' income, than to lose a thousand francs a year by continuing it on the scale to which you have reduced us? Why were you jealous of our poor little Almanac venture, which in any case was one of our specialities?'

'Well now, Madame, why didn't you warn us in advance? We would not have trodden on your heels,' one of the two brothers graciously replied – the one who was known as 'tall Cointet'.

'Come now, gentlemen, you only began your almanac after Cérizet had told you that I was producing mine.' As she made this sharp retort she looked straight at tall Cointet and made him lower his gaze. This was a clear proof of Cérizet's treachery.

This particular Cointet, who was in charge of the paper-mill and the business side, was much more able commercially-speaking than his brother Jean. The latter ran the printing-works with much intelligence, but this function could be compared with that of a colonel, whereas Boniface was a general whom Jean acknowledged as his commander-in-chief. Boniface, a lean and wizened man with a face as yellow as a church taper though it was marked with red blotches, having tight lips and eyes like a cat's, never lost his temper. He listened with sanctimonious calm to the grossest insults and his voice was always meek in reply. He went to Mass, confession and communion. Behind smug manners and an almost flabby demeanour he concealed the tenacity and ambition of a priest and the avidity of a tradesman thirsting for wealth and consideration. As early as 1820, tall Cointet coveted everything that the middle classes were finally to obtain from the Revolution of 1830. He was full of hatred for the aristocracy and indifferent as regards religion. In fact his piety was about as sincere as Bonaparte's revolutionary zeal had been. He bowed his spine with marvellous flexibility before the nobility and the administrative authorities: in their presence he was lowly, humble and obsequious. In fine, we may depict this man by revealing a characteristic whose significance will be fully appreciated by people accustomed to business dealings: he wore blue-tinted spectacles in order to mask his eyes, on the pretext of preserving his eyesight from the dazzling reflection of light in a city where earth and buildings are white and where high altitude intensifies the glare of the sun. Although he was only of slightly more than average height, he seemed tall because of his leanness, a spareness which showed that he was of a nature to accept an overwhelming burden of work and that he had a mind in a perpetual state of ferment. The finishing touch to his shifty cast of countenance was provided by a head of long, lank grey hair, cut in clerical style, and also by the kind of clothes he had worn for the last seven years: black trousers, black stockings, black waistcoat and a *lévite* (the Southern French word for a frock-coat) of chestnut-brown cloth. He was called 'tall Cointet' to distinguish him from his brother, 'stout Cointet', whose nickname expressed the contrast both of stature and capabilities between the two brothers, even though the one was as redoubtable as the other. In fact, Jean Cointet, a comfortably fat man with a Flemish type of face, though it was tanned by the Angoulême sun, small and stocky, as pot-bellied as Sancho Panza, with his broad shoulders and his perpetual smile, stood out in strong contrast to his elder brother. Jean not only differed from his senior in cast of countenance and brand of intelligence, but also professed almost liberal opinions: he belonged to the Left Centre, only went to Mass on Sunday and was on excellent terms with the Liberal tradespeople. Some business men in L'Houmeau maintained that the difference of outlook between them was merely a pretence. Tall Cointet cleverly exploited his brother's show of guilelessness and used Jean as one might use a cudgel. Harsh words and brutal decisions were repugnant to Boniface's benignity of manner and fell to Jean's lot. He was in charge of the Tantrums Department, lost his temper and came out with outrageous proposals which made those of his brother seem more acceptable: thus, sooner or later, they achieved their common purpose.

With her womanly intuition Eve was quick to divine the characters of this pair, and she remained on guard in the presence of such dangerous adversaries. David, already primed by his wife, listened to his enemies' proposals with an air of profound distraction.

'Settle the matter with my wife,' he said to the two Cointets as he left the glazed office to return to his little laboratory. 'She knows more about my printing business than I do. I'm busy with a concern which will prove more lucrative than this sorry concern, one through which I shall make good the losses I have suffered thanks to you.'

'How will you manage that?' asked stout Cointet with a laugh.

Eve gave her husband a glance to recommend him to be prudent.

'You'll all be paying tribute to me, you and all other consumers of paper,' David replied.

'What then is the object of your research?' asked Benoît-Boniface Cointet.

After Boniface had let out this question in a mildly inquisitive manner, Eve again looked at her husband to urge him to make no reply or at most a non-committal one.

'The object of my research is the manufacture of paper at fifty per cent below the present cost-price.'

He went off without seeing the look which the two brothers exchanged. It conveyed the following dialogue: 'This man was bound to be an inventor: you can't have a head and shoulders like his and remain idle.' – 'Let's get in on this.' – 'But how?' asked Jean.

Eve spoke out loud. 'David', she said, 'is only doing with you what he does with me. When I get curious he no doubt remembers that my name is Eve and makes the same off-hand reply. After all, it's only a project.'

'If your husband can bring off this project he'll certainly make his fortune more quickly than by printing. I'm no longer surprised to see him neglecting that set-up,' Boniface continued, turning towards the deserted workshop where Kolb was rubbing his bread with a clove of garlic. 'But it would not suit us to see this office in the hands of an active, bustling and ambitious competitor. And that's why we might come to an understanding. If for example you agreed for a certain sum to hire your plant to one of our journeymen who would work for us in your name – it's often been done in Paris – we would keep the fellow sufficiently occupied to pay you a very good rent and make small profits for himself . . . '

'That depends on the sum,' Eve Séchard replied. 'How much do you offer?' she asked, showing by the look she gave Boniface that she saw through his plan completely.

'How much are you expecting to get?' Jean Cointet quickly asked.

'Three thousand francs for six months.'

'But my dear lady, you were talking of selling your printing-office for twenty thousand francs,' Boniface replied in dulcet tones. 'The interest on twenty thousand francs is only twelve hundred francs at six per cent.'

Eve was abashed for a moment and fully realized the value of circumspection in business negotiations.

'You will be using our presses and our type,' she rejoindered. 'I have proved to you that I am still capable of putting them to profitable use. And we have rent to pay to Monsieur Séchard Senior, who doesn't exactly shower gifts on us.'

After two hours of haggling Eve obtained two thousand francs for the half-year, a thousand of them to be paid in advance. When all was settled, the two brothers informed her that they intended to lease the printing-office apparatus to Cérizet. Eve was unable to restrain a start of surprise.

'Isn't it better to employ someone who knows his way round the works?' stout Cointet asked.

Eve showed the two brothers out without replying, but she made up her mind that she would herself keep Cérizet under close observation.

'There we are then! Our enemies are inside the citadel!' David laughingly said to his wife when, as they sat down to dinner, she showed him the documents which had to be signed.

'Well, after all,' she said. 'I can answer for the loyalty of Kolb and Marion. The pair of them will keep an eye on everything. Besides, we are getting an income of four thousand francs a year for a working plant which was costing us money, and I can see that it will take you a year to realize your expectations.'

'You were cut out, as you told me on the Charente weir, to be the wife of a man with an inventive turn of mind!' said Séchard, giving her hand a tender squeeze.

David had now enough money to meet his household expenses for the winter. But he was under constant observation from Cérizet, and had become a dependant of tall Cointet without appreciating the fact.

'They're in our hands!' the manager of the paper-mill had said to his brother the printer as they left the house. 'The poor creatures will get into the habit of drawing the rent from their printing-press. They'll reckon on it and pile up debts. In six months' time we'll refuse to renew the lease, and then we shall see what this genius is made of. We'll offer to extricate him by going into partnership with him for the exploitation of his invention.'

If any astute businessman could have seen tall Cointet as he uttered the words 'by going into partnership', he would have acknowledged that even the dangers attendant upon a contract of marriage are less than those one incurs in contracting a business alliance. The situation was already grave enough with these ruthless hunters tracking down their prey: would David and his wife, having only Kolb and Marion to help them, be able to counter the wiles of a Boniface Cointet?

7. The first thunderbolt

WHEN the time came for Madame Séchard's confinement, the note for five hundred francs which Lucien had sent, together with a second payment from Cérizet, was enabling them to cover all their expenses. For the time being Eve's jubilation, and that of her mother and David, who had all been fearing that Lucien had forgotten them, was as great as the joy they had felt on hearing of Lucien's initial successes, for his entry into journalism had created even more of a stir in Angoulême than in Paris. And so, having been lulled into a false sense of security, David felt positively staggered when he received a devastating letter from his brother-in-law which ran as follows:

My dear David,

I have negotiated with Métivier three bills under your signature, payable to me, and post-dated one, two and three months respectively. Between this transaction and suicide I have chosen the former, a terrible expedient which will no doubt cause you great embarrassment. I shall be explaining what straits I am in and I shall moreover try to return the money to you when the bills fall due.

Burn this letter and say nothing about it to my sister and mother, for I confess I have counted on the heroism of which you have so often given proof.

In despair,
Your brother-in-law,

LUCIEN DE RUBEMPRÉ.

'Your poor brother,' David told his wife, who by then was up and about again, 'is in frightful difficulties. I have sent him three drafts for a thousand francs each, to be redeemed in one, two and three months. Make a note of it.'

Then he took himself off to the fields in order to avoid giving the explanations his wife was about to ask of him. But Eve, talking over this ominous statement with her mother, and already disquieted by the silence her brother had maintained during the last six months, was filled with such forebodings of evil that, in order to dispel them, she resolved to take a step which despair alone could have dictated to her. The Baron de Rastignac's son had come to spend a few days with his family and had spoken so disparagingly of Lucien that the news he brought from Paris, with the commentaries made on it as it passed from mouth to mouth, had come through to the journalist's mother and sister.

Eve went to see Madame de Rastignac and begged the

favour of an interview with her son, to whom she confided all her fears and of whom she asked the truth about Lucien's predicament in Paris. She was promptly informed about his liaison with Coralie, the duel with Michel Chrestien resulting from his treachery towards d'Arthez, in short all the details of Lucien's career – envenomed by the wit of a dandy who managed to give his hatred and envy a colouring of pity by adopting the friendly tones of a fellow-provincial concerned about the future of a local celebrity and professing sincere admiration for the talent of a son of Angoulême, now so cruelly compromised. He spoke of the misdeeds by which Lucien had forfeited the protection of very influential personages and which had led to the cancellation of an ordinance conferring on him the name and escutcheon of Rubempré.

'Madame, if your brother had taken good advice, he would today be on the road to ennoblement and married to Madame de Bargeton. But what else could be expected? . . . He deserted and insulted her! She has now become Madame la Comtesse Sixte du Châtelet – to her great regret, for she loved Lucien.'

'Can that possibly be true?' Madame Séchard exclaimed.

'Your brother is a young eagle blinded by the first sunbeams of luxury and fame. When an eagle falls, who can tell into what deep abyss it will plunge? A great man's fall is always in direct ratio to the heights he had reached.'

Eve returned to her house appalled by this last remark, which pierced her heart like an arrow. All that was most vulnerable in her was wounded to the quick, and at home she maintained the deepest silence, though many a tear dropped on to the cheeks and forehead of the child she was nursing. Nevertheless, one does not easily renounce illusions inspired by family loyalty and cherished since infancy. And so Eve placed no reliance on Eugène de Rastignac: she wanted to hear what a true friend would have to say, and therefore she wrote a moving letter to d'Arthez whose address Lucien had given her at the time when he had been so enthusiastic about the Cénacle. This is the reply she received:

Madame,

You ask me for the truth concerning the life your brother is leading in Paris. You wish to be enlightened about his future. Also, in order to make sure of a candid reply, you repeat to me what Monsieur de Rastignac had told you, asking me if such facts are true. In so far, Madame, as my own relations with Lucien are concerned, what Monsieur de Rastignac told you in confidence calls for rectification.

Your brother was ashamed of what he was doing. He came to show me his review of my book, telling me he could not bring himself to publish it despite the danger which a person very dear to him would incur if he disobeyed the orders given by his party. Alas, Madame, it is a writer's task to understand human passions since he stakes his reputation on depicting them: and so I realized that when a man has to choose between mistress and friend, it is the friend who must be sacrificed. I made it easier for your brother to carry out his misdeed by myself correcting his murderous article and giving it the stamp of my approval.

You ask me if I still feel any esteem or friendship for Lucien. That is a difficult question to answer. Your brother is on a path which may lead him to perdition. At the moment I am still sorry for him, but soon I shall deliberately forget him, not because of what he has done already but because of what he is likely to do. Your Lucien has poetry in him but is no real poet. He's a dreamer, not a thinker; he makes a great to-do but is not creative. Forgive me for saying so, but he's an effeminate little person who loves to show off – and that is what is wrong with most Frenchmen. And so Lucien will always sacrifice his best friend in order to make a parade of wit. He would willingly sign a pact tomorrow with the devil himself if this pact promised him a few years of brilliance and luxury. Has he not already done worse than that by bartering his future against the transitory pleasure of living openly with an actress? At present the youth, beauty and devotion of this woman – for she adores him – blind him to the dangers of a situation which neither reputation, nor success, nor prosperity will induce society to tolerate. So then, whenever a new temptation comes his way, your brother will think only – as he is doing just now – of the pleasures of the moment. Be assured of this: Lucien will never take to crime: he's too weak-minded. But he would accept a ready-made crime and share the profits without having shared the dangers, and all people, even scoundrels, stand aghast at that. He will despise himself; but he would do the same again when need arose, for he lacks will-power and will always take the bait when pleasure or the satisfaction of the most trifling whims are in question. He's lazy, like all men of poetic temperament, and thinks he's clever enough to juggle difficulties away instead of overcoming them. He'll be courageous and cowardly by turns, and is no more to be applauded for his courage than blamed for his cowardice: Lucien is like a harp whose strings become taut or slack according to the weather conditions. He might well write a fine book in an angry or happy mood and yet be indifferent to the success he has longed for.

During the early days of his stay in Paris he came under the ascendancy of an unscrupulous young man who had such skill and experience in coping with the difficulties of literary life that he was dazzled. This trickster won Lucien over completely and dragged him into a disreputable way of life on which, unfortunately for him, love cast its spell. When admiration is too easily gained it is a sign of inherent weakness: a tight-rope walker and a poet should not be paid in the same currency. We all of us felt hurt because Lucien admired intrigue and literary knavery more than the courage and honourable conduct of those who advised him to accept combat instead of filching success, to leap into the ring instead of taking a job as a trumpeter in the band.

Society, Madame, by a strange turn of whimsy, is full of indulgence towards young men of such a nature: it takes a liking to them and lets itself be captivated by the tinsel of their surface qualities. It demands nothing of them, condones all their faults, accords them the prerogatives due only to mature characters and sees only their advantageous points: in fact it makes spoilt children of them. On the other hand, it shows unbounded severity to people of rounded and forceful character. In so acting society appears to be outrageously unjust, but perhaps its attitude can be justified on a higher plane. It lets the buffoons amuse it without asking them for anything but enjoyment, and then promptly forgets them; whereas, if it is to bend the knee before real greatness, society expects it to be as munificent as the gods. Everything has its special law: the eternal diamond must be without blemish, the momentary creations of fashion have a right to be frivolous, wayward and flimsy. And so perhaps Lucien, despite his mistakes, will meet with marvellous success. It will suffice for him to exploit some happy vein or find himself in good company; but if he meets a Lucifer he will hurtle down into the nethermost hell. He offers a brilliant assemblage of fine qualities, but they are embroidered on too slight a ground: age wears off the floral designs and one day only the fabric remains; and if that is shoddy only rags and tatters are left. So long as Lucien is young he will be popular; but what will his position be when he is thirty? That's the question which those who really love him must ask themselves.

If I had been alone in thinking thus of Lucien, perhaps I should have tried to avoid causing you so much grief by my sincerity; but apart from the fact that platitudinous evasion of the questions your anxiety has prompted seemed to me to be unworthy of you – your letter is a cry of anguish – and of myself, although you hold me in too great esteem, those of my friends who knew Lucien are un-animous in passing the same judgment. I saw therefore that it was my duty to make the truth clear, however terrible it may be. Any-thing may be expected of Lucien, the best as well as the worst. This single sentence sums up the tenor of my letter and expresses what we think. If the vicissitudes of life – his life is at present very wretched and at the mercy of chance – should bring this dreamer back to you, use all your influence to keep him in the bosom of his family, for until he has acquired some stability of character Paris will always be a danger to him. He used to call you and your hus-band his guardian angels. No doubt he has forgotten you, but he will remember you at the time when, buffeted by the tempest, he will have no other refuge than his family. And so still keep a place for him in your heart, Madame: he will need it.

Accept, Madame, the sincere tribute of a man who well knows your invaluable qualities and has too much respect for your maternal solicitude not to offer you herewith his obeisance in signing him-self

Your devoted servant,
D'ARTHEZ.

Two days after receiving this reply, Eve's milk dried up and she had to hire a wet-nurse. Having made a god of her brother, she now looked on him as a man brought to de-pravity by the misuse of excellent faculties; in fact she saw that he was wallowing in the mire. A noble creature like her-self could admit of no compromise with the probity, scruples and principles so piously observed in family life – and in the heart of the provinces family life still retains its purity and radiance. So David had been right in what he had foreseen. When, in one of those heart-to-heart talks in which a loving couple can say all they feel, Eve told him the sorrowful news which had brought a leaden pallor to her white brow, he found soothing words to say to her. Although tears came to his eyes at the thought of his wife's lovely breasts running dry through grief and the sight of a mother in despair because she could not fulfil her maternal function, he calmed her fears and revived some hope in her.

'You see, my darling, it's your brother's imagination that has led him astray. It's only too natural for a poet to expect to be clothed in purple and fine linen. He's so eager for all the enjoyments of life! He's like a bird caught in the snare of brilliance and luxury; and he's so ingenuous about it that, even if society condemns, God will forgive him.'

'But he's ruining us!' the poor woman exclaimed.

'He's ruining us today, just as some months ago he came to our rescue by sending us the first-fruits of his pen!' In making this reply the kind-hearted David realized that despair was taking his wife too far and that her love for Lucien would soon reassert itself. 'About fifty years ago Sébastien Mercier said in his *Tableau de Paris* that the products of the brain, literature, poetry, the arts and the sciences, can never provide a living. Being a poet, Lucien has rejected the experience of four centuries. The kind of crops watered, not with rain, but with ink, are only harvested – if ever – ten or twelve years after seeding-time, and Lucien has taken the leaves for the sheaves. At any rate he will have learnt something about life. After being first of all duped by a woman, he was bound to be the dupe of society and false friendship. He has paid dearly for his experience, that's all. There's an old saying: "So long as a prodigal son comes back home with two ears and honour intact, all is well!"'

'Honour!' cried the unhappy Eve. 'Alas! In how many virtues has Lucien been found wanting!... Writing against his conscience! Attacking his best friend! Living on an actresss! ... Showing himself with her in public! Reducing us to beggary!'

'Oh! that's not all ...' David exclaimed. Then he stopped short: he had almost let out the secret of his brother-in-law's forgery. Unfortunately Eve noticed this hesitation and was left with a vague anxiety. 'Not all? What do you mean?' she asked. 'And where shall we get the three thousand francs we have to pay?'

'In the first place,' David continued, 'we shall soon be renewing Cérizet's lease for the running of our printing-office. During the last six months the fifteen per cent which the Cointets allow him on the work he does for them have brought him six hundred francs, and he's made five hundred francs with the town work.'

'If the Cointets know that,' said Eve, 'perhaps they won't take the lease on again. They'll be afraid of him. Cérizet's a dangerous man.'

'Well, what do I care!' cried Séchard. 'In a few days' time we shall be rich! And, my darling, once Lucien is rich he'll lead an exemplary life.'

'Ah! David, my love, my love, what an admission you've just made! According to you, when Lucien's down on his luck there's no crime he won't commit! You have the same ideas about him as Monsieur d'Arthez. A man must be strong if he wants to rise in the world, and Lucien is weak . . . What good would even an angel be if he can't resist temptation?'

'Well, men of his kind are at their best only when they're in their proper environment, their proper sphere and climate. Lucien's not a fighting man: I'll do the fighting for him. Come and take a look! I'm too close to results not to tell you all about the way I'm getting them.' He drew from his pocket several octavo sheets of white paper, flourished them triumphantly and laid them in his wife's lap.

8. A glance at paper-making

'A REAM of this paper, royal format, will not cost more than five francs,' he said, inviting Eve, who showed childlike surprise, to handle the specimens.

'Tell me, how did you make these samples?' she asked.

'With an old hair-sieve I got from Marion.'

'But you're not satisfied with them yet?'

'It's not a problem of manufacture: it's the cost price of the pulp. Unfortunately, darling, I'm only one of the latest to have entered on this difficult path. Back in 1794 Madame Masson tried to produce blank paper from printed paper. She succeeded, but at what a cost! Round about 1800, in England, the Earl of Salisbury, like the Frenchman Seguin in 1801, was trying to use straw for the manufacture of paper. The sheets you are holding were made from our common reed *arundo phragmitis*. But I intend to use nettles and thistles because, in order to keep down the cost of the raw material, recourse must be had to vegetable substances which grow in marshes and infertile soil and therefore are very cheap. The whole secret lies in finding a way to treat these plants. So far I have not discovered a simple enough process. Never mind! In spite of the difficulty, I'm sure I can confer on paper-making in France the same privilege as our literature already enjoys and establish a French monopoly equivalent to the monopoly which the English have in steel, coal and earthenware. I want to be in paper-manufacture what Jacquard was in the weaving industry.'

Eve rose to her feet, moved with enthusiasm and admiration by David's simple explanation. She opened her arms, pressed him to her heart and leaned her head on his shoulder.

'You're rewarding me as if I'd already discovered the process,' he said.

Eve's only response was to raise her lovely face all bathed in tears: for a moment she was unable to utter a word.

'It's not the man of genius that I'm hugging,' she said, 'but the man bringing consolation. One star has fallen, you show me one that is rising. Over against the grief I feel at the abasement of a brother, you are setting the great-heartedness of a husband. Greatness will certainly come to you, as it came to Graindorge, Rouvet, Van Robens and the Persian who introduced the cultivation of the madder-wort into France; as also to all the men you mentioned, whose names are still unknown because they did good unostentatiously by perfecting an industrial process.'

*

'What are they up to?...' Boniface was asking. Tall Cointet was walking with Cérizet in the Place du Mûrier and watching the shadows of husband and wife outlined against the muslin curtains of their living-room. The latter came there regularly at midnight to spy on the slightest activities of his former employer.

'It's clear enough,' replied Cérizet. 'He's showing her the paper he's made this morning.'

'But what's he making it of?' asked the paper-manufacturer.

'I just can't guess,' Cérizet replied. 'I made a hole in the roof, climbed on to it and saw my gaffer boiling his pulp all night long in a copper cauldron. It was no use my examining the supplies he had heaped up in a corner. All I could see was that his raw material looked like stacks of tow.'

'Go no further,' Boniface Cointet said to his spy in sanctimonious tones. 'It would be dishonest!... When Madame Séchard proposes to renew your lease for the running of the printing-office, tell her you want to become a master-printer. Offer her half the value of the licence and stock; and if they accept, come and see me. In any case, let things drag out ... They have no money.'

'Not a sou?' Cérizet asked.

'Not a sou,' tall Cointet echoed. – 'I have them!' he said to himself.

The firm of Métivier and the Cointet firm combined the function of bankers with their business as commission agents in paper supply, paper-manufacture and printing: be it said that they were careful not to pay any licence for their banking activities. Taxation authorities have not yet found a way to keep such close surveillance on trading concerns as would enable them to force all those who carry on banking surreptitiously to take out a banking licence, which, in Paris for example, costs five hundred francs a year. None the less the

Cointet brothers and Métivier between them, although in this capacity they were what are called 'maroons' at the Stock Exchange, handled no less than some hundreds of thousands of francs each quarter in the money markets of Paris, Bordeaux and Angoulême. It so happened that on that very evening the Cointet firm had received from Paris the bills for three thousand francs which Lucien had forged. Tall Cointet had immediately made this debt the basis of a formidable machination directed, as we shall see, against the poor, long-suffering inventor.

9. Provincial solicitors

NEXT day at seven in the morning Boniface Cointet was taking a walk along the mill-race which drove his enormous paper-mill and deadened all speech with the roar it made. He was waiting for a young man of twenty-nine who had six weeks' standing as a solicitor at the Angoulême County Court: his name was Petit-Claud.

'Were you at the college of Angoulême with David Séchard?' tall Cointet asked after saying good morning to the young solicitor, who had taken good care to answer the rich manufacturer's summons.

'Yes, monsieur,' Petit-Claud replied, walking in step with Cointet.

'Have you met him since then?'

'Not more than twice since his return from Paris. There were no opportunities. On week-days I was either deep in office work or attending at court. Sundays and holidays I carried on my studies, for I had only myself to depend on.'

Tall Cointet gave a nod of approval.

'When David and I met again, he asked me what I was doing. I told him that after taking my law degree at Poitiers I had become chief clerk to Maître Olivet and that sooner or later I hoped to succeed to his post ... I was much better acquainted with Lucien Chardon who now styles himself

Monsieur de Rubempré, the lover of Madame de Bargeton, our great local poet: in short, David Séchard's brother-in-law.'

'Consequently you can go and tell David that you are qualified and offer him your services.'

'That isn't done,' the young solicitor replied.

'He has never been to law and has no solicitor. That can certainly be done,' Cointet replied, peering through his glasses at the little solicitor.

Pierre Petit-Claud was the son of a tailor in L'Houmeau and had been cold-shouldered by his school-fellows, so that a certain amount of bile seemed to have passed into his bloodstream. His face had the blurred and murky colouring which speaks of childhood sicknesses, late hours imposed by poverty and – almost always – resentful feelings. Colloquial speech provides adjectives to depict this young individual in two words: he was snappy and prickly. His cracked voice was in keeping with his sour looks, frail appearance and the indeterminate colour of his magpie eyes. Napoleon once observed that magpie eyes are a sign of dishonesty. 'Look at so-and-so,' he said to Las Casas at Saint Helena, speaking of a confidant whom he had been obliged to dismiss for embezzlement. 'I don't know how I could have been mistaken for so long: he has the eye of a magpie.' And so, after tall Cointet had scrutinized this skinny, pock-marked little solicitor, with hair so sparse that one could scarcely tell where cranium left off and forehead began, when he saw him striking the pose of a sophisticated man with one hand on his hip, he said to himself: 'He's the fellow I need!' In fact Petit-Claud, having had his fill of disdain, eaten up with a gnawing desire to push himself forward, had been bold enough, penniless as he was, to buy his employer's practice for thirty thousand francs, counting on marriage to furnish him with this sum. As was customary, he expected his employer to find him a wife, for a predecessor always has a motive for making a match for his successor in order to get the money for his practice. But Petit-Claud relied even more on himself, for he was not without a certain superiority, rare in the provinces, though hatred was the ruling principle behind it. The more a man hates, the greater the efforts he will make.

There is a great difference between Parisian and provincial solicitors, and tall Cointet was too clever not to take advantage of the petty passions to which petty lawyers are prone. In Paris, a solicitor of some repute – there are many of them – has some of the qualities of a diplomat by virtue of the numerous affairs with which he has to deal, the importance of the interests involved and the wide scope of the issues confided to him; all this exempts him from the temptation to make a living out of legal shifts and tricks. Legal procedure, whether it is used as an offensive or defensive weapon, is no longer for him what it had been in former times – a source of lucre. In the provinces the opposite is true: solicitors go in for what Paris lawyers call 'nibblings', a superabundance of pettifoggeries which load their accounts with costs and use up a lot of stamped paper. A provincial solicitor is taken up with these trivialities. His concern is to pile up costs, whereas a Paris solicitor thinks only of his 'retainer'. This honorarium is what a client owes, over and above costs, to his solicitor for the more or less skilful management of his affairs. The State takes half of the costs, whereas the retainer is his entirely. Let us face this fact: the fees paid rarely square with those which are asked for – reasonably so – for the services a good solicitor can render. Solicitors, doctors and barristers in Paris are like courtesans with their casual customers, extremely careful not to put too great a strain on their clients' gratitude. Two admirable *genre* pictures worthy of Meissonier might be made of a client before and after his case is concluded, and no doubt a society of emeritus solicitors would bid a high price for them.

There is yet one more difference between a Paris and a provincial solicitor. The former rarely pleads, although he sometimes addresses a judge sitting in chambers. But in 1822, in most country districts (since then advocates have multiplied like rabbits), solicitors were also advocates and conducted their own cases. From this twofold function results a twofold responsibility which confers on a provincial solicitor the intellectual defects of a barrister without relieving him of his onerous obligations as a solicitor. He therefore becomes a gas-bag and loses that lucidity of judgement which is indispensable for the conduct of affairs. Through this doubling of parts an exceptional man often finds himself reduced to the status of two mediocre men. A solicitor in Paris, since he does not spend himself making speeches in court and rarely pleads on one side or the other, is able to preserve his sanity of judgment. True, he ranges his legalistic artillery and ransacks his arsenal to find the ways and means which the pros and cons of jurisprudence can furnish, but he allows himself no delusions over the case in hand, even though he is making every effort to win it. In a word, thinking goes to the head much less than talking. A man can talk himself into believing what he says, whereas it is possible to act against one's own opinion while still holding to it and successfully conduct a bad case without maintaining that it is a good one, which is what an advocate does when he pleads. And so there are many reasons for a provincial solicitor turning out to be a mediocre person: he becomes involved in petty squabbles, takes on petty cases, makes his living on costs, misuses the code of procedure . . . and he pleads! In brief, he has many shortcomings. Consequently, when a noteworthy man is found among provincial solicitors, he stands head and shoulders above the rest.

'I imagined, Monsieur, that you had sent for me to talk of your own affairs,' Petit-Claud replied, and the look he cast on tall Cointet's impenetrable spectacles gave added point to this remark.

'Let's come to the point,' answered Boniface Cointet. 'Listen.' After uttering this one word, pregnant with confidential statements, Cointet went and sat down on a bench and invited Petit-Claud to do the same.

'When Monsieur du Hautoy passed through Angoulême in 1804 to take up his consular post at Valencia, he met Madame de Sénonches who was then Mademoiselle Zéphirine.

'– And a daughter was born to them,' Cointet added in a whisper to his interlocutor. 'Yes,' he went on as he saw Petit-Claud giving a shrug. 'Mademoiselle Zéphirine's marriage with Monsieur de Sénonches followed close upon this secret confinement. The daughter, who was brought up in the country by my mother, is Mademoiselle Françoise de La Haye, now looked after by Madame de Sénonches who, as is usual in such cases, poses as her godmother. As my mother, a farmer's wife and a tenant of Mademoiselle Zéphirine's grandmother, Madame de Cardanet, knew the facts about this sole heiress of the Cardanets and the Sénonches – the senior branch – I was commissioned to turn to account the small sum which Monsieur François du Hautoy intended eventually to make over to his daughter. I made a fortune out of these ten thousand francs which today amount to thirty thousand. Madame will certainly provide her ward with a wedding trousseau, silver and a modicum of furniture. And I, my boy,' said Cointet, giving Petit-Claud a tap on the knee, 'I can get the girl for you. If you marry Françoise de La Haye, you'll add a large part of the aristocracy of Angoulême to your clientele. This bar sinister alliance will open out a magnificent future for you . . . They'll be satisfied to marry her to a solicitor-advocate: I know they won't ask more than that.'

'What must I do?' asked Petit-Claud with avidity. 'Maître Cachan is your solicitor.'

'Yes, and I'm not going to drop Cachan all of a sudden for you. You'll only have my legal business later,' said tall Cointet . . . 'What are you to do, my friend? Why, you take over David Séchard's affairs. The poor devil has three thousand francs to pay us in bills: he won't be able to pay them, and you'll defend him against legal proceedings in such a way as to load him with enormous costs . . . Have no misgivings: go ahead, pile up the incidental expenses. Doublon, my bailiff, whose job it will be to carry out the proceedings with Cachan behind him, won't do things by half . . . A wink's as good as a nod . . . Well now, young man? . . . '

The two men looked at each other for a time in eloquent silence.

'Mark this: you and I have never met,' Cointet continued. 'I've said nothing to you. You know nothing about Monsieur du Hautoy or Madame de Sénonches or Mademoiselle de La Haye. But when the time comes, in two months, you will ask for this young person's hand in marriage. Whenever we have to get together you'll come here in the evening. No letter-writing.'

'So you want to ruin Séchard?'

'Not entirely. But we've got to hold him in prison for a time.'

'What's your purpose?'

'Do you think I'm fool enough to tell you? If you've sense enough to guess, you'll also have sense enough to keep quiet.'

'Old Séchard's a rich man,' said Petit-Claud, who already had a glimmering of Boniface's purpose and saw that it might be thwarted.

'The old man won't give his son a farthing in his lifetime, and he has no intention of passing on just yet.'

'I'll take it on,' said Petit-Claud, having made a prompt decision. 'I'm not asking you for guarantees. I'm a lawyer. If you made a fool of me we should have accounts to settle.'

'That rascal will go far,' Cointet thought as he said goodnight to Petit-Claud.

10. *A free public lecture on dishonoured bills for those unable to meet them*

THE day after this colloquy, on 30 April the brothers Cointet presented the first of the three bills Lucien had forged. Unfortunately the draft was handed to poor Eve, who recognized Lucien's imitation of her husband's signature. She called David and asked him point-blank: 'Did you sign this bill?'

'No,' he said. 'Your brother was so hard-pressed that he signed it for me.'

She returned the bill to the cashier of the Cointet firm and told him: 'We cannot meet it.'

Then, feeling faint, she went to her bedroom, with David following.

'My dear,' she said to him in a failing voice, 'hurry to Messrs Cointet. They will show you some consideration. Ask them to wait, and also remind them that when Cérizet's lease is renewed they will owe you a thousand francs.'

David went straight away to face his enemies.

A foreman-printer may always become a master-printer, but an able typographer is not necessarily a business man. And so David, who was out of his depth, remained dumb-struck before tall Cointet when, after having, with choking voice and racing heart, somewhat clumsily faltered out ex-cuses and made his request, he received the following reply. 'This is not our concern. We hold the bill from Métivier. Métivier will pay us. Apply to Monsieur Métivier.'

'Oh!' said Eve on hearing of this reply. 'Once the bill is returned to Monsieur Métivier we can be easy in our minds.'

The next day, the bailiff, Victor-Ange-Herménégilde Doub-lon, brought David the protest at two o'clock, a time at which the Place du Mûrier is crowded with people; and, although he was careful to talk to Marion and Kolb only at the entrance to the alley, the protest was none the less a matter of common knowledge by that evening among the tradespeople of Angoulême. In any case, how could the hypocritical formali-ties resorted to by Maître Doublon, whom tall Cointet had recommended to show the greatest consideration, have saved Eve and David from the commercial ignominy resulting from a suspension of payment? Let us look into the matter. Even a lengthy disquisition will seem too brief. Ninety per cent of our readers will find the following details as appetizing as the spiciest news-item. They will offer new proof of the truth of this axiom: there is nothing about which people are more ignorant than what they ought to know: the workings of the law!

Indeed, to the immense majority of Frenchmen, a good description of one part of the machinery of banking could be as interesting as a chapter of a book on travels abroad. When a merchant sends a money order from the town in which his premises lie to a person living in another town, as David was supposed to have done for Lucien's benefit, he converts a very simple operation, that of a negotiable instrument drawn between two merchants for business purposes, into something resembling a bill which one exchange draws on another. Thus, by accepting Lucien's three drafts, in order to recover the sum advanced, Métivier was obliged to send them to Messrs Cointet, his correspondents in Angoulême. Hence an initial charge on Lucien designated as *commission for change of place*, which worked out at so much per cent on each draft irrespective of discount. The Séchard notes had thus passed into the category of Bank transactions. One would hardly believe to what extent the function of banker, joined to the august title of creditor, alters conditions for the debtor. Thus, 'on the Bank' (note this expression), once a bill transferred from Paris to Angoulême remains unpaid, the bankers owe it to themselves to draw up what in law is called a 'Return Account' – such an account, if we may risk a pun, as never any novelist gave of the most breathtaking adventures. For these are the ingenious clowneries authorized by a certain clause in the Commercial Code, and an explanation of them will show how many atrocities are concealed behind the terrible word *legality*.

As soon as Maître Doublon had registered his protest he took it in person to the Cointet brothers. The bailiff had an account with these Angoulême sharks and allowed them credits for six months which tall Cointet dragged on for a year by his method of settlement, although month after month he would say to his equally shark-like assistant: 'Doublon, I suppose you want some money.' And there was more to it than that. Doublon favoured this powerful firm with a rebate, and thus it made a gain on each process served: just a trifle, a mere nothing – one franc fifty per protest!

Tall Cointet sat down calmly at his desk, took out a little sheet of paper with a thirty-five centimes stamp on it, and chatted with Doublon the while in order to obtain information about the actual situation of certain tradespeople.

'Well now, are you satisfied with little Gannerac?'

'He's not doing badly. After all, a haulage contractor . . . '

'Yes, but in fact he's having to do quite a lot of hauling. They say his wife is spending a lot of his money.'

'*His* money?' exclaimed Doublon with a leer.

Then the shark, who had just finished ruling lines on his sheet of paper, wrote out in a round hand the sinister heading beneath which he drew up the following account:

RETURN ACCOUNT AND COSTS

To a draft for ONE THOUSAND FRANCS, dated from Angoulême on the tenth of February, eighteen hundred and twenty-two, drawn by SÉCHARD junior to the order of LUCIEN CHARDON styled DE RUBEMPRÉ, passed to the order of MÉTIVIER and to our order, payable on the thirtieth of April last, protested by DOUBLON, bailiff, on the first of May eighteen hundred and twenty-two.

Principal	1000.00 *frs.*
Protest..	12.35
Commission at one-half per cent	5.00
Brokerage at one-quarter per cent	2.50
Stamp for redraft and this return	1.35
Interest and postage	3.00
	1024.30
Exchange transference at one and one quarter per cent	13.25
	1037.45

One thousand thirty-seven francs and forty-five centimes, for which sum we reimburse ourselves by our draft on sight on Monsieur Métivier, rue Serpente, Paris, to the order of Monsieur Gannerac, of L'Houmeau,

Angoulême, the second of May, eighteen hundred and twenty-two.

COINTET brothers.

Underneath this little memorandum, drawn up with the skill that comes from sheer habit – for he was still chatting with Doublon – tall Cointet wrote the following declaration:

We the undersigned, Postel, licensed apothecary of L'Houmeau, and Gannerac, haulage contractor, tradesmen of this city, certify that the charge for exchange between Angoulême and Paris is one and one-quarter per cent.

Angoulême, the third of May, eighteen hundred and twenty-two.

'Look, Doublon, do me the pleasure of going to Postel and Gannerac, ask them to sign this declaration and bring it back tomorrow morning.'

And Doublon, well up in these instruments of torture, went off as if it were the simplest of matters. Clearly, even if the protest had been delivered, as it is in Paris, in a sealed envelope, all Angoulême would have been well informed about the unhappy state of poor Séchard's affairs. And how many accusations of indifference were levelled against him! Some said that his ruin was due to the excessive love he bore his wife. Others blamed him for being too fond of his brother-in-law. And what fearful conclusions they drew from these premises! One should never devote oneself to the interests of one's relatives! There was approval and admiration for the severity which old Séchard was showing to his son.

Now, let any reader who for any reason whatsoever has neglected to 'honour his obligations' look closely at the perfectly legal proceedings thanks to which, in ten minutes, 'on the Bank', twenty-eight francs can be made to accrue from a capital sum of one thousand francs.

In the above 'Return Account', the first item alone is beyond dispute.

The second item covers what was due to the Inland Revenue and the bailiff. The six francs levied by the Treasury for registering the debtor's discomfiture and providing stamped paper will keep that abuse going for a long time still! You should know, moreover, that this item gave a gain of one franc fifty centimes to the banker thanks to the rebate made by Doublon.

The commission of one-half per cent, with which the third item is concerned, is levied on the ingenious pretext that not

526

to receive payment is equivalent, 'on the Bank', to discounting a bill. Nothing could be further from the truth: no two things are more alike than disbursing a thousand francs and not getting them back. But anyone who has offered money orders for discount knows that, over and above the six per cent legally due, the discounter exacts, under the unpretentious name of commission, so much per cent; and that represents the interest which, in addition to the legal rate, comes to him through his ingenuity in exploiting his capital. The more money he hopes to make, the more he demands. It is therefore wiser to get fools to discount one's bills. But *are* there any fools 'on the Bank'?

The law obliges the banks to have the rate of exchange certified by a stockbroker. In 'places' unfortunate enough not to have a stock exchange a couple of business men act in lieu of the stockbroker. The commission known as brokerage due to the stockbroker is fixed at one quarter per cent of the sum stated in the protested bill. It has become usual to count this commission as paid to the business men who replace the stockbroker; but the banker simply slips it into his cash-box. Hence the third item in this fascinating account.

The fourth item covers the cost of the sheet of stamped paper on which the 'Return Account' is drawn up; also the stamp for what is so ingeniously called the re-draft, that is to say the new bill drawn by the banker on his colleague in order to recoup himself.

The fifth item comprises the cost of postage and the legal interest on the sum for so long as it is missing from the banker's coffers.

Finally the exchange transference, the very purpose for which banking exists, represents what it costs to draw one's money in a different 'place' or 'domicile'.

Let us now make a closer analysis of this account, judging by which, according to Punchinello's way of computing in the Neapolitan *chanson* so dramatically sung by Lablache, fifteen plus five makes twenty-two! Clearly the signature of Messrs Postel and Gannerac was a matter of mutual accommodation: when need arose, the Cointets wrote a certificate for Gannerac and Gannerac did the same for the Cointets: as the well-known proverb goes: 'You scratch my back and I'll scratch yours.' The brothers Cointet, having a running account with Métivier, had no need to draw bills on him. No draft passed between them ever added a single line to the credit or debit side.

In reality then this fantastic account could well be whittled down to the thousand francs owed, the protest, amounting to thirteen francs and interest for one month at one half per cent: in all perhaps one thousand and eighteen francs.

If a banking house has an average of one 'Return Account' *per diem* on a value of one thousand francs, it draws in twenty-eight francs every day by the grace of God and the rules of banking. A formidable kind of royal levy invented by the Jews in the twelfth century and operative today over both monarchs and their subjects! In other terms then, a thousand francs bring in twenty-eight francs a day to the banking house or ten thousand two hundred and twenty francs a year. Multiply by three the average number of these 'Return Accounts' and you reach an income of thirty thousand francs drawn from fictitious capital. That is why nothing is more tenderly cared for than these accounts. Had David Séchard come along to pay off his draft on the third of May or even the day after the protest, Cointet brothers would have told him: 'We have returned your draft to Monsieur Métivier!' – even though the protest might still have been lying on their desk. The 'Return Account' becomes operative on the very evening of the protest.

And this, in provincial bankers' language, is called 'making the money sweat'. Postage for letters alone produces about twenty thousand francs per annum for the Keller bank which has a correspondence stretching over the whole wide world. Return Accounts pay for Madame la Baronne de Nucingen's box at the *Italiens*, her carriage, clothes and cosmetics. Letter postage is so much more a scandalous abuse because bankers deal with ten similar matters in one ten-line letter. Strangely enough, the Inland Revenue takes its share of this premium extorted from misfortune: the Treasury waxes fat on commercial failures! As for the Bank, from the vantage-point of its counters it flings an eminently reasonable question at a debtor: 'Why can't you meet your obligations?' Alas! There is no answer to this. It follows then that the tale of items in a Return Account is a tale full of hair-raising fictions which debtors who ponder over these informative pages will henceforth hold in salutary awe.

On May the fourth Métivier received the Return Account from Messrs Cointet with instructions to take relentless proceedings against Monsieur Chardon styled de Rubempré.

11. Lucien under distraint

A FEW days later Eve received, in reply to a letter she had written to Monsieur Métivier, the following note which put her mind completely at rest:

TO MONSIEUR SÉCHARD JUNIOR, PRINTER IN ANGOULÊME

I am in receipt of your esteemed letter of the fifth instant. I understood from your explanation relative to the unpaid draft of the 30th ultimate that you drew it to oblige your brother-in-law Monsieur de Rubempré, who lives on a sufficiently lavish scale for it to be doing you a service to force him to pay: his situation is such that he need not let the proceedings against him continue for long. If your honoured brother-in-law does not settle the debt I shall rely upon the loyalty of your firm, and I sign myself, as always,

Your devoted servant,
MÉTIVIER.

'Well,' said Eve to David, 'at any rate my brother will learn from these proceedings that we have not been able to pay.'

What a change in Eve this remark betokened! The growing love inspired in her by David's character, which she was coming to know better and better, was taking the place of brotherly affection in her heart. But ... to how many illusions was she not saying good-bye?

Let us now see how the Return Account fared on the Paris exchange. A third endorser – this is the commercial term for one who holds a bill through transmission – is legally entitled to proceed solely against that person amongst the various debtors for the bill who he thinks will most promptly repay him. By virtue of this option Lucien was sued by Monsieur Métivier's bailiff. The stages of this action, quite a useless one as it turned out, were as follows: Métivier, the Cointets' catspaw, was well aware that Lucien was insolvent, but *de facto* insolvency can only exist *de jure* once it has been established as a fact. So then the impossibility of getting payment from Lucien was established in the following manner.

On 5 May Métivier's bailiff gave notice to Lucien of the Return Account and the protest made at Angoulême, citing him to the Commercial Court of Paris to be informed of a number of facts, one of them being that as a merchant he would be liable to imprisonment for debt. When Lucien, living as he was the life of a hunted stag, came to read this gibberish, he also received notification of a judgment made against him *in absentia* at the Commercial Court. His mistress Coralie, knowing nothing about all this, had supposed that Lucien had been lending money to his brother-in-law, and she handed all the writs over to him too tardily, at one and the same time. An actress sees too many actors taking the parts of bailiffs in light comedies to take legal documents seriously. Tears came to Lucien's eyes: he was moved with pity for Séchard, ashamed of his forgery and desirous to pay up. Naturally he consulted his friends about means of gaining time. But when Lousteau, Blondet, Bixiou and Nathan told him what little attention a poet should pay to the Tribunal de Commerce – a jurisdiction set up by shopkeepers – this particular poet was already under the threat of distraint. On his door was pinned the little yellow placard whose jaundiced colour washes off on to concierges, has an astringent effect on the facilities of credit, strikes fear into the heart of all caterers and above all chills the blood of poets sensitive enough to become attached to the sticks of wood, rags of silk, piles of dyed wool, in short the baubles which go by the name of furnishings. When the bailiffs came to fetch Coralie's furniture, the author of *Les Marguerites* went to see a friend of Bixiou, a solicitor names Desroches, who laughed when he saw Lucien alarmed at such a trifle.

'It's nothing to worry about, my friend. I suppose you want to gain time?'

'As much time as possible.'

'Well then, apply for a stay of execution. Go and see a friend of mine, Masson, an attorney at the Commercial Court. He will renew the stay of execution, represent you at that court and challenge its competence to judge your case. There won't be the slightest difficulty about that, for it's well known you are a journalist. If you're summoned before the Civil Court, come and see me and I'll take your case on. I undertake to dispose of the people who want to vex our beautiful Coralie.'

On 28 May Lucien, cited before the Civil Court, lost his case more promptly than Desroches had expected, for the proceedings against him were being vigorously pursued. When a new distraint was set in motion, when the yellow placard was once more gilding the pilasters of Coralie's door and there was a new threat to take away the furniture, Desroches, feeling a little foolish at having 'his fingers nipped', as he put it, by a colleague, demanded another stay of execution, claiming, rightly enough, that the furniture belonged to Coralie. He called for a hearing in chambers, and as a result of this summary procedure, the chairman of the Court reopened the case. Judgment was delivered in favour of Coralie as being the owner of the furniture. Métivier appealed, and on the thirtieth of July his appeal was dismissed.

On 7 August, Maître Cachan received by stage-coach an enormous file of documents with the heading: MÉTIVIER *versus* SÉCHARD AND LUCIEN CHARDON.

The first of these documents was the following dainty little memorandum, the accuracy of which is guaranteed, since it is copied from the original:

Bill to date *30 April* ultimate, drawn by Séchard junior to order of Lucien de Rubempré (*May 2*). Return account: 1037.45 frs.

May 5. Notice of return account and protest with summons to appear before the Commercial Court of Paris on May 7	8.75
May 7. Judgment by default and order for attachment	35.00
10 May. Notification of judgment	8.50
12 May. Order to pay	5.50
14 May. Inventory of distraint	16.00
18 May. Appending of placard	15.25
19 May. Insertion in journal	4.00
24 May. Report of verification prior to seizure of chattels, including application for stay of execution by Monsieur Lucien de Rubempré	12.00
27 May. Order of Court in session, referring parties to Civil Court upon application for renewal of stay of execution	35.00
28 May. Summary citation of case before the Civil Court by Métivier represented by counsel	6.50
2 June. Judgment after hearing, ordering Lucien Chardon to pay costs of Return Account and assigning to plaintiff costs for proceedings before the Commercial Court	150.00
6 June. Notification of the aforesaid	10.00
15 June. Warrant of execution	5.50
19 June. Inventory with view to distraint and appeal therefrom by Mademoiselle Coralie claiming proprietory right in the furniture and requesting urgent hearing in chambers for stay of execution	20.00
Order from presiding judge, referring parties to special hearing in chambers	40.00
19 June. Order adjudging property of furniture to the said Mademoiselle Coralie	250.00
20 June. Appeal by Métivier	17.00
30 June. Dismissal of above appeal	250.00
Total	889.00

Bill to date 31 May with Return Account	1037.45
Notification to Monsieur Lucien Chardon	8.75
	Total	1046.20
Bill to date 30 June with Return Account	1037.45
Notification to Monsieur Lucien Chardon	8.75
	Total	1046.20

With these documents went a letter in which Métivier instructed Maître Cachan, solicitor, Angoulême, to take full legal proceedings against David Séchard. Maître Victor-Ange-Herménégilde Doublon accordingly summoned David Séchard to appear before the Commercial Court of Angoulême on July third and pay the total sum of four thousand eighteen francs and eighty-five centimes, the amount due for the three bills and the costs so far incurred. The morning of the day when Doublon was to present Eve with the injunction to pay what was for her an enormous sum she received a staggering letter from Métivier:

TO MONSIEUR DAVID SÉCHARD, PRINTER, ANGOULÊME,

Your brother-in-law, Monsieur Chardon, is a man of notorious bad faith and has registered his furniture under the name of the actress with whom he is living. You ought, Monsieur, to have loyally informed me of these circumstances to spare me from taking futile legal proceedings, for you did not answer my letter of May tenth. Do not therefore take it in evil part if I ask you immediately to reimburse me for the three bills of exchange and all my expenses.

Yours truly,
MÉTIVIER.

Having had no further news of her brother, Eve, who knew little about commercial law, had been supposing that he had atoned for his crime by paying off the forged bills.

'My dear,' she said to her husband, 'hurry off to Petit-Claud. Explain our position and ask him what we should do.'

12. *'Your house is on fire'*

'MY friend,' said the unfortunate printer as he rushed head-
long into the office of his former schoolfellow, 'I little knew,
when you came to tell me of your appointment and offer me
your services, that I should so soon find myself in need of
them.'

Petit-Claud studied David's fine face – that of a thinker –
as he sat opposite him in an arm-chair, without listening to his
account of matters with which he was more familiar than the
man who was explaining them. Noticing Séchard's anxious
air as he entered, he had said to himself: 'We've done the
trick!' Such a scene is often enacted in a lawyer's office. Petit-
Claud was wondering: 'Why are the Cointets persecuting
him?' It is part of the mentality of solicitors to pierce through
to the innermost thoughts of their clients as well as those of
their adversaries: they have to see both back and front of the
judicial weft.

'You want to gain time,' Petit-Claud at last answered when
David had finished. 'How much time? Something like
three or four months?'

'Get me four months and I shall be saved!' cried David,
who looked on Petit-Claud as a ministering angel.

'Very well. They shall not lay hands on any of your furniture, and they shall not arrest you for three or four months . . .
But it will cost a lot of money,' Petit-Claud added.

'Oh! What does that matter?' cried Séchard.

'You're expecting payments to come in? Are you sure of
them?' the solicitor asked, almost surprised at his client's
readiness to fall into the trap set for him.

'In three months' time I shall be a rich man,' the inventor
replied, with all the self-assurance of an inventor.

'Your father's not yet in the churchyard,' said Petit-Claud.
'He prefers to remain in his vineyard.'

'Do you think I'm counting on my father's death?' David
replied. 'I'm on the track of an industrial process which,

without one thread of cotton, will enable me to manufacture a kind of paper as substantial as Holland paper at fifty per cent of the present cost of cotton pulp . . . . '

'That means a fortune,' exclaimed Petit-Claud, at last tumbling to tall Cointet's plot.

'A great fortune, my friend, for in the next ten years ten times the amount of paper consumed today will be needed. In our century journalism is going to become a mania.'

'No one knows your secret ? . . . '

'No one, except my wife.'

'You have not divulged your project, your programme to anyone . . . to the Cointets for example ? '

'I told them about it, but only in vague terms, I believe !'

A flash of generosity shot through the embittered soul of Petit-Claud, and he made an attempt at reconciling interests, those of the Cointets, his own, and David's.

'Listen, David. We are old school friends. I'll stand up for you. But make no mistake: your defence against legal pursuit will cost you five or six thousand francs ! . . . Don't run the risk of losing your fortune. I believe you'll be obliged to share the profits of your invention with one of our manufacturers. Come now ! You'll think twice about it before you buy or build a paper-factory . . . Besides, you'll have to take out a patent . . . All that will take time and money. Maybe the bailiffs will swoop down on you too soon in spite of the evasive action we're going to take . . . '

'No, I'll stick to my secret !' David replied with all the ingenuousness of a scientist.

'Well, your secret will be your life-line,' Petit-Claud continued, thwarted in his first, his honest intention to avoid a law-suit by compromise. 'I don't ask to know what it is. But mark my words: try to work underground. Let no one see you or get an inkling of your process of manufacture, or else your life-line will be torn from your grasp . . . An inventor is often a simpleton at bottom. You will be thinking too much of your secret process to be able to think of everything. Sooner or later people will suspect the purposes of your researches, and you have paper-manufacturers all around you !

You'll be like a beaver hemmed in by hunters: don't let them get your skin!'

'Thank you, my dear friend. I have told myself all that,' Séchard exclaimed. 'But I'm grateful to you for showing so much caution and solicitude! ... I'm not the only person concerned in this venture. I myself could be content with twelve hundred francs a year, and some day my father will surely leave me at least three times that amount ... My life is taken up with loving and thinking – a blissful life ... My concern is for Lucien and my wife, and it's for them I'm working ...'

'Come on then, sign me this power of attorney, and give your mind only to your researches. When the day comes for you to go into hiding to avoid arrest, I'll warn you the day before. And let me tell you this: don't let anyone inside your house unless you're as sure of them as you are of yourself.'

'Cérizet has refused to renew his lease for the running of my press, and that's why we're a bit worried about money. So the only persons I have left are Marion, Kolb who's like a watch-dog for me, my wife and my mother-in-law.'

'Take my advice,' said Petit-Claud. 'Don't trust even your watch-dog.'

'You don't know him,' David exclaimed. 'Kolb is like a second self to me.'

'Will you let me put him to the test?'

'Yes,' said Séchard.

'Well, good-bye. But send the charming Madame Séchard along to me: I simply must have power of attorney from her. And reflect upon this, my friend: your house is on fire.' By saying this to his old schoolfellow, Petit-Claud was warning him of all the judicial catastrophes which were about to descend on him.

'There I am then, with a foot in both camps,' Petit-Claud said to himself after showing his friend David to the door.

A prey to the vexations due to lack of money, a prey to the worry caused by his wife's state of mind – reduced to despair as she was by Lucien's infamous conduct – David was still pondering over his problem. It had so happened that, as he was on his way from his house to see Petit-Claud, he had absent-mindedly been chewing a nettle stalk which he had steeped in water as a means for somehow or other retting the stalks he was using as material for his pulp. He was trying to find a process equivalent to the various kinds of attrition effected by soaking, by weaving or by ordinary wear-and-tear on anything of which the end-product is thread, linen or rag-stuff. As he made his way home, quite satisfied with his talk with Petit-Claud, he realized that he had a ball of pulp in his mouth. He took it out, rolled it out in his hand, and found that it made a better pulp than any of the compounds he had produced hitherto; for the principal defect in pulps made from vegetable matter is that they lack adhesiveness. Straw for instance produces a brittle, half metallic and rustling paper. Chance discoveries like this are only made by bold researchers into natural causes.

He told himself that he would use a machine and a chemical agent to carry out the operation which he had just accomplished automatically. And he appeared before his wife in a state of jubilation, believing that he had scored a triumph.

'My angel, don't worry any more!' said David, noticing that his wife had been crying. 'Petit-Claud guarantees us a few months' respite. There will be expenses but, as he said when he showed me out, all Frenchmen have the right to keep their creditors waiting provided that in the long run they repay capital, interest and costs! . . . Well, we'll do that.'

'And keep alive?' said the unhappy Eve, who saw all the difficulties ahead.

'Ah! That's a point!' David answered, pulling at his ear – an inexplicable gesture, but one customary with all people who find themselves in a quandary.

'Mother will take charge of our little Lucien and I can go back to work,' said Eve.

'Eve! My beloved Eve!' David exclaimed, taking his wife into his arms and clasping her to his heart. 'Eve, a short distance away from here, at Saintes, in the sixteenth century, lived one of France's greatest men, for he was not only the inventor of enamelling, but also the glorious forerunner of Buffon and Cuvier: a simple-hearted man who discovered the science of geology before they did! Well, this man, Bernard de Palissy, was a passionate enthusiast for research. But he had his wife, his children and all the neighbours of his quarter against him. His wife made him pay her for his tools . . . He wandered about the countryside misunderstood and hounded, and people pointed their fingers at him! . . . Whereas *I* have a wife who loves me!'

'Loves you very much,' Eve replied with the serene accents expressive of love which is sure of itself.

'So then I can put up with everything that Bernard de Palissy had to put up with: the man who made the faience of Ecouen, the man whom Charles the Ninth saved from the Saint Bartholomew massacres and who, in the end, when he was old, but rich and loaded with honours, gave public lectures to the whole of Europe on 'the science of clays', as he called it.

'So long as my hand has strength enough to hold a smoothing-iron you shall want for nothing!' poor Eve exclaimed in accents expressive of the deepest devotion. 'At the time when I was Madame Prieur's forewoman I was friendly with a very good girl, a cousin of Postel, Basine Clerget. Well, Basine has just told me, when she brought home the laundry, that she is taking over from Madame Prieur. I'll go back and work for her!'

'You won't stay there long!' David exclaimed. 'I've found what I was after . . . '

For the first time, the sublime certainty of success which keeps inventors in good heart and encourages them to press on in the virgin forest of the land of discovery was greeted by Eve with a smile which was almost sad. David's head drooped in a gesture of despondency.

'Oh my dear! I'm not mocking or laughing at you. I'm not doubting you,' said the lovely Eve, falling on her knees before her husband. 'But I do see how right you were to be very secretive about your experiments and hopes. Yes, my dear, an inventor must hide from everyone the painful travail which is to lead him to glory, even from his wife. A wife is always a wife. Your Eve has been unable to refrain from smiling on hearing you say, for the seventeenth time in the last month: "At last I've got it!" '

David began to laugh so heartily at himself that Eve took his hand and reverently kissed it. It was a moment of delight: one of those roses, symbolic of love and tenderness, which one finds blooming alongside the most arid paths of misery, and sometimes even at the bottom of a precipice.

13. A contrast in loyalties

EVE'S courage increased the more misfortune raged against them. Her husband's great-heartedness, his ingenuousness as an inventor, the tears she sometimes discerned in the eyes of this man of feeling and imagination, all of this developed in her an extraordinary power of endurance. She had once more recourse to an expedient which she had already found to be so successful. She wrote to Monsieur Métivier asking him to advertize the sale of the printing-office, offering to pay their debt from the price obtained for it and begging him not to ruin David by creating unnecessary costs. Métivier paid no heed to this moving letter: his chief clerk replied that in Monsieur Métivier's absence he could not take it upon himself to call a halt to the proceedings, for that was not usually the way his employer conducted his affairs. Eve offered to renew the bills and pay all the costs, and the clerk agreed to this provided that David Séchard's father furnished a guarantee by endorsing them. Eve then went on foot to Marsac, accompanied by her mother and Kolb. She confronted the aged vine-grower. She used her charm, and brought smiles to his wrinkled old face; but when, with trembling heart, she mentioned the endorsement, his drink-sodden countenance showed a sudden and complete change.

'If I give my son a chance to put his hand to my lips ... I mean to the edge of my cash-box ... he'd push it right down into my guts and drain them dry. All children have an itch to get their fingers into their father's purse ... How did *I* manage? I never cost my parents a farthing. Your printing-works isn't a going concern. The only printing that's done there is by the rats and mice ... You're a pretty girl, you are, and I like you. You're a careful, hard-working wife. But what about my son? ... You'd like to know what David is? I'll tell you. He's a good-for-nothing, a scholar! If I'd left him to himself as I was left to myself and not had him taught reading and writing, if I'd made a "bear" of him like his Dad was, he'd be drawing interest now on his capital. Oh, he's my cross in life, that lad is. It's pity he's the only one: I'm too old to pull off another copy! What's worse, he's making you unhappy.'

Eve's gesture at this was a protest of absolute denial. 'Yes he is,' he went on in answer to this gesture. 'You've had to take a wet-nurse because worry has dried up your milk. You see, I know all about it! You've been taken to court and the whole town's shouting about it. I was only a "bear". I'm no scholar. I never had a foreman's job at the Didots, a first-rate printing-firm. But I've never had a summons! D'you know what I say to myself as I work away in my vineyard, looking after the vines and picking the grapes and doing my little jobs? I say to myself: "You poor old fool. You're slaving yourself to death pinching and scraping, and you'll have a fine lot of property. Well, it'll all go to the bailiffs and lawyers ... or else be chucked away on hair-brained ideas." See here, my girl, you're the mother of that little boy who looked to me just the spit of his grandfather when I was holding him at the font with Madame Chardon. Well, think less about Sé-chard and more about that little scamp ... You're the only one I put any trust in ... You could stop him frittering away my goods and chattels, the poor little bit I've saved up ... '

'But my dear Papa Séchard, your son will be your pride and glory. One day he'll make a fortune for himself and he'll have the Cross of the Legion of Honour at his buttonhole.'

'How's he going to get that?' the vine-grower asked.

'You'll see! But in the meantime three thousand francs wouldn't ruin you ... With three thousand francs you could put an end to this law-suit ... All right, if you've no confidence in him, lend them to me. You'll get them back. I'll give you a mortgage on my dowry, on the work I'm going to do ... '

'So David Séchard's being sued!' the vine-grower exclaimed, astonished to learn that what he had supposed to be a slander was the truth. 'That's what comes of being able to sign your name! And what about my rent? ... Very well, young woman, I'll have to go to Angoulême to get things straight and have a talk with my lawyer, Maître Cachan ... You did right to come here ... Forewarned is forearmed!'

After a debate lasting two hours Eve was obliged to go off defeated by the unanswerable argument: 'Women know nothing about business.' She had gone there with a vague hope of success; she was almost a broken woman as she made her way back from Marsac to Angoulême. She reached home just in time to receive notice of the judgement ordering Séchard to pay Métivier in full. In the provinces, even to have a process-server at one's door is an event, but Doublon had been coming much too often recently for tongues not to be wagging in the neighbourhood. Consequently Eve no longer dared leave her house for fear of hearing people whispering as she went by.

'Oh! My brother, my brother!' the poor woman cried as she rushed through the alley and went upstairs. 'I could only forgive you if it had been a question of ... '

'Alas!' said David as he came to meet her. 'It *was* a question of avoiding suicide.'

'Then let's say no more about it ever,' she replied in a gentle tone. 'The woman who took him off into the maelstrom of Paris is criminally to blame! ... And your father, David, is absolutely pitiless! ... We must suffer in silence.'

A timid knock on the door cut short a tender remark which was on David's lips, and Marion presented herself dragging the tall, sturdy Kolb through the first room.

'Madame,' she said. 'Kolb and I knew that Monsieur and Madame were in a big fix. We have eleven hundred francs saved up between us. We thought that they couldn't be better invested than with Madame ... '

'Viz Matame,' Kolb repeated with enthusiasm.

'Kolb!' cried David Séchard. 'You and I will never be parted. Take a thousand francs on account to Cachan, the solicitor, but ask for a receipt. Kolb, let no power on earth wring a word from you about what I'm doing, the hours I spend away from the workshop or what you might see me bringing back. And when I send you looking for herbs – as I do – don't let a single soul see you ... My good Kolb, they'll try to get round you and perhaps offer you a thousand or ten thousand francs if you'll talk ... '

'Efen if zey offeret me millionss, I voult not say von vort! I vass a soltier ant I know zat orterss are orterss.'

'Well, I've warned you. Off you go, and ask Monsieur Petit-Claud to witness the delivery of the money to Monsieur Cachan.'

'Yes inteet,' said the Alsatian. 'Von tay I hope I vill pe rich enough to gif hiss gown a goot dustink, zat man of tchustice! I to not like hiss face!'

'Kolb's a good man, Madame,' said the stout Marion. 'He's as strong as a horse and as mild as a lamb. Just the kind of man to make a woman happy! And mark you, he's the one who had the idea of investing our wages like this. He calls them *vaitches*. Poor man! He talks funny, but he thinks all right, and anyway I can always take his meaning. He's thinking of working extra at some other job so as not to cost us anything ... '

Séchard looked at his wife and said: 'It would be worth getting rich if only to be able to reward such kind souls.' To Eve this was a very natural idea, for she was never astonished to find other people as noble-hearted as herself. Her attitude would have shown the most stupid people, and even cold-hearted persons, what a lovely disposition she had.

'You'll be rich, my dear Monsieur David. Things are going to turn out all right,' Marion exclaimed. 'Put it like this: your father has just bought a farm and is giving you the rent for it ... '

In these circumstances, were not the words Marion uttered, in order to minimize the merit of her action, a sign of exquisite tact?

14. Keeping the fire going

LIKE all man-made things, French legal procedure has its defects. None the less, like a two-edged sword, it is useful both for defence and attack. In addition it has an amusing feature: if two solicitors are on good terms with each other (they can be so without exchanging two words since they understand each other through the simple routine of the procedure they follow), a law-suit in that case is like war as waged by the first Maréchal de Biron who, when his son, during the siege of Rouen, proposed a plan for taking the town in two days, replied: 'You're in a hurry to get home, aren't you?' Two generals can make a war drag on for ever by making no decisive moves and sparing their troops in accordance with the method followed by Austrian generals, whom the Aulic Council never reprimands for letting a plan of action miscarry in order that their soldiers need not miss a meal. Petit-Claud and Doublon went one better than any Austrian general – they modelled themselves on an Austrian of ancient times, Fabius *Cunctator*!

Petit-Claud, who was as unreliable as a mule, was not slow to recognize all the advantages of his position. Once tall Cointet had guaranteed that all his costs would be paid, he set his mind on hoodwinking Cachan and showing the paper-manufacturer how clever he was by creating difficulties for which Métivier would have to foot the bill. Unfortunately for the glory of this young Figaro of the legal confraternity, the historian must glide over the field of his exploits as swiftly as if he were treading on live coals. But no doubt one single memorandum of costs, typical of Parisian procedure, will suffice for this history of contemporary manners. Let us therefore imitate the style of the bulletins of the Grande-Armée. The more succinct our account of Petit-Claud's feats, the better this page of exclusively judicial information will be for the understanding of the story.

Summoned before the Commercial Court of Angoulême

on 3 July, David failed to appear: on 8 July he was notified that judgment had been passed against him. On the 10th, Doublon issued the order to pay and, on the 12th, made an attempt at distraint which Petit-Claud opposed by serving Métivier with a new summons for that day fortnight. The next day Métivier, objecting to such long delay, countered with a peremptory summons and, on the 19th, obtained a judgment rejecting David's demand for stay of execution. This judgment, notified point-blank on the 21st, authorized an order to pay on the 22nd, a writ for David's arrest on the 23rd and the drawing-up of an inventory for distraint on the 24th. Then Petit-Claud put the brake on this feverish haste for distraint by applying to the Court of Appeal for another stay of execution. This appeal, repeated on the 15 July, meant that Métivier's case had to go to Poitiers.

'So far so good!' Petit-Claud said to himself. 'The matter will remain at that stage for quite a time.'

Once the storm had been diverted to Poitiers and the case was in the hands of an advocate of the appeal court briefed by Petit-Claud, this two-faced champion of the Séchard cause induced Eve to take summary proceedings against David for the separation of their estates. To use the current legal jargon, he 'expedited' the affair so as to obtain the judgment of separation on 28 July, inserted it in the *Courrier de la Charente*, gave due notification of it and, on 1 August, the settlement of Madame Séchard's claim was officially carried through: it recognized her as her husband's creditor for the paltry sum of ten thousand francs which the loving David had acknowledged as her dowry in the marriage contract. In discharge of this debt he made over to her the stock-in-trade of the printing-office and the household furniture.

While Petit-Claud was thus safeguarding the family goods and chattels, he was also successfully establishing at Poitiers the contention on which he had based his appeal. He was arguing that David ought not to be liable for the costs incurred in the Paris proceedings against Lucien de Rubempré, because the Civil Court there had judged that they fell to Métivier's charge. This view of the matter, adopted by the

Court, was embodied in an order which confirmed the decisions taken against Séchard junior by the Commercial Court of Angoulême while making a rebate on the Paris costs which were charged to Métivier, thus balancing a portion of the costs between the contending parties in recognition of the point of law which had motivated the Séchard appeal. This decision, notified on 17 August to Séchard junior, was implemented on the 18th by a summons to pay the capital, the interest on it and the costs incurred, and by a writ for distraint on the 20th. At that juncture Petit-Claud intervened on Madame Séchard's behalf and claimed the furniture as belonging to the consort, whose property had been formally sequestrated. What is more, Petit-Claud brought Séchard senior, now his client, into the case, for the following reason:

The day after his daughter-in-law's visit, the vine-grower had come to Angoulême to consult his solicitor, Maître Cachan, on means to be adopted in order to recover his rent payments, jeopardized by the legal wrangles in which his son was involved.

Cachan told him: 'I cannot act for the father while I am suing the son. But go and see Petit-Claud. He's a very able man and will probably serve you even better than I could.' And when they met in court, Cachan said to Petit-Claud: 'I've sent old Séchard to you. Take him on instead of me on a give-and-take basis.' – In the provinces as in Paris, solicitors do one another these mutual services.

The day after old Séchard had entrusted his interests to Petit-Claud, tall Cointet came to see his accomplice and said: 'Try and teach old Séchard a lesson! He's the sort of man who'll never forgive his son for landing him in for a thousand francs' costs: a disbursement like that will dry up any generous impulse in his heart, even if he had one!'

'Go back to your vineyards,' Petit-Claud told his new client. 'Your son is in difficulties. Don't sponge on him by eating his food. I'll send for you when the time comes.'

And so, in Séchard's name, Petit-Claud claimed that the presses now under seal were real estate thanks to the purpose they served, the more so because the building itself had been

545

a printing-office since the reign of Louis XIV. Cachan, indignant on Métivier's behalf – after finding that Lucien's furniture in Paris belonged to Coralie, Métivier was now discovering that David's furniture in Angoulême belonged to his wife and father (some cutting remarks were made about this at the hearing) – proceeded against both father and son with a view to demolishing their claims. 'Our aim,' he vociferated in Court, 'is to unmask the frauds of these men who are building up a most formidable defence-work of bad faith and entrenching themselves behind the clearest and most straightforward articles of the Code. And for what purpose? To avoid paying three thousand francs which have been rifled from the unfortunate Métivier's coffers. And people dare to accuse the discount-brokers! . . . In what times are we living? . . . In fact, I ask you, gentlemen, is there not a general scramble to lay hands on one's neighbour's money? . . . You will certainly not sanction a claim which would bring immorality into the very heart of justice! . . . ' The Angoulême court, moved by Cachan's eloquent plea, gave a judgment, after a full hearing, which ceded the ownership of only movable furniture to Madame Séchard, rejected the claims of Séchard senior and flatly ordered him to pay four hundred and thirty-four francs and sixty-five centimes in costs.

'Old Séchard is good for the money,' the solicitors said with a laugh. 'He insisted on putting his foot in it. Let him pay! . . . '

Notice of the judgment was given on 26 August, which meant that the presses and appurtenances of the printing-office could be put under distraint on the 28th. The placards were duly posted. An order was applied for and obtained for the sale to take place on the premises. An announcement of the sale was inserted in the newspapers, and Doublon flattered himself that he would be able to proceed with the verification of the inventory and hold the sale on September 2nd.

David now owed Métivier, by formal judgment and valid writs of execution – quite legally in fact – the lump sum of five thousand two hundred francs and twenty-five centimes exclusive of interest. He owed Petit-Claud twelve hundred francs plus his fees, the figure for which, by analogy with the noble trustfulness of a cabman who has driven fast to satisfy his customer, was left to his generosity. Madame Séchard owed Petit-Claud about three hundred and fifty francs, and fees into the bargain. Old Séchard's debt came to four hundred and thirty-four francs and sixty-five centimes, and Petit-Claud also demanded three hundred francs from him in fees. The whole thus amounted to some ten thousand francs.

Apart from the use these particulars may serve in enabling foreign nations to witness the play of judicial artillery fire in France, it is highly desirable that our Parliamentary legislators, supposing of course that legislators have time for reading, should know how far the abuse of legal procedure can go. Should not some minor enactment be speedily passed which in certain cases would forbid solicitors to let costs exceed the sum with which the law-suit is dealing? Is there not something absurd in subjecting a property of one square metre to the same formalities as govern a piece of land worth a million? This very terse account of all the phases through which the Séchard proceedings passed will enlighten readers about the value of such terms as *rules of procedure*, *justice* and *costs*! All this is double Dutch to the vast majority of Frenchmen. It is all part and parcel of what the legal confraternity calls 'setting a man's business on fire'. David's printing type, five thousand pounds in weight, was worth two thousand francs for the metal it contained. The three presses were worth six hundred francs. The rest of the plant might just as well have been sold off as scrap-iron or mouldy wood. The household furniture would have fetched a thousand francs at most. Thus, of values belonging to David Séchard and representing a total of about four thousand francs, Cachan and Petit-Claud had made a pretext for extorting seven thousand francs in costs without reckoning in future perquisites – and the buds in blossom promised very fine fruit, as will be seen. Certainly legal practitioners in the kingdom of France and Navarre – those in Normandy above all – will accord their esteem and admiration to Petit-Claud. But will not good-hearted people spare a tear of sympathy for people like Kolb and Marion?

While this conflict went on, Kolb, sitting in a chair by the alley door so long as David did not need him, carried out his duties as watch-dog. He took in the official writs, though always under the surveillance of one of Petit-Claud's clerks. When placards announcing the sale of the printing-house stock were affixed, Kolb tore them down as fast as the bill-poster stuck them up. He even rushed through the town to do the same there, crying out the while: 'Ze scountrelss! . . . Plaquink so goot a man! . . . Ant zey call zat tchustice!' In the mornings Marion was earning fifty centimes turning a wheel in a paper-mill and she used them for the daily expenses. Madame Chardon had uncomplainingly resumed the exhausting vigils of her profession as a nurse, and every weekend she handed her wages over to her daughter. She had already made two novenas, but was astonished to find God deaf to her prayers and blind to the gleam of the candles she lit.

15. Climax

ON 3 September Eve received the only letter Lucien wrote to her after the one in which he had announced the circulation of the three bills drawn on his brother-in-law and which David had concealed from his wife.

'And this is only the third letter I've had from him since he left us!' Lucien's afflicted sister said to herself as she hesitatingly unsealed the fatal screed. At that moment, she was giving her child his milk – she was bottle-feeding him, for she had not been able to afford to keep on the wet-nurse. One can imagine the state she was in after reading the following letter; David also, whom she woke up. After spending the night at his paper-making, the inventor had gone to bed at about daybreak.

My dear sister,

Two days ago, at five in the morning, one of God's loveliest creatures breathed her last: the only woman who was capable of loving me as you, David and my mother love me, and who added to such affectionate feeling what a mother and sister could not give – all the bliss of passionate love! Coralie sacrificed everything to me and probably died because of me. For me, who at present haven't even the money for her funeral! She would have consoled me for the fact of being alive; you alone, dear angels, will be able to console me for her death. This innocent-hearted girl has, I believe, received absolution from her Maker, for she died a Christian death.

Oh, Paris! ... My Eve, Paris is at once the glory and all the infamy of France. I have lost many illusions here, and I shall lose many more as I go about begging for the little money I need in order to bury an angel's body in consecrated ground!

Your unhappy brother,
LUCIEN.

P.S. I must have brought you much sorrow through my frivolity: one day you will know all and forgive me. In any case, you need not worry. When he saw that Coralie and I were in such straits, a worthy merchant of the name of Camusot whom I had caused much cruel affliction, undertook, so he said, to settle this affair.

'The letter is still wet with his tears!' said Eve to David, and she looked at him with so much pity that some gleam of his former affection for Lucien showed in his eyes also.

'Poor boy, he must have suffered very much if he was loved as he says he was,' exclaimed the man who had found happiness in marriage.

And both husband and wife forgot their own sorrows, faced as they were with this cry of incomparable grief. At that moment Marion rushed in and said: 'Madame, here they are! ... Here they are!'

'Who?'

'That demon Doublon and his men. Kolb is struggling with them. They are going to sell us up.'

'No, no, they shall not sell you up, don't be alarmed!' cried Petit-Claud in a voice which echoed through the room leading to the bedroom. 'I have just launched an appeal.

We must not submit to a judgment which taxes us with bad faith. To gain time for you, I have allowed Cachan to go on blathering. I'm sure of getting the better of him again at Poitiers.'

'But how much will it cost us?' asked Madame Séchard.

'Legal fees if you win, a thousand francs if we lose.'

'Good Heavens!' poor Eve cried. 'Isn't the remedy worse than the disease?' – When he heard this cry of innocence, now clear-sighted thanks to the glare judicial procedure was casting on their predicament, Petit-Claud stood quite abashed, so impressed he was by Eve's beauty.

At this juncture old Séchard put in his appearance. He had been summoned by Petit-Claud. The presence of this old man in the young couple's bedroom, with his grandson in his cradle smiling amid all this sorrow, gave the finishing touch to this scene.

'Papa Séchard,' said the young lawyer, 'You owe me seven hundred francs for having intervened in this case; but you will claim them as against your son and add them to the rent payments due to you.'

The old vinegrower was alive to the stinging irony which Petit-Claud's air and tone of voice conveyed as he made this remark.

'It would have cost you less to have stood surety for your son!' said Eve as she came forward from the cradle to embrace the old man.

David, overwhelmed at the sight of the crowd which had gathered in front of his house, to which Kolb's scuffle with Doublon's assistants had attracted many people, tendered a hand to his father without wishing him good-day.

'Seven hundred francs! How can I owe you that?' the old man asked Petit-Claud.

'In the first place, because I have acted for you. Since it's a question of your rents, as far as I am concerned you and your debtor are jointly responsible. If your son doesn't pay me the costs for this, you'll have to pay them . . . But that's a trifling matter. In an hour or two they'll try to get your son in prison. Will you let him be taken there?'

'How much does he owe?'

'Something to the tune of five or six thousand francs, apart from what he owes you and what he owes his wife.'

The old man, now suspicious of all and sundry, looked round at the touching spectacle before his eyes in this blue and white bedroom: a lovely woman in tears over her son's cradle, David, at last bending under the weight of his afflictions, and the solicitor, who had perhaps brought him to this pass in order to entrap him. The 'bear' then decided that they were staking on his paternal benevolence, and he was afraid of being exploited. He went over to fondle the child who stretched out his tiny hands to him. In the midst of all this anxiety the tiny boy, who was wearing a little embroidered bonnet with a pink lining, was the object of as much attention as the son of an English peer.

'All right,' the old grandfather blurted out. 'Let David manage as best he can. All I'm thinking of is the baby, and his mother will back me in this. David's such a scholar that he'll surely manage to pay his debts.'

'I'm going to translate your feelings into plain language,' said the solicitor with a sarcastic air. 'See now, Papa Séchard, you're jealous of your son. Listen to the truth: it's you who put David in his present predicament by selling him your printing-works for three times its real value and you've ruined him by making him pay this exorbitant price. It's a fact. Don't shake your head. The price the Cointets paid for the periodical – and you pocketed the whole of it – was all your printing-press was worth ... You hate your son, not only because you've fleeced him, but more so still because you've made him a far better man than you are. You're making a pretence of prodigious love for your grandson in order to disguise the bankruptcy of your feelings for your son and daughter-in-law who might cost you money *hic et nunc*, whereas your grandson will need your affection only when you're *in extremis*. You fondle that little one so that you may appear to love someone in your family and not be taxed with hardheartedness. That's all there is to it, Papa Séchard.'

'Is that why you sent for me, in order to tell me that?' the old man said in blustering tones, looking round in turn at the solicitor, his daughter-in-law and his son.

'Monsieur Petit-Claud,' cried the unhappy Eve, 'are you dead set on ruining us? Never has my husband complained about his father.' – The vine-grower cast a mocking glance at his daughter-in-law – 'He has told me a hundred times that you're fond of him in your way,' she said to the old man, for she was able to understand why he was so much on his guard.

Complying with tall Cointet's instructions, Petit-Claud was completing the task of embroiling father and son so that the father should not extricate his son from the cruel situation in which he found himself. 'The day when we get David in prison,' tall Cointet had told him the evening before, 'you will be introduced to Madame de Sénonches.' The understanding born of affection had given enlightenment to Madame Séchard, who tumbled to the lawyer's show of severity as easily as she had sensed Cérizet's treachery. The reader will readily understand David's air of surprise. He could not fathom why Petit-Claud knew so much about his father and his affairs. The honest printer knew nothing about the connivance between his solicitor and the Cointets. Nor did he realize that the Cointets were hand in glove with Métivier. David said nothing, and the old vine-grower took this as an insult. And so the solicitor took advantage of his client's astonishment in order to withdraw.

'Good-bye, my dear David. I warn you: imprisonment for debt cannot be invalidated by appeal. That is the only recourse left to your creditors, and they'll make use of it. And so, get away from here!... Or rather, if you'll take my advice, go and see the brothers Cointet. They have capital, and if you've brought your invention to completion and if it comes up to expectations, go into partnership with them. After all, they're very decent people ...'

'What invention?' old Séchard asked.

'Well now, do you think your son's such a fool as to have given up his printing without having something else in mind?' the solicitor exclaimed. 'He's on the way, he tells me, to discovering a process for manufacturing a ream of paper for three francs. The present cost is ten francs ...'

'One more trick for catching me,' old Séchard cried. 'You're all as thick as thieves. If David has made an invention like that he doesn't need me. He'll be a millionaire! Good-bye, my friends. Nothing doing.' And the old man clattered down-stairs.

'You must go into hiding,' said Petit-Claud to David as he ran after old Séchard with a view to getting him still more exasperated. The diminutive solicitor caught up with the grumbling vine-grower at the Place du Mûrier and escorted him as far as L'Houmeau. As he left him he threatened to serve him with a writ for the costs due to him if he was not paid within a week. Old Séchard replied: 'I'll pay them if you can find some way for me to disinherit my son without cutting out my grandson and daughter-in-law!' And he abruptly took leave of Petit-Claud.

'How well tall Cointet understands these people! ... Yes, he was right! Having to pay seven hundred francs will prevent the father from paying the seven thousand francs which his son owes!' Such were the little solicitor's reflections as he made his way to Angoulême. 'Nevertheless I must not let Cointet get the better of me. It's time I asked this wily old paper-manufacturer for something more than words.'

'Well, David my dear, what are you thinking of doing?' Eve asked her husband when old Séchard and the solicitor had left them.

'Put your biggest pan on the fire, my girl,' cried David to Marion. 'I've solved the problem.' On hearing these words, Eve took up her hat, shawl and shoes in a fever of excite-ment. 'Get your clothes on, my friend,' she said to Kolb. 'You shall go with me, for I must know if there's a way out of this inferno ... '

'Monsieur David,' Marion exclaimed once Eve had gone. 'Do be reasonable, or Madame will die of grief. Earn some money to pay what you owe, and after that you can spend all the time you like searching for your treasure ... '

'Be quiet, Marion,' David replied. 'The final difficulty will be overcome. I shall get the two patents I need: the one for invention, and the one for improvement.'

The patent of improvement is a plague for inventors in

France. A man spends ten years of his life researching into a new industrial process, a machine, some discovery or other; he takes out his patent and believes he has everything under control. Then he finds a competitor on his heels, and if he has not foreseen every contingency this man perfects the invention by adding a screw, and thus takes it out of his hands. The fact of inventing a cheap pulp for papermaking did not clinch the matter: others might improve on the process. David wanted to allow for every possibility so that the fortune for which he had striven in such adverse circumstances should not be snatched from his grasp. Holland paper (paper made entirely from linen rag still keeps this name although it is no longer made in Holland) is only lightly-sized. If it became possible to size the pulp in the vat with a fairly cheap size (that is in fact what is done today, but the process is still imperfect) there could be no further 'improvement'. For a month then David had been trying to size his pulp in the vat and was thus aiming at two simultaneous discoveries.

Eve went to see her mother. By a lucky chance, Madame was nursing Madame Milhaud, the Deputy Public Attorney's wife, who had just presented the Milhaud family at Nevers with an heir presumptive. Eve distrusted all the ministerial officials and had had the idea of consulting the legal champion of widows and orphans about her position and asking him if she could extricate David by standing surety for him and liquidating her own rights; but she was also hoping to learn the truth about Petit-Claud's ambiguous dealings.

Impressed by Madame Séchard's beauty, the magistrate received her not only with the consideration due to a woman, but also with a kind of courtesy to which she was not accustomed. At long last the poor woman read in the magistrate's eyes an expression which, since her marriage, she had only read in Kolb's eyes. That, for beautiful women like Eve, is a criterion for judging men. When some ruling passion, or self-interest, or old age puts a chill in a man's eyes and quenches the gleam of complete deference which is ablaze in a young man's eyes, a woman then conceives mistrust for such a man and begins to watch him closely. The Cointets, Petit-Claud, Cérizet, every man in whom Eve had divined hostility, had looked at her with a dry, cold eye. She therefore felt at ease with this magistrate. But although he gave her a gracious hearing, a few words from him sufficed to crush all her hopes.

'It is not certain, Madame,' he said, 'that the Court of Appeal will reverse the decision limiting to movable furniture the cession which your husband has made to you of all he possessed in satisfaction of your claim. The privilege you enjoy ought not to serve as cover for fraudulence. However, since as a creditor you will be entitled to your share in the price obtained for the articles distrained, and since your father-in-law will have a preferential claim for the amount of rent due, there will be, once the court has made its order, matter for still further contestation in regard to what in legal terms we call a *contribution*.'

'But in that case Monsieur Petit-Claud is bringing us to ruin?'

'Petit-Claud's procedure in this affair,' the magistrate went on, 'is in conformity with the instructions of your husband who, according to his solicitor, wants to gain time. In my view it would perhaps be better to withdraw the appeal and, when the auction comes off, to buy in the apparatus most necessary for the running of your business: you to the limit of what should be restored to you, and your father-in-law for the amount of his rents ... But that would be rushing things too much for the lawyers: they are battening on you!'

'In that case I should be in the hands of Monsieur Séchard senior, to whom I should owe rent for the apparatus and rent for the house. But my husband would still be subject to prosecution from Monsieur Métivier, who would have scarcely got anything back.'

'That is so, Madame.'

'So then our position would be even worse than it is now ...'

'The law, Madame, comes down in the long run on the creditor's side. You received three thousand francs, and it goes without saying that you must pay them back.'

'Oh, Monsieur, do you think we are capable of . . . ' – Eve stopped short on realizing the danger her brother might incur if she exonerated David and herself.

'Oh, I well know that there are obscurities in this case, both as regards the debtors who are honest, scrupulous and even high-minded people . . . and as regards the creditor, who is merely a man of straw.'

Eve was appalled and gave the magistrate a bewildered stare.

'You must realize,' he said, looking at her with an undisguisedly sly expression, 'that we magistrates have plenty of time for reflecting on what is happening before our eyes as we sit listening to the learned counsels' speeches.'

Eve went home in despair at having made no headway. That evening, at seven, Doublon brought the court order giving notice of David's impending arrest. Thus, at this moment, the proceedings against him reached their climax.

'From tomorrow onwards,' said David, 'I shall only be able to go out at night.'

Eve and Madame Chardon burst into tears. For them, to go into hiding was a disgrace.

16. Imprisonment for debt in the provinces

ON learning that their master's liberty was threatened, Kolb and Marion were so much the more alarmed because they had long since recognized that he was completely guileless. They were so concerned for him that they came to see Madame Chardon, Eve and David under the pretext of asking how their devotion could be put to good effect. They arrived just at the moment when these three persons, for whom life had been so simple until then, were weeping at the thought of having to keep David in concealment. How indeed could they elude the invisible spies who from that instant would be watching every move of this lamentably absent-minded man?

'If Matame vill vait tchust a qvarter off an hour, I vill to a pit of reconnoitrink in ze enemy camp,' said Kolb. 'You vill see zat I know my way apout, efen if I look like a Tcherman. But I am a true Frentchman, ant I am cunnink enough.'

'Yes, Madame, let him go,' said Marion. 'He only wants to protect Monsieur; that's all he's thinking of. He's ... what shall I say? ... a real Newfoundland dog.'

'Go, my good Kolb,' said David. 'We still have time to come to a decision.'

Kolb went off quietly to the bailiff's house, where David's enemies, in counsel together, were devising means to lay hands on him.

To put debtors under arrest in the provinces is as exceptional and abnormal an occurrence as could be imagined. To begin with, every person is too well known for anyone to take so odious a step. Creditors and debtors have to live out their whole lives face to face. Moreover, when a defaulting trades-man is contemplating bankruptcy on a large scale – in the provinces business ethics are uncompromisingly severe against this kind of legal robbery – he takes sanctuary in Paris. To some extent Paris is to the provinces what Belgium is to France: almost inaccessible hide-outs can be found there and the process-server's writ has no validity outside his legal area. In the second place, there are other impediments which make it virtually null and void. For instance, the law estab-lishing the inviolability of the domicile holds good without exception in the provinces; a process-server is not entitled, as he is in Paris, to make ingress into a third person's house in order to apprehend a debtor. Our legislators deemed it necessary to make exception for Paris because there the same building regularly houses several different families. But in the provinces, even in order to intrude into the debtor's own domicile, the process-server must have a *juge de paix*[1] with him. Now this magistrate, who has control over the process-server, is more or less free to grant or refuse his cooperation. It must be said in praise of these *juges de paix* that this obli-gation weighs heavily with them and that they are unwilling

1. A paid magistrate who deals with minor civil and criminal cases: not to be confused with the English 'justice of the peace'.

to serve blind passion or personal vindictiveness. And there are other no less grave obstacles tending to mitigate the wholly useless cruelty of the law on arrest for debt through the operation of moral scruples which often modify and almost nullify the laws. In large cities there are plenty of depraved, unprincipled wretches who are ready to serve as informers. But in a small town everyone is too well known to put himself in the pay of a bailiff. Anyone, even in the lowest strata of society, who lent himself to this kind of baseness would be obliged to leave the town. And so, the arrest of debtors not being, as in Paris and other great centres of population, a privileged function like that of the 'Gardes du Commerce', it becomes an exceedingly difficult operation of legal procedure, a battle of wits between the debtor and the process-server, and the stratagems devised have occasionally provided very amusing news-items for the newspapers.

The elder Cointet had not wanted to appear in person, but stout Cointet, who made out that he was acting for Métivier, had called on Doublon with Cérizet, now one of his compositors, whose cooperation had been acquired by the promise of a thousand-franc note. Doublon had two of his own men to assist him, so that the Cointets already had three bloodhounds to keep watch over their prey. Moreover, when it came to the act of arrest, Doublon was entitled to employ the police militia which, by the terms of the court decisions, is obliged to give its support to the bailiff who calls for it. These five persons were therefore assembled at that very moment in Maître Doublon's private office, situated on the ground-floor of the house and adjoining the main office.

Access to this office was given by a fairly wide paved corridor which formed a sort of alley. The house had a single-leaf door, on either side of which were the gilded escutcheons of the Court in the centre of which BAILIFF was inscribed in black letters. The two windows of the office opening on to the street were protected by stout iron bars. The private room looked out on to a garden in which the bailiff, a votary of Pomona, himself cultivated his espaliers with great success. The kitchen stood opposite the office, and behind it ran a staircase leading to the upper storey. The house itself stood in a little street behind the law-courts, then under construction, but only to be finished after 1830. These details are not without utility for the understanding of what happened to Kolb. The Alsatian had had the idea of presenting himself to the process-server on the pretext of betraying his master – in order thereby to find out what traps were to be laid for him and circumvent them. The cook opened the door and Kolb expressed the desire to talk to Monsieur Doublon on business. Vexed at being disturbed while she was washing up, the woman opened the door of the office and told Kolb, whom she did not know, to wait there for Monsieur, who was at that moment holding consultation in his inner room. Then she went and informed her master that a man wanted to speak to him. The word 'man' so evidently meant 'peasant' that Doublon said: 'Let him wait!' Kolb sat down close to the door of the private room.

'Now then,' said stout Cointet, 'how do you propose to proceed? If we could nab him tomorrow morning it would be so much time gained.'

'Nothing could be easier.' cried Cérizet. 'He's quite rightly called the Gaffer. He makes gaffes in plenty.'

On recognizing stout Cointet's voice and above all on hearing these two remarks, Kolb immediately guessed that they were talking about his master, and his astonishment increased when he picked out Cérizet's voice.

'A fellow who hass eaten his preat!' he exclaimed, horror-stricken.

'Now, friends,' said Doublon, 'this is what we have to do. We'll spread our men round at wide intervals, from the rue de Beaulieu and the Place du Mûrier in every direction, so that we can follow the Gaffer (I like that nickname) without his noticing, and we'll keep on his track until he's got into the house where he proposes to hide. We'll leave him for a few days until he feels secure, then we'll pounce on him some day before sunrise or sunset.'

'But what's he up to just now? He might slip away,' said stout Cointet.

'He's at home,' said Maître Doublon. 'I should know if he went out. I have one of my practitioners (bailiffs call their assistants by this honorable title) on watch in the Place du Mûrier, another at the corner of the law-courts, another thirty yards away from his house. If our quarry came out they would give a whistle, and he wouldn't have taken three steps without my already knowing it thanks to this telegraphic means of communication.'

To hear this was a piece of luck on which Kolb had not reckoned. He quietly left the office and told the servant: 'Monsieur Touplon vill pe encatchet for a lonk time. I vill kom pack early in ze mornink.'

The Alsatian, who had been a cavalryman, had been seized with an idea which he immediately proceeded to carry out. He hurried to a man he knew who hired out horses, chose a horse, had it saddled, and returned at full speed to his master's house, where he found Eve plunged in grief.

'What is it, Kolb?' the printer asked on seeing the Alsatian in a state of mind which was both jubilant and disturbed.

'You haf scountrelss all rount you. Ze best sink iss to hite ze master. Has Matame tought off somevere to put Monsieur out off ze vay?'

The honest Kolb told them of Cérizet's treachery, the ring of spies circling the house and the part that stout Cointet was playing in the business. He also gave them some foreknowledge of the tricks these men were likely to devise against his master, and this threw a very sinister light on David's predicament.

'Then it's the Cointets who are suing you,' poor Eve, quite dumbfounded, exclaimed. 'Since they're paper-manufacturers they're out after your secret.'

'But what can be done to keep David out of their clutches?' asked Madame Chardon.

'If Matame can fint some little place for Monsieur to hite in,' said Kolb, 'I untertake to get him zere vizout anypoty efer knowink.'

'Wait till night-fall,' Eve replied, 'and go and stay with Basine Clerget. I'll go and arrange it all with her. In a case like this Basine will stand by me through thick and thin.'

David recovered his wits and found his tongue at last. 'The spies will follow you. We must find a way to warn Basine without either of us going there.'

'Matame can go zere,' said Kolb. 'Zis iss my plan: I vill go out viz Monsieur and ve vill traw ze vistlerss avay on our tracks. Turink zis time, Matame vill go ant see Matemoisselle Clerchet ant vill not pe followet. I haf a horse, Monsieur vill rite pehint me. Ze tefil take me if zey catch us!'

'Very well . . . Good-bye, my dear,' the poor woman cried, throwing herself into her husband's arms. 'None of us will come to see you, because that might lead to your arrest. We must say good-bye for the whole duration of this voluntary imprisonment. We'll write to each other by post. Basine will put yours in the letter-box, and I'll address mine to you in her name.'

As they went out David and Kolb heard the spies whistling and drew them off to the bottom of the Porte Palet where the horse-dealer lived. There Kolb took his master on the crupper and recommended him to hold on tight.

'Vistle avay, vistle avay, goot frients,' cried Kolb. 'I make foolss off all off you. You vont catch an olt cafalryman!'

And the old cavalryman spurred on into the country at a speed which necessarily made it impossible for the spies either to follow them or to guess where they were going.

Meanwhile Eve went to see Postel on the ingenious pretext of consulting him. After stomaching the insulting kind of pity which is prodigal only of words, she left him and reached Basine's house without being seen. She confided her griefs to her and asked her for succour and protection. Basine, who for greater precaution had drawn Eve into her bedroom, opened the door of an adjacent dressing-room which had a hinged skylight through which no eye could peer. The two friends opened up a small fire-place whose chimney-pipe ran parallel with the one belonging to the workshop in which the laundresses kept a fire going to heat their irons. Eve and Basine spread some shabby blankets on the floor-tiles to muffle any noise that David might inadvertently make. They gave him a trestle-bed to sleep on, a stove for his experiments, and a table and chair for sitting down to write. Basine promised to bring him food at night, and since no one ever found their way into this room, David could defy all his enemies, and even the police.

'There we are then,' said Eve, embracing her friend. 'He's safe now.'

She returned to Postel's house in order, so she said, to clear up some doubt which had brought her back to consult so learned a juryman in the Tribunal du Commerce, and she got him to escort her home while she listened to his whinings. 'You wouldn't be in a mess like this if you had married me!' This was the burden of every sentence the little apothecary uttered. When he was home again, Postel found his wife in a fit of jealousy because of Madame Séchard's remarkable beauty. Furious at the politeness her husband had shown, Léonie was only pacified by the opinion the apothecary claimed to hold about the superiority of red-headed over dark-haired women. The latter, he maintained, were like beautiful thoroughbreds which always had to be kept in the stable. No doubt he put up a good show of sincerity, for the next day Madame Postel was in a simperingly affectionate mood.

'We can set our minds at rest,' Eve said to her mother and Marion, whom she found, to use Marion's own expression, still 'all of a flutter'.

When Eve cast an involuntary glance into the bedroom, Marion told her: 'They've gone.'

17. An obdurate father

'VERE shoult ve go?' asked Kolb, when they were a few miles along the main road to Paris.

'Marsac,' David answered. 'Since we're half way there I'm going to make a last appeal to my father's feelings.'

'I myself voult razer leat a tcharche against a pattery of cannonss. Monsieur's fazer hass no heart.'

The old pressman had no faith in his son. Like all working-class people, he judged by results. In the first place he would not admit that he had despoiled David. In the second place, without taking into account the fact that times had changed, he thought to himself: 'I made him boss of a printing-office, the same as I had been myself. He knew a lot more about it than I did, and yet he couldn't make a go of it!' Totally incapable of understanding his son, he passed judgement on him and assumed a sort of superiority over this highly intelligent man by telling himself: 'After all, I'm saving up food and drink for him.'

Kolb and David arrived at Marsac at eight o'clock and caught the old fellow as he was finishing dinner and therefore on the point of going to bed.

'So the beaks still let you come to see me*' he said to his son with a bitter smile.

'How can you ant my master efer come togezzer?' cried the indignant Kolb. 'He iss flyink high in ze skiess and you are alvays vine-pippink . . . Gif him vat he neets! Zat iss vat a fazzer iss for!'

'Now, Kolb, be off, and stable the horse with Madame Courtois so as not to bother my father with it. And learn this fact: fathers are always in the right.'

Kolb went off growling like a dog who, though scolded by his master for his vigilance, lies down – but only under protest. Then, without revealing his secret process, David offered to give his father the clearest possible proof of his discovery and proposed that he should have a stake in the concern in return for the money David now needed in order to shake free from legal pursuit, so that he might give himself up to the exploitation of his invention.

'Come on now, how can you prove you can make fine paper out of nothing and one which will cost nothing?' the ex-typographer demanded, throwing his son a drunken, but astute, inquisitive and avid glance, which was like a flash of lightning darting through a rain-cloud; for the old 'bear', keeping to his long-established practice, never went to bed without his 'night-cap', consisting of two bottles of excellent old wine at which, as he put it, he took a sip now and then.

'That's an easy matter,' David replied. 'I have no paper on

me. I came here to get away from Doublon and, happening to be on the way to Marsac, I thought I could certainly find in your house the facilities which even a money-lender would give me. I have nothing here but the clothes I stand up in. Shut me up in a sealed-up out-house which no one can enter and in which no one can see me. And then . . . '

'What!' said the old man, casting a terrible glance at his son. 'You won't let me watch you while you work?'

'My father,' David replied. 'You have proved to me that in business fathers don't exist . . . '

'So you don't trust the man who brought you into the world.'

'It's not that. I don't trust the man who robbed me of the means of living in it.'

'You're right! Everyone for himself!' said the old man. 'Very well, I'll put you in my store-room.'

'I shall take Kolb in with me, and you'll give me a cauldron to make my pulp,' David continued, without noticing the look his father shot at him. 'Then you'll go out and find me some artichoke and asparagus stalks, stinging nettles and reeds which you'll cut from the banks of your little river. Tomorrow morning I shall come out of your store-room with some magnificent paper.'

'If you can do that,' cried the Bear, with a hiccough, 'I'll give you maybe . . . I'll see if I can give you . . . dammit, I'll give you twenty-five thousand francs – on condition that I get the same amount back every year.'

'Put me to the test, I accept it!' cried David. 'Kolb, get on your horse, ride over to Mansle, buy me a big hair-sieve from the dry cooper and size from a grocer and get back as quickly as you can.'

'Come on, have a drink,' said his father, setting a bottle of wine, some bread and some left-over cold meat in front of his son. 'Get your strength up and I'll go and find you your supply of rags – green rags! May be they're a bit too green! Like the grapes the fox was after!'

Two hours later, at about eleven o'clock, the old man was shutting up his son and Kolb in a little room backing on to his store-room, roofed with gutter-tiles, where he kept the utensils needed for distilling the wines of Angoulême which, as is well known, furnish all the brandies supposed to come from Cognac.

'Why! It's as good as being in a factory,' said David. 'Wood and basins, just what I need.'

'Well, see you tomorrow,' said old Séchard. 'I'll shut you in and let my two dogs loose. That way I'll be sure no one will bring in any paper. Show me the sheets tomorrow and I declare I'll be your partner. Then everything will be straight and above-board.'

Kolb and David let him shut them in and spent about two hours crushing and preparing the stalks with the help of a couple of planks. The fire burned bright and the water boiled. But at about two in the morning Kolb, less busy than David, heard a sound of heavy breathing which ended in a drunken hiccough. He took one of the two candles and began looking all around. Then he caught sight of old Séchard's purple face blocking up a small square aperture cut out of the door leading from the store-room to the distilling-room and concealed behind empty casks. The wily old man had let his son and Kolb into the distilling-room through an outer door which was used for rolling out barrels for delivery. The inner door enabled puncheons to be rolled from the storeroom into the distillery without taking them round the courtyard.

'Ah, Papa Séchard! You are tcheatink, you vant to svintle your son ... Shall I tell you vat you're toink ven you trink a pottle of goot vine? You are qvenchink ze tirst off a scountrel.'

'Oh, father!' said David.

'I came to find out if you needed anything,' said the vine-grower, almost sober by now.

'And it iss for our sakes zat you haf brought a little latter?' said Kolb, clearing the way to the door and opening it. The old man was in his shirt-sleeves and standing on a step-ladder.

'You might break a limb!' cried David.

'I think I must be a sleep-walker,' said the shamefaced

old man as he climbed down. 'The way you don't trust your father gave me bad dreams. I dreamt you were in league with the devil to do something that just can't be done.'

'Ze only tefil here iss your lof for little colt coinss,' said Kolb.

'Father, go back to bed,' said David. 'Shut us in if you like, but don't bother to come back. Kolb will be on guard.'

At four o'clock David came out of the distilling-room after clearing away all traces of his operation and brought his father about thirty sheets of paper whose fineness, whiteness, consistency and strength left nothing to be desired and had as its water-mark the stronger and weaker threads of the hair-sieve. The old man took these samples and put his tongue to them like any old 'bear' accustomed since youth to use his palate as a test of paper. He felt them in his hands, crumpled them, folded them and tried out all the tests which typographers make on paper in order to assess its quality. Although he could find no fault, he was reluctant to admit defeat.

'We must see how it stands up to the presses!' he said, in order to avoid praising his son.

'Vat a schtranche man!' cried Kolb.

The vine-grower, now chilled down, made a pretence of hesitancy and covered it with a show of paternal dignity.

'I don't want to deceive you, father. I think that this paper is still likely to cost too dear, and I want to solve the problem of sizing it in the vat. That's the only improvement I still have to make.'

'Ho! Ho! You're trying to take me in!'

'However . . . can I tell you this much? I can certainly do the sizing in the vat, but so far the size doesn't mix evenly with the pulp and makes the paper as rough as a brush.'

'Very well, perfect your process of sizing in the vat and you shall have my money.'

'My master vill nefer see ze colour of your money!' said Kolb. It was evident that the old man wanted to pay David out for the humiliation he had suffered the previous night. His attitude grew even colder.

'Father,' said David after sending Kolb away. 'I have never borne a grudge against you for having put an exorbitant

566

price on your printing-office and making me buy it on your own valuation. I have always remembered you were my father. I have said to myself: let an old man who has toiled hard and brought me up better than I had a right to expect enjoy the fruits of his labour in peace and in the way he likes. I even surrendered my mother's estate to you and uncomplainingly accepted the debt-encumbered existence to which you reduced me. I promised myself I would make a fine fortune without being a burden to you. Well, I have been through fire and water to make my discovery and have made it, deprived of my daily bread and tortured with debts which I had not myself incurred. Yes, I have struggled on patiently until my strength was exhausted. You ought perhaps to come to my help ... But don't bother about me. Think of my wife and the little child! ... ' (At this point David could not hold back his tears) 'and give them aid and protection. Will you be less generous than Marion and Kolb who have given me their savings?' As he made this appeal he saw that his father was as cold as one of his imposing-stones.

'And you want more still?' the old man exclaimed without feeling the slightest shame. 'Why, you'd swallow up the whole of France ... Nothing doing! I'm too ignorant to dabble in inventions. All the dabbling would be done on me. The "monkey" shan't eat up the "bear",' he said, reverting to printing-office slang. 'I'm a vine-grower, not a banker. And besides, mark my words, no good can come of father and son doing business together. Let's have dinner – you shan't say I don't give you anything at all! ... '

David was one of those men of intense feeling who thrust their sufferings deep down and hide them from those who are dear to them, so that when grief overflows, as his did now, they have reached the limit of endurance. Eve had well understood this trait in her husband's fine character. But his father only looked on this flood of grief welling up from David's heart as the commonplace wailings of a child trying to get his own way with his parents: he attributed his son's extreme dejection to the shame born of failure. When they parted, father and son were at loggerheads.

David and Kolb were back about midnight in Angoulême

which they entered on foot as warily as thieves bent on burglary. At about one in the morning David slipped unobserved into Mademoiselle Basine Clerget's house, the inviolable sanctuary his wife had prepared for him. Once inside, David was to be guarded by the most resourceful kind of compassion, that of a working-class girl. The next morning Kolb boasted that he had helped his master to escape on horseback and had only left him after seeing him into a public vehicle which was to take him to the environs of Limoges.

A considerable amount of raw material was stored in Basine's cellar, so that Kolb, Marion, Madame Séchard and her mother need have no open contact with Mademoiselle Clerget.

18. The pack pauses before the kill

Two days after the scene with his son, old Séchard, who had three weeks to wait before he could begin harvesting his grapes, came bustling to see his daughter-in-law, under the spur of avarice. He could not sleep, so anxious was he to find out if there was any chance of a fortune in David's invention. He intended to keep a weather-eye open, to quote his expression. He installed himself on the floor above his daughter-in-law's apartments in one of the little attic rooms he had reserved for his own use, and he lived there with his eyes shut to the penury from which his son's household was suffering. They owed him rent and the least they could do was to feed him! He saw nothing strange in having his meals served on tin-plate. 'That's how I started,' he answered his daughter-in-law when she apologized for not being able to serve him on silver.

Marion was forced to pledge her credit to the shopkeepers for every commodity the household consumed. Kolb took work with masons for a franc a day. The time soon came when only ten francs remained to the unhappy Eve who, in David's interests and those of her child, was sacrificing her last resources so as to give a good welcome to the vine-grower. She still hoped that her endearing ways, respectful affection and resignation would touch the miser's heart, but she found him always unmoved. In the end, seeing the same coldness in his eyes as in those of the Cointets, Petit-Claud and Cérizet, she tried to observe his character and divine his intentions: labour in vain! Old Séchard made himself unfathomable by maintaining a state of semi-intoxication. Drunkenness is a veil of double thickness. Under cover of tipsiness, as often shammed as real, the wretched man tried to worm David's secret out of Eve. At one moment he would wheedle and at another intimidate her. When Eve replied that she knew nothing, he said: 'I'll buy an annuity and drink all my money.' These degrading altercations wearied his poor victim and in the end, in order not to show disrespect to her father-in-law, she gave up talking to him. But one day, driven to extremities, she said: 'Anyway, father, there's a simple way of getting all you want. Pay David's debt, he'll return home, and you can come to an agreement.'

'Ah! So that's all you want of me,' he exclaimed. 'It's as well I know that.'

Old Séchard had no faith in his son, but he believed in the Cointets. He went to consult them, and they set out to dazzle him with the prospect of millions of francs to be made out of his son's researches.

'If David can prove that he has succeeded,' said tall Cointet, 'I'll not hesitate to turn my paper-factory into a company and go in fifty-fifty with him for his invention.'

The distrustful old man gleaned so much information when taking glasses of cognac with the journeymen-printers, he so effectively sounded Petit-Claud while playing the imbecile that in the end he came to suspect the Cointets of hiding behind Métivier. He credited them with the plan of ruining the Séchard press and getting him to pay the debt by dangling the invention before him as a bait, for as a simple working-class man he was unable to guess at Petit-Claud's complicity or the plot they were hatching to possess themselves sooner or later of this splendid industrial secret. At last the old man, exasperated at his failure to make his daughter-in-law talk or even to find out from her where David was hiding, decided one day to break open the door of the work-shop in which the rollers were cast, having now discovered that it was there that David had been conducting his experiments. He came downstairs early one morning and started tampering with the lock.

'Hey! Papa Séchard, what are you up to?' shouted Marion who had got up at dawn to go to the factory where she was working. She made one leap to the damping-shed.

'I'm at home here, am I not?' the old man said shame-facedly.

'Come off it! Are you taking to burglary in your old age? . . . And yet you're still sober . . . I'm going to tell the mistress about it straight away.'

'Don't say anything, Marion,' the old man begged her, pulling two six-franc pieces out of his pocket. 'Here . . .'

'I'll say nothing, but don't try that on again!' said Marion, wagging a finger at him, 'or I'll tell all Angoulême about it.'

As soon as the old man had gone out, Marion went upstairs to her mistress. 'Look, Madame, I've squeezed twelve francs out of your father-in-law.'

'How did you manage that?'

'Would you believe it? He was trying to take a peep at Monsieur's pans and supplies, hoping to find out the secret. Oh, I knew there was nothing left in the little kitchen, but I pretended to think he was going to rob his son. That scared him, and he gave me twelve francs to keep quiet.'

Just then Basine joyfully brought her friend a letter from David and handed it to her in private. It was written on magnificent paper.

My beloved Eve,

My first letter written on the first sheet of paper my process has produced is for you. I have succeeded in solving the problem of sizing in the vat! One pound of pulp costs twenty-five centimes, even supposing that the produce I use has to be grown on good land. So a twelve-pound ream of paper will use up three francs' worth of sized pulp. I am sure of reducing the weight of books by one-half. The envelope, the letter itself and the samples enclosed were made separately.

All my love. Much-needed wealth will come our way and bring us happiness.

'Look at these,' said Eve, handing the samples to her father-in-law. 'Give your son the price you get for your vintage and let him make his fortune. He'll repay you ten times over. He has reached success!'

Old Séchard immediately hurried round to the Cointets. There every sample was tested and meticulously examined. Some of them were sized, others not; they each had a price-label on them ranging from three to ten francs the ream. Some of them were of metallic hardness, others were as soft as Chinese paper, and there were some which had every possible shade of whiteness. Jews valuing diamonds would not have had a more avid glint in their eyes than these three men.

'Your son is on to a good thing,' said stout Cointet.

'All right then, pay off his debts,' said the old pressman.

'Certainly I will, if he'll take us into partnership,' tall Cointet replied.

'You're a pair of brigands!' the ex-'bear' retorted. 'You're suing my son in Métivier's name and you want me to do the paying. That's what it adds up to. Well, my fine gentlemen, I'm not such a fool!'

The two brothers looked at each other, but managed to conceal the surprise they felt at the miser's shrewdness.

'We're not millionaires,' stout Cointet rejoindered. 'We can't afford to discount bills for fun. We should be only too glad if we ourselves could pay cash for the rags we buy, but we still have to get them on credit.'

'What is needed is a wholesale experiment,' tall Cointet coldly replied. 'What has succeeded in a saucepan may fail in large-scale manufacture. Set your son free of debt!'

'Yes, but once my son is free will he take me as a partner?'

'That's no business of ours,' said stout Cointet. 'Do you imagine, my good man, that when you have given your son ten thousand francs you'll have finished? A patent of invention costs two thousand francs and will involve journeys to Paris. Also, before you start advancing capital, it would be well, as my brother has said, to manufacture a thousand reams and risk whole vatfuls in order to make a check. Mark my words, there's nobody one should be more wary of than inventors.'

'I myself,' said tall Cointet, 'prefer to have my bread ready baked.'

The old man spent the night ruminating over this dilemma: 'If I pay David's debts he'll be free, and once he's free he needn't take me on as a partner. He knows very well I swindled him in our first partnership, and won't feel like starting a second one. So it's in my interest to keep him in prison and down on his luck.'

The Cointets knew old Séchard well enough to be sure that he would keep up with them in the chase. Each one of them was thinking: 'In order to found a company based on a secret process, experiments are needed. In order to make these experiments, David Séchard must be solvent. But once he's solvent he'll be out of our power.' And each of them was making his own mental reservations. Petit-Claud was saying to himself: 'After my wedding I'll pull along with the Cointets, but until then I'll keep a tight rein on them.' Tall Cointet told himself: 'I'd rather keep David under lock and key and have him under my control.' Old Séchard told himself: 'If I pay his debts my son will just thank me and say good-bye.'

As for Eve, with her father-in-law pestering her and threatening to drive her from the house, she refused either to reveal where her husband was sheltering or to advise David to accept safe-conduct. She was not sure that she would be able to find him a second hiding-place better than the first, and so she replied to her father-in-law. 'Set your son free and you shall know everything.' Not one of the four schemers, who were sitting as it were at a sumptuous table, dared begin the banquet, so much did each one fear that the other might get ahead of him. So they all watched one another in mutual suspicion.

19. A bride for Petit-Claud

A few days after David had gone into hiding, Petit-Claud had come to see tall Cointet in his paper-mill.

'I've done my best,' he said. 'David has voluntarily retreated into a prison we can't locate and he's peacefully working to perfect his process. If you haven't yet reached your goal it's no fault of mine. Are you going to keep your part of the bargain?'

'Yes, if we're successful,' tall Cointet replied. 'Old Séchard has been in Angoulême for several days and has come to ask us questions about the manufacture of paper. The old miser's sniffing round his son's invention and wants to make something out of it. Therefore there's some hope of forming a partnership. You are the solicitor of both Father and Son ...'

'You must be the Holy Spirit and lay hands on them!' Petit-Claud continued with a smile.

'Yes,' Cointet replied. 'If you can manage either to put David in prison or to get him into our power by means of a deed of partnership, you shall marry Mademoiselle de La Haye.'

'So that's your *ultimatum*, as the English say?'

'*Yes*,' said Cointet, in English, 'since we're talking foreign languages.'

'I'll give you mine in plain French,' Petit-Claud curtly replied.

'Indeed! Let's hear what it is,' Cointet retorted in a tone of curiosity.

'Introduce me tomorrow to Madame de Sénonches, make a positive arrangement for me, in short fulfil your promise, or I'll pay Séchard's debt, sell my practice and become his partner. I'm not going to be duped by you. You've just been frank with me, I'll be the same with you. I've proved my mettle: you must do the same. So far you've made all the winnings. Unless you give me some pledge of good faith I'll overcall your hand.'

Tall Cointet took up his hat, his umbrella, and, maintaining his jesuitical cast of countenance, he went out, telling Petit-Claud to follow him.

'You'll see, my dear friend, whether I've prepared the way for you or not,' said the tradesman to the solicitor.

The astute and wily paper-manufacturer had been quick to realize the danger he was running, and had recognized that Petit-Claud was one of those men with whom one has to play a straight game. Already, in order to keep abreast with him and salve his conscience, he had made a few quiet hints to the former consul-general on the pretext of giving an account of Mademoiselle de La Haye's financial situation.

'I've a match in view for Françoise, for in these days, with a dowry of only thirty thousand francs, a girl mustn't expect too much,' he said with a smile.

'We'll have a talk about it,' Francis du Hautoy had replied. 'Now that Madame de Bargeton has left Angoulême, the standing of Madame de Sénonches has changed for the better: we can marry Françoise to some worthy elderly country gentleman.'

'And she'll misbehave,' said the paper-manufacturer, putting on his chilly air. 'Come now, marry her to a capable, ambitious young man, one you'll help to get on, one who'll put his wife in a good position.'

'We'll see,' Francis had repeated. 'Before all else we must consult her godmother.'

After Monsieur de Bargeton's death, Louise de Nègrepelisse had put her residence in the rue du Minage up for sale. Madame de Sénonches, considering herself meanly-lodged, persuaded Monsieur de Sénonches to buy the house which had been the cradle of Lucien's ambitions and the opening scene of this story. Zéphirine de Sénonches had conceived the plan of succeeding Madame de Bargeton in the kind of royalty the latter had enjoyed, holding a salon and in fact playing the great lady. A schism had occurred in the high society of Angoulême between those who, when Monsieur de Bargeton fought his duel with Monsieur de Chandour, maintained that Louise de Nègrepelisse was innocent and those who believed the slanders spread about by Stanislas de Chandour. Madame de Sénonches opted for the Bargetons and began by winning over all the adherents to their cause. Then, when she was settled in her new residence, she took advantage of the routine habits of many people who had come there year in year out for an evening of cards. She held an at-home every evening and won a decisive victory over Amélie de Chandour, who posed as her rival. Francis du Hautoy thus found himself in the very centre of the Angoulême aristocracy and let his hopes go so far as to think of marrying Françoise to the aged Monsieur de Séverac, whom Madame du Brossard had failed to capture for her daughter. The return of Madame de Bargeton, now wife of the prefect of Angoulême, encouraged Zéphirine's ambitions for her darling godchild. She told herself that the Comtesse Sixte du Châtelet would use her credit on behalf of a woman who had championed her cause. The paper-manufacturer, who had Angoulême at his fingertips, sized up the difficulties at one glance; but he resolved to get over them by a stroke of audacity that Tartuffe alone would have permitted himself. The little solicitor, very surprised that his associate in sharp practice was keeping his part of the bargain, left him to his meditations as they proceeded from the paper-mill to the mansion in the rue du Minage. When they reached the landing, the two uninvited visitors were halted by the announcement: 'Monsieur and Madame are at lunch.'

'Nevertheless,' said tall Cointet, 'tell them we are here.'

And the devout tradesman, immediately admitted on the strength of his name, introduced the advocate to the affected Zéphirine, who was lunching privately with Monsieur Francis du Hautoy and Mademoiselle de La Haye. Monsieur de Sénonches had gone off, as usual, to open the hunting season with Monsieur de Pimentel.

'Here, Madame, is the young solicitor-advocate I spoke to you about, who will undertake to relieve you of the tutelage of your beautiful ward.'

The ex-diplomat scrutinized Petit-Claud who for his part was casting sideward glances at the 'beautiful ward'. Zéphirine, with whom neither Cointet nor Francis had ever broached the subject, was so surprised that her knife and fork fell from her hands. Mademoiselle de La Haye, a shrewish sour-faced, skinny little person with an ungraceful figure and insipid blond hair, was exceedingly unmarriageable despite her aristocratic little airs. The formula *of unknown parentage* on her birth certificate in reality barred her from the sphere in which the benevolence of her godmother and Francis was trying to establish her. Mademoiselle de La Haye, ignorant of her situation, was inclined to be fastidious: she would have refused to marry even the richest tradesman in L'Hou-meau. The meaningful grimace which contorted her features was reciprocated, as Cointet noticed, by Petit-Claud himself. It looked as if Madame de Sénonches and Francis were at one in wondering how they could get rid of Cointet and his pro-tégé. Cointet took in the whole scene and begged Monsieur du Hautoy to grant him a moment's audience. He accompanied the diplomat into the salon.

'Monsieur,' he said to him in plain terms, 'paternal affec-tion is making you short-sighted. You will find it difficult to marry your daughter. And, in your common interest, I have made it impossible for you to draw back out of this, for I love Françoise as one loves one's ward. Petit-Claud knows all the facts!... His unbounded ambition is a guarantee of your dear girl's happiness. In the first place Françoise will be able to do anything she wants with her husband. But you, with the aid of the Prefect's wife who is coming back to Angoulême, will make a public attorney of him. Monsieur Milhaud has definitely been promoted to Nevers. Petit-Claud will sell his practice, it will be easy for you to obtain him a post as assis-tant deputy attorney, and he'll soon become public attorney, then president of the tribunal, a Parliamentary deputy, and...'

When they had returned to the dining-room, Francis be-haved charmingly to his daughter's suitor. He gave Madame de Sénonches a warning glance and brought this presentation scene to an end by inviting Petit-Claud to dinner the following day so that they might talk matters over. Then he escorted the tradesman and the solicitor as far as the courtyard while he told Petit-Claud that, on Cointet's recommendation, he was inclined, with Madame de Sénonches, to ratify everything which the custodian of Mademoiselle de La Haye's fortune had arranged for the happiness of their little angel.

'Good Heavens, how ugly she is!' said Petit-Claud. 'I'm trapped . . . !'

'She has an air of distinction,' Cointet replied. 'But if she were beautiful would they let you marry her? Why now, my dear fellow, there's more than one small land-owner who'd ask nothing better than her thirty thousand francs, the patronage of Madame de Sénonches and that of the Comtesse du Châtelet – the more so because Francis du Hautoy will never marry and this girl is his heiress . . . Your marriage is a foregone conclusion!'

'How do you make that out?'

'This is what I have just told Du Hautoy,' tall Cointet continued, and he informed the solicitor of his bold move. 'My dear man, Monsieur Milhaud, they say, is about to be appointed public attorney at Nevers. You'll sell your practice, and in ten years' time you'll be Keeper of the Seals. You've nerve enough not to shrink from doing any services the Court will require of you.'

'Very well. Meet me tomorrow, at half past four, at the Place du Mûrier,' the solicitor replied, fascinated at the prospect of such a future. 'I shall have seen old Séchard, and we'll fix up a deed of partnership which will make Father and Son the property of the Holy Spirit, namely the Cointet firm!'

20. *The Curé has his say*

AT the moment when the old Curé of Marsac was climbing the slopes of Angoulême in order to inform Eve about her brother's condition, David had been in hiding for eleven days only two doors away from the house which the worthy priest had just left.

When the Abbé Marron emerged on to the Place du Mûrier, he found the three men there, each of them remarkable in his own way, who were bringing all their weight to bear on the present and the future of the poor self-constituted prisoner: old Séchard, tall Cointet and the little shrimp of a solicitor. Three men, three kinds of covetousness, but each kind as different as the men themselves. The one had hit upon the idea of trafficking in a son, another in a client, and tall Cointet was purchasing all this infamy while flattering himself that it would cost him nothing. It was about five o'clock, and most of the people who were then going home to dinner paused for a moment to look at these three men.

'What on earth can old Papa Séchard and tall Cointet have to say to each other?' asked the most inquisitive among them.

'No doubt they're talking about the poor devil who's leaving his wife, mother-in-law and child without a crust of bread,' someone replied.

'That's what comes of sending one's children to learn their trade in Paris!' said one of the local philosophers.

'Well now, what brings you here, Monsieur le Curé?' cried the vine-grower, who had spotted the Abbé Marron the moment he came into the square.

'I've come on behalf of your family,' the old priest answered.

'Another of my son's crackpot notions?' said Séchard senior.

'It would cost you very little to make them all happy,' said the priest, pointing up to the window between the curtains of which Madame Séchard's lovely head was visible. At this moment Eve was quieting her crying child by rocking him up and down and singing a lullaby.

'Do you bring news of my son?' asked David's father. 'Or, better still, some money?'

'No', said the Abbé. 'I'm bringing your daughter-in-law news about her brother.'

'News of Lucien?' cried Petit-Claud.

'Yes. The poor young man has walked the whole way from Paris. I found him at Courtois's mill half-dead with fatigue and misery. Indeed, he's very unhappy.'

Petit-Claud raised his hat to the priest and took tall Cointet's

arm as he said out loud: 'We're dining with Madame de
Sénonches, it's time we got ready.' When they were a few
paces away he whispered to him: 'Catch the duckling and
you'll soon catch the duck. We'll use Lucien as a decoy.'

'I've got you a wife, now you get me married!' said tall
Cointet with some attempt at humour.

'Lucien was at school with me and we were friends! ...
Within a week I shall learn quite a lot about him. Have the
banns published and I undertake to clap David in jail. Once he's
in the lock-up, my mission is fulfilled.'

'Ah!' tall Cointet quietly exclaimed. 'The great thing would
be to take out the patent in our own name!' The skinny little
solicitor gave a start as he heard this remark.

At that moment Eve saw her father-in-law and the Abbé
Marron coming in. The latter, with a single word, had just
brought the judicial drama to the point of climax.

'Look now, Madame Séchard,' the old 'bear' said to his
daughter-in-law. 'Here's our curé who's no doubt come to tell
us some pretty stories about your brother.'

'Oh!' poor Eve cried with her heart in her mouth. 'Whatever can have happened to him now?' This exclamation was
expressive of so much pain suffered and so many fears of all
kinds that the Abbé was quick to say: 'Set your mind at rest,
he's alive.'

'Would you be good enough, father,' said Eve to the old
vine-grower 'to go and fetch my mother so that she can hear
what Monsieur l'Abbé has to tell us about Lucien?'

The old man went off to find Madame Chardon and told
her: 'You'll be learning lots of funny things from the Abbé
Marron. He's a decent man although he's a parson. No doubt
dinner will be late. I'll come back in an hour's time.' And the
old man, callous about everything except the clink and glitter
of gold coins, quitted the old woman without noticing the
effect his brutal announcement had on her.

The misfortune weighing on her two children, the mis-
carriage of all the hopes she had set on Lucien, the unexpected
deterioration in the character of one so long believed to be
energetic and honest, in short all the events of the last eighteen

months had already changed Madame Chardon beyond recognition. She was noble in heart as well as birth, and she worshipped her children. Consequently she had known m ore suffering in the last six months than ever since she had lost her husband. Lucien had had the chance of becoming a Rubempré by virtue of a royal ordinance, of giving a new start to the family, of reviving its title and escutcheon, of becoming a great man! And he had fallen into the mire. She was harder on Lucien than his sister was, and had regarded him as a reprobate since learning about the forged drafts. Mothers sometimes wilfully deceive themselves; but they always know through and through the children they have brought up from the cradle. In the discussions between David and his wife over the hazards Lucien was running in Paris, Madame Chardon might seem to have shared Eve's illusions about her brother, but she trembled lest David might be right, for what he said tallied with what her maternal awareness told her. She knew her daughter's delicate sensitiveness too well to be able to voice her forebodings and was therefore obliged to keep them to herself, a thing which only truly loving mothers can do. On her side Eve was terrified to observe the ravages which grief had wrought in her mother, to see her passing steadily and continuously from old age to decrepitude. So mother and daughter alike kept up the noble pretence of believing what each of them knew to be false. For the unhappy mother the uncouth vine-grower's remark was the last drop needed to fill the cup of her afflictions, and Madame Chardon was stricken to the heart.

And so, when Eve told the priest: 'Monsieur, this is my mother,' and when the Abbé gazed on her face, as chastened as that of an aged nun, framed in hair which had turned completely white, but beautified by the mild and calm expression of pious resignation characteristic of women who walk this vale of tears, as the phrase goes, in submission to God's will, he fully understood the sort of life these two creatures had been living. He no longer felt pity for Lucien, who had put them on the rack, and he shuddered as he guessed what tortures they had gone through.

'Mother,' said Eve, wiping her eyes, 'my poor brother is quite near to us. He's at Marsac.'

'But why isn't he here?' asked Madame Chardon.

Then the Abbé related everything Lucien had told him about the misery of his journey and his adversities during his last days in Paris. He described the poet's anguish on learning what effect his imprudent acts had had in the bosom of his family and his apprehensions about the reception they might give him if he came home.

'Has he come to the stage of doubting us?' said Madame Chardon.

'The unhappy young man has made his way towards you on foot, suffering the most terrible privations, and he is coming back in the right frame of mind for entering on the humblest path in life and making amends.'

'Monsieur l'Abbé,' said the sister, 'in spite of all the wrong he has done us, I love my brother as one cherishes the remains of one who is no more; and to love him like this is still to love him more than many sisters love their brothers. He has reduced us to utter poverty, but let him come back and share with us the meagre crust of bread we still have, all in fact that he has left us with. Ah! If he had not gone away, Monsieur, we should not have lost all that we treasured most in life.'

'And he was brought back in the carriage of the woman who snatched him away from us,' cried Madame Chardon. 'He went away inside Madame de Bargeton's barouche, sitting beside her, and came back in the boot!'

'What can I do to help you in the situation you are in?' asked the worthy priest, hard put to it to know what to say as he left.

'Oh, Monsieur l'Abbé!' Madame Chardon replied. 'One can get over money troubles, they say. But only the patient himself can cure this sort of affliction.'

'If you had influence enough to persuade my father-in-law to help his son, you would save a whole family,' said Madame Séchard.

'He has no faith in you and it looked to me as if he was very exasperated with your husband,' said the old priest whom the vine-grower's rambling discourse had brought to consider the Séchard affairs as a wasps' nest into which he should take care not to step.

His mission accomplished, the priest went back to dinner with his grand-nephew Postel, who dissipated his old uncle's modicum of goodwill towards the Séchards by siding, like everybody in Angoulême, with the father against the son.

'There are ways of coping with spendthrifts,' little Postel said by way of conclusion. 'But with those who dabble in experiments there's no escaping ruin.'

THE 'FATAL MEMBER OF THE FAMILY'

21. *The prodigal's return*

THE Abbé Marron's curiosity was completely satisfied, and that, in all French provinces, is the chief motive behind the excessive interest people take in one another. That evening he informed the poet of everything that was happening in the Séchard household, making out that his journey had been a mission prompted by the purest charity.

'You have put your sister and brother-in-law in debt to the tune of ten or twelve thousand francs,' he said as he finished. 'And no one, my dear sir, has such a trifling sum to lend to his neighbours. In the Angoulême region we are not rich. I thought much less money was at stake when you told me about your drafts.'

Lucien thanked the old man for his kindness and said: 'The words of forgiveness you bring me from them are what I most treasure.'

Next day, very early, he left Marsac for Angoulême, where he arrived about nine, a walking-stick in his hand, wearing a short coat somewhat damaged by the journey from Paris and black trousers with faded streaks in them. Moreover his worn-out boots plainly showed that he belonged to the needy brotherhood of pedestrians. And so he did not close his eyes to the effect which the contrast between his departure and his return would have on his fellow-citizens. But, with heart still quivering from the remorse which had gripped him when he listened to the old priest's report, he accepted this punishment for the moment and resolved to look the persons he knew straight in the face. He even persuaded himself that he was a hero. Such self-deception is a primary reaction in poetic natures like his.

As he walked into L'Houmeau his mind was divided between the shame of his home-coming and poetic memories of former times. His heart beat faster as he went by Postel's door but, very fortunately for him, Léonie Marron was alone in the shop with her child. Vanity was still so strong in him that he was glad to see that his father's name had been painted out. Since marrying, Postel had had his shop redecorated and had had PHARMACY printed over the door, as is done in Paris. As he climbed the slope of the Porte-Palet Lucien was feeling the effect of his native air; the weight of his misfortunes was lifted from his shoulders and he said to himself with delight: 'So I'm going to see them once more!' He reached the Place du Mûrier without meeting a soul: an unforeseen piece of luck for a man who formerly had stalked about triumphantly in his home-town. Marion and Kolb, standing sentry at the door, rushed upstairs shouting: 'He's here!' Lucien once more saw the old printing-press and the old courtyard, found his sister and mother on the stairs, and they flung their arms round him, for an instant forgetting their misfortunes in this embrace. A family almost always comes to terms with misfortune; its members make their bed in it, and hope enables them to put up with the hardness of it. Lucien was a living picture of despair, but it had its poetic side: the sun had tanned his face as he tramped the highroads; deep melancholy was imprinted on his features and cast its shadows on the poet's forehead. This transformation denoted so much suffering that at the sight of the marks misery had left on his countenance the only possible feeling was pity. The dreams which the Séchard family had cherished at Lucien's departure gave place to the sad reality of his home-coming. In spite of the joy she felt, Eve's smile was like that of a saint in the throes of martyrdom. Grief imparts sublimity to the face of a very beautiful young woman. The gravity of Eve's expression, which had replaced the complete artlessness Lucien had seen written on it when he left for Paris, spoke to him with too much eloquence for him not to feel a pang of sorrow. And so the first effusion of feeling, so impulsive, so natural, was followed by a reaction on both sides: everyone was afraid to speak. However Lucien could not help looking round for the person who was missing from this reunion. At this glance, which Eve well understood, she burst into tears, and Lucien followed suit. As for Madame Chardon, she remained wan and apparently impassive. Eve stood up, went downstairs in order to avoid speaking harshly to her brother, and called out to Marion: 'My dear, Lucien is fond of strawberries. You must find some ... !'

'Oh! I well knew you would want to give Monsieur Lucien a treat. Don't worry, you shall have a nice little lunch and a good dinner too.'

'Lucien,' Madame Chardon said to her son. 'You have much to atone for here. You left us so that you might become the pride of the family, and you have plunged us into penury. You have almost broken the tool in your brother's hands which was to make his fortune, though he was only thinking of that for the sake of his new family. And that is not all you have broken ... ' There was a terrible pause and Lucien's silence implied the acceptance of this maternal rebuke. 'You must take to hard work,' she continued more kindly. 'I don't blame you for trying to re-establish the noble family to which I belong; but such an enterprise calls for a great deal of money and pride of feeling; you had neither the one nor the other. You have changed the faith we had in you to distrust. You have destroyed the peace of this patient and hard-working family, which already had a hard enough furrow to plough ... To first misdeeds a first forgiveness is due. Don't commit any more. At present we find ourselves in very difficult circumstances: be prudent, do what your sister tells you. Misfortune is a schoolmaster whose harsh lessons have borne fruit in her: she has lost her gaiety, she's a mother, she's carrying the whole household burden out of devotion to our dear David. Finally, thanks to your misdeeds, she has become the only consolation I have left.'

'You might have shown even more severity,' said Lucien as he embraced his mother. 'I accept your forgiveness, because I shall never put myself in a position to need it again.'

Eve returned and, seeing how bowed down her brother was,

realized that Madame Chardon had been talking to him. Her goodness of heart brought a smile to her lips. Lucien responded with tears which he quickly restrained. Personal presence acts like a charm and transforms the starkest hostility between lovers or members of a family however strong the motives for discontent may be. Is this because affection marks out tracks in the heart which one loves to take to again? Is it a phenomenon belonging to the science of magnetism? Does reason aver that people must either never meet again or forgive one another? Whether it is reasoning or physical or spiritual causes which produce this effect, it must be a common experience that a beloved person's glances, gestures and actions revive a lingering tenderness in those he has most offended, grieved or ill-used. The mind may be loath to forget, self-interest may still feel the hurt, but the heart becomes enslaved anew in spite of everything. And so poor Eve, as she listened until lunch-time to her brother's confidences, could not mask the expression in her eyes when she looked at him, nor her tone of voice when she spoke from her heart. Once she realized the basic facts about literary life in Paris she understood how it had been possible for Lucien to suffer defeat. The poet's joy as he fondled his sister's baby, his boyishness, his happiness at seeing his home-town and his own people once more, mingled with the deep chagrin he felt on learning that David was in hiding, the melancholy words which escaped from his lips, his emotion on seeing, when Marion served the strawberries, that in the midst of her distress his sister had remembered his liking for them: all this, and even the mere fact that the prodigal brother had to be housed and looked after, turned this day into a festive occasion. It was as if misery had called a truce. As for old Séchard, he reversed the course of the two women's feelings by saying: 'You're making as much fuss of him as if he were bringing you loads of money.'

'Why, what has my brother done that we should not make a fuss of him?' cried Madame Séchard, anxious to conceal her brother's shame.

Nevertheless, once the first tender demonstrations were over, they were brought back to a sense of reality. Lucien soon noticed the difference between the affection Eve was now showing him and that she had once bestowed upon him. David was held in deep honour, whereas Lucien was loved *in spite of everything*, as a mistress is loved no matter what disasters she has caused. Respect, a necessary foundation for our feelings, is a solid stuff providing them with the kind of confident certainty on which they thrive: this was lacking between Madame Chardon and her son, also between brother and sister. Lucien felt deprived of that entire trust they would have placed in him if he had not fallen into dishonour. The opinion d'Arthez had expressed about him, one which Eve had adopted, could be divined in her gestures, looks and tone of voice. Lucien was an object of pity. As for being the pride and glory of his family and the hero of the domestic hearth, all such fine hopes had vanished for ever. They were sufficiently afraid of his light-headedness not to tell him where David was hiding. Eve, impervious to Lucien's caresses – prompted by curiosity, for he wanted to see his brother-in-law – was no longer the Eve of L'Houmeau for whom, in the past, one glance from Lucien had been an irresistible command. Lucien talked of making amends for his wrong-doing and boasted that he would be able to rescue David. Eve replied: 'Keep out of it; our adversaries are the most perfidious and cunning people you could find.' Lucien shook his head as if to say: 'I have joined battle with Parisians . . . ' His sister countered this with a look which signified: 'Yes, and lost!'

'They no longer love me,' thought Lucien. 'I see that in family as in social life one must be successful.'

From the second day onwards, as he tried to fathom why his mother and sister had so little confidence in him, the poet was seized with a thought, not of aversion, but of petulance. He applied the standards of Parisian life to this chaste provincial life and forgot that the patient mediocrity reigning in this household, so sublime in its resignation, was the work of his hands. 'They are *bourgeois*, they can't understand me,' he told himself, and thus drew apart from his sister and mother and Séchard, whom he could no longer deceive as regards his character or his future prospects.

Eve and Madame Chardon, whose sense of divination had

been awakened by so many shocks and misfortunes, detected Lucien's most secret thoughts, felt that he was misjudging them and saw that he was becoming estranged. 'How Paris has changed him!' they said to each other. They were at last reaping the harvest of the selfishness which they themselves had cultivated in him. On both sides this touch of leaven was bound to ferment and it did ferment, but chiefly in Lucien, who knew how much he was to blame. As for Eve, she was certainly the kind of sister to say to an erring brother: 'Forgive me for the wrongs *you* have done . . . ' But when a spiritual union has been as perfect as it had been between Eve and Lucien in early life, any blow dealt at so beautiful and ideal a sentiment is mortal. Whereas criminals make peace with one another after some play with their daggers, people who love each other fall out irretrievably for a look or a word. The secret behind estrangements which often seem inexplicable can be found in the memory of a well-nigh perfect union of hearts. One can live on with mistrust in one's heart when the past affords no picture of pure and unclouded affection; but for two beings who in the past have been perfectly at one, life becomes intolerable as soon as looks and speech have to be kept in careful control. That is why great poets kill off their Pauls and their Virginias as they emerge from adolescence. Could you imagine Paul and Virginia having a quarrel?

Let us note, to the credit of Eve and Lucien, that material interests, although they had suffered such grievous damage, played no part in quickening a sense of injury. With the blameless sister, as with the blameworthy poet, personal feeling was alone involved. And so it was likely that the slightest misunderstanding, the most trivial disagreement, a new blunder on Lucien's part, might tear them asunder or give rise to one of those quarrels which create an irreparable breach in family life. Reconciliation over money disputes is possible: when feelings are hurt there is no remedy.

22. *An unexpected triumph*

THE next morning Lucien received an issue of the Angoulême newspaper and turned pale with pleasure when he saw that he was the subject of a leading article, one of those *Premiers-Angoulême* imitated from the Paris press by an estimable news-sheet which, like a provincial Academy or a properly brought-up young lady, as Voltaire puts it, never got itself talked about.

Let Franche-Comté take pride in having given birth to Victor Hugo, Charles Nodier and Cuvier; Britanny for having produced Chateaubriand and Lamennais; Normandy for its Casimir Delavigne; Touraine because it can lay claim to the author of *Eloa*. Today the province of Angoulême, where already, under Louis XIII, the illustrious Guez, better known as de Balzac, had been one of our fellow-countrymen, need not envy any of those provinces, nor yet Limousin, which nurtured Depuytren, nor yet Auvergne, the home of Montlosier, nor Bordeaux, which has been lucky enough to engender so many great men. We too have a poet! The author of those fine sonnets entitled *Les Marguerites* has made his name not only as a poet but also as a prose-writer, since we are indebted to him for a splendid novel: *The Archer of Charles the Ninth*! One day our nephews will be proud of their fellow-countryman Lucien Chardon, a rival of Petrarch!!!' [In the provincial journals of those times, exclamation marks were like the *hurrahs*! which greet the *speeches* made at *meetings* in England.]

Despite the brilliant success our young poet has met with in Paris, he has remembered that the Hôtel de Bargeton was the cradle of his triumphs, that the aristocracy of Angoulême had been the first to applaud his poetry, that the consort of Monsieur le Comte du Châtelet, our Prefect, had encouraged the first steps he took in the cult of the Muses. He has returned to our midst! . . . The whole of L'Houmeau was stirred yesterday when our Lucien de Rubempré arrived there. The news of his return has everywhere aroused the liveliest excitement. It is certain that the city of Angoulême will not lag behind L'Houmeau in doing honour to a man who, in the fields both of journalism and literature, has gloriously represented his native town in Paris. As both a religious and a royalist poet Lucien has stood up to partisan fury; and now, i t is said, he has come home to rest from the fatigue of a struggle which would exhaust even athletes of stronger build than men of poetry and reverie.

With an eminently politic motive in view, one which we applaud, one which, it is said, Madame la Comtesse du Châtelet was the first to conceive, the question has arisen of restoring to our great poet the name and title of the illustrious Rubempré family, of which Madame Chardon, his mother, is the sole inheritor. To rejuvenate in this way, by dint of talent and renewed glory, our old families when they are on the point of dying out, is a fresh proof of the steady purpose of His Majesty, the immortal creator of the *Charte*, which he expressed in the words: *let us unite and forget*!

Our poet is staying with his sister, Madame Séchard.

In the column of local news were the following items:

Our Prefect, Monsieur le Comte du Châtelet, who already holds an appointment as Gentleman-in-Ordinary of the Privy Chamber, has been appointed Councillor of State with special duties.

Yesterday all the civic authorities came to pay their respects to Monsieur le Préfet.

Madame la Comtesse Sixte du Châtelet will be at home on Thursdays.

The Mayor of L'Escarbas, Monsieur de Nègrepelisse, representing the junior branch of the d'Espards, father of Madame du Châtelet, recently gazetted Count, Peer of France and Commander of the Royal Order of Saint-Louis, is, according to report, nominated to preside over the electoral college of Angoulême for the forthcoming elections.

'Look at this,' said Lucien, taking the journal to his sister. After attentively reading the article, Eve returned the sheet to Lucien with a pensive air.

'Well, what have you to say about it?' asked Lucien, astonished at her reticence, which to him looked like coldness.

'My dear,' she replied, 'this journal belongs to the Cointets, who can insert absolutely any articles they choose and are only obliged to print what is sent them from the prefectural and episcopal offices. Do you suppose that your former rival, now Prefect, is generous enough to sing your praises in this way? Are you forgetting that the Cointets are suing us in Métivier's name and undoubtedly want to force David to let them share in the profits from his discoveries? ... From whatever source this article comes, I find it disturbing. Here, formerly, you excited nothing but hatred and jealousy and were slandered by virtue of the proverb: "No man is a prophet in his own country." And now everything is changed in a twinkling!'

'You don't know the self-pride of provincial towns,' Lucien replied. 'In one little southern town they even went out to the city gates to welcome a young man who had won the first prize in a national competition and treated him as a great man in embryo!'

'Listen to me, my dear Lucien, I don't want to preach you a sermon. I'll say everything in one single word: here you must be on your guard about the slightest things.'

'That's true enough,' Lucien replied, though he was surprised to find his sister so unenthusiastic. He himself was at the height of joy at seeing his mean and shameful return to Angoulême metamorphosed into a triumph.

'You're not impressed by this small tribute which is costing us so dear!' Lucien exclaimed after an hour of silence during which something like a storm was gathering in his heart. Eve's only answer was the look she gave him, one which made him ashamed to have made such an accusation.

A few moments before dinner, a commissionaire from the prefecture brought a letter addressed to Monsieur Lucien Chardon which seemed to justify the poet's vanity and show that society was competing for him with his family. It was an invitation:

Monsieur le Comte Sixte du Châtelet and Madame la Comtesse du Châtelet have the pleasure of inviting Monsieur Lucien Chardon to do them the honour of dining with them on the fifteenth of September following.

R.S.V.P.

A visiting-card was enclosed:

LE COMTE SIXTE DU CHÂTELET

Gentleman-in-Ordinary of the Privy Chamber, Prefect of the Charente, Councillor of State

'You're in favour,' old Séchard said. 'They're talking about you in the town as if you were a somebody ... Angoulême and L'Houmeau are arguing about which of them shall weave garlands for you.'

'My dear Eve,' Lucien whispered to his sister. 'I'm in absolutely the same position as I was in L'Houmeau the day I was invited to go to Madame de Bargeton's: I haven't evening clothes for the Prefect's dinner.'

'You're surely not going to accept this invitation?' Madame Séchard cried out in alarm.

An argument ensued between brother and sister about whether he should accept or not. Eve's provincial good sense told her that a man should only show himself in society with smiling face, proper evening clothes and impeccably groomed. But she concealed what she was really thinking: 'What will this dinner with the Prefect lead up to? What can high society in Angoulême do for Lucien? Isn't some conspiracy being hatched against him?'

Lucien ended up by saying to his sister, before they went to bed: 'You don't know how much influence I have. The Prefect's wife is afraid of me as a journalist. Besides, the Comtesse du Châtelet is still Louise de Nègrepelisse at heart. A woman who has recently obtained so many favours could save David! I'll tell her about the invention my brother has just made, and it would be child's play for her to obtain a grant of ten thousand francs from the Government!'

At eleven o'clock that night, Lucien, his sister and mother, old Séchard, Marion and Kolb were awakened by the city band reinforced by the regimental one; they found the Place du Mûrier full of people. Lucien Chardon de Rubempré was being given a serenade by the young people of Angoulême. Lucien stood at his sister's window and, after the last piece of music, said amid the deepest silence: 'I thank my fellow-citizens for the honour they are doing me. I shall try to make myself worthy of it. They will forgive me for not saying more: I am so moved that I could not go on.'

'Long live the author of *The Archer of Charles the Ninth*!'
'Long live the author of *Les Marguerites*!'

'Long live Lucien de Rubempré!'

After these three salvos shouted out by a number of voices, three laurel wreaths and three bouquets were adroitly thrown through the apartment window. Ten minutes later the Place du Mûrier was empty and silence reigned once more.

'Ten thousand francs would be more use,' said old Séchard, turning the wreaths and bouquets over with a supremely derisive air. 'Well, you've given them marguerites, they're giving you bouquets in return. You're doing well in the flower trade.'

'That's how you appreciate the honours bestowed on me by my fellow-citizens!' cried Lucien, whose countenance, from which all melancholy had vanished, was positively beaming with satisfaction. 'If you had any knowledge of men, Papa Séchard, you'd realize that moments like this only occur once in a lifetime. Such triumphs can only be due to genuine enthusiasm! ... This, my dear mother and my good sister, wipes out many disappointments.' Lucien embraced his mother and sister in the way people do embrace at moments when their joy overflows so abundantly that they simply have to pour it out into a friendly heart. – Bixiou had once remarked: 'If an author intoxicated with success hasn't a friend, he goes and embraces his concierge.'

'Come now, my dear child,' Lucien said to Eve, 'why are you crying? ... Ah! it's with joy!'

'Alas!' Eve said to her mother when they were alone and before they went back to bed: 'In every poet, it seems to me, there's a pretty woman of the worst sort.'

'You're right,' her mother replied, shaking her head. 'Lucien has already forgotten not only his own troubles, but ours too.'

Mother and daughter parted without daring to express all their thoughts.

23. How the triumph had been staged

IN countries where the sentiment of social insubordination – egalitarianism – is rampant, any triumph is a miracle, and, like certain other miracles for that matter, it does not come off without the co-operation of expert stage-managers. Out of ten ovations obtained by men still living and offered to them with patriotic acclamation, nine are due to causes quite alien to the achievements of those thus honoured. Was not Voltaire's triumph on the stage of the Théâtre-Français in reality that of the eighteenth century philosophic movement? In France a triumph is only possible when the garland placed on the triumphant person's head is a garland for all and sundry. And so the two women's presentiments were well-founded. The success of the provincial 'great man' was too little in keeping with the moral stagnation of Angoulême not to have been engineered through self-interest or by the agency of an enthusiast for stage-managing: a perfidious operation in either case. Eve's misgivings – like those of any woman indeed – were a matter of intuition and not reasoned out logically. She asked herself as she fell asleep: 'Who in Angoulême is fond enough of my brother to have stirred up local feeling? Besides, *Les Marguerites* are not yet in print, and how can he be congratulated on success which is yet to come?'

In fact this triumph was the work of Petit-Claud. The day when the parish priest of Marsac announced Lucien's return, the solicitor was dining for the first time with Madame de Sénonches, so that she might receive the formal request for the hand of her ward. It was one of those family dinners whose formal purpose is brought out more by the clothes worn than by the number of guests. It may be an intimate affair, but one knows it is a stage performance, and the motive for it is written plain on every face.

Françoise was dressed as for shop-window display. Madame de Sénonches had given great care to her toilet and looked like a ship with all its pennons flying. Monsieur du Hautoy was wearing a dinner-jacket. Monsieur de Sénonches, whom his wife had informed by letter of Madame du Châtelet's impending visit – the first she was to make at their house – and of the formal presentation of a suitor for Françoise, had come home from Monsieur de Pimentel's manor. Cointet, in his best maroon suit with its clerical cut, was sporting on his shirt-frill a diamond worth six thousand francs – a rich trades-man taking his revenge on an impoverished aristocracy. Petit-Claud, close-shaven, well-kempt, spick and span, had still not been able to shed his dry little air. It was impossible not to liken this skinny little lawyer, in his close-fitting garments, to a cold-blooded adder; but hopefulness had so much heightened the gleam in his eye, there was so much frostiness in his looks and so much starch in his demeanour that he just managed to achieve the dignified bearing of an ambitious little public attorney. Madame de Sénonches had begged her close friends not to say a word about this first interview between her ward and a prospective husband, or about the presence of the Prefect's wife: in consequence she expected her salons to be crowded.

In fact, Monsieur le Préfet and his wife had made their official calls by leaving cards, reserving the honour of personal calls as a means of action. Therefore the Angoulême aristocracy was worked up to so high a pitch of curiosity that several persons from the Chandour camp were proposing to present themselves at the 'Hôtel Bargeton', which they carefully refrained from calling the 'Hôtel Sénonches'. Proofs of the credit the Comtesse du Châtelet enjoyed had awakened many ambitions, and besides that she was said to have changed so much for the better that everyone was bent on forming his own judgement about her. Petit-Claud, having heard from Cointet on the way to the house the great news of the favour Zéphirine had obtained from the Prefect's wife, namely the privilege of introducing dear Françoise's future husband to her, felt sure of being able to take advantage of the embarrassing position in which Louise de Nègrepelisse found herself thanks to Lucien's return.

Monsieur and Madame de Sénonches had committed them-

selves so heavily in buying their house that, like typical provincials, they did not think of making the slightest alterations.
And so Zéphirine's first word to Louise, as she advanced to
meet her when she was announced, was: 'My dear Louise,
look ... You are still at home here!' She pointed to the
little crystal chandelier, the panelling and the furniture which
once had fascinated Lucien.

'That, my dear, is what I should least wish to remember,'
Madame la Préfète graciously replied as she looked round at
the assembly.

Everyone avowed that Louise de Nègrepelisse bore no
resemblance to what she had been. The Parisian world in
which she had lived for eighteen months, the first happy days
of married life, which had transformed the woman as Paris
had transformed the provincial, the kind of dignity conferred
by prestige, everything resulted in the Comtesse du Châtelet
resembling Madame de Bargeton as a girl of twenty resembles
her mother. She was wearing a charming lace bonnet trimmed
with flowers and negligently fastened with a diamond-headed
pin. Her English hairstyle set off her features admirably,
softened the contours of her face and gave her a more youthful
appearance. She wore a daintily-fringed dress of light silk
with the bodice in point lace, a creation by the celebrated
Victorine which was excellently moulded to her figure. Her
shoulders, under a pale-coloured fichu, were veiled by a scarf
of gauze, skilfully draped round her rather long neck. As a
finishing touch, she was toying with the pretty trinkets which
provincial women find it fatally difficult to manage: a charming little *cassolette* hung by a chain from her bracelet, and in
one hand she was holding her fan and a folded handkerchief
without a trace of self-consciousness. The exquisite taste
revealed in these slightest details, her pose and mannerisms,
copied from the Marquise d'Espard, showed that Louise had
studied the Faubourg Saint-Germain with scientific thorough-
ness.

As for the elderly beau of Imperial times, marriage had
ripened him like a melon – the sort which, green one day, turns
yellow in a single night. The male guests, discerning on his

wife's face the bloom and freshness which Sixte had lost, whispered typically provincial pleasantries from ear to ear, with all the more gusto because all the women were enraged at the way the former queen of Angoulême was reasserting her supremacy: the tenacious intruder had to act as scapegoat for his wife. Except for Monsieur and Madame de Chandour, the defunct Bargeton, Monsieur de Pimentel and the Rastignacs, the salon was almost as crowded as on the evening when Lucien had given his recital: my lord bishop also arrived with his vicars-general trailing behind him.

Petit-Claud, impressed at the sight of the Angoulême aristocracy, in whose midst, four months ago, he had despaired of ever finding himself, felt his hatred for the upper classes abating. He thought the Comtesse Châtelet was ravishing and he said to himself: 'She's just the sort of woman to get me the post of deputy public attorney!'

Halfway through the evening Louise, after chatting for some time with each of the ladies in turn, suiting the tone of her conversation to the importance of the person concerned and to the attitude he or she had adopted concerning her elopement with Lucien, withdrew into the boudoir with the bishop. Thereupon Zéphirine took Petit-Claud, whose heart was racing, by the arm and showed him into the boudoir in which Lucien's misfortunes had begun and in which they were about to reach their consummation.

'This, my dear, is Monsieur Petit-Claud, and I will recommend him to you the more keenly because anything you do for him will no doubt redound to my ward's advantage.'

'You are a solicitor, Monsieur?' asked the august daughter of the Nègrepelisses as she scanned Petit-Claud.

'Alas, yes, *Madame la Comtesse.*' Not once in all his life had the tailor's son had the opportunity to use these three words, so he savoured them well as he spoke. 'But,' he went on, 'I am dependent on Madame la Comtesse to obtain for me a standing in the public prosecution department. They say Monsieur Milhaud is transferred to Nevers . . . '

'But is not one first of all assistant deputy, then deputy attorney?' asked the Comtesse. 'I should like you to be deputy attorney straight away . . . But before taking steps to obtain this favour for you, I must be quite certain of your devotion to the legitimate monarchy, the Church, and above all to Monsieur de Villèle.'

'Oh, Madame!' said Petit-Claud, drawing close in order to speak in her ear. 'I am a man whose absolute obedience to His Majesty can be relied on.'

'That is what we need today,' she rejoindered, drawing away from him in order to make him understand that she wanted no more of such confidential utterances. 'If Madame de Sénonches continues to favour your suit you may count on me,' she added, making a regal gesture with her fan.

'Madame,' said Petit-Claud as he saw Cointet appearing at the door of the boudoir: 'Lucien is home again.'

'What of that, Monsieur?' the Comtesse replied in a tone which would have paralysed the organs of speech in any ordinary man.

'Madame la Comtesse does not take my meaning,' Petit-Claud continued in the most respectfully formal language. 'I wish to give her a proof of my devotion to her person. How does Madame la Comtesse desire the "great man" of her making to be received in Angoulême? There is no middle way: he must be either an object of contempt or of adulation.'

Louise de Nègrepelisse had not thought of this dilemma, in which she was obviously concerned more on account of her past than her present. Now the success of the plan the solicitor had conceived for securing Séchard's arrest depended on the feelings which the Comtesse bore Lucien at that moment.

'Monsieur Petit-Claud,' she said, putting on an air of great haughtiness and dignity, 'you wish to belong to the Government. Learn then that its first principle must be never to be in the wrong, and that women, more even than ministries, have the instinct for power and the sense of their own dignity.'

'That is exactly what I was thinking, Madame,' he briskly replied, observing the Countess with close attention without appearing to do so. 'Lucien is coming home in utter destitution. But, if he is to receive an ovation here, I can use that very ovation to compel him to leave Angoulême, where his sister and brother-in-law David are being hotly pursued by the law.'

A slight tremor on Louise de Nègrepelisse's countenance betrayed her pleasure, which she was trying to repress, on hearing this. In surprise at seeing her thoughts so well divined, she looked hard at Petit-Claud as she flicked her fan open: Françoise de La Haye was coming in, and that gave her time to think out her reply.

'Monsieur,' she said with a meaningful smile, 'it won't be long before you are a public attorney ... ' Without committing herself, she was making the position clear.

'Oh, Madame!' cried Françoise as she came up to thank the Prefect's wife. 'And so I shall owe you my life's happiness!' Leaning towards her patroness with a girlish gesture, she whispered to her: 'To be the wife of a provincial solicitor would be like dying in a slow fire!'

As for Zéphirine, if she had thrown herself at Louise, it was because she had been urged to do so by Francis, who was not without a certain knowledge of the bureaucratic world. 'During the early days of any accession, whether that of a prefect, a dynasty or even a development company,' the former consul-general had said to his mistress, 'one finds people all agog to do one service. But it doesn't take them long to find out that patronisation has its drawbacks: and then they freeze. Just now Louise will take steps on behalf of Petit-Claud that in three months' time she wouldn't take even for your husband.'

'Has Madame la Comtesse thought,' asked Petit-Claud, 'of all the obligations our poet's triumph will impose on her? She will have to receive Lucien during the week or so this adulation lasts.'

The Prefect's wife gave a little nod of dismissal to Petit-Claud and stood up in order to go and chat with Madame de Pimentel whose face was showing at the boudoir door. Impressed by the news that Louise's worthy father had been raised to the peerage, the Marquise had deemed it advisable to pay deference to a woman who had so cleverly increased her prestige by committing what was practically a lapse from virtue.

'Tell me, dear, why you bothered to get your father into the Upper House?' the Marquise asked in the course of a confidential conversation during which she was virtually dropping curtseys to the superiority of 'her dear Louise'.

'My dear, this favour was the more readily granted me because my father has no other children and will always vote for the Crown. But if I have any male children I can count on the eldest inheriting his grandfather's title, escutcheon and peerage.'

Madame de Pimental, who had hoped to get her husband raised to the peerage, was chagrined to perceive that there was no chance of her making use of a woman whose ambitions were already reaching out to her prospective children.

'I've won the Prefect's wife over,' Petit-Claud was saying to Cointet as they left, 'and I promise you your deed of partnership . . . In one month I shall be assistant deputy attorney, and you will have Séchard where you want him. Now try and find someone to buy my practice – in five months I've made it the best one in Angoulême.'

'All you needed was a leg-up,' said Cointet. He was almost jealous of what he had done for Petit-Claud.

So now the reason for Lucien's triumph in the town of his birth is made plain. Following the example set by the 'King of the French' who abstained from avenging the injuries done to him as Duke of Orleans, Madame du Châtelet was ready to forget the insults she had received in Paris as Madame de Bargeton. Her object was to patronize Lucien, crush him under the weight of her patronage and get rid of him in a respectable way.

Petit-Claud had learnt through gossip the whole story of what had happened in Paris, and he easily sensed the undying hatred which women bear to the man who has not been clever enough to love them at the time when they wanted to be loved.

24. A rare kind of devotion

THE day after the ovation which vindicated Louise's past, Petit-Claud, intent on turning Lucien's head completely and getting him in his power, called at the Séchards' with six young men of the town, all former friends of Lucien at the College of Angoulême. They formed a deputation sent to the author of *Les Marguerites* and *The Archer of Charles the Ninth* by his fellow-scholars, to invite him to a banquet they wished to give to the great man who had emerged from their ranks.

'Why, it's you, Petit-Claud!' Lucien exclaimed.

'Your return here,' said Petit-Claud, 'has stimulated our self-pride, and we have felt in honour bound to club together and arrange a splendid dinner for you. The headmaster and assistant masters will be there, and by the way things are going, we're likely to have the civic authorities there too.'

'For what day?'

'Sunday next.'

'That would be impossible,' the poet replied. 'I can't manage it until ten days from now . . . But then I'd willingly accept.'

'Very good, we're at your command. We'll have it in ten days' time.'

Lucien behaved charmingly to his former comrades, and they showed him almost respectful admiration. He chatted for about half an hour with much wit, for he felt he was placed on a pedestal and wanted to justify the opinion his home-town held of him. He thrust his thumbs into the arm-holes of his waistcoat and held forth like a man looking at things from the height on which his fellow-citizens have set him. He was modest and affable, like a genius in undress. He voiced the complaints of an athlete exhausted by his wrestling-bouts in Paris, stressing his disenchantment and congratulating his comrades on having stuck to their native hearth, and so on. They were all under a spell when they left him.

Then he took Petit-Claud aside and asked him the truth about David's affairs, blaming him for the sequestration in which his brother-in-law was living. He tried to be clever with Petit-Claud, and Petit-Claud did his best to give his old schoolfellow the impression that he, Petit-Claud, was a paltry little provincial solicitor without any kind of finesse.

The present constitution of human societies, infinitely more complex in its machinery than that of ancient societies, has resulted in a subdivision of the faculties at man's command. Outstanding people in former times had to be men of many parts, they were relatively few in number and shone out like beacons amid the nations of antiquity. Later, though faculties became specialized, quality was still comprehensive in its field of action. Thus a 'past master in guile' like Louis XI could adapt his cunning to any and every situation. But today quality itself has become subdivided. For instance, each particular profession has its own special brand of cunning. A wily diplomat conducting an affair in the depths of a province may very well find himself duped by a mediocre solicitor or even a peasant. The most cunning journalist may turn out quite a simpleton in commercial matters, and Lucien was, nor could he help being, a puppet in Petit-Claud's hands. It goes without saying that the mischief-making advocate had himself written the article which forced the city of Angoulême to take its cue from its suburb, L'Houmeau, in celebrating Lucien's return. Lucien's fellow-citizens, those who had assembled in the Place du Mûrier, were workmen from the Cointets' printing-office and paper-mill, in company with the clerks employed by Petit-Claud and Cachan and a few school comrades. Having once more become, in the poet's eyes, his old school friend, the solicitor was right in thinking that in due time his comrade would blurt out the secret of David's hiding-place. And if David came to grief through Lucien's fault, Angoulême would no longer be habitable for the poet. Therefore, in order to get a better hold on him, he posed as Lucien's inferior.

'How could I have failed to do my best?' Petit-Claud asked Lucien. 'The interests of my old classmate's sister were at stake. But, in the law-courts, there are situations in which one is bound to come off badly. On the first June David asked me to guarantee him peace and quiet for three months. He won't be in danger until September, and even so I have managed to keep all his goods and chattels out of his creditors' grasp. For I shall win the Appeal Court suit and obtain judgment to the effect that a wife's privilege is absolute and that, in this particular case, no fraud is involved. As for you, you have come back in unhappy circumstances, but you're a man of genius . . . ' Lucien made the gesture of a man who feels that the censer is swinging too near his nostrils. 'Yes, my dear friend,' Petit-Claud went on. 'I've read *The Archer of Charles the Ninth*. It's not a mere publication, it's a great piece of writing! The preface could only have been written by one of two men: Chateaubriand or yourself!'

Lucien accepted this eulogy without revealing that the preface was by d'Arthez. Ninety-nine out of a hundred authors would have done the same.

'And yet you didn't seem to be known here!' Petit-Claud continued with a pretence at indignation. 'Once I took stock of the general indifference, I conceived the idea of stirring all these people up. It was I who wrote the article you have read . . . '

'What, it was you who . . . ' cried Lucien.

'Myself. Angoulême and L'Houmeau were vying with each other, I gathered some young people round me – your old schoolfellows – and arranged for yesterday's serenade. Then, once our enthusiasm was under way, we launched the idea of a subscription dinner. I said to myself: "Even though David's in hiding, at least Lucien shall have his tribute!" – I've done even better,' he went on. 'I've seen the Comtesse Châtelet and made her realize she owes it to herself to extricate David. She can and must do it. If David really has invented the process he told me about, it won't ruin the Government to support him, and what a feather in a prefect's cap to be able to claim his share in so great a discovery by virtue of the timely protection he granted to the inventor! That's the way to get talked about as an enlightened administrator! . . . Your sister's afraid of the sputtering of our judicial musketfire! She's even frightened of the smoke it raises . . . War in the courts costs as dear as on the battle-field; but David has stuck to his guns, he's in control of his secret. He can't and won't be arrested!'

'I thank you, my dear friend, and I see that I can confide my plan to you. You will help me to bring it off.'

Petit-Claud looked at Lucien with his gimlet-shaped nose screwed up to resemble a question-mark.

'I want to save Séchard,' said Lucien with an air of self-importance. 'I am responsible for his misfortune. I will put everything right. I have more power over Louise than ... '

'Who is Louise?'

'The Comtesse Châtelet.' Petit-Claud made a gesture.

'I have more power over her than she herself realizes,' Lucien continued. 'Only, dear friend, if I'm to make it felt in Government circles, I need clothes ... '

Petit-Claud made another gesture as if to offer his purse.

'Thank you,' said Lucien, shaking Petit-Claud's hand. 'In ten days from now I shall pay a call on Madame la Préfète and return your call.'

They parted with comradely handshakes.

'He's a poet right enough,' Petit-Claud thought to himself. 'He's crazy!'

'Say what you like,' Lucien was thinking as he returned to his sister's room. 'When it comes to friends, there are none like old schoolmates.'

'Well, Lucien,' said Eve. 'What has Petit-Claud promised you that you should show him so much friendship? Beware of him!'

'Of him?' cried Lucien. 'Listen, Eve,' he went on, as if in response to a sudden idea. 'You no longer believe in me, you distrust me, you may well distrust Petit-Claud. But in twelve or fifteen days' time you'll change your mind.' This he added with a fatuous smirk.

25. The pride of his province?

LUCIEN went up to his bedroom and wrote a letter to Lousteau:

My friend,

Of the two of us I alone, probably, remember the thousand francs I lent you. But I know only too well, alas, the situation you will be in as you open this letter, not to add straight away that I'm not asking for them back in gold or silver. No, I ask them from you in the shape of credit, as one might ask Florine for them in the shape of pleasure. We have the same tailor, so you can have a complete outfit of clothes made for me in the shortest possible time. I'm not exactly in Adam's birthday suit, but I can't show myself in public. Here, the honours due by the *département* to Parisian celebrities were awaiting me, to my great astonishment. I'm to be guest of honour at a banquet, no more and no less than a deputy of the Left might be. Do you understand now why I must have evening clothes? Promise me this payment. Make it your concern. Use your power as a writer of puffs. In short, write a new scene between Don Juan and his creditor: his name was *Sunday*, and I simply must have some Sunday garments. I've nothing but rags: that's the point to start from!

It's September and the weather's magnificent. *Ergo*, see to it that I receive by the end of this week some smart outdoor wear: a morning coat, dark bronze-green, three waistcoats, one yellow, the second a fancy one in Scottish tartan, the third completely white. Also three pairs of trousers likely to impress the ladies, one in white English material, the second in nankeen, the third in fine black cashmere; finally a black evening coat and a black satin waistcoat.

If by now you have picked up some new Florine or other, ask her to choose me two fancy cravats. All that will be easy: I'm counting on you, on your resourcefulness. I'm not worried about the tailor. But, my dear friend, as we have often had cause to regret, the intelligence born of poverty (surely the worst bane in the life of that epitome of mankind, the Parisian), an intelligence so fertile in ways and means as to cause even Satan some surprise, has still not hit on a device for getting a hat on credit. When we have started a

605

fashion in hats costing a thousand francs we shall be able to get them on credit; but until then we must always have enough coins in our pockets to pay cash for them. Oh! What harm the Comédie-Française has done us with its catch-phrase *Lafleur, put some money in our pockets*! And so I am well aware of the difficulty you'll have in satisfying this request. To what the tailor provides add a pair of boots, a pair of dancing-shoes, a hat and six pairs of gloves. I know I'm asking the impossible, but isn't a literary man's life one long series of impossible achievements? This is all I have to say to you: perform this miracle by writing a great article or a scandalous little one, and I'll regard your debt as well and duly paid. It's a debt of honour, my friend, of twelve months' standing: you'd blush at it if you were capable of blushing.

Joking apart, my dear Lousteau, I'm in a serious position. Judge of it by this one piece of information: the Cuttle-fish has put on flesh, she's married to the Heron, and the Heron is Prefect of Angoulême. This appalling couple can do a lot for my brother-in-law whom I've landed in an appalling situation: he's being hounded for debt and is in hiding as a result of a bill of exchange I drew . . . So it's up to me to reappear before Madame la Préfète and regain some ascendancy over her. Isn't it terrible to think that David Séchard's fortune depends on a handsome pair of boots, some grey open-work silk stockings (don't forget them either) and a new hat? . . . I'm going to pretend that I'm ill and in pain and retire to bed like Duvicquet, so that I need not respond to the attentions of my fellow-citizens. These same fellow-citizens, my dear, gave me a very fine serenade. I'm beginning to wonder how many fools it takes to make up the term *fellow-citizens* now that I have learned that the enthusiasm of this provincial capital was sparked off by a few of my old school-friends.

If you could insert in your *News Items* a few lines about my reception, you'd raise my stature here by the thickness of several boot-heels. It would also make the Cuttle-fish feel that I have, if not friends, at least some credit in the Parisian press. Since I'm not giving up any of my hopes, I'll do the same for you one day. If you wanted a good leading article for some periodical or other, I have time to think one out at leisure. I'll say nothing more, my dear friend, than this: I'm counting on you, as you also can count on the man who signs himself

Entirely yours,

LUCIEN DE R.

P.S. Send everything by stage-coach, labelled 'to be called for'.

This letter, in which Lucien once more assumed the tone of superiority reawakened in him by his recent success, took his mind back to Paris. He had been steeped for six days in the absolute calm of provincial life; now his thoughts reverted to the brighter side of his afflictions. He felt vague regrets, and for a whole week the Comtesse Châtelet was the sole object of his reflections. In short, he attached so much importance to his reappearance in society that when, late one evening, he went down to collect the parcels he was expecting from Paris, he experienced all the anguish of uncertainty – like a woman who has staked her last hopes on a pretty dress and is in despair over getting it.

'Ah! Lousteau! I forgive you for all your treachery,' he said below his breath as he noticed by the shape of the parcels that everything for which he had asked had been despatched. He found the following letter in the hat-box:

My dear boy,

The tailor behaved very well but, as your penetrating hindsight helped you to foresee, the cravats, hats and silk stockings you ordered cost us serious heart-searchings, for it was no use searching our pockets. As we agreed with Blondet, someone could make a fortune by setting up a shop in which young people could buy things for next to nothing, for in the end the goods we don't pay for cost us very dear. For that matter, our great Napoleon said, when the lack of a pair of boots halted him in his race to India: 'The easiest things never get done.' Anyway, all was going well except for your footwear ... I could see you dressed up, but no hat; in a fine waist-coat, but without shoes! I even thought of sending you a pair of mocassins which an American gave Florine as a curiosity. She offered us a lump sum of forty francs to be gambled with for your needs. Nathan, Blondet and I were so lucky, since we were not gambling on our own account, that we won enough money to take the Torpedo,[1] Des Lupeaulx's former ballet-girl, out to supper. Frascati certainly owed us that. Florine undertook the purchases: she has added three fine shirts. Nathan offers you a cane. Blondet, who won three hundred francs, sends you a gold chain. The ballet-girl joined in with a gold watch the

1. Electric ray or numbfish: the nickname given to Esther van Gobseck (destined to be Lucien's next mistress) because of her electrifying beauty. See *Splendours and Miseries of Courtesans*.

size of a forty-franc piece which some imbecile gave her, though it doesn't go! 'It's trumpery stuff,' she told us, 'like what he had from me!' Bixiou, who joined us at the Rocher de Cancale, elected to include a bottle of *eau de Portugal* in the package we're sending you from Paris. And, in his deep bass voice and with the middle-class portentousness he takes off so well, our star comedian added: 'If that can ensure his success, so be it!'

All this, my dear boy, shows how much we love our friends in misfortune. Florine, whom I've been feeble enough to forgive, asks you to send us a review of Nathan's latest work.

Good-bye, my son. I can only pity you for having gone back to the chemist's bottle you came out of before you made an old comrade of

Your Friend,

ETIENNE L.

'Poor fellows! They even gambled for me!' he said to himself, quite touched.

Sometimes, from insalubrious regions or those where one has suffered most, come wafts of air which seem to be laden with the perfumes of Eden. In a humdrum life the memory of sufferings brings an indescribable pleasure. Eve was stupefied when her brother came downstairs in his new clothes: he was scarcely recognizable.

'I can now go for a walk in Beaulieu!' he exclaimed. 'They won't say of me: "he came home in tatters!" Look, here's a watch you can have. It really is mine. Besides, like me, it's out of order.'

'What a child you are!' said Eve. 'One can't be cross with you for long.'

'Do you think then, dear girl, that I asked for all that with the silly idea of cutting a figure in Angoulême? I don't care a rap for all that!' he said, thrashing the air with his cane, which had a pommel of chased gold. 'I want to repair the harm I've done: that's why I'm in battle array.'

Lucien's success as a well-dressed man was the only real triumph he was to achieve, but it was a tremendous one. Envy loosens as many tongues as admiration freezes. Women raved about him, men talked scandal about him, and he might well have exclaimed, like Sedaine in his song, 'It's all because of the clothes I'm wearing!' He left two cards at the Prefecture and also paid a visit to Petit-Claud, but he happened to be out. The next day, the day of the banquet, all the Paris newspapers had the following lines in their news item from Angoulême:

ANGOULÊME. The return of the young poet whose beginnings were so brilliant, the author of *The Archer of Charles the Ninth*, which is the only historical novel in France not imitated from Sir Walter Scott, the preface to which is an event in literature, has been singled out for an ovation as flattering to the city as it is to Monsieur Lucien de Rubempré. Angoulême has lost no time in giving a patriotic banquet in his honour. The new Prefect, very recently installed, has associated himself with this public demonstration by acclaiming the author of the *Marguerites*, whose budding talent had been so warmly encouraged by Madame la Comtesse du Châtelet.

In France, once an impetus is given nothing can stay its course. The colonel of the regiment stationed in Angoulême produced his regimental band. The proprietor of the Bell, the famous hostelry of L'Houmeau, who was also its *maître d'hôtel*, and whose consignments of truffled turkey travel as far as China and are despatched in most magnificent porcelain, took charge of the catering: he had decorated his great dining-hall with hangings whereon intertwined bouquets and laurel wreaths made a superb display. By five o'clock forty people, all in formal dress, were assembled there. Lucien's fellow-citizens were represented by a crowd of over a hundred people, attracted for the most part by the presence of the bandsmen in the courtyard.

'All Angoulême is here!' said Petit-Claud, taking his stance at the window.

'I just can't understand it,' Postel was saying to his wife, who had come to listen to the band. 'Why, the Prefect, the Receiver-General, the Colonel, the manager of the Gunpowder Factory, our M.P., the Mayor, the Headmaster, the manager of the Ruelle foundry, the Chairman of the Court, the Public Attorney, Monsieur Milhaud, all the town authorities are here!'

When all were seated at table, the band struck out with variations on the tune of *Long live the King, long live France!* – an air which never became popular. It was then five o'clock. At eight the appearance of dessert – sixty-five dishes, the *pièce de résistance* being a Mount Olympus in icing sugar with a chocolate figure of France on top – was a signal for toasts to begin.

'Gentlemen,' said the Prefect, rising to his feet: 'The King! The lawful monarchy! Is it not to the peace which the Bourbons have restored to us that we owe the generation of poets and thinkers thanks to whom France still holds pride of place in literature?'

'Long live the King!' shouted the guests, among whom the supporters of the Government were in great force.

The venerable headmaster stood up. 'To our young poet,' he said, 'to the hero of the day, who has combined the grace and poetry of Petrarch, in a form of verse which Boileau declared was so difficult, with the talent of a prose-writer!'

'Bravo! Bravo!'

The Colonel stood up. 'Messieurs, let us drink to him as a Royalist, for the hero of this feast has had the courage to defend the right principles!'

'Bravo!' said the Prefect, giving the cue for applause.

Petit-Claud stood up. 'All Lucien's comrades drink to the glory of the College of Angoulême and its venerable head-master who is so dear to us, and to whom we must express gratitude for all he has contributed to our successes!'

The old headmaster, who had not expected this toast, wiped his eyes. Lucien stood up. The deepest silence ensued, and the poet turned pale. At this instant the headmaster, who was on his left, placed a laurel wreath on his head. Everyone clapped. There were tears in Lucien's eyes and a break in his voice.

'He's drunk,' the future Public Attorney of Nevers whispered to Petit-Claud.

'Not with wine,' the solicitor replied.

'My dear fellow-citizens, my dear schoolfellows,' said Lucien at last. 'I could wish that the whole of France might witness this scene. Thus it is that men are nurtured, thus it is that great works and great deeds are accomplished in our country. And yet, seeing what little I have done and what great honour I am receiving, I can only feel embarrassed and entrust to the future the task of justifying the acclamation I am receiving today. The memory of this moment will give me new strength for struggles to come. Allow me to single out for your homage the lady who was both my first Muse and my protectress, and to drink also to my native city. And so then, to the beautiful Comtesse Sixte du Châtelet and the noble city of Angoulême!'

'He didn't do too badly,' said the Public Attorney with a nod of approval. 'Our toasts were pre-arranged. His was improvised.'

At ten o'clock the guests went away in groups. David Séchard, hearing the unaccustomed music, asked Basine what was going on in L'Houmeau. She replied: 'They are giving a banquet in honour of your brother-in-law Lucien.'

'I'm sure,' he said, 'that he must have regretted that I couldn't be there!'

At midnight, Petit-Claud escorted Lucien back to the Place du Mûrier. There Lucien said to the solicitor: 'My dear, we are friends for life!'

'Tomorrow,' said the solicitor, 'my contract of marriage with Mademoiselle de La Haye is being signed at the house of her godmother, Madame de Sénonches. Do me the pleasure of coming. Madame de Sénonches has asked me to bring you, and you will meet the Prefect's wife, who will feel very flattered by your toast – no doubt she will have heard about it.'

'I had my motive for that,' said Lucien.

'Oh! you'll save David.'

'I'm sure I shall,' the poet replied.

At this moment David appeared as if by magic. And this is how it came about.

26. The snake in the grass

DAVID was in an impossible position: his wife absolutely forbade him either to receive Lucien or to let him know where he was hiding. Meanwhile Lucien was writing him affectionate letters telling him that in a few days' time he would have atoned for his misdeeds. Now Mademoiselle Clerget had handed David the two following letters and explained to him the motive behind the celebrations of which the music had reached his ears.

Darling, just go on as if Lucien were not here. Don't worry about anything, but get this idea firmly fixed in your dear head: our safety depends entirely on the impossibility of your enemies finding out where you are. I am in the unhappy position of having more confidence in Kolb, Marion and Basine than in my brother. Alas! My poor Lucien is no longer the ingenuous, tender-hearted poet we once knew. It's precisely because he's trying to meddle in your affairs and presuming to get our debts paid (out of pride, my dear David) that I fear him. He has had some fine clothes sent him from Paris and a hundred francs in gold – in a beautiful purse. He put them at my disposal and we are living on them. At last we have one enemy less: your father has left us. We owe his departure to Petit-Claud who got wise to Papa Séchard's intentions and brought them to naught by telling him that henceforth you would do nothing without Petit-Claud's advice, and that Petit-Claud himself would not let you cede any part of your invention without a preliminary indemnity of thirty thousand francs: fifteen thousand to begin with to clear off your debts, and fifteen thousand which you would get unconditionally whether you succeed or not. I can't make out what Petit-Claud is after.

Love and kisses to you, those of a wife to her unhappy husband. Our tiny Lucien is well. It's lovely to see this little flower coming into bloom in the midst of our domestic storms! Mother is praying hard as usual and would embrace you almost as tenderly as

Your own Eve.

As can be seen, Petit-Claud and the Cointets, alarmed by old Séchard's peasant cunning, had got rid of him, the more

612

easily because his grape-harvest was calling him back to his Marsac vineyards. Lucien's letter, enclosed in Eve's, ran thus:

My dear David,

All goes well. I am armed *cap-à-pie*. I'm beginning my campaign today and in two days' time I shall have covered some distance. With what pleasure I shall embrace you when you are free and clear of the debts I saddled you with! But I am hurt and saddened for life at the mistrust my sister and mother continue to show me. Don't I already know you are hiding in Basine's house? Every time she comes to our house she brings news of you and your answers to my letters. Anyway it's obvious that Eve had only her laundry friend to rely on. I shall be very near you today and cruelly grieved not to have you with me at the banquet which is being given me. Local patriotism in Angoulême has earned me a small triumph. It will be forgotten in a few days, but the joy you felt would be the only sincere one. Anyhow, a few more days, and you will entirely forgive the man who values more than any mundane glory the privilege of being

Your brother,

LUCIEN.

David's heart was sharply torn between these two contending forces, unequal though they were, for he adored his wife, and his friendship for Lucien had diminished now that he felt less esteem for him. But solitude can effect great changes in strength of feeling. A man who is alone and a prey to pre-occupations like those in which David was immersed gives in to thoughts which would have no purchase on him in the normal routine of life. Thus, as he read the letter Lucien had written amid the fanfares of his unexpected triumph, he was profoundly touched at the words of regret which he had hoped Lucien would express. Tender-hearted people are unable to resist such minor manifestations of sentiment, and think they mean as much to others as to themselves. They are like the last drop of water which overflows a brimming cup. And so, as midnight approached, no entreaties from Basine could prevent David from going to see Lucien.

'No one,' he told her, 'is about at this time in the streets of Angoulême. I shall not be seen and they can't arrest me at night. Even if I did meet anyone, I could use the means devised by Kolb to get back to my hiding-place. And besides, it's much too long since I kissed my wife and child.' Basine yielded to these specious arguments and let him leave the house.

In consequence, just as Lucien and Petit-Claud were saying good-night to each other, David came up and cried: 'Lucien!' The two brothers fell into one another's arms, weeping. The emotion which surged up in Lucien sprang from the kind of friendship which nothing can destroy, by which men always lay insufficient store, but which they blame themselves later for having betrayed. David was feeling the urge to forgive. This generous-hearted, noble-minded inventor desired above all to have things out with Lucien and dispel the clouds overcasting the affection between brother and sister. With such sentimental considerations in mind he had lost sight of the dangers arising from his financial situation.

Petit-Claud said to his client: 'Go to your house, and at least make the most of your imprudence by embracing your wife and child! And mind no one sees you!'

'What a pity!' he exclaimed as he stood alone in the Place du Mûrier. 'Oh! If only Cérizet were here!'

Just as the solicitor was making this aside while walking along the boarded enclosure built round the square in which, today, the Law-Courts proudly stand, he heard someone knocking on a board behind him, like the pounding of knuckles on a door. 'I *am* here,' said Cérizet, speaking through a chink between two badly-joined boards. 'I saw David leaving L'Houmeau. I already had an idea where he was hiding. Now I'm sure, and I know where we can nab him. But if we're to set a trap for him I must learn something about Lucien's plans, and you've gone and sent them home. At any rate stay here on some pretext or other. When David and Lucien come out again, bring them near where I am. They'll think they're alone and I shall hear what they say when they part company.'

'You're a clever devil!' Petit-Claud said in a low voice.

'God help us!' Cérizet retorted. 'What wouldn't a man do to get what you've promised me!'

Petit-Claud moved away from the fence and as he paced round the Place du Mûrier he looked up to the windows of the room in which the Séchard family was assembled and fixed his mind on the future as if to give himself courage, for Cérizet's stratagem might make a knock-out blow possible. Petit-Claud was a thoroughly shifty, treacherous, two-faced man, one of those who never swallow any bait that the present holds out or let themselves get caught up in any attachment once they have studied the vagaries of the human heart and the twists and turns of self-interest. That is why, from the beginning, he had placed little faith in Cointet. In the eventuality of his marriage project failing without him having grounds for accusing tall Cointet of double dealing, he had thought out a way of causing him trouble. But now that he had succeeded at the Bargeton mansion, he was playing fair with Cointet. The scheme he had held in reserve had now become superfluous and would jeopardize the political situation to which he aspired.

These are the foundations on which he had wished to base his future importance. In L'Houmeau Gannerac and some other big tradesmen were beginning to form a Liberal committee connected by business relationships with the leaders of the Opposition. The accession to power of the Villèle cabinet, accepted by the moribund Louis XVIII, had heralded a change of tactics in the Opposition: now that Napoleon was dead, they were giving up the dangerous method of conspiracies. The Liberal party was organizing a system of law-abiding resistance. It was aiming at getting control in the constituencies in order to reach its goal by winning over the masses. Petit-Claud, born and brought up in L'Houmeau as a rabid Liberal, was the life and soul and also the secret counsellor of the Opposition in the Lower Town, kept under as it was by the aristocracy of the Upper Town. He had been the first to see the danger of allowing to the Cointets the monopoly of the Press in the Charente valley, where the Opposition needed an organ in order to keep abreast with other towns.

'Let each of us give Gannerac a five-hundred franc note,' said Petit-Claud, 'and he will have over twenty thousand francs to buy the Séchard printing-office. We'll lend this sum to the purchaser and so control the running of it.' The solicitor got this idea adopted with a view to thereby strengthening his position as regards both Cointet and Séchard, and naturally his eye fell on Cérizet as being the sort of scoundrel he could make into a stout supporter of the Liberal party.

'If you can find out where your former boss is and deliver him into our hands,' he had said to Séchard's former compositor, 'we'll lend you twenty thousand francs to buy his printing-works, and probably you'll be put in charge of the journal. So get busy.' More certain of the activity of a man like Cérizet than of that of all the Doublons in the world, Petit-Claud had then promised tall Cointet that David should be arrested. However, once he had begun to cherish the hope of becoming a magistrate, he foresaw that he might have to turn his back on the Liberals; but he had so successfully worked up the L'Houmeau people that the funds needed for the purchase of the printing-works were in hand. Petit-Claud resolved to let things take their natural course. 'Bah!' he had told himself. 'Cérizet will break some Press law or other and I'll take advantage of it to display my talents.'

He went up to the printing-office door and said to Kolb, who was standing guard. 'Go upstairs and tell David to get away while he can, and see you take all possible precautions. It's one o'clock, I'm going home.'

When Kolb moved from the doorstep Marion took his place. Lucien and David came out: Kolb walked a hundred paces ahead of them and Marion a hundred paces behind. While the two brothers were passing alongside the boarding, Lucien was talking animatedly to David.

'My dear David,' he said, 'my plan is exceedingly simple; but how can I talk about it before Eve? She would never understand the means I shall adopt. I'm sure that Louise has deep down in her heart a desire that I shall be able to re-awaken, and I want her solely in order to avenge myself on that imbecile of a prefect. Once we are lovers, if only for a week, I shall persuade her to ask the Ministry to allot you a subsidy of twenty thousand francs for your researches. Tomorrow I shall be seeing the creature again in the little boudoir where our love affair began – according to Petit-Claud, nothing has been altered there. I'll do a bit of acting. And so, the day after tomorrow, in the morning, I'll send you word by Basine to tell you whether I've been hissed or clapped . . . Do you understand now why I wanted clothes from Paris? One can't play a role like that in rags.'

At six that morning, Cérizet came to see Petit-Claud.

'Tomorrow at midday,' said the Parisian, 'Doublon can get ready to pounce. He'll catch our man, I guarantee that. You see, I have a hold on one of Mademoiselle Clerget's laundry-girls.'

After Cérizet had disclosed his plan, Petit-Claud hurried to the Cointets. 'Arrange matters so that by this evening Monsieur du Hautoy will have decided to make over his estates without usufruct to Françoise, and in two days' time you'll be signing your contract with Séchard. I won't get married until a week after the signing, and so we shall have kept strictly to the terms of our little agreement: *give and take*. But let's keep a close watch this evening on what happens at Madame de Sénonches' house between Lucien and the Comtesse du Châtelet, for everything depends on that. If Lucien is hopeful of success through the Prefect's wife, David's in our hands.'

'I can see you'll be Keeper of the Seals one day!' said Cointet.

'Why not, if a man like Peyronnet could do it?' said Petit-Claud, thereby showing that he had not yet entirely cast his slough as a Liberal.[1]

27. *Lucien takes his revenge*

THE dubiousness of Mademoiselle de La Haye's status ensured the attendance of most of the nobility of Angoulême at the signing of her marriage contract. The poverty of this future *ménage*, which had no wedding settlements behind it,

1. Peyronnet had begun his career as a provincial advocate. He was one of the most unpopular Conservative ministers.

quickened that sort of interest which society likes to show, for with beneficence as with ovations the case is the same: a show of charitableness bolsters self-esteem. Therefore the Marquise de Pimentel, the Comtesse du Châtelet, Monsieur de Sénonches and two or three habitual visitors to the house gave Françoise several presents which were much talked of in the town. These dainty trifles, added to the trousseau Zéphirine had been preparing for a year, to the godfather's jewellery and the customary gifts from the bridegroom, soothed Françoise's feelings and pricked the curiosity of several mothers who who brought their daughters along. Petit-Claud and Cointet had already observed that the Angoulême nobility was tolerating the presence of both of them on their Olympian heights as a necessity, since one of them was the steward of Françoise's fortune, her deputy guardian, while the other was as indispensable for the signing of the contract as a condemned criminal would be at a hanging. And yet, although when the wedding was over Madame Petit-Claud would still have the right to visit her godmother, the bridegroom realized that he would find it difficult to obtain admission, and he had made up his mind to force his way into this arrogant society. Ashamed of his low-class parentage, the solicitor made his mother stay behind at Mansle where she was living in retirement, asking her to say she was ill and give her consent in writing. Somewhat humiliated to be there without parents or patrons, having no one to sign on his behalf, Petit-Claud was consequently very happy to introduce, in the person of the celebrated Lucien, an acceptable friend, whom in any case the Comtesse wanted to see again. So he called for Lucien in a carriage. For this memorable evening the poet had groomed himself in such a way as to assert an incontestable superiority over all the men present. Madame de Sénonches had singled him out as the guest of the evening, and the interview between the two estranged lovers was to provide one of those scenes which are much savoured in the provinces. Lucien was now being lionized; he was said to be so handsome, so changed, so wonderful that all the society women of Angoulême were agog to see him again. In conformity with the fashion reigning during this period, to which we owe the transition from the former ballroom breeches to the ignoble trousers of our day, he had put on black, tight-fitting trousers. Men's clothes were still cut close to the figure, to the great despair of skinny or misshapen people: Lucien's proportions were those of a Phoebus Apollo. His grey silk open-work stockings, his elegant shoes, his black satin waistcoat, his cravat, everything in fact was scrupulously fitted, one might say moulded to his person. His fair, abundant, wavy hair enhanced the beauty of his white forehead, round which the curls rose with elaborate gracefulness. His eyes were sparkling with self-assurance. The beauty of his small, feminine hands was so enhanced by his gloves that one might have thought that they should never be seen bare. He modelled his deportment on the famous Parisian dandy de Marsay, holding in one hand his cane and hat, which he did not lay down, and using the other to make the rare gestures with which he gave effect to his remarks.

He would have liked to slip into the salon in the manner of those celebrities who, out of false modesty, would stoop even when they passed under the Porte-Saint-Denis. But Petit-Claud had only one friend with him and made all he could out of the fact. Almost pompously he led Lucien to Madame de Sénonches in the centre of the gathering. As he made his way forward, the poet heard murmurs which in former times would have put him into a flurry. But he kept a cool head: he was sure that, singly, he was equal to the whole crowd of Angoulême olympians.

'Madame,' he said to Madame de Sénonches, 'I have already congratulated my friend Petit-Claud, who has in him the makings of a Keeper of the Seals, on being so fortunate as to become allied to you, however tenuous may be the bonds between a godmother and her god-daughter.' He said this as if he were launching an epigram, and his point was well taken by all the ladies, who were listening without appearing to do so. 'But, on my own account, I rejoice at an occasion which enables me to offer you my homage.'

He said this unconstrainedly, striking the attitude of a great lord on a visit to humble folk. As he listened to Zéphirine's embarrassed reply he cast an appraising glance round the salon as a prelude to making an impression. So he was able to give graceful bows and appropriate smiles to Francis du Hautoy and the Prefect, who returned his salute. Then at last he walked over to Madame du Châtelet whom he pretended to have just noticed. This encounter was so decidedly the event of the evening that the marriage contract, to which people of mark were to append their signature after being ushered into the bedroom either by the notary or by Françoise, was forgotten. Lucien took a few steps towards Louise de Nègrepelisse, and with that Parisian gracefulness which was now, since her return, only a thing of memory for her, he said in a fairly audible voice:

'Is it to you, Madame, that I owe the invitation which procures me the pleasure of dining at the Prefecture the day after tomorrow?'

'You owe it, Monsieur, to your renown alone,' Louise dryly replied, somewhat shocked by Lucien's aggressive turn of phrase, which he had thought out in order to wound the pride of his former patroness.

'Ah! Madame la Comtesse,' said Lucien with an air which was both subtle and fatuous. 'I could not bring the man enjoying this renown to you if he's in your bad books.' And, without waiting for an answer, he wheeled round on perceiving the bishop, to whom he gave a dignified bow.

'You were almost prophetic, my lord,' he said in a charming voice, 'and I shall try to make your prophecy come true. I consider myself happy to be here this evening, since I am thus able to pay you my respects.'

Lucien then engaged his lordship in a conversation lasting ten minutes. All the ladies were looking on him as a nine days' wonder. His unexpected impertinence had left Madame du Châtelet speechless. As she saw that Lucien was a subject of admiration for all the ladies; as she followed, from group to group and from person to person, the whispered report of the words they had exchanged and the way Lucien had rebuffed her with his apparent disdain, she felt a spasm of self-pride gripping her heart.

'If he didn't come tomorrow, after making such a remark,' she thought, 'what a scandal it would be! Why is he so proud? Can it be that Mademoiselle des Touches is in love with him? ... He's so handsome! They say she rushed to him in Paris the day after the actress died! ... Perhaps he came back home to save his brother-in-law and found himself in our carriage at Mansle through a traveller's mishap. He looked us up and down, Sixte and myself, in a singular way that morning.'

Myriad thoughts raced through her head and, unfortunately for her, she gave free rein to them as she watched Lucien chatting with the bishop as if he were a monarch holding court. He gave no salutes and waited for people to come to him, looking round with a versatility of expression and an ease of manner worthy of his model de Marsay. He did not leave the prelate even in order to go and greet Monsieur de Sénonches as he came into view. After ten minutes of this, Louise could stand it no longer. She rose to her feet, walked up to the bishop and asked him: 'What is being said to you, my Lord, to make you smile so often?'

Lucien took a few tactful paces backwards in order to leave Madame du Châtelet with the prelate.

'Ah! Madame la Comtesse, this young man has much wit! ... He has been telling me that all his strength came from you.'

'I at least am not ungrateful, Madame!' said Lucien, giving the Comtesse a reproachful look in which she found some charm.

'Let us talk things out,' she said, beckoning Lucien towards her with a flick of her fan. 'Come this way with my Lord! ... He shall be our judge.' She pointed to the boudoir and led the bishop to it.

'She's enlisting his lordship in a strange kind of profession!' said a woman belonging to the Chandour allegiance in a voice loud enough to be heard.

'Our judge?' said Lucien, looking turn by turn at the prelate and the Prefect's wife. 'Does that mean that one of us is a guilty person?'

Louise de Nègrepelisse sat down on the sofa in her former boudoir. After making Lucien sit down on one side of her

621

and the lord bishop on the other, she began to speak. Lucien did his former love the honour of not seeming to listen, a thing which both surprised and pleased her. He assumed the attitude and gestures of La Pasta in *Tancredi* when she is about to sing *O patria*! . . . The expression on his face was such that he seemed to be singing the famous cavatina *del Rizzio*. Finally Coralie's pupil managed to squeeze out a few tears.

'Oh Louise, how I loved you!' he murmured in her ear without attending either to the prelate or the conversation once he saw that the Comtesse had noticed his tears.

'Dry your eyes, or you might disgrace me here once again,' she said, turning round to him with an aside which shocked the bishop.

'And once is enough,' Lucien replied with vehemence. 'Such a word, coming from the cousin of Madame d'Espard, would dry the tears of a Magdalen. My God! . . . For an instant my memories, my illusions, my adolescence came back to me, and you are . . . '

His lordship hastily regained the salon, realizing that his dignity might be compromised if he stayed with this pair of former lovers. Everyone made a point of leaving the Prefect's wife and Lucien alone in the boudoir. But a quarter of an hour later Sixte, annoyed by the chatter and laughter and tiptoeing to the threshold of the boudoir, entered it with a more than anxious air and found Lucien and Louise in animated conversation.

'Madame,' Sixte whispered to his wife, 'you know Angoulême better than I do. Ought you not to keep Madame la Préfète and our official responsibilities in mind?'

'My dear,' said Louise, eyeing her censor with a haughtiness that made him tremble, 'I am talking to Monsieur de Rubempré about matters which are important for you. It's a question of rescuing an inventor who is about to fall victim to the basest form of intrigue, and you must come to our help . . . As for what those ladies may be thinking of me, you shall see how I shall comport myself in order to congeal the poison on their tongues.'

She left the boudoir leaning on Lucien's arm and took him

along to sign the contract of marriage with all the audacity of a great lady. 'Shall we sign it together?' she said, offering him the pen. He let her show him the place where she had signed so that his signature could be next to hers.

'Monsieur de Sénonches, would you have recognized Monsieur de Rubempré?' said the Comtesse, thereby forcing the insolent huntsman to acknowledge Lucien.

She took Lucien back to the salon and sat him between herself and Zéphirine on the formidable divan in the middle of the room. Then, like a queen on her throne, she began, at first in a low voice, an intentionally vivacious conversation which was shared by a few of her old friends and several women who were deferentially hovering about her. Soon Lucien, who had become the centre of an admiring circle, was launched by the Comtesse on the theme of life in Paris. The satire he made of it was improvised with incredible verve and spangled with anecdotes about celebrated people: real conversational titbits of the kind which provincials lap up greedily. They admired him for his wit, just as they had admired him as a personable man. Madame la Comtesse Sixte du Châtelet was so patently making a lion of Lucien, so cleverly bringing him out like a woman delighted with the instrument on which she is performing, giving him cues with so much apropos, canvassing approval for him with such compromising glances, that some of the ladies began to regard the coincidence of Louise's and Lucien's return to Angoulême as proof of deep love labouring under a misunderstanding on both sides. It was perhaps a lovers' quarrel which had occasioned her untoward marriage with Châtelet; forthwith a reaction of feeling set in against the latter. 'Well,' Louise whispered to Lucien at one o'clock in the morning before rising from her seat. 'We shall meet again the day after tomorrow. Do me the pleasure of being punctual.'

The Prefect's wife left Lucien with a slight but friendly bow, and went to say a few words to Sixte, who was looking for his hat.

'If what Madame du Châtelet has just told me is true, my dear Lucien, you may count on me,' said the Prefect, starting off after his wife who was leaving without him, as she used to do in Paris. 'From tonight your brother-in-law may consider himself out of danger.'

'Monsieur le Comte certainly owes me that,' Lucien smilingly answered.

'There you are, he's trumped our trick!' Cointet whispered to Petit-Claud, who had witnessed this parting. Petit-Claud, dumbfounded by Lucien's success, stupefied by his brilliant wit and graceful demeanour, was watching Françoise de La Haye, who was looking very admiringly at Lucien with an expression which seemed to say to her betrothed: 'I wish you were more like him.'

An exultant gleam flashed over Petit-Claud's face. 'The Prefect's dinner isn't till the day after tomorrow,' he said. 'We still have one day. I'll answer for everything.'

'Well, dear friend,' said Lucien to Petit-Claud, as they walked back at two in the morning. 'I came, I saw, I conquered! In a few hours Séchard will be very happy.'

'That's all I wanted to know,' thought Petit-Claud.

'I imagined you were merely a poet. You're a Lauzun[1] into the bargain! That makes you twice a poet,' he replied, giving Lucien a handshake. It was the last one they were ever to exchange.

28. *The peak of disaster*

'Eve, my dear,' said Lucien, waking his sister up. 'Good news! In one month David will be out of debt.'

'How so?'

'Well, my Louise of former days has peeped out from behind Madame du Châtelet. She loves me more than ever and is getting her husband to report to the Ministry of the Interior in favour of our discovery! . . . And so we haven't more than

1. Lauzun: a seventeenth century nobleman, courtier and, to some extent, adventurer; a man of wit but no stability. For a time in favour with Louis XIV, he fell into disgrace and was imprisoned for ten years.

a month of tribulation – time enough for me to avenge myself on the Prefect and make him the happiest of husbands!'

Eve thought she was still dreaming as she listened to her brother.

'When I saw the little grey salon again in which I had trembled like a child two years ago, when I examined the furniture, the painting and people's faces, the scales fell from my eyes! How one's ideas change in Paris!'

'Is that a good thing?' asked Eve, at last understanding what her brother was talking about.

'Come now, you're still asleep. We'll have a chat after breakfast,' said Lucien.

Cérizet's plan was exceedingly simple. Although it was one of those chancy ruses adopted by provincial bailiffs for the arrest of debtors, it was bound to succeed, for it was based as much on knowledge of Lucien's and David's characters as on their hopes. Among the little laundresses over whom he ruled like a Don Juan by playing them one against the other, the Cointets' compositor, temporarily seconded for special tasks, had picked out one of Basine Clerget's ironing-girls, one almost as beautiful as Madame Séchard, whose name was Henriette Signol and whose parents were small vine-growers living on their holding five miles away from Angoulême, on the road to Saintonges. Like all peasants, the Signols were not sufficiently well-off to keep their only child at home, and they had destined her for domestic service as a chamber-maid. In the provinces a chamber-maid must be able to starch and iron fine linen, and the reputation of Basine's predecessor, Madame Prieur, was such that the Signols apprenticed their daughter to her and paid for her board and keep. Madame Prieur belonged to the old breed of provincial employers who feel that they stand *in loco parentis*. She treated her apprentices as members of the family, took them to church and kept a conscientious eye on them. Henriette Signol, a buxom, dark-haired young woman with long, bushy hair, had the magnolia complexion which many Southern girls possess. That is why Henriette was one of the first working-girls whom Cérizet singled out. But since she belonged to a family of honest land-workers her only motives for yielding to him were jealousy, bad example, and the seductive phrase 'We'll get married!' which Cérizet whispered to her once he had become the Cointets' assistant compositor. Learning that the Signols owned vineyards worth ten or twelve thousand francs and a habitable house, the Parisian lost no time in making it impossible for Henriette to become another man's wife. The amours of the beautiful Henriette and little Cérizet had reached this stage when Petit-Claud talked of making him the owner of the Séchard printing-press by holding out the prospect of a kind of limited partnership whose purpose was to put a halter round his neck. The compositor was dazzled and his head was turned. Mademoiselle Signol now looked like standing in the way of his ambitions and he began to neglect the poor girl. In her despair Henriette clung the more closely to the Cointets' little compositor because it seemed as if he intended to drop her. Once he discovered that David was hiding in Mademoiselle Clerget's house, the ex-Parisian changed his ideas about Henriette, but not his behaviour to her. He proposed to exploit for his own ends the kind of lunacy which takes hold of a girl when she needs to marry her seducer if she is to hide her dishonour.

That very morning when Lucien was designing to reconquer Louise, Cérizet informed Henriette of Basine's secret and told her that their fortunes and marriage depended on discovering the spot in which David was hiding. Once instructed, Henriette had no difficulty in recognizing that the printer could not be elsewhere than in Mademoiselle Clerget's dressing-room. She thought that this bit of spying was quite harmless, but by involving her in this initial co-operation Cérizet had already made her his accomplice in treachery.

Lucien was still asleep when Cérizet, having come to Petit-Claud's office to find out what had happened at the reception, was listening to the lawyer's account of the trivial though important events which were to throw Angoulême into a turmoil.

'Has Lucien written any letter to you since his return?' the Parisian asked after giving a satisfied nod when Petit-Claud had finished.

'Here's the only one I have,' said the solicitor, handing Cérizet a few lines which Lucien had written to him on his sister's writing-paper.

'Right!' said Cérizet. 'Ten minutes before sunset, let Doublon lie in wait at the Porte-Palet. Let him post his gen-darmes and keep them hidden, and you'll get your man.'

'Are you sure of the arrangements you've made?' asked Petit-Claud with a close look at Cérizet.

'I'm trusting to chance,' said the former street-urchin. 'But chance is a downright scoundrel and doesn't like decent people.'

'You must pull it off,' the solicitor said curtly.

'I shall pull it off. It's you who have pushed me into this muck-heap, and you may well give me a few bank-notes to wipe myself clean ... But, Monsieur,' the Parisian added, detecting an expression on the solicitor's face which displeased him, 'if it turned out that you had taken me in, if you don't buy the printing-works for me within a week ... well, you'll leave a young widow behind you.' The former street-arab said this quietly with a murderous look.

'If we get David under lock and key by six o'clock, come at nine to Monsieur Gannerac's house, and we will settle your affair,' the solicitor peremptorily replied.

'It's a bargain: you'll get what you want, Guvnor!' said Cérizet.

Cérizet was already an expert in the industry which con-sists in washing out paper, one which today is endangering the interests of the Inland Revenue. He washed out the four lines Lucien had written and replaced them by what follows, forging Lucien's handwriting with a skill which promised a lamentable social future for the compositor.

My dear David,

You can go and see the Prefect without fear. Your affair is settled. What's more, you can come out of hiding immediately. I'll meet you on the way, to explain what line you should take with the Prefect.

Your brother,

LUCIEN.

At noon Lucien wrote a letter to David, telling him that the soirée had been a success and assuring him of the Prefect's protection. That very day, he said, du Châtelet would be sending the Minister a report on the invention: he was enthusiastic about it.

Just as Marion brought this letter to Mademoiselle Basine on the pretext of delivering Lucien's shirts for laundering, Cérizet, whom Petit-Claud had warned about the probability of this letter, took Mademoiselle Signol out for a walk on the banks of the Charente. No doubt a debate ensued in which Henriette's honesty put up a long resistance, for the stroll lasted two hours. Not only, Cérizet argued, were the interests of their child at stake, but also their future happiness and prosperity. What he was demanding was only a trifle: he was careful not to tell her what the consequences would be. What alarmed Henriette was the exorbitant price that had to be paid for this trifle. Nevertheless, in the end Cérizet persuaded his mistress to fall in with his stratagem. At five o'clock, Henriette was to go out, then return and tell Mademoiselle Clerget that Madame Séchard wanted to see her immediately. Then, a quarter of an hour after Basine had left, she was to go upstairs, knock at the dressing-room door and hand over the forged letter to David. After that Cérizet was staking everything on chance.

Eve, for the first time in over a year, felt that the iron grip in which neediness had held her was relaxing. She had some hope at last. She too wanted to enjoy her brother's company, show herself in public on the arm of the man who was adulated in his home-town, adored by the women and loved by the haughty Comtesse du Châtelet. She smartened herself up and proposed to take a walk in Beaulieu after dinner, arm in arm with her brother. At that time in September the whole of Angoulême goes out to take a breath of fresh air.

'Oh! It's the beautiful Madame Séchard,' a few voices exclaimed on seeing Eve.

'I would never have believed she would show herself in public,' one woman said.

'The husband's in hiding, the wife flaunts herself,' said

628

Madame Postel, loud enough for the poor woman to hear.

'Oh! Let's go back home. I shouldn't have come out,' said Eve to her brother.

A few minutes before sunset, the murmur of an assembled crowd rose from the slope leading down to L'Houmeau. Lucien and his sister, seized with curiosity, made their way in that direction, for they heard several people from L'Houmeau talking to one another as if some crime had just been committed.

'Likely enough it's a thief who's just been arrested ... He's as pale as death,' said a passer-by to the brother and sister as he saw them hurrying down in front of the swelling crowd.

Neither Lucien nor his sister had the slightest apprehension. They watched the thirty-odd children and old women, the workmen leaving their workshops and walking ahead of the gendarmes whose braided caps were conspicuous in the middle of the central group. This group, with a mob of about a hundred people behind it, was moving along like a storm-cloud.

'Oh!' said Eve. 'It's my husband!'

'David!' cried Lucien.

'It's his wife!' said the crowd of people, moving aside.

'But who or what brought you out?' Lucien asked.

'Your letter,' David answered, looking deathly pale.

'I knew it!' said Eve, and she fainted away.

Lucien lifted his sister up, two people helped him to carry her home, and Marion put her to bed. She had not come to by the time the doctor arrived. Lucien was then forced to admit to his mother that he was the cause of David's arrest, for he could not fathom the misunderstanding due to the forged letter. Thunderstruck by his mother's maledictory glance, he went upstairs to his room and locked himself in.

29. *A last farewell*

ANYONE who reads the following letter, written in fits and starts in the course of the night, will gain some idea of Lucien's agitation of mind from the disjointed statements thrown together one by one.

My beloved sister,

We saw each other just now for the last time. My mind is made up irrevocably. And this is why: in many a family there is a fatal being who, for that family, is a sort of blight. That is what I am in our family. This is not an observation of my own, but one made by a man with much experience of the world. We were supping, a gathering of friends, at the Rocher de Cancale. Among the many pleasantries exchanged this man, who was in the diplomatic service, told us that a certain young woman, who to everyone's astonishment had remained unmarried, was suffering from 'father-sickness'. He then developed his theory about family sicknesses. He explained to us how, without such and such a mother, such and such a household would have prospered, how such and such a son had ruined his father, how such and such a father had destroyed his children's future and the consideration they could have enjoyed. This social thesis, although jestingly sustained, was supported by so many examples in a matter of ten minutes that I was struck by it. This one truth made up for all the witty but extravagant paradoxes with which journalists amuse one another when they've no one to make a fool of.

Well then, I am the fatal being in our family. With a heart full of tenderness I behave like an enemy. I have requited all your devotion with evil. The latest blow I have dealt you, unintentionally, is the cruellest of all. Whilst I was leading an unworthy life in Paris, a life full of pleasure and misery, mistaking comradeship for friendship, giving up true friends for people who wanted and were bound to exploit me, forgetting you or only remembering you in order to bring evil upon you, you were modestly plodding along, making your way slowly yet surely towards the prosperity which I in my folly was trying to take by storm. While you were going from good to better, I was launching out into a disastrous way of life. Yes, I am a man of inordinate ambition, and it prevents me from following a humble career. I have tastes and have known pleasures the mere memory of which poisons the enjoyments within my reach, though in times past they would have satisfied me. Oh my dear Eve, I judge myself with more severity than anyone. I condemn myself and feel no pity for myself. The struggle for life in Paris calls for enduring strength, and my will-power only works in fits and starts; my brain only functions intermittently. I am so afraid of the future that I don't want to have a future, and I find the present unbearable.

I did want to see you again but I should have done better to have stayed away for ever. Yet to go on living far from home with no means of subsistence would be a folly which I will not add to all my other follies. Death to me seems preferable to a frustrated life; and in whatever circumstances I can imagine for myself my overweening vanity would make me do stupid things. Some creatures are like noughts in arithmetic: they need a positive number in front of them so that the zero they represent becomes a ten. I could only acquire some value by marrying a person of strong, relentless will. Madame de Bargeton was certainly the wife I needed and I missed my destiny by not leaving Coralie for her. David and you would have been excellent pilots for me, but you are not forceful enough to master my weakness which so to speak shies at domination. I like an easy, trouble-free existence, and when I want to get out of an awkward situation I'm capable of a cowardice which could take me to extremities. I was born to be a prince. I have more mental adroitness than is needed for success, but it only works spasmodically: in a career which so many ambitious persons follow the prize is won by the man who husbands his wit and still has some left at the end of the day. I should do evil, as I have just done here, with the best intentions in the world. Some men are made of oak; I'm perhaps only an elegant shrub trying to be a cedar.

This disparity between my capacity and my desires, this lack of equilibrium will always bring my efforts to naught. There are many such people in literary circles, thanks to this continual disproportion between will-power and desire. What destiny would await me? I can see what it would be when I call to mind certain well-established reputations in Paris which I saw fall into oblivion. On the threshold of old age I should be older than my years, without fame or fortune. Everything in me at present recoils before an old age of that sort: I don't want to be, socially speaking, a cast-off garment. Dear sister, whom I worship as much for your recent severity as for your early tenderness, if we have paid dearly for the pleasure I have had in seeing you and David again, later on perhaps you will think that no price was too high to pay for the last joys given to a poor creature who loved you! . . .

Make no search for me, and don't try to find out what has become of me. What intelligence I have will at least have helped me to do what I want to do. To resign myself, dear angel, would be to commit suicide every day. I have only resignation enough for one day, and I shall make use of it this very day.

2 a.m. Yes, my mind is made up. So good-bye for ever, dear Eve. I find some sweetness in the thought that from now on I shall be living only in your hearts. I shall have no other grave and I ask for no other. Good-bye once more. This is the last adieu you will receive from

Your brother,

LUCIEN.

After writing this letter Lucien went noiselessly downstairs, laid it on his nephew's cradle, imprinted a last kiss, moist with tears, on the brow of his sleeping sister and left the room. As day was breaking he put out his candle and, after taking a last look at the old house, very quietly opened the door into the alley. But in spite of the care he took, he awakened Kolb who was sleeping on a mattress on the workshop floor.

'Who goess zere!' cried Kolb.

'It is I,' said Lucien. 'I'm leaving, Kolb.'

'It voult haf peen petter if you hat nefer come,' Kolb muttered to himself, but loudly enough for Lucien to hear him.

'It would have been better if I had never come into the world,' Lucien replied. 'Good-bye, Kolb. I bear no grudge against you for having the same thought as myself. Tell David that in my dying breath I shall regret that I could not give him a farewell embrace.'

By the time the Alsatian was up and dressed, Lucien had closed the door of the house and was walking down towards the Charente along the Beaulieu promenade, clad as if he were going to a banquet, for his clothes from Paris and his elegant dandy's outfit were to be his funeral garments. Impressed by Lucien's tone and final words, Kolb thought of going to find out if his mistress knew about her brother's departure and if she had said good-bye to him; but seeing that the house was plunged in deep silence he concluded that this departure had been agreed upon beforehand and went back to bed.

30. *A chance encounter*

CONSIDERING the gravity of the subject, very little has been written about suicide, and no study has been made of it. Perhaps it is a malady that cannot be studied. Suicide results from a feeling which if you like we will call self-esteem in order not to confuse it with sense of honour. The day when a man despises himself, the day when he sees that others despise him, the moment when the realities of life are at variance with his hopes, he kills himself and thus pays homage to society, refusing to stand before it stripped of his virtues or his splendour. Whatever one may say, amongst atheists (exception must be made for the Christian view of suicide) cowards alone accept a life of dishonour. There are three kinds of suicide: firstly the kind which is no more than the last bout of a long-lasting sickness and surely belongs to the domain of pathology; secondly suicide born of despair; thirdly suicide which is reasoned out. Lucien was proposing to kill himself through despair and reasoning: from these two kinds of suicide retreat is possible. Pathological suicide alone is irrevocable; but often the three causes come together, as in the case of Jean-Jacques Rousseau.[1]

Once he had made his resolve, Lucien fell to deliberating about the means: as a poet he wanted to make a poetic end. He had first of all thought of simply throwing himself into the Charente; but as he walked down the slopes of Beaulieu for the last time he could hear in advance the hubbub his suicide would arouse and visualize the appalling spectacle of his body, swollen and deformed, being dragged from the

1. The theory that Rousseau committed suicide has long been exploded.

water and the inquest which would follow: as is the case with a number of suicides, his self-esteem looked beyond death. During the day he had spent at Courtois's mill he had walked along the river and had noticed, not far from the mill, one of those round pools such as are formed along a small water-course, whose tremendous depth is emphasized by the calmness of the surface. The water is neither green, nor blue, nor yellow: it looks like a mirror of polished steel. The edges of this basin presented neither blue nor yellow flags, nor the wide leaves of the water-lily; the grass on the bank was short and close, and it was surrounded by weeping willows, all of them picturesquely spaced. One could easily guess that it was un-fathomably deep. Anyone with the courage to fill his pockets with stones must inevitably drown in it, and his body would never be recovered. 'This spot,' the poet had said to himself while admiring the pretty scene, 'would be a delicious one to drown in.'

The memory of this came back to him just as he was reaching L'Houmeau. So he made his way towards Marsac, his mind full of final and funereal thoughts, but firmly resolved to use this means of keeping his death secret, not to be the subject of an inquest, not to be buried in earth, not to be seen in the horrible state of drowned men coming up to the surface. He quickly arrived at the foot of one of those slopes too frequently found on the roads of France, and especially between Angoulême and Poitiers. The stage-coach from Bordeaux to Paris was speeding along and no doubt the passengers would soon be getting down in order to walk up this long hill. Lucien did not want to be seen, so he hurried down a little sunken lane into a vineyard where he began to pick flowers. When he returned to the main road he had in his hand a big bunch of stonecrop, a yellow flower which grows on the pebbly soil in vineyards. He emerged just behind a traveller dressed entirely in black, with powdered hair, wearing shoes of Orleans calf-skin with silver buckles, his face tanned and seamed as if it had been accidentally scorched when he was a child. This traveller, in a patently clerical garb, was walking slowly and smoking a cigar. On hearing Lucien jumping on the road from the vineyard, the stranger turned round and seemed to be struck by the poet's profoundly melancholy beauty, his symbolic bouquet and his elegant clothes. He looked like a hunter coming upon a prey long and vainly tracked. In naval fashion, he waited for Lucien to reach him and slackened his pace as if he wished to survey the plain below the slope. Lucien did likewise and noticed a little barouche drawn by two horses and a postilion who was leading them.

'You have let the stage-coach pass by, Monsieur. You will lose your seat unless you care to get into my carriage to catch up with it, for the stage-coach goes quicker than the local omnibus.' The traveller pronounced these words with a markedly Spanish accent and his offer was made with exquisite courtesy. Without waiting for a reply, the Spaniard took a cigar-case from his pocket, opened it and offered Lucien a cigar.

'I am not travelling,' Lucien replied, 'and I am too near the end of my term of life to allow myself the pleasure of smoking.'

'You are hard on yourself,' the Spaniard rejoindered. 'Although I am an honorary canon of Toledo cathedral, I treat myself now and then to a little cigar. God gave us tobacco to quiet our passions and soothe our grief . . . You seem to have some sorrow, or at least you are carrying an emblem of sorrow, like that sad deity, Hymen. Come . . . all your woes will fly away with the smoke . . .'

'Forgive me, father,' Lucien dryly replied. 'No cigar-smoke can blow away my sorrows.' As he spoke, his eyes became wet with tears.

'Young man! Can it be divine providence which prompted me to take a little exercise to dispel the drowsiness that over-takes those who travel in the mornings, so that by offering you consolation I can fulfil my mission here below? . . . But what sorrows can you have at your age?'

'Your consolations, father, would be in vain. You are Spanish, I am French. You believe in the precepts of Holy Church. I am an atheist . . .'

'*Santa Virgen del Pilar!* . . . You are an atheist!' the priest exclaimed, passing his arm through Lucien's with maternal eagerness. 'Why, that's one of the curious phenomena I promised I would study in Paris! In Spain we do not believe in atheists ... It's only in France, and only when one is nineteen, that one can have such opinions.'

'Oh! I'm an out-and-out atheist. I don't believe in God, or in society, or in the possibility of happiness. Take a good look at me, father, for in a few hours' time I shall no longer exist. I shall never see the sun again!' said Lucien, somewhat bombastically, pointing to the heavens.

'Come now, what have you done that you should die? Who has sentenced you to death?'

'A sovereign court: myself!'

'Child that you are!' cried the priest. 'Have you committed murder? Does the scaffold await you? Let's reason things out. If, as you say, you want to return to nothingness, everything on earth is a matter of indifference to you.'

Lucien gave a nod of assent.

'Well then, why can't you tell me your troubles? ... No doubt some love affair which has gone wrong? ... '

Lucien gave a very significant shrug.

'You want to kill yourself to avoid dishonour or because life has lost its meaning? Very well, you can kill yourself as easily at Poitiers as at Angoulême, or at Tours as easily as at Poitiers. The quicksands of the Loire do not give back their prey ... '

'No, father,' Lucien replied. 'I have found what I want. About three weeks ago I came upon a most attractive harbour where a man disgusted with this world can come ashore in the next one.'

'The next world? ... I thought you were an atheist.'

'Oh, what I mean by the next world is my future metamorphosis into an animal or a plant.'

'Have you an incurable illness?'

'Yes, father.'

'Ah, we're coming to it,' said the priest. 'And what is it?'

'Poverty.'

The priest looked at Lucien with a smile and said to him,

with infinite grace and an almost ironical smile: 'A diamond has no idea of its value.'

'Only a priest,' cried Lucien, 'could flatter a man who is destitute and intends to die!'

'You will not die,' the Spaniard firmly declared.

'I've often heard,' Lucien retorted, 'of people being robbed on the highway, but never of their being enriched.'

'You are going to hear of it,' said the priest after ascertaining that his carriage was far enough away for them to go on walking along together.

31. The story of a favourite

'LISTEN,' said the priest, chewing away at his cigar. 'Your poverty could scarcely be a reason for dying. I need a secretary, since mine has recently died in Barcelona. I find myself in the same situation as Baron Gœrtz, the famous minister of Charles the Twelfth of Sweden, who arrived without a secretary in a small town when he was making for Sweden as I am making for Paris. He met a goldsmith's son, remarkably handsome, though certainly not so handsome as you. Baron Gœrtz found this young man intelligent – just as I find you with the hallmark of poetry on your brow. He took him into his carriage, just as I am going to take you into mine; and this youngster, whose lot was to burnish plate and make jewellery in a small provincial town like Angoulême, became his favourite – just as you will be mine. Once at Stockholm, he installed him as secretary and put a great burden of work upon him. This young secretary spent his nights writing, and like all hard workers he contracted a habit: his was to chew paper. That of the late Monsieur de Malesherbes was to blow smoke in people's faces, and incidentally he did this one day to some important person or other who had a law-suit depending on his report. Our handsome young man began with blank paper, but he grew tired of that and took to masticating manuscripts, which he found more tasty – people didn't smoke so much then as they do today. Finally the little secretary, passing from one flavour to another, acquired the habit of munching parchment. At that time Russia and Sweden were negotiating a treaty which the Swedish States-General was forcing on Charles the Twelfth, just as in 1814 Europe was trying to impose a peace treaty on Napoleon. The basis of these negotiations was a treaty the two powers were drawing up on the subject of Finland. Gœrtz entrusted the original document to his secretary, but a slight difficulty arose: the treaty was no-where to be found. The States-General imagined that the Minister had hit on the idea of suppressing the document in order to serve the King's passion for war. Baron Gœrtz was accused of this: his secretary then owned up to having eaten it. He was brought to trial, found guilty and condemned to death.... However, since you've not come to that pass, have a cigar and smoke it while we wait for our barouche.'

Lucien took a cigar and lit it at the priest's cigar in Spanish fashion, thinking as he did so: 'He's right. I've plenty of time to kill myself.' The Spaniard continued:

'It's often just when young people are most in despair about their future that their luck turns. That is what I wanted to tell you, but I preferred to prove it by an example. The handsome secretary, condemned to death, was in so much more desperate a plight because the King of Sweden was powerless to re-prieve him since he had been sentenced by the Swedish States-General. But he was ready to wink at an escape. The good-looking little secretary got away in a barge with a few crowns in his pocket and came to the court of Kurland armed with a letter of recommendation from Gœrtz to the Duke, to whom the Minister explained the misadventure and his protégé's mania. The Duke appointed the young man secretary to his major-domo. The Duke had spendthrift habits, a pretty wife and a major-domo: three causes of ruin. If now you were to imagine that this personable young man, after being sentenced to death for having eaten the Finnish Treaty, shook off this depraved taste, you know nothing of the hold a vice has on men: even the threat of execution won't stop them indulging in a pleasure of their own invention.

'How does a vice get such a strangle-hold? From its inherent strength or from human weakness? Are there certain cravings which border on insanity? I can't help laughing at the reformers of morals who try to combat such disorders with eloquent exhortations. There came a time when the Duke, alarmed at his major-domo's refusal to satisfy his requests for money, asked to see the account-books. A foolish notion! There's nothing easier than to produce an account: that's not where the difficulty lies. The major-domo handed all the documents to his secretary so that he could draw up the balance-sheet of the Kurland Civil List. He settled down to this task and sat up all night to finish it. Half-way through, the little paper-eater discovered that he was masticating a receipt for a considerable sum of money, signed by the Duke himself. Panic-stricken, he stopped before he had eaten his way through the signature, ran and flung himself at the feet of the Duchess, explained his mania to her and implored his sovereign lady to shield him – what's more, this took place in the middle of the night! The young clerk's beauty made such an impression on Her Grace that, when she became a widow, she married him.

'Thus, right back in the eighteenth century, in a country where armorial bearings were all that mattered, a goldsmith's son became a sovereign prince! . . . He did even better for himself: he became Regent at the death of Catherine the First, ruled over the Empress Anne and set out to be the Richelieu of Russia. Well, young man, learn this fact: you may be better-looking even than Biron, but I'm worth more than Baron Gœrtz although I'm only a canon. Come along, get in! We'll find you a Duchy of Kurland in Paris; or, if we can't find a duchy, at any rate we'll find a duchess.'

The Spaniard slipped his arm through Lucien's, literally forced him up into the carriage, and the postilion closed the door on them.

'Now talk, I'm listening,' said the Canon of Toledo to the stupefied Lucien. 'I'm an old priest to whom you can tell everything without risk. So far no doubt you've only devoured your patrimony or Mamma's money. You've done your little moonlight flit and, bless us! you're all sense of honour right down to the tip of your pretty, dainty little boots! . . . Come, make a clean confession; it will be absolutely as if you were talking to yourself.'

Lucien felt he was in the situation of the fisherman in an Arabian tale who, trying to drown himself in mid-ocean, is borne down into a country under the sea where he is made king. The Spanish priest seemed so genuinely affectionate that the poet did not hesitate to open his heart to him. And so, as they travelled from Angoulême to Ruffec, he recounted his whole life, leaving out none of his misdeeds and finishing up with the latest disaster for which he was responsible. At the moment when he was ending his story, the more poetically delivered because Lucien was repeating it for the third time in a fortnight, they arrived at a point on the road near Ruffec, where the Rastignac family had their domain. The first time he mentioned this name, the Spaniard gave a start.[1]

'It's from there,' said Lucien, 'that young Rastignac set out. He's certainly not up to my standard, but he's had better luck than I have.'

'Ah!'

'Yes, that quaint little country seat is his father's manor. As I told you, he became the lover of Madame de Nucingen, the wife of the famous banker. As for me, I gave myself over to poetry. He was more clever and went in for more solid things.'

The priest halted his barouche, wishing out of curiosity to walk along the little avenue from the main road to the manor-house. He looked at it all with more interest than Lucien would have expected from a Spanish priest.

'So you know the Rastignacs?' Lucien asked him.

'I know everyone in Paris,' said the Spaniard, getting back into the carriage.

1. As *Splendours and Miseries of Courtesans* makes clear, Herrera, who was the master-criminal Vautrin in disguise, had already made an unsuccessful attempt to capture Eugène de Rastignac (see *Old Goriot*). Hence his interest in the Rastignac domain.

32. *A history lecture for the ambitious – by a disciple of Machiavelli*

'AND so, for lack of ten or twelve thousand francs, you were going to drown yourself. You're a child, you know nothing of men or things. A man's destiny is worth whatever price he puts on it, and you value your future at only twelve thousand francs. Well, I shall presently pay a higher price for you. As for your brother-in-law's imprisonment, that's a trifle. If the good Monsieur Séchard has made a discovery, he'll be a rich man. Rich people have never been put in prison for debt. You don't seem to me to be well up in history. There are two kinds of history: official history, all lies, the history which is taught in schools, history *ad usum delphini*. Then there's secret history, which explains how things really happened: a scandalous kind of history.

'Let me tell you briefly another little story you've never heard. An ambitious young man, a priest, wanted to get into public affairs and became the sycophant of a favourite – a queen's favourite. The favourite took an interest in the priest and promoted him to the rank of minister by getting him a seat on the Council. One evening, one of those men who think they're doing a service (never do a man a service without his asking), wrote to tell the ambitious young man that his benefactor was in danger of his life. The King was angry at having a master, and the next day the favourite was to be murdered if he showed himself at the palace. Well now, young man! What would you have done on receiving such a letter?'

'I should have gone straight away to warn my benefactor,' Lucien promptly replied.

'You're certainly still the child your life-story has shown you to be,' said the priest. 'The man in question said to himself: "If the King is ready to commit a crime, my benefactor is done for. I must pretend I received this letter too late." And he slept until it was time for the favourite to be murdered.'

641

'But he was a monster!' said Lucien, suspecting that the priest's intention was to test his moral rectitude.

'All great men are monsters,' the Canon replied. 'That man was Cardinal Richelieu, and his benefactor was the Maréchal d'Ancre. You see you don't know your history of France. Was I not right in telling you that the history taught in schools is a collection of dates and facts which in the first place are extremely dubious and which have not the slightest significance? What use is it to you to have heard of Joan of Arc? Have you ever drawn the conclusion that if France had at that time accepted the Angevin dynasty, the Plantagenets, two united peoples would be ruling the whole world today; and that the two islands in which all the political disturbances of Europe are fomented would be two provinces of France? . . . And have you studied the means whereby the Medicis, once simple merchants, came to be Grand-Dukes of Tuscany?'

'A poet, in France, doesn't have to be as learned as a Benedictine.'

'Well, young man, they came to be Grand-Dukes in the same way as Richelieu came to be a minister. If you had searched history to find out the human causes of events instead of learning "facts" by heart, in tabloid form, you would have deduced your own principles of conduct from it. From what I have just chosen haphazard from the collection of genuine facts, this law emerges: look upon men, and women particularly, as mere tools, but without letting them realize it. Worship as if he were God himself the man who, being higher placed than you, can be of use to you, and don't leave him until he has paid dear for the servility you have shown him. In short, in your dealings with the world, be as ruthless as a Jew, be as base as he is; if you want to gain power, do what he does to gain money. And mark this too: have no more concern for a man in disgrace than you would if he had never existed. Shall I tell you why you must behave in this way? You want to dominate society, don't you? You must begin by obeying society and studying it closely. Scholars study books, politicians study men, their interests and the motives for their acts. Now the world, society and the common run of men are fatalists: they bow to the accomplished fact. Do you know why I'm giving you this little lecture on history? It's because I believe you to be inordinately ambitious.'

'Yes, father, I am.'

'I could see that,' the Canon went on. 'But at the moment you're saying to yourself: "This canon from Spain is inventing anecdotes and squeezing the juice out of history in order to prove to me that I've been too virtuous."'

Lucien smiled at seeing his thoughts so well divined.

'Well, young man! Let's take a few commonly accepted facts of history. One day France is practically conquered by the English and the King has only one province left. Two persons emerge from the common people: a poor girl, that same Joan of Arc I was talking about, and a burgher named Jacques Cœur. She offers her sword and the prestige of her maidenhood, he offers his gold, and the kingdom is saved. But the girl is captured . . . The King, who could have ransomed the girl, lets her be burnt alive! As for the heroic burgher, the King allows him to be accused of capital crimes by his courtiers, who swoop down on all his property. The spoils torn from this innocent man, pursued, hemmed in and struck down by justice, enrich five noble houses . . . And this man, the father of the Archbishop of Bourges, leaves the country never to return, without a penny of his French belongings and having no other money of his own except what he had entrusted to Arabs and Saracens in Egypt. You may reply that such examples of ingratitude belong to the distant past, that they are separated from the present by three centuries of public education, that the skeletons of that period belong to the realm of fable. Well, young man, do you believe in France's latest demi-god, Napoleon? He kept one of his generals in disgrace, was reluctant to make a marshal of him and never willingly made use of his services. His name was Kellermann. Why did Napoleon behave like this? Kellermann saved France and the First Consul on the field of Marengo by a dashing cavalry charge which was applauded amid the blood and fire of battle. This heroic charge was never mentioned in army despatches. The reason for Napoleon's coldness towards Kellermann is the reason for the disgrace which befell Fouché and Prince Talleyrand: it's the ingratitude of Charles VII and Richelieu all over again, the ingratitude . . . '

'But, father, supposing you save my life and make my fortune, you're making my burden of gratitude to you a very light one!'

'Little scamp,' said the Abbé with a smile, tweaking Lucien's ear with an almost royal familiarity, 'if you showed me ingratitude you would then prove yourself a strong man and I should bend the knee before you. However you're not yet at that stage. You've been just like a school-boy, in too much of a hurry to become one of the masters. That's what's wrong with Frenchmen in your generation: they've all been spoiled by Napoleon's meteoric success. You're leaving the service because you couldn't get the epaulettes you want. But have you concentrated all your desire and actions on a single purpose?'

'Alas, no!' said Lucien.

'You've been what the English call *inconsistent*,' the Abbé continued with a smile.

'Does it matter what I *have* been, if I can no longer *be* anything?'

'Let there be behind all your fine qualities a force which is *semper virens*,' said the priest, wanting to show that he knew a little Latin, 'and nothing in the world will stand against you. I am already quite fond of you . . . '

Lucien gave an incredulous smile.

'Yes,' the stranger went on in answer to this smile. 'I'm as interested in you as if you were my son, and I have enough power to be able to speak to you frankly. Do you know what I like about you? You've made a clean breast of your past and so can listen to a lecture on morals which you won't get anywhere else; for men in the herd are even more hypocritical than they are when self-interest forces them to act apart. That's why one spends a good deal of one's life weeding out what one has allowed to grow in one's heart during adolescence. This operation is called gaining experience.'

As he listened to the priest Lucien was thinking: 'This man is some elderly politician delighted to amuse himself as he travels along. The whim has taken him to muddle the ideas of a poor young wretch whom he found on the verge of suicide. He'll drop me once he's had his little joke ... But he's an expert in paradox and strikes me as being quite a match for Blondet or Lousteau.'

Despite so sage a reflection, the diplomat's effort at corruption made a deep impression on a man only too disposed to welcome it, and its effect was the more devastating because it was supported by well-known facts. Caught in the spell of this cynical conversation, Lucien was all the more inclined to cling on to life again because he felt as if he had been snatched by a powerful arm from a suicide's watery grave.

In this respect, the priest was obviously fighting a winning battle. And so, from time to time, a mischievous smile had seasoned his historical sarcasms.

33. *A lecture on ethics – by a disciple of Mendoza*

'IF your treatment of ethics in any way resembles your views on history,' said Lucien, 'I should very much like to know what the motive is for the charity you seem to be showing me at present.'

'That, young man,' he replied with the astuteness of a priest who sees that his wiles are succeeding, 'is the concluding point in my sermon, and you will allow me to hold it in reserve, otherwise we shall be together for the rest of the day!'

'Very well, talk ethics to me,' said Lucien, thinking to himself: 'I'll try and bring him out.'

'Ethics, young man,' said the priest, 'begin with law. If religion alone were at stake, there would be no need for law: religious peoples have few laws. Above civil law there is political law. Well, would you like to know what a politically-minded man finds inscribed above the door-way to this nineteenth century of yours? In 1793 Frenchmen invented popular sovereignty and it ended up in imperial absolutism. So much for our national history. As for morals, Madame Tallien and Madame de Beauharnais behaved in much the same way, but Napoleon married the one and made her your Empress, and never admitted the other to his court although she was a princess. Napoleon was a Jacobin in 1793; in 1804 he donned the Iron Crown. From 1806 onwards the ferocious champions of 'Equality or Death' acquiesced in the creation of a new nobility, which Louis XVIII was to legitimize. The emigrant aristocracy, which lords it today in its Faubourg Saint-German, behaved worse still: it took to usury, commerce, pastry-making, cooking, farming and sheep-rearing. In France then, in politics as well as ethics, all and sundry reached a goal which gave the lie to their beginnings: their opinions belied their behaviour, or else their behaviour belied their opinions. Logic went by the board, both with the people in power and private individuals. So you no longer have any ethics. Today, with you, success is the ruling motive for all the action you take of whatever kind. Deeds therefore are nothing in themselves: they exist entirely in the ideas other people have about them. Hence, young man, another precept: put up a fine outward show! Hide the reverse of the coin, but keep the obverse bright and shining. Discretion, a watchword for ambitious persons, is also that of the Society of Jesus to which I belong: adopt it as yours. Great people commit almost as many despicable deeds as the very poor, but they commit them under cover and make a parade of virtue; and so they remain great. Humble folk keep their virtues under cover and only expose their misery to the light of day; and so they are despised. You hid what was great in you and only showed your sores. You flaunted your actress-mistress in public and lived with her in her rooms. There was nothing reprehensible in this; everybody recognized that you were both perfectly free to do as you liked; but you were flouting social conventions and failed to win the respect which society accords to those who observe its rules. If you had left Coralie to this Monsieur Camusot or if you had kept your relations with her secret, you would have married Madame de Bargeton and you'd now be Prefect of Angoulême and the Marquis de Rubempré.

'Change your tactics. Make a display of your beauty, grace, wit, poetic talent. If you indulge in minor infamies, do it within four walls. From then on you'll no longer be guilty of tarnishing the back-cloth in the great theatre which we call the world. Napoleon had a phrase for this: "Wash your dirty linen in private." There is a corollary to this second precept: *form* is all-important. Understand clearly what I mean by *form*. There are uneducated people who, under the pressure of need, steal a sum of money with violence from somebody else: they are dubbed criminals and brought to justice. An impecunious genius invents a process which will bring him a fortune if he can exploit it: you lend him three thousand francs (like the Cointets who took over your debt of three thousand francs in order to despoil your brother-in-law), you persecute him into ceding you the whole or part of his secret, and you only have your conscience to reckon with: your conscience won't bring you to the Court of Assizes. The enemies of social order take advantage of this contrast in order to yelp at justice and, in the name of the people, get angry because a burglar or a chicken-stealer in an inhabited area is sent to the galleys, whereas a man who ruins whole families by fraudulent bankruptcy gets off with a few months' imprisonment at the worst. But these hypocrites know full well that by sentencing the burglar the judges are upholding the barriers between rich and poor. If these were overthrown social order would come to an end. Whereas the bankrupt, the clever rogue who diverts an inheritance, the banker who brings a business to ruin in order to line his pockets, is merely an instrument by which fortunes change hands.

'Thus, my son, society is forced, for its own sake, to make distinctions; that is what I want you to do for your own sake. The great point is to measure up to the whole of society. Napoleon, Richelieu and the Medicis measured up to their century. Present-day society no longer worships the true God, but the Golden Calf! That is the religion of your Charter, which politically speaking takes no account of anything but property. Is that not tantamount to saying to every subject: "Try and get rich"? . . . Once you have managed to make a fortune in a legal way and have become the wealthy Marquis de Rubempré, then you'll allow yourself the luxury of a sense of honour. You'll then make such a parade of scrupulousness that no one will dare to accuse you of ever having fallen short of it, even though you had done so in the process of getting on. – Not that I would ever advise that!' the priest added, taking Lucien's hand and patting it.

'What then must you get into that handsome head of yours? Just this simple idea: set yourself a splendid goal, but don't let anyone see what means you adopt and the steps you take to reach it. You have been acting like a child: be a man. Do what a hunter does. Lie in wait, lie in ambush in the world of Paris. Keep on the watch for a lucky chance which will bring you your quarry. Spare neither your person nor your so-called dignity, for we are all at the beck and call of something, perhaps a vice, perhaps a need. But observe the law of laws: secretiveness!'

'You horrify me, father!' said Lucien. 'This sounds to me like a code for highwaymen.'

'You're right,' said the Canon, 'but it's not of my invention. That's the way upstarts have reasoned, both the dynasty of Austria and the dynasty of France. You have nothing: you're in the same situation as the Medicis, Richelieu and Napoleon when they first conceived their ambitions. These people, my boy, reckoned that their future had to be paid for with ingratitude, treachery and the most flagrant inconsistencies of conduct. Who wants all must dare all. Let's reason it out. When you sit down to a game of *bouillotte*, do you argue about the rules? They exist, you accept them.'

'Well now,' thought Lucien. 'He knows how to play *bouillotte*.'

'How do you behave over a game of *bouillotte*?' asked the priest. 'Do you practise that finest of all virtues, openness? Not only do you hide your hand, you even try to make your opponents believe that you're going to lose the game when you're sure of winning it. In short, you dissimulate, don't you? ... You lie in order to win a hundred francs! ... What would you say of a player who was generous enough to inform the others that he held four aces? Well, an am-

648

bitious man who wants to follow the precepts of virtue while he's struggling along in a career in which his antagonists scrap them, is a child to whom hardened politicians would say what card-players say to the man who throws his honours cards away: "Monsieur, you should never play *bouillotte*." Is it you who make the rules in the ambition-game? Why did I tell you to measure up to society? Because in these days, young man, society has gradually arrogated to itself so many rights over the individual that the individual finds himself obliged to fight back against society. There are no longer any laws, merely conventions, that is to say humbug: nothing but *form*.'

Lucien made a gesture of astonishment.

'Ah, my child,' said the priest, fearing that he had shocked the unsophisticated young man. 'Did you expect to find the angel Gabriel in an Abbé whose shoulders have to bear all the iniquity in the diplomatic tug-of-war between two kings? I'm an intermediary between Ferdinand VII and Louis XVIII, two great kings who both owe their thrones to shrewd scheming ... I believe in God, but I have even greater belief in our Order, and our Order only believes in the temporal power. To strengthen the temporal power, our Order supports the Church Apostolic, Catholic and Roman, that is to say the sum total of sentiments which keep the common people in bounds. We are the modern Knights Templars, and we have our doctrine. Like that of the Templars, our organization was broken up for the same reasons: it had measured up to society. You want to be a soldier? I will be your commanding officer. Obey me as a wife obeys her husband, as a child obeys her mother, and I guarantee that in less than three years' time you'll be the Marquis de Rubempré, you'll marry into one of the noblest families in the Faubourg Saint-Germain and one day you'll have a seat on the bench of Peers. At this moment, if I had not amused you with my conversation, what would you be? An undiscoverable corpse deep down in a bed of mud. Well, use your imagination as a poet ... ' (At this point Lucien gazed at his protector with curiosity.) 'The young man sitting here in this barouche with the Abbé Carlos Herrera, honorary

649

canon in the cathedral chapter of Toledo, secret envoy of his Majesty Ferdinand VII to His Majesty the King of France, bearing a despatch in which the former probably says: "When you have freed me from my enemies, have all the people I am humouring at present hanged, including my envoy so that he will really be a secret one" . . . this young man,' said the stranger, 'has nothing in common with the poet who has just died. I've fished you out of the water, brought you back to life, and you belong to me as a creature belongs to its creator, the afreet to the genie, the icoglan to the sultan, the body to the soul! My strong arm will maintain you on your road to power, and yet I promise you a life of pleasure, honour and continuous festivity . . . You'll never lack for money. You will shine and show off while I, bending low in the mud of the foundations, shall be propping up the brilliant edifice of your fortune. I myself love power for power's sake! I shall always be happy to see you enjoying the things which are forbidden to me. In short, I shall live in you! . . . And in any case, the day when this pact between a human being and a demon, a child and a diplomat, no longer suits you, you can still go and find some little pool, like the one you mentioned, to drown yourself in: you'll be slightly more or slightly less than what you are today – an unhappy or a dishonoured man.'

34. *A Spanish profile*

'THAT was not one of the Archbishop of Granada's homilies!' Lucien exclaimed as the barouche drew to a halt at a relay post.

'I don't know what title you would give to this educational digest, my son – I'm going to adopt you and make you my heir – but it's the code for ambitious people. God's elect are few in number. There's no choice: either one must bury oneself in a monastery – and there too the world is often to be found in miniature – or one must accept this code.'

'Perhaps it's better not to know all that,' said Lucien in an attempt to sound the spiritual depths of this formidable priest.

'What!' the Canon rejoindered. 'After playing your game without knowing the rules, you would give it up just when you're holding strong cards, with a dependable sponsor to back you? And don't you even want to take your revenge? Have you no desire to climb on the backs of the people who chased you from Paris?'

Lucien shuddered, as if these terrible, nerve-shattering sounds came from some bronze instrument or a Chinese gong.

'I'm only a humble priest,' the man continued, and a malignant expression appeared on his sun-tanned face. 'But if I had been humiliated, vexed, tortured, betrayed and sold as you have been by the rogues you told me about, I should feel like an Arab of the desert! . . . Yes, I would give myself over body and soul to vengeance. I wouldn't care whether I ended my life on a gibbet, under the rack, impaled or guillotined as they do it in your country. But I wouldn't let them cut off my head until I'd trampled my enemies underfoot.'

Lucien remained silent. He was no longer anxious to 'bring the priest out'.

'Some men descend from Abel, some from Cain,' said the priest by way of conclusion. 'I'm a mixture of both: Cain to my enemies, Abel to my friends, and woe to him who awakens the Cain in me! . . . After all, you're a Frenchman. I'm a Spaniard and a canon into the bargain!'

'He's more of an Arab than anything!' thought Lucien, scrutinizing the protector that Heaven had just sent him.

The Abbé Carlos Herrera had nothing about him that betokened the Jesuit or any member of a religious order. He was stout and short, with broad hands and broad chest, herculean strength and a glance that terrified, though it could be softened into mildness at will. His bronzed complexion, which allowed nothing to show of what went on inside him, inspired repulsion rather than attachment. A head of fine, long hair, powdered in the Talleyrand style, gave this strange diplomat the appearance of a bishop; moreover his blue ribbon, fringed with white, from which hung a cross of gold, was indicative of an ecclesiastical dignitary. His black silk stockings set off the curve of his athlete's legs. His exquisitely spotless clothes bespoke a personal fastidiousness which one does not always find in priests, particularly in Spain. A tricorne figured on the front of his carriage, which was blazoned with the arms of Spain. Although there was much that was repulsive in his physiognomy, this effect was attenuated by his manners which were at once brusque and ingratiating; and it was evident that for Lucien the priest was doing his best to be seductive, wheedling, almost feline. Lucien noted all these details with an anxious air. He felt that this instant must settle the question of life or death for him, for they had come to the second relay stage after Ruffec. The Spanish priest's latest words had set many chords in his heart vibrating; and, be it said to Lucien's shame and that of the priest who, with perspicacious eye, was studying the poet's handsome face, they were the most harshly resonant since they responded to sentiments of depravity. Lucien could see himself in Paris once more, snatching again at the reins of domination which his unskilled hands had let fall, and taking his revenge! The comparisons he had recently been making between provincial and Parisian life – his most urgent motive for suicide – were fading from his mind. He would be back again in congenial surroundings, but this time under the aegis of as deep and wicked a schemer as Cromwell.

'I was alone before: now there will be two of us,' he was thinking.

The more he had laid bare his past misdeeds, the more interest the cleric had shown. His indulgence had increased in proportion to Lucien's misfortunes, and he had shown no astonishment. None the less Lucien wondered about the motives of this conductor of royal intrigues. He first of all took refuge in a commonplace explanation: the generosity of Spaniards! A Spaniard is generous, an Italian will poison you out of jealousy, a Frenchman is frivolous, a German is ingenuous, a Jew is despicable, an Englishman is noble-hearted! Reverse these propositions and you will come nearer to the truth. The Jews have cornered the supply of gold, but they are great composers, great actors, great singers. They build palaces, write works like the *Reisebilder*, they are admirable poets. They are more powerful now than ever they were; their religion is accepted, and finally they lend money to the Pope! Germans are so given to hair-splitting that in their most trivial dealings with a foreigner they stipulate for a contract. Frenchmen have been clapping their hands for fifty years at the stupidities proffered by their National Theatre; they go on wearing inconceivable hats and only accept a change of government on condition that it remains the same! The English flaunt their perfidiousness in the face of the whole world, and their rapacity is equally horrible. The Spaniards, who once possessed the gold of the two Indies, are penniless. There's no country in the world where less poisoning takes place than in Italy and where manners are so easy and so courteous. Spaniards have lived much on the reputation of the Moors.

When the Spaniard climbed back into his barouche, he whispered to the postilion: 'You must go as fast as the mail-coach: three francs for you if you make good speed.'

As Lucien was hesitating to climb in, the priest said: 'Come along.' Lucien got in on the pretext of trying an *argumentum ad hominem* on him.

'Father,' he said. 'A man who has just, in the coolest way in the world, reeled off maxims which most middle-class people would regard as profoundly immoral . . .'

'They *are* immoral,' said the priest. 'That, my son, is what Jesus Christ said: "It must needs be that offences come." And that is why society shows such great horror at them.'

'A man of your calibre will not be astonished at the question I am going to put.'

'Go ahead, my son!' said Carlos Herrera. 'You don't know me. Do you think I would take a secretary before I knew that he was principled enough not to rob me? I'm quite happy about you. You still have all the innocence of a man who's capable of committing suicide at twenty. What's your question?'

'Why are you interested in me? What price are you asking for my obedience? Why are you offering me so much? What do you expect to get out of it?'

The Spaniard looked at Lucien and began to smile.

'Let's wait until we get to a hill. We'll walk up it and talk in the open. In this carriage we might be overheard.'

Silence reigned for some time between the two travellers, and the speed at which they tore along contributed to what we might call Lucien's moral intoxication.

'Father, here's a hill,' said Lucien, awakening as from a dream.

'Right! Let's walk,' said the priest, shouting to the postilion to halt.

And they both of them jumped down.

35. Why criminality and corruption go hand in hand

'My child,' said the Spaniard, taking Lucien by the arm. 'Have you pondered over Otway's *Venice preserved*? Have you understood the deep friendship between man and man which binds Pierre to Jaffeir, makes them indifferent about women and alters all social relationships for them? ... I'm putting that question to the poet in you.'

'The Canon knows something about drama too,' Lucien thought to himself. 'Have you read Voltaire?' he asked.

'I've done better than that,' said the Canon. 'I put him into practice.'

'Don't you believe in God? ...'

'So now I'm the atheist!' said the priest with a smile. 'Let's get down to facts, my boy,' he went on, putting his arm round Lucien's waist. 'I'm forty-six. I'm a nobleman's natural child, and so I have no family; and yet I have a heart. But learn this, write it down in your impressionable brain: man is terrified of solitude. And of all solitudes, moral solitude is what terrifies him most. The early anchorites lived with God and were inhabitants of the most populous world of all, the spiritual world. Misers live in a world of fantasy and self-gratification. A miser stores everything, even his sex, in his brain. Man's first thought, whether he's a leper or a convict, infamous or diseased, is to have someone whose destinies are wrapped up in his. To satisfy this urge, a vital one, he brings all his strength, all his might, all his energy into play. Without this over-ruling desire, would Satan have found any companions? – One might write a whole poem which would be a curtain-raiser to *Paradise Lost*, itself an apologia for rebellion.'

'Such a poem would be the *Iliad* of corruption,' said Lucien.

'Well now, I am alone and I live alone. Though I wear the habit I have not the heart of a priest. My weakness is self-devotion. I live by self-devotion, and that's why I'm a priest. I'm not afraid of ingratitude, but I myself am a grateful man. The Church means nothing to me: it's just an idea. I have devoted myself to the King of Spain; but one cannot love the King of Spain: he's my protector and lives on a higher plane. I want to love a creation of my own, shape it, mould it to my purposes so that I may love it as a father loves his progeny. I shall ride about in your two-wheeler, my boy, I shall enjoy your successes with women, I shall say: "This handsome young man is myself! This Marquis de Rubempré, I made him and set him in the aristocratic world. His greatness is my work; he speaks or keeps silent at my prompting and consults me on every matter." That is what the Abbé de Vermont was for Marie-Antoinette.'

'He brought her to the scaffold!'

'That's because he didn't love the Queen!' the priest retorted. 'He only loved the Abbé de Vermont.'

'Must I leave a trail of desolation behind me?' said Lucien.

'I have plenty of money. You can draw on it.'

'Just now I would do much in order to extricate Séchard,' Lucien replied in a voice which no longer suggested suicidal intentions.

'Say one word, my son, and tomorrow he'll get the money needed to set him free.'

'What! You would give me twelve thousand francs?'

'Child that you are! Don't you see that we're doing ten miles an hour? We shall dine in Poitiers. There, if you are willing to make this pact with me, to give me one single proof of obedience – I admit it's asking a lot – well, the stage-coach to Bordeaux will take fifteen thousand francs to your sister.'

'Where are these fifteen thousand francs?'

The Spanish priest gave no answer, and Lucien thought: 'I've got him there! He was making fun of me.'

A minute later, the Spaniard and Lucien had silently climbed back into the carriage. Silently the priest put his hand into the pocket of his carriage, and drew out of it a leather bag, resembling a game-bag, of the kind divided into three compartments with which travellers are familiar. He pulled out a hundred Portuguese sovereigns, plunging his broad hand into it three times and each time bringing it out filled with gold coins.

'Father, I'm yours!' said Lucien, dazzled at the sight of this torrent of gold.

'Child!' said the priest, tenderly kissing Lucien on the forehead. 'That's only a third part of the money contained in this bag – thirty thousand francs, apart from travelling expenses.'

'And you travel alone?'

'What does that matter?' said the Spaniard. 'I have drafts on Paris for more than three hundred thousand francs. A diplomat without money is like what you were not so long ago: a poet with no will-power.'

36. On the brink of surrender

WHILE Lucien was stepping into the carriage of the self-styled Spanish diplomat, Eve was getting up to feed her son. She found the fatal letter and read it. A cold perspiration broke out on her face still moist with morning sleep. She turned dizzy and called for Marion and Kolb.

To her question: 'Has my brother gone out?' Kolb replied: 'Yes, Matame, pefore it vass taylight.'

'Keep absolutely quiet about what I am telling you,' said Eve to the two servants. 'My brother has no doubt gone out to put an end to his life. Hurry off both of you, make cautious enquiries and look along the river bank.'

Eve remained alone, in a state of terrible stupefaction.

She was still in the same mental turmoil when Petit-Claud made his appearance, at about seven o'clock, to talk business with her. At such moments as these, one is ready to listen to anybody.

'Madame,' said the solicitor, 'our poor David is in prison and he is coming to the predicament I foresaw at the beginning of this affair. I advised him then to go into partnership with his competitors the Cointets for the exploitation of his invention, since the Cointets are in a position to provide the means for carrying out an enterprise which, as far as your husband is concerned, is only a project as yet. And so, yesterday evening, as soon as I heard of your husband's arrest, what did I do? I went to Messrs Cointet with the intention of obtaining concessions from them which you would find satisfactory. If you try to safeguard your invention, your life will go on as it is now: nothing but legal wrangles. You'll lose your battle and in the end, worn-out and disappointed, you'll come to an arrangement with some moneyed man – to your detriment perhaps – which I should like to see you make – to your advantage – with the Cointet brothers. Thus you will spare yourselves something of the privations and anguish an inventor suffers in his struggle against capitalist greed and the indifference of society. Let's see now! If the Cointets settle your debts ... if, once your debts are paid, they also give you a sum which will be well and duly yours whatever the merit or future prospects of the invention, allotting to you, which goes without saying, a certain share in the profits from exploitation, would you not be in a happy position?

'You thus become, Madame, owner of the printing-office plant, which no doubt you will sell. It will certainly fetch twenty thousand francs: I can guarantee to find you a purchaser at that price. If by your deed of partnership with the Cointets you acquire fifteen thousand francs, your assets will come to thirty-five thousand francs, and at the present rate of interest that would bring you an income of two thousand francs a year. One can live on that in the provinces. And note also, Madame, that you would still have possible future returns from the partnership in question. I say "possible", for the venture might fail. Well then, this is what I am able to obtain: firstly, David's complete deliverance, secondly fifteen thousand francs as an indemnification for his researches without the Cointets being able to make any sort of counter-claim even if the invention were unproductive, and thirdly a company formed by David and the Cointets for the exploitation of a patent which would be taken out after experiments had been made – jointly and in secret – on his process of manufacture. And it would be formed on the following basis: the Cointet brothers will incur all the expenses, David's capital contribution will be the purchase of the patent, and he will have one quarter of the profits. You are a woman of good judgement and sound sense – not a usual thing with very beautiful women like you. Think over these proposals and you will find them very acceptable . . . '

'Oh, Monsieur!' poor Eve cried out in desperation, melting into tears. 'Why did you not come to me yesterday evening to propose this compromise? We should have avoided dishonour and . . . something much worse besides.'

'My discussion with the Cointets who, as you must have suspected, are hiding behind Métivier, only ended at midnight. But what then has happened since yesterday evening that could be worse than our poor David's arrest?'

'This is the appalling news I discovered when I got up,' she replied, holding out Lucien's letter to Petit-Claud. 'You are now proving to me that you take an interest in us, that you are a friend to David and Lucien. I've no need to ask you to keep this secret.'

'Don't worry in the slightest,' said Petit-Claud, reading and returning the letter. 'Lucien won't kill himself. After being the cause of his brother-in-law's arrest, he had to have some reason for leaving you, and this strikes me as being merely an exit speech in theatrical style.'

The Cointets had achieved their ends. After persecuting the inventor and his family, they were seizing the moment when lassitude resulting from such persecution brings a longing for repose. Not all researchers have the tenacity of the bull-dog who dies with his prey between his teeth, and the Cointets had methodically studied the characters of their victims. For tall Cointet David's arrest was the final scene in the first act of this drama. The second act had begun with the proposition that Petit-Claud had just made. Like a skilful player in a game of chess, the solicitor regarded Lucien's impulsive move as one of those unhoped-for chances which decide the issue. He saw that Eve was so completely put in check by this event that he resolved to make use of it to win her confidence, for now he fully realized the influence she had over her husband. Therefore, instead of plunging Madame Séchard into still deeper despair, he tried to reassure her, and he was clever enough to steer her towards the prison while she was in her present state of mind, believing that, once there, she would persuade David to agree to the partnership with the Cointets.

'David told me, Madame, that he only wanted to make money for you and your brother, but it must be clear to you now that it would be madness to try and enrich Lucien. That young man would devour three fortunes.'

Eve's attitude showed plainly enough that the last of her illusions about her brother had vanished, and so the solicitor made a pause in order to convert his client's silence into a kind of assent.

'Thus, in this question,' he resumed, 'you and your child are alone concerned. It's for you to decide if an income of two thousand francs is enough to make you happy, without counting what you will inherit from old Séchard. Your father-in-law has long since been piling up an income of seven or eight thousand francs irrespective of the interest he draws from his capital. So after all you have a fine future before you. Why worry?'

The solicitor left Madame Séchard to reflect on this prospect, one which, on the previous evening, tall Cointet had quite skilfully prepared. 'Go and dangle before their eyes the possibility of laying hands on a sum of money,' the shark of Angoulême had said to the solicitor when he had come to tell him of David's arrest. 'When they have got used to the idea of pocketing some money, we shall have them. We'll do some bargaining, and bit by bit we'll bring them down to the price we're ready to pay for the invention.' This remark to some extent conveys the gist of the second act in this financial drama.

When Madame Séchard, broken-hearted through her apprehensions over her brother's fate, had dressed and gone downstairs to visit her husband in prison, she was full of anguish at the thought of passing through the streets of Angoulême by herself. Though he felt no concern for his client's distress, Petit-Claud returned to the house to offer his arm: he had been brought back by a somewhat Machiavellian motive, that of winning credit for a tactful gesture which Eve very much appreciated. He accepted her thanks without undeceiving her. This little attention, coming from so hard and unyielding a man, and at such a moment, modified the judgements that Madame Séchard had made on Petit-Claud hitherto.

'I'm taking you the longest way round,' he said, 'so that we shall not meet anybody.'

'This is the first time, Monsieur, that I have not had the right to hold my head up as I walk along. That fact was harshly brought home to me yesterday . . . .'

'It's the first and last time.'

'Oh! I shall certainly not stay in this town.'

'If your husband were to agree to the proposals which I have practically settled with the Cointets,' Petit-Claud said to Eve as they arrived at the prison gate, 'let me know. I should immediately come with Cachan's authorization for David's release. It's not likely that he would have to go back to prison.'

This remark made in front of the gaol was what the Italians call a *combinazione*. This word expresses the indefinable act whose ingredients are a modicum of perfidy with a blend of legality, the choice of an opportune moment for a permissible fraud, a virtually lawful and well-planned piece of knavery. According to the Italians, the Saint Bartholomew massacre was a political 'combinazione'.

37. *The effect of a night in gaol*

FOR the reasons set forth above, detention for debt is so rare a judicial fact in the provinces that most French towns have no debtors' prison. When that is so the debtor is shut up in the same prison as people held on suspicion, people accused of minor or major offences and those who have already received sentence – such being the various legal stages by which those who are popularly known as *criminals* are brought to book. So David was temporarily lodged in one of the lower cells in the Angoulême gaol. Once his name had been entered with a statement of the sum which the law allows for the prisoner's monthly food bill, David found himself in front of a stout man, the man who holds more power over those incarcerated than the King himself, namely the gaoler. In the provinces, one never meets with a gaoler who is thin. To begin with, his post is almost a sinecure. Secondly, a gaoler is like an innkeeper who has no overhead charges; he feeds himself well by feeding his prisoners very badly – moreover he lodges them, as an innkeeper does, according to their means. This man knew David by name, mainly through the latter's father, and he was trusting enough to give him good accommodation although David was penniless.

The prison at Angoulême dates from the Middle Ages and has not gone through any more changes than the Cathedral. Still called the House of Justice, it is backed by the magistrates' court. It has the standard type of entrance: a door studded with nails, solid-looking, well-worn, low, and so much the more cyclopean in its construction for having one eye in the middle – the spy-hole through which the gaoler takes stock of the inmates before opening the door. A corridor runs along the front on the ground-floor, and on to this corridor a number of cells open, having high canopied windows which draw their light from the prison yard. The gaoler occupies a lodging separated from the cells by a vault which divides the ground-floor into two halves; and at the end of it one can see, once one is through the wicket, a grill shutting off the prison-yard. The gaoler led David into a cell close to the vault whose door stood opposite his lodging. He wanted to be near a man who, in view of his special situation, might be company to him.

'It's the best cell,' he said when he saw that David was stupefied at the sight of this den.

Its walls were of stone and somewhat damp. There were iron bars at the very lofty windows. An icy chill struck up from the flag-stones. David could hear the rhythmic steps of the warder on sentry-go as he paced up and down the corridor. This sound, as monotonous as the boom of the tide, dins into one every minute the thought: 'There's a guard outside! I'm no longer free!' All such details have a prodigious cumulative effect on the morale of honest people. David saw that the bed was execrable; but incarcerated people feel so violently upset during their first night that they do not notice how hard their couch is until the following night. The gaoler was gracious and in a natural tone proposed that David should walk about the prison-yard until night-time. His torture was only to begin when he went to bed. Prisoners were allowed no light, and a permit from the Public Attorney was needed to exempt a prisoner for debt from this regulation, which evidently only applied to those in the hands of criminal justice. The gaoler was kind enough to admit David to his fire-side, but he had to be shut up at last, at bed-time.

Then the poor man realized the horrors of prison and was revolted at the brutality of its routine. But, thanks to a re-action common enough among thinking men, he cut himself off from this solitude, escaping into one of those dreams in which poetic minds have the power to indulge during their waking hours. In the end the unhappy man came round to reflecting about his affairs. Prison gives a tremendous impetus to examination of conscience. David asked himself if he had fulfilled his duties as head of a family, wondered what state of desolation his wife must be in and why, as Marion had suggested, he might not earn enough money to be able to carry out his researches at leisure.

'How,' he asked himself, 'can I stay in Angoulême after such a disgrace? If I get out of prison, what will become of us? Where shall we go?' He felt misgivings about his paper-making process, the sort of poignant misgivings which only other inventors would have been able to understand. From one doubt to another David came to a clear view of his predicament, and he told himself what the Cointets had told Papa Séchard, what Petit-Claud had just told Eve: 'Supposing all goes well, what will happen when the invention is tried out? I need a patent, and that means money! I need a factory for experiments on a large scale, and that means divulging my secret! Oh! How right Petit-Claud was!'

From the darkest prisons such shafts of light proceed.

'Anyway,' said David as he fell asleep on the wretched camp-bed with its horrible mattress of extremely coarse brown cloth, 'no doubt I shall see Petit-Claud in the morning.'

Thus David had worked himself into the mood for listening to the proposals of his enemies by the time his wife came to report them to him. After embracing her husband and sitting down at the foot of the bed, for there was only one chair of the most squalid sort, her regard fell on the hideous bucket standing in a corner and on the walls bespattered with the names and apophthegms which David's predecessors had scrawled on them. Then, at the sight of her husband sharing the plight of criminals, the tears began to flow from her reddened eyes – she still had some tears left in spite of all those she had shed.

'It's to this then that a desire for glory can bring one!' she cried. 'Oh my angel, give up this career ... Let's follow the beaten track without trying to get rich quick ... It needs so little to make me happy after so many sufferings! ... And if you knew everything! ... The disgrace of this arrest is not our worst misfortune! ... Read this.'

She handed over Lucien's letter which David ran through quickly. In order to quiet his fears, she quoted the scathing remark Petit-Claud had made about Lucien.

'If Lucien has committed suicide, all is over by now,' said David. 'And if all is not over, he won't kill himself. As he says himself, his courage wouldn't last longer than a single morning.'

'But how can we stand this anxiety?' Lucien's sister cried, ready to forgive almost everything at the thought of her brother's death.

Then she repeated to her husband the proposals Petit-Claud had made a pretence of obtaining from the Cointets. David accepted them immediately with obvious pleasure.

'We shall have enough to live on in a village close to L'Houmeau, and all I ask for is a peaceful life,' the inventor exclaimed. 'If Lucien has chosen to punish himself by dying, we shall have enough money to live on until my father dies. If Lucien is still alive, the poor boy will manage to conform to our modest circumstances ... The Cointets will certainly reap the profit from my discovery; but after all what do I matter in comparison with my country? ... I'm only one man. If everybody benefits from my invention, well, I am content. Look, my dear Eve, we're neither of us cut out for business. We have neither the greed for gain nor the reluctance to let any money slip through our fingers, even when we have every right to it. These two kinds of avarice may be virtues in a tradesman: they are called prudence and business acumen!'

Delighted at this unanimity, one of the most fragrant flowers which bloom from mutual love – for it is impossible that two beings who love each other should not see eye to eye in their interests and points of view – Eve asked the gaoler to send a note to Petit-Claud telling him to set David free and informing him of their mutual consent to the basic points of the projected arrangement. Ten minutes later Petit-Claud came to David's horrible cell and told Eve: 'Go home, Madame, we will follow you.'

'So then, my dear friend,' said Petit-Claud, 'you let them catch you! How did it come about that you were so foolish as to leave your sanctuary?'

'How could I not leave it? This is what Lucien wrote to me.'

He handed Cérizet's forgery to Petit-Claud, who took it, read it, gazed at it, felt the paper and went on talking business while he folded the letter and slipped it into his pocket as if through absent-mindedness. Then the solicitor took David by the arm and left the prison with him, the bailiff's warrant for release having been brought to the gaoler during the conversation. When he was back home David felt as if he were in Heaven: he wept like a child as he hugged his little Lucien and found himself back in his own bedroom after three weeks of duress, the last hours of which, according to provincial standards, had brought disgrace upon him. Kolb and Marion had returned. Marion had learnt in L'Houmeau that Lucien had been seen walking along the road to Paris beyond Marsac. His dandyish clothes had been noticed by country people who were bringing produce to market. Kolb had ridden on horseback along the high-road and in the end had learned that Lucien, whom the Abbé Marron had recognized, was travelling post in a barouche.

'What did I say?' exclaimed Petit-Claud. 'He's not a poet, that young man: he's a serial novel!'

'Travelling post,' Eve was saying. 'But where's he going to this time?'

'Now,' said Petit-Claud to David, 'come to the Cointets. They're waiting for you.' 'Oh, Monsieur!' cried the beautiful Madame Séchard. 'I implore you to defend our interests as best you can. Our whole future is in your hands.'

'Madame,' said Petit-Claud, 'would you like the discussion to take place here? I'll leave David with you. The Cointet brothers will come here this evening, and you'll see if I know how to defend your interests.'

'Oh, Monsieur!' said Eve. 'You would be doing me a real service.'

'Very good. Then we'll be here this evening about seven.'

'I am very grateful,' Eve replied with a look and tone of voice which showed Petit-Claud how far he had gone in gaining his client's confidence. 'Have no fear,' he added. 'You can see I was right. Your brother is a long way from suicide. Well now, perhaps by this evening you'll have a small fortune. A serious purchaser has come forward for your printing-works.'

'In that case,' said Eve, 'why not wait before binding ourselves to the Cointets?'

'You're forgetting, Madame,' Petit-Claud replied, seeing that he had made a dangerous avowal, 'that you won't be free to sell your printing-works before paying Monsieur Métivier, for all your plant is still under distraint.'

Petit-Claud went home and sent for Cérizet. Once the compositor was in his office, he took him aside into a window-recess.

'Tomorrow,' he whispered to him, 'you'll be owner of the Séchard press, with enough influence behind you to obtain the transfer of the licence ... But you don't want to finish up in a convict-prison, do you?'

'Here! What do you mean? *convict-prison*?' Cérizet stammered.

'Your letter to David was a forgery, and I hold it ... If Henriette were questioned, what would she say? ... But I don't want to bring you to ruin,' Petit-Claud quickly added on seeing Cérizet turn pale.

'There's still something you want me to do?' the Parisian exclaimed.

'Yes indeed. This is what I expect of you. Listen carefully. In two months you'll be a master-printer in Angoulême ... but you'll owe the money for your press, and it will take you more than ten years to pay it back! ... You'll be working a long time for those who found you the capital! And what's more you'll have to act as figure-head for the Liberal party ... I myself will draw up your deed of partnership with Gannerac, and I'll do it in such a way that one day you'll have the printing-works to yourself ... But if they found a newspaper, if you become managing-editor, if I become deputy Public Attorney here, you'll arrange with tall Cointet to insert in your newspaper some articles of such a nature as to get it confiscated and suppressed. The Cointets will pay you generously to do them that service. It's true you'll be sentenced and get a taste of prison, but you'll pass for an important and persecuted man. You'll become a somebody in the Liberal party, a Sergeant Mercier, a Paul-Louis Courier, a small-scale Manuel.

I won't ever let your licence be cancelled. Finally, the day when the journal is suppressed, I'll burn this letter in front of you . . . It won't have cost you a lot to make your fortune . . .'

The popular classes have very erroneous ideas about the legal ins and outs of forgery, and Cérizet, who had imagined himself already in the dock, breathed again.

'In three years from now I shall be Public Attorney in Angoulême,' Petit-Claud continued. 'You might well have need of me. Think it over.'

'It's agreed,' said Cérizet. 'But how little you know me! Burn this letter in front of me, and trust to my gratitude.'

Petit-Claud scrutinized Cérizet. There ensued one of those eye-to-eye duels in which the regard of the scrutinizer is like a lancet probing deep into the soul and in which the eyes of the man trying to show how trustworthy he is provide an interesting spectacle.

Petit-Claud made no reply. He lit a candle and burnt the letter, saying to himself: 'He has his fortune to make!'

'I'll serve you hand and foot,' said the compositor.

38. A day too late

DAVID waited in a state of vague disquietude for the conference with the Cointets. What was worrying him was neither the discussion of his interests nor the debate about the deed to be drawn up, but the opinion the paper-manufacturers were likely to form about the work he had done. He found himself in the situation of a dramatic author in front of his critics. His pride as an inventor and his anxieties at the moment when he was approaching his goal threw all other feelings into the shade. At last, about seven in the evening – just when Madame la Comtesse Châtelet was taking to her bed on the pretext of a migraine and leaving her husband to do the honours of the dinner, so afflicted she was by the contradictory news circulating about Lucien – Cointet the Stout and Cointet the Tall came with Petit-Claud to the house of the rival who was delivering himself over to them bound hand and foot. First of all a preliminary dilemma had to be faced: how could a deed of association be drawn up without David's process being revealed? And once David's process was divulged he would be at the Cointets' mercy. Petit-Claud stipulated that the deed should first be drawn up. Then tall Cointet asked David to show samples of his products, and the inventor offered them the latest sheets he had made, guaranteeing that the cost price would be low.

'Very well, there we are!' said Petit-Claud, now that the groundwork for the deed was complete. 'You can form your company on these data, inserting a dissolution clause in case the terms of the patent are not fulfilled when the process is put into fabrication.'

'It's one thing, Monsieur,' tall Cointet said to David, 'it's one thing to make samples of paper on a small scale in a private workshop with a small mould, another thing to carry out manufacture on a large scale. Judge of this by one simple fact. We manufacture coloured papers and, for the dyeing process, we buy parcels of identical colour. For example, the indigo we use to blue our post-demy is delivered to us in boxes in which every cake of dye comes from the same lot. And yet we have never been able to produce two vatfuls of exactly the same shade. Phenomena which we can't account for occur in the preparation of our material. Any change in the quantity and quality of pulp used immediately complicates the problem. When you had your ingredients (I'm not asking you what they are) measured into your pan, they were under your control. You could work evenly on every portion of them, bind them, macerate them, knead them at will and make a smooth mixture of them. But who can guarantee that in a vatful of five hundred reams the same thing will happen and that your process will be successful?'

The glances which David, Eve and Petit-Claud exchanged were eloquent with unspoken thoughts.

'Take an example which offers some sort of analogy,' said tall Cointet after a pause. 'You cut two bundles of hay from your meadow, and you put them close packed in your room without letting the grass throw off its heat, as the peasants say: fermentation takes place but causes no accident. Would you rely on this experiment and stack two thousand bundles in a wooden barn? ... You know very well that the hay would catch fire and that your barn would burn like matchwood.

'– You're an educated man,' Cointet continued. 'What's your conclusion? So far you have cut two bundles of hay, but we should be afraid of setting our mill on fire if we packed two thousand into it. In other words we might waste many a vatful, incur losses and find ourselves with nothing in our hands after spending a lot of money.'

David was flattened. It was a case of Practice talking in positive terms to Theory, which only uses the future tense.

'Devil take me if I sign such a deed,' stout Cointet cried out in brutal tones. 'Boniface, you may waste your money if you like: I'm keeping mine ... I'll pay Monsieur Séchard's debts and offer him six thousand francs into the bargain ... Or rather,' he said, taking himself up, 'three thousand francs in bills of exchange payable in twelve or fifteen months ... That's quite enough money to risk ... We have twelve thousand francs to take over on our account with Métivier. That will come to fifteen thousand francs! ... Why, that's all I would pay for the discovery in order to exploit it all by myself. – So that's the windfall you were telling me about, Boniface ... Well, no thank you. I thought you had more sense. No indeed, that's not what I call business.'

'For you,' said Petit-Claud, without being alarmed by this outburst, 'the question comes down to this: are you willing to risk twenty thousand francs to buy a process which might make you rich? Why, gentlemen, risks are always proportionate to profits. It's staking twenty thousand francs against a fortune. A gambler puts down a louis at roulette in order to get back thirty-six, but he knows his louis is gone. Do likewise.'

'I must have time to reflect,' said stout Cointet. 'I'm not so clever as my brother. I'm a plain, simple fellow who knows only one thing: how to produce a prayer-book for one franc and sell it for two. I can see ruination coming from an invention which is only at the experimental stage. The first vatful will be a success, the second a failure; you'll go on with it, you'll let yourself be dragged along, and when you've got one arm caught in that sort of machinery your whole body will follow.' He told the story of a Bordeaux merchant who was ruined because he tried to cultivate a tract of the Landes on the word of a scientist. He thought of half a dozen similar examples, both industrial and agricultural, in the districts of the Charente and Dordogne. He flew into a rage, refused to listen any more, and Petit-Claud's objections increased instead of calming his irritation. 'I prefer to pay more for something more certain than this invention and make only a small profit,' he said with a glance at his brother. And he ended up by saying: 'In my opinion, none of this work has gone far enough for a deal to be based on it.'

'But after all,' said Petit-Claud, 'you didn't come here for nothing. What do you offer?'

'To free Monsieur Séchard of debt and, in case of success, pay him thirty per cent of the profits,' was stout Cointet's sharp reply.

'Come now, Monsieur,' said Eve, 'What are we to live on all the time the experiments are being made? My husband has been put to the shame of arrest. He can go back to prison. There's nothing more to be said. We will pay our debts.'

Petit-Claud laid a finger on his mouth as he looked at Eve.

'You're being unreasonable,' he said to the two brothers. 'You've seen the paper, Séchard senior told you that his son, shut in by himself, had made some excellent paper in a single night, with ingredients which must have cost very little ... You came here with a view to buying. Will you buy or not?'

'Look now,' said tall Cointet, 'whether my brother is willing or not, I myself will take the risk of paying Monsieur Séchard's debts. I will give six thousand francs, cash down, and Monsieur Séchard will have thirty per cent share in the profits. And if within the space of one year he has not fulfilled the conditions which he himself will set down in the deed, he will return the six thousand francs, we shall retain the patent, and we'll recoup ourselves as best we may.'

'Are you sure of yourself?' asked Petit-Claud, drawing David aside.

'Yes,' said David, caught in the toils and trembling lest stout Cointet should put an end to the parley on which his future depended.

'Very well, I'll draw up the deed,' said Petit-Claud to Eve and the Cointets. 'Each of you will have a duplicate for this evening and you can ponder over it the whole of tomorrow morning. Then tomorrow evening, at four, when I've finished at court, you will sign it. You gentlemen will please call in the Métivier documents. I shall write and halt the suit in the Court of Appeal, and we will give notification of our reciprocal withdrawals.'

Séchard's commitments were drawn up in the following terms:

AGREEMENT BETWEEN THE UNDERSIGNED,
etc . . .

Monsieur David Séchard junior, master printer in Angoulême, having declared that he has invented a method for giving a uniform gloss to paper in the vat and for reducing the cost of manufacture of every kind of paper by more than fifty per cent by the introduction of vegetable matters into the pulp, whether by mixing them with the rag-stuff used up to the present day or by using them without the addition of rag-stuff, a Company is hereby formed between Monsieur David Séchard and Messrs Cointet brothers for the exploitation of the patent of invention to be taken out in regard to these processes on the following terms and conditions . . .

One of the clauses in this deed completely deprived David Séchard of his rights in case he did not fulfil the undertakings set forth in this carefully worded document drawn up by tall Cointet and agreed by David.

When Petit-Claud brought the deed the next morning at seven-thirty, he informed David and his wife that Cérizet was offering twenty thousand francs for the printing-works. The deed of sale could be signed that evening.

'However,' he warned them, 'if the Cointets learnt about this purchase, they would be quite capable of refusing to sign your deed, continuing their persecution and selling you up . . .'

'You're sure Cérizet will pay?' asked Eve, astonished to see the conclusion of a transaction of which she had despaired and which, three months earlier, would have been their salvation.

'I have the money in my house,' he flatly replied.

'But it's a piece of magic,' said David, asking Petit-Claud for an explanation of this lucky event.

'No, it's simple enough. The tradesmen in L'Houmeau are going to found a newspaper.'

'But I barred myself from doing that,' cried David.

'*You* did, but not your successor ... In any case,' he went on, 'don't worry about anything. Sell, pocket the price, and leave Cérizet to extricate himself from the conditions of sale – he'll find his way out all right.'

'That I can well believe,' said Eve.

'If you have barred yourself from founding a newspaper in Angoulême,' Petit-Claud continued, 'Cérizet's financial backers will found one in L'Houmeau.'

Eve, dazzled by the prospect of possessing thirty thousand francs and of being freed from want, now only looked on the deed of partnership as a secondary hope. And so Monsieur and Madame Séchard gave way over one point in the deed of association which gave rise to a final discussion. Tall Cointet demanded the right to take out the patent of invention in his own name. He succeeded in establishing the point that, once David's financial rights were perfectly defined in the deed, it mattered little in which partner's name the patent was registered. Stout Cointet terminated the argument: 'It's my brother who is paying for the patent and finding the expenses for the journey to Paris, and that means another two thousand francs! Let him take it out in his own name or there's nothing doing.'

And so the Shark won all hands down. The deed of partnership was signed at about half past four. By way of pin-money, tall Cointet presented Madame Séchard with a set of silver forks and spoons with fluted handles and a fine Ternaux shawl – to help her to forget the fire and fury of the discussion, as he put it! But scarcely were the contracts exchanged, scarcely had Cachan handed Petit-Claud the cancellation order and the other documents, as well as the three terrible bills forged by

Lucien, when Kolb's voice echoed in the staircase, preceded by the deafening clatter of a van from the stage-coach office which halted in front of the door.

'Matame! Matame! Fifteen tousant francs!...' he shouted. 'Sent from Poitiers in tchenuine money py Monsieur Licien.'

'Fifteen thousand francs!' cried Eve with arms raised on high.

'Yes, Madame,' the carrier said, coming forward. 'Fifteen thousand francs brought by the Paris–Bordeaux stage-coach, and to be sure it was a heavy load! I've a couple of men downstairs who are bringing up the sacks. They are sent by Monsieur Lucien Chardon de Rubempré ... I'm bringing up a little leather bag in which there are five hundred francs in gold for you, and likely enough a letter too.'

Eve read the following letter as in a dream:

My dear sister,

Here are fifteen thousand francs.

Instead of committing suicide, I have bartered my life. I belong to myself no longer. I'm nothing more than the secretary of a Spanish diplomat. I'm his creature.

I'm beginning a terrible existence all over again. Perhaps I should have done better to drown myself.

Good-bye. David will be free, and with four thousand francs he can no doubt buy a little paper-mill and make a fortune.

Give no more thought – that is what I wish – to

Your unfortunate brother,
LUCIEN.

'My son is fated, as he wrote in his letter,' said Madame Chardon as she watched the sacks being piled up, 'to bring disaster, even when he does good.'

'We've had a narrow squeeze!' tall Cointet exclaimed when he arrived at the Place du Mûrier. 'One hour later, those glittering coins would have cast their sheen on the deed of partnership and our man would have shied off it. In three months' time, as he has promised us, we shall know how we stand.'

That evening at seven o'clock, Cérizet bought and paid for

the printing-press, the rent for the previous quarter remaining chargeable to him. The next day Eve sent fourteen thousand francs to the Receiver-General, in order to buy an income of two thousand francs in her husband's name. Then she wrote to her father-in-law asking him to find a small property at Marsac for ten thousand francs as a basis for her personal fortune.

39. *The history of a business venture*

TALL Cointet's plan was formidably simple. From the very beginning he had decided that it was impossible to size paper in the vat. The only real method for making a fortune seemed to him to be the addition of vegetable matter to rag pulp. He therefore proposed to take the following line with David: cheapness of pulp was unimportant, the great problem being that of sizing in the vat.

His motive was that at the present time paper-manufacture was almost solely concerned with those kinds of writing-paper known as crown, fancy note-paper, foolscap and post-demy, all of which of course have to be sized. For a long time these had given Angoulême paper-making its reputation. And so this speciality, a monopoly which Angoulême manufacturers had enjoyed over long years, justified the Cointets in their exactions: we shall see that sized paper had no real place in their speculations. The demand for writing-paper is extremely restricted whereas that for unsized printing paper is almost unlimited. During the journey he made to Paris in order to take out the patent in his own name, tall Cointet was thinking of making deals which would result in great changes in his methods of manufacture. He took up his quarters at Métivier's house and gave him instructions for robbing other paper-makers of their custom with the newspapers in the space of one year, by dropping the price per ream to so low a level that no mill could compete, and promising every journal a whiteness and quality superior to the finest 'sorts' in use up to then. Since supply-contracts with newspapers are forward deals, a certain period would be needed for *sub rosa* intrigues with the editorial managements in order to secure this monopoly; but Cointet reckoned that this would give him time to get rid of Séchard while Métivier was obtaining contracts with the leading Paris newspapers whose consumption was then reaching a figure of two hundred reams a day. Naturally Cointet gave Métivier a proportionate financial interest in these supplies so as to have an able representative in the Paris market and save himself time in travelling. Métivier's fortune, today one of the most considerable in the paper trade, originated in this transaction. The supply of paper for the Paris Press fell into his hands for ten years without any competition being possible. Tall Cointet, his mind at ease about his future market in paper, returned to Paris soon enough to attend the wedding of Petit-Claud, whose practice was sold and who was awaiting the appointment of his successor in order to take up Monsieur Milhaud's post, which had been ear-marked for him as the Comtesse Châtelet's protégé. The Assistant Deputy Public Attorney in Angoulême was appointed Deputy Public Attorney at Limoges and the Keeper of the Seals sent one of his protégés to the public prosecutor's department in Angoulême. Thus the post of Deputy Attorney remained vacant for two months and this interval was a kind of honey-moon for Petit-Claud.

While tall Cointet was away, David first of all made a batch of unsized news-print paper which was far superior to the kind then in use. Then he made a batch of splendid vellum for de luxe printing which the Cointet press used for an edition of the diocesan prayer-book. The raw material had been prepared by David himself in secret, for he would have no other workers with him than Kolb and Marion. On Cointet's return the outlook changed completely: he examined the samples of paper manufactured and was only moderately satisfied.

'My dear friend,' he said to David. 'Angoulême does all its trade in post-demy. What we need to do before anything

675

else is to produce the finest post-demy at fifty per cent of the present cost.'

David attempted to make a vatful of sized pulp for post-demy but only obtained a very rough paper on which the size was unevenly distributed. The day when this experiment was finished, after handling one of the sheets, David retired into a corner in order to gulp down his disappointment in solitude. But tall Cointet came up to him, treated his partner with charming affability and soothed him. 'Don't be despondent,' he said, 'Carry on! I'm not a bad sort, I understand how you feel, and I'll see this through! . . . '

'Really,' David said to his wife when he went home to dinner. 'We're dealing with decent people. I never thought tall Cointet could be so generous!' And he told her what his perfidious partner had said.

The experiments continued for three months. David slept at the paper-mill and observed the results to be obtained by varying the composition of his pulp. At one moment he attributed his lack of success to the mixing of rag with his material and made a vatful from his own ingredients alone. At another he made an attempt at sizing a vatful wholly composed of rag. Continuing his work with admirable perseverance under the watchful eye of tall Cointet, whom the poor man no longer distrusted, he tried one homogeneous material after another until he had gone through the whole range of his ingredients, combining them with all the different kinds of size. For the first six months of 1823 David lived in the paper-mill with Kolb, if it can be called living to take no care for food, dress or appearance. He battled with his difficulties so desperately that any other men than the Cointets would have been lost in admiration, for this intrepid fighter was moved by no thought of self-interest. The time came when he had no other desire than to win through. With extraordinary discernment he studied the strange properties of substances when they are transformed by man into products answering to his requirements, Nature itself being broken in as it were and its secret resistances quelled. From this he deduced the great laws governing human industry, observing that creations of this sort can only be achieved through obedience to that ulterior relationship between things which he called the second nature of substances. At last, by the end of August, he succeeded in producing a paper, sized in the vat, absolutely similar to the kind which is in production at present and is used as proof-paper in printing-presses, although the 'sorts' are not uniform and the sizing is not always dependable. This result, a fine one in 1823 considering the stage paper-making had then reached, had cost ten thousand francs, and David had good hopes of solving his remaining difficulties.

But then strange rumours spread round Angoulême and L'Houmeau to the effect that David Séchard was ruining the brothers Cointet. After consuming thirty thousand francs in experiments, so it was said, in the end he was only producing very bad paper. The other manufacturers, alarmed at this, were sticking to their old-fashioned processes and, being jealous of the Cointets, they spread the tale that this ambitious firm was on the verge of ruin. As for tall Cointet, he was ordering machines for manufacturing paper in reels while letting it be supposed that these machines were needed for David Séchard's experiments. None the less this dissembler was mixing the ingredients indicated by Séchard in his pulp while still urging him to concern himself only with sizing in the vat. He was sending Métivier thousands of reams of newsprint.

When September came, tall Cointet drew David aside, and when he learnt that David was planning to make a conclusive experiment, he persuaded him to give up the struggle.

'My dear David,' he said in amiable tones. 'Go and visit your wife at Marsac and rest from your labours. We don't want to ruin your health. What you regard as a great triumph is still only in its initial stages. We will now pause awhile before we go in for further experiments. Be reasonable: look at the results. We're not only paper-manufacturers, we're also printers and bankers, and people say you are ruining us ... '

David Séchard made a sublimely ingenuous gesture as a protest of good faith, and tall Cointet responded to it in this fashion: 'Fifty thousand francs thrown into the Charente aren't going to ruin us, but we don't want to have to pay cash for everything we buy because of the slanders which are being circulated at our expense. We should be forced to put a stop to our operations. This brings us back to the terms of our contract and calls for reflection on both sides.'

'He's right!' David said to himself. Immersed as he was in his large-scale experiments, he had given no thought to the actual running of the paper-mill.

He returned to Marsac. During the last six months he had been visiting Eve every Saturday evening and leaving her on the Tuesday morning. Old Séchard had given her some good advice, and she had bought a house called La Verberie, just in front of her father-in-law's vineyards, with three acres of garden and a vineyard inside the old man's domain. She was living with her mother and Marion – very economically, because she was still short of five thousand francs to complete the purchase of this charming property, the prettiest in Marsac. The house stood between courtyard and garden. It was built of white chalk-stone, roofed with tiles and embellished with carvings, with which one can be lavish without great expense since chalk-stone is so easy to cut. The pretty furniture she had brought from Angoulême looked prettier still in these country parts, where no one then made the slightest show of luxury. In front, on the garden side, stood a row of pomegranates, orange-trees and rare plants which the previous owner himself, an old general who had died under the ministrations of the Abbé Marron, had cultivated.

David and his wife were playing with little Lucien under an orange-tree, with old Séchard looking on, when the bailiff of Mansle in person brought a summons from the Cointet brothers to their partner for the setting-up of a court of arbitration to which, by the terms of their deed of association, any contention had to be referred. The brothers Cointet demanded the restitution of their six thousand francs, the patent rights, and any future rights in its exploitation – as compensation for the exorbitant expenses they had incurred without results.

'They make out you're ruining them!' the vine-grower said to his son. 'Well, that's the only thing you've ever done that I find pleasing.'

At nine next morning Eve and David were in the ante-room of Monsieur Petit-Claud, who had now become the champion of widows and the protector of orphans. It seemed to them that all they could do now was to follow his advice.

The magistrate gave a wonderful reception to his former clients and insisted that Monsieur and Madame Séchard should do him the pleasure of lunching with him.

'So the Cointets are claiming six thousand francs from you!' he said with a smile. 'What do you still owe on the price of La Verberie?'

'Five thousand francs, Monsieur. But I have two thousand towards it,' Eve replied.

'Keep your two thousand francs,' Petit-Claud answered. 'Let's see, five thousand ... You need another ten thousand to get comfortably settled in. Very well, within two hours the Cointets will bring you fifteen thousand francs ... '

Eve made a gesture of surprise.

' ... in return for your renouncing all the profits from the deed of partnership, which you will dissolve on friendly terms. Will that suit you?'

'And we shall really have a legal right to the money?'

'Quite legal,' said the magistrate, still smiling. 'The Cointets have caused you trouble enough. I'm going to put an end to their pretensions. Listen to me: I'm now a magistrate and must tell you the truth. Well, the Cointets are swindling you here and now; but you're in their hands. You might win the suit they're bringing against you if you decided to fight them. But do you still want to be at law with them ten years hence? Expert valuations and arbitrations will be multiplied and you'll run the risk of getting the most conflicting opinions ... And besides,' he said with another smile, 'I can't think of any solicitor who could defend you. My successor isn't up to it. Come now, an unsatisfactory settlement is better than even a sound case.'

'I'll accept any settlement that will leave us in peace,' said David.

'Paul!' Petit-Claud shouted to his servant. 'Go to Monsieur Ségaud, my successor ... ' – 'While we are lunching,' he said to his former clients, 'Ségaud will see the Cointets, and a few hours hence you'll leave for Marsac, ruined, but easy in your minds. From ten thousand francs you'll still get five hundred francs' interest, and you'll live happy on your little estate.'

Two hours later, as Petit-Claud had predicted, Maître Ségaud arrived with two deeds duly signed by the Cointets and fifteen thousand francs in notes.

'We owe a lot to you,' said Séchard to Petit-Claud.

'But I've just ruined you,' Petit-Claud replied to his astonished ex-clients. 'I repeat, I have ruined you – you'll see that in course of time. But I know you: you prefer ruin to a fortune which might come too late.'

'We're not interested in that, Monsieur, we thank you for having shown us the way to happiness,' said Madame Eve. 'We shall always be grateful for that.'

'Good Heavens, don't give me your blessing!' said Petit-Claud. 'You're making me feel remorseful. But I do believe that today I have put everything right. It's thanks to you that I became a magistrate. And if anyone should feel grateful, it's myself . . . Good-bye!'

40. Conclusion

As time went on the Alsatian changed his mind about Papa Séchard, who in his turn took a liking to the Alsatian, finding in him a kindred spirit, with no notion of reading or writing, and easy to make drunk. The erstwhile 'bear' taught the erstwhile cuirassier to tend the vineyard and sell the produce: he trained him, with the idea of leaving his children a man who had his head screwed on right. For, in these latter days, he entertained great and childish fears for the future of his property. He had taken the miller Courtois into his confidence:

'You'll see,' he said, 'what will happen to my children once I'm underground. Lord save me! I go all a-tremble when I think of their future.'

In March, 1829, old Séchard died, leaving about two hundred thousand francs in real property. Added to La Verberie, this made a magnificent estate which Kolb had been running very competently for the last two years.

David and his wife found nearly three hundred thousand gold coins in their father's coffers. Public opinion, as always, so much exaggerated old Séchard's hoard that it was valued at a million all over the Charente region. From this inheritance, with their own fortune added to it, Eve and David drew an income of about thirty thousand francs a year, for they waited some time before investing their funds and were able to buy Government stock after the July Revolution.

It was not until then that the whole Charente area and David Séchard came to realize the extent of tall Cointet's fortune. Tall Cointet, several times a millionaire, after being a Deputy, is now a Peer of France and, so they say, will be Minister of Commerce in the next cabinet. In 1842 he married the daughter of one of the most influential statesmen under the present dynasty, Mademoiselle Popinot, the daughter of Monsieur Anselme Popinot, a Parliamentary Deputy of Paris and Mayor of a Paris *arrondissement*.

David Séchard's invention was assimilated into French manufacture as food is assimilated into the body of a giant. Thanks to the introduction of other materials than rag-stuff, France is able to manufacture paper at a cheaper rate than any other European country. But Holland paper, as David Séchard predicted, no longer exists. Sooner or later, no doubt, it will be necessary to set up a Royal Paper Factory on the same lines as the Gobelins tapestry, Sèvres porcelain, the Royal Soap-Works and the Royal Printing-Press, which up to now have survived the attacks made on them by middle-class vandals.

David Séchard has a loving wife, two sons and a daughter. He has had the good taste never to talk about his experiments. Eve has had the good sense to make him renounce the disastrous vocation of inventor, that of a Moses consumed in the burning bush of Horeb. He cultivates literature as a relaxation while living the happy, leisurely life of a landowner developing his estate. Having said good-bye once and for all to glory, he has sensibly taken his place in the class of dreamers and collectors. He is given to entomology and research into the as yet secret metamorphoses of insects only known to science in their final transformation.

Everyone has heard of Petit-Claud's success as Attorney-General. He is a worthy rival of the famous Vinet of Provins, and his ambition is to become First President of the Royal Court of Appeal in Poitiers.

Cérizet has often been sentenced for political offences, but he has been talked about a lot. As the boldest of the Liberal Party's forlorn hopes, he bears the nickname of Plucky Cérizet. Constrained by Petit-Claud's successor to sell his Angoulême printing-office, he turned to the provincial stage in search of a new career which his talent for acting might make a brilliant one. His relations with a young actress drove him to Paris in quest of medical treatment, and there he tried to cash in on his favour with the Liberal Party.

As for Lucien, his return to Paris belongs to the domain of the *Scenes of Parisian Life*.

1835–1843.

MORE ABOUT PENGUINS
AND PELICANS

Penguinews, which appears every month, contains details of all the new books issued by Penguins as they are published. From time to time it is supplemented by *Penguins in Print*, which is our complete list of almost 5,000 titles.

A specimen copy of *Penguinews* will be sent to you free on request. Please write to Dept EP, Penguin books Ltd, Harmondsworth, Middlesex, for your copy.

In the U.S.A.: For a complete list of books available from Penguins in the United States write to Dept CS, Penguin Books, 625 Madison Avenue, New York, New York 10022.

In Canada: For a complete list of books available from Penguins in Canada write to Penguin Books Canada Ltd, 2801 John Street, Markham, Ontario L3R 1B4.

BALZAC

Honoré de Balzac (1799–1850) was the author of a cycle of novels, the *Comédie Humaine*, that analyse the motives underlying human action. In his remorseless reality and the minute documentation of his characters he foreshadowed the Realism of Flaubert and Zola.

OLD GORIOT

This story of the intersecting lives of a group of people living in a boarding-house forms a profound indictment of Paris society.

EUGÉNIE GRANDET

In provincial Saumur, after the Revolution, the miser Grandet lives with his daughter, Eugénie. The tragedy that follows the arrival of her cousin Charles is described by Balzac with irony and psychological insight.

A HARLOT HIGH AND LOW

The harlot of the title is no more than a pawn in a game of wits. The novel is dominated by Vautrin, the Satanic genius at the heart of the web, and one of the great characters of world literature.

COUSIN BETTE

Bette is a poor relation of the rich and vulnerable Hulot family. She dreams of destroying the people on whose patronage she is forced to rely.

Also published:

THE BLACK SHEEP

SELECTED SHORT STORIES

URSULE MIROUËT